For the first time, all 3 books in DDC Morgan's stunning Reg Calloway trilogy in one stunning volume.

Weighing in at a mighty 680 pages and with a new introduction by the author, this beautiful volume is definitely one to treasure.

Includes

- Blood & Cinders
- Pills & Soap
- Rope & Canvas

Blood & Cinders

London 1949. Speedway fever runs high.

Its stars are the working class heroes of a Blitz-torn city emerging from the ravages of war. With cash in their wallets and hoards of adoring fans, these dirt-track chancers enjoy a life of speed, celebrity and sex.

But as Bermondsey Bullets defend their league title, they are rocked by the death of star rider Des Fenton in a mid-race smash.

It's the start of a new and dangerous chapter for stadium security boss Reg Calloway, as he's dragged into the dark side of life at the track, with echoes of his own troubled wartime past.

Pills & Soap

Six months after his adventure in *Blood & Cinders*, Reg Calloway finds himself working as head of security for a London film studio turning out low-budget Brit flicks.

When the studio boss's car is blown up, Special Branch suspects Irish terrorists are responsible but Calloway doesn't buy it. He saw a woman fleeing the scene. Finding the woman and uncovering her connection to the case becomes his obsession.

Calloway's under pressure from all sides - Special Branch and his studio bosses are convinced that the IRA are behind the bomb but when the terrorists give Calloway an ultimatum to find the real bomber or else, he knows for sure that the mysterious woman who fled the scene is the real key to everything.

His investigation takes him into the dark side of the London film business - its exploitation of starlets, its underworld connections and its Faustian star makers who trade young souls for broken dreams.

As Calloway delves into some of the seediest recesses of 1950s London he risks everything in an attempt to find the truth and see that justice, in some form, is served.

Rope & Canvas

When speedway superstar Bert Webber asks his old friend Reg Calloway for help Reg is reluctant to get involved.

Webber's brother-in-law is dead, seemingly the victim of a simple road traffic accident, but if the dead man was in a crash just north of London why was there a flyer for a clip-joint in Berlin and a ticket for the city's U-Bahn tucked in his pocket?

Ten years in the military police and six in the Intelligence Corps have taught Calloway that things are not always as they seem, and with Webber happy to pay him a pretty penny to investigate further, Reg puts aside his initial misgivings and determines to find the truth, wherever it lies.

So begins a high-speed, high-octane thriller which propels Calloway through a post-war world of female wrestlers, wall-of-death riders, Berlin gangsters and the shadowy spy-masters he thought he'd escaped forever.

"Up there with the very best examples of British Post-War noir – a towering achievement…"

"With each new book, the calloway series is developing into a tour de force of british noir – a must-read…"

"A terrific addition to the english mean streets school…"

"A gem of a find and highly recommended."

"As I read, I had that feeling that I haven't had since I read Chandler for the first time."

"A fantastic read, stylishly written."

"Exciting, gripping and enjoyable - what more could you want!"

This edition first published 2022 by Fahrenheit Press.

ISBN: 978-1-914475-60-3

10 9 8 7 6 5 4 3 2 1

www.Fahrenheit-Press.com

F 4 E

Grit, Spit & Brilliantine

By

DDC Morgan

Fahrenheit Press

Introduction

It started with a friend's junk shop purchase thirty years ago, a framed set of cigarette cards featuring speedway stars of the thirties and forties. With their bullet helmets, worn, chiselled faces and very British teeth, they were unlikely looking sporting stars. But stars they were, earning big enough money to leave behind their dirty jobs in the workshops, the factories or the haulage yards, for a life of celebrity, with all the trappings (and, no doubt, temptations) that came with it. There was a story there, although it was another three decades before I would write it.

It was January 2017 and politics on both sides of the Atlantic had lurched angrily to the right, reviving narratives seldom heard in the mainstream political sphere since the time those jug-eared speedway riders were risking their necks on the track. Those two ideas collided and from that collision Blood & Cinders emerged, written on a tablet in twenty-minute bursts, all that my shortish commute would allow. It was set in a lost part of London, a Speedway stadium, the kind you would have found in every London neighbourhood and regional city in the middle of the last century. My wife and I discovered the remains of one once, close to our home, a few fragments of the concrete stands still visible and an oval of scrubby parkland that had once been the track. This became the fictional Bermondsey Stadium, home of 'The Bullets', with Reg Calloway its track security officer. Calloway's world is a post-war world of damaged people, showbiz opportunists and bomb-site urchins. I remembered the bomb-sites of my own childhood in the sixties and seventies, not in London but in a provincial east coast port (also a big speedway town), overgrown with ivy and the all-invasive buddleia. As a young journalist I covered the redevelopment of the last City of London bomb-site as late as the mid 1990s. They were part of the landscape of my early life and as a writer I felt quite at home among them, in a part-researched, part-imagined London of the late 1940s and early 1950s.

Calloway's world is the world of the common people, the world where the lords and ladies of cosy crime fiction seldom go (unless it's to misbehave). These are purposefully working class stories for the most part (drawing much inspiration from historian Ken Worpole's book *Dockers & Detectives*, which explored the popularity of hard-boiled American crime writing and the UK's emerging 'lowlife' fiction among British working people in the early twentieth century). Calloway drifts from job to job, taking low-grade security roles at rundown venues that offer entertainment to the masses, in an age before every home had a television. Fairgrounds, boxing rings, flea-pit cinemas and wrestling arenas are his preserve, each with their own intrigues that need 'a man with your skills, Reg' to sort out.

Reg is of the damaged generation. I remember them from my early childhood, friends of my grandparents, wounded visibly or imperceptibly, their trauma talked about knowingly in hushed tones ('he was at Anzio', 'he was on the Burma railway'). Reg bears his scars on the inside, the anger, the loss, the regret, clouding his judgement, boiling over into rage. Less the conquering hero, more an inconvenient truth.

This trilogy is Calloway's odyssey, fuelled by warm beer and fry-ups, reeking of sweat and cigarettes and not without violence. And Reg will, I'm sure, return. He's not finished with me yet.

DDC Morgan, August 2023

BOOK ONE: BLOOD & CINDERS

ONE

When Des Fenton hit the barrier at seventy miles an hour, his bike had bucked him, thrown him and snapped him like a twig. This wasn't meant to happen to Des. Dashing Des had the luck of the devil. He was Pattie Moxon's lucky star. In twenty years of speedway riding he'd never copped more than a few broken fingers. Des was good. Des was the Bullets' ace. Quick off the tape, king of the first bend. Nothing could touch him. Until tonight.

He had hit the barrier head-first, crumpling like a jack-in-the-box in reverse, before flopping face down onto the cinders. The stretcher bearers of the St John Ambulance knew it was a bad one. They sprinted across the centre green and over the track towards the prostrate rider, looking fearful. Pattie, the Bullets' boss, followed close behind. She too knew it was bad. She'd been in the business long enough. She threw her fur coat to the ground and knelt by Fenton's side as the St John's men examined him. One of them looked up at her and shook his head.

The heat had started well. Fenton was first off the tape, taking the lead on the first bend and holding it like it was his divine right. His teammate Ray Simpkins was a hair's breadth behind. He hugged the star's rear wheel like a hound at heel until their two wheels touched in the third lap. Fenton and his motorcycle spasmed as one, as if shocked by a high voltage current. Twenty thousand fans let out a collective gasp that bounced off the stadium walls. His wife let out a shriek that could be heard above the crowd. She scrambled out of the VIP box and ran towards the scene in quick faltering steps. She'd seen him come off before, but this wasn't the same. This one was bad. A speedway wife knows the difference.

Ken Kilminster knew the difference too, as he quickly ushered his photographer onto the track, hoping this might be the story that would make his career as a speedway correspondent. As the first flashbulb popped, it lit up Simpkins standing at the edge of the track watching, a cigarette dangling from his lower lip.

Simpkins had been twitchy that night. Uptight and tetchy. Something on his mind. Something that had been building for a while. Fenton clapped him on the back and wished him luck before the heat. Simpkins had blanked him. Now he stared blankly in the glare of the floodlights, as the ambulance crew eased Fenton's limp body onto the stretcher and covered his face with a blanket. He watched Pattie consoling Fenton's wife, who was gasping hysterically, her hand to her cheek and tears welling in her eyes. He saw Kilminster, notebook in hand, his pudgy fist squeezing a pencil stub as he captured the moment in shorthand. And he watched the stretcher bearers lift Fenton into the ambulance and slam the doors, leaving no doubt that this was Dashing Des's last race.

A hush descended on the stadium, the cheering and chanting of the crowd turned to ghoulish whispers as the ambulance drove slowly over the centre green towards the main gates. Simpkins flicked his cigarette butt towards it as it passed, spat the cinder dust from his mouth and walked back towards the dressing rooms. 'Not your night, was it Des?' he muttered under his breath.

TWO

Reg Calloway wished the morning over. He'd seen enough burials for one lifetime. He'd spent the past hour waiting for a break in the proceedings so he could smoke. When he lit a Navy Cut he realised he had company.

'Did you know Des well?'

'Only as a name over the tannoy.'

She leaned in to accept a light, letting the small veil of her mourning hat brush his cheek. He caught her scent but couldn't name it. It was a long time since he'd bought perfume for a woman.

'A great loss to the club,' she said.

'Not to mention to his wife. I hope he was insured.'

Dashing Des, star rider of Bermondsey Bullets, always drew a big crowd. Today was no exception. They had lined the streets from the stadium to the cemetery. Fifteen thousand had turned out to watch the funeral procession. Men, women, children. So many women, all made up and in their best coats. Dashing Des was the Bullets' ladies' man. Roguish good looks chiselled into a well-worn face. All flash suits and too much brilliantine. He'd walk onto the track before each fixture in top hat and tails, a red carnation in his lapel. He looked swell and had a swagger to match. The crowd would sing Putting on the Ritz as he plucked the button-hole from his lapel and threw it into the stands. The women would reach out to snatch it. They were all Des's girls.

'I value my riders, Mr Calloway. They're all insured. And the club will make a contribution to the widow.'

'Very generous, I'm sure. What is it they call speedway promoters? Merchants of manslaughter?'

'They know the risks. And they live well. They enjoy the spoils.'

Calloway stole a glance at her. He put her past thirty and then some, like him, but she wore it well. Clothes from town, hair too he reckoned, and good shoes. Very good. Nothing you'd find on the local women. Shoes were always a tell. They set off her calves and ankles. She noticed him looking but didn't react. She was Patricia Moxon, speedway aristocracy. He was a glorified commissionaire.

He had walked in false solemnity ahead of the cortège. He didn't know Fenton in anything but name and he cared little for the Bullets. But as track security officer he was obliged to join in, taking his place alongside the promoter, the pit crews and the county commander of the St John's Ambulance. The procession reached the cemetery, the Bullets flanking the hearse in race jackets and leathers. They rode slowly, revving staccato to stay steady. Calloway counted six, three riders a side, plus Fenton in the hearse. One rider missing from the team of eight.

In the four months since taking the job, Calloway had grown to hate the stadium. It was a tinny colosseum for a shilling's worth of vicarious danger to punctuate a dreary existence. Fans came from the docks and the railways and the Peek Freans biscuit factory, scarves around their necks and rattles in hand, ready to sing oft-sung anthems to their adopted heroes. Their four-stroke gladiators. Their champions of the cinders. A pint or two in the Dun Cow before the races, then saveloy and pease pudding from George's Hole in the Wall on the way home. A ritual to blot out the grimness of life on the ration.

Calloway watched Fenton's widow as she dismounted the funeral car. Tight-jawed, more numb than sorrowful, her tailored black two-piece worn like armour to shield emotion. It was the onlookers who cried tears, perhaps for Des Fenton, more likely for loved ones lost to the war, to the Blitz or to the hardship of their tenement lives. Their collective grief on this crisp April Saturday had purpose. Have a good cry, love. Get it all out. Dashing Des's reckless demise was the spark to ignite a tankful of hurt.

As the final mourners passed through the cemetery gates, a woman stepped forward from the crowd and fell in line. About twenty, with a doll face and dyed-blonde hair, she wore a dark grey suit with a full skirt over rounded hips and a narrow-waist jacket. She wore it well but wore it local. This was New Look style through the shop windows of the Old Kent Road. Too full in the shoulders, padded in the bust, with clumsy stitching that lacked the finesse of its couture inspiration. The birdcage veil of her pillbox hat hid little of her common good looks. She gave the crowd something new to gawp at. She held her head proud, her small lips pursed with a hint of defiance.

The riders peeled off and parked their motorcycles in two neat lines flanking the cemetery road. They removed helmets and bowed heads. They snuck looks at the young woman and exchanged glances with their teammates. All except Simpkins. His head hung lower than the others, his eyes fixed on the damp bitumen of the road.

Calloway watched Patricia Moxon and the widow exchange the meaningless words the situation required. Hushed and insincere but better than morbid silence. Only then did Fenton's widow notice the young blonde who now stood at Calloway's side. The widow's eyes flashed through her veil. Her body squared up as dignity fought the urge to advance. Patricia Moxon gripped her arm, the meaning clear. Don't, love. Whoever she is. Calloway looked sideways at the young women. She stared purposefully into the middle distance with parade ground detachment. Oblivious, the undertakers' men beckoned the riders to the hearse to lift the coffin. It broke the line of hostility from the widow to the blonde. The county commander of the St John's Ambulance sighed, relieved that a scene had been avoided. Calloway caught his eye and raised a quizzical eyebrow. The commander shrugged. Pat Moxon saw the exchange. She flickered disapproval.

The proceedings were dismal, the eulogy long and inauthentic, the priest working to a script prepared from the customary fag-end biography of a man he knew little of. The widow wept a little but her composure held out. Calloway was grateful.

Between the eulogy and the lowering of the coffin, a grey mist drifted in from the river and under its shroud, the young woman had withdrawn unnoticed. Calloway looked for her among the headstones and the vulgar statues that mocked them, but she was gone.

'Who was the bottle blonde?' he asked when the formal proceedings were over.

Patricia Moxon shrugged, as if indifferent to his question. 'Perhaps she's the other woman.'

'So there is one?'

'They're speedway stars, Mr Calloway. Odds on there's another woman, on the side or just for the night.'

'Nice boys then.'

She considered this, drawing on a cigarette she held between well-manicured fingers and exhaling with deliberation.

'They enjoy taking risks. It goes with the job.'

Calloway glanced back up the cemetery road. The undertakers' men were rearranging the floral tributes and the grave diggers shovelled earth into the hole. He could see their breath as they panted from the exertion. Spring had yet to clock on for its shift. Moxon pulled the collar of her fur coat tight against the chill. A handsome woman, Calloway thought, and expensively dressed, but in a way that said she wasn't born to it. The lady Pat enjoyed new money. Beneath the couture there was a grafter.

The riders buckled helmets and mounted their bikes. Matchless, Triumph, the mighty Vincent, marques etched in gold and chrome polished mirror-bright. Their four-cylinder engines pounded brutally through the hush as the Bullets left the cemetery two abreast. Moxon and Calloway stood aside to let them pass.

A car was waiting outside the cemetery gates, its engine running. Moxon gestured to it. 'Where do you live? I'll drop you off.'

The invitation seemed premeditated. Calloway tried to duck it.

'No thank you, ma'am. I'd prefer to walk.'

She snorted. 'Don't be silly.'

She held the door for him. He accepted and eased his big

frame into the back seat. It felt awkward going first. He was used to holding the door for ladies. She flicked a gloved hand, waving him to the far side of the seat before sliding in next to him. The driver asked for instructions. Calloway gave his address. He caught a look of disapproval on Moxon's face. She must have known his street. The driver nodded with a shortfall of enthusiasm. He was thin, shabby and smelled of coal tar soap. He gripped the wheel with nicotine-stained fingers, nails chewed short. His Burton's suit was ready for retirement. Calloway knew this type. A demobbed drifter down on his luck. Someone you wouldn't lend money to.

'Does he drive you everywhere?'

'Good lord, no,' she said, removing her beret and shaking her hair loose. 'The Bullets are good but they're not that good.'

'Why the chauffeur today?'

The title was generous.

'An excuse for a quick exit. I didn't want to hang around for the wake. I've seen them drink, and worse. Best I don't hang around. What the manager doesn't see, if you get my drift.'

The car swept past Saturday shoppers along New Cross Road, a bustling normality against the strange rubble landscape that was post-war London. The Kinema was showing Hollywood movies again, now the tax dispute with America was over. Now showing: The Sands of Iwo Jima. Coming soon: I was a Male War Bride. Still suffering the hangover of war yet revelling in the glory and the romance.

The car swung a sharp right at the Marquis of Granby. Pat Moxon leaned into Calloway on the turn. He felt her warmth through the flannel of his suit and caught her scent again - jasmine and roses.

'I need to talk to you, Mr Calloway. I suppose you'd call it a security matter.'

'Someone been skimming your turnstile take?'

'Something rather delicate, about the team. I'd appreciate your help.'

The driver caught a look at them through the rearview mirror, his interest piqued. Calloway returned the look. The driver read the signal and feigned disinterest.

'I work for the stadium, ma'am. This sounds like a club matter.'

She slipped off her shoes, then leaned forward in her seat to massage her feet. They were small and neat, her painted toes visible through the sheer silk of her stockings.

'I lease the stadium, Mr Calloway. I'd say you work for me.'

'Then I'd say you share me with the greyhounds on Saturdays.'

She laughed and sat back in the seat, toying with the expensive-looking pearls around her neck.

'Come to see me on Monday. We can't talk now in any case.'

The driver shuffled in his seat. Calloway tapped him on the shoulder.

'You can drop me here. I'll walk the rest.'

The car pulled up alongside the curb, just short of the turning into Calloway's street. Patricia Moxon looked out of the side window with seeming disinterest, as if noticing the place for the first time. Calloway sensed she knew the area well, but it would be unbecoming of speedway royalty to admit it. It was an unloved street, bombed into unintended blocks and connected by cleared sites, the rubble on some still to be removed. The exposed flanks of party walls lacking their neighbours bore a clumsy patchwork of paper and paint. Fireplaces floated in pairs at each floor level, like the plaintiff eyes of vagrants. It was a street of single rooms and lightless basements.

'Are you married, Mr Calloway?'

He climbed out of the car, placed his big hands on the dusty roof and leaned in to reply.

'Put it this way. If I broke my neck like one of your riders, there'd be no widow to mourn me. And no other woman.'

She smiled with what might have passed for warmth.

'You should do something about that.'

He turned away. 'Goodbye, ma'am.'

'Goodbye, Mr Calloway.'

Calloway glanced backwards as he walked towards the dilapidated street and caught the driver sneering.

THREE

They were filming at the track. A Pathé news crew had set up close to the inner boundary. With speedway stars back in the ascendant, there was appetite for newsreel in the cinemas. The crew was meant to interview Des Fenton. Pat Moxon had substituted Bert Webber, her number two rider since young Billy Riley started losing form at the start of last season. Webber didn't have Fenton's swagger, nor his rough diamond looks, but he was cocky and tenacious. The director had him making repeated broadsides, trailing dirt then stopping in front of the camera. The show-off in Webber was enjoying himself. The cameraman had to wipe the lens with each take and the producer tutted, picking cinder specks from the Harris tweed of his overcoat.

Webber removed his helmet for the interview and the director had him perch casually on the seat of his motorcycle while he answered questions. They rehearsed some lines beforehand with Pat providing the words for her rider. Webber removed a glove and scraped his hand across his head to sweep his hair back. He was no matinee idol. He was a snaggle-toothed grease monkey, wiry and bow-legged like a jockey, with the dull parchment skin of a chain smoker. But his hair was thick and lustrous and his eyes were steely and keen, his pupils darting shiftily like beetles on a hot plate.

'Oh yes, there's money in speedway racing and a good rider can make five thousand a year if he gets the breaks. It's a risky old game and you've got to have guts, but I wouldn't swap it for the world.'

He spoke the lines in a self-conscious monotone, oblivious to the rhythm of punctuation. Patricia Moxon coached him off-camera between the retakes. With each successive take he would fluff the lines, each time in a different place.

Reg Calloway leaned on a stand rail and watched the scene play out. A female member of the Pathé crew was adjusting Webber's scarf, untying the outlaw-style bandana favoured by the riders and knotting it into a rakish foulard. Webber wriggled like a child whose mother had spat on a hankie to wipe the smut off his face.

The frustration on the small rider's face grew with each successive retake. The producer feigned patience, but it was wearing thin.

'I'd be alright if it wasn't for that fucking camera putting me off me stroke.'

Moxon's voice echoed off the empty concrete stands. 'We'll have less of that language Bert Webber!'

Webber jumped, as if some all-seeing goddess of speedway had spoken.

'I've warned you before. None of your effing and blinding on my track. Otherwise you'll go straight back where I found you.'

Calloway crossed the stands towards her. 'So where did you find him?'

'The arse end of Rotherhithe, via The Hammers for a couple of seasons. They might tolerate his uncouth ways at West Ham but I'm not having it here.'

Webber gave it one last take before dismissing himself with a shrug and wheeling his machine towards the starting line.

'Still, he won the London Cup in forty-seven. Fearless little fella. An old-style leg trailer. It's a miracle he still has all his limbs.'

'Missing a finger, though.'

'You're observant. And two toes on his left foot. But that's small change for a rider like him.'

The film crew were setting up for cutaway shots at the side of the track. Webber was summoning two of the Bullets' crew, gesturing that he needed a push-off.

'They tell me Bob Danvers-Walker is going to narrate it,' said Moxon. 'I hope he does a better job than poor Bert. Do you follow the news, Mr Calloway?'

He nodded. 'On the radio and in the papers. I'm not one for

the news theatres.'

'I don't blame you. Full of courting couples and queers. Still, good luck to them. It's not like there's many places they can do it.'

She was blunt, Calloway gave her that.

'You wanted to talk to me.'

She didn't respond. She was distracted. Two riders were ripping up the track with practice laps and Moxon was seeing something in their riding she disapproved of. He waited for her to answer. His impatience showed and she noticed.

'We've not spoken much have we, Mr Calloway?'

'Not much, ma'am, no. I look after the stadium. You look after the club. It suits me that way. I've not much time for the antics of these maniacs.'

She flicked her cigarette onto the stand and ground it into the concrete with her heeled shoes.

'You make me wonder why you're here at all.'

He had wondered the same thing himself in the few months since taking the job. But he knew the answer. Peacetime didn't suit him and opportunities to make a living were scarce. God knows the war hadn't been kind to him, but the past three years had been worse. He'd stuck with the army until forty-six. He had had no place else to go at the time. After the episode in Nuremberg, there had been no choice but to leave.

'I look after the pen, ma'am. Don't expect me to love the animals.'

She laughed.

'Some of them are beasts at that. But I like that in a man, Calloway. It suits me well. This game's about aggression as much as skill.'

'I think I've seen enough aggression, ma'am.'

She offered him a cigarette, which he accepted. She had a man's cigarette case embossed with the initials PRM and a matching lighter. They looked expensive but not ostentatious.

'You're right. I did want to talk to you.'

She turned to lean back on the railing. She closed her eyes and inclined her head to face the mid-morning sun, which had broken through the cloud. A wolf whistle cut through the noise from the track. Without opening her eyes, Pat said: 'Get back on that bike, O'Donnell. You've been slow off the tape for the last two fixtures. You of all people need the practice.'

The rider O'Donnell was stretched out on the upper tier of the stands in full leathers, taking the last drags of a cigarette held inwards between his oil-stained thumb and finger.

'But baby, the view from here is too damn good.'

'You'll get a view of the back of my hand in minute. Get your overpaid Yank arse down to that starting line or you'll be back in Pasadena before you can say Chattanooga Choo-choo.'

The rangy American put on a show of looking hurt, then lolled his way down each tier of the stands blowing kisses at his boss. She shot him a look, the kind a foreman gives when he's caught an apprentice smoking on his shift.

'They're still overpaid and over here then, ma'am.'

'And the other, I've no doubt, Mr Calloway.'

She watched O'Donnell as he straddled his bike like a western hero saddling up and shouted instructions for his push start to the track crew.

'I brought him over in forty-six. I needed some glamour in the team. His face has been advertising shaving soap since we won the league.'

'I've seen the posters. Do you take commission?'

'He gets to keep his fee. It pays for his lifestyle. He's got expensive tastes that one.'

She watched the American ride laps, pulling Looney Toons faces at the crew on the home straight.

'Outwardly they behave as if nothing's happened. But Des Fenton's death has rattled them.'

'Surely that's not surprising.'

'You'd think not, but this is a tough old life and not without its tragedies. Riders take the rough with the smooth. Deaths are few and far between, thank the Lord, but when they happen, well there's a sort of heroic acceptance of the inevitable.'

'But not this time?'

She shook her head. 'They're talking.'

'Saying what?'

She lit another cigarette and took a long and deliberate drag on the hot tar. 'They're poring over the details. The track conditions, the speed Des was coming out of the turn, why Ray Simpkins was on his tail the whole time.'

'It's the Bullets' first fatality. They're bound to be rattled. Anything show up on the club's investigation?'

'The track conditions were fine. We'd laid new cinder over the summer and the depth was tested at the start of the race. Deeper than the requisite six inches. The chief mechanic confirmed both bikes were in proper condition when they left the pits. Des Fenton was in good shape too. The trainer confirmed it. So was Simpkins.'

Moxon had installed a gym at the stadium and put the Bullets on a fitness regime. A former Charlton Athletic trainer put them through their paces twice a week and kept fitness records.

'Have your insurers investigated?'

'Yes, and the association. Neither found anything untoward.'

She turned and looked across to the track. The American rider was performing tricks for the cameras. She drew on the cigarette and exhaled hard.

'I've been around this business a long time, Mr Calloway. This is something different.'

'Different how?'

She paused for a moment, as if reluctant to continue. 'They're saying Des Fenton's death wasn't an accident.'

The statement hit him like a punch to the guts.

'Who's saying?'

She ignored the question. He pressed her. 'Who is saying this to you?'

'I can't tell you. I was told in confidence.'

'You were told that Ray Simpkins ran Fenton off the track deliberately? That's a serious allegation. It's a matter for the police.'

'I don't want the police involved. I want it not to be true.'

Calloway let this sink in. He changed tack. 'What's Ray Simpkins saying?'

'He's keeping his head down for the most part.'

'Was there something between Simpkins and Fenton? Bad blood?'

'Competition certainly, but that's not unusual. And they were different types. Fenton was gregarious. The life and the soul. Simpkins is quieter, a bit surly when he wants to be. The chippy type.'

'Did he resent Fenton's success?'

'Not so you'd notice. They were business-like around one another, but wouldn't call them pals.'

'Always like that?'

'They became distant over the last few fixtures, maybe since the end of last season.'

'You don't run a man off the track for being distant.'

'Maybe not, but I need to know more, Mr Calloway. If something's not right, I need it dealt with and dealt with quickly.'

She looked towards the track at the practicing riders. 'I can't have a jinx on the club, not this season. I've too much to lose. I need you to make some enquiries.'

'Why do you think they would talk to me?'

'You strike me as the persuasive sort. And I've asked around about you, what you did in the war. There's more to you than filling the fire buckets and locking the gates.'

She didn't know the half of it, he thought.

'I work for the stadium not the club. If there's anything in this, which I doubt, it's club business.'

It wasn't the answer she wanted.

'What do you earn, Calloway? Don't bother answering, I've read your personnel file. It takes you a month to earn what my riders can make in a night. If you help me, I'll pay you what I pay them, from now until the end of the season.'

Calloway snorted. 'Worth that much to you?'

'For the right result.'

'And what if I get the wrong result?'

'Then we'll need to fix that.'

He was inclined to leave it right there. But Patricia Moxon could be persuasive too. She was all persuasion from where he stood. She worked hard at it. From the fit of her dress to the height of her heels, her boldness of speech and her confident tone. Even the studied way she held a cigarette.

'I'll make some enquiries but I won't take your money. I'm not one of your prize stallions and I won't be bought.'

'It's good money, Calloway.'

'I've no need for it.'

She raised an eyebrow. It was plucked to the width of a pencil point. 'You could spend it on proper digs. I don't see you as the "furnished room for single gentleman" type.'

'It suits me fine.'

He stubbed his cigarette against the metal stand rail. O'Donnell clunked past them in lead-soled boots and sat on the stands a few yards away. He ran his fingers through the pile of helmet-sweaty hair on his big skull.

'Give me a week,' Calloway said. 'If I don't find anything, I suggest you draw a line under it. Tell your lads you've ordered a safety review. Any suggestions where I should start?'

Moxon looked over at the snaggle-toothed Webber, who chatted cheerily to the mechanics in the pits.

'Start with Bert. He knows everyone's business and he likes to talk. Whatever you find out, you tell me first. No one else.'

Calloway nodded an acknowledgement. She looked him up and down. Six foot and broad, with a firm jaw and all his own teeth. Dark hair shorn short, Brylcreemed close to his scalp in the no-nonsense fashion of an ex-NCO. Barrel-chested, with strong-looking hands balled into fists by his side. A powerful man, but in control, at least that's how he appeared to her.

'You know I'd never thought of you as a stallion, Reg.'

She took a long last draw on the lipstick-stained stub of her cigarette. Then she winked.

'Well not until now anyway.'

The American laughed. Calloway wasn't the laughing kind.

FOUR

Local women shouted at a thick-set man who stood at the front step of his narrow, smog-blackened house. He wore old suit trousers with braces over an unwashed vest, which showed off broad shoulders and taught, muscled arms. Thirty years old or so, his thinning black hair was combed flat across his scalp, with jagged, uncombed tufts sticking out where he had slept. He said nothing, staring back with mean detachment. Still in his hand was the wooden post which he'd used just a minute ago to strike a stray dog repeatedly on its head, as the stunned creature skulked motionless beneath the blows. The dog now crawled in deranged circles on half-crouched legs, blood dripping from its mouth onto the dusty stone paving.

Reg Calloway and Bert Webber had watched the scene play out from the table they were sharing in a cafe on the opposite side of the street. Neither seemed shocked, just distracted by the brutality of it. Webber broke the silence.

'That's Wally Whitby. I used to work with him down the rope factory. That was before the war.'

Even from across the street, Calloway recognised the look on Whitby's face, expressionless but with a certain kind of mania behind the eyes. He'd seen that look on men during the war.

'Whoever he is, he's a troubled soul.'

Webber took a slurp of tea and nodded. 'He was on the Burma railway. Never been the same since he come back from that POW camp. Fucking Japanese. I was in North Africa me'self. Them Italians weren't a bad lot. Half of 'em didn't want to be there. Same as us really.'

The two men ate fried food, smearing grease and egg yolks

around thick plates. Webber spoke while he ate, saliva smacks punctuating his bad grammar, which he delivered cheerily.

'Was you overseas, Mr Calloway?'

Calloway nodded. 'Europe mostly. Normandy, the Ardennes, Germany.'

'What was you?'

'Army.'

'Same here. Service Corps. Driver. Not a bad mechanic too as it happens. You?'

'Airborne.'

Webber sat up, his eyes alight. 'Paratrooper?'

Calloway put his knife and fork together and lit a cigarette from the plain gunmetal case he had carried throughout the war.

'Gliders.'

Webber frowned. 'Blimey. Fucking death traps.'

Calloway flicked ash into a chipped metal Players ashtray, which stood in a moat of slopped tea on the pale blue Formica of the tabletop.

'Yep. I reckon they killed more of my lot than the enemy. What with that and the jeeps rolling over.'

Webber rolled his eyes and nodded. 'I don't know why they got rid of the Tillies. Granted they wasn't so good on rough ground, but on the roads those old utility cars handled like a proper motor.'

Webber slurped his tea and used the barbed end of a broken matchstick from the ashtray to pick tiny gobbets of bacon from the crevices between his crooked yellow teeth.

'Jeeps. They looked flash enough, but you couldn't trust 'em on the bends.' He sniggered. 'A bit like Six Gun O'Donnell.'

The waitress passed their table, half sashay, half slouch. Webber wolf whistled as she passed. The waitress turned and Bert leered. She stuck out a hip, crossed her arms and glared.

'That house coat's a bit on the snug side, Vera. Showing off your curves something lovely.'

She raised a thick eyebrow then threw a sodden grey cloth in the small man's direction.

'Who pulled your chain, Bert Webber?'

Webber caught the cloth like a fielder and let out a wheezy smoker's laugh.

'See you Sunday, Vera,' he shouted.

'Not if I see you first.'

She was about Webber's age, thirty-five but looking forty, with cheap lipstick on plump lips. A floral wrap-over housecoat restrained an ample bosom and clung to her hips. She had a menial seductiveness, the stuff of rushed encounters in back rooms. Groping and giggling with milk-stout breath. A thought forced its way into Calloway's head, base and filthy. He shook it off.

'One of your fancy women, Bert?'

'Leave it out. That's Vera, me sister-in-law. Coming to our place Sunday with her husband Stan for dinner.'

Dinner meaning lunch, Calloway noted. Just as tea meant supper. He'd used the same lexicon before the army and over time was re-educated into the ways of the mannered classes after his temporary commission. That and don't drink tea with your food. Webber looked his sister-in-law up and down as she walked back to the counter.

He leaned forward and whispered. 'Not that I wouldn't mind.'

Calloway had Webber down as the talker of the team, at least when he wasn't in front of a camera. There was no training on Tuesdays so Calloway had taken him for breakfast. The cafe was the rider's choice. It was dimly lit and a fog of cheap tobacco and smoking lard hung in the air. Webber was at home here, not like the places up West where his teammates would go to swank, as he put it. This place was favoured by drivers from the bus garage and posties from the sorting office. Painters and decorators, skilled men. The unskilled labourers had their own caffs, places the young Bert would go before the war when he worked at the factory. This was his concession to the rarefied life of a speedway rider with cash in his pocket. It was a very small concession. But Webber was content with this modest rung up the ladder, shunning the ostentation of his fellow track stars.

'Tell me about O'Donnell.'

'Typical Yank. A bragger. When he's not telling you why he's the club's best rider, which he ain't, he's telling you about getting his leg over. A different bird every Saturday. Acts like a movie star and they fall for it too.'

'Working his way through the fans?'

'Nah, his tastes are more upmarket. He goes dancing in town. Says he's good at that an' all.'

Calloway let him talk, mostly harmless anecdotes about his teammates. Calloway interjected with prompts until the conversation, virtually one-sided once the little man got into his stride, reached the death of Des Fenton.

'Des was a good rider and he knew that circuit better than any of us. He was with the Bullets in the thirties, before Pat took it over. He'd rode at Catford, under Eddie Dandridge, before the club moved to Bermondsey. He was the first one to really master the new track. The Dustbin Lid, they call it. Shortest track in the country. Tight as a gnat's arse, pardon my French. All bends and no straights. One big fuckin' broadside all the way round. The away clubs hate it. They're used to more straight riding in a lap. That's the Bullets' advantage. We know our own track and when we're away, well, it's a bleeding luxury. Room to breathe if you know what I mean.'

Webber lit a new cigarette from the burned down butt of the one that dangled from his dry lips. Calloway ordered two more teas.

'Shame Des Fenton didn't have more room the night he died. Did you see the accident?'

'Nah, just heard.'

'So what happened?'

The small rider stubbed the butt of his last cigarette onto the dirty breakfast plate in front of him.

'Des was bombing down the back straight. Simpkins was hanging onto his tail. Ray's front wheel touched Des's rear and sent him into a skid. Des couldn't pull out of it. He piled into the back of the Harringay rider, Alfie Biggs. Biggs hit the barrier but was okay. Fenton was thrown over his handlebars and landed smack on his head. Dead on the spot. Broken neck.'

The waitress, Vera, banged the teas down onto their table.

Webber spooned in three sugars then slurped noisily. Pans crashed in the kitchen, followed by profanities. An old man with a veined and mottled face at the table opposite jumped. He peered with rheumy eyes over the counter into the kitchen. Amused by the sound of the ensuing argument, he grinned with too-white false teeth, a present from the National Health.

'There's a rumour Fenton's death wasn't an accident,' said Calloway.

Webber looked out of the cafe window as if distracted. The man who had beaten the dog had disappeared into his house leaving his neighbours on the pavement to gossip. There was tut-tutting and shaking of heads.

'I know. I've heard,' he said.

'Who from?'

He evaded the question. 'It's going around.'

Calloway pressed him. 'Around where? Around who?'

Webber didn't budge. 'Just around.'

Webber fidgeted and looked around the room. Calloway lowered his voice and leaned across the table. 'Any truth in it?'

Webber shrugged, showing discomfort at the question. 'I'm keeping out of it. It wasn't my race. I was in the pits with Hale, the chief mechanic. I'd come off me'self in the previous heat. Nothing serious, but me handlebars needed adjusting. I didn't see nothing of the accident. Just heard the commotion after Des came off.'

'Is Ray Simpkins a good rider?'

'Rocket Ray? Good as any. Was on good form start of last season. Got right sluggish halfway through and finished fourth on points overall. He's not rode so well this season either.'

'How was his riding in the heat?'

'The heat? Fenton copped it. He was showing a bit of muscle. Quick off the tape but not enough to get out front. It's been a while since he could beat Des to the first bend.'

'Was he being reckless?'

'Like I said, I was in the pits.'

Calloway changed tack. 'How did Simpkins get on with Fenton?'

'Alright I s'pose. Simpkins isn't exactly the friendly type. A bit on the chippy side you might call it.'

'That's what Pat Moxon said. Was he chippy with Fenton?'

'Fenton's flash ways got on his nerves. Nothing serious. I can only recall them ever having one barney.'

'What about?'

Webber thought for a moment. He rubbed the stump of his missing finger. 'You remember Joe Smoke? No, thinking about it, that was before your time.'

The small rider leaned back and rocked on the legs of his chair. 'There was this tramp. A proper smokey Joe, hence the name we give him. Blackened face and stank of wood smoke like he'd been burning a brazier on a bomb site. He had a big scar down one side of his face, all laced up. It looked like a fork of lightning. Army deserter, we reckoned. Anyway he used to kip under the west stand. He'd made himself a little camp out of old crates and blankets up one corner where it was dark. He'd come and go through a hole in the fence down by the railway line. We never knew he was there at first. He'd been there ages before the management realised. Then they turned a blind eye for a bit. He wasn't any bother and the last fella to do your job was a bit on the slack side. When he wasn't swinging the lead, he was half pissed. The manager, that is. Fell asleep at his desk one night with the safe open and Saturday night's takings there for anyone to help himself to. Prat. So one day this Joe Smoke came out of his hole and hung around the track when we was practicing. Des Fenton took the piss at first then he got talking to him.'

He was in his stride now. Calloway pushed him gently. 'Talking about what?'

'Dunno, but it happened on and off for a few weeks, Des and Joe Smoke having little chats. After a bit Ray Simpkins started to get the nark about it. Telling Des not to encourage him. Des carried on until this one time Simpkins has a right old go at the tramp. Telling him to fuck off and not to come back. Making a right fuss. Des Fenton wasn't having this and they started having a go at each other.'

'What happened then?'

'A bit of shovin'. Seemed to blow over. Joe Smoke never came back and Simpkins and Fenton kept out of each other's way. They've sort of stayed that way since. A bit distant. Whatever it was I suppose it's resolved itself now, with Des being gone.'

'Did this tramp every show up again?'

Webber shook his head. 'Nah. Not seen him since. They patched up the hole in the fence and took down his camp and burned it.'

'Where do you think he went, this Joe Smoke?'

'Probably on a bomb site somewhere. Or up the spike.'

Calloway looked quizzical. 'Spike?'

'Carrington House, the men's hostel.'

Webber grinned to himself then sang, husky and croaking.

'Dimly the lights of the city are gleaming,
Drear is the night and so cold.
Grimly the walls of the workhouse are frowning,
Frowning on mis'ry untold.'

He chuckled to himself. 'Thinking about it, Carrington House might be a bit upmarket for him.'

'And you've no idea what Fenton and the tramp used to talk about?'

'No, mate. You can't hear nothing on that track when there's bikes going round. He did show Des some pictures once though. Old Joe had these photographs in this grubby old album.'

'Speedway photographs?'

Webber shrugged.

'Did you ever see this album up close?'

The other man recoiled. 'You're joking. I wouldn't go near him. He stank of piss. I'm surprised Fenton had anything to do with him, what with all his flash ways.'

Calloway paid the bill and left half a crown tip on the table. Vera spied it from across the room.

'Thanks, lovely. You can come again.'

Calloway doubted he would. As the two men stood to leave, he said to Webber: 'Why didn't Billy Riley show up for Fenton's funeral?'

Webber rubbed at the stump of his missing finger. 'Said he

was ill.'

'You think he was?'

'Dunno. It was odd that he didn't show up. Didn't show for training on Monday neither.'

They left the cafe and walked across the street, passing the house where the incident with the dog had occurred. There was a trail of dark red blood leading down a passageway to the side of the house. Somewhere the dog lay dying.

FIVE

Wednesday. The Bullets at home to Wembley. Twenty-five thousand pale white faces crammed into the stands. Flat caps and hair oil. Girls crushed against the barriers, arms hanging over the sides trailing black-and-red scarves. Gas rattles clapping out a machine-gun brat-a-tat. Young voices chanting in unison over the tinny crackle of the tannoy.

'One-two-three-four, who are we for? B-U-L-L-E-T-S, Bullets!'

Expectant faces hoping for the first glimpse of the riders. Banners and flags, the black flying bullet emblem of the home team waved euphorically, as if in some rally for a people's empire.

Calloway shouted orders to his staff. Boys had climbed the tannoy tower for a better view. They clung keenly to the scaffold, their chins resting on the cold metal. He sent men to bring them down. He didn't want a child breaking their neck on his watch.

The stand lights dimmed. A hush descended. A single spotlight beamed into the darkness, bathing the home riders in a sphere of white light. The crowd let out a roar. The tannoy blared Marching Along Together as the riders strode two abreast across the inner track and onto the manicured oval of grass within the circuit. They walked with the slow swagger of heroes, helmets slung by their sides swinging on the straps. Polished race leathers glistened, silk scarves shimmered.

Webber led the team, waving to the crowd. O'Donnell blew kisses to the girls, who shrieked a collective retort. The track crews took up their positions alongside the St John's Ambulance, who stood like sentinels in black uniforms with blancoed cross straps at regular stations around the inner perimeter. Their furled blankets and stretchers lay in ordered rows ominously beside them.

The pit crews swarmed around the riders' machines, rear wheels spinning as they made their pre-race checks. They adjusted gear ratios to suit the track conditions. The riders entered the pits to the din of the engines, conferring with their crews in short shouted bursts. They fastened helmets, strapped on lead boots and slapped each other's backs for luck.

Marshals in white coats busied around the start line. Crew members in matching buff overalls and black berets paired up to give push starts. Engines fired up, filling the air with methanol. Castrol R, the smell of speedway. The first four riders nudged up to the tape. Chromium forks and silver spokes signalled like mirrors in the bright track light, which hung over them in a lattice of black wire. Webber and the South African rider, Jack Duiker, were first up for the Bullets, against the two Wembley Lions. Webber wore the blue race cap, Duiker the red. They edged their machines back and forth along the start line, digging into the dirt with their heels. The start marshal gave the signal and the tape snapped upwards. The four machines lunged forward in unison like a single mechanical being. Within three seconds they were leaning into the first bend, lead boots down and rear wheels showering cinders. Then three seconds of straight before screaming into the return bend.

Calloway looked on from the tower. His eyes tracked the black-and-red race jackets of Webber and the South African. Their opponents had the edge. As the four riders passed the final lap flag, the Bullets lagged by a motorcycle's length. The crowd screamed encouragement, desperation in their blood-lust roar. Webber responded, riding with pure aggression, throwing his bike into the final bend, his left leg trailing so that the toecap of his boot dug grooves in the dirt. It failed to count and as the chequered flag waved, Webber finished third to the two Lions ahead, with Duiker inches behind him. The cheering turned to a deflated groan as the riders left the track. Calloway saw Moxon in the pits, her body tense, her face contorted. Riders and crew kept clear. They knew this look.

The tower door opened and a uniformed commissionaire, breathless from running, called over to Calloway. 'There's trouble under the west stand, down by gate five. I think you need to come.'

They double timed along the underside of the tiered concrete, jostling fans. Calloway signalled to two of his boys to leave their gates and follow them.

'What's happening, Sid?'

The commissionaire, fifty, ruddy-faced and unfit from too much standing around, spoke between gasps.

'Cosh boys, sir. About ten of 'em. Started cutting up rough in the buffet. Some of the regulars turfed 'em out and now there's a standoff.'

A small crowd had formed a ring around the commotion. Calloway pushed his way through.

At one end a gang of youths jittered, their mouths tensed and eyes set firm on the group of burly older men that faced them. Some of the youths held weapons, a leather cosh, a bike chain, no knives Calloway noted, despite the stories he'd heard. They wore jackets cut long in the body in herringbones and flecks, some with velvet pocket flaps. High-waist trousers, narrow at the ankles with loud socks in plaid and spots. They dressed like cavalry officers, Calloway thought, only cheaper and nastier. Their matching hair was long and piled high on top. They were fifteen or sixteen years old at most. The men that had them cornered, dockers by the looks of them, were in their thirties and forties, just looking for an excuse to exert their rightful seniority over theses sneering pretenders. Calloway stepped between the two camps. The older men would be quicker to see reason. They would also be the most dangerous if things kicked off. He tackled them first.

'At ease, gentlemen. Don't let this spoil your night out,' he said, and then more quietly, 'Make some room and we'll have these little bastards out of here. You've done your bit, now go and enjoy yourselves.'

The older men exchanged looks, weighing up whether they should comply. One of them stepped forward to face Calloway.

'These little fuckers need a good talking to.'

The shortest of the mob, he was broad-shouldered and packed with muscle. His shirt was half unbuttoned beneath his jacket revealing an old swallow tattoo on his freckled chest. A seaman, or used to be, and a leader. The rest squared up behind him, acknowledging his superiority. Bold enough to pick a fight on two fronts, he was staring Calloway down, challenging him to his face.

'Language, gentlemen. Speedway's a family night. Now I need you to let me do my job.'

But there was pride at stake here and principle. The older men had confronted the younger to establish a natural order among the local males. Calloway's intervention was denying them justice. He signalled to the security staff to standby, which they did without enthusiasm. They didn't relish the thought of taking on both groups. Calloway spoke softly to the sailor.

'Look around you, pal. Girls, kids, their mums and dads. It's no place for a fight. Do the decent thing. Let us deal with this.'

The sailor looked to one side thinking and ran a big stub-fingered hand through his wiry blonde hair. He looked back at Calloway and nodded. Calloway turned to the youths.

'Now I can call the police or you can leave with my lads and save yourselves a lot of bother.'

'Who the fuck are you, cunt?'

He was the tallest of the group, standing with what passed for a chest all puffed out, his acned chin jutting forward. A bike chain swung by his side from his bony hand.'

Calloway leant forward and whispered in the cosh boy's jug ear.

'I'm the cunt that's going to stop these big lads here turning you and your mates into a pool of piss on the floor. If you leave now, standing tall, you'll save face. If you don't, the St John's Ambulance will be taking you out on a stretcher and all your mates will get to watch.'

The boy snapped 'Fuck off' and swung the chain at Calloway who sidestepped to avoid it. He kicked the boy's legs from under him so that he toppled back onto the concrete. The older men moved forward but their leader signalled to them to stay. Calloway bent down and hauled the boy off the deck by the lapels of his cheaply tailored coat and slapped him twice, good and hard across the face. The boy lay stunned, unhurt and unsure of his next move. Then he grinned, a forced grin for the benefit of his mates. He stared up at Calloway, cocky and defiant. Calloway should have left it there, but the switch had flicked. The switch that sent him back to the war, to the things he'd seen and the things he'd done. The stadium faded to the edge of his consciousness and his past closed around him. It was an angry past and the anger found a way out through his fists. The boy on the ground spasmed with the first blow. The second blow was harder and the face that recoiled from it had changed. It was not the boy's face. It was a face from the past, imprinted on Calloway's memory. A loathsome face. He raised his fist a third time. A hand on his shoulder snapped him back to reality.

'That's enough now, Mr Calloway. I think the boy's learned his lesson.'

It was Les Birkett, the most senior commissionaire and Calloway's effective number two on the security staff. An old and even-tempered veteran who commanded respect, not least from his boss. Calloway lowered his arm and rose to his feet, panting. He faced the boy's gang mates.

'Anyone else?'

His violence had them rattled. Some looked terrified. They shuffled and looked to their leader on the ground who offered no response, just rubbed his pockmarked chin and muttered profanities through split lips. The sailor spoke to the boys with a calmness he'd not shown up to now.

'Alright lads, we've had our fun. Now piss off before this big fella here calls the Old Bill and we all get a night in the cells.'

Birkett shouted to his lads to open up gate five and nodded towards the boys.

'See these gentlemen the off the premises,' he said. 'They won't be coming here again.'

Calloway took a slow walk under the stands. Ruddy-faced Sid caught him up and fell in beside him.

'Nasty little Herberts,' he wheezed. 'If they were mine, they'd get a taste of the strap. If their fathers were here now I'd give 'em a piece of my mind an' all.'

'Too many boys without fathers these days. And mothers too busy holding house and home together to keep them on the rails. That's the trouble with war, Sid. We're too busy remembering the dead to see what it's done to the living.'

'The back of my hand, that's what they'd get.'

And they'd probably return the favour, thought Calloway, looking for an excuse to be alone. He told Sid to check on the turnstiles and ducked under the tunnel that led to the circuit. The engine noise echoed off the bare concrete walls. He crossed to the outer track, leant on the wire mesh fence and pulled out his cigarette case. Four riders lined up at the tape. He recognised the lanky American O'Donnell from his height, even as he sat astride the skeletal bike. Calloway picked a discarded programme from the ground and opened it. The second Bullets rider was Chip Bellman according to the list of heats.

The tape shot up and Bellman took an early lead. The fans roared. Calloway turned to face them. It was a capacity crowd, crammed into the stands, pressed against the fences by the weight of the bodies behind them. Penned like livestock. To Calloway there was an obscenity about it. An unwelcome echo of his past. He turned again to face the track as Bellman came out of the bend showering cinder. Calloway spat the dust from his mouth. Bellman held his lead for another lap with the American close on his tail. The crowd sensed a much-needed win. They sang Oranges and Lemons, Clanger Bellman's given anthem. Their hope was short lived. O'Donnell wobbled out of the final bend hitting Bellman's rear wheel. It sent the machine sliding sideways across the path of the oncoming Wembley rider, throwing Bellman into a roll. He lay still where he fell until the second Wembley bike clipped him. He jolted as if given an electric shock. Two of the track crew leapt from their stations to remove the bike while the St John's Ambulance lifted the downed rider off the dirt and onto a stretcher.

Calloway had seen enough. Maniacs, the lot of them. He'd

spend six years in Europe hoping to God that he and his colleagues would be spared death or wounding. This lot threw themselves in harm's way willingly for a few thousand a year. And their fans cheered them on as they went. He tossed the programme onto the ground and walked back through the tunnel towards his office. Giggling girls with plump faces and head scarves stuffed their mouths with hot dogs. Calloway caught the sickly whiff of fried onions. Two young boys in hand-me-down shorts and snake belts sang 'One-two-three-four, who are we for...' then screamed 'Bullets!' over the ear-splitting clack of the gas rattles in their grubby hands.

The altercation with the youths had rattled him. He regretted slapping the boy. As a gesture to appease the older men and a warning to the younger ones, it was effective enough in diffusing the situation. That was his job after all. But the violence came too easily to him, as it had in the past. He thought of the man he'd watched beating the dog. They weren't so different.

Bert Webber slouched in the doorway of the riders' dressing room, smoking and staring at nothing. Sweat trickled from his hairline making streaks in the smuts on his face. He had an expression like a slapped child. Calloway gave him a What's up? look.

'It's a fucking rout. The Lions have won every heat bar one.' He sucked hard on the fag. 'Clanger's bust up his wrist so he ain't gonna be fit to race for weeks. Pat's doing her nut.'

Calloway wished he hadn't asked. He shrugged and left him to it. Not his problem.

By eleven o'clock silence was descending on the emptying stadium. The main gates clanged in the distance as his lads shut up for the night. Calloway made his final rounds and tested each door. The surgery, the workshop, the supporters' club kiosk. As he approached the door of the riders' changing rooms, he heard rhythmic knocking and audible voices from within. Clasping the handle, he eased the door open.

'Christ, Calloway. You picked your moment.'

Jack Duiker was naked save for motorcycle boots and a red spotted neck scarf. Beneath him on the team's massage bench, a young woman half his age wearing his leather jacket and his goggles over her mussed-up hair. Her dress and shoes lay in a pile on the floor next to an empty gin bottle.

'If you'd like to finish what you're doing, Mr Duiker, I'd like a word,' Calloway said. 'And you,' he nodded to the young woman, 'what's your name, love?' 'Maureen,' she replied. 'Maureen Baxter.' 'You need to be out of here Maureen,' he said. He took a bunch of keys from his pocket and unlocked the door to an adjoining room. 'Get yourself dressed in there. It's not much but at least it's private.' She scooped the pile of clothing from the concrete floor and staggered into the adjoining room, closing the door behind her. Duiker slid off the bench. Calloway turned to face him. 'Not on my watch Duiker, you got that?' Duiker rolled his eyes and nodded. The bestial rapture on his face of moments before had turned to an irritable sulk. He pulled on suit trousers and a vest and leaned back against the lockers.

'So you wanted a word, Mr Calloway. You going to give me a lecture now?'

'Stow it, Duiker. I'm not in the mood. I want to talk about Des Fenton.'

'Ah, pretty Pattie's got you sniffing around hasn't she. You're the boss lady's little bloodhound. You want to know about Fenton? Okay, Calloway, I'll tell you about Dashing Des. He was no gentleman.'

'That's quite some condemnation coming from you.'

The rider pulled a pair of expensive-looking shoes from the locker behind him and dropped them carelessly onto the floor. He pushed a foot inside each one without bothering to bend down, treading the backs down as he did so.

'The fans might have adored him, but all they saw was his public face. Wearing that fucking top hat. Beneath all that Dashing Des bullshit was a different guy altogether, I can tell you. He was a bloody bastard.'

'He seemed popular enough.'

'Popular? He was a speedway star. A real ace, I don't deny. The fans hung round him like flies on shit. That doesn't mean he was great bloke.'

Duiker tugged at the trodden-down shoe backs with his oil-stained fingers, swearing under his breath, then laced the shoes up. He spat on the palm of his hand and wiped smudges off the toe caps.

'So what kind of bloke was he?'

The South African swivelled to face him.

'He had to have something on you. Something that gave him the upper hand. If he found your weakness, he'd use it. He could be a right devious little shit. He was...' he groped for the word, '...manipulative.'

'Did he find your weakness?'

Duiker laughed. 'He thought he had.'

Calloway nodded in the direction of the door behind which the girl was dressing. 'Notching up autograph hunters?'

'I wouldn't be the first.'

Duiker pulled a pack of Navy Cut from his suit jacket, which hung on the peg behind him. He flicked a Zippo lighter and took a long drag.

'It wasn't that. It was something else. Something from the old days back in South Africa before the war.'

'Tell me.'

'It's no great secret. I did time. A couple of years inside. Stealing cars. I was just a kid and I've not stepped out of line since. Des Fenton found out. He'd taunt me with it, joking at first. Seeing how I'd react. Then he threatened to tell Pattie Moxon.'

'Or else what?'

'He didn't get the chance to tell me that. You see, Pat already knew. Nothing much gets past her. She couldn't care less, provided I kept my nose clean over here. All she cares about is whether riders win or lose. I'm a winner, Calloway. I'm one of her golden boys.'

'Not tonight you weren't.'

'We all have off nights.' He nodded towards the inner door. 'And hey, my night didn't turn out so bad.'

'I hope young Maureen feels the same way once she's sobered up. So why didn't Fenton push his luck?'

'Because I told him Pat knew about me and I also told him I'd tear him a new arsehole if I ever heard him mention it again. I had to give him a proper warning. He backed off. He was a coward. It wasn't Pat I was worried about anyway. It's that I was getting good press. A rider with good press gets good money. I couldn't afford for any old dirt on me spoiling that. You know what, Calloway? There's a cigarette card with my face on it. That buys you a lot in this game.'

'A cigarette card, eh? That's quite an accolade. You must be very proud.'

'Get out of it.' He snorted up a gobbet of phlegm and swallowed it. 'Do you buy this story that Fenton's death wasn't an accident?'

'Is that what people are saying?'

'The only person saying it is Pattie Moxon as far as I'm aware.'

The girl stepped back into the dressing room, fully dressed and her hair back into some semblance of style. She moved awkwardly towards the door, swaying a little on her heels and avoiding eye contact with the two men.

'Don't forget your autograph book,' Duiker said.

Calloway waited for the door to swing closed.

'So why is Pat Moxon suspicious?'

Duiker shrugged. 'Search me.'

'You've been with the team over two years. You must have some idea.'

Duiker stood up and stretched. Then he picked up the gin bottle and held it to the light, checking for any last drops. Disappointed, he tossed it onto the pile of soiled towels in the corner.

'Listen, do you know how easy it is to come off a bike in this game? How easy it is to hit another rider? We're doing seventy miles an hour around a dirt track the size of a cat's arsehole with one gear and no brakes. The only thing stopping us from sliding all the way from here to the shit house is our left fucking leg. Accidents happen, mate. Sometimes riders die. It's tragic, but it doesn't make it someone's fault.'

He flicked his cigarette onto the dressing room floor and

stubbed it out with his shoe.

'Pat just can't accept she's lost her prize pony.'

SIX

Ray Simpkins slammed a beaten-up toolbox on the workbench. He pulled a spanner from the tray.

'I do my own maintenance. Always have,' he said, as if responding to an unspoken criticism.

It was the morning after the mid-week fixture. Calloway had waited until Simpkins was alone in the stadium workshop and shown up uninvited. He watched Simpkins working on the skeletal JAP motorcycle, which was raised up on a wooden lift table.

'Don't trust the mechanics?'

'My bike. My life. Simple as that.'

He was about five foot eight and slim built. His face was thin with mean features. A sharp nose, narrow eyes, narrow lips. He had red-brown hair, thinning at the sides, which he Brylcreemed back without a parting. There were navy tattoos on his forearms and the kind of scars that a man who falls off motorcycles for a living tends to collect.

'Des Fenton looked after his own bike too, didn't he?'

Simpkins held the butt of a roll-up cigarette between his thumb and forefinger and drew hard on the damp end with compressed lips.

'That was his living. At least before speedway. Had a workshop under the arches down Deptford. Stands to reason he'd do his own work.'

He gripped the roll-up in his teeth and worked on the bike's rear wheel.

'He'd have the mechanics running round after him though. He was good at ordering people about. Lording it over them.'

'Ever lord it over you?'

Simpkins crouched behind the JAP, checking the wheel alignment by sight. 'Not likely.'

'Did the two of you get on?'

Simpkins shrugged. 'We were teammates.'

'That's not the same thing.'

'We were teammates, like I said. We didn't have much in common. He was flash and liked to get around. I keep myself to myself.'

He leaned back against the bench, blinked hard and stretched his neck muscles. The sinews tautened through pale white skin. He looked as if he could use more sleep.

Calloway stood in the workshop doorway and watched the rider work. By now word had gone round that Calloway was conducting his own investigation, so he was direct with his questions.

'What happened the night Fenton was killed?'

'Why d'you wanna know?'

'My stadium. My business.'

Simpkins sighed. His irritation showed. He turned towards Calloway and spat shreds of tobacco from the wet fag end onto the workshop floor. The workshop smelled of grease but it was tidy and well lit. Tools hung in orderly rows on pinboard along the far wall. Alfie Hale, the Bullets' chief mechanic, was a stickler for order. A true engineer. This was Alfie's place. With the shop to himself, Simpkins used it with an air of surly contempt. He tossed tools around noisily and dropped debris onto the floor. His locker door hung open. The bright pendant lighting illuminated a gallery of oil-smudged pinups. Simpkins liked a fuller figure. The adjacent locker had a broken lock, Calloway noted.

'I told Pat, like I told the association and the insurance, I got too close to his tail. He went into a skid, hit the rider in front and came off. Accidents like that happen all the time. This time someone died. That's all.'

Simpkins wiped his oily palms on a rag. He wore buff army overalls like the track crews, with the top half rolled down and tied at the waist, his torso covered by a vest. His chest was broad for a man his build and his arms were muscle-packed. He dropped the rag onto the bench.

'They say you hung on his tail the whole race.'

'What was I supposed to do, keep a polite distance? You don't know much about speedway, do you Mr Calloway?'

'It makes a lot of noise and sometimes people die. But maybe you could enlighten me on its finer points.'

Simpkins gripped a heavy-looking wrench and adjusted it. It gave him somewhere to look.

'When you're out there on the track, you don't think, not in the normal sense. You just go with it. We talk about tactics but really we just ride. When that tape goes up it's like throwing yourself off a cliff edge. Something inside you takes over. Sixty seconds later, the chequered flag goes up. Everyone cheers. It's instinct that keeps you going but by the time you've slowed up, it's just the blur of a memory.'

He turned to face Calloway, the heavy wrench hanging by his side, just like the chain in the hand of the cosh boy. He wore a similar expression too.

'You want to know why I clung onto his tail?' His tone smacked of provocation. 'I've got no fucking idea.'

'It must be difficult for you, knowing you killed a teammate.'

Calloway knew he was prodding at a raw nerve. He wanted a reaction.

'Difficult? How d'you think I felt riding alongside the hearse Saturday? Knowing his wife was in the car behind, looking at me.' He prodded his chest with an oil-stained finger. 'Me, Calloway. The rider that put her husband in the ground. How's that supposed to feel?'

'How well do you know Fenton's wife? Close were you?'

'What's that supposed to mean? I hardly knew her at all. He'd bring her to the club's annual dinner, that sort of thing. She never had much time for me and the feeling was mutual, seeing as you ask. I was too common for her, with her pearls and her semi-detached.'

'Probably makes it easier for you.'

'I might be common but I'm not callous.'

That's not how he looked to Calloway. The tensed lips, the narrowed eyes, the inability to look you in the eye unless it was to confront you. A hint of sneering resentment was constant in his manner.

'Did you see much of Fenton outside the track?'

Simpkins tossed the wrench back on the workbench. 'No more than the other lads. The usual drink in the members bar if we'd had a good night. I'm not one for socialising.'

'What are you one for?'

'I mind my own business.' He looked Calloway in the eye. It could have been a warning. Calloway ignored it.

'You and Fenton ever argue?'

'No. Why should we?'

'This is a tough old game, so I've heard. There's bound to be fallings out.'

'Well there wasn't between me and him. What are you getting at?'

'I have to write a report.'

'Why would me and Fenton arguing be in your report?'

'You said you didn't argue.'

'And we didn't.'

Calloway changed tack. 'What did you do before speedway?'

Simpkins seemed relieved by the diversion. 'Merchant navy, since I was fourteen. Started off shipping coal from Wandsworth to South Shields for the gas company. Then war broke out and one of my mates signed on for the convoys. I decided to go with him.'

He drew up phlegm and spat on the workshop floor. 'Worst decision of my life, looking back on it.'

'How come?'

Simpkins relaxed a little. He dropped the hard man act, but he didn't lose the surliness. That was ingrained.

'I was on a five-thousand tonner running between Liverpool and New York.'

He glanced over at the plus-size pinup on his locker door with a predatory sneer.

'I met a lot of American girls. Those Yank bints know how to put out, if you know what I mean. Then the Admiralty put the kibosh on that. Sent us to the Arctic, making runs to Murmansk. We had a pretty clear run for the first few crossings. Then the Kriegsmarine deployed more U-boats and started hunting in packs. We'd try evading them, zig-zagging you know, but we couldn't avoid them in the end. We were hit about fifty miles off the Norwegian coast. The starboard engine had started playing up so we'd stopped to fix it. We lost our escort because the fucking navy said they couldn't spare a corvette. Had to protect the convoy, they said. So we were on our own just floating there, like a turd in a toilet bowl. It wasn't long before a wolfpack found us. Put two bloody great holes in our hull. Once we started taking on water, that was it. It was all over so quick. No time to launch the lifeboats. Half a dozen of us made it clear on a Carley float.'

'How long were you adrift?'

'About three days. We were picked up by a German cruiser.'

'You were lucky then.'

'Was I? I spent the next four years in a prisoner of war camp.'

'Unlike the rest of your crew.'

Simpkins thought about this. He forced a smile like a sulking child who's been made to thank the host at a birthday party.

'Yeah. We were treated alright as it happens. But there's only so much football and cards you can play before you go stir crazy. It did my nut in.'

He started tinkering with the bike again.

'And after the war?'

'Drifted for a bit. Didn't want to see another ship, not from the inside anyway. Got work up the Surrey Docks.'

'How did you get into speedway?'

'I started coming here to watch, when the stadium opened up again after the war. I got talking to some lads in the pits and one thing led to another. They were short of younger riders at the start. There was no speedway after 1939 so the club was a bit on the old side. Bellman was nearly fifty even then. Pat gave me a tryout. I'd done a bit of riding during the war so I knew my way around a bike. I must have impressed her.'

‘Is there much motorcycling in the merchant navy?’

Simpkins shot Calloway a look. The hard man act was back. ‘I bought myself a bike in Liverpool, to use when I was on leave. Have you got enough for your report now?’

Calloway planted himself on a stool and lit up. ‘Almost. What do you know about the dosser that used to sleep under the stands? The one they called Joe Smoke.’

Simpkins thought too long about the question. He shuffled where he stood and busied himself with tools without using them. When he replied, he sounded like one of the Three Stooges playing the innocent.

‘Yeah, I remember him. That’s was a few months back. The last bloke who did your job slung him out.’

‘Did you ever speak to him?’

He shook his head with too much emphasis. ‘Why would I?’

‘Fenton used to talk to him. What was that about?’

Simpkins scoffed. ‘Fenton would talk to anyone if he thought there was some reflected glory in it. What’s this got to do with the accident?’

‘I’m reviewing security. We can’t have unauthorised personnel hanging around the stadium.’

‘’Spose not. And while we’re at it, I can’t have you hanging round here. I’ve got work to do if you don’t mind, Mr Calloway.’

Simpkins slammed tools around to make his point. Calloway backed off. He’d heard enough to know he wasn’t getting straight answers. He returned to his office. Wally Gurney, one of the pit crew, was there waiting. There was a toolbox on Calloway’s desk, like the one Simpkins had been lugging around but in better condition.

‘What’s this, Wally?’

‘Des Fenton’s tools. I dunno what to do with ’em. Not sure his wife will want ’em. Mr Hale said to bring ’em to you.’

‘Where did Des keep these?’

‘In his locker in the workshop. Only the door was bust and I was worried, well you know, light fingers.’

‘Do you have many light-fingered folk round here?’

Gurney looked sheepish. ‘One or two. They don’t mean

nothing by it. Just use what's there sometimes.'

'It's the same with scotch in the members bar.'

Gurney grinned through crooked yellow teeth embedded in his dull parchment face.

'When did you notice the locker door was bust?'

'This morning when I got in. I've been lugging this toolbox round with me since.'

'Who was around?'

'Just me and Rocket Ray. He always works on his bike Thursdays.'

'Was Ray there when you arrived?'

'Yeah.' Gurney hesitated. 'I reckon he was first in. Listen, I'm not saying anything. Just thought you better have Des's tools for safekeeping.'

Calloway had been in London long enough to know the code. Grassing was worse than thieving. Gurney's hesitation said as much.

'Good man, Wally. This stays between us.'

Gurney shuffled off, visibly relieved to be leaving the security boss's office.

Calloway sat behind the big metal desk and opened the toolbox. He removed the tools one by one and laid them on the desktop. It was a standard mechanic's toolkit. Good-quality tools by the looks of them but well used. He also removed several receipts and laid these flat on the table. He ran his hand over the bases of the expanding tool trays and pulled out stray nuts and bolts until only the butterfly nuts in each corner of the toolbox floor remained. There were three receipts. One for inner tubes, one for gaskets and one for two bottles of chemicals, acetic acid and ammonium thiosulphate. He put the first two receipts back in the box along with the tools and slipped the third into his jacket pocket.

There were files on his desk too that morning. Manila folders containing the Bullets' points tables for last two years plus the current season to date. He had requested them from Patricia Moxon and she must have sent a lad up to his office to drop them off. He lit a cigarette and turned the pages one by one.

In forty-seven the Bullets finished fifth out of seven in Division One. Last year they were National League champions. This was the title Moxon was so keen to defend. Calloway read down the club results for each fixture. The Bullets started last season with outstanding results, a run of unbroken wins and stellar points averages for the top riders. Things had wobbled badly during July and August but they had clawed back some of their form by the Autumn, in spite of noticeably poor performances by Simpkins and Riley. Bert Webber and Des Fenton had led an assault on Belle Vue in the last two fixtures of the season and clinched the trophy. There were photos of the team celebrating their victory, in dusty leathers with white teeth grinning through cinder-blackened faces. Fenton beamed, Webber sniggered, Billy Riley smiled like a self-conscious boy in his school photo. Ray Simpkins forced an uncomfortable smirk.

This season told a different story. The club hadn't won a single fixture. True there had been some strong individual rides, with Bert Webber a clear contender for the season's star man, but Moxon was right. What victories they enjoyed as individuals belied the team's performance.

Calloway took a wooden ruler from his desk drawer and read across the individual scores. He compared each rider's results with those of their team members. He looked especially at the performance of riders paired with each other in each heat. He pulled out the small black police notebook he carried in the inside pocket of his suit jacket and made notes. Names and numbers. He slipped the notebook back into his jacket alongside the receipt he'd taken from Fenton's toolkit.

There was a pattern in the numbers that needed an explanation.

SEVEN

Calloway slept in on Saturday. At least he tried to. Sleep didn't come easily to him and the sounds of the house starting its day were especially intrusive this morning. He lay in bed gazing at the ceiling of his single basement room, imagining the domestic chaos in the flat above, where the young war widow Mrs Cobb was failing to keep breakfast on the table. Children's feet thumped on bare boards as the widow's two young boys fled from the scolding their mother struggled to make heard. A minute before, there had been the sound of breaking crockery, a reflex smack, leading to tears then rebellion. Calloway wished the noise would stop. At the same time the pang of regret for the family life he'd been denied pained him.

The Cobb family chaos clashed with the comforting sounds of morning. Milk bottles jangled on the stone steps above the door to his basement. Women in the street exchanged cheery good mornings and reported on their plans for the day. Bicycle bells rang as boys left home for their half-day Saturday shifts. But echoes of his past did their best to drown out the pleasing normality of the present and on mornings like these he relied on a routine of distractions. He abandoned his lie-in and took a gramophone record from the collection he kept on a makeshift shelf on the chimney breast. The plain card record sleeve felt soft with damp. There was only one dry wall in the room and that was reserved for a curtained off wardrobe and rail on which he hung his clothes. An old army habit. Dry clothes trumped everything, in this case even a prized collection of heavy shellac discs.

A gentle Mahler symphony rose from the inadequate speaker

of the portable HMV radiogram he had guarded zealously in the final weeks of war. He lit the single gas ring to boil water for coffee and tied the cord tightly on his old wool dressing gown before venturing into the light of morning to retrieve the newspaper carelessly dropped into the basement well outside his door. He was glad to have his own entrance. It spared him too many encounters with the neighbours in his building. The overwrought Mrs Cobb and her fatherless children, the painted Miss Logan whose past career in the theatre was as dubious as her frequent gentleman callers, and the O'Sheas, who Calloway knew only through the obscenities they exchanged during booming, unrestrained arguments that were the talk of his street.

The music soothed him as he took in the news from the paper. The signing of the Treaty of London had formalised the Council of Europe, which was to sit in Strasbourg. Winston Churchill claimed it as a victory in his campaign for European integration. Calloway had seen firsthand the consequences of a divided Europe and wished this new council every success. He trusted Mr Churchill's judgement, but as a nation we weren't taking any chances. A separate item confirmed peacetime conscription would be introduced under the National Service Act, with the first lads getting their call-up papers in two years' time. Pattie Moxon better make the most of her novices before they swap their leathers for battledress, Calloway thought. What with that and the signing of the North Atlantic Treaty the previous month, it felt to Calloway like we were back on a war footing. Victory in Europe seemed more like a temporary ceasefire while the powers that be swapped a couple of the sides around.

He filled a basin with warm water from the kettle and strip-washed over the stone sink. He shaved in the small mirror which hung on a nail over the sink, focusing on the task in hand and avoiding his own eye, as was his habit. Then he dressed in one of the clean shirts Mrs Cobb had brought down the previous afternoon. She topped up her meagre widow's pension by taking in laundry, a menial service but more savoury Calloway suspected than one Miss Logan provided to callers.

After breakfasting late on boiled eggs, he left the house. Bert

Webber, who in the past few days had become a benign source of information on the Bullets' movements, had told him Billy Riley habitually took a pint with his sister in the snug of the Four Bells at opening time on a Saturday. Calloway wanted a chance encounter. Riley's failure to show as an outrider at Fenton's funeral a week ago needed an explanation. So too did the numbers in the Bullets' points tables.

Calloway ordered a pint of Courage and settled himself in the public bar with a view of the snug. He was the sole customer save for three Caribbeans in bus company uniform who sat in silence at a table in the corner. The barman, Wilf, with whom Calloway was on nodding terms from his occasional post-work drink, gazed at the three men, transfixed. 'What d'you reckon then?' he said.

'About what?'

Wilf, a diminutive elf of a man with a jutting chin and oversized ears, nodded to the three men in the corner.

'The darkies. They've started coming here from the bus garage. Been working the night busses. I wasn't sure whether to serve 'em at first, but they don't cause no trouble. What d'you reckon?'

Calloway had read about the Jamaicans and the Trinidadians who had arrived at Tilbury the previous year on the Windrush. Like Wilf the barman, these were the first he'd seen in the neighbourhood.

'I reckon you've got three new customers, Wilf. And someone to drive your busses.'

The pub started to fill up, as workers clocked off from their half-day shifts. They trailed the smell of sweat and industry as they trooped to the bar shouting orders to Wilf and the barmaid, Dinah, a robust and red-faced woman with arms like a docker. The customers eyed the three Caribbeans with suspicion as they entered. Some muttered quiet words, but were soon distracted by their first pint of the weekend.

Calloway ordered a second pint and nodded along with Wilf's narrow world views with a grudging interest. It passed the time, but wasn't the type of company he'd choose. Mind you, he was no longer sure what type of company he would have preferred. His life after the army had become increasingly solitary as the years progressed.

The chat in the pub turned to Millwall and became more heated as drinks were downed. True to Bert Webber's word, Calloway saw Billy Riley slip through the far door and into the snug, accompanied by a pale but pretty girl. Riley bought a pint for himself and a milk stout for his sister and the pair settled themselves at a table. They conversed in an unhurried, almost bored way, but they looked content. They were comfortable in each other's presence and looked pleased to be away from the throng that had filled the public bar. Calloway let them enjoy their drink for now. He would wait for Riley to order a second round before approaching him.

As he waited, the far door opened and a well-dressed woman walked into the crowded bar. Heads turned, cutting animated conversations short. Calloway recognised her from the funeral. Des Fenton's widow. Her outward suburban respectability drew looks from the regular clientele, whose common masculinity made the well-dressed woman more out of place than the three black bus drivers who drank quietly in the corner. Ignoring the looks, and a few coarse mutterings, the widow slipped into the snug. From his vantage point at the bar, Calloway watched her approach Riley, who excused himself to his sister and followed the widow back into the public bar. She looked agitated, verging on combative. As they spoke, Riley appeared uncomfortable. He responded calmly but tensions were clearly rising. Calloway wished he could hear their words, but the hubbub in the bar made that impossible. The widow pointed a finger threateningly at the boy rider, who responded plaintively. The drinkers nearest the pair watched the escalating argument. Riley turned to leave but the widow grabbed him by the arm and pulled him back. She mouthed at him in anger and he responded in kind before wrenching himself from her grasp and heading for the snug, slamming the door behind him. Fenton's widow stood for a moment, weighing up whether to follow him. Instead she pushed her way through the cluster of onlookers and left.

Calloway slid his big frame off the bar stool and nudged his way through the crowded room to where the scene had taken place.

'What was all that about?' he asked a two of the drinkers who'd been closest to the scene.

'Search me, chief, but the lady wasn't happy,' said one. The other chipped in, 'Said he owed her money.'

His mate snickered.

'I'd give her money.'

'Save yourself the trouble, Spike. Her sort don't put out. Too busy polishing their silverware.'

The man called Spike winked. 'I'd give her something to polish.'

Calloway left them to their ribaldry. He'd spent his army career keeping out of conversations like that. It had earned him the nickname Reverend for a while, until the stripes on his arm earned him more respect, to his face at least.

He crossed the public bar into the snug.

'Hallo Billy. It thought I saw you come in.'

Riley was surprised by the sudden appearance of the security boss.

'Didn't know you drank in here, Mr Calloway.'

'You know how it is, Billy. I found myself at a loose end.'

He was a good-looking man of twenty or twenty-one Calloway estimated, with dark, well-cut hair swept back from his face. His hairline formed a sharp V on his forehead pointing downwards to two dark, deep-set eyes. With a slender nose and strong, chiselled jawline, his classic good looks were a stark contrast to the back-street rakishness of the better-looking Bullets.

Riley was courteous. 'This is my sister Doreen, Mr Calloway.'

The young women smiled awkwardly. 'I only come here on Saturdays,' she offered, as if making the point that she didn't frequent pubs habitually.

'Nice quiet spot in here. Away from the rabble.'

'It's the only time I get to see Billy these days. The rest of the time its speedway, speedway, speedway.'

'Not easy having a star in the family, eh Billy? I expect you get stopped all the time. Even in here.'

Riley smiled politely but looked uncomfortable. Calloway couldn't tell whether his sister knew about the altercation with Fenton's widow. Doreen answered for him.

'I can't say I'm not proud, Mr Calloway. But I'd be lying if I said I wasn't scared for him when he's out there on the track.

'Dangerous business.'

Doreen sipped her stout. Its head was as pale as her freckled face. 'Seeing that poor Mrs Fenton just now. How she must be feeling.'

Riley looked at Calloway like he owed him an explanation. 'Des's wife popped in here, as it happens.'

Calloway played dumb. 'Joined you for a drink?'

'No, just wanted to say thank you. I sent flowers.'

It hadn't looked like gratitude to Calloway.

'Billy couldn't make it to the funeral. He wasn't well.'

Riley shrugged in acknowledgement. There was an awkward silence. Calloway broke it. He had noticed Doreen had laid a coloured team scarf on top of her coat, which was folded on the seat beside her. But it wasn't the familiar red and black of the Bermondsey club.

'Not a Bullets fan then?' he said pointing at the scarf.

'That's the Rattlesnakes. Billy is a club patron. We're going along to support them later, aren't we Bill?'

Riley explained and Calloway feigned interest.

'You should come along,' said Doreen. 'They're away to Peckham Stars at East Surrey Grove. It's just up the road. Starts at two thirty but they're always late.'

Riley cut in, too quickly Calloway thought. 'I'm sure Mr Calloway has better things to do Doreen.'

Calloway made a play of thinking about the offer for a moment. He clapped Riley on the back. 'Like I said, I'm at a loose end today. I think I might just come along.'

Doreen seemed pleased. Her brother managed a courteous smile, which looked like it hurt.

East Surrey Grove was a street in name only. The Blitz had replaced its familiar built forms with a boulevard of rubble and dust. Calloway found it by following the elated screams of a thousand children huddling five deep around an oval of track, marked by a border of single bricks laid end to end. The stadium was no more than a picket fence and a hundred yards of bunting, with a blackboard and chalk to keep score. This was cycle speedway, a bomb-site sport improvised in the rubble. Riders lined up at a makeshift start line of knicker elastic stretched between white painted posts. They wore skid lids and race jackets like their motorised counterparts, with white socks turned over the tops of long boots. They shielded their faces from the dust with bandanas worn bandit style over their nose and mouth. Their bikes were stripped bare, with long cow-horn handlebars and no brakes.

Billy Riley was at the start line. Young fans pushed and shoved to get a closer look. Pure joy beamed from their undernourished faces. They chanted 'Riley, Riley, he's our man, if he can't beat them no one can.' Riley signed autographs and ruffled hair. With his lightweight American clothes and tortoise shell sunglasses, he was a bomb-site idol. He made his way down the line of riders from both teams, slapping backs and mouthing words of encouragement. Riley's sister watched him from the sidelines, with the same look of pride she'd shown in the Four Bells. Next to her a small boy with knotted hair stood on a broken chair to chalk Peckham Stars and Rotherhithe Rattlesnakes on the blackboard in his best block capitals. He left blanks for the scores. The boy jumped down and handed Riley the flag. As guest of honour he would start the first race. The riders lunged forward at the drop of the flag. They pedalled hard and took the corners with abandon, their worn down boots churning up dust. They were older than the fans, lanky teens, lean as whippets. Supporters cheered them as they passed with the shrill voices of children. Their excitement lit up the drab colosseum of street backs and half-demolished homes.

Doreen spotted Calloway across the track and waved. She tugged her brother's sleeve and gestured towards the big man who stood incongruously amid a sea of short trousers, scuffed knees and hand-knitted jerseys. Riley didn't seem to share his sister's enthusiasm at Calloway's arrival.

The heats continued in quick succession. Small boys and girls mobbed the winners each time they passed the homemade checkered flag. Riley walked around the poorly roped off perimeter of the track and shook hands with the handful of adults present. They seemed to know him. Calloway took this as his cue. He crossed the track between heats.

'Quite a show you put on here, Billy.'

Riley hid behind his courteousness. 'I can't claim the credit but I support where I can. It's good to see these kids enjoying themselves. Even if it's in the middle of all this mess.' He gestured to the barely discernible remains of the street, with its jagged half walls and overrunning buddleia. 'Mind you,' he chuckled, 'they probably did half this damage themselves. What the Germans didn't destroy, this lot would have taken care of after. Smashing up abandoned homes was the local sport, before the skid kids started up. That's why I encourage 'em. These kids need something.'

He pointed to one of the riders.

'See the tall kiddy with the Rattlesnakes bib? His house took a direct hit with his mum and sister still in it. Six weeks later his old man went down on a tanker crossing the Atlantic. He lives four to a room in a Corporation flat with his auntie now. She doesn't want him, poor sod. But he's wanted here you see. These kids love him. Listen to 'em cheer.'

It was true. They cheered like war had just ended. They lined the tacky little circuit five deep to get a better view of the lanky teen riders. They chanted like Bullets fans chanted, minus self-consciousness. Pure joy mixed with bomb-site mischief. The young ones screamed like pint-sized banshees. The older ones snuck behind the rubble to smoke cadged cigarettes. Urchins' paradise.

Riley watched keenly, doing his best to ignore Calloway. He hoped he would leave. Calloway spoke above the din.

'Why did Irene Fenton come looking for you in the Four Bells, Billy?'

'I told you at the pub. To thank me for the flowers I sent.'

'Long way to go for that, don't you think?'

'Said she was passing.'

'She didn't look grateful from where I was sitting.'

The realisation Calloway had watched the scene spread over Riley's face. The look didn't suit him. Calloway pressed the point. 'In fact she looked quite upset with you, Billy. Everything alright between you two?'

'She was upset, sure. Still grieving I s'pose.'

'Perhaps she was upset you didn't show at her husband's funeral.'

'I was ill.'

'I thought you might have toughed it out, Fenton being a teammate. Were you and him close?'

'We got on.'

'Not good mates though?'

'Not particularly.'

'Des Fenton didn't seem to have many mates, from what I've heard. Why do you think that was?'

'He was popular enough.'

'With the fans, sure. Not too many pals among the Bullets though.'

'S'pose not.'

'I've yet to hear good word about him, in fact. I hear he liked to have the upper hand. Did he have the upper hand over you, Billy?'

Riley flushed red. Anger tugged at his good looks for a few seconds before he composed himself. 'He was a cocky sod. Yeah, he liked to have the upper hand. I s'pose that's what stardom does to some people. It never bothered me.'

The boy with the knotted hair rubbed the scores out with the sleeve of his jumper and chalked up new ones. Riley's sister whispered in his ear. He repeated the process this time with the scores added correctly.

'You a gambling man, Billy?'

Riley screwed up his face. 'What's that got to do with anything?'

'Ever had a wager with Fenton?'

'Why would I do that?'

'Friendly rivalry. A bit of fun.'

'Not me.'

'Ever borrow money off him?'

The anger flashed again and this time it won. Riley snapped. 'I don't need to borrow from anyone. I do alright.'

Calloway gave no ground. 'It's just that I heard you owed his missus.'

'You heard wrong. What's with all the questions? This isn't about track security.'

'I have to make a report.'

'Yeah, well, you're barking up the wrong tree. There was nothing between me and Des Fenton and nothing between me and his missus.'

'Whose tree should I bark up, Billy? You see there are rumours.'

Riley nodded. 'I've heard. I dunno what's got into Pat. An accident's an accident. But she ain't letting go. It's not like her.'

'What is like her?'

'Hard as nails that one. Whenever one of us gets bust up she's all "there, there, now get over it and get back on that track". This time she's scared of her own shadow.'

'She's lost her star rider. She's bound to be out of sorts.'

'Star rider?' He sniffed. 'Star turn, more like. He was flash off the track. Nothing special on it.'

Calloway had found a raw nerve. He prodded it. 'He saw you off more than once. You've not been able to touch him since the middle of last season.'

Calloway had studied the results from Moxon's file. This was one of the stories the numbers told.

'Just tactics, that's all.'

'Oh come on, Billy. You were Pattie's rising star this time last year. You mean to say your loss of form is tactical. Get away. You're as hungry for glory as the best of 'em. You just can't cut it anymore.'

Riley turned on him. 'Oh, so you're suddenly an expert.'

'I can read the scores.'

'Yeah? Well read 'em to someone who gives a damn. What d'you come here for anyway? You're not interested in all this.'

'Your sister invited me, remember.'

'Too polite for her own good.'

'She's a nice girl. And you're a good man, Billy, I can tell. But you're not being straight with me.'

'Aren't I?' Riley looked him in the eye. His defences were up. 'Well that's too bad.'

A cheer went up from the dirt track. The tiny Rattlesnakes fans huddled around their star rider as he raised a cheap and tarnished trophy above his head. He was tall and confident, a diamond in the rough. This could have been Riley a few years back, Calloway thought. But unlike Riley, this kiddy had nothing holding him back.

EIGHT

Saturday. Greyhound night. Calloway watched the track-side bookmakers setting up. The main gates were not yet open and the stadium was quiet, save for the shouts of staff and the barking of excitable dogs.

The bookies set up easels for their chalkboards, hung their cash bags and fastened their decorative nameplates on top. One of them fumbled and dropped a butterfly nut, which bounced along the concrete landing at Calloway's feet. He bent to pick it up, turned it over in his fingers and flicked it into the air, catching it in his palm like a tossed coin. He handed it to the bookie who nodded his thanks.

'Thanks, chief. Tricky little buggers.'

Butterfly nuts weren't permanent fixings, it occurred to Calloway. So why were there four of them fastening the base of Des Fenton's toolbox?

He walked to his office, locked the door behind him and lifted the toolbox from the floor beside the filing cabinet and onto the desk. He pulled out the tools in handfuls and dumped them on the desktop. Then he twisted off the butterfly nuts one by one. He took one of Fenton's screwdrivers and used it to lever up the metal panel from the base. Between the panel and the floor of the box was a void an inch deep. It concealed a small marbled notebook and a brown envelope, unsealed and bound by an elastic band. He snapped off the band and removed the contents of the envelope. There were bank notes to the value of four hundred fifty pounds. He placed these on the desk. He then opened the notebook. There were handwritten notes on the first few pages, with three names at the top: Ron Sampson, Jack Ladbroke, Frank Belper. Calloway didn't recognise the names. They weren't Bullets men. The name Ron Sampson was underlined. Beneath the names was a list:

1943
Marlag Westertimke/Amerhsam
Genshagen, Berlin
Totenkopf/Belper
1944
Hildesheim
Dresden/Division Nordland
Lodz
Chelmno
1945
Lubeck

On the two pages that followed there was a ledger of dates and payments, starting in July 1948. The last entry was four days before Fenton's accident. Calloway looked down the column and made a rough calculation. The numbers added up to the four hundred fifty pounds in the envelope.

He put the cash back into the envelope, fastened it with the elastic band, and locked it in his safe. He took the notebook and dropped it into his desk drawer, then refastened the false panel to the base of the toolbox, replaced the tools and slid the box into the footwell of the desk where it was concealed from view.

They were testing the tannoy when he returned to the track. The sound of the announcer bounced off the concrete of the empty stands. The bookies nodded as he passed.

'All good, Mr Calloway?' shouted one.

'All good,' he replied, joining in the weekly ritual, which endorsed the track-side bookmakers' legitimacy.

The Saturday night crowd was gathering at the turnstiles. A tall and severe-looking commissionaire watched them from the top of the steps, which led up to the circuit.

'They're an excitable lot tonight, Mr Calloway. Millwall won at home. We can expect high spirits.'

'The high-spirited ones will still be in the Royal Archer, Les. This lot are the early birds. The Dandelion & Burdock brigade.'

Les Birkett acknowledged with a nod but failed to crack a smile. Good humour wasn't his strong point, but his dourness carried an authority which suited his role. At six foot one with a heavy build, the big ex-infantryman's presence was enough to dissuade the most high-spirited punters from any roughhousing. And the North African and Italian campaign ribbons sewn to his uniform testified to the hard-earned toughness of the former regimental sergeant-major.

Small talk wasn't Birkett's strong point either, so Calloway asked him a question outright.

'How well did you know Des Fenton, Les?'

He answered obliquely. 'Fenton? Bad business that accident.'

Birkett surveyed the line of punters at the turnstiles, his head swivelling on his sinuous neck like a gun turret seeking a target. He prided himself on his ability to spot trouble.

'Know him? Nope. No more than the rest of 'em.'

'Did he serve in the last shout?'

Calloway knew from past conversations that the one thing Les Birkett could be relied upon to know about a man was his war record.

'Gunner. Royal Artillery.'

'Overseas?'

'Manned an ack-ack battery at Dover. Cushy billet. Probably went home for his tea.'

'Dover, eh? Long way from Berlin.'

The old Regimental Sergeant Major looked quizzical. 'Sir?'

'Don't worry, Les. Thinking aloud.'

Calloway left Birkett to surveil the crowd, adding a brisk, 'As you were, sar'nt-major' as he left. This got him a smile.

They were training novices at the track the following Monday. Calloway watched from the stands as a pro rider demonstrated cornering, hitting full speed on the straight and letting momentum carry the bike into the bends. The novices paid close attention to the moves as the rider glided over the cinder with the aplomb of a veteran. Even with his scant interest in speedway, Calloway was impressed. He couldn't tell which

Ranger this was. Their face was masked by a white silk scarf leaving only a slit between scarf and helmet. After two more laps the pro jerked the bike into an abrupt skid, stopping inches short of the novices.

The rider was Pat Moxon. She removed her helmet, tugged down the white scarf and raked her fingers across her tied-back hair. She leaned on the handlebars to address the would-be Bullets.

'You've got to get out of those corners fast, which means backing off the throttle to control wheel spin. If you hit that dirt with too much gas your bike will take off. Wait until you feel the grip of the track, then you give it a handful. Got it?'

The novices nodded like dutiful children.

'Right.' Moxon pointed to the slack jawed lad at the front. 'You. Show me what you've learned.'

She dismounted the bike and handed it to him. 'I've warmed the seat for you.'

The novices sniggered. The boy flushed red.

'Four laps then pass the bike to the next lad. Off you go.'

Moxon crossed the track to where Calloway stood leaning on the stand rails. She swaggered, swinging the helmet by its strap and tugging down the zip of the heavy black Lewis Leathers jacket.

'I know what you're thinking.'

'Go on.'

'It's no job for a lady.'

'It's no job for anyone with an ounce of sense.'

She leaned on the rail next to him, watching the young riders practice. 'I decided I'd better start training them myself. With Des gone, Clanger Bellman out of action and Billy Riley riding like a wet weekend, I've got to breed some new talent.'

'How long have you been riding?'

'That's like asking a lady her age. Let's just say long enough.'

'Why don't you race?'

She laughed. The laugh said he was being naive. 'Women don't race, not anymore. They banned us in 1930. Speedway's a man's game, Mr Calloway, like everything else in this life. Unless it involves screaming kids or dirty dishes.'

She smiled at him, as if forgiving him his naivety, and offered him a cigarette from her monogrammed case. He accepted.

'Why did they ban women?'

'Modesty, Mr Calloway. A female rider took a fall at Wembley and broke her collar bone. The St John's Ambulance had to cut some of her clothes away by the track to treat her. The crowd got an eyeful. This was deemed most improper by the men that controlled the sport. That's all it took for them to ban us all.'

She hollered instructions across the track to one of the novice riders. She shook her head, unimpressed by his performance.

'What did you do then?' asked Calloway.

'After the ban, I took to demonstration riding. Showing off between races. A novelty act, or as good as. Pretty Pattie Moxon, Queen of the Dirt Track.'

'I bet there's a cigarette card with your face on it.'

She dropped the smile. 'Oh, there's more than that, believe me.'

She drew hard on the cigarette and exhaled slowly. 'So Calloway, you've had your week. What have you found out for me?'

'Nothing to suggest Fenton's accident was anything other than that.'

Moxon looked displeased with the answer. She fingered the string of pearls she wore under the leathers.

'So nothing up with the team?'

'Oh there's something up with the team. Plenty, I would say. But nobody's killed anyone yet. Not deliberately.'

The novice was demonstrating the wrong way to corner. His machine bucked beneath him, throwing him into a heap on the cinders. Moxon shouted words of encouragement, then turned to Calloway.

'So tell me.'

'They're a cagey lot for the most part. And you're right, something's got them spooked, some of them at least. Fenton wasn't well liked and there's no love lost between him and his teammates.'

'Why?'

'He was flash, manipulative, liked to have the upper hand. Qualities not conducive to camaraderie in my experience.'

He sensed this struck a chord but she was trying hard not to show it. 'That could apply to anyone in this business. Anything specific?'

'Two things. Fenton and Simpkins fell out over a tramp that used to doss down under the stands. I don't know why but Simpkins is denying it. And I saw Billy Riley in an argument with Fenton's widow, over money apparently, although he won't admit it. Any of this make any sense to you?'

Moxon shook her head.

'There's one more thing. Fenton had built a false bottom into the toolbox he kept in the workshop. He'd hidden four hundred fifty pounds cash and a notebook showing payments adding up to the same amount. The last entry was just before his accident.'

'Was he running a book?'

'Unlikely. The payments were for regular amounts. And there was a list of dates and place names which I can't figure out. Dates during the war, towns in Germany and Poland, and German military units by the looks of them.'

Calloway knew this for sure. As a member of an airborne field security section during the war, he had a good working knowledge of enemy formations. The Totenkopf Division was notorious. He had no recollection of a Division Nordland.

'Did Fenton spend any time in Germany after the war?'

Moxon considered this. 'Speedway started up in Germany quite soon after the war. Mainly forces clubs setting up impromptu dirt tracks. Then the locals joined in. It's big over there now. I know Fenton's racing career pretty well. He never raced in Germany. He was with the Bullets all through the thirties, then did his best not to get called up.'

'He was a gunner according to Les Birkett, but didn't make it past Dover. Had a good war by all accounts.'

'Sounds like Des. Probably bribed someone to keep it that way. He was always a bit on the wide side. He got back into racing pretty soon after speedway started up again. He's been with the Bullets since. Never ridden in Germany. Nor Poland for that matter. They only started speedway again last year. What do you make of it, this notebook and the money?'

'Not a lot right now. But I know someone who might make sense of the dates and names on that list. I can give them a call.'

'Do that,' she said, then added, 'I know you said you'd work for gratis for a week. I need to start paying you now.'

'I won't take your money.'

She looked him up and down. 'It won't make you any less the man, Reg. Or do you have trouble with lady bosses?'

'Can't say I've had one. I'll treat this as a stadium matter. My wages will cover the time.'

'Suit yourself. But allow me one thing?'

'Like what?'

Moxon glanced back to the track. Another novice had the bike this time and was showing promise. She seemed to approve.

'I have a party invitation this evening, in the West End. I'm short of a date. You seem like you could do with a night out. Care to join me?'

His instinct was to pass. But for the first time in a long while he ignored it. She was right. He'd spent too many nights with his records, polishing his shoes and listening to groans of Miss Logan and her gentleman callers. And he hated to admit that Patricia Moxon had started to appeal to a side of him that he'd buried away since the war.

'I'd hate to think of you at a party on your own. Not that I imagine you would be for very long.'

'A compliment? So there is a gentleman under there. I knew that parade ground manner was just an act.'

'Don't be so sure.'

She gave him an address in Mayfair. There was definitely money in speedway.

'Call for me at eight. And leave that demob suit at home.'

'I think there's still a blazer in the back of my wardrobe.'

Probably damp, it occurred to him.

'Fine. Now run along and polish your buttons. And make that phone call. Whatever's going on, I want it cleared up.'

He clicked his heels. 'Yes, ma'am.'

Calloway strode back to his office with a lightness in his step. Part of him felt buoyed by her invitation. Another part of him already regretted accepting it.

It took Calloway an hour of calls to various government departments before he tracked down Sammy Mackay. They had stayed in touch for a while after Calloway left the army, but not to the extent that he had a current address or phone number. He had outsmarted a succession of officious telephonists with half-truths and a confident tone, until he was put through to an extension within one of Whitehall's less-public departments.

'Reggie? Good God man, how did you find me here?'

Calloway recognised the familiar tone of the gentrified Scot. 'Peasant cunning, Sammy.'

'Oh yes. It makes up for lack of breeding.'

'That and grammar schools.'

Mackay scoffed. 'Not so sure about that. What are you up to?'

'Stadium security officer.'

Through the earpiece Calloway heard the sound of a match striking, followed by the smack of lips sucking on a pipe, drawing in air.

'You work at a dog track?'

'Dogs and motorbikes.'

'Oh dear me.'

'Didn't have much choice, Sammy.'

The line crackled as Mackay paused.

'I suppose not. That Nuremberg business was a damn shame. You only did what any of us would have done.'

'Yes, but without the benefit of breeding.'

'I suppose class does have its advantages. Christ, I sound like a Bolshevik.'

Calloway heard breathy chuckling. Mackay was the jovial type, on the surface at least. Beneath the joviality was a ruthless operator.

'No one's going to mistake you for a red, Sammy.'

'That's a comfort, especially in this place, although I suspect I wouldn't be alone.'

'Careful, Sammy, they might be listening.'

'Very possibly,' he whispered, then chuckled some more. 'To what do I owe the honour?'

'I'm after a favour.'

'That's not like you. You were always the stoic, self-reliant type. Well, fire away.'

'I need you to make sense of something for me. Something up your street. Relating to the last shout. Got a pencil?'

'The departmental budget can just about stretch to one. I use it to clean out my pipe.'

Calloway read out the dates, place names and the two German divisions from the marbled notebook. He heard the tapping of a pipe on teeth through the earpiece.

'Not meaning much to me so far, old man.'

'How about Ron Sampson, Jack Ladbroke and Frank Belper? They may relate to someone named Amersham.'

Mackay was silent for a moment. His tone had changed. The joviality was gone. 'Still not ringing any bells, I'm afraid. Do you know their units or ranks?' He paused for a second. 'Or where they might be now?'

'No, but I'm guessing you have access to the registry. Dig around for me, will you.'

'I remember when I used to give a you the orders. Should I ask what this is about?'

'Probably nothing. Call it a character reference.'

'For a greyhound?'

'Got it in one, Sammy.'

Calloway gave Mackay his contact details and hung up.

NINE

Patricia Moxon's mansion block was the kind people with interesting lives lived in. Double-fronted modernism, with curved bays, metal windows and travertine steps up to a grand entrance flanked by miniature conifers. The street number was carved large into stone relief in Broadway lettering. It said movie-star chic a little too loudly. Calloway imagined her neighbours were single folk of private means who dined out, threw parties and crashed borrowed sports cars. It wasn't the kind of place for a coal miner's son with a soon-forgotten battlefield commission and a blazer from Alkit. But the blazer, crisp white shirt and Tootal cravat earned him a respectful welcome from the building's doorman, who addressed him as sir and directed him to Moxon's apartment via the small cage lift.

She answered the door with a cocktail cigarette in one hand and a crystal tumbler of what looked like gin in the other.

'Reggie. Just the man I need.'

She turned her back to him. Her cocktail dress was unfastened, revealing a band of soft white flesh pushed upwards over a tightly cinched bra strap.

'Zip me up, will you love. My nails are still drying.'

He leant into her, eased up the zip and fastened the clasp, the backs of his fingers glancing over the smooth nape of her neck. He smelled the same fragrance she wore at Fenton's funeral.

'Fix yourself a drink. It's gin or gin.'

She drew on the gold filter of her cigarette waved it towards a bar in the corner of the room.

'Gin is fine,' he said.

'Ice in the bucket. The big pineapple. Tacky, I know. A gift from GI friend who was posted to Hawaii.'

She disappeared into what he assumed was the bedroom.

The pineapple was alone in its tackiness. The rest of the flat was decorated in an understated style. Clean, modern, quite masculine, he thought. Like a Hollywood director's office, at least the way they're depicted in films, but with overstuffed bookshelves. He looked over the book spines. Modern editions of American novelists, Steinbeck, Faulkner, some Chandler. Virginia Woolf, Hardy, the Brontës. Some art books.

The gramophone told a different story. Caribbean rhythms and sexual double-entendres. Calloway had never heard this music.

He shouted towards the open bedroom door. 'What the hell are you listening to?'

'Do you like it? It's Lord Kitchener.'

She sounded distracted. He imagined her in front of the dressing table mirror applying lipstick.

'The field marshal?'

'The calypsonian.'

'It's obscene.'

'All in the mind, darling. He's a wonderful man. I was introduced to him in a club in Soho. Straight off the boat. A friend and I spent a fascinating weekend in Notting Hill tracking down his records. I learned to smoke reefers. Isn't he wonderful?'

'I prefer your books.'

'Help yourself. But don't expect to spend the night in reading.'

She appeared at the door. 'Well, will I do?'

She wore an expensive-looking black cocktail dress, with a plunging neckline and tightly cinched waist. The dress clung in a way that held his attention too long. She noticed him stare but stood in the doorway regardless, hands on her hips, fingers with newly painted nails smoothing over wrinkles in the shiny fabric.

'You look very nice,' was all he could manage.

She shot him an exaggerated scowl. 'Damned by faint praise. For that you can fix me another drink.'

He poured two gins and failing to find a mixer, dropped ice

into the straight liquor.

'There's a bottle of angostura behind the bar. Splash in a couple of drops for me, will you?'

'Did you learn that in the navy?'

'What, pink gin? No, but I've drunk with a few sailors in my time.'

She joined him on the angular, chromium-framed sofa, and slid across the polished leather to within a foot of him. The sofa was a triumph of style over comfort. She turned to him and chinked glasses.

'We're officially off duty. You can stop calling me ma'am now.'

'Are you Pat or Patricia?'

'Oh strictly Pat. Pattie sounds patronising and Patricia sounds like my mother. I'm calling you Reggie by the way.'

'As you wish.'

She swivelled sideways, crossed one leg over the other and swung her foot in time with the music. Calloway was about to make conversation when the doorbell rang. Pat didn't seem surprised. She patted him on the knee.

'I'll only be a moment.'

She crossed the room and walked down the apartment's generous hallway to open the door. The caller was a middle-aged man with watery blue eyes and a drinker's nose. A whisky man. He wore a tweed suit with brown suede brogues. The suit had been expensive and was now well-worn in. His tie may have been regimental. Calloway couldn't tell from where he sat. His greying hair was inches too long, swept back over his ears and tickling his shirt collar. He held a small package in his puffy hand.

Moxon took the package without looking. She took something from a handbag on the hall stand and passed it to the caller in return. She exchanged a few words, which he acknowledged with a knowing nod, before closing the door. She called back to Calloway.

'Amuse yourself for a moment, will you.'

Then she disappeared into a room off the hallway, which he judged from its chequered tiling was a bathroom. She emerged a few minutes later straightening her skirt. She strode down the hallway and rejoined him.

'Now, about this do,' she said, draping an arm over the back of the sofa and leaning into him. Her foot tapped to the calypso rhythm, double time.

'We're going to Dennis Robinson's place in Belgravia. An old friend. He's a talent scout for Centurion Pictures. Recruits girls for their charm school. He swans around like a minor aristocrat but don't be fooled. His father was a bus driver from Maidstone. Still can't hold a knife and fork properly. He always throws a party for his latest cohort of starlets. A sort of passing out parade when they've stopped dropping their aitches and mastered the rudiments of RP.'

'Sounds like a cattle market.'

'Don't knock it, Calloway. Plenty of single young ladies with all the attributes.'

She sounded excitable. She prodded his bicep through the sleeve of his blazer. 'We might even find you a girl.'

'I thought I was your date. Or have I been demoted to chaperone already?'

'We're both free spirits, Reggie. Let's see what the night brings.'

She crossed room to the gramophone swaying a little in time to the rhythm.

'I'll change this for something that won't offend your puritanical streak. What do you fancy?'

'I like the German romantic composers.'

She screwed up her face like she'd smelled a bad smell.

'Dreary. We'll have jazz. Anyone who doesn't like Duke Ellington isn't allowed in here. It's the door policy.'

'Do you get many through the door here?'

She shot him a hurt look, then winked. 'That's my business. Let's talk about you.'

She spoke quickly and was now far more animated than when he'd first arrived. 'You like the German romantic composers and you're interested in books. You're not married when you really should be by now and you walk around like smiling is on the ration and you've run out of coupons. You don't have any friends that I'm aware of and you don't like letting people inside that hard shell sewn into the lining of the demob suit you're still wearing. So I'm guessing you're suffering either a bad war or a broken heart.'

'Try both and you might just be getting somewhere.'

She knew how to read a man. He changed the subject. 'You've an impressive library.'

She seemed pleased he had noticed. 'Thanks. I'd never read a book in my life until I was thirty.'

'What happened then?'

'The war came and I joined the ATS.'

'You got an army education?'

He had the Army Education Service to thank for filling the gaps in his own half-baked schooling.

She tutted. 'You think I had time for that? I was a dispatch rider. Working all hours. They billeted me with a pale young thing who had dropped out of Cambridge to fight the fascists. I'd be so full of adrenaline after riding all day I used to read her cast-off novels to get to sleep. I got a taste for it and haven't stopped since.'

'Does she still lend you her books?'

He doubted it, if the affluence her flat reflected was anything to go by.

She shook her head and took a sip of the pink gin.

'One night during the blackout she swerved to avoid a policeman on a bicycle. Wrapped her bike around a lamppost and died on the spot. It sounds silly when you tell it like that.'

'There's nothing silly about war. Just blood, death and bad dreams.'

She stubbed out the lipstick-stained filter of the cocktail cigarette in a large metal ashtray and with her other hand waved the tumbler in circular motions.

'Fix us both one for the road. We'll see if we can't get through to the real Reggie Calloway before the evening's out. Have you eaten?'

He shook his head as he mixed the drinks.

'Good. We'll meet Dennis at a Greek restaurant in Dean

Street. His crowd always goes there before a party. I prefer Italian food but there's not been much of that around since the riots drove the Eyeties out. Italy's loss has been the Cypriots' gain.'

She talked as though he'd never eaten out in his life. He suppressed rising irritation.

'Will any of the Bullets be there tonight?'

'Only the house-trained ones, which narrows it down a bit. O'Donnell's bound to be there. Try keeping that one away. Brains in his trousers, or pants as he'd call them. Maybe Billy Riley. He scrubs up well and likes a night up West, although he's been a bit of a stop-at-home of late.'

'Something not right with that one.'

She nodded agreement.

'He does have a haunted look these days. But let's not talk shop. This is your night out.'

He passed her the drink and their fingers touched for second.

'Reckon I can allow myself just the one.'

He flagged them a cab to Soho, which wove its way through Kodachrome streets. London was alight again, now the ban on electric signs had been lifted. The city shone its colours into the night with pent-up defiance. He paid the cab fare and held the door for Pat as they entered the restaurant. The noise inside could compete with the stadium on speedway night. Excitable diners showing off and waiters playing up their foreign accents at full volume. Pat spotted Dennis Robinson and his crowd. They sat at the biggest table in the place, with a loud red gingham tablecloth and candles stuck into wine bottles.

'Pattie darling! Queen of the cinders! Come sit next to me.'

Robinson shouted across the room, shoving a male guest over and pulling up another chair in between them. He was late thirties and tanned, with hair cut en-brosse. He wore a broad-shouldered dog tooth sports jacket, the long collar of his primrose yellow shirt splayed California style revealing a hairless chest.

'And who's this big brute?' He looked Calloway up and down. 'Sit yourself over there fella, next to the delightful creature that's doing her best not to fall out of that rather common dress.'

A cutesy-faced girl with scarlet lips and dyed-blond hair that was lacquered brittle screwed up her face and threw a breadstick at Robinson. He caught it like an arrow through the heart and mugged death throes.

They ordered and ate. The food was good. Calloway joined in the chat. The girl next to him was a charm school graduate with leading lady ambitions. If her acting was as fake as her conversation, she wasn't going far. Pat kept catching his eye from across the table. He couldn't tell if she felt sorry for him or was worried he'd show her up in front of her cheap show business friends. Either way, her concern irritated him.

By eleven they'd left. Pat had picked up the bill he noticed and Robinson seemed happy to let her. She'd refused Calloway's own offer to contribute for both of them. The group divided up and took cabs to Belgravia. Robinson had the first two floors of a Nash-style townhouse. It was grandiose, scuffed and sparsely furnished. The flat was already full and the music cranked high. Calloway got the impression this was a place where bright things came and went. Pat had been right about the Centurion girls. Fresh from the charm school mint, all hips and bust, they talked self-consciously with professional smiles to men of varying ages. Some of the girls danced with eager young men, heavily Brylcreemed in sports jackets and twills. The girls danced like they were auditioning.

Pat took his arm and paraded him around the room making introductions. She called the people friends although he doubted they were. A shrill wolf whistle cut through the noise. O'Donnell gave Moxon and Calloway a film star's wave. He was leaning in a window alcove, his arm locked around the waist of one of Centurion Pictures' hopefuls. Of all the girls in the room, she looked like the one most likely. She had Betty Grable's legs, Jayne Mansfield's curves and Jean Harlow's hair, which tumbled down in platinum waves from her hairline to her cleavage. Her full lips looked pumped to bursting, like the rest of her. The nostrils of her turned-up nose flared slightly into an almost predatory sneer.

'O'Donnell's a fast worker.'

Moxon looked in the direction of the rider and the starlet.

'And an ambitious one too. That bombshell is Robinson's squeeze. They have quite an open relationship by all accounts, so old Six Gun might get lucky. But she usually aims higher when she plays away. Not sure my boy's speedway-star credentials will cut it.'

Other men in the room looked on enviously as O'Donnell tightened his grip on the bombshell's waist. A sharp suited and skinny young man with jet black hair and eyebrows that gave him a look of permanent mischief crossed over to them, trying his best to cut in. Calloway couldn't hear his patter but it looked slick and well-practiced. It made the bombshell laugh. She pinched his cheek. The skinny young man swooned. O'Donnell looked irritated and steered the girl towards the adjoining room. The young man made a quick about turn, swiped a wine bottle from the window sill and glided over to a lone brunette who was flicking disinterestedly through the host's record collection. He started up his patter again.

An hour passed. Calloway made small talk with a bunch of people he'd be in no hurry to meet again. Pat excused herself and Calloway poured himself another drink. A strong arm slapped him on the back.

'How's that investigation of yours, Calloway?'

It was O'Donnell. He had lost the blonde and sounded drunk.

'Detected any foul play?' He slurred the last two words in a bad English accent.

'I'm off duty,' said Calloway.

He waved the bottle at the big American. 'Can you fit any more in there?'

O'Donnell thrust his empty glass forward. 'Fire away.'

Calloway poured neat scotch. O'Donnell belched and raised his glass.

'Salute.' He necked the scotch in one. 'Spider tells me you were airborne.'

'Spider?'

'Webber. All you Limeys have nicknames, right? What's yours?'

'Cab.'

O'Donnell whooped. 'As in Calloway? Yeah!'

The drunken American started to sing:

'The jim, jam, jump on the jumpin' jive,

'Makes you like your eggs on the Jersey side,

'Hep hep!

'You like your eggs on the Jersey side Calloway?'

'If I knew what it meant. I was intelligence, attached to the 6th Airborne Division.'

'Intelligence, that figures. I was with the 82nd. All the way from Normandy to the Rhine.'

'I'm surprised we didn't run into one another.'

'It was a big war.'

O'Donnell swayed but not in time to the music. He clapped a hand on Calloway's shoulder and pointed across the room with the other.

'Mr intelligence guy, you should talk to that one over there. She could tell you a few things about the late James Fenton.'

It was the young woman who had appeared at the funeral. She was dancing with a round and ruddy-faced man in his fifties. He was dancing as close as his gut would allow. Beads of sweat popped on his forehead as he pawed at her with pudgy fingers. In the absence of moonlight and romance, she managed a polite grimace.

'Who is she?'

O'Donnell shrugged.

'I dunno, but I've seen her around with Fenton in places where his wife was strangely absent. Places like nightclubs. They seemed to get along.'

O'Donnell spied a face in the crowd, a female face. He knocked back the scotch and slurred, 'So long Cab' in Calloway's direction. He left humming the Jumpin' Jive.

Calloway crossed the room towards the dancing couple.

He tapped the fat man on the shoulder. 'Mind if I cut in?'

The fat man looked put out. 'Actually I do, squire. Push off, will you.'

Calloway gripped the man's fleshy arm. He squeezed so it hurt. 'But it's the gentleman's excuse me.'

He used a tone that ruled out any argument. The fat man complied, mouthing to himself as he retreated rubbing his arm. Calloway took the woman's hand and led her. He danced well, with a lightness of step which belied his big frame. The woman looked relieved to be shot of the fat man, but uncertain what to make of Calloway's intrusion.

'Forgive me, but you looked like you needed a change of partner.'

'Did I? And how would you know that?'

'He didn't seem like your type.'

'Really? So what is my type?'

'Oh I don't know, someone a bit more flash. A racing driver perhaps.'

He spun her under his arm and she responded, a half beat behind the rhythm. She was dancing under the influence.

'Or a speedway rider.'

She pulled back from him but he was too strong. He spun her again and felt her stiffen.

Her eyes narrowed and her lips tensed. 'Who the hell are you?'

'I should have introduced myself. My name's Calloway. I work at Bermondsey stadium. I saw you at Des Fenton's funeral.'

'Yes, I was there,' she said, as if responding to an accusation. Then she composed herself, as much as the drink would allow. She was remembering her charm school training. 'I'm Liz. Liz Francis.'

'Did you know Fenton well, Liz?'

'Des and I were friends.'

'Good friends?'

She started laughing. She was drunk and past caring.

'If you mean lovers, then yes. Oh don't look so shocked. We were going to get married.'

'I'm not shocked, but Mrs Fenton might have been.'

She let out a bored-sounding hiss. 'I couldn't care less.'

'Did Des care?'

'He was going to leave her. He promised me he would. He kept putting it off but he promised he would tell her that night. The night of the accident.' She laughed again. It was a dark laugh.

'So that was us finished.'

Calloway watched her retreat into the thoughts in her head. She was full of anger, grief and cheap wine. It wasn't a good look on a would-be starlet.

'How long had you and Fenton been going together?'

'It would have been two years next month. He was putting money aside for a flat. For the two of us. We were going to live up West.'

'Putting money aside? Fenton earned more in a month than most of us earn in a year. He could have paid for a flat without putting anything aside.'

'He wanted to keep the money separate from her. She had her claws into everything he earned. For her pearls and her nice house in the suburbs. He said he had a sideline that she didn't know about.'

Calloway thought of the cash in Fenton's toolbox.

'What kind of sideline?'

'He wouldn't tell me. Told me not to worry about it. Just said he had it all arranged.'

The tempo of the music had slowed. They danced closer and she leaned into him, rolling carelessly to the rhythm. He could feel fatigue and resignation in her limp body.

'How did you and Fenton meet?'

She looked up at him as if awoken from sleep. 'Through Dennis Robinson. I was at the Centurion charm school. Dennis invited me to a party here. Pat Moxon brought Des and some of the Bullets along. I didn't know he was married at first. Then I saw a photo of him and Irene in Speedway Gazette. Silly I know but I'd started buying the speedway press to read about Des. I must sound like a schoolgirl.'

'You're not much older.'

Her face hardened. 'I'm old enough.'

'So you're an actress?'

She shook her head and looked disdainfully around the room at the charm school hopefuls. 'I dropped out of the Centurion school. Convinced myself I was going to be the wife of a speedway star. Des saw I was alright, financially. And I've done some modelling.'

Calloway could imagine and he didn't imagine couture. 'Did Des get you into that?'

She shook her head, as if the suggestion was improper. 'Dennis fixed me up. Some glamour work.'

'Very tasteful I'm sure. So what now?' He nodded towards the other partygoers. 'Are you looking for the next Des Fenton?'

He felt her body tense as they danced. 'You're quite insensitive, did you know that?'

'It has been said.'

The needle zipped across the record that was playing and the music stopped abruptly. Robinson appeared and shoved his face between Calloway and Liz as they danced.

'Showtime, lovelies. Follow me if you would.'

He still looked immaculate but up close he smelled of neat liquor and too much cologne.

Calloway looked at Liz and shrugged. She seemed to know the form and led him into the hallway towards the stairs. Other revellers were heading in the same direction. They looked furtive. Robinson whispered in new ears along the way and the group grew, Pied-Piper style, to a dozen or so. At the piper's behest, they crammed into a darkened bedroom. It was void of furniture, save for some tea chests of what Calloway assumed were the occupant's still unpacked belongings. With a flourish of showmanship, Robinson drew back a dusty Persian rug. Beneath it, a hole of around three inches in diameter had been bored in the heavy floorboards. The people lined up and took turns in crouching down and peering into the room below. One of them was Billy Riley. They stifled giggles and exchanged salacious looks, except for Riley who looked awkward. It was Calloway and the girl's turn. She passed, rolling her eyes as though she'd seen this show before. Calloway peered into the circle of light. The skinny young man with the mischievous eyebrows was crouched on a bare mattress in the room below. This time he was naked save for his socks. Beneath him, the brunette he'd been making a play for earlier was doing a poor impression of rapture. Someone in the audience kicked a tea chest. There was shushing and laughing out loud. The skinny man looked up, in the direction of the noise. He spotted the spy hole and shook his fist at the ceiling.

'Robinson, you utter bastard!' he cried, as the brunette scrabbled on the floor for her clothes.

There was more laughing. It was the greatest show on earth, judging by the look on Robinson's satisfied face. Calloway pushed his way out of the room. Riley was ahead of him. Liz Francis had disappeared.

Calloway followed Riley as he made his way downstairs and into the dimly lit hallway. Riley stopped to talk to a young man about his age. He was a similar height and build, but better bred from the look of him. He had the sandy hair and healthy complexion of privilege. They knew each other but not well, Calloway sensed from the exchange. Calloway couldn't hear them over the sound of the gramophone, which had started up again, but their conversation had the air of conspiracy. The pair made to leave a moment later. Calloway found his trench coat in the pile that had formed beneath the bulging mass of garments on the hall stand and followed them, but at a distance.

TEN

It had rained and the streets gleamed mirror-black under the streetlights. Riley and the sandy-haired man flagged a lone taxi as it passed. Calloway hung back in a doorway and strained to hear their destination. They were too far away to be audible above the tick-tick of the taxi's diesel engine. Calloway watched as the twin red dots of the cab's tail-lights faded to a faint glow in the distance. Then a second taxi approached. Calloway stepped into its path and flagged it with a raised hand as the tail-lights of Riley's cab turned into a side street. He barked instruction to the driver to catch it up and follow.

The streets were empty. It was past two am. It made the tail easier. The cars passed through Victoria, around the back of the palace and along Piccadilly. They circled the statue of Eros and headed down Shaftesbury Avenue until the cab in front cut left into Wardour Street. It snaked its way through a tangle of Soho side streets before pulling up next to a darkened passageway. Calloway let his taxi continue for thirty yards before stopping. He paid the driver who took his cash with a knowing look. This was Soho after hours. Men didn't come here at this time of night for the Greek food.

Calloway double timed back to the passageway. En route he was propositioned from a darkened doorway by a woman in a fur that was as tired looking as her painted face. She smelled of Ma Griffe. He waved her off. Her scent followed him to the corner of the passageway.

The passage was poorly lit and empty, but there was music coming from a doorway set back a little with a spy hole. There was a small printed card pinned to the doorframe. It promised "all night gaiety in London's bohemian rendezvous". Beside it was a bell push. Calloway pressed it. He heard scratching at the spy hole then a bolt slid back. The door opened slowly, casting a swathe of red hued light onto the wet paving. A large man appeared in silhouette, his features emerging as Calloway's eyes adjusted to the light. He was big and foreign, Maltese most likely, who looked like his sole job at the establishment was to keep people like Calloway out.

'Are you a member?' the big doorman asked, with a heavy accent. More a warning than a question. Calloway mugged embarrassment. It bought him time to peer into the club over the shoulders of the goon. Through the reddened glow he could see a small and busy room, cheaply decorated like a Bedouin tent, with oriental throws over old sofas, low tables and lamps with red shades. The clientele were mostly men, draped over the sofas or leaning against the room's roughly painted wooden pillars, talking enthusiastically. There were a handful of women too but, Calloway noticed, they had size-nine feet and Adam's apples. Billy Riley and his friend were ordering drinks at a makeshift bar. Riley looked more relaxed than he had at Robinson's party. The other young man seemed to know everyone.

'I think I've made a mistake,' said Calloway, playing up the embarrassment.

The doorman gave a grudging nod and closed the door. Calloway heard the bolt slide back.

A voice from behind him gave him a start. He caught the smell of Ma Griffe again.

'Not your cup of tea then luvvie?'

Calloway shook his head.

'Are you sure you don't want some company? It's a filthy night.'

He did want company, but not this kind. The company he craved could never be. It left an empty place in his heart, which grew colder as the years wore on. Nothing the whore could offer could fill the gap, no matter how extensive her repertoire. He declined her invitation and started to walk. He'd reached the Embankment before it occurred to him to hail a taxi. It was the time of night for refusing fares south of the river but Calloway wasn't having it. He made this known when he barked his address, like an NCO to an errant private. The cabbie took the hint. It earned him a decent tip when they pulled up in Calloway's street a half hour later.

The basement room was as dismal as he'd left it. Perhaps he needed oriental throws and some red lamps. He should ask Miss Logan for advice. He laughed to himself as he sat on the narrow, creaking cot and pulled off his brogues. He was too alert for sleep. He poured himself a slug of London gin from the bottle he kept behind a curtain on a shelf under his old stone sink. The burn of the gin on his throat was comforting. He switched on the portable gramophone and chose a record while its valves warmed up. The heated valves smelled like burning dust. It brought back memories. Two peopled intertwined in the sanctuary of a requisitioned villa in Germany, soothed by gentle music away from the carnage of war. He poured a second shot of gin, necked it in one go and drifted off, fully clothed. The violin concerto soothed him even now, but the soothing was bittersweet.

He woke around eight. He'd slept poorly. It was cold in the basement and his damp clothes clung to him. He lit the old oil heater. It emitted a thick chemical smell, but it took the chill off the cold spring morning. He made tea and drank it black and sweet. Then he changed into fresh clothes, hanging the old set on the rail behind the wardrobe curtain. He heard the telephone in the main hallway above ring and Mrs Cobb's footsteps cross her ground floor room and enter the hallway. Small feet followed her excited by the sound of the shrill telephone bell. He heard her shout 'hush' to her boys before answering. Then the front door opened and feet padded down the stone steps outside and into the basement well. Calloway opened the door, anticipating the knock.

'It's the stadium, Mr Calloway. They say they need to speak to you urgently.'

The two boys clung to her legs and peered nosily into

Calloway's room. He thanked her and followed the three of them back up the steps and into the hall. One of the boys stuck out his tongue. The other scowled.

'Calloway, it's Pat.'

She sounded tense. 'Morning, ma'am.'

'You can cut that out. Look, you need get yourself down here. There's been a break in.'

'Where?'

'The workshop lockers, my office, your office.'

'What's been taken?'

'I can't tell. The safes look to be untouched. But they've gone through the filing cabinets and desk drawers.'

'Have you called the police?'

'They're on their way. You need to be here when they arrive.'

'I'll be there in fifteen minutes.'

'Good.' She hesitated a moment. 'Calloway, I'd be grateful if you didn't mention the matter you and I have been looking into.'

'They could be connected.'

'They could equally be nothing of the sort. I don't want to set hares running. It's not good for the club.'

He thought about telling her where to go. He was head of security, not some cloak-and-dagger stooge.

'Understood, ma'am.'

He drove to the stadium and parked in Canal Road. A police Wolseley was already parked in front of the main gate. Les Birkett was there too. He looked uncomfortable on seeing Calloway arrive.

'They're waiting in your office sir.'

'Give me the gen on the break in first, Les.'

Birkett cleared his throat. 'Well, they must have come in overnight sir, They cut the fence.'

'Who was on nights?'

'Archie Hook sir. He...'

The old soldier hesitated.

'Spit it out, Les. I don't have time for tall tales.'

'I found him asleep, sir. Under the stands. Had an empty bottle of single malt in his hand.'

'Single malt? We must be paying him too much.'

'I've read the riot act to him sir.'

Calloway's anger rose. He let it show. 'You'll do more than that, Birkett. Get rid of him.'

'Sir?'

'A night watchman needs to watch. At night. He drank himself unconscious and slept. Get rid of him.'

Birkett frowned, his camaraderie fighting with his sense of duty.

'As you wish, sir.'

Birkett turned on his heels. Calloway called him back. 'Archie was with you in Italy wasn't he?'

'Anzio, sir. A right old mess that was. Ted machine guns had us pinned down on the beach.'

'Ted?'

'The Tedeschi, sir. It's what the Eyeties called the Jerries. We sort of picked it up along the way. Archie was caught in a shell hole with three pals. The other three copped it. Those MG42s took their heads clean off their shoulders. Archie's not been right since. He takes a drink to calm his nerves, sir.'

Calloway sighed and let the anger subside. He was too soft by half.

'Let him down gently, Les. I'll find him four weeks' pay and put in a good word for him for his next job. But I want him out, alright?'

'Yes, sir. There's one other thing sir.'

'What?'

'It wasn't Archie's bottle, sir. He said he found it in his hut, next to the kettle and the tea. I think someone knew he liked a drink and left it for him.'

'To knock him out deliberately?'

'It seemed to have had the desired effect.'

'Let's keep that to ourselves for now. Go and check the bar, the workshops and Miss Moxon's office. See if anything's been taken.'

Birkett turned on his heels and left, swinging his arms in parade ground time.

There were two uniformed officers in Calloway's office. One looked like he ate the other one's dinner habitually. The big one had sergeant's stripes. The skinny one looked straight out of Hendon. His uniform fitted him like a hand-me-down. Calloway took stock. The place had been turned over. The door lock had been jemmied and the doorframe was splintered. Drawers hung open. Files lay splayed on the lino. The safe was closed and looked untouched. He introduced himself as security officer.

'Security officer, eh?' the sergeant chuckled. 'Not your day then is it, sir?'

Calloway bristled. 'When I want a laughing policeman I'll go to the end of the pier.'

This drew a smirk from the boy copper. The cheer drained from his sergeant's face. 'Alright sir, alright. Now perhaps you can tell me what's been taken.'

Calloway pulled out his handkerchief and used it to open the safe. He felt stupid doing it, like something Basil Rathbone would do in one of those preposterous films. The weekend's turnstile and bar takings had been banked the day before and the petty cash was still there. So was the cash from Fenton's toolbox. He checked the filing cabinet. The marbled notebook was gone. It was the only thing missing. He turned to the police.

'Nothing missing as far as I can see. They probably heard the night watchman coming and scarpered. Kids, most likely. We get a few in here from time to time looking for things to nick.'

'Nothing gone form the safe?'

Calloway shook his head. Les Birkett appeared at the door. He gave a respectful nod on seeing the uniforms, before giving the laughing policeman and his malnourished apprentice the once over. The look on Birkett's face said they didn't pass muster.

'The bar's still locked, sir. The workshop's been broken into but Hale says nothing's been taken. Just one of the lockers prised open, but that was empty he says.'

Calloway rolled his eyes so the policeman could see him. 'This isn't a professional job, sergeant. More like vandalism. I think we can stand you boys down. I certainly don't think we should waste CID's time on a bit of high jinks like this. The stadium can deal with it.'

Birkett looked unsure. The sergeant looked relieved. He had one less thing to do. Calloway waited until the police had left before quizzing Birkett on the details.

'Which locker was broken into?'

'Des Fenton's. Nothing taken though. There was nothing to take. Mr Hale had already had it cleared.'

'I know. That's Fenton's toolbox there,' said Calloway nodding to the upturned box on the floor. 'How about Pat's office?'

'The door's been jemmied and it looks like Juno Beach on D plus one, but she says everything's still there.'

'A couple of chancers most likely. Ghoulish souvenir hunters looking for a piece of Fenton memorabilia. We'll get the doors and the fence patched up.'

'What about the whisky bottle sir?'

'I reckon Archie has a secret admirer. I'm not convinced it's connected to the break in.'

Birkett didn't buy this but Calloway was security officer. He was happy to let the buck stop with him.

'Right you are, sir,' he said, then hesitated. 'Do you still want me to give Archie his cards?'

Calloway sat on the edge of his desk and pulled out his cigarette case. He lit one and drew on it hard. 'Give him a final warning. But no second chances, Les.'

Birkett smiled, relieved.

'Thank you, sir.' He turned to leave. 'Oh, Miss Moxon has asked to see you in her office.'

Moxon's office was in the same state as Calloway's. She sat behind her desk, which was strewn with papers from rifled files. The lino told a similar story. Framed photos of Bullets' line-ups through the years had been pulled from the walls, their glass lying in splinters on the floor.

'Some date you proved to be.' She blew cigarette smoke his way. 'Last time I looked you were all over that little blonde piece.'

'I thought we were free spirits.'

'It certainly seems that way,' she snorted, righting an upturned ashtray and stubbing her cigarette out hard.

'She was Fenton's mistress,' said Calloway.

She raised her eyebrows. 'Available then.'

He shrugged this off. 'Fenton was planning to leave his wife. He was putting money aside for a flat. He had a sideline apparently. Something he kept from Irene. I don't know what.'

'That might explain the cash you found.'

He nodded.

'And the notebook that went missing in last night's break in. Seems like this was the only thing that did.'

She looked concerned. 'Did you share that with the police?'

'You told me not to. I sent them away. Blamed it on vandals.'

She leaned back in the chair. She looked tired. 'So I can rely on you for something at least. So what next?'

'I'm going to follow up the Joe Smoke angle. That connects Fenton and Simpkins somehow.'

For now he was keeping Billy Riley and the all-night gaiety at London's bohemian rendezvous out of the picture.

'Do that. Take off for a day. But hurry it up will you. You've had your week and we're none the wiser.'

He clicked his heels. 'Understood, ma'am.'

'Stop it. Call when you've got something to tell me.'

He acknowledged her with a half-hearted salute.

'Oh and Reg.' Her tone had softened.

'Ma'am?'

She held his eye for a few seconds too long. 'Thank you. I do appreciate your help you know.'

He turned to leave. 'Keep working on that Pat. You might just end up sounding sincere.'

ELEVEN

Carrington House was a sanctuary for single men who were down on their luck. A big brick fortress with a hundred tiny windows, it reminded Calloway of a military prison. He caught the smell of cabbage and carbolic as an earnest-looking man in his forties greeted him with a tolerant smile, introducing himself as the manager of the hostel. He had the demeanour of a disgraced clergyman. Calloway explained that he was trying to trace a rough sleeper. He described Joe Smoke and his scar. The manager's nostrils flared like he smelled something worse than cabbage.

'A vagrant? I'm not sure why you've come here.'

'I thought this was a spike.'

The manager recoiled. 'It certainly is not. This is a gentlemen's hostel. We provide clean and decent lodgings for working men. Quite respectable and not all of them labourers.' He puffed out his pigeon chest with an awkward pride. 'Some of our residents are from the clerkly classes.'

Calloway had already taken a dislike to him.

'That's not what they say round here.'

'People can be very judgemental,' he said, meaning people like Calloway. 'What's your interest in this gentleman?'

'We believe he may be an army deserter.'

'Are you with the army?'

'Field security.'

The best lies were the half lies based on a version of the truth.

'I see.' He seemed satisfied with the answer, to Calloway's relief.

'It's possible this man was looking for accommodation last

summer.'

The manger considered this with the air of a man who really had better things to do. 'It's true that vagrants do come here looking for a bed or a hot meal. We can accommodate some. It all depends on...' he grappled for words becoming of the manager of respectable lodgings '...their state of mind. We have to think of the welfare of our residents.'

'So if they look mad or dangerous you turn them away?'

'A rather indelicate way of putting it, but yes.'

'And when they're turned away, where do they end up?'

'Bomb sites and abandoned buildings most likely. That's the harsh reality. And London has plenty of both these days.' He hesitated for a moment and thought some more. 'Actually I do remember the man you describe. That scar is hard to forget. He was very confused. He didn't make a lot of sense and his behaviour was unsettling. We couldn't help him here. We're not that sort of establishment.'

'Unsettling how?'

'He was rambling and incoherent. Fragments of memories mostly. Some moments of lucidity.'

'Did he say anything lucid when you turned him away?'

The manager took umbrage. 'Look, we're not equipped to deal with men in his condition. It's tragic I appreciate. Men like him need help and it's just not there for them a lot of the time. But we can't help everyone. Carrington House isn't a place for men like him. Our guests are hard-working, capable men in need of a helping hand. Your vagrant was way beyond our capabilities.'

'I appreciate that, but any thoughts you may have would be of tremendous help.'

'He was a deserter you say? Well that would make sense. I remember he talked about the marshes. There is a place, you see. I know it only by reputation.'

He described it and gave Calloway directions. It was an hour's drive at least. Calloway took Pat Moxon at her word and set aside the rest of the afternoon. He drove south east along the A2. London gave way to cheap suburbia before hitting Kent, not the Garden of England part. This Kent was a mess of gravel pits and quarries and scrubby fields with scrubbier livestock. The place was held together with rusting barbed wire and corrugated iron, with uninviting roadhouses for light relief. Following the hostel manager's directions, he turned north before Dartford and headed for the river. From there he navigated by instinct. If there had ever been signposts here then they had not been replaced after their removal during the war, under a plan to fox the enemy based on the assumption the German army couldn't read a map.

Short haul trucks spilling aggregates terrorised the narrowing roads. The surrounding terrain was barren and soggy, the air smelled of dust and chemicals. A cold spring sun was going down behind him. It lit up a string of abandoned coastal defences, which peeked from the overgrown marshland. Thank God we'd never had to rely on them, Calloway thought. He'd seen the Atlantic Wall the Germans had built in France. The Germans had built well. They had slave workers to do it. We had built pillboxes with all the defensive capabilities of a public convenience.

The road petered out, ending at a rotting five-bar gate, which gave way to a raised track through the open marsh. He cut the engine, took the torch from the glove compartment and left the car. He walked along the track towards the river, grey and cold in the distance. There was a brittle silence, broken only by the swish of the breeze through the reeds and the steam whistles of cargo vessels navigating the estuary. As the sun sunk lower in the sky behind him, the way ahead was turning to grey.

He had walked a quarter mile before he saw the first camp, an elaborate bivouac which had expanded over time, made of heavy canvass, crates and salvaged iron sheeting. Its owner peered through the half light at him over the smoke of a small camp fire. He wore a filthy greatcoat over layers of clothing. His face was hard and weather worn.

Suspicion flickered in his eyes before the opportunism kicked in. 'Got an oily?'

A roll-up already hung from his cracked lips. Calloway pulled three cigarettes from his case. The man held his hand out as if this was payment due to him and slipped them into the greatcoat pocket.

'What do you want?' he wheezed.

'What makes you think I want anything?'

'You're not here for the view. You police?'

'Not police. I'm looking for a friend.'

'No friends here.'

He drew up a gobbet of phlegm and spat into the embers.

'I'm looking for an old army pal. He dropped out of sight. I want to see him again.'

The man looked wary. 'So you say.'

'My friend has a scar on his face, a big scar, shaped like a fork of lightning. He was sleeping rough in London then came out here seven or eight months ago.'

He cocked an eye, sensing another opportunity. 'An army pal, eh? Got any more of those smokes?'

Calloway handed out another three cigarettes from his case. The man in the greatcoat pocketed them with the others.

'Mad Carew,' he said.

'What's that mean?'

'We call him Mad Carew. After the rhyme.'

He stared out over the estuary and began to recite, like a drunken music hall act with an audience of one.

'There's a one-eyed yellow idol
'To the north of Kathmandu;
'There's a little marble cross below the town;
'And a broken-hearted woman
'Tends the grave of "Mad" Carew,
'While the yellow god for ever gazes down.'

He gave a small bow from where he squatted and said, 'You won't get much sense out of him. Speaks in tongues half the time.'

'So he camps out here?'

'Camps? He's a gentlemen of property.'

He pointed with a blackened finger towards a squat concrete cube just visible through the reeds.

'You see that pillbox? That's Mad Carew's castle.'

He laughed to himself until the laughter turned to coughing.

The embers hissed with another gobbet of phlegm. Calloway continued down the sodden path. His shoes were soaked by now and the turn-ups of his suit trousers felt wet against his ankles. Eyes followed him as he walked, all with the same look of suspicion. Some had shelters like the one he'd just seen, others just simple bivouacs. The hostel manager had described it as a colony. Deserters had hidden out in the remote marshland during the war. Some had stayed, making homes among the abandoned defences. He'd counted half a dozen colonists before reaching the pillbox.

Up close he could see it was brick built with a concrete slab roof a foot thick. There were rifle loops on all sides and an aperture for a door on the landward wall. Discarded tins, bottles and the detritus of a sorry existence littered the doorway. Flies buzzed around him as he approached. Then he caught the stench. Something he'd not smelled since the war, when he'd smelled it far too often.

By now the light was all but gone. He lit the torch and took cautious steps through the doorway on crouched legs. Joe Smoke had been dead at least a week. Calloway had seen enough corpses to know. Flies darted in and out of his mouth, which hung open as though singing his own eulogy. His eyes stared at the underside of the concrete from his scarred and soot-blackened face, which was stiff from advanced rigor mortis. The concrete roof was heaven's foot-thick defence against an unwanted spirit. Joe's soul was consigned to an eternity in the North Kent marshes, hanging like fog over the stinking estuary mud. His dead hand clutched a half-drunk bottle of meths as if in celebration of the fact.

The stench was overpowering. Calloway choked back the urge to wretch. With his torch in one hand he rifled through the vagrant's few possessions. A tobacco tin, an empty and rusting paraffin lamp, soiled blankets and some dog-eared pornography. He opened up the dead man's greatcoat. The stench of the bloated corpse grew more intense. He shone the beam of the torch along the body. There was a deep poacher's pocket sewn to the inside of the rough wool fabric of the coat. He slid in his free hand and withdrew a book. It was the photo album Webber had described.

Calloway backed away from the corpse, ducked through the doorway and gasped down the damp mashland air. Setting the album on the remains of a brick outer wall, he shone the torch on it and turned the pages. A dozen pages in he found perhaps twenty small three-by-five prints. They were the kind of photos army buddies took, but it wasn't the army he'd expected.

TWELVE

It was past nine when he returned to his basement room. He poured a slug of gin and settled himself at the undersized drop-leaf table, which served as his desk and dining table. He set the photograph album on the table. The green sugar paper leaves were damp from successive winters spent in makeshift shelters. The pages tore as Calloway turned them.

The photos showed the same two men. The first few pages were cheery shots of comrades in arms, in bars, with girls, or sightseeing in unfamiliar towns. The backdrops were European, Central or Eastern. Images of military mobilisation followed, the two comrades posing on the tailgates of trucks or from the windows of railway carriages. The final two pages showed scenes only possible once war has desensitised its participants. Trophy shots, posing with their human prey like big game hunters. Rifles on hips, boots on the bodies of their kill, smiling for the camera. Civilians hanging from trees, nooses cinched beneath contorted gargoyle faces, with the two pals pointing, grinning or mocking the still-warm dead. And in every photo the they wore the same uniforms, which Calloway knew well. They were Waffen SS.

The photographs were water stained an indistinct, but some were clear enough for him to make out the insignia worn by the two men. The SS runes on their collar patches and death's head cap badges were clear enough. The cuff titles were typical of Waffen SS units although their script was illegible in the photos. It was the right-hand collar tab that Calloway couldn't make out. Three heraldic lions stacked vertically against a black background. Unit recognition had been part of his job as a sergeant in the Intelligence Corps and he could spot most units from the manuals he had committed to memory. But he'd never seen the three lions insignia before.

He turned the pages again from the beginning and this time read each of the handwritten captions. Though the ink had smudged, he recognised place names and dates from the notebook he'd found in Fenton's toolbox. Three photos were missing from the final page of the album, with only the small black photo corners and captions remaining.

Calloway tried to connect the photographs with the two riders, but neither Fenton's nor Simpkins's war records tallied with the locations, most of which were further east than the western Allies had advanced by 1945. They would have been under the control of the Red Army. There were other explanations of course. The album might have been seized from a POW who had been withdrawn from the eastern front to repel the Allies' westward advance. But the connection would need to be deeper if it was to link Fenton, Simpkins and the tramp in a way that was worth the two of them falling out.

He removed each photo from the album and stacked them in a deck. He took an envelope from the drawer and stuffed the photos inside. Then he licked the flap of the envelope to seal it, taking a swig of the gin to wash away the taste of the glue. Fumbling in a draw he picked out two drawing pins and used these to pin the envelope to the wooden underside of the portable radiogram cabinet. He stood back and looked at the gramophone from across the small basement room. Even with the cabinet opened to play records, the envelope was not visible.

The next morning he called Sammy Mackay from his office. Mackay answered in a musical brogue.

'Sammy, it's Cab.'

'I was about to call, but you've saved His Majesty's Government the tuppence.'

'The stadium coffers will cover it.'

'Yes, I'm sure there's money in dog racing. Now about your names and places. I've done some digging and frankly old man, it's something you might want to leave be.'

'Why?'

'You always were so wonderfully blunt. I can't go into detail but ties in with a bit of departmental business, if you get my drift. Pretty low-grade stuff but not worth meddling in. It could all get horribly complicated.'

Calloway ignored this. 'What can you tell me about a Waffen SS unit with three lions on its collar tabs?'

He heard irritation in Mackay's voice. 'Last time I had anything to do with the Waffen SS I was interrogating one of their Obersturmfuhrers from the Das Reich division. You stood behind him like a terrier that had cornered a fox. I had to stand you down as I recall. I always thought you enjoyed your job a little too much.'

Calloway let the comment go. 'So what can you tell me? Three lion insignia and a shield on the forearm.'

'What's on the shield?'

He could tell Mackay knew the answer already but was probing to see how much Calloway knew. Calloway had failed to make the emblem out. The watermarking and foxing on the photo was too bad.

'You tell me.'

There was silence on the end of the line for a moment, then a deep sigh. 'Cab, where have you seen all this?'

'Photographs.'

Another silence followed by a muffled humming. Mackay was smothering the receiver with his hand while he spoke to someone else. He came back on the line. 'Look, take my word for it, this is something that really shouldn't be your concern. You were in the game. You know how this works. Let it go, old man.'

Calloway didn't let it go. 'If it affects the security of my stadium and those that use it, then it's very much my concern. Goodbye, Sammy.'

He ended the call, left the office and walked down to the track. A couple of the Bullets were doing laps. Simpkins hung over the guard rail watching. He saw Calloway cross the centre green. As he approached, Simpkins flicked his cigarette onto the concrete and turned to walk away. Calloway stopped him.

'We need another talk.'

'I've said all I need to.'

'I'll decide that.'

The rider shrugged. His insubordination was well practiced.

'So talk,' he said.

Both men ducked to avoid the spray of cinders as the two practicing riders passed.

'I need you to be straight with me,' Calloway said. 'I know there was bad blood between you and Des Fenton. You fell out over the tramp that slept under the stands, the one they called Joe Smoke. I'm guessing you knew him. I'm also guessing Fenton knew that you knew him and this bothers you. Fenton wasn't well liked but you seemed to have more reason to dislike him than most. I don't know why yet. You need to tell me.'

Simpkins shouted above the clatter of the motorcycle engines. One of the riders had pulled up. A mechanic was making adjustments to his machine as the rider revved the engine.

'I don't need to tell you anything.'

Calloway stood to his full height. He was a head taller than the Simpkins. 'Oh, I think you do, Raymond. Because right now people are saying you ran Des Fenton off the track deliberately. Personally I don't believe it. But there are rumours and they're getting louder. Soon they will be so loud that the police will get to hear them and then, whether those rumours are true or not, you son will be in a lot of bother.'

Simpkins smirked. He stretched his neck and shoved his chin forward. 'So maybe I didn't like Fenton. He was a flash bastard, if you want my opinion. I remember the tramp, sure. Doesn't mean I know him. Is that all you've got? Not much of an investigation, is it?'

Calloway could see through the bravado. He played his hand.

'The tramp had a photo album. I've seen it.'

Simpkins switched off the surliness. He looked worried for a moment. Calloway noticed and pressed the advantage.

'Those photos don't make happy viewing, Ray. A couple of kamerads from the Waffen SS slaughtering their way across Europe. They were good at that. I met a few myself, although the boys in these photos were from a unit I don't recognise. Three lions on their collar patches. Strange that some tramp who hung around here had an album like that. Mean anything to you, does it?'

Simpkins lit a cigarette and tried to look disinterested. Calloway recognised the discomfiture beneath the sham.

'So what am I German now? This is bollocks and you know it.'

'What I know is that there were place names and dates under those photos. I found the same places and dates in a notebook hidden in Fenton's toolbox. The notebook was stolen from my office.'

The rider drew on the cigarette with tensed lips. Calloway sensed he was getting somewhere. Then a thought seemed to flicker behind Simpkins's eyes. 'Why don't you ask Joe Smoke about it?' he asked.

He sneered as if he'd scored a point with the question.

Calloway answered deadpan, 'Joe Smoke is dead.'

The rider smiled. He stood back from the stand rail and turned to face Calloway square on. 'Then I'd say you've hit a dead end. Best to forget about it I reckon.'

'Perhaps I should.' Calloway clapped a hand on the small rider's back and leaned in towards him. He spoke quietly into his ear. 'The problem is, Raymond, you're not the first person to tell me that today. And that just spurs me on.'

THIRTEEN

The away team rider slid a dozen yards along the rough cinder track before hitting the perimeter fence feet first. Sparks flew as his lead-soled boots scraped the metal posts. The crowd oooh'd and aaah'd. This was injury as entertainment. The ambulance crew scrambled across the track with a stretcher, as the remaining three riders scudded down the back straight at full throttle. The pit crews lifted the buckled bike out of the race's path. The three riders passed within feet of the stretcher party before it reached the centre ground and laid the injured man down. Calloway watched from the tower. The whole operation had taken less than twenty seconds. A lap later the checkered flag flew. Billy Riley took first place, O'Donnell second. Riley removed his helmet and waved to the crowd. They chanted 'Billy, Billy, he's our man', waving their scarves and cranking their gas rattles, which clacked like an ack-ack battery in an air raid. Riley played to the crowd. He made a victory lap, head held high, waving regally as he passed. O'Donnell followed, a respectful bike's length behind his winning teammate. He made the six-gun sign with his thumb and forefinger, firing off imaginary rounds into the night sky above.

The Bullets had ridden well. They had clinched a victory over the visitors by a narrow points margin and the crowd responded in full voice. The spectre of Des Fenton's death seemed to have departed, for the last few heats at least. Pat Moxon seemed pleased with her boys. She strutted around the pit in her fur coat like a lioness in her den. Riley was the man of the moment. There was much back slapping and ruffling of hair from his teammates. Later a horde of autograph hunters gathered outside the riders' changing room. Mostly girls. Calloway's men struggled to hold them back, such was the frenzy.

'I swear some of 'em pissed 'emselves,' said Sid Tanner, the ruddy-faced commissionaire, once the autograph hunters had dispersed. He was a man of few words and most of them indelicate.

Riley, to his credit, signed every book. He valued his supporters and treated them with respect. Duiker should take note, Calloway thought.

A good night for the Bullets meant a late night in the members bar. The lights still shone brightly through the long picture window above the west stand, which gave the more discerning punters a panoramic view of the track. Calloway would leave them to their celebrations for another half hour before closing the bar. He made his rounds. As he passed the members changing rooms, he saw Billy Riley coming towards him. He had bailed from the celebrations early.

'Hallo, Billy. You've had a good night.'

Riley didn't look pleased to see him. Since their talk at the cycle speedway, he had been avoiding the security boss.

'Not bad, I s'pose.'

'Not bad? A return to form I would say.'

'We all have our good nights.'

'Yes, but this is the first good night you've had since the middle of last season. What's changed Billy?'

Riley shrugged. 'I guess my luck just turned.'

Riley made to leave but Calloway blocked him.

'I don't believe in luck Billy. I prefer numbers. I've been studying the Bullets' form. Your results make interesting reading.'

'I didn't think you were a speedway fan, Mr Calloway.'

'I'm a recent convert. I've been following a couple of riders in particular and one of them is you. Your results puzzle me. You were flying high at the start of last season, none of the riders could touch you, home or away. Then something happened.'

Riley made a play of looking nonplussed. Calloway continued.

'Your form tailed off, Billy. But not across the board.'

'What do you mean?' Riley's voice wavered.

'You started losing to one rider in particular.'

Sweat beads popped beneath Riley's hairline. 'I had a run of bad luck, that's all. Every rider does.'

'Maybe. But you were only unlucky when you were paired with Des Fenton. The trouble is I don't believe in luck. I think you were pulling races, Billy. I'd like to know why.'

Riley flushed, half anger, half disbelief. 'That's rubbish. Sure, I had a bad season. I didn't just lose to Fenton.'

'True, up to a point. But when you were paired with another Ranger, your luck held up pretty well.'

Calloway looked to the side and ran his big hand through his hair. 'Ah, but there I go again talking about luck when I said I don't believe in it. Your numbers show above average form in all your races except for those when Fenton rode with you. You lost every one of those races. That's not bad luck. The pattern is too obvious. I think you were pulling races and Fenton was behind it. I think his widow was in on it too. She wasn't in the Four Bells to thank you for the flowers last week, Billy. I watched the altercation between you. I'll wager you weren't ill for her husband's funeral either. You were keeping out of her way.'

Riley rolled his eyes. 'What are you on about? Pulling races! This isn't boxing, Calloway. Riders don't take a fall in the third round, like they do in the films. You're seeing things that aren't there.'

'Perhaps. I'm sorry to have brought this up when you should be celebrating. I meant to talk to you at Dennis Robinson's party, but as I recall, you left early.'

The colour drained from Riley's face. He swallowed hard. 'I wasn't enjoying the party. I don't like Robinson, as it happens, or his friends. They're a bunch of fakes. Me and a mate went looking for a late-night drinking club.' He pulled a cigarette from the pocket of his blouson jacket and lit it. Calloway noticed his hands were trembling. 'Is that allowed, Mr Calloway?'

'It's allowed.'

'Look can't you just drop this Fenton business. Whatever Pat's got you chasing, it's got nothing to do with me.'

‘I’d like to drop it. Genuinely I would. But when there’s something not right on that track, or in this stadium, well that becomes my business. Things need explaining.’

Riley pushed past Calloway. ‘Just blow, will you.’

The security boss called after him. ‘Des Fenton and Ray Simpkins fell out over some photographs. Do you know anything about that?’

Riley stopped dead. Cautiously he turned to face Calloway. ‘Photographs?’

The rider’s mouth was dry and his voice rasped.

‘From the war. German soldiers.’

Riley’s face relaxed. ‘Before my time, Mr Calloway. I spent my war in the shelters. I was even too young for the Home Guard.’

Two autograph hunters came bowling along the underside of the stands. They had spotted Riley and were offering up their autograph books to the one-time star rider. They were pursued by Sid Tanner. He was a furlong behind and wheezing. Riley made the most of the diversion. He played the star and signed the books. Calloway dismissed Tanner with a wave of his hand and told the fans their time was up. They skipped away, grinning. Calloway leaned in towards Riley and whispered, ‘You need to trust me Billy, for your own good.’

FOURTEEN

The Fentons lived the mock Tudor dream. Their suburban house was a contrived apology for the humble roots they had earned enough to disown. Every house in the street told the same story. This was Merrie England with an Alvis in the drive. Calloway knew these avenues, although not in this town. He had visited his better-off school friends in similar surroundings back home, the perks of a grammar school education, sometimes finding yourself a guest in a home where your tea was called dinner and the lav was indoors. His own father called it bourgeoise. The foreign words he used were Marxist. At the time Calloway didn't care. These houses were warmer, the mothers more fragrant and the food more plentiful. He'd learned a new etiquette from his encounters with the middle classes. His father called it 'putting on airs'. He was a coal miner, a socialist and a staunch union man. About this time Calloway resolved never to follow his father down the pits. The army had been his escape.

Irene Fenton greeted him with an unfelt smile. Courtesy came with the house but it was as fake as the half-timbered facade. Calloway returned it in kind. She invited him into the front room. The chintz was fighting a style war with the American dream. The three-piece suite and curtains were a riot of pastel flora. The bar was Broadway in miniature. Chromium-framed photos of speeding bikes and scenes from the stadium lined the walls, an odd substitution for the customary Haywain and hunting prints. The Fentons' wedding photo stood on the bar, next to the soda siphon. Fenton wore battledress with Royal Engineers' insignia.

He was one stripe up. Irene had done her best with dreary utility fabric. The picture gave no hint of celebration. This was a cheap wartime marriage. The trappings of motor sport stardom were a few years off.

They drank tea from china cups. Irene made small talk with the tight vowels of a telephonist. She held the cup with her pinkie extended. Her lips left a perfect pink bow on the rim. Calloway turned on the bedside manner. It was the best the jaded ex-sergeant could muster.

'I know this is a difficult time for you, Mrs Fenton. I will keep this short. There are some questions I need to ask as part of my investigation into your husband's accident.'

She gave him a condescending smile. 'It's no trouble, Mr Calloway. The Bullets was Des's life. He would want me to help you.'

There was no fragility in her voice, nor any hint of stoicism. She was hard, plain and simple.

'How did your late husband get on with his teammates?'

'What, my Des? He was the life and soul. Everyone loved Des.'

There was a hint of bitterness. It made him think of Liz Francis.

'Were there tensions with any teammates? Grudges or differences?'

She placed the cup and saucer down on the table between them and took a cigarette from the dark wood cigarette box beside it. Calloway offered her a light and she accepted.

'He got on with most of them. There were a few who resented his success.'

'Was Ray Simpkins one of them?'

She drew on the cigarette and spoke as she exhaled. 'You don't believe the rubbish about the accident do you?'

'What rubbish is that?'

'That it wasn't an accident.'

'I don't believe anything yet.'

'That's Pat Moxon, that is. Spreading rumours. She thinks the intrigue will be good for business. You know why people flock to the speedway, Mr Calloway?' She toyed distractedly with the cup on its saucer. 'For the accidents. The smash-ups. The broken limbs.'

She glanced at the speedway photos on the walls as if she suddenly resented them being there. 'And the prospect of a death on the track. I've been a speedway wife long enough to know.' She corrected herself. 'A speedway widow now.'

She rose from the armchair and walked over to the window, pulling aside the net curtain and gazing into the street. It looked like bad amateur dramatics, a scene Noel Coward might have written while drunk. Calloway didn't doubt her grief. He just wasn't convinced by the play acting. He knew the real Irene Fentons of this world. They greeted death with savage emotion. They wailed and sobbed and cried, 'Why my Des? Why do the good die young?' Then they spoiled for fights. The claws came out and the accusations flew. Calloway sensed this grief was deeply suppressed in the widow Fenton. She had left that past behind, locked it inside her electroplated suburban shell and buried the key under the rose bushes in her garden.

'He was my Dashing Des, Mr Calloway. And now he's gone. I don't care what others thought of him.'

'What did Billy Riley think of him?'

She stiffened at the name, only slightly, but enough for Calloway to detect. He had learned to read the small signs during interrogations.

'I'm not sure Des had much to do with Billy. They weren't close.'

'Is that why Riley failed to show up for your husband's funeral?'

She leaned forward and stubbed her cigarette into the ashtray. The veins on the back of her hand protruded as she ground the stub into the heavy glass.

'You'll have to ask him.'

She pursed her lips revealing the lines of a lifelong smoker beneath her makeup and powder.

'I've not seen him since before Des's accident, and then only in passing. As I said, we didn't mix with people like him.'

'People like him?'

She skirted the question. 'I have no interest in Billy Riley's business and I'm sure he had no interest in ours. Like I said, I've not seen him.'

Calloway looked down, cradling his hands in his lap. 'That's odd, Mrs Fenton. You see I like a drink of a lunchtime, usually in the Four Bells on New Cross Road, and I'd swear I saw you speaking to Riley there last Saturday. In fact the two of you seemed to be arguing over something. What might that have been?'

She stood and straightened the skirt of her two-piece. It was a signal. 'I don't go to pubs, Mr Calloway. Especially not in New Cross. If you don't mind I'm really not feeling too well. My Des's not been in the ground ten days and now all these questions, well it's all a little too soon.'

She gestured to the door and he rose to leave. He'd heard enough. As he crossed the room he picked up the wedding photograph.

'Royal Artillery. Did your husband serve overseas? Germany, for instance?'

She shook her head. 'Des was stationed in Kent. Anti-aircraft duties.'

She took the photograph from his hands and replaced it on the bar. 'He would come back home whenever he could. We met at the New Cross Empire one Saturday night. He asked me to dance. He was a good-looking boy. I knew him from speedway. He rode before the war you see. He wasn't as big a name then of course.'

'Did Pat Moxon manage him in those days?'

Femton's widow scoffed. Her accent slipped. 'Her? She was just a just a show rider. Tarting herself around the circuit doing tricks.'

'Of course. That was when Mr Dandridge was promoter.'

Irene Fenton put on a playground voice: 'Pretty Pattie Moxon, Queen of the dirt track. Believe me, that one's no better than she should be.'

Calloway let this ride. He glanced around the walls. 'These are very good photos, Mrs Fenton. Someone has a real eye for a picture.'

'Des took them. Photography was hobby with him. When he had the time of course.'

'He takes a good photograph.'

'Took a good photograph,' she corrected.

Calloway thanked the widow for her time. They exchanged polite goodbyes. As he drove away he thought of Billy Riley and the exchange with Irene Fenton in the pub, the exchange she had just denied. He thought of Riley at the Soho club and the photos on Fenton's wall that the deceased rider had taken himself with an obvious talent for capturing the moment. And he remembered Duiker's claim that Fenton always liked to have something on you. On the Riley-Fenton front at least, things were starting to fall into place.

It was almost midnight. The pubs had long since called time and locked up. In the moonless night the streetlamps struggled against the blackness. A train whistle blew in the distance. The last train home. Otherwise the street was quiet.

Calloway had been waiting in a doorway, which gave him a view down the cobbled path beside the railway viaduct. Satisfied now that the street was deserted, he walked slowly towards the path, keeping a hand his raincoat pocket to ensure the tools inside did not clink against one another. In his other hand he held an old No. 4 battery lamp not yet lit.

The cobbled path was uneven and smelled of motor oil. The railway arches were infilled with corrugated iron, within each a peeling wooden door wide enough to take a car. Some had enamelled signs nailed to them for Castrol oil and Champion spark plugs. The fourth arch along had a painted sign above the door with white lettering that was just visible through the darkness: J Fenton, Motor Mechanic, with the phone number TID 0621. Checking behind him to see that he'd not been followed by a drunk looking for somewhere to piss, he twisted the selector switch on the side of the lamp and turned it on. It cast a red glow through its coloured filter, enough for him to examine the padlock which fastened the doors. He withdrew a small jemmy from his coat pocket and slid it between the wood of the door and the padlock bracket. He worked slowly and gently, easing the bar a fraction of an inch at a time to avoid the noise of scraping metal in the darkness. Then from behind he heard voices. He stopped work, extinguished the light and flattened himself against the doors as best he could.

'You're having a fucking laugh aren't you?'

It was a woman's voice, coarse and husky from too many cigarettes. She sounded drunk.

'You don't think I'm going down there with you. It stinks of petrol and Christ knows what.'

Calloway made out two figures at the end of the path, silhouetted against the glow of the streetlamps. The second figure was male and swaying, steadying himself against the woman as the pair stumbled towards the first of the railway arches. The man-made plaintiff grunts, barely able to form the words through his inebriation. He sounded pathetic and the woman cackled in derision.

'Come on then. If this is what you want.'

The silhouetted woman leaned with her back to the doors, hitched up her skirt and hooked one leg around the man. He had by now unbuttoned himself and was pushing his groin towards her in faltering jerks.

'What do you need, a map or something? Give it here.'

She grabbed between his legs and guided him into her. The doors banged against the frame as the pair bucked, bestial in their drunkenness. The woman mocked him with insincere encouragement as he went at her, frustrated with his own ineptitude. Before long he let out a yelp, high pitched and feeble. She patted his back as he slumped against her, like a disinterested mother consoling a sobbing child, before pushing him away and straightening her clothes. They stumbled off.

Calloway stayed flattened against the doors until the pair had disappeared from view.

He resumed his work on the lock. He put his full weight behind the jemmy. The bracket snapped off easily, its screws wrenched quietly from the damp wood. Calloway slid the jemmy back into his coat and eased his way through the crack in the door, pulling it closed behind him. He turned the selector switch of the lamp to its normal position and shone a beam of white light through the darkness.

The workshop was tidy, the workbenches clear and tools hung in neat rows from pinboard. The trolley jack on the shop floor was squared away under the bench and all the drawers of the metal tool cabinets were closed, with small patches of rust bubbling up through their drab paintwork. The cans on the shelves were arranged neatly and the tyres on the racks above his head were lined up in order of size. The whole place was preserved in aspic, presumably as a fall back in the event Des Fenton's speedway career took a turn for the worse and he needed to go back to his old job.

In the centre of the floor were five loosely laid, oil-blackened planks covering a small inspection pit, just large enough for a man to crouch in. Calloway eased up one of the planks and shone his torch into the void. It was empty. He rifled through the draws and shelves and found nothing you wouldn't expect of a well-equipped mechanic.

At the back of the railway arch was a wooden screen with glazed wood panels. It was a typical workshop office, for paperwork and the telephone, but its windows were blacked out with paint on the inside of every pane. Calloway's heart rate increased. He had expected to see such a place and the discovery felt good. He tried the door, which was locked. A simple domestic lock. The key was most likely on a hook somewhere but he couldn't waste time looking for it. If the cobbled path outside was a favourite place for locals to fuck in the dark, there was a chance another two would come along before the night was out. Maybe even the same woman. He took the jemmy and levered it into the crack between the wooden door and its frame. He gave it a shove. The wood splintered with a crack, much louder than he expected. He stopped and listened. From the path outside he heard the rattling of doors. He judged the sound to be coming from the workshop in first arch, nearest the street corner. Above the rattling he heard a tentative whistling, a popular tune he recognised but couldn't name. He stepped quietly towards the doors, avoiding the lose planks over the inspection pit, and peered through the chink between the door and the frame. Against the glow of the distant streetlight he saw the outline of a police helmet. A copper making his rounds, checking doors. He whistled as he worked his way along the path, trying each door in sequence. He was too close for Calloway to slip away unseen. He looked back into the workshop for a hiding place. He eased up the first plank of the inspection pit, then heard a voice from the end of the path. He froze, gripping the heavy raised plank in his hand.

'Is that you 453?'

A young and surprised-sounding voice replied. 'Yes, Sergeant. Just checking locks on the workshops. They're buggers round here for swiping tools.'

The sergeant cleared his throat in disapproval. 'Language unbecoming, 453. Language unbecoming.'

'Sorry, Sergeant.'

'So lad, anything to report?'

'No, Sergeant. All correct.'

'Then get yourself down to Comet Street. Our old friend Ida is making a right old commotion. One of her clients is too drunk to find his wallet.'

'On my way, Sergeant.'

Calloway heard heavy footsteps disappear into the distance. He replaced the plank over the inspection pit and moved to the office door. He entered in darkness, closed the door behind him and felt along the doorframe for a light switch. With the blacked-out window-panes and door closed, it would be safe to turn on the light. He felt the cold brass switch cover under his palm and flicked the switch. The room lit up blood red. A darkroom safelight shone from a pendant in the ceiling. There was a bench along the far wall with three shallow rectangular trays in a row. An old photographic enlarger stood beside them. On a shelf behind were bottled chemicals. He peered at the labels, already knowing what they read. Acetic acid and ammonium thiosulphate, the same as on the receipt he'd found in Fenton's toolbox.

Photographic prints hung from a cord above the bench. Speedway shots. Riders captured mid-race. Team shots and crowd scenes, like the ones in Fenton's living room. There was a metal filing cabinet on the adjacent wall. He tried the drawers, which were unlocked. There were files inside. Receipts, bills, accounts and catalogues for motors spares. The darkroom doubled as a working office. As he crouched to close the bottom drawer, he saw a tool cabinet like the one in the main workshop tucked beneath the bench. It was far enough back not to be visible when standing. He pulled it into the centre of the room and tried the drawers. They were locked. He took a screwdriver from his pocket and used it as a lever. The metal rim of the cabinet bent easily, enough for him to remove the draws without unlocking them. There were photographic prints inside, in a batch bound with elastic. He slid off the band and rifled through each print in turn.

He recognised Liz Francis, even without her clothes. The first few shots were cheesecake pinups, risqué but nothing that would frighten the censor. The rest were pornography. Francis acting out Fenton's private fantasies. Performing acts he doubted wife Irene would to be cajoled into. The second draw had several bundles of prints, each with a set of negatives labelled with names, locations and dates. The names belonged to men. The dates were within the last three years. Each set of prints told a similar story. Men meeting in public places, talking, laughing, but furtively, then touching and kissing. Some went further. The shots were taken from a distance, blurred through magnification but with the parties still recognisable. One of them was Billy Riley.

Calloway gathered up the prints and negatives and stuffed them into his coat pocket. There was a third draw, jammed shut. He pulled out the jemmy and used brute force on it. Inside was an envelope, old and dog-eared, some initials and the date September 1934 scrawled across it in pencil. Calloway pulled the set of prints and the strip of negatives from inside. The images showed the same eye for depravity Fenton has used for his private shots of Liz Francis. But the model was someone else entirely.

FIFTEEN

It was two am. The curtains on his basement window were drawn shut. They had been open when he left. From behind them he saw the glow of a torch moving around his room. He descended the basement steps, treading lightly. The door was open an inch. There were wood splinters sticking out from the frame. He drew the jemmy from his pocket, a lightweight crowbar a foot long, heavy enough to break a man's nose or put a dent in his skull. He let his eyes adjust to the darkness in the basement well before easing open the door an inch at a time. He placed his steps close to the skirting to avoid the loose boards creaking. In the near darkness of his single room he made out a figure, male, five foot ten perhaps, rifling through drawers. There was ten feet between the two of them. Calloway would need to be fast if he was to land the first blow. He raised the crowbar and sprang forward. The floorboards creaked, the intruder turned and dropped the torch, raising his arm to parry the blow. He swivelled his body, grabbed Calloway's forearm and braced it for an elbow break. Calloway stamped down hard on the man's shin, failing to snap the bone but causing enough pain for the intruder to loosen his grip. Calloway broke free. He grabbed the man's head with both hands and raised his knee. There was a sharp crunch as the knee slammed into his jaw. The man buckled. As he slumped to the ground, he reached inside his jacket and pulled out a Webley service revolver. Calloway flung himself at the intruder. It was harder to shoot a man at close quarters. He made a half turn and crashed his forearm down on the other man's gun hand. The revolver fell to the floor, illuminated by the beam of the torch. Calloway snatched it up. The intruder made for the door and Calloway followed.

Outside a car was waiting, engine running but headlights doused. The intruder shouted to the driver and fell into the passenger seat clutching his injured arm. The driver revved hard, slipped the car into gear and pumped the accelerator. Calloway gripped the butt of the heavy Webley in both hands, raised it to his eye line and aimed for the car's tyres. He fired off three rounds which echoed through the silence like iron doors slamming. The first two missed. The third burst a rear tyre as the car was making its sharp turn into the adjacent street. The driver lost control and the car piled headlong into a shop window, showering glass. Calloway strode towards it, the Webley still raised and the passenger door in his line of sight. Through the rear windscreen he saw the outline of the driver slumped over the wheel. There was movement in the passenger seat. The passenger leapt out, like a paratrooper on a green light. Calloway fired another round, which went wide. His target ran with adrenaline-charged energy towards the creek. Calloway pocketed the Webley and followed. He had twisted his ankle in the scuffle. A searing muscle pain shot through his calf. He pressed on at a fast hobble, favouring his good leg and trailing the bad.

Calloway was breathing hard, swallowing down the damp creekside air in big gulps. The other man was finding it hard to run, hampered by injuries from the fight or the car crash. They ducked through the courtyards of municipal flats, clawing through washing lines and crashing into bins, before emerging onto the Lower Road. Out of nowhere Calloway heard the screech of brakes. A lone car hit the man he pursued before skidding to a halt. The man rolled off the bonnet like a barrel off a dray. He landed feet first and the momentum carried him forward. He recovered by reflex and continued to run. The car driver leaped from his vehicle and into Calloway's path. He started to shout in angry panic. Calloway barged past him and ran towards the escaping man, gritting his teeth against the pain of the twisted ankle. They cut through a passageway between the backs of the old sailors cottages. The hard cobblestones jarred his injured leg. The intruder had slowed his pace. His injuries were taking their toll too. By the time they reached the river,

Calloway had gained ground. There was twenty feet between them. As they rounded the corner of the dock wall, the silhouetted bulk of Paynes Wharf loomed into view. Beside it a dark alley, at its end only the Thames. There was no exit save for a leap into the stinking river. Calloway knew this. The intruder clearly didn't. He stopped dead and for a second and contemplated a leap into the high tide. This was Calloway's chance. He gripped the Webley barrel first and clubbed the other man across the side of the head with the butt. The pistol's lanyard ring gouged a deep wound across his scalp, but the blow failed to floor him. He struck Calloway's windpipe hard with the side of his flattened hand. The big man choked. From the corner of his eye Calloway saw his attacker reach down and draw a stiletto from an ankle sheath. It was a Fairbairn-Sykes knife and it had only one purpose, killing a man quickly and efficiently. He lunged towards Calloway in a move well practiced from the manual. Calloway took a reflex step to the side, stumbling against the wharf steps. The attacker lunged again. Calloway was trapped between the high wharfside and the steps. He still held the Webley and in a single move swivelled it on his palm, found the trigger and squeezed. The blast echoed between the high dock walls. His assailant slumped. The knife dropped from his hand, the black metal hitting the cobblestones with a dull clatter. The man grasped the wound in his gut with both hands and let out a wounded animal squeal. Calloway raised the pistol with a straightened arm and put the remaining bullet through his skull.

Calloway made a circuit of the neighbourhood to approach his street from the south. He clung to buildings, hiding in their shadows. Every hundred yards he stopped in a doorway or passage to surveil the route ahead. He couldn't risk an encounter with 453 or his sergeant. Not at three am with a blood-spattered trench coat furled under his arm.

He dumped the dead man's body into the river. There had been no way of weighting it down. He just had to hope it would drift with the tide and not end up back in the same place, though this was entirely possible. Throughout history Deptford was a place bodies washed up. The currents brought them home. It was the resting place of the drowned. The Webley had sunk like a rock. He had wiped off his fingerprints then grasping the angular barrel in a handkerchief had hurled it as far as his muscles, weakened from the fight and the inevitable come-down from adrenalin, would allow. He did the same with the knife. He took comfort knowing these at least wouldn't be found. The river would ingest them, deep within its mud-lined gut.

His street was empty as he approached it. At the far end he could see a huddle of figures around the spot where the car had crashed. The car was gone, leaving a gaping whole in the shopfront, as if the window, with its glass-shard teeth, had swallowed it whole. Some of the figures were in uniform. Police, possibly young 453 and colleagues. Some looked half dressed, no doubt the shop owners. It was too soon for the vehicle to have been towed. The driver must have recovered and fled the scene in the crumpled car. This was not good. It meant a living witness, however culpable in the break in. As Calloway approached his house, the front door opened. Miss Logan bade a practiced farewell to a caller. He wore the cheap suit of a commercial traveller. He looked flushed and embarrassed. Miss Logan was wearing a dressing gown. It was silk and frayed at the neck and cuffs, its colours faded in the chink of light from the hallway. Beneath the gown she was naked, the outline of her ageing and undernourished frame showing through the thin material. As her caller left, she saw Calloway approach. She appeared to see nothing surprising in the hour of his arrival. She was a night bird and assumed he was too.

'You missed all the fun, Mr Calloway.' For a moment he wondered what fun she meant. 'Gun shots, a car crash, it was like the St Valentine's Day Massacre.'

'Did you see it?'

'No, luvvie. Didn't get to the window in time. I was a bit indisposed.'

He didn't doubt it. He played her along. 'The papers are right, Miss Logan. It's a crime wave. Too many guns brought back from the war. Too many folk knowing how to use them.'

She drew the robe closer together and made a half-hearted attempt to straighten her hair.

'We learned a lot of things in the war that we've brought with us into peacetime,' she sighed, before drifting back into the house and closing the door.

His basement room was a mess, his few possessions strewn across the floor. His collection of gramophone records had borne the worst of it. Shattered discs lay on the lino like haphazard tiles. He checked the gramophone, sliding his hand inside the cabinet and feeling for the envelope with Joe Smoke's photographs. They were still where he'd pinned them.

He stripped bare and scrubbed himself down in front of the stone sink. Then he lay on the bed still damp, letting the air cool him. He felt an overpowering tiredness. The fatigue of combat. He fell into a fitful sleep and dreamt.

It was 1945. There were three of them. McNally driving, Calloway riding up front, a Sten gun on his lap, and Cox the wireless operator in the back, his lanky six-foot frame twisted into the jeep's mean back seat. They drove at speed through a dense pine forest. Dangerous country for a lone, un-armoured vehicle. The three men sat upright and alert, their eyes scanning the forest walls and the road ahead. They had met no resistance since leaving their unit in Wesel. The enemy was in retreat and in poor shape. The remnants of the German 89th infantry division pulling back from the Rhine. Calloway had orders to investigate an enemy camp beyond the forest near Bergen. RAF reconnaissance photographs suggested there was a barracks. Calloway, McNally and Cox were to approach from the south west, assess its strength and report by wireless to 6th Airborne Division headquarters.

Two miles from the map reference they had been given, they slowed the jeep, mounted the verge on the roadside and drove beyond the first few lines of trees. The three men shouldered their weapons and dismounted. McNally and Cox unrolled a camouflage net and dragged it over the vehicle. Calloway checked the map. It showed a network of forestry tracks they could navigate on foot, out of sight of the road. He marked a route in cinograph pencil on the transparent cover of the map case. The track was damp and rutted and made for slow going. It was still early, a grey mist hung above the track in the forest half-light. They trod silently and cautiously, stopping at intervals to check ahead for signs of the enemy. It took an hour to reach the clearing Calloway had marked as their observation point. As the cover of the forest gave way to open ground, they crouched low then lay on the damp ground. The barracks was six hundred yards in front of them.

It was the smell they noticed first. A smell of death so strong it burned their throats.

Through binoculars Calloway could see the perimeter fence, but the last of the morning mist hung low and prevented a proper view. Behind the fence, a grey mass masked the huts behind. It seemed to ripple gently in the breeze, a tarpaulin he thought at first, stretched between the concrete fenceposts. As the mist drifted from the dead ground in front of him, the mass took on its true form. There were people pressed against the wire, three or four deep. They wore simple oversized uniforms, some with caps, most had shaved heads. Their faces were gaunt and androgynous. All of them looked close to death.

Calloway swore under his breath.

'What is it, Sarge?'

McNally had known Calloway too long to call him sir after his promotion. He also knew him well enough to sense something was very wrong.

'I'm not entirely sure.'

All Calloway knew was that this wasn't war. It was something altogether more terrible.

SIXTEEN

It took a day for the first medical units to arrive. They were ill prepared to deal with what they found. Starvation and typhus on a mass scale. The medics were equipped for battlefield medicine, not this. A neutral zone around the camp was declared to stop the spread of disease. The Royal Engineers did their best to establish basic sanitation and the medical corps oversaw the building of temporary medical facilities.

Calloway and colleagues who had arrived from 316 Field Security Section processed the guards. The kommandant and his cohort of SS officers seemed resigned to the point of nonchalance. Most were drunk. They cooperated in line with the expectations of their rank. When questioned they exhibited a kind of defiance, the bravura of schoolboys about to be caned. The other ranks had mostly fled. Those that remained milled about without purpose until one of the medical corps officers set them to work piling the corpses.

Several days later 316 Section was recalled to division with orders to proceed as planned to the Baltic. Calloway suggested to his CO that he remain at the camp with a small intelligence detachment. There were offices here full of documents, filed with the meticulousness of Nazi bureaucracy. The kommandantur had made no effort to destroy them. Calloway wondered whether they were proud of their work. And the kommandant's staff had yet to be interrogated, save for questioning necessary to help with the handover to the British forces. The CO gave Calloway orders to remain.

The interrogations had proved fruitless, the SS officers' defiance turning to silence when questioning moved beyond routine subjects. Calloway handed them to the military police. With McNally, Cox and three others, he spent the days that followed working through the files. They held reports on the running of the camp. They were written with utter detachment, like the accounts of a well-run business. Between the carefully typed lines, the carbon copies and rubber stamps, the unwritten human cost of this terrible place became clearer to Calloway as he read. The intelligence was of no military use. This was not a military establishment in any conventional sense, yet it had very efficiently been producing a level of cold brutality rarely found in battle.

Calloway received instructions from the Army Legal Service to send the processed documents back up the line to divisional headquarters. They would be used as evidence for war crimes trials following the German surrender that now seemed inevitable.

Calloway and his men took turns helping the medics, under the direction of a medical corps major who was trying his best not to let the near futility of his efforts show. The spread of typhus could not be halted and feeding the starving was not simply a matter of giving them food. Their bodies couldn't handle normal nutrition. He heard talk that Bengal Famine Powder might help, if the supply lines could provide such a thing.

The mortality rate from starvation and disease was running at five hundred a day. Civilian doctors and nurses from neighbouring towns had been drafted in to assist the medical corps personnel. Some showed a genuine willingness to help, whether through compassion or guilt. Others looked like the whole affair was an inconvenience. There were also volunteers from among the inmates, mostly from the overflow camp nearby, where newer prisoners had been held. They were generally fitter, healthier and more able to assist. Calloway noticed one volunteer in particular. A woman of around twenty-eight, perhaps thirty. The overflow camp had not ravaged her looks, as the main camp would have done in time. She still had hair as dark and lustrous as her eyes. Though clearly undernourished, she had not succumbed to the emaciation that characterised the inmates of the main camp. She wore a simple dress from the bundles of confiscated clothing they had found piled high in one of huts. In spite of its gruesome provenance, she wore it well, with elegance and poise. When they worked together in the makeshift infirmary, Calloway couldn't help but watch her. In time she noticed and would return his look, but briefly and with no indication as to whether his attention was welcome. Their first interaction was unspoken. He had found her resting after a shift in the typhus ward. He offered her a cigarette, which she accepted without acknowledgement. They smoked together in silence, before she returned to her work on the ward. It became a routine, which continued for a while, with neither speaking. In these silences Calloway found himself hoping that she found them as comforting as he did. Small moments of purity amid the horrors.

One evening he was returning to the room in the hut he had made his billet and office, when he noticed her standing in his path, as if she had been waiting for him. She turned and walked towards the far perimeter of the camp. Though no words were spoken, he knew she intended for him to follow. It was an hour past dusk and the rows of huts were lit up against the dark and empty sky. He followed her past the special camp, the star camp, the camp for Hungarian Jews and the clothing store, until they reached a larger, more substantial building with a tall brick chimney. Calloway recognised it as the camp crematorium. He followed her inside. There was just enough light to see. She stood in the sickly yellow glow of the electric light, which shone through the high windows. Still she said nothing, but he knew she had brought him here for a reason. There was something she wanted him to see. He let his eyes adjust to the half-light and looked around him. It could have been any abandoned factory, a foundry perhaps. There were trolleys and tools, shovels and piles of coal for the furnaces and long-handled tongs with jaws wide enough to grip a man's head. The oven doors hung open, the furnaces piled high with ash. A deep layer of ash and cinders carpeted the floor below them.

It was then Calloway noticed a figure, shrouded in sacking, huddled against the brick half walls of an empty coal bay. He looked to the young woman for affirmation that this was the thing he was supposed to find. She stared back expressionless. Calloway reached forward and removed the sacking. Beneath it was a man, alive and trembling. He wore the striped uniform and yellow star of an inmate. He sat on the floor with his knees raised and his arms clasped around them. His head was low, his chin pressed deep into his chest so that Calloway could not see his face. Calloway spoke to him softly, but the man buried his head deeper. Gently, Calloway leaned forward and raised the man's head by the chin so that he could better see his face. The man's flesh felt warm and pudgy, his face full and rounded. It wasn't the face of an inmate. It was too healthy, too well fed. The eyes were keen and alert, lacking the despair he'd seen around him every day since arriving at the camp. Calloway then realised what he'd been shown. He grabbed the man by the collar and dragged him across the concrete floor into the light cast by the window. He pushed up the loose sleeve of the uniform. The man's wrist was blackened with coal dust. Calloway rubbed it away. There was the tattoo, but it was different to the tattoos that branded the camp inmates. This was an SS blood group tattoo. The man now knew he had been discovered and the mask of fear fell from his face. In its place the same school-bully defiance the other SS men had shown under interrogation. This was enough for Calloway. He fell on the man with his full weight. He knelt hard on his shoulders, pinning him to the ground. He started pounding with his fists. He split the man's nose and broke his teeth. With repeated blows he pulped his face until his lips split so many times they pared away from his jaw. He grabbed him by the hair and slammed his head onto the concrete floor, again and again. With each blow the impact become softer, as the skull smashed into a patchwork of bone fragments and hair. He continued his savage attack until he realised the body beneath him had become limp.

Calloway stood, panting like an animal. Only then he realised the woman was standing beside him. She was calm, almost impassive, despite his savagery. She looked down at the bloodied corpse and spoke.

'He ran the overflow camp. He hurt me. He hurt all the women.'

She reached down and tore a wide strip of fabric from the hem of her dress. Taking Calloway's big hands in hers, she used the soft material to wipe the blood and cinders from his fists.

Her name was Miriam, he later found out, and she was twenty-nine. She was from Breslau, where she had taught music in a school. She fled to France while travel for Jews was still possible, settling in Paris and earning a meagre living as a private tutor to the children of affluent French families. When the Germans invaded in 1940, she was taken in by one of her clients and lived as the family governess. Monsieur Berteaux, the head of the house, was a man of resource and influence, with friends in both the resistance and among the occupying army. He arranged false papers for Miriam. In return she became his mistress, a role she did not want but in time came to accept. Madame Berteaux came to accept it too, after very soon discovering her husband's infidelity with the young Jewess, as she took to calling her. These were not times to be leaving the security of a marriage, especially one to a man who enjoyed the privileges and relative security of having friends on both sides.

The arrangement lasted for almost four years, until Berteaux's duplicity became his undoing. He was arrested and sent to Natzweiler-Struthof, a labour camp in Alsace. With no more need to harbour her husband's mistress, Madame Bertaux turned Miriam in to the Paris Gestapo, claiming she had been duped by her husband into believing the girl's new identity was bona fide. The Gestapo believed her story and Miriam was transported east with other French Jews. She spent a month or more in transit before arriving at the overflow camp.

After the incident in the crematorium, Calloway and Miriam had started to talk, in snatched moments while helping in the infirmary. He had learned her story a little at a time as he grew to earn her trust. Neither mentioned the death of the relief camp kommandant.

One afternoon, as his work on the camp files neared completion, Calloway left McNally in charge and took a jeep into the nearby town. It had been a pleasant enough place in its day he imagined, but now looked drab and uncared for. But it had avoided any significant bomb damage and its town square retained that gemutlich charm that seemed obligatory in the provinces here. The townspeople in contrast were joyless. They eyed the jeep with suspicion, with looks that implied that their indifference to the horrors of the neighbouring camp was about to catch up with them.

As he left the main square, he noticed a villa at the top of the road ahead. Three storeys with a chalet roof and well-tended window boxes. The whitewashed walls were clean and bright, as if five years of war had never happened. It stood in stark contrast to its neighbours. He drove the jeep through the gates and parked on the drive. This too was well maintained and the adjacent lawn with its beds of brightly coloured flowers was edged with precision by a skilled gardener.

He dismounted the jeep and rang the doorbell. A woman answered. She was thirty-five perhaps, handsome and well dressed. She looked Calloway up and down with an air of superiority and an expression that suggested his stained battle dress and mud-caked boots offended her. Only now he realised how shabby he had become after his days at the camp, where the punctiliousness of military life had given way to humanitarian expediency. He pushed past her despite her protestations. The house was well furnished showing little sign of wartime hardship. There was heavy oak furniture and polished silverware and a baby grand by the window of the drawing room. He crossed the room leaving a trail of mud on the expensive Persian carpet and picked up a framed photograph that stood on the piano. The husband, he assumed, wearing the uniform of an SS Obergruppenfuhrer.

The woman continued with her protestations, with a righteous indignation she was too arrogant to accept was no longer deserved. Calloway tossed the photograph to the floor. The woman gasped as the glass broke in the frame. He noticed a full decanter of what looked like brandy. He poured a glass and swallowed it on one gulp. The warm liquor burned his throat. It emboldened him. He searched the house room by room before coming to the couple's bedroom. It was light and airy with a cool breeze from an open widow, rippling newly pressed curtains. He rifled through the drawers and wardrobes, deaf to the woman's objections. He picked out clothes, which were all laundered and pressed, and laid them on the bed.

'I'm requisitioning this property. You have twenty-four hours to leave. Take what you need but leave these.' He gestured to the clothes he had selected.

'But where will I go?'

It was a complaint more than a question.

'I don't care.'

He took Miriam to the villa whenever he could. It was their private sanctuary. They feasted on tinned food from larder and drank from what remained of the Obergruppenfuhrer's cellar. Miriam wore the dresses Calloway had chosen. They weren't entirely to her taste, but she forgave him. The luxury of water to bathe in and clean clothes to wear was the best gift he could have given. In return, she gave him music. She played piano and picked records to play on the gramophone. Like good Nazis the Obergruppenfuhrer and his wife eschewed the Jewish composers, although a Mahler symphony seemed to have survived the ideological purge. And Calloway learned to appreciate Beethoven, Schumann and Strauss.

When they first made love it had happened quite naturally. Neither had made overtures. Both felt it was right, savouring the passion and the tenderness that circumstance had denied them for years. Then to sleep in clean sheets just for a few hours, inured from the continuing misery of the liberated camp, brought them a comfort that was beyond value. Though he never said as much, in his head Calloway was imagining a life for them both, away from the camp and the war.

At first he didn't notice the pain she was in. She hid it well. But the more she relaxed in his presence, the more she let it show. And though they continued to enjoy those moments of tenderness in the sanctuary of the villa, Calloway knew this happiness wasn't lasting.

She died from an internal haemorrhage, the surgeon explained to Calloway. He was German and had been transferred from a civilian hospital in Duisburg. His English was poor and he struggled to find the words at first.

'A result of appalling violation,' he managed to say.

A week later Calloway rejoined 316 Section. He wished he had a photograph of Miriam. Instead he returned to the villa one last time and took gramophone records of the music she had taught him to love.

SEVENTEEN

Rough hands shook him awake.

'Christ Mr Calloway. What happened here? You have a party?'

Calloway's eyes adjusted to the light. It was Bert Webber. He stood amid the chaos of the turned-over room, shaking his head. Calloway sat up, feeling the dull ache of bruising from the fight.

'What the hell are you doing here, Bert?' he grunted.

'Pattie sent me. She was worried, with you not turning up for two days. Not like you, chief. Everything alright?'

Two lost days. He cursed himself inwardly. He thought he was over this. He had kept himself from going under for more than two years now. He had convinced himself he'd beaten it.

'Everything's fine. Flu, that's all,' he lied.

'Rough kind of flu. Did it break your door in and turn your place inside out?'

Calloway ignored him. He waved vaguely towards the gas ring. 'Coffee?'

'Coming up, chief. Looks like you need it.'

Webber looked uncertainly at the coffee pot on the shelf. 'How do you make coffee?'

'Tea then.'

Webber lit the gas and filled the old enamel kettle. He started to pick the records up from the floor.

'Leave them.'

'It's no bother. There's a few still alright.'

Calloway snapped. 'I said leave them.'

Webber shrugged. He turned his back and spooned tea into the pot. Calloway crossed the room and splashed water on his face, drying himself on the tea towel. Webber passed him a cup of the treacle-brown brew. He noticed the scabbed-over cuts on Calloway's knuckles.

'Sorry, Bert. Out of sorts.'

Webber slurped his tea. 'Yeah. Alright. But you better get yourself down the stadium. Pat's doing her nut.'

'Pat can wait.'

He sent Webber away and did his best to clean up the room. He gathered up the shards of shellac from the floor. All but a few of the records were broken or scratched beyond being playable. He should have been angry. Instead he just felt numb. The anger would come later.

He called the stadium from the hallway phone. Les Birkett answered.

'Les, it's Calloway.'

'Yes, sir. Everything alright sir?'

Calloway ignored the question. 'Is Billy Riley at the track today?'

'I believe so sir.'

'Get him for me, will you. And when you've done that, find Pat Moxon and tell her I'll meet her tomorrow. Call me at home with the time and place.'

Birkett was not the type to question an instruction. 'Will do, sir. Now if you'll just hold on, I'll fetch Mr Riley.'

Calloway heard the clunk of the receiver on the desktop. In the distance he could hear the roaring engines of the riders practicing. He waited ten minutes before Riley came to the phone. He sounded wary.

'It's Calloway. We need to speak. Can you meet me tonight?'

'I've got nothing to say to you.'

'You've no need to worry, Billy. I just need to talk. It's important.'

'Why would I be worried?'

'I think you know why. I just need to talk. Sort a few things out between us. I don't want to have to take this to Pat.'

There was silence for a moment. 'Alright. I'll meet you at nine, but not near here.' He suggested a meeting place. 'You know where that is?'

'I can find it.'

Calloway hung up. A woman's voice behind him said: 'You look very pale, luvvie. Another late night?'

It was Miss Logan. She was done up like a fashion plate. Only the fashion was two decades late. She examined him through kohl-rimmed eyes and frowned with her Cupid's bow lips.

'You need a holiday, darling,' she said, placing a gloved hand on his arm. 'Or a good woman.'

He allowed himself a laugh. Many a true word. She muttered something about having a lunch date and tap-tapped down the hallway and out of the front door.

Calloway went back to his basement. His half-drunk tea was lukewarm. He reached under the sink for the gin and poured the last of the bottle into the cup, then downed it in one. He let the alcohol work its way through his veins. He lay on the bed and made a mental report. Some facts connected, others didn't. The Fenton-Riley connection was clear now. The Fenton-Simpkins connection was obscure, save for a handful of wartime photos which had meant something to both of them, something that put Simpkins behind the theft of the notebook and a series of lies when questioned. The photos, or at least their subjects, were also important enough for Sammy Mackay and his birdwatchers to fire a warning shot across Calloway's bow. The intruder connected with the photographs too, although had failed to find them. He was professional. More henchman than thief. He carried a service revolver and a commando knife. Even in this so-called crime wave, those were not the tools of a work-a-day burglar. Who the henchman and his driver worked for was unclear. It could have been Simpkins or Mackay, Riley at a push. Now he was dead, floating down the Thames with a hole in his forehead that Calloway had put there. It was the big loose end that he couldn't leave untied.

He parked near the river in a street of bombed-out shells awaiting demolition. The sun had long set and the sky loomed dull-grey over the estuary. The fumes of the approaching ferry hung heavy in the damp night air, mingling with the soot of the power station. Across the water, the masts of giant freighters in the Royal Docks cast a skeletal semaphore against the fading light. He crossed the street towards the blackened brick cupola that marked the entrance to the foot tunnel. The lift was stopped for the night. He stepped into the spiral of the descending stairs.

The tunnel was empty. The last of the dock workers had headed south for the night. The dim electric lighting buzzed and flickered. Midway through the tunnel he heard footsteps ahead. Heavy steps which echoed off the white ceramic walls. Then the steps seemed to double time. There were two men approaching, one ahead of him, another behind. Dockers or seamen he judged from their clothing. The man ahead stopped. He was a pug-faced bruiser, five foot ten and barrel-chested, with muscled arms and ham-hock fists. He was big enough to block the tunnel all by himself.

'Are you Calloway?'

His Liverpudlian accent was deep and phlegmy.

'Are you going to let me by?' Calloway replied.

'Answer the question, pal. Are you Reg Calloway?'

Calloway looked behind him. The other man was short and wiry, with dark leathery skin and swallow tattoos on his neck and hands. He would be the dangerous one. He'd compensate for his size by fighting dirty.

'If I'm Calloway, what then?'

'Then I've got a message for you.'

'So pass it on and get out of my way.'

'Steady, pal. I don't see reinforcements showing up any time soon.'

'Who says I need them?'

'Fighting talk, eh?'

The big man laughed to himself and spat between his feet. The small man behind said nothing. Calloway braced himself.

'Billy Riley's changed his mind. He doesn't want to see you. And if you keep on at him the way you've been doing, well...'

He heard movement from behind and felt a sharp blow to the kidneys. He'd been expecting it and had tensed to deflect it. The pug face followed up with a punch to his jaw. It had weight behind it but no technique. His attackers paused, waiting for his reaction. The blows were warnings. If they intended a beating they would be all over him by now. Calloway put his full weight onto his right leg and stamped hard on the small man's shin. A cry of agony echoed down the tunnel. The pug face swung at him. Calloway sidestepped. Pug face lost his balance and stumbled forward. Calloway aimed a rabbit punch at his neck. The big man slumped. He crouched on all fours, gasping. From the corner of his eye Calloway caught the glint of a blade. The small man gripped a knife in his tattooed hand. He danced on light feet looking for an opening. He knew what he was doing. The small man lunged forward with the knife. Calloway stepped back but the blade connected. He the felt pain as blood seeped from a gash in his forearm. Behind him, the big man struggled to his feet. He grabbed Calloway's arms and used his weight to anchor him where he stood. The blade flashed beneath the electric light. Calloway tried to remember his training, but his head spun too much with adrenaline. He struggled in the grip of the pug face, his heel aiming for the big man's shin bone but stamping thin air instead. Calloway saw the sinews in the knife man's neck tighten as he prepared for the kill.

A voice hollered down the tunnel.

'Don't, Charlie! Put the fucking knife down.'

It was Riley.

The small man stood firm, his knife hand poised.

'Call off your dogs, Riley. I'm not here to make trouble for you,' Calloway shouted.

The two men looked to Riley for instruction.

'Charlie, Ron. It's alright. Let him go.'

Charlie slipped the knife into the pocket of his reefer jacket. Pug-faced Ron loosened his grip on Calloway's arms and shoved him in the direction of the tunnel's southern stairway.

The pub was a hole. It stood alone on the street corner, having defied the bombing of the docks that it served. The dim streetlight lit up a grim facade with peeling paintwork beneath a single, smog-black upper floor. Etched glass windows screened the interior from passing eyes. A babble of voices hit them as they walked through the doors. The place was full. It was a drab place, a comfortless dock pub. The clientele wore the same reefer jackets and wool caps as pug-faced Ron and his friend. They knew Riley. They acknowledged his arrival with turned heads and subtle nods. They eyed Calloway with curiosity and suspicion.

Ron turfed two drinkers off a table and gestured to Riley and Calloway to sit. The displaced drinkers raised little objection. The pug face and the knife man Charlie had a reputation here. A fat landlady with a music hall laugh poured them pints from the crowded bar. Charlie brought them over, laid them on the table, then left them to talk. They kept a watch on Calloway from the bar.

'An odd choice for a man of your means, Billy.'

'I prefer my own kind.'

'Been to sea often have you?'

On the surface it was a typical dock pub. Seamen and dockers, loud and drunk. But there were others here too. Better dressed men, out of place but clearly at home. And the talk was different. Part Silvertown, part Soho, ports of call with hints of polari. It was the looks Calloway noticed. An interrogator learns to read the small signs, the sideways glances and the eye contact. He'd seen the same looks on the faces of the men in Fenton's photographs. When patrons left, they left in pairs.

Riley downed half his pint and set the glass down.

'I suppose we had better talk.'

He looked down at the table like he was expecting the worst.

Calloway leaned forward and spoke, as quietly as the noise around them would allow. 'I know Fenton was blackmailing you. I've seen the photographs. Tell me what he wanted.'

Riley took another gulp of beer. 'He threatened to send copies to Ken Kilminster.'

'Police?'

Riley shook his head. 'He writes for Speedway Gazette. He's always down the track. Sweaty bloke with a bald head. Smells of moth balls. Fenton used to go crawling round him. Glory hunting.'

Calloway recognised Kilminster from the description.

'Would Speedway Gazette run that kind of thing?'

'No, but Ken is a stringer for the Sunday Pictorial. They'd lap it up. Fenton wanted a third of my winnings for keeping quiet. He also told me I was never to win a race when I was paired with him.'

'What did you do?'

'I paid him, didn't I? And I pulled back on races. I was at the top of my game when he first got onto me. The next star rider. But it was him who shot up the tables. Left me as an also-ran.'

'And you never told anyone?'

'Are you having a laugh? Of course I fuckin' didn't. It would have been the end of my career, not to mention two years in jail with the nonces. Do you know what they do to people like me inside?'

His voice had risen to a shout. He looked around to see who might have heard him. He needn't have worried. The hubbub in the bar drowned out their conversation.

'I only told Charlie and Ron so they'd warn you off.'

Calloway glanced at the dried blood on his sleeve. 'They did a pretty good job.'

'Look, I never knew Ron would pull a knife on you. They were only supposed to rough you up a bit. It was a stupid idea.'

Riley gulped down the rest of his pint. He looked scared.

'Are you going to tell the police?'

Calloway shook his head. 'I've seen a lot of bad things in my time Billy. Those pictures aren't one of them.'

He pulled the prints and negatives from his pocket and slid them across the table. 'Take them and burn them.'

Riley looked doubtful, as if he didn't believe his boss's head of security. Calloway passed him a second bundle.

'There's a list of names on the back. Do you recognise any of them?'

Riley read through the list. He raised his eyebrows at a couple of the names. 'One or two.'

'Tell them you've burned the lot. I'm not interested in you or the others. I'm only interested in Ray Simpkins.'

Riley looked puzzled. 'Why Ray?'

'Fenton had something on him. He was taking money from him and getting him to pull races, same as you. Is Ray like the other men on that list?'

Riley laughed. 'You're joking aren't you? Ray Simpkins? He's a proper cunt chaser. Spends his winnings on whores. Real rough ones an' all, from what I've heard.'

'Rough enough to blackmail him over?'

'Nah. He boasts about it. He's a dirty bastard.'

'Then Fenton must have had some other kind of dirt on him. Simpkins's score card shows the same tail off in form as yours. All the signs point to him making regular payments to Fenton. The only way I can connect them is through the tramp that used to doss down under the stands. The tramp had photos from the war.'

'Photos of Simpkins?'

'No, Germans. SS soldiers.'

'Fuckin' hell.'

'Can you think of anything that might make sense of all that?'

Riley shrugged. 'Honestly, Mr Calloway, if I could I'd tell you.'

The young rider paused to take it all in. 'Why do you need to know, Mr Calloway? Fenton's dead isn't he?'

'Pat knows something was up. She thinks the accident was suspicious.'

Riley rolled his eyes. 'Seriously? Speedway's a dangerous game. We all know the risks. We don't get many deaths in the sport, but when they happen, it's not like anyone's surprised.'

'That's what I thought at first. But when I started asking around, well Billy, it felt like I'd kicked the hornets' nest. You ever see Fenton and Simpkins arguing? Or talking about the war?'

Billy thought about it. 'I didn't spend much time with them two, to be honest. Didn't like 'em. Even before, well you know. I like a drink with the fellas but it's usually with Bert and Six Gun, sometimes the skipper, if his missus will let him out.' He sniggered at this. 'They're good blokes. Bert's everyone's mate and O'Donnell, well he's a bit flash, but he's got your back, you know?'

Riley noticed Calloway's glass was empty. 'You want another? It's the least I can do.'

Calloway accepted. Riley signalled two more pints to Ron who was maintaining a keen watch from the bar. They sat in silence for a moment, then Calloway noticed Riley turning something over in his mind.

'There was this one time, thinking about it. Something a bit odd, if you know what I mean.'

'Tell me.'

'We were away to White City. The Rebels. A few of us were having a post-race drink-up. We'd lost as it happens, but they were being, you know, gracious about it. One of 'em knew Simpkins from before the war. Ray's not local, you see. He's west London, from Acton way. This Rebel rider, I forget his name, kept calling Simpkins blackshirt.'

'Blackshirt? Meaning fascist?'

'Yeah. Said he remembered him when he was following Mosely around. Simpkins denied it, but this Rebel rider kept on. Pulling his leg, but a bit serious about it too.'

'What happened?'

'Simpkins told him to fuck off and left.'

'Did anyone mention this again?

'Nah. By the end of the night we were all too pissed to remember. It's not like it was a big deal. There was enough of 'em around before the war.'

'Blackshirts?'

'Yeah. My old man knew a few round here.'

'Was he one?'

Riley choked. 'Christ, no. He was practically a communist. Told me he fought the fascists in Cable Street.'

'A man of principle.'

'Yeah. He had a lot of principles. Not all of 'em worked in my favour.'

He looked reflective. 'He was shop steward for the union at Surrey Docks. That was until a bomb got him. Direct hit. He was helping unload aggregates for the Mulberry harbours. Mum never got over it. She died of lung cancer a year later. Me and my sister looked after each other after that. We were both underage, but my sister managed to convince the Peabody Mum was still alive. That way we got to stay in the flat.'

As they spoke, Charlie and pug face Ron walked up to their table.

'Everything alright Billy?' the pug face asked.

Riley slipped the photographs into the pocket of his blouson jacket. He smiled at Calloway.

'Yeah, everything's fine.'

EIGHTEEN

The hotel bar was a jazz-era throwback with a drinks list to match. Every cocktail told a story which came at a price. The decor was Tinseltown on the Strand. Chrome, walnut and zigzags. Calloway could hear his father's voice. A cocktail bar? Who d'you think you are lad, Franchot bloody Tone?

'We could have met in my office,' he said.

Pat was already seated with a drink in front of her. He guessed it wasn't her first. 'Or mine.'

She was reminding him she was still the client, even though he'd refused her money.

'Sorry for dragging you here but I had to meet with a couple of chaps from Ealing Studios.'

She enjoyed saying this, he could tell.

'They want to make a film.'

'Another newsreel?'

'No, a proper feature film. They've bought the rights to some book or other, about speedway riders. They want to film it at the stadium, use the Bullets for the race scenes.'

More bloody show business. Calloway heard his father's voice again. This time he agreed with him.

'Can I be in it?'

She laughed. 'A big brute like you?'

She sipped from her drink. It was pale pink and had a cherry in it. The cherry matched her lipstick.

'They're thinking of casting that young Dirk Bogarde.'

'Good is he?'

'Well he's a looker. No offence.'

A waiter came over. Calloway ordered the most expensive cocktail on the list.

'Not too ill to drink then.'

She put the cocktail stick to her lips and bit on the cherry. 'This film would be good for the club. Good publicity. But I don't want this Fenton business hanging over it.'

'No, you don't. It's dirty business.'

She seemed unsettled by the word.

'Dirty how?'

'Fenton was running a blackmail racket. I found a stash of photographs in his workshop, photographs of men importuning. Enough to put them in jail. One of them was Billy Riley.'

He waited for a reaction but she didn't seem surprised. She took it in and let him continue.

'Billy was paying him a third of his winnings and letting him win races. I've found evidence to suggest Ray Simpkins was doing the same, but for different reasons.'

'What reasons?'

'I don't know yet. But Fenton had something on Simpkins, something he'd learned from a dosser that used to sleep under the stands. I went looking for him. I found him dead. He'd drunk himself to death on meths down by the estuary. I found photographs on him from the war.'

'Photos of Simpkins?'

Calloway shook his head. 'Photographs of SS soldiers.'

It was the first thing he'd said that seemed to surprise her.

The waiter brought Calloway's drink and set it down on the table. He was worn and sallow-faced, his white steward's jacket too big for his skinny frame. Pat waved her empty glass at him. He acknowledged the order with a servile nod and withdrew to the bar.

'Simpkins has denied any knowledge, but he's lying. Somehow those photos connect him to something he'd sooner keep quiet about. Something serious. And he's not the only one who wants it kept quiet.'

'Meaning?'

'Someone broke into my flat. A professional. My guess is they were looking for the photographs. I caught them at it before they had a chance to find them.'

She looked shocked this time. 'What happened?'

'Best you don't know. But this is more than a spat between teammates.'

'And the accident?'

'Probably just that. An accident. Granted, one that was convenient for Simpkins. But even if Simpkins did intend to run Fenton off the track, it would be nigh on impossible to prove.'

'Even if Fenton was blackmailing him?'

Calloway nodded.

'So I just forget about it?'

'The accident? Yes. That's the answer you wanted, wasn't it?'

She looked annoyed. 'Yes, Reg, that was the answer I wanted.'

'Then I'm happy to oblige, at least on that front. It's the dirt Fenton had on Simpkins you need to worry about.'

But it was Calloway that needed to worry. The dead burglar could wash up at Deptford steps where all the bodies wash up, right on his doorstep, shot through the forehead at point-blank range. He may have been seen, he may have left fingerprints during the fight. It would be hard to argue self-defence if it came to it. More likely he'd be dealt with through less-formal means.

His mouth was dry. He drank the expensive drink. It was hard liquor with a drop of something to take the edge off it. He felt the alcohol course through his veins. It calmed him.

'So what do we do now?'

'You do nothing. I need to brace Simpkins. I also need to call a friend of mine. Someone else that's lying to me.'

She toyed with her drink, buying time. She had something to ask him, something he was expecting. 'The photographs you found in Des's workshop.'

'What about them?'

'Were they just of men? Blackmail photos of queers?'

'No. Fenton liked to photograph women too. Only much closer up.'

She lit a cigarette. 'What have you done with them?'

'They're safe.'

He felt a frost descend. She had dropped her cocktail bar act. 'I need those photos, Reg.'

'I'm keeping everything until I've sorted this business out.'

He didn't trust her. He didn't trust anyone right now. He was holding the cards and this wasn't the time to play them. Her face tensed. She lit a cigarette and drew on it hard.

'How much do you want?'

Calloway scoffed. 'Don't insult me.'

'If not money, then what else?'

'I want to deal with the Simpkins situation. Like you asked. I'll tie up the loose ends afterwards.'

Liz Francis lived with her mother and three younger siblings in a tenement flat on the Old Kent Road. Bert Webber had given Calloway the address. Like Billy Riley said, Bert was everyone's friend. The tenement was cramped. It smelled of a place where people slept and fried food in the same room. Washing hung from a line across the room. Children's vests and pants, grey and frayed, nylons and women's underwear, cheap and worn out.

Liz was embarrassed to see him. She had answered the door in a dressing gown. It was three in the afternoon and she had slept in her make-up. She kept him at the door, making excuses. He'd insisted they speak in private. She made him tea and they sat at a mean-sized table, penned in by two iron beds and an old stone sink. The sink was full of dishes. Calloway struggled to squeeze his big frame into the space. She put two cups without saucers on the table in front of them. There was a film of grease on the surface of the tea.

She pulled the dressing gown tight across her and made a half-hearted attempt to tidy her hair.

'Late night?' he said.

'Working. Didn't get home until five.'

'Night shift was it?'

'You could call it that. I'm a waitress at a club.'

'A gentleman's club?'

'Believe me, they're not gentleman.'

She held the tea with both hands. Her painted nails were chipped.

'So this is me.'

She waved a hand around the dismal room. 'Des said he'd take me away from all this.'

'Men say a lot of things.'

'Don't I know it.'

She lit a cigarette and tossed the match into a filthy ceramic ashtray. It was a present from Margate.

'He didn't seem in any hurry though.'

'You told me he was raising the money for a flat.'

'So he said. I'm beginning to wonder. Anyway, you can't miss what you've never had I suppose.'

'Did he tell you how he was raising the money?'

'Just said it was a sideline. Something different to the speedway.'

Calloway supped the tea reluctantly and looked around the room. He guessed Liz and her mother shared one bed and the children shared the other. Neither beds were made. There was an un-emptied pot beneath one.

'I need to tell you something Miss Francis. It might shock you.'

She raised a pencilled eyebrow. 'I'm not easily shocked, Mr Calloway.'

'Des Fenton was a blackmailer. Homosexuals mostly. Irene Fenton was in on it, but not all of it. Fenton kept one of his victims from her. His teammate, Ray Simpkins. He wasn't like the others. Fenton had another kind of dirt on him. Something going back to the war. My guess is he kept this from his wife so he could use the money he extorted from Simpkins to pay for the flat he promised you.'

He gave her time to take it in. She folded her arms and looked down at the grubby table. 'Des Fenton was a bastard.'

'But you were lovers.'

'The two aren't exclusive. Des was charming, generous when he felt like it, exciting to be with. He took me to parties and restaurants and clubs. He showed me off, it was flattering. I 'spose I knew he would never leave Irene. She had her claws into him too deep. He didn't have the balls. But I kidded myself willingly, imagined a life, you know. A nice flat up West, glamorous friends, being photographed on his arm. The speedway star's beautiful wife.'

She corrected herself. 'Second wife.' She glanced around the cheerless room. 'I mean, look at the alternative.'

A baby screamed in the next door flat. It could have been in the room with them. Its mother screamed back. Then a man's voice shouted. A door slammed. The mother started sobbing.

'Did you know Fenton was a blackmailer?'

She shook her head. 'No, but it doesn't surprise me. He'd often let on that he knew people's secrets. It was bit of thing with him, you know? "See him over there", he'd say. "I could tell you a thing or two". He got a kick out of it. Probably said things about me too.'

Calloway didn't doubt it. He'd seen the photographs. Fenton seemed the type that might show them around.

'Did Des ever mention anything about Ray Simpkins to you?'

She shrugged. 'He didn't like Ray. Didn't have a good word for him. They were chalk and cheese.'

'And he never talked about the war? Never suggested he knew a thing or two about Ray?'

She shook her head. 'Sorry.'

The baby next door was wailing, competing with the clang and clatter of the trolley busses in the street below. Children's feet in heavy boots rumbled along the tenement balconies where two women argued. The smell of damp and bad cooking was all pervading. The place made the pit village back-to-backs of Calloway's childhood seem as genteel as the Fenton's suburban idyll.

'Fenton processed his blackmail photos in a darkroom at his workshop. I went there. I found these.'

Calloway took the photos of Liz from his raincoat pocket and laid them on the table. She snatched them up and rifled through them. Her hands trembled. She tossed the pictures back on the tabletop. They fanned out as they landed, the pin-ups on top, the explicit poses underneath, the worst of their depravity visible to them both.

'Alright, so you've seen them. I'm not proud of them. He said he'd take publicity shots, to help with my career. I was still at the

Centurion school and couldn't afford to pay for a professional shoot. Des took a good photograph. Of course I accepted. He had borrowed a flat from a friend. A nice flat. We went there one evening. It was all set up. He kept telling me to have a drink. Said it would relax me. Bring out the best in the photos. After a while I said I'd drunk too much but he kept insisting. He started asking me to do things. Things I didn't want to do. As you can see, he got his way.'

She picked up one of the explicit shots and held it up so Calloway could see. 'That's not me, Mr Calloway. That's Des Fenton.'

She threw the photo down. 'He was a bastard.'

Anger gripped at her face through the smeared make-up. But if he was expecting tears, he was wrong. She was full of fight. Calloway gathered up the prints, pulled the negatives from his pocket and added them to the pile.

'Destroy them all. You're worth more than that and you know it. Fenton's gone. Forget him and move on.'

'Move on?' She laughed. 'Do you know how hard it is to get out of a place like this? Do you think I want to be here? The charm school was my big chance. I've got the looks, I've got the figure.'

He couldn't help but look her up and down.

She saw him. 'Yeah. In case you hadn't noticed.'

She shook her head and sighed. 'I thought I'd got the talent too. Who was I kidding? Like it or not, if a girl like me wants out, chances are she has to find a man. Des seemed like that man, at least at first.'

She stubbed the cigarette out hard. 'Boy, can I pick 'em.'

He had no advice to give. No suggestion of a way out, although God knows he wished he had one. He managed a sympathetic look, which made him seem weak.

'I'm sorry,' she said. 'You're not seeing me at my best.'

'I wouldn't say that. At least I'm seeing you. Not the charm school hopeful, or Fenton's mistress or the girl in those photos.'

He offered her another cigarette.

'I prefer this version.'

She looked down, embarrassed. 'Thanks. But I reckon you're the only one.'

He sipped his tea. He felt obliged to. It wasn't so bad.

'Where's the family?'

'Mum went up to the World Turned Upside Down. They'll have called time by now, so Christ knows where she's ended up.'

She rolled her eyes. 'Or who with. The boys will be out smashing up bomb sites and scrounging cigarettes.'

They sat in awkward silence until she spoke again, 'Des fucking Fenton.'

Calloway stood up to leave. She stopped him. 'Wait.'

She hesitated, then stepped over to the little mantlepiece above the cast-iron fireplace. There were papers in a plain wooden rack, the sort prisoners of war used to make. She rifled through them, coupons, leaflets, a letter or two.

'Des asked me to look after this. Said it was insurance.'

She passed Calloway a sealed envelope. 'He told me not to open it.'

'Do you know what it is?'

'I don't know and I don't want to know. You take it. Perhaps it will help with whatever it is you're trying to find out.'

He thanked her and slipped the envelope into the inside pocket of his suit jacket.

She turned to face him as she opened the door. 'Thanks for listening Mr Calloway. Not many do. Men don't want to hear that sort of thing.'

He thought about the times he had spent in the villa in the small German town.

'You're welcome,' he said. 'I liked having someone to listen to.'

The greasy tea had turned to acid in his stomach. He couldn't remember the last time he had eaten. He felt nauseous and light-headed. He took a trolley bus to Deptford and ate pie and mash at Manze's, soaked in thick green-white liquor.

He had settled himself in a booth at the rear of the shop with his back to the wall. He pulled the sealed envelope from the pocket of his jacket, wiped his knife clean on the edge of the plate and slid it under the flap. There were three photographs inside, the missing shots from the vagrant's album. He examined them under the harsh overhead lighting.

The same uniformed men, only three of them this time. The first photo was taken in a field hospital. One soldier lay on a cot, his face half covered with a dressing but managing to grin. His two comrades squatted either side him, giving the thumbs up to the camera. The injured soldier and the comrade to his right had featured in the all of the photographs Calloway had removed from the album. The face of the third soldier was overexposed and indistinct. The second photo was taken subsequently, the injured man recovered with his healed wound visible. The three were rounding up civilians at gunpoint. Again, the third face was obscured. The civilians held their hands in the air. Two old men, one too frail to walk unaided, being assisted by the other. Two women, alike enough to be mother and daughter. And a child of no more than ten, in shorts with loose socks bunched around the ankles of his stick-thin legs. In the final photo, the three SS men stood with their arms extended, aiming pistols at the heads of the two old men and the child, who kneeled in front of them on the mossy floor of a pine forest. A few feet beyond the kneeling men, three shovels stood in the ground next to the grave they had been used to dig. In the background, a group of Waffen SS soldiers looked on as spectators.

Calloway held this last photo up to the light and squinted to better see the detail. He saw that the three executioners were smiling as they squeezed the triggers. He could also see that one of them, holding his pistol to the frail old man's head, had a lightning-fork scar on his face. And this time he could clearly see the face of the soldier that held his gun to the head of the child. It was Ray Simpkins.

NINETEEN

He parked behind the Fenton's Alvis. Overnight rain had left a patina of soot-black circles on the polished maroon coachwork. He saw the front room curtains twitch. Irene Fenton opened the door moments later and crossed the paved driveway towards him. Her expression was lacking the suburban propriety of his previous visit.

'What do you want?'

No chance of tea in china cups this time. This was the un-gentrified Irene, the Kentish twang of her south east London accent cutting through the quiet of the morning like a rusty scythe.

'I need to talk to you again Mrs Fenton.'

She stood toe-to-toe with the big man, arms crossed, chin jutting forward like an unvoiced threat.

'I've told you all I know. Now please leave. You've no business here.'

'I wish for your sake I hadn't.'

'For my sake?'

'For your sake, Mrs Fenton. You see blackmail carries a sentence of up to fourteen years. I imagine Holloway prison would come as quite a shock after the leafy suburbs.' Although, judging by the look on her face right now, he suspected she might just get by inside. 'I'm sure your neighbours would agree.'

By now other curtains twitched in the street. Irene noticed them.

'Shall I carry on, Mrs Fenton?'

She dropped the fighting stance. They went inside, into the kitchen this time. It was pristine and looked like an advertisement. He settled himself on a chrome-legged chair.

'Sit down, Mrs Fenton.'

'I'd rather stand.'

'As you wish. I won't waste time. You ran a blackmail racket with your husband. Ran it, or at least were complicit in it. You blackmailed homosexuals with incriminating photographs. You said yourself, your late husband took a good photograph. Seems he put his talents to use.'

She rolled her eyes. 'This is rubbish.'

'Is it? Your husband had a darkroom at the back of his workshop. He kept the photographs and negatives there. I've seen them. In fact I have them.'

She frowned, disbelieving.

'The workshop's all locked up.'

'I'm the resourceful type.'

'I don't know anything about this.'

'Then you won't mind if I go to the police. I have to, you see. It's track business. I'd be negligent if I didn't.'

'I said I know nothing about this.'

'You knew enough to squeeze Billy Riley for money in the Four Bells last Saturday.'

Her eyes flashed. The muscles in her jaw tensed. 'You can't prove that.'

'Actually, Mrs Fenton, I can. Billy Riley made a statement for my report. He signed it.'

She shook her head. 'He'd never do that. It would be the end of his career.'

'Very possibly. But he's prepared for the consequences. The lad's had enough you see. He wants the whole thing to be over.'

She clenched her fists, digging her manicured nails into her palms. 'He'll deserve everything he gets. He's a dirty little queer. They're all dirty queers. Des hated them, hated their type. He hated Billy the most. He couldn't stand having a dilly boy for a teammate.'

'And rather than report him, he decided to blackmail him. Him and half a dozen others. That's hardly the moral high ground.'

She spat her retort. 'They deserved it. Hit them in the wallet where it really hurts, that's what my Des said. Prison's too good for their sort. A nancy boys' holiday camp, he called it.'

Calloway felt his anger rise. Veins pulsed in his head. He had seen homosexuals at the camp in Germany. The faded pink triangles sewn to their lousy prison jackets. The hollowed-out faces filled with desperation and confusion. He'd been ambivalent up to then. He'd used the words everyone used, sniggered when others sniggered, called them nancy boys along with the rest. He wasn't scared of them, but he'd no great concern for their lot in life. The camp changed that. He saw the humanity in all its victims. The Jews, the communists, the gypsies and the queers. It was the common denominator that trumped the prejudice.

'Spare me the moral crusade. Now sit down.'

She ignored him, out-staring him with hating eyes. He leapt to his feet and grabbed her by the arm, dragged her across the showroom-bright lino and pushed her down hard on the chair opposite his. She bared her teeth like a cornered animal.

'If you lay a hand on me again I swear I'll...'

'Shut up and listen. You're going to jail, Mrs Fenton. A cold filthy women's prison. I have evidence and a witness, enough to put you away for years. Long, cold, ugly years, far away from the niceties your filthy racket has been paying for. You have one chance to avoid that happening. One chance, if you do exactly what I ask.'

She threw her head back and laughed, play acting derision. 'If you think I'm going to sleep with you, you've got another think coming.'

'Don't drag me down to your level. Now listen. Do you have writing paper and an envelope?'

She nodded.

'Fetch them.'

When she returned from the living room he made her sit again and dictated a letter. She started to write then stopped. 'What's this about?'

'Just write.'

'What if I refuse?'

'Then you'd better hope there's a hard-as-nails brass inside

Holloway that will be your friend. Of course she might want something in return.'

She hissed, 'You're a bastard.'

'They say the same about your Des, as it happens. Now write.'

She did as she was told, gripping the fountain pen hard and scratching the letters into the velum paper as if to spite him.

'Sign it.'

She looked up. Her eyes narrowed and her tensed lips showed white through her lipstick. 'I'm not signing this. It makes no sense.'

He leaned back in the kitchen chair. He didn't speak until he had her full attention. Then he spoke calmly and quietly, 'There's an ex-army sergeant-major on my staff, reliable sort he is. He's at the stadium right now with my report in an envelope addressed to CID and ready to take to New Scotland Yard. He's instructed to deliver the report at three o'clock sharp today.'

Calloway looked at his watch.

'He'll be preparing to leave now I reckon. I've got about five minutes to call him from the phone in your hall and stand him down. Sign that letter and I'll make the call. Refuse and you take your chances in a court of law.'

He crossed his arms and waited. She picked up the pen and scrawled a signature.

'I hope you burn in hell.'

He crossed the room to the hallway and closed the door behind him. He dialled the stadium number and asked to be put through to security. Les Birkett answered.

Calloway spoke quietly, 'Les, go to the personnel files and find me an address.'

From the kitchen he heard crying. A deliberate, self-pitying wail for his benefit. Birkett retuned a few minutes later and Calloway memorised the address. Calloway didn't mention the report to Birkett. There was no report. There was no signed statement from Billy Riley either. He returned to the kitchen. He found her with her head in her hands, sobbing, but not so much that her make-up ran, not even so much as a smudge.

'You can stop that. I'm not interested.'

He grabbed her hand roughly and thrust the pen in it. 'Now write this address.' She complied. He sealed the letter, slipped it into his inside pocket and left her to her crying. On the drive back to the stadium he stopped a post office, bought a thrupenny stamp and posted the letter in the local mail slot. The next collection was four pm. With luck the letter would arrive tomorrow.

He drove to the stadium and parked in Canal Road. Les Birkett saluted as he passed through the main gates. Curiosity showed on the old NCO's face. Calloway blanked him. He was in no mood for conversation. As he approached his office, he saw movement behind the frosted glass panel of the door. Slowly and silently he tested the door. It was unlocked, when it shouldn't have been. He gave the door a shove and stepped inside.

Pat Moxon sat at his desk rifling through the drawers.

'Find anything?'

Her expression implied she had every right to search his office. 'Your filing's impeccable. A proper shiny arse.'

He shook his head. 'I did my reporting in the field. No desks to jockey there.'

'A man of action, clearly,' she leaned back in his chair, 'but very few words.'

'I speak when I'm spoken to, ma'am.'

'Don't start that again.'

He pulled a cigarette from his case and lit up. 'As you wish. Find what you were looking for?'

'You know I didn't.'

She was right. The last set of Fenton's photographs were in the safe along with the contents of Joe Smoke's album and the 'insurance' shots that Liz Francis had given him. Moxon would get them when he was ready. Right now there were still questions that needed answering about the whole affair. Until he had answers, he was trusting no one.

'Tried the bottom drawer yet?'

'I was rudely interrupted.'

'There's a bottle of Johnnie Walker in there and a couple of glasses. Pour us one each.'

'Is the sun over the yard arm?'

'It's over the west stand and I need a drink. I imagine you do too.'

She poured two glasses and waved one in front of him. 'Promise not to walk out on me this time? You still haven't redeemed yourself for leaving me at the party. Dennis drove me home four sheets to the wind. Nearly killed us both. Not the best end to an evening, what with that and his wandering hands.'

'I was following Riley and his man friend. It's how I tumbled the blackmail angle.'

'A proper Dick Barton.'

She passed him the glass. 'Chin-chin.'

The whiskey tingled through his veins. He relaxed into the chair. She dipped a finger into her glass and put it to her lips, holding his stare as she did so.

'So what's your story, Calloway? Was stadium security a lifelong ambition?'

'No, just the result of a lifelong need to eat. I was discharged in forty-eight. Honourably, in name if not in deed.'

'A bad boy were you, Reg?'

'I'll let the angels decide. My conscience is still unsure. Let's just say there was a war criminal who went to trail a little less hale and hearty than when I picked him up. I was escorting him to Nuremberg. On the way there he happened to say the wrong thing to the wrong man.'

Compared to the guard on the crematorium floor, the Nuremberg incident was nothing. The difference was Calloway let the man live and suffered the consequences.

'It seemed like a good time to leave the army. At least that's what my CO suggested, and in no uncertain terms. So I went home, if you can call it that. The army had been my home since grammar school. The war had been my life since thirty-nine. I had about as much in common with that tiny pit village than one of your Bullets has with a district nurse on a bicycle. I was offered a desk job by the coal board on account of my education and my short-lived commission.'

He shook his head dismissively. 'I packed a bag the next day and got as far away from that place as I could. I was down to the last few pounds of my demob money when I ran into an old pal from my unit. He was running security at a greyhound stadium on the south coast. He'd heard on the grapevine that Bermondsey was looking for the same. I knew nothing about the place and even less about speedway or dogs. But I knew how to keep people in line. The rest you know.'

He drank some more of the whiskey. It felt good. She poured him another glass. Sleep tugged at his consciousness. The fatigue of the past few days was taking its toll. He craved the onset of a gentle stupor. He wanted to relax, enjoy the company of a woman. But it didn't come naturally anymore. And he was still unclear how Pat Moxon fitted into the story. He scrunched up his eyes and blinked himself back to a safe state of alertness.

'So why no Mrs Calloway?'

It was a fair question, given his age, but one he was loathe to answer. He'd never spoken of Miriam and those precious weeks in the villa to anyone. It was a memory locked in the music he played to remember, the music that filled a very private place inside him. He'd allowed no one in, never wanted a shoulder to cry on nor a sympathetic ear. But as he sat in the gloomy office with the lady boss, a part of him that needed to pour it all out, lay the burden down if only for the duration of two cheap whiskies in glasses filched from the members bar.

'There was a future Mrs Calloway, once.'

'What happened?'

He stopped himself. The shell hardened around him once more. He felt safer inside it.

'A lot of things, not many of them good. What about you?'

'Me?' she huffed. 'Yet to meet a man good enough, Reg.'

He nodded in the direction of the circuit. 'You've got the pick of the league.'

She knocked back the whiskey. 'Never love a speedway rider. I learned that lesson the hard way.'

'So why buy a whole team of them?'

She thought for a moment, then laughed. 'To prove a point.'

'To who?'

'Where shall I start? The ones that said girls don't ride. The ones that put me down when I did, the ones who denied me the credit and the ones that banned us from the sport.'

'That's quite a list.'

'That's only the half of it. Then there's the goosing, the groping, the promises in return for favours and the name calling when the favours are denied. Shall I go on?'

'I think you've made your point.'

'I've every right to, believe me.'

'Let's drink to that then.'

He pushed his glass across the desk towards hers and she refilled both. As she poured, he said: 'What made you suspect Fenton's accident might have been deliberate?'

He'd surprised her. She tried hard not to show it. 'There were rumours.'

'Word has it you started them.'

'Why would I do that?'

She was trying to sound casual but her tone was defensive. She looked away. She took a cigarette from her case and lit it with his desk lighter, inhaling deeply. When she turned to face him she was composed again. She pushed the glass towards him.

'I know them well enough, Reg. It's not what they were saying, it's what they were holding back. There was something wrong. You said yourself Des and Ray Simpkins were known to have fallen out.'

'It's a big jump from that to running a man off the track.'

'Des was a blackmailer. He had something on Ray. A convenient accident would be a good way out.'

'But you didn't know that when you asked me to look into this.'

'Then let's call it intuition.'

He left it there, but he wasn't buying it. She diverted the conversation, rummaging through the open drawers of his desk and pulling out a well-thumbed paperback.

'Zane Grey? Like a good western, Reggie?'

'Not especially. Bert Webber lent it to me. He's a big fan so he tells me. Read every one.'

'Bless him. He makes three thousand a year and still eats at the Civic Restaurant. Refuses to leave his prefab.'

She smiled with rare and genuine warmth. 'Fame hasn't changed that one.'

'I'd call that a virtue.'

His limbs felt heavy with the drink. He stood and stretched, walked to her side of the desk and took the book from her hand, dropping it back into the drawer and nudging it closed with his knee. She stood to face him, close enough for him to smell her scent and feel her warmth. He felt her breath on his face, the smell of the whiskey and cigarettes tingling his nerves. Her hand slid into his. She looked him in the eye and held his gaze, half tempting, half taunting.

'I need those photographs, Reggie. I beg you.'

Her closeness felt too good. He shook her hand free.

'You're not the begging kind.'

'I've tried money. What more can I offer you?'

'Nothing I'm prepared to take.'

She withdrew, poured the last of the whiskey into her glass and knocked it back.

'You'll get the photographs when I've dealt with Simpkins. I expect to see him tomorrow night. I'll sort things out, one way or another.'

'Then I guess I'm in your hands. But leave him in one piece, eh? I need him to race on Friday.'

He thought of the three photographs Liz Francis had given him.

'I can't promise that,' he said.

TWENTY

The heavy motorcycle rumbled over the cobbles down the dark mechanic's path. It was past midnight and deserted. The low throb of the engine bounced off the viaduct walls. The rider cut the engine, then it was quiet save for the distant screech of freight train wheels on metal rails further down the track.

Calloway heard the bike arrive. He had settled himself on a chair at the back of Fenton's workshop with a clear view of the big double doors in the railway arch. He sat in the darkness with a hip flask for company. He'd been there an hour, listening out and watching the chink of light between the doors for signs of movement. A man's shadow appeared in the chink. The figure hesitated, eased the door ajar and stepped inside.

Calloway had rigged an inspection lamp to face the doors. He flicked the wall switch. Ray Simpkins flinched and squinted through the glare. He could make out Calloway's shape but couldn't identify him.

'Where's Irene?'

'It's just me, Raymond.'

Simpkins recognised the voice. His eyes adjusted.

'Oh. You doing her dirty work, Calloway?'

'It's my dirty work, Ray.'

'Why'd she write to me then?'

'I wrote to you. She just held the pen. Sit down.'

Calloway gestured to a chair in front of him and tossed the hip flask at Simpkins. The rider caught it by reflex.

'Have a drink, Ray. We're going to have a chat you and I. See if we can't sort this little problem out.'

Simpkins squared up, stretching his jockey-like frame to full height. 'You know what your little problem is? You can fuck off, that's what.'

Calloway looked the lean rider up and down. 'Nine stone eight I reckon. Perhaps nine two without the motorcycle gear.'

Simpkins looked perplexed.

'They say Mr Pierrepoint can tell a man's weight just by looking at him. He needs to know the weight, you see, to know what length of rope to use, how long a drop from the trapdoor. He's very precise apparently. He's not vindictive. He likes a quick, clean, instant death. Painless they say, although they can't be sure, can they? He's busy mind. You might have to wait a while, in the condemned cell. A long wait, all by yourself, with a rope at the end of it.'

Calloway crossed the workshop and leaned forward. He spoke softly into the other man's ear. 'Very busy of late Mr Pierrepoint, what with this gun crime epidemic and the trips back and forth to Germany to hang the war criminals.'

Simpkins tensed. The sinews tautened in his neck.

Calloway continued. 'I met him once, at Hamelin prison in December 1945. I watched him execute eleven SS guards from a camp I had helped to liberate. I was no stranger to death, not after six years of war, but I'd never witnessed that many deaths in a single day. I suppose it would have been shocking had Mr Pierrepoint not been so professional. He hooded every one of them personally before pulling the lever. Most died instantly, but not all. The ones who took longer were harder to watch.'

Simpkins's bravura ebbed. He slouched into the chair and took a swig from the hip flask.

'Of course they wouldn't hang you in Germany. You're one of ours. Wandsworth, I imagine. Not too far from here, eh? I wonder if any Bullets fans would come to watch.'

The rider summoned some nerve. 'What the fuck are you on about?'

'Don't play the innocent, Simpkins. We're way past that stage. This is about you doing as I say and maybe, just maybe mind, saving your own wretched hide. I have the evidence see. The photographs. The ones your old mate Joe Smoke carried with him like some macabre trophy of your wartime adventures. There's one in particular, one of the three photographs Fenton kept for himself. The one he used to skim your winnings, the one that bought him points each time he finished ahead of his teammate Ray on the track.'

Simpkins tried to swallow but couldn't. He uncapped the flask and drained it. Calloway noticed his hands had started to tremble.

'What do you want?'

Calloway stood over him, hands in his pockets. 'Did you bring the money?'

'What makes you think I've got that kind of money?'

'What's this, Ray's a laugh? Spare me, son. I've never liked comedy. I know you're good for five hundred, even after Fenton skimmed his percentage.'

Simpkins coughed up a gobbet and spat at Calloway's feet. He managed a laugh. 'Christ, you're no better than him.'

'Perhaps not. But you're in no position to preach morals.'

Simpkins glared, defiant.

'Go whistle for your fuckin' money.'

The rider had not expected the blow. By the time he felt the smack of Calloway's fist he was already on the floor. When the big man's foot slammed into his guts, Simpkins's survival instinct took over. The rider gagged down the bile that rose in his throat. He summoned energy and scrambled to his feet. Calloway was ahead of him. He grabbed the rider in a neck lock and yanked him up, then pushed him face down on the workbench. He kept him there, twisting his arm to breaking point behind his back while he patted him down. He found the money zipped into a pocket of Simpkins's leathers. He kicked the rider's legs away and dragged his featherweight frame across the oil-soaked floor, dumping him back in the chair.

'Let's start again. Three men. One I don't recognise, one with a scar on his cheek and one that's quite clearly you, standing in a forest in Waffen SS uniforms executing geriatrics, cripples and children. I need this to make sense.'

Simpkins spluttered. The slam to the bench had split his lips and loosened his teeth. His nose leaked blood and mucus. He mumbled, but the words wouldn't form. Calloway barked.

'Speak up son! Let's hear it!'

The bust-up rider spat half-formed obscenities. Calloway's patience wore thin. There was a basin bolted to the workshop wall and in it a can catching drips from a leaking tap. Calloway picked up the can and doused Simpkins in the rusty water. The water shocked him into lucidity.

His screamed words echoed around the archway. 'They were rats. Fucking vermin!'

Something snapped inside Calloway. He bolted to the workbench, took up a wrench and swung it at the seated rider. A clanging blow caught the edge of the metal chair between Simpkins's legs. The rider snapped to attention. His face showed real fear this time.

'Tell me everything or I swear to God I'll kill you myself.'

Calloway tossed the wrench onto the concrete and grabbed Simpkins by the collar of his motorcycle jacket.

'You're a traitor and a war criminal with enough evidence to see you hang. Personally I'd like nothing better, believe me. I spent a lot of time putting scum like you on the end of a rope and you know what, Raymond? I enjoyed every minute of it.'

He loosened his grip on the stunned rider. 'Now the money keeps me from going to the police, but they're not the ones you need to worry about. There's others have an interest in you, son. And now they have an interest in me too. For both our sakes, I need to know why.'

He pulled his chair closer and sat, legs spread and hands on his knees. He leaned in and lowered his voice to a whisper. 'You tell me and I might just let you disappear. Lose yourself. You can clear your bank account and get the next steamer out of Tilbury. But I want answers, understand?'

Simpkins nodded keenly, his slitted eyes fixed on Calloway's.

'So tell me how a cabin boy from Acton ended up in a forest in Poland with a swastika on his cap and a Luger in his ratty little paws.'

TWENTY-ONE

They had drifted for three nights. Seven men with oil-blackened faces clinging to the Carley Float. The rest of the crew had gone down with the freighter. A U-Boat, loose from its pack and hunting alone, had snapped the five-thousand-ton vessel like a brittle twig, setting its cargo of munitions ablaze and lighting the clear night sky as if it were day. Men burned or drowned or choked on oil. Some swam for it but were dragged down by the vortex of the sinking vessel, the still-spinning screws dicing them to pieces.

For a day and a half the first mate, a solid Bristolian with a thick greying beard that aged him beyond his years, had kept his fellow survivors active physically and mentally with songs and filthy stories. But by midday on their second day adrift, even his reserves were all but used up. As he and the others drifted into a desperate half-sleep, Simpkins had watched the horizon, alert with fear, his young eyes sweeping back and forth for signs of funnel smoke.

It was near dusk when he spotted the fine wisp of black against the purple sky. A cruiser perhaps, or a frigate, too far away to tell if it were one of ours. He screamed and waved his numb, skinny arms, deluded by exhaustion into thinking he could be heard. He slapped and punched at the sailors who lay slumped over the float, urging them to join in. They rallied at the prospect of rescue, caring little about the allegiance of their rescuers. To the joy of his comrades the first mate produced a Very pistol from the pocket of his sodden bridge coat and with fumbling frozen fingers slid a distress flare into the chamber. His crew as the bright crimson light streaked across the now dark sky. A lone firework, celebrating what remained of their hope. Then, following Simpkins's stare, they too looked to the horizon at the faint outline of the distant vessel.

They clung to the float in silence as they watched for a sign their flare had been seen. Some prayed, others muttered desperate encouragement as though the ship were a dog on which they'd bet their shirts.

Then one man cried out: 'He's changing course! Praise the lord if he ain't changing fuckin' course!'

A cheer went up. They flailed their arms in frantic semaphore. They whistled and hollered, their different dialects blending into a harmony of hope. It was true. The vessel had altered course, turning to port and heading towards them, waves breaking on its prow in the moonlight as it sliced through the black peaks of the sea. As its shadowy bulk loomed closer, an Aldiss lamp flashed a dit-dit-da message in morse. The first mate hushed his men so that he could better concentrate on the signaller's instruction.

A stoker broke the silence. 'For fuck's sake guv, what's he saying?'

The first mate's shoulders dropped.

'I don't know, stoker. He's saying it in German.'

A stab of reality intruded. Every man had heard the rumours. Machine gunning survivors, not picking them up. They knew the U-Boats did it. Why shouldn't the rest of the Kriegsmarine fleet? Their collective minds raced. Why change course just to shoot us up? We're going to die anyway, from cold or dehydration. Why not just steam ahead and leave us? They'll do the decent thing, surely. They've got to. It's the Geneva Convention isn't it? But whose gonna report 'em if they break it? They make their own rules out here.

Desperation won out. They continued to holler and wave their frozen arms.

'It's a cruiser. Leipzig Class by the look of it.'

'They're lowering the nets!'

They jabbered thorough trembling lips and chattering teeth.

'Thank fuckin' Christ.'

'If there's a cosy little bunk in a POW camp, I ain't complaining.'

'Get to it, lads. Paddle with your hands.'

The tiny Carley float bumped alongside midships, the bullying waves buffeting the little raft against the iron wall of the cruiser's hull. They had little enough strength to climb the nets. The German sailors hauled them up and over the rails, barking in guttural pidgin English. Six men fell limply onto the deck, their clothing sodden with sea water, oil and excrement. A seventh man floated on the waves below them, claimed by the cold minutes before rescue.

Simpkins lay flat, his arms spread like a crucifix, his narrow chest heaving as it sucked in the damp sea air. He stared at the stars thanking a god he barely believed in for this uncertain salvation. He felt a rough hand shake him. It yanked him upright and wrapped a blanket around his shoulders. Simpkins grabbed it with trembling hands and pulled it tight around his teenage frame. The same hand, gentler this time, held the back of his head and pushed a flask to his lips.

'Brandy,' the German sailor said in English. 'Drink it.'

The cruiser docked in Stavanger in Norway a day later. The British seamen had been held below deck and fed black bread and jam, which the Germans called marmalade, washed down with lukewarm ersatz coffee. From Stavanger boarded a troopship to Aarhus in Denmark. Simpkins blagged a pack of cards from a burly military policemen in Aarhus. Their Kriegsmarine guards called the MP kettenhund meaning chained dog, after the silly little breast plate that hung around the neck of his oversized wax greatcoat on a quarter-inch chain. On the train out of Aarhus they practiced their German, shouting kettenhund and barking like dogs. Their navy guards laughed and offered them cigarettes, while being graciously beaten at gin rummy for the next five hundred kilometres.

They were interned in Marlag X-B, a navy prison camp north east of Bremen, with other merchant marine captives. Dutch, Danes, Norwegians and Americans billeted in huts according to their nationality. They were treated in accordance with the

Geneva Convention, fed and watered, worked but not abused and spent their free time playing football and keeping fit. They wrote letters home and enjoyed the Red Cross parcels when they arrived. No one thought of escape. Here they could sit out the war away from the U-Boats and the merciless ocean, while their pay accumulated back home.

The winter that followed was harsh. Temperatures dropped below freezing and the stoves in their flimsy barracks proved ineffective. The cold penetrated their clothing and the thin blankets on their bunks. It brought inertia and apathy towards the pursuits that had distracted them in the preceding season. Morale sunk and tensions rose. Simpkins's natural surliness and his growing irritability earned him a reputation as a troublemaker. Few allowances were made for the fact he was not yet nineteen. His mouth got him into fights and he fought back hard. A scrappy bantam weight who had few limits, he fought with feet and nails and teeth and could bring down the heftiest of sailors through sheer nastiness. His violence earned him nights in the cooler, his Kriegsmarine guards tiring of the disruption. They wanted a quiet war.

Camp conditions worsened. Germany was in retreat on the eastern front and resources were short. Too short to waste on foreign prisoners when supply lines were disrupted and troops at the front were the priority. Dissent spread among the prisoners, every man's emotions on a hair trigger which Simpkins knew how to squeeze. Whatever the dispute, be it over food or cigarettes or fuel, he would taunt fellow inmates with the old national rivalries. The Yanks came in late, the Danes gave up early, the Norwegians were quislings. He called them communists and Jews, revelling in his old blackshirt rhetoric, which since the outbreak of war he'd felt obliged to suppress. Before long he was isolated, his own crew members turning their backs on him. The stoker and a burly winchman once tried to knock sense into him, with a lengthy if restrained beating behind the latrines after curfew. It had little effect, silencing the lad for a week or so before his old ways came back with a vengeance. He took a razor to the stoker in the washhouse and might have cut his throat had not the guards heard the commotion and cornered him with fixed bayonets.

Simpkins sat his time out in the cooler muttering obscenities and harbouring grudges. It was a long sentence. Three weeks on half rations. No one had been banged up that long. Simpkins wore the fact as a badge of honour. His retribution would be harsh. He planned it each night on the hard floor of the dark and draughty cell.

He was released a week early and escorted to the guardhouse by the same two guards that had intervened in the fight. A lecture he imagined, from a pompous reservist officer who would read him the riot act. This didn't happen. Instead he was shown to a small and warm room with a roaring stove in the corner and a table and two chairs. The guards told him to sit, then one disappeared. The other held a big Mauser rifle at readiness and scowled. Simpkins scowled back. The second guard returned with a tray and set it on the table. Hot coffee, a sandwich and a pastry that could have been strudel had Simpkins known the name for it.

'Eat,' said the guard nodding at the tray, before the pair withdrew, locking the door behind them.

Simpkins ate like an animal. It was the best food he'd had for months. He pushed chunks of it into his mouth and slurped the coffee so fast it dripped down his face onto the table, leaving streaks in the dirt from a fortnight of not washing. When he'd finished he sucked his fingers one by one for every last sticky morsel. He belched loudly and deliberately, then dragged his chair over to the stove and warmed himself.

An hour passed and as Simpkins nodded into half sleep, the key turned in the door and a man entered. A smartly dressed civilian who spoke perfect English and introduced himself as Amersham. He was around thirty, foppish almost, with lustrous parted hair and a neat pencil moustache. He described himself as an Englishman and a friend. He had a battered leather briefcase bearing the initials JA from which he produced a hand bill.

'Can you read?' he asked.

Simpkins nodded. Amersham passed him the hand bill and

said: 'Have a read of this.'

The young seaman was curious enough to comply. As he read, the man lit a cigarette from an expensive silver case. It was embossed with a swastika. He laid the case on the table so that Simpkins could clearly see the emblem.

'Well,' said Amersham, 'what do you make of that?'

Simpkins pushed the bill back across the table and helped himself to a cigarette from the case. Amersham lit it for him.

'I reckon there's truth in that.'

Amersham smiled. It was a long time since anyone had smiled at the young sailor, save for the forced pouts of the whores he spent his wages on.

'I reckon there is too,' he said.

Amersham leaned back, crossed his legs and draped an arm over the back of the chair. 'How would you like to get out of here, help me fight the real enemy? The Jew bankers and the Bolsheviks. The people who will bring our great nation to its knees.'

Simpkins looked confused. 'Which nation?'

Amersham grabbed his forearm and gave it a squeeze. 'England of course. The greatest nation. The nation that will become even greater when it joins the Thousand Year Reich. We need men like you, Simpkins. Strong patriotic men. Men that can lead the new order when the Germanic people unite to defeat those that would drag us down.'

Simpkins warmed to Amersham. He was a toff but he talked sense. He talked like Mr Mosely.

'There are plenty like us you know. In every POW camp. Men that can see the truth behind our so-called allies' lies. They've dragged us into an unnecessary war. Our comrades are dying because of a Jewboy communist lie. You know what I'm talking about, Raymond. We're the same, you and I. British to the core.'

The young seamen's eyes narrowed. He peered at the toff, cautious but curious.

'Was you a blackshirt?'

'A fascist, certainly. A proud one too. Fought alongside Franco in Spain in thirty-six.'

'I was a blackshirt. Youngest in the London area they reckoned. I lied about me age to get in. Done the same with the navy.'

Amersham nodded his approval.

'I knew you were a good 'un. That's why I'm here. Now listen.'

He learned forward and lowered his voice. He made Simpkins an offer. If he accepted, he would be released with immediate effect and would accompany Amersham to Berlin. There would be drinking and whoring, then he would be set to work. Honourable work, for which he would be rewarded and respected.

Amersham left the young seaman to think it over. He would be back in an hour for his answer. When he left the room Simpkins read the hand bill again.

As a result of repeated applications from British subjects from all parts of the world wishing to take part in the common European struggle against Bolshevism, authorisation has recently been given for the creation of a British volunteer unit.

The British Free Corps publishes herewith the following short statement on the aims and principles of the unit.

1. The British Free Corps is a thoroughly British volunteer unit conceived and created by British subjects from all parts of the empire who have taken up arms and pledged their lives in the common European struggle against Soviet Russia.

2. The British Free Corps condemns the war with Germany and the sacrifice of British blood in the interests of Jewry and international finance, and regards this conflict as a fundamental betrayal of the British people and British Imperial interests.

3. The British Free Corps desires the establishment of peace in Europe, the development of close friendly relations between England and Germany and the encouragement of mutual understanding and collaboration between the two great Germanic peoples.

4. The British Free Corps will neither make war against Britain or the British crown, nor support any action or policy detrimental to the interests of the British people.

Published by the British Free Corps

That evening Simpkins was on a train to Berlin.

TWENTY-TWO

Berlin was not the holiday Simpkins had been promised. Amersham had disappeared and his Waffen SS handler seemed disinterested in the young Englishman in his charge. He was issued with a uniform bearing the insignia of the British Free Corps, three heraldic lions on the collar tabs and a Union Jack shield on the forearm. It brought curious looks in bars and not a little hostility when he found himself in the air raid shelters alongside terrified Berliners, the RAF doing its worst in the sky above them.

He was left largely to his own devices during the first month, spending much of his time visiting the zoo and drinking in the Tiergarten, in the shadow of the enormous flak tower. He spoke enough German to order beer and food, learned in the navy from his visits to Hamburg before the war. His whorehouse German was passable too. He found a brothel off Potsdamer Strasse which satisfied his taste for big girls with few boundaries. He was paid the wage of a SS-Shutze and with little else to spend it on, became a regular visitor on speaking terms with all the girls and a few of their customers too.

He had no real desire for active service. It was enough for him to be out of the camp and enjoying freedom, with the benefit of a uniform which carried authority if not respect in all quarters.

Amersham returned to Berlin and Simpkins was summoned to a meeting in the Reich Main Security Office, a monstrous grey building on Prinz-Albrecht-Strasse. The young able seaman, whose experience of formality did not extend beyond refraining from spitting in the paymaster's office, was awed by the place. Sharp young men with earnest faces strode with purpose along polished corridors, darting in and out of endless rows of doors. There were women too, some of them lookers Simpkins thought, but a bit on the frumpy side in their serious grey uniforms.

He reported to room B16 and gave his name to a pimply clerk in an oversized Sharfuhrer's uniform, seated behind an Olympia typewriter the size of an armoured car. The clerk eyed the British shield on Simpkins's forearm suspiciously. He checked his day-book, running his finger down a row of names.

'Yes, you may enter,' he said.

Simpkins reached for the door handle. The clerk cleared his throat. 'Knock first.'

Simpkins sneered. He may have swapped sides in the fight against the reds and the Jews, but this little twerp was still a Jerry. He acknowledge the request by rolling his eyes, before knocking twice. A voice behind the door he recognised called 'Herein!'

The office was generous and well furnished. It smelled of sweet tobacco. A uniformed SS Obersturmbannfuhrer sat behind a mahogany desk, a small pipe dangling from the corner of his mouth. He was lean and fit, with well-cut hair and a tolerant smile. Behind him, a portrait of the Fuhrer stared down at Simpkins as if questioning his legitimacy. The newly inducted Shutze thought about giving the Nazi salute. He remembered Will Hay in that film The Goose Steps Out and decided against it.

'Raymond, old man!'

Amersham looked him up and down. 'My, my, look at you. A credit to the Reich.'

Amersham was draped over a chair in front of the Obersturmbannfuhrer. He held a cigarette high and away from his immaculate suit. He patted the seat of the adjacent chair.

'Sit yerself down then.'

The young Shutze looked apprehensive.

'Come on, we're all friends here.'

To Simpkins the toff looked liked a nancy, but he'd always found it hard to read the posh ones. A Rottenfuhrer at the Lichterfelde barracks said Amersham was shacked up with a Berlin whore. A proper dirty bastard he was.

The SS officer pushed an ornate cigarette box towards

Simpkins and gestured for him to smoke. Amersham produced the silver swastika lighter.

'This is Otto Bauer. He's the real boss. I'm just the tart who lures the boys in.'

Simpkins managed a deferential nod to the German behind the desk.

'Now Otto has a job for you. You see he's been running this holiday camp just outside the city for chaps like you.'

'Like me?'

'Chaps that recognise the Bolshevik threat and the influence of the Jewboys that pull the strings. At this camp they're well fed, they play sports, get a few trips into town to chat up the frauleins, that sort of thing. Otto's been showing these British POWs that their German foes are actually quite decent folk after all. Now the next stage is to persuade them to join the corps. That's where you come in. You will be our recruiting sergeant.'

'Sergeant?'

'Well, Sturmann at least.'

Amersham turned to Bauer. 'Comes with a pay rise I expect.'

The officer nodded.

'Do I have to live at this camp?' asked Simpkins. He had enjoyed his weeks at the barracks and not least its proximity to his adopted whorehouse. The camp sounded like a backwards step. Amersham shook his head.

'You'll be a regular visitor. You can boast about the freedoms you enjoy as a member of the corps. You'll also need to stir them up a bit. Appeal to their patriotism. Convince them that fighting the red is an Englishman's duty. You were a blackshirt, Raymond. This should be right up your street.'

This whole business was still strange to the former able seaman. But the role of recruiter sounded preferable to a posting to the eastern front.

'Alright,' he said, helping himself to another of the Obersturmbannfuhrer's cigarettes.

'Good man!'

Amersham clapped him on the back.

'Get yerself up to the camp at Genshagen as soon as you like.

We'll find you some transport.'

He was issued with a brand new RT125 fresh from the Auto Union factory in Chemnitz. The peoples' motorcycle, the clerk at the SS motor transport depot had called it. Simpkins had never ridden a motorbike, but took immediately to the little two-stroke machine. A six-foot Teuton would have dwarfed it. Simkins's small jockey frame sat well in the saddle.

The recruiting drive did not go well. The POWs were content enough with their more comfortable conditions and suspicious of the Free Corps proposition. Even those who had been fascists before the war could not reconcile their patriotism with the prospect of a traitorous defection to the enemy. But Simpkins's efforts were not entirely without success. A young infantry private called Wood was a willing listener. A fellow Londoner, not much older than Simpkins, he too had followed Mosely and his blackshirts. His profound antisemitism led him quite effortlessly towards Nazi ideology. Before the outbreak of war he had more than once confessed to being pro-Hitler and only stopped his overt support for national socialism through fear of internment. Although a reluctant conscript into the British army, he had seen action in Italy and Sicily and had developed a taste for battle. In fact he enjoyed killing, not for the sensation of taking a life – he was not a psychopath – but for the feeling of power that his low status in both civilian and military life otherwise denied him. Simpkins recognised a kindred spirit and fixed on Wood as his best chance of success. He was coming under pressure from Bauer for results. The pair would go drinking and whoring in Berlin, Woods perched uncomfortably on the back rack of Simpkins's motorcycle, his legs trailing. While they drank together they fired each other's passion for the ideology of their adopted masters. They became committed Nazis and soon Wood was wearing the same uniform as Simpkins, with three lions on his collar and the union flag on his forearm. Together they continued their recruiting drive, but with little success. Acknowledging that the soft sell of the holiday camp was yielding few results, and under increasing pressure from the Fuhrer himself, Bauer resorted to other means –

maltreatment and blackmail, the methods of the press-gang. These new techniques worked. Two dozen prisoners from Genshagen were conscripted into the Free Corps and transferred to its new headquarters in Hildesheim, under the command of Hauptsturmfuhrer Richter.

Frank Joseph Belper was a Waffen SS Hauptscharführer assigned to the Free Corps as an instructor. The son of Birmingham factory foreman, he had grown up in the industrial town of Smethwick, benefiting from a passable education and, in time, a good understanding of politics. A former blackshirt and fervent Nazi sympathiser, he had risen through the ranks of the British Union of Fascists to become one of Mosely's trusted men on the ground in the Midlands. At the outbreak of war, faced with the prospect of internment by the British, he fled to Europe and made his way to Germany, his goal being to enlist in the German armed forces and fight for the Reich. The Nazi authorities were suspicious of him at first, but through persistence he had convinced the Reich Main Office of his allegiance to the fatherland. He was accepted into the Totenkopf division of the SS in the spring of 1940 and posted to the Eastern Front.

Belper was unhinged. With his close-cropped hair and his manic stare, his face resembled a prison mugshot. His taste for violence and his unbridled hatred might under other circumstances have put him in a psychiatric institution. In the SS he found an organisation that could accommodate and indeed value the worst extremes of his behaviour. He proved a smart and determined Nazi, whose seething antisemitism was put to use at Sobibor concentration camp in Poland, where he served as a guard. He enjoyed his work, boasting to Wood and Simpkins later that he had personally killed twenty-seven Polish Jews. His extremism was unnerving, even to now-committed Nazis like Wood and Simpkins. But they were drawn to Belper. He was a charismatic and they became willing followers. In time they became something akin to friends.

At Hildesheim, the Free Corps recruits settled into a routine of training and recreation. Belper drove them hard and could be brutal. But the evenings made up for the rigours of training, when the young Englishmen enjoyed the local hospitality and the attentions of curious local women. An English boyfriend soon became not just a novelty but a prize, a situation that the Free Corps members exploited.

Belper, Wood and Simpkins eschewed these outings, preferring to drink by themselves and use the local brothel. When they drank together, Belper would spew out beer hall rhetoric and as the evenings wore on he became darker, turning from politics to the mechanics of killing. These beer-fuelled talks became a regular fixture and in time Wood and Simpkins became desensitised to the near psychosis of Belper's keenness for destruction. They became converts to the collective madness of Nazism.

Amersham's grand plan to recruit a legion of Englishmen could not be fulfilled. His early attempts to drum up support from disillusioned POWs saw him driven from their camps by an angry rabble. When Free Corps recruitment was passed to the Waffen SS, they too failed to rouse a following. Even with their more coercive tactics, the Free Corps numbers never reached more than fifty. It was decided they should be absorbed into regular fighting units and posted east. The Hildesheim contingent were told they would be sent to the pioneer school in Dresden for training as assault engineers, then integrated into Division Nordland, the Scandinavian volunteer unit of the Waffen SS. Belper was reluctant to waste his talents on regular soldiering, even if this was under the auspices of the Waffen SS. He had a different plan for himself and his two English friends. He had become quite well connected with personnel in SS Obergruppenfuhrer Ernst Kaltenbrunner's office. He was able to persuade them to post the three of them to one of the remaining Einsatzgruppen, an SS death squad charged with the mass killing of Jews, gypsies, partisans and intellectuals.

By the time of the German surrender in May 1945, Ray Simpkins had personally executed one hundred twenty-seven men, women and children.

TWENTY-THREE

Simpkins was alert now. He sat on the edge of the chair in the spotlight of the inspection lamp, telling his story with rising enthusiasm. At first he had seemed reluctant to shed the burden of the past half-decade of secrecy. Now he was revelling in it, the hero of his own story. Calloway had seen this before. There comes a point in any interrogation where the subject feels an uncontrollable need to confess. Not through duress, but to release themselves from the strictures of their own deceit. Calloway let him talk.

'We fell in with the Einsazgruppe in Lodz. We took part in the actions, rounding up Jews from the ghetto and packing them off to the camps. Some we had to deal with there and then, if there wasn't any transport.'

He made it sound like any regular job. He could have been a postal worker or a railway porter or a haulage clerk from the matter-of-factness of his tone.

'Then we moved further east. By the time the Russians were close to overrunning us we were at the camp at Chelmno, supervising the Sonderkommando. They were the prisoners we'd got exhuming the bodies from the mass graves and cremating the remains so the Russians wouldn't discover them. We had to deal with the Sonderkommando once they were done. Frank was given that job to supervise, on account of his experience at Sobibor. After that we dispersed.'

'Dispersed?'

'You know, every man for himself. Get the fuck away and cover our tracks. We ditched the SS uniforms for regular army ones. There were enough German dead around to take 'em off of. We were lucky. The Free Corps didn't have blood group tattoos like the other SS. The only thing we had to worry about was the language, but by then me and Wood had picked up enough German to get by and anyway the eastern front was full of foreigners, volunteers like. Danes, Norwegians, Hungarians, even Russians. We stuck together, me, Belper and Wood. Frank spoke German like a native and he was a canny bugger too. He got us back as far as the Elbe, which the British had reached. We could see the 11th Armoured Division from the other side of the river. We nicked some old civvies and wandered towards the British lines. Told 'em we were POWs who'd been banged up in a Stalag. Me and Woody anyway.'

'What about the third man, Belper?'

'He took off by himself. He wanted to avoid the allies. He was regular SS and had the tattoo. He said he'd burn it off with a hot iron then pull the same POW stunt as us.'

'Did you ever see him again?'

'Belper? Nah. Don't think I'd want to, to be honest. He was alright, after a fashion, but he was a nutter.'

'Shame that didn't occur to you before he persuaded you to join a death squad.'

Simpkins shot Calloway a look of defiance. 'I don't regret it. I'd do it again. I might have to. You read the papers lately? There's reds in the government and blackies coming over by the boat load. Then there's the Jews. Killing our troops in Palestine while over here they're buying up all the houses. The fight ain't over, Calloway. There's gonna be blood. Mark my words.'

Calloway felt his anger rise. The veins drummed on either side of his head.

He took a long deep breath. 'When did come you back to England?'

'Late forty-five. Me and Woody got back to London but he was right twitchy. He wanted to drop out of sight.'

'But you came back as British POWs. You'd got away scot-free.'

Simpkins shook his head. 'The trouble was this. When we was in the Free Corps they told us to change our names. I was Ron Samson, Woody was Pat Ladbroke.'

Sampson, Ladbroke and Belper. The three names on the

notebook hidden in Fenton's toolbox. Names Fenton had been given by the tramp, Wood.

'It was a precaution, so we could come back to England after the allied surrender and not get flak for joining the other side. I could go back to me own name because no one knew I'd joined the corps. When Amersham took me out of the Marlag the other prisoners were told I'd been taken to a bad boys camp 'cause I attacked that stoker. It was different for Woody and the Genshagen lot. Their old mates knew they'd gone to the holiday camp. Wouldn't have been long before the military police clocked that.'

'And Belper didn't take an alias.'

'That's right.'

Simpkins seemed curious how Calloway knew this.

'He was regular Waffen SS. Half German too. He joined up under his own name and kept it. That's another reason he scarpered.'

'So where did you and Wood lay low?'

'We fell in with some deserters. They were in the same boat as us, but for different reasons. I tagged along for a while. We camped out mostly. I couldn't hack it for long. I like me home comforts, you know. Cash in me pocket, beer in me hand and a bit of female company. I went back to London and worked up the docks for a bit.'

'Then Pat Moxon gave you a try out.'

He nodded. 'I knew me way around bikes by that stage. I hung onto that little RT as long as I could. I got a real taste for riding. I traded up bikes and acted as despatch rider for the Einsatzgruppe.'

The word sounded odd from the mouth of the little London bike jockey.

'They gave me a big bastard Zundapp. I could barely get me leg over it at first. What I'd give for one of them now, eh? But there's no way you could ride a Kraut bike here. Not since the war.'

He sniggered. 'No one would talk to me.'

Calloway reckoned Simpkins had worse reasons not to be

talked to.

'Then me and Wood got our hands on a BMW sidecar combination. It had an MG42 mounted up front. That's a very efficient weapon, I can tell you.'

He sneered at Calloway, taunting him. 'Saved the squad a lot of time and effort, that MG42 did.'

Calloway snapped. He made to grab the rider by the collar, raising his fist as he did so. A noise in the alley stopped him. Heavy footsteps approaching the workshop. Then the rattling of the lock. Calloway lowered his hand and gestured to Simpkins to keep quiet. Half comprehending, the small rider compiled. The workshop door opened a chink and a uniformed figure leaned in. Calloway swore. That bloody policeman again, 453, the young constable who had disturbed him when he was searching the place last time. Doing his rounds, trying doors and finding this one open. Simpkins turned. He saw the police uniform. He spat at Calloway.

'You dirty fucker. You set me up.'

His small frame sprung from the chair and leapt towards the door. Calloway tried to grab him but couldn't get a grip on the tough leather of his jacket. The rider threw himself at the copper, wrenching off his helmet and landing a head butt on him. The crunch of bone echoed around the railway arch and the young policeman rolled back like a kellyman, clutching his face. Blood from his nose seeped through his fingers. Calloway tipped the lamp over with force so the bulb smashed on the concrete floor. Hidden by the darkness he made for the door, leapt over the now-prostrate constable and followed the sound of Simpkins's boots down the cobbled path. Ahead of him a pale moon glowed behind fast moving clouds. In the moonlight the faint outline of the baroque church mocked its humble surroundings, the railway arches and the half-bombed streets with the all-pervading buddleja tearing their brickwork. Moments later he heard a police whistle behind him. He banked on 453 being too unsteady from the blow to keep pace. He prayed the young copper didn't have the wherewithal to jump on the big Matchless Silver Hawk Simpkins had left behind. Ahead he could just make out the silhouette of the rider turning into Church Street. Simpkins ran with the familiar monkey gait of the speedway rider, hobbled by the stiff racing leathers and rigid-soled boots. It allowed Calloway to gain ground. The pair crossed Church Street towards the creek, only a few yards between them now.

The streets narrowed. They were dark and featureless, a hotchpotch of cottages, small warehouses and jerry-built lean-tos blending into the gloom. Calloway drew deep breaths of the damp creekside air. It smelled of soot and decay. He was out of shape and his chest heaved painfully. Simpkins disappeared down a snicket between two low brick buildings. It was just wide enough to take the rider's monkey-boy frame. Calloway squeezed himself into the gap and did his best to run. The walls seemed to narrow as he neared the chink of grey light at the end of the passage. He stumbled over the discarded flotsam underfoot and snagged his clothes on the coarse brickwork. Reaching the banks of the creek, he drew breath and scanned the narrow creekside path in both directions. To the north, only the lone chimney of the power station. Simpkins was heading south towards the mill. Calloway summoned the reserves of his strength and gave chase. The path had petered out and the two men slid along the damp grass border of the open riverbank. He heard Simpkins curse at the tangle of barbed wire and planks that blocked the path ahead. Calloway was within feet of him when the monkey-boy leaped feet first onto the riverbank and started to wade through the sucking mud.

In the distance the roar of an engine and the shrill ting-a-ling of a police car's bell. Young 453 had summoned help. Too far away to worry about. Calloway jumped into the creek and followed Simpkins, heaving himself out of the mud with each step and plunging back in again. The young rider was lighter and leaner and had gained ground. Calloway's big frame seemed to sink deeper into the mud with each step. His chest hurt deeply, phlegm rose in his gullet and his windpipe constricted. His leg muscles cramped, pinning him upright in the mud like a scarecrow swaying in the wind. Inside his head a white light was threatening to engulf him. He fought against it and lost. When he came to, minutes later face down in the mud, Simpkins was gone.

TWENTY-FOUR

Two young boys pissed against the corrugated-iron fence. Calloway cuffed their heads midstream.

'Do that again and you're banned.'

The boys skulked off, zipping up their shorts with piss-wet fingers.

Bouncer and babysitter, that's all he was. Pattie Moxon's strong-arm boy and wet nurse to her paying punters. His cigarette hissed as he flicked it into the pool of urine. He'd not slept and his nerves were ragged. The thought of Simpkins evading justice had torn at him through the night. As he lay restless on the old iron cot, he saw the little rat rider's defiant face smirking at him.

'The fight's not over, mark my words.'

As he teetered on the edges of sleep that never came, the rat face merged into the mess of the SS guard he'd beaten on the crematorium floor, his pulped lips grinning through the gore.

'They were rats. Fucking vermin!'

He'd been called to the stadium that morning. The police had found Simpkins's Silver Hawk and were asking questions. Calloway denied knowledge.

'You'll probably find him drunk in a whorehouse,' he had offered as an explanation. The police didn't buy it. They were CID, a cut above the laughing policeman and his sidekick who had visited after the burglary. The detectives knew what they were doing. And 453 had identified Simpkins from his publicity photos as the man in the race leathers who had head butted him at the workshop. The detectives quizzed Calloway on who the second man might have been, the one who followed Simpkins into the night. Calloway was confident he'd not been recognised by the dazed constable. It was unlikely he'd been seen behind the harsh beam of the inspection lamp and when the lamp smashed, the darkness had hidden him as he bolted.

Part of him wanted to hand the whole thing over to the two detectives. The photographs, the notebook, the five hundred pounds and an account of Simpkins's confession, however much coercion was employed in its extraction. But as Basil Rathbone might say in one of those ridiculous mysteries, there was the difficult matter of the body in the Thames with a .445 calibre hole in its forehead. As loose ends go, that was a pretty big one still to be tied off. He had no plan other than to lay low, get on with his day job and wait for the fish in the Thames to do the rest. It wasn't a comforting plan.

He walked past the already-crowded stands towards the turnstiles. The fans were doubly eager tonight, shoving forward to buy their tickets.

'Full house tonight, sir. Bursting at the seams we'll be.'

Les Birkett stood sentinel at the turnpikes, his chest puffed out more than usual.

'Special night, Les. We've got royalty in.'

Birkett allowed himself a chuckle.

'Hardly royalty, sir. But he is very comical.'

The big ex-RSM was uncharacteristically chipper. He was even humming to himself. The Chinese Laundry Blues.

Calloway's fixed smile was hurting his face. The night was a big one for Pat Moxon and her twenty-five thousand paying punters, but on top of the Simpkins business, he could have done without it. He maintained only the facade of enthusiasm the job demanded. Inside, anxiety was eating at his stoicism. He wanted the whole affair brought to a conclusion. With Simpkins gone this looked unlikely. He cursed Pat Moxon under his breath for bringing him into the whole sordid business.

There was a different kind of excitement inside the stadium. The presence of a screen star at the track heightened the euphoria, the crowd desperate for a glimpse of the unlikely matinee idol with the jug ears and the horse teeth.

Calloway took his position in the commentary box. The

commentator wore a dinner suit and had an extra layer of oil on his thinning hair. His cologne smelled like chemicals. He moistened his lips and held the big microphone close to his face.

'It's a big night tonight folks! The highlight of the season. Our VIP guest will be arriving soon and I want you to give him a rousing Bullets welcome.'

A cheer went up automatically, as if someone just pulled a lever.

'But first, time to introduce the real stars of the show...'

The commentator's sidekick, a pimply lad with bottle-end spectacles placed the gramophone needle into the groove of a worn shellac disc. Marching Along Together echoed around the stands.

The crowd roared like a reflex, conditioned by the ritual of countless Wednesday night fixtures. There was comfort in the certainty of it all. Calloway didn't begrudge them. The poor sods had survived six years of war and emerged into a world of shortage and dereliction. But they left it all behind at the turnstiles. He envied them. He craned his neck and eased his aching shoulders.

The spotlight followed the riders across the centre green. Billy Riley led them out with renewed swagger, waving to the crowd and enjoying it. Female fans blew kisses. He spotted Calloway in the commentary box and gave him a knowing nod. The Bullets lined up along the home straight, their opponents joining them to polite applause. Bert Webber was missing from the line-up. The announcer switched to amateur dramatics.

'Oh no folks. One of the riders seems to be missing. Where can he be?' he asked the crowd, sounding as convincing as a children's radio presenter who had failed the audition. 'Perhaps his motorcycle has broken down.'

The announcer passed the mic to the pimply boy and dashed for the door.

The spotlight swept over the green towards the pits. Bert Webber sat astride his motorcycle, behind him a squat figure in an astrakhan coat and mirror bright shoes pushed the bike onto the cinder track, helped by two of the pit crew. He mugged effort, tipping up his homburg and wiping his brow. His grinning horse teeth shone in the spotlight's beam. The crowd were hysterical. Driven by the collective consciousness of the sports crowd, they broke into song as one.

'If there's one thing that I like, it's riding around on a motor-bike.'

The man in the astrakhan coat let go the bike and waved with both hands, acknowledging his song.

'I once won first prize two and six, I know all the dirt track dirty tricks.'

Calloway snorted. The song was imbecilic.

The announcer was on the podium now, at the edge of the centre green. He looked out of breath. Smoothing down his oily hair with one hand, he raised another microphone to introduce the VIP.

'Ladies and gentlemen, boys and girls, give a rousing Bullets welcome to the boy from Wigan, Mr George Formby!'

Formby took the mic, a cigarette dangling from the side of his mouth. He threw them a catchphrase.

'Turned out nice again!'

Euphoria filled the stadium. The experience was religious. A picture-house deity with a hymn book of innuendo, right there in the flesh. He received the adulation with a bow as the supporters sang.

'In a fifty mile race I am the best, I ride five miles and skid the rest.'

Pat Moxon led the star down the line of riders like the bride's mother at a wedding. Calloway wondered whether her fixed smile hurt as much as his did. Formby glad-handed the Bullets, cracking jokes and pulling faces. Calloway had seen enough. He left the commentary box and crossed to the lighting gantry. It was the best vantage point for surveilling the crowd. From here he could spot trouble, not that there was much at a typical fixture. But tonight wasn't typical. The crowd were excitable and there was a VIP on the bill. Formby's wife and manager, Beryl, had reviewed security arrangements with Calloway personally. He like her. She was professional and not what he'd imagined from a show business type.

He kept a pair of old infantry binoculars in an oilcloth bag which hung from the gantry's tubular steel railing. Slinging the webbing strap around his neck, he scanned along the rows of spectators looking for the usual signs. Excitable kids, angry drunks or a knot of youths in the latest garb. Or the cosh boys from last Wednesday spoiling for a rematch. He saw nothing untoward. He looked up towards the members bar with its elongated window overlooking the track, like an aquarium for un-exotic specimens. Three men caught his attention. They weren't the usual types who sipped their pale ale and marked their race cards with pencil stubs. Two wore belted trench coats and sat facing the window. They were big and stony-faced with inexpressive eyes. Planted firmly in their seats, they sat straight-backed not touching their drinks. He recognised the type. Not police. More like former NCOs doing strong-arm work. It spelled bad news. A third man had his back to the window. He was smaller in build and wearing a dark suit too good for his surroundings. Though his face was not visible there was something about his build and his movements that was familiar to Calloway.

The first heat got underway. The four riders hit the dirt track, pushed off by their pit crews and accelerated into their warm-up laps. The smell of methanol filled the stadium. Calloway leant over the rail of the lighting gantry straining to get a better view of the members bar through the binoculars. Framed by his field of view the three men rose from their seats and wove their way through the regular punters towards the exit. It was then he caught a glimpse of the third man's face. A few pounds heavier with less hair and a neat new moustache, but still recognisable. It was Sammy Mackay.

Calloway descended from the gantry and headed towards the members bar exit. What the hell was Mackay doing here? If he wanted to pick up Simpkins he would send the police. The rat rider's wartime treason carried a death sentence but was a criminal matter, not something for Mackay and his security service goons. And there was nothing to suggest Mackay could make a connection between the name Ron Sampson that Calloway had mentioned when they spoke and the Bullets rider Simpkins. Odds on Mackay was looking for Calloway himself, and an explanation for the missing house breaker. It wasn't something Calloway looked forward to explaining, even to Sammy.

The three men were weaving through the crowd towards the rear of the west stand. Calloway picked up their trail, hanging back so he was obscured by the throng. He pushed past the tightly packed punters mumbling apologies. They were oblivious. The next heat was underway and all eyes were on the track. Behind him the announcer's voice raised an octave, broadcasting excitement to the crowd. Riley first off the tape and holding his lead. Webber close behind and gaining ground on the visiting riders. Five points for the taking. Mackay and the two NCO types ducked under the stand. They were heading for Calloway's office. He followed them, keeping two or three spectators between himself and the three men. But the crowd thinned out the closer they got to the office, depriving him of cover. He needed a vantage point from which to observe them unseen. He slipped between the supporters club and the workshop, into a small passage littered with cigarette butts and hotdog wrappers. From here he could climb the gantry that held up the north stand. The steel lattice work of the upright supports served as a ladder. He'd had to coax kids down from it in the past with the threat of a clipped ear.

Twenty feet up he hooked an elbow around one of the uprights and wedged his brogues into the angles of the cross bracing. It gave him a clear view of the door to his office, above the heads of Mackay and his strong-arm boys. One of the boys tried the door, which Calloway kept locked. He withdrew a small canvas tool roll from the pocket of his trench coat and selected a pair of wood-handled lock picks. He worked the lock as the other two men shielded him from the eyes of any passing spectators. It popped open with an audible click. Mackay and the second goon ducked inside while the third man kept watch. He lit a cigarette and tried to look like he should be there.

There would be nothing for them to find in Calloway's desk, unless they were fans of Zane Grey or in need of a drink so much they would drain the peg of whiskey he and Pat Moxon had left in the bottle two nights ago. And unless they'd brought explosives, which he doubted, SS Shutze Wood's sick photo collection were secure inside the heavy Banhams safe.

A collective gasp went up from the crowd, muffled by the underside of the stand above him. The announcer adopted his well-practiced shocked tone. Riley had over-banked and hit the cinders and Webber had lost his lead to the visiting rider. The marshal was allowing the race, four-two to the away club.

Mackay and the second NCO type emerged from the office as casually as they could manage. Their faces said they'd found nothing. The three headed back towards the track. They would be looking for Calloway now. A part of him wanted to stay where he was, hidden in the dark underside of the north stand. But he was already aching from the strain of clinging to the upright steel. He couldn't maintain that for the remaining ninety minutes of the fixture. He had to keep moving, away from Mackay and his friends. It should be easy enough to disappear with twenty-five thousand in tonight. At least he hoped.

When the three men were beyond his line of sight, he eased himself back down the lattice work of steel, shaking his numbing arm back into life. From the track, he heard the relieved tone of the announcer.

'It's alright folks. Billy Riley is on his feet. He's on his feet and walking back to the pits. Give us a wave Billy!'

Riley must have obliged. The crowd cheered in return. The rider would be heading for the surgery with Doc McArdle, the club medic. It seemed as good a place as any for Calloway to make for. He would be out of sight behind closed doors for a while.

The lights were on behind the frosted glass pane of the surgery door. He tried the handle, which was locked. He pulled the pass key from the leather loop on his belt, unlocked the door and entered.

Pat Moxon sat on a bench in a corner of the empty surgery,

her skirt hitched up and the soft white flesh of her thigh exposed above the dark silk of her stocking top. She was guiding the needle of a syringe into a green-blue vein. She looked up as Calloway entered the room.

'Don't look so judgemental, Reg. It's just a little pick-me-up.'

'From your gentleman caller in the tweed suit?'

'He's a Harley Street doctor.'

'I'm sure he is.'

He watched her as she eased the plunger of the syringe into the barrel. The needle left a tiny red puncture wound on her pale skin as she withdrew it. She placed the empty syringe into a small velvet-lined case and slid it into her handbag. Then she stood up and eased the tight-fitting skirt back down over her thighs, straightening out the creases with a wiggle of her hips.

'Get a good eyeful, did you Reg?'

'Something for your nerves, ma'am?'

'If you want to call it that. Put it this way, it's the George Formby Cup, it's ours for the winning but I'm fielding three novices, Clanger's laid up with his broken wrist, Fenton's riding with the angels and now Simpkins has gone AWOL. What the hell have you done with him? I told you not to hurt him.'

'And I didn't. Well not as much as I'd like to have done. He's a very bad lot that boy. Worse than you could imagine.'

'I can imagine quite a lot.'

'Not like this.'

She flicked her cigarette butt onto the concrete and stubbed it out with her toes. 'Fenton?'

Calloway shook his head. 'An accident. Plain and simple.'

'Then what else?'

Les Birkett appeared in the doorway, his white-topped commissionaire's cap touching the doorframe.

'They're doing photographs, Miss Moxon. You're needed on the track.'

'Christ, I have to go.'

She pulled a compact mirror from her bag and checked her lipstick. Then she took out a small half-moon-shaped perfume bottle and dabbed a drop behind each ear with her forefinger.

'Les, tell them I'm coming! And you,' she dropped the perfume bottle into the bag and turned to Calloway, 'You'll have to save your Bulldog Drummond stories for later. My office, once the stadium's clear.'

She pushed past him leaving a trail of Shalimar on the stale surgery air. She bumped past Riley at the door without apology and sashayed off.

'She means well,' said Calloway.

'Sometimes I wonder,' Riley replied.

'Not just me then.'

The young rider limped to the examination table and peeled off his race leathers, wincing. Calloway fetched him a beaker of water from the tap in the corner. Riley necked it down, the cold water running down the sides of his jaw leaving trails of clean flesh in the cinder smut. McArdle, a stocky balding man of fifty with horn-rimmed glasses and a shiny black, slug-like moustache, patted the bench. Riley lay back in his underwear while the medic worked him over with his big muscular hands. When he'd finished the examination, he stepped back satisfied.

'Someone up there likes you, Billy. Another lucky escape,' the medic said.

Riley looked up at him, expectantly. 'Fit to ride, Doc?'

The medic nodded. He took some powders from the cabinet and mixed a preparation of aspirin and caffeine in a glass of water. He passed it to Riley.

'Drink up, then chase it with this.' He poured a slug of cheap medicinal brandy from a bottle in the cream enamel cabinet. Riley drank the two liquids in succession.

'Now get your leathers back on, son. You're back in the race.'

Riley struggled into the stiff leather clothing and pulled on the red race jacket with its black flying bullet emblem. He saluted the doc as he left, easing himself stiff-legged through the surgery door, swinging his lead soles by their straps. Before the door could swing shut, O'Donnell appeared. He stood framed in the doorway, a giant among the Bullets with his rangy five-foot-eleven frame.

The medic rolled his eyes. 'Gawd, not another one. What

happened to you?'

'Nothing Doc, go take a walk. I need to talk to Calloway here.'

'Haven't you got a heat to win?'

'I'm done for the night. Straight deuces all. Not a single race win. I'm gonna sit here with Calloway and bask in my own mediocrity.'

The Doc rolled his eyes again, took a nip of the medicinal brandy and left as he was asked. When they were alone O'Donnell said: 'I've got a message from Birkett. He says some old friends are looking for you only he didn't think they looked the kind of friends you'd want to meet anytime soon.'

'An officer type and two goons?'

'I'd say that's a fair description. Limey officer, mind. Stupid little moustache.'

'My old CO. The fact he brought two goons means he's not here to reminisce.'

'Birkett thought as much. Told me to tell you on the QT while he kept them busy.'

'A good man, that Les.'

'He's certainly got a nose for trouble. What's the deal, Calloway? Something to do with Simpkins blowing town?'

He needed an ally. He couldn't hide from Mackay and his friends all night. They were too good. They'd catch up with him sooner or later. His best chance was to meet them, bluff his innocence and buy time. If they caught him running there would be no telling where he'd end up. Some basement under an abandoned country house with very thick walls and two ex-Guardsmen to bounce you off them. If he could buy time he could slip away, but he would need help. O'Donnell seems like a good sort. He'd just have to trust the lanky American.

Calloway told O'Donnell the Simpkins story, minus the Riley angle, the photographs Pat Moxon was desperate to get her hands on and the fact he'd put a bullet through the head of one of Sammy's black bag men. When he'd finished all O'Donnell could say was: 'Dirty limey motherfucker.'

Calloway nodded. 'Yep, that about covers it.'

'So who are the goons, police?'

Calloway shook his head. 'Sammy's military intelligence. The other two will be army muscle. There's something behind Simpkins's story that runs deeper than aiding the enemy.'

'That's deep enough.'

'Yes but it's history. If Sammy Mackay's involved, there's another angle I haven't worked out. Something still current. What I do know is I can't avoid him all night.'

O'Donnell clapped a hand on Calloway's shoulder.

'Listen man, if there's anything I can do, then name it.'

He made it sound like a drunk doing the old pals act, but Calloway knew he meant it. There was a half-baked plan in his head. He poured them both a slug of brandy from the medicinal supply in the doc's cabinet and let the plan bake a while longer.

'Who are the most popular Riders with the fans?'

'Since Fenton died? Well Riley's got the looks and I got the animal magnetism, baby.'

'I can work with those qualities. Now listen. First you've got to take a message to Les Birkett. Then you get hold of Riley and the pair of you do exactly what I'm about to tell you.'

When he finished he poured them both another shot for luck. 'You reckon you're up to that?'

O'Donnell gave the high sign and chinked his glass against Calloway's.

'As we say in the 82nd, All the way!'

TWENTY-FIVE

'Evening, Sammy. Getting a taste for the dirt track?'

Mackay and his two goons were back at their table by the big window of the members bar. The goons' expressions hadn't changed.

'You know I think I might be. Once you get the hang of it, well, it's really quite thrilling. Although the chaps do spend a lot of time sliding along on their arses. Strange little men. I do hope they don't get too badly hurt.'

'And your friends seem to be enjoying themselves.' He nodded to the two stone-faced goons. 'Do they speak?'

'They're more the physical type.'

'Unlike you, Sammy. Never liked to get your hands dirty.'

'No, that was always your job, Cab. You liked it rather a lot, I seem to recall.'

'That was then. Times were different.'

But it wasn't just then. He was still quick to violence. Too quick for civilian life. Like the Burma railway victim he'd watched beat the dog, there was a rage inside him that would fester until it burst. It was best not to be around him when it did.

Sammy was the only one touching his drink. The other two each sat with a full glass of Britvic on the Formica table in front of them, next to a copy of the night's race card. Through the big window behind them, George Formby was presenting the cup. Moxon was watching with forced grace as the Lancashire comedian handed the trophy to the visiting club. Calloway hoped her pick-me-up was easing the pain.

'So I'm glad we've caught up, Cab. You've been treading on my turf rather.'

'I doubt that. There's nothing I do here that would interest your department. Unless the Russians are recruiting greyhounds now.'

'I wouldn't put it past them. No, it's people I'm interested in. Three in particular. Sampson, Ladbroke and Belper. The names you mentioned when we spoke. How does a washed up ex-sergeant running a dog track come by those names, Cab?'

'Novice riders, doing tryouts. I check their bona fides for the club boss. We get some chancers through here. The boss likes to know what she's buying.'

'And the places, Genshagen, Hildesheim?'

'We get services types trying out. Dispatch riders who rate themselves. I ask where they served. Check they're not spinning a yarn.'

'That's very diligent.'

'I was taught by the best, Sammy.'

Mackay took the compliment with mock grace. 'And these novices, Sampson, Ladbroke and Belper.' He waved the red-and-black race card. 'Not on the team?'

'Didn't make the grade. The boss is very strict.'

'Ah, yes.' He peered at the cover of the race card. 'Miss Patricia Moxon, Managing Director of South London Speed Stars.' He tossed the card onto the table. 'Never saw you working for a lady boss, Cab. What on earth is that like?'

Calloway shrugged. 'Like working for a male boss but in higher heels.'

Mackay laughed and shook his head in disbelief. 'What's the world coming to? I need to watch my back, clearly. Some popsie from the WRACs might be after my job.'

'And might do it better.'

'Well, I suppose anything goes, like the song says.'

Mackay leant over the table and spoke into Calloway's ear. He dropped the supercilious tone. 'I need some fucking answers, Cab. If you don't give me them, then we'll have to dig them out of you.' He gestured to the two goons, who were staring blank-faced at Calloway. 'Like I said, they're more the physical type. You should get on well.'

There was a commotion at the doorway to the bar. Right on

cue, God bless them. O'Donnell and Riley pursued by fifty excitable supporters, young girls mostly, holding out race cards for autographs. Another twenty from the bar ran over to join them, arms outstretched. Their young voices rose to fever pitch. O'Donnell made a play of fending them off, but his face was egging them on. He spotted Calloway and led the crowd towards the table where the four men sat. Irritation showed on Sammy's neat little face. From behind, Les Birkett laid a hand on Calloway's shoulder, true to the plan.

'Apologies gentlemen, but Mr Calloway is wanted down at the track. A security matter. Urgent, I'm afraid.'

Calloway rose from his seat. One of the goons grabbed his forearm and tried to pull him back down. O'Donnell stumbled into the goon and a swarm of supporters with red-and-black scarves engulfed them like bees round the hive. Calloway pushed through the swarm towards the exit. Mackay and the goons were pinned to their seats by the screaming fans. Calloway looked back as he left the bar. O'Donnell winked. He raised a hand showing five fingers and mouthed 'five minutes'.

Calloway's heavy shoes clattered down the iron stairs. He snaked his way through the crowd who were by now heading to the exit gates. He had to barge through, drawing looks of consternation and shrill protests in soft south east London accents. He was heading for the workshop. O'Donnell had left a set of race leathers and a helmet inside, the biggest he could find. Calloway hoped the riders' garb would conceal him for long enough to meet O'Donnell at the rear gates. Here he would be waiting with his road bike, a big Vincent Black Shadow, its near-thousand cc engine running. If they could make it out of the stadium before Sammy and his men, they would be clean away.

The workshop was unlit. Calloway entered into the darkness, with just enough glow from the high windows for him to make out the helmet and leathers draped over the bench. As he crossed the room, he saw movement in his peripheral vision. A darkened figure moving quickly towards him, something glinting in its hand. Then an artillery shell burst inside his head. And then another. He saw white light and heard a noise so loud he buckled at the knees and fell hard onto the oily concrete, clutching his skull for fear it would explode into a thousand fragments. More blows came, from boots this time, to his guts and to his face. Pain dragged at his consciousness with barbed claws. His senses were failing. He heard a voice singing an imbecilic song. He recognised it as Ray Simpkins's.

'I once won first prize two and six, I know all the dirt track dirty tricks.'

The ground was slick. An upturned can of Castrol oozed rank-smelling fuel to engulf him. It soaked into the fabric of his suit, seeped into his hair and clung to the exposed flesh of his hands and face. His legs jerked in spasms as his heels slid around on the workshop floor. His fingers clawed at the legs of the workbench, desperately seeking a grip but failing.

He sensed he was alone now. The smell of burning fuel filled the room. He felt heat, intense burning heat. Acrid smoke crawled its way into his lungs as he gasped through searing chest pain. Then there was another voice. A familiar voice. An American. He felt strong hands dragging his ankles, his inert frame gliding slowly through an oily sea. More voices, angry this time. Shouts and scuffling. Then a heavy body falling onto his, sending his pain right off the dial. He gasped more of the acrid fumes into his lungs. Then a calm, quiet blackness pulled him down through the hard concrete, bone fragment by bone fragment, and into the netherworld below.

TWENTY-SIX

He came to on the hard metal floor of some kind of truck. Beside him another body, a dead weight that buffeted against him as the vehicle took corners. He was hooded and his hands were tied. He couldn't find a piece of him that didn't hurt when he moved. He sensed a presence over him, perhaps two people, the sound of breathing and the smell of cigarette smoke cutting through faint diesel fumes.

They drove for another hour at least, Calloway drifting in and out of consciousness, an overwhelming fatigue dragging him into bouts of fitful sleep. At first, in his waking moments, he heard other vehicles passing them at regular intervals. Now they seemed alone on quiet roads.

The truck stopped. He heard the driver exchange words with another voice outside, as you would with a sentry. The vehicle drove on, slower this time, before pulling up. He heard the rasp of the handbrake being applied and the metallic clink of small chains being released as the tailgate was dropped. The body next to him was dragged out first. Out cold or dead, it made no sound. There were heavy footsteps and the sound of a door opening, then swinging shut. Minutes later, the footsteps returned. Arms grabbed him roughly and dragged him over the tailgate. By reflex his legs felt for the ground. He attempted to stand but his legs gave way. Two heavy-footed men frogmarched him in the direction of the door he had just heard slam. They yanked his outstretched arms over their shoulders to keep him upright as his feet dragged along the hard concrete beneath them.

Inside the building the air was stale and damp. He could smell the fug of abandonment, even through the dusty canvas of the hood. It was cold too, the kind of cold you only get in places that haven't been heated for months. Ahead of him keys clanked in a lock and a heavy door screeched on his hinges as it was opened. Beyond the door the smell was worse.

They dumped him on what felt like a wooden bunk. The pain he felt all over suddenly grew more intense, as his injured body connected with the hard surface under it. He sensed another presence in the room. He felt practiced hands probe him, like the doc had done to Reilly on the examination bench. Then a rough hand yanked off the hood. The room was dark, except for the beam of a pen-torch in the hand of the man examining him. He raised each eyelid in turn with a calloused thumb and shone the torch into Calloway's eyes. The two other men stripped off his jacket, causing a shaft of pain to spread down his arms and across his ribs. Calloway yelped like an animal. He felt the pressure of a cuff over his bicep and heard the puff of a blood pressure gauge being pumped then released. He felt a hand on his wrist and the light touch of fingers taking his pulse to the faint ticking of a wristwatch.

His examiner then fumbled in a case and tinkered with an instrument Calloway could not make out in the darkness. A sound like a small bottle top being unscrewed, a short pause and the tap-tapping of a fingernail against something small and glass. Hands fumbled with his limp forearm. The needle of a syringe bee-stung through the fabric of his bloodied shirt. A thousand tiny ants scurried through his arteries. He felt becalmed. Then the eddying wooden surface under him seemed to swallow him whole.

He woke. A barbed wire skullcap was clawing its way into his brain. Pressure and pain. His limb joints constricted like rusting monkey wrenches in the hands of an angry mechanic. Simpkins at the workbench tossing tools around. There was light in the cell now, a big floodlight illuminating the Bullets as they saluted the crowd. He heard Marching Along Together inside his head. He scrunched up his eyes against the glare. His eyeballs felt pumped to bursting. He tried to summon proper consciousnesses but just kept drifting. He felt his bicep. It felt bee-sting sharp, like the puncture wound in Pattie Moxon's soft white thighs. Pat was there, standing over him, her skirt hitched up. She spoke with the voice of Liz Francis. 'Des Fenton was a bastard.'

Hours passed. Perhaps days. A window in his consciousness opened, but whatever was outside was fog bound. He shifted where he lay and tried to audit the damage. The hurt had shifted. The truck he'd arrived in had parked on his chest and dumped a ton of cinders into a chute in his forehead. A light blinded him. A golden, heavenly light rising up from the maggot-ridden body of the tramp Wood, permeating the concrete roof of the pillbox and spouting skywards to the stars. He tried to raise an arm to shield his eyes but it wouldn't budge. He was filled with concrete, the more he tried to move the more it solidified. He lay still and breathed hard. The air was damp and dusty. Floodlit dust specs floated around him. He scrunched his eyes to shut out the light. They felt over-ripe and mushy. It made him nauseous. The dust cloud smothered him. It suffocated his consciousness. He faded out again.

Giant hands shook him awake. He complied. He struggled to his feet like a rusted-up automaton. The body was working half capacity. The brain was still dormant save for enough nerve endings to instruct his limbs. They shuffle-marched him along a corridor. He heard himself singing Marching Along Together. His joints ground metal, his blood supply had hit the reserve tank. He felt his head bobbing like a kellyman. His bare, aching feet scraped on the gritted floor. His toes tingled with a million tiny agonies.

Then came a moment of clarity, as if a gallon of new blood had flooded his brain. He was alert, but he knew it would not be for long. He felt the urge to act, almost by reflex. He lashed out. A red haze frenzy took over. He struggled free and swung at the biggest of the two men holding him. It was a mistake. They pushed his face into the painted brick wall. His lips splayed and he tasted damp dust. The man he'd struck made a swift retort. Calloway's kidneys took a well-practiced jab. His nerve endings crescendoed pain. He kicked back, aiming for a shin. A bone snap would have given him an opening. But he donkey-kicked thin air with bare feet. A second kidney blow made his legs buckle. His body slimed down the wall in an ooze of hurt.

They scooped him up and dragged him through an open door into an interrogation cell. Two metal chairs flanked a tarnished metal table. They dumped him on one of the chairs. He fell like a half-full sack. The big hands grabbed his wrists and snapped on cuffs. There was enough light for him to recognise the two men. Mackay's stooges. They muttered too indistinctly for Calloway to make out. The words meant nothing but the tone was menacing, a prelude to something worse to come. It came. An elbow jack-hammered into his jaw. The crack echoed around his skull. He tasted his own blood. Then the door slammed. He was alone in the room, save for the spectre of his own private terror.

He must have slept as he sat. When he awoke Sammy Mackay was seated in the chair opposite, rocking back on its legs while he puffed on a pipe. There was a heap of pipe ash in an ashtray on the table in front of him. There was also an unopened packet Players Navy Cut, Calloway noticed.

'About time,' said Mackay. 'You certainly were out for the count.'

'I generally am when I've been beaten by professionals and pumped full of junk.'

Mackay raised an eyebrow. 'Happened to you before?'

'Fuck off, Sammy. Give me a cigarette.'

Mackay tossed the unopened packet at him.

'And take off the manacles. I'm not going anywhere.'

Mackay waved his head from side to side as if deciding whether this was a good idea. He dug in his pocket and fished out a key. He gestured to Calloway to hold out his hands, then unlocked the cuffs. Calloway rubbed some life back into his wrists and lit himself a cigarette. The hot tar burned his lungs but it felt good. His head swam with the right kind of giddiness this time. Mackay spoke without his characteristic superciliousness, the way he used to speak in the field.

'I had hoped that we could have avoided this. But you left me no choice, Cab.'

‘I’m difficult like that.’

‘I don’t know who you’re trying to protect.’

‘Would it shock you if I said the reputation of the club?’

‘Those motorbike jockeys? Are you kidding?’

Mackay laughed. ‘Or is it your boss, the lady Patricia?’

He quoted from the race card.

‘Managing Director of South London Speed Stars. I suppose she’s not in bad shape for an old boiler, but really, Cab, are you that shallow?’

Calloway felt the urge to defend her but he bit his tongue. It wouldn’t make any difference, not with Mackay.

‘What do you want?’

Mackay leant over the table and looked him in the face. Calloway knew the look. This would be the crux of it.

‘I want to know what names Ron Sampson and Pat Ladbroke go by these days.’

‘Why?’

‘A matter of national security.’

‘You’ll have to do better than that.’

Mackay thought about this. He sighed. ‘I suppose I could have asked my boys to beat it out of you, but you always were a stubborn old shit. And strong as an ox.’

‘Intelligence from torture isn’t reliable Sammy. I reckon your lot should have realised that by now.’

‘It never stopped you trying.’

Calloway shrugged. It made his shoulders hurt. ‘Perhaps I enjoyed it, like you said.’

Mackay sighed again more deeply this time. He sat back in the chair and sucked on the pipe.

‘You’re still covered by the Act, Cab. If what I’m about to tell you goes beyond this room, I’ll make sure you swing for it.’

Calloway shifted his weight in the chair. He recalled the kidney punches. Two swollen kidneys made sure he was reminded.

‘I may be a fool, but I’m not a traitor, Sammy. Your official secrets are safe with me. Say what you’ve got to say.’

Mackay clasped his hands together on the desk and leaned forward. He looked liked the headmaster at a second-rate private school about to share the benefit of his wisdom with a disinterested pupil.

'You called me with three names. Sampson, Ladbroke and Belper. Three men who went by these aliases were members of the British Free Corps. Nazi volunteers. You had the names of Free Corps barracks and a description of their insignia, which I'm guessing came from the photographs we found in your safe.'

'Go on.'

'We've been trying to find Sampson and Ladbroke, but we've never known their true identities.'

'Why go to the trouble? For a charge of assisting the enemy? Even if you found them they'd be out of jail within five years.'

'We're not interested in their Free Corps membership. As you say, they would barely get more than a slap on the wrist if they had good lawyer. There's more to it.'

'Like membership of an Einsatzgruppe?'

Mackay waved a hand dismissively. 'Oh we know about that too. Nasty business, but hardly in the interest of national security. That's all in the past.'

'Unless you're a Jew, or a gypsy, or a homosexual, or a communist. I imagine that sort of nasty business is still very much part of their present.'

Mackay gave a condescending nod. 'Of course, Cab, you probably feel that more than most of us, what with that poor little Jewess you fell for. What a sentimental brute you are. But really, the war crimes trials are done and dusted. Waste of time digging around in that old nonsense again.'

Calloway had never felt more like punching someone.

'We found Frank Thomas Belper in Berlin. He was passing himself off as a German under the name Franz Baumann, working in the Russian sector. He'd burned off his blood group tattoo but we identified him from the records that survived from Prince-Albrecht-Strasse. The Nazis were so wonderfully bureaucratic. Unlike the other two, Belper was regular SS. He transferred to the Free Corps later. He was also a very bad boy indeed. We had enough evidence to get him an appointment with Mr Pierrepoint. It seems when faced with the end of a rope his willingness to die for the fatherland dissipated somewhat. We saw in him the makings of an asset. We tossed him back and made sure he found gainful employment within the state apparatus. He's been supplying us with intelligence ever since. Not chicken feed. Good quality gen. He's one of our best sources in the Soviet sector.'

'And to protect his cover, you want his two old Free Corps pals out of the way.'

Mackay nodded. 'Something like that.'

'Is that really necessary? What are the chances of them identifying him? He's behind the Iron Curtain. It's not as though their paths are going to cross.'

'That all depends what they're up to. But of course you'd know that, wouldn't you Cab? That's why we brought you here. You and that bloody American.'

The second body on the truck floor, out cold.

'O'Donnell's here?'

He realised it was O'Donnell who had dragged him from the workshop when Simpkins had left him to burn. Mackay's men must have snatched him too.

'Is that his name? I was trying to work it out from that little pamphlet I picked up at your stadium. Yes, he's here and bloody awkward it is too. If the cousins find out we're holding one of theirs there will be an almighty stink.'

'So let him go. He stumbled into this. It's not his lookout.'

'Actually you got him into this. That's your lookout. He'll get the same deal I'm about to offer you.'

'Go to hell.'

Mackay stood up and stretched. He checked his watch. 'Tiresome, Cab. Very, very tiresome. I'm half inclined to ask my men to beat some sense into you after all.'

'Be my guest.'

Calloway couldn't hurt more than he did.

Mackay leaned against the painted brick wall, sunk his hands into his pockets and stared at the filthy floor.

'The East Germans are forming a new ministry for state security. Franz Baumann is tipped for a top job in one of its departments, something called the Administration for Struggle Against Suspicious Persons. I do love these ideological names. It seems Herr Baumann's peculiar talents have been recognised. Essentially, he'll be spying on westerners, some of whom of course will be working for us. Well, you can see what a useful sort he's going to be.'

Now it made sense. Sammy had recruited a butcher as his favourite errand boy. The psychopath Belper would be deep within East Germany's intelligence apparatus with a direct line on which foreign agents were under suspicion. Even Calloway could see the value of protecting such a source.

'Find Sampson and Ladbroke. I don't care how you do it. Then we'll do our best to leave you and the American alone.'

'And if I refuse?'

Sammy let out one of his theatrical sighs. 'Then there's something else I should mention. I sent a black bag team to your flat to see what they could find. Two men. Only one came back. He described a man your height and build pursuing him and his colleague down the street. Four days later the river police fished the other man out of the Thames at Rotherhithe. He'd been shot at point-blank range with his own revolver.'

Calloway shrugged. 'There's a gun crime epidemic. Haven't you heard?'

'Your neighbourhood is a godforsaken place but I'm assuming executions aren't a daily occurrence. And don't even think of crying self-defence. Point blank, Calloway, dead centre, through the forehead, close enough for powder burns even that toxic river water couldn't wash away.'

Mackay pocketed his pipe, picked up the Navy Cut and lit one, tossing the pack back across the table. Calloway took another and shared the light. Mackay pulled on the cigarette and exhaled hard.

'I miss these. I took up the pipe because they're better for your health. Not the same though.'

He savoured the rough tobacco for a moment before continuing.

'We look after our own kind, Calloway. We don't need a court of law to do it. We're a long way from anywhere and no one knows you're here. Don't make me spell it out.'

They took Calloway back to his cell. It was light and he could see through the windows of the abandoned building. Outside was the vehicle he'd arrived in, a rugged light truck with a tilt cover and big suspension. Beyond it, a runway overgrown with weeds, next to that the familiar shape of Quonset huts, paint peeling on their curved corrugated tin roofs. In the distance a control tower, its windows broken and its distinctive Mickey Mouse camouflage fading. The runway was long, stretching as far as he could see. An old bomber station he presumed. He was most likely in the guardhouse.

One of Mackay's heavies shoved him into the cell and slammed the heavy door shut. He heard the key turn in the lock.

He lay on the hard bench. Above him the faint crying of crows cut through a howling wind. An east wind, he surmised. He would be in one of those featureless flatlands in Lincolnshire, Cambridgeshire or Norfolk. There would be nothing as far as the eye could see except black earth and intermittent rows of poplar trees, an ineffective windbreak against a biting wind blowing straight off the Ural Mountains two thousand miles to the east.

In the gloomy half-light of the cell he read the graffiti on the grey painted brickwork. Obscene sketches and Hitler caricatures. He dozed a little and dreamed half dreams. Shutze Wood's photographs flashed behind his closed eyes like a depraved magic lantern show. He heard Simpkins's voice carried on the wind outside.

'They were rats. Fucking vermin!'

He jumped up and banged on the cell door.

'Mackay, you bastard! Come here Mackay!'

Heavy footsteps echoed down the corridor and the key turned in the lock. The two heavies entered with Mackay behind them.

'What's all this, Cab? Had a bad dream?'

'Pat Ladbroke's real name is Wood. He was an infantry private with the British Expeditionary Force. He lived as a tramp and drank himself to death on meths. I saw his corpse. Ron

Sampson's name is Ray Simpkins. He's a speedway rider. He rides for the Bullets, or at least did. I braced him and he confessed to his wartime exploits. Then he did a runner.'

'So he's at large?'

Calloway nodded. 'I can find him. Release me and O'Donnell and we'll bring him in.'

Sammy shook his head and laughed.

'Bring him in? I don't want him, Cab. I want him out of the picture altogether. Make that happen and you might just get to go back to your dog track with your big American friend. Are you up to it?'

'You said yourself I was always quite good at that sort of thing.'

'Is Simpkins dangerous? It's not that I care for your safety or anything. I just need to know you can do the job without fucking up.'

It was Calloway's turn to laugh, but it hurt him to do so. 'You mean more dangerous than beating a man my size half to death and setting fire to the stadium? Yes, I'd say so, wouldn't you?'

'Is he armed?'

'Considering half of all demobbed servicemen came home with a Luger as a souvenir, I'd say there's a fair chance. And he'd probably have more emotional attachment to a German weapon than most of them. He seemed to have enjoyed using one.'

'I can get you firearms. Do you know men who can use them?'

'Men? What am I doing, raising a posse? Do you like the novels of Zane Grey, Sammy?'

'If you go this alone, you'll fail. A manhunt is a team play.'

Calloway nodded. 'I've got some friends.'

'Good. You'll be strictly freelance on this. You realise if you're caught we'll disown you?'

'I had assumed as much.'

'But better that than the alternative, eh?'

'Fuck off, Sammy. I'll need a vehicle too. Like the one I arrived here in.'

Mackay recoiled at this. 'You're not having my Land Rover.'

'Land what?'

‘Rover’s new overland vehicle. Like a jeep, only it doesn’t roll over at the sight of a bend. I’ve been waiting two years for one.’

‘I want it.’

Quite suddenly Calloway found himself desperately in need to ask Mackay a question. ‘How is the stadium?’

His old commanding officer looked incredulous. ‘Well I’m no expert but I reckon you’ll need a new workshop. Everything else is still standing.’

‘And the spectators?’

‘Your boys got them out, so I’m told.’

He felt a pang of relief he hadn’t expected. But in this whole disgusting business, the stadium had become some kind of constant he could cling to. When he’d first arrived in post he had arranged a fire drill with the stadium staff and fire brigade crews from the divisional headquarters at New Cross. He’d timed the fire crews at nine minutes from station to stadium gates. The drill had paid off. He felt a warmth inside that overcame the hurt from the beatings. For the first time since leaving the army, he felt like he belonged.

TWENTY-SEVEN

There were four of them in the Land Rover. Calloway, O'Donnell, Webber and Birkett. Webber drove. It was more than they could do to stop him. He gave a running commentary as they rumbled down the Kentish lanes. How the vehicle handled, its responsiveness, the suspension. He was in his element behind the wheel of the newly designed marque.

O'Donnell had raised the posse, like the sheriff in one of Webber's westerns. He picked military men. He played on their sense of outrage at the London boy turned Nazi. All three volunteers thought they would be handing Simpkins over to the authorities. Only Calloway knew of the deal he'd made with Mackay. He would honour that alone. The other three need never know.

Calloway was playing a hunch, but an informed one. This wasn't the first time Simpkins had gone to ground. He'd lost himself in the marshes once before, with Wood and the deserters. Calloway wagered he'd do it again.

As the road petered out he recognised the gate where he'd parked previously.

'We're out of road, Bert. Pull her up just ahead.'

Webber drew close to the gate and applied the handbrake. He killed the engine and doused the headlights.

'Sweet as a nut,' he said, patting the dashboard with his four remaining fingers.

The four men disembarked. Calloway dropped the tailgate and hauled a long canvass bag from the deck. He unbuckled the webbing straps. There were two Webley service revolvers, a Browning HP and a MkIII Lee Enfield.

O'Donnell whistled. 'Planning to start a war Calloway?'

'Let's hope we don't have to.'

He had worried O'Donnell would blame him for ending up in a cell at the bomber station. Sammy was right. Calloway had got the innocent American into this. But O'Donnell's grudge was with Simpkins. He saw the whole affair as a betrayal by a teammate and it hurt.

Calloway handed a Webley to Bert Webber and tucked the second one in his own waistband. O'Donnell grabbed the Browning automatic.

Webber smirked. 'Wouldn't you prefer a six shooter?'

'What, to thirteen rounds in the clip? Are you kidding?'

'Who's starting a war now?' said Birkett dourly, sliding the bolt back on the Lee Enfield and putting a round in the chamber.

Calloway was firm. 'No war. No cowboy antics. Use the weapons as a deterrent or in self-defence at the absolute worst. No one's leaving this place with hole in them that God didn't put there.'

Webber sniggered.

Calloway took Birkett to one side. 'You don't have to do this, Les. You've earned your stripes and then some. You've nothing to prove.'

The old RSM bristled. 'With respect, Mr Calloway, I've spent the last four years watching those punters file through the turnstiles with no more action to be had than bollocking them for dropping litter. This feels like the life I remember and if you think I'm too old for it, just try fucking stopping me.'

Calloway clapped him on the back. 'Then keep watch here, Les. Secure the exit route. If Simpkins bolts for the road, your job's to stop him.'

'You're Johnny on the spot, Birkett,' said O'Donnell. 'Make it count.'

Calloway beckoned the three men to him. 'So Birkett's holding the rear. The remaining three will fan out, one man on the path, such as it is, and two either side at fifty-yard intervals. If you see something, holler. The rest of us will close in. Don't go taking on Simpkins alone. He's unpredictable and fights dirty.'

'You think the 82nd fights clean?'

'Stow the bravura. There's to be no unnecessary risks.'

Webber raised his hand. He gestured towards the estuary. 'The light's fading and that looks like a pea-souper blowing in. The biggest risk is that we end up clobbering one of our own.'

'We'll use a sign and countersign. If you see another man, give the sign. If he gives the wrong response, you'll know he's not one of us. That doesn't mean it's Simpkins. I've been here. There's a colony of vagrants. Don't get the wrong man.'

'So what's the sign?' asked Webber.

O'Donnell offered one. 'The call is, "How d'ya like your eggs?", the response is, "On the Jersey side". That's one for Cab.'

'That'll have to do,' said Calloway.

Webber was right. A thick mist was blowing in from the river. The light had all but gone and above them a full moon glowed through the cloud cover.

'Time to move. Best of luck, gentlemen.'

O'Donnell stopped them. He put a hand to his lips for quiet. All four strained to hear above the rising wind. In the distance they heard the faint rumble of a motorcycle engine. As the engine noise grew louder, Calloway made out a single headlamp weaving its way through the lanes towards them. He instructed the men to scatter, each finding cover and readying their weapons. As the motorcycle approached, its headlamp picked up the reflectors of the Land Rover casting a faint red glow over the mist. It was a heavy bike which crunched over the gravel of the path as it pulled to a halt. The rider killed the engine and dismounted, crossing to the Land Rover and peering through the side windows. Then the figure stepped back and removed its helmet. Recognising the rider the four men broke cover. A female voice broke the silence.

'Jesus. What do you think you look like? A bunch of bloody Boy Scouts.'

Calloway ran forward, anger rising in his veins. 'What the hell are you doing here Pat?'

'What am I doing here? I could ask the same of you. Have you seen yourselves? Like Karno's bloody army.'

'You need to leave.'

'Oh, I'm going nowhere mate. Not till I've yanked that Simpkins by the ear back to my stadium. No rider goes AWOL on me, not on the night of the George Formby Cup.'

Calloway let out a frustrated growl. 'How the hell did you know about this?'

Moxon looked at Webber. Even in the darkness the small rider looked sheepish.

'You don't want to tell him your secrets, believe me.'

She shook her hair loose and pulled down the zip on her leathers. She turned to Calloway.

'So do you have a plan or are you going to run around all night like a big girl's blouse?'

There would be no arguing with her, Calloway knew that much. He ran through the plan. Moxon seemed to approve.

'Right. So I'll take the left flank and that way we can cover an extra fifty yards between us.'

Webber raised his hand. Moxon sighed. 'Yes, Bert?'

The small man stuttered. 'If you see someone, you say "How d'ya like your eggs?". That way we'll know it's you.'

'Oh behave yourself, Bert Webber. I'll do no such thing.'

Undeterred, Webber raised his hand again, this time looking at Calloway. It was Calloway's turn to sigh.

'We haven't got a gun for Pat, Mr Calloway.'

Moxon let out an incredulous squeal. 'Who do you lot think you are, the Texas bloody Rangers. If someone comes near me I'll knock his teeth out. It wouldn't be the first time. Guns my Aunt Fanny!'

Birkett signalled the end of the conversation, laying his rifle on the bonnet of the Land Rover and lighting a cheroot. 'You lot better get going then. You've lost the light. Best just get on with it.'

Calloway led them forward, then as agreed they spread out at intervals. From the estuary the sound of a steam whistle carried on the wind.

It was boggy underfoot, more so than last time. There had been rain. The four picked their way through the long grass, eyes sweeping from side to side and peering through the mist which surrounded them now on all sides. Overhead, gulls cried. Then Calloway heard a voice singing a bawdy shanty. He looked down. A blackened face peered up from a bivouac and cackled, 'Fuck me, it's a will-o'-the-wisp.'

Calloway pressed on. He'd lost sight of the path and was using the moon to navigate as best he could. It lit up the fog through breaks in the fast-moving cloud, like a lighthouse beam rotating. To his left he heard muffled profanities. Webber finding a ditch the hard way, he imagined. His own boots were sodden now too and a fine film of moisture clung to his jacket. The mist was turning to mizzle. He felt it trickling down his neck and into his shirt collar. Through the occasional break in the mist he made out the pin-prick of a torch beam from one of the other hunters. They should have left the torches behind. They were no use in these conditions. All they would do was advertise their presence to Simpkins and risk giving him a head start.

Through the gloom he made out the outline of a low structure. As he drew closer he recognised it as the shelter of the man he'd given cigarettes to. It was securely fastened and as Calloway drew nearer, he heard the snoring and muttering of a fitful sleep from inside. As he passed, as light footed as he could, he saw the last embers of the sleeping man's fading campfire glowing through the ash.

The shelter gave him a bearing. A quarter mile ahead was the tramp Wood's pillbox. He played a hunch and headed for it, keeping the moon in a constant position above him to stay on course. Conditions underfoot deteriorated. It was slow going now and took him a quarter hour to cover the distance. Clouds covered the moon fully, ahead only a grey-black darkness. He trod deliberately and carefully, then paused. Two eyes glared thorough the mist, as if from the face of an invisible demon. The rifle loops in the pillbox, lit from inside. Joe Smoke's castle had a new king.

Calloway advanced at a crouch, steadying himself with this fists on the sodden ground that rose in clumps the nearer he drew to the tiny blockhouse. He pulled the Webley from his waistband and slid off the safety catch that nestled discreetly above the trigger on the weapon's cold metal body. He hugged the damp walls of the building listening for movement inside. The rising wind bounced off the bricks and drummed against his ears making it hard to hear. He scrambled around to the front. A crack of light shone down the side of the hessian sack that served as the pillbox door. Still no sound from inside that Calloway could hear above the wind. He rose to his feet and steadied himself. Adrenaline coursed through his veins and his heart pounded in his still-aching chest. In a snap, he ripped down the sack and lunged through the blockhouse door, pistol arm extended. No one inside. Joe Smoke's corpse was gone and the fug of death had dissipated. The place had been cleaned out and was arranged in a soldierly fashion, with a Primus stove, water canteen and a bedroll stowed along the far wall. A tilly lamp hung from a rusting hook on the underside of the roof. In its glow Calloway noticed a kitbag, stuffed to capacity, leaning against the sidewall to his left. The new king of the castle was going somewhere and soon.

He ripped the kitbag open and tugged out its contents. Spare clothing in small sizes, wash kit and a small tool roll of motorcycle tools. Buried at the bottom an envelope of cash, plenty of it, in sterling and French francs. Against the same wall, a jacket hung from a nail in the brickwork. He recognised it as Simpkins's. He rifled the pockets. Loose cash, a switchblade and a dozen 9mm cartridges. Also a folded slip of paper. He unfolded it and held it up to the light of the quietly roaring lamp. A line scrawled in pencil read The Channel Queen, Ramsgate, midnight, followed by today's date. He pocketed the note.

He crawled out of the pillbox and stretched his aching body to full height. Gripping the revolver in readiness he swept three hundred sixty degrees, using his peripheral vision to more clearly see through the darkness. Simpkins was out there, perhaps observing him right now.

The wind had dropped leaving an eerie silence. He edged back to the walls of the pillbox and dropped to a crouch. He heard the sound of sodden ground being trodden underfoot and strained to hear from which direction it was coming. The blackness was disorientating. Before he could get a fix on the nearing footsteps, the hard butt of a pistol stuck him from behind. There was a flash inside his head and he buckled. A figure pushed past him and ducked into the blockhouse. He heard scuffling as the figure hastily gathered up the strewn kit. Calloway thought he heard the chink of the dozen brass cartridge cases being pocketed. Then, like a will-o'-the-wisp, the small figure fled from its cave in the direction of the road a half mile behind them.

Calloway struggled to his feet, a searing pain from ear to ear and a ringing inside his skull. He levelled the Webley to his eye line and aimed at the faint outline of the running man illuminated against the moonlit mist. He fired two rounds which cracked like thunder through the silence. The will-o'-the-wisp ran onwards. Calloway aimed again and fired two more rounds. The wisp-like shadow stopped, turned and spat fire of its own. The first round ricocheted off the pillbox wall before Calloway had seen the muzzle flash. The second round caught his left shoulder and slammed him back against the hard brick wall. As he slumped he saw the wisp turn, then disappear into the darkness. He slid his hand under his shirt and checked the wound. It was light, just nicked flesh, arteries intact. Behind him he heard shouting – O'Donnell voice, then Webber's.

Calloway drew breath and hollered, 'Fall back to the truck, he's heading for the road!'

He stuffed his handkerchief under his shirt as a makeshift swab and followed O'Donnell and Webber's voices back towards the gate where they'd left Birkett. Birkett would have heard the shot and would be covering the marshes with the big .303. Calloway hoped the old soldier's eyesight was up to it. In these conditions it would be just as easy to fire on one of his own.

The three men met at the path and ran together towards the road. There was no sign of Pat Moxon. By now Calloway had figured she could take care of herself. He pictured Simpkins being dragged along by the ear, his two front teeth missing. Then another image of Moxon flashed through his mind, water-stained and faded like one of the sick photos from the tramp Wood's album. She lay in a ditch half naked with a bullet through her head, a trickle of blood running down her dead face and seeping into the silk of her torn slip. Amid the pain of exertion he found the strength to run faster.

As the three men neared the road the outline of the Land Rover loomed into view. But between them and the gate a fourth figure crouched in the reeds.

O'Donnell gave the sign to halt. Webber whispered, 'Is it Pattie?'

'I can't tell. Too far ahead and too dark.'

O'Donnell drew back the slide and put a round in the Browning's chamber. Ahead of them a shot rang out and the muzzle flash lit up the crouching figure of Simpkins. He bolted for the gate and fired twice more. Someone flicked a switch and the Land Rover's big headlamps lit up the marshes like a stage set. Calloway scrunched up his eyes to peer through the glare, looking for Birkett. There was no sign of the old RSM, nor any sound from the .303.

In silhouette against the beam of the lights, Simpkins raised the pistol again, this time in his direction. Two more shots rang out. Under this covering fire the small rider scrambled over to the reeds and tossed clumps of foliage aside. Beneath the camouflage was a motorcycle. Simpkins kicked it into life.

O'Donnell spat: 'That's my fucking Vincent.'

They heard the deep clunk of the gears engaging before the powerful bike crashed through the rotting gate, passed the Land Rover and headed for the road.

Birkett lay propped against the nearside wheel of the small truck. Moxon crouched over him, using her scarf as a compress to stem the flow of blood. Birkett looked up at Calloway.

'Bastard fucking winged me before I could loose off a round.'

Moxon shouted at Webber, 'Bert, hold this, press as hard as you can.'

She passed the compress to Webber and crossed over to Calloway and O'Donnell. 'He'll live, if we get him to a doctor right now. You know where Doc McArdle lives?'

O'Donnell nodded.

'Then you and Bert take the Land Rover and get him over there pronto. You drive, Bert needs to hold that compress tight.'

Webber called across to them, 'It's a fucking bullet wound, Pat. What if Doc calls the police?'

'Tell the old soak if he wants to keep his job, he'll keep this to himself.'

'Will he do that?' Calloway asked.

'He will if he wants me to keep quiet about the backstreet abortion clinic he runs on the side.'

She grabbed Calloway by the arm. 'Now you, come with me.' She nodded towards her motorbike. 'If were going to catch the little bastard up, we've got to get going. Any idea where he's heading?'

'Ramsgate, for midnight.'

She looked at her watch. 'Come on then, get on the back.'

Calloway stopped. Only then did it occur to him he'd be riding pillion. He sensed the other men were watching him.

Pat cocked her head and raised an eyebrow. 'Unless you can ride a motorcycle, Reg.'

She knew he couldn't. They both knew she was the professional rider. He fought with his pride and won by a slim margin. He climbed onto the rear seat of the motorcycle.

'Hold me tight, Reg,' she shouted above the noise of the gunning engine. 'I won't break.'

TWENTY-EIGHT

They picked up Simpkins's tail-light a mile ahead. He was throwing himself into the bends and Moxon did the same, in spite of the additional weight on the mean passenger seat of her Series C Rapide.

'Lean in, Reg, you're like a sack of coal back there.'

He pressed himself closer to her and gripped her waist, pushing his chin into the crook of her neck below the line of the tightly buckled helmet. For a second he felt her nuzzle closer. The rain was heavier now and the visibility worsened. She tugged the flyers' googles down off the helmet and onto the bridge of her nose.

She turned her head and shouted above the roar of the slipstream, 'Is he meeting a boat?'

They were touching eighty miles an hour and the oncoming rush of air sucked the words from his chest.

Calloway shouted back, 'Crossing the Channel on a contraband run I reckon. One of those fast-motor vessels. A ration-buster fetching brandy and God knows what back from France. Simpkins will try and lose himself in Europe, maybe even head to Germany. He speaks the language.'

The small red tail-light faded in and out of the mizzling rain. Moxon dropped a gear and squeezed more power from the throttle. She clamped her legs around the tank and merged with the machine.

The cry of the wind had risen to a scream. She could no longer hear him. The two motorcycles cut through darkened towns and villages, their whirring wheels spraying rainwater over the slick bitumen of the empty streets. Rochester, Chatham, Rainham, places Calloway knew from maps but had never been.

They left the streetlights behind. Their eyes adjusted to the darkness, but at best visibility was down to the two dozen yards of their headlamp's beam. The full moon was lost behind thick cloud now. The distant red dot of the tail lamp disappeared.

Calloway shouted above the scream of the engine, 'Have we lost him?'

Moxon responded with a clunk from the gearbox and a shriek of acceleration. They powered through the darkness for another half mile. Then something glinted in the headlamp a hundred yards ahead. Moxon cried out.

'Jesus Christ, hold on.'

Simpkins had stopped dead, broadsiding the Black Shadow to block the single-track road. He sat astride the motorcycle gripping his pistol with both hands. Two shots flashed from the barrel. The first went wide, whistling past Calloway's head. The second clipped Moxon's helmet sending a spark off the metal cowl into the darkness. There was no room to brake. She accelerated and lugged the heavy bike up and onto the verge to the side of them. Their back wheel struggled to grip the grass and the soft earth beneath. Moxon decelerated, then revved once more, manoeuvring the bike back onto the road and gliding to a halt. Simpkins was back on the Vincent. He accelerated past them and disappeared into black night ahead.

Moxon gunned the engine aggressively, let the clutch out and gripped the bike hard as it lunged forward in pursuit of the Black Shadow. Calloway's head snapped back with the inertia.

'Lean in for Christ's sake Reg! You'll have us off.'

He complied, clasping her around the waist and pushing his head into the crook of her neck. The rain eased as they passed through Faversham. They were able to keep the tail-light in sight for another half hour. Calloway's damaged frame ached in new places but he held tight to Moxon, their bodies and the motorcycle moving as one.

They entered Ramsgate from the west, both motorcycles cutting a swathe through the red neon haze cast by the sign of the grand Odeon cinema. The posters advertised Adam's Rib. Calloway managed a laugh. Ahead of them the harbour lights glistened. Moxon dropped a gear and squeezed more life from the Rapide's hot engine. Their rear wheel skidded on the slick wet cobbles as they descended through the deserted coastal town. They were close enough to Simpkins now to see the beam of his headlamp lighting the wet road that led to the western arm of the harbour. As they approached the Royal Parade and dropped down towards the harbour wall, Calloway loosened his grip on Moxon and peered at his watch under the streetlight. Five minutes to midnight. Sensing the urgency, Pat dropped another cog and gave the throttle every last drop.

They were closing on Simpkins. The two motorcycles shot along the long curving arm of the West Pier towards the lighthouse, its constant red light soaking the two machines in a wash of blood red.

The bike ahead was yards from the end of the harbour wall and showing no signs of stopping. Simpkins gripped the throttle with his right hand and swivelled his body back towards them, his left arm outstretched. He let fly the last rounds in the pistol's clip. Calloway saw sparks glance off the harbour wall to their right. Simpkins's motorcycle wavered, his body snapped back attempting to wrest control of the big Vincent and failing. The bike glanced off the lighthouse, flinging Simpkins's bare head into the curved brickwork. They saw a red spay of blood against the harbour lights before the Black Shadow dragged its unconscious rider over the end of the jetty and down into the black water below.

Moxon pulled up just ahead of the jetty's end and both she and Calloway dismounted, running to the water's edge and peering down into the spume that crashed against the stone harbour wall. Bike and rider were gone, swallowed by the Channel that was to have been the young traitor's escape.

Moxon took Calloway's hand and led him back to the motorcycle.

'We need to leave here, find somewhere for the night.'

Calloway continued staring at the water. Ray Simpkins' angry little saga had reached its end. It gave Calloway no satisfaction, just a cold sense of relief that the job had been done.

They rode to the top of the town and found a guest house with its lights still on. Pat fed the elderly landlady a line about a motorcycle holiday and a blown gasket. It seemed to work, even if the last guest remaining awake in the lounge raised an eyebrow at their lack of luggage.

She led him to the room and locked the door behind them. He walked to the window and stared down towards the harbour. Behind him he was aware she was undressing. He heard the unzipping of race leathers and smelled the sweet scent of Shalimar cutting through the musk of the rough black hide.

She crossed the room to the window and eased off his jacket and waistcoat, now sodden with rain. Then she circled him with her bare arms and unbuttoned his shirt, slipping it down over his shoulders and onto the floor. His handkerchief, caked in congealed blood, fell onto the worn rug. He heard her wince in sympathy. She pressed herself against his bare back and clasped her arms around him tightly. She was warm. She traced a line down his chest and over his clenched stomach with her fingernail.

'What are you doing?' he asked.

'Helping you make up for lost time,' she whispered.

He turned to face her. She was naked save for an oil-stained slip and stockings snagged by the zip of the leathers. Her hair was mussed, her lipstick smudged. The small puncture mark left by the syringe had faded.

He cupped her chin in his mud-streaked hand and pulled her lips onto his. From the harbour he heard the bells of a police car, its flashing light casting a blue neon glow onto the damp-stained ceiling of the cheap guest house room.

TWENTY-NINE

He woke to the sound of gulls crying in the sky above. The sun was rising, flooding cool white light through the open-curtained windows. Pat's head lay on his chest. Her arm rested on his stomach, her nails tracing shapes down his side.

'Are you awake?' she asked.

'Yes.'

A thought was tugging at him. He voiced it. 'There never were any rumours about Simpkins running Fenton off the track.'

She stopped stroking him. 'I needed those photos. When Fenton died it was my last chance to get them. I reckoned someone like you would find them, given the opportunity. The circumstances of Des's death created the opportunity I needed.'

'So you were prepared to accuse an innocent man of murder?'

She scoffed. 'Ray Simpkins was hardly innocent.'

'But you didn't know that when you dragged me into this business.'

She rolled off him, reached for her cigarettes on the bedside table and lit two of them. She put one between his lips and drew hard on the other.

'No harm would have come to him. It was an accident, plain and simple. You said so yourself. There was no evidence. Nothing that would stand up. The police weren't going to take a few rumours seriously.'

She laid her head back onto his chest. 'I knew he was a nasty piece of work long before Bert told me about this Free Corps business. I had no great qualms about spreading some gossip.'

Calloway pushed her head away. 'Ray Simpkins tried to kill me. He tried to burn down your stadium. Do you have qualms about that?'

She sat up and laid the ashtray on her lap. 'I didn't think things would get out of hand like that. Christ, I know they all think I'm a hard-nosed bitch, but I'm not that hard.'

He should have been angry. God knows he had reason. He'd been beaten to a pulp, threatened with death and shot at. Even by his standards that was beyond the call.

'Tell me about the photographs,' he said.

She turned to face him. 'Have you seen them?'

He nodded. She laughed. 'And you're still here.'

'Did Fenton take them?'

She let out a deep sigh.

'It was a long time ago. The early thirties. I was a show rider down at Catford. Des was the star of the home team there. We became lovers.'

She tutted at herself. 'I liked them flash in those days. I was young. Too young to know better. And they were mad times, Calloway. Des and his gang were hell raisers. Parties, drinking, snow. A blizzard of snow. I didn't need any encouragement. I was wild. When you risk your neck on a motorbike, recklessness becomes a way of life. I didn't care.'

She climbed out of bed and walked naked to the window.

'I love the sunrise. I like to think it wipes the slate clean from the previous day.'

The previous day's slate was quite a full one, Calloway thought.

'Des bought a camera. A good one and all the darkroom kit. He said he'd take publicity photos for the club.'

She laughed to herself. 'Publicity photos my arse. He was peddling smut. He had expensive habits and his speedway winnings didn't cover them. That workshop he's got down in Deptford? That was decked out like a boudoir back then. All plush and gold paint. He'd pick up girls, young ones mostly. Brasses some of them, but not always. Sometimes just girls. Wide-eyed and susceptible. He'd get them high as a kite and photograph all manner of depravity.'

'And you were one of them?'

She shook her head slowly. 'I wasn't like the others. I was

Des's girl. He persuaded me to do a private session, just for him. I was high as a kite myself most of the time, what with the snow and the booze. I didn't need a lot of persuading. I suppose I kidded myself that sort of thing was normal. I'd be lying if I said I hadn't developed a taste for decadence. My judgement was a little off, you might say. I did two or three shoots in the end. Des would be flying too and we'd be getting up to all sorts, once he'd put the camera down'

'So what happened?'

'Des and I didn't last. I knew I had to calm down. My health was starting to suffer and my riding was turning to rat shit. I quit the snow and the booze for a while and got my life back together. Des didn't seem so great when I was sober. He found someone else and I wasn't too cut up about it. Then one day down at the stadium I caught some of the young riders sniggering. I asked them to share the joke and they fumbled around trying hide something from me. Des had been selling my pictures. Pretty Pattie Moxon, Queen of the dirt track, dirtier than you've ever seen her. That night I went looking for him. I searched all his old haunts and found him pawing a couple of young tarts in a club up west. I threatened to kill him. He just laughed. He said if I didn't want those photos all over the speedway scene I'd better play nice. That's when the penny dropped. With those pictures he would always have a hold over me. It's no coincidence Des had a glowing career, Reg. Sure he was a good rider, one of the best, but he always enjoyed a big helping hand from yours truly whenever he needed it.'

She turned away from the window to face him. 'He betrayed me Reg. He betrayed my trust. And I've been paying for it ever since.' She threw back her head and laughed. 'I suppose I was the start of his career as a blackmailer.'

Calloway crossed to the window and wrapped his arms around her. She tensed and bit hard on her lip. Then she spat, 'He may have owned my reputation, but I owned his fucking neck.'

'That's all in the past,' he said. 'For good. The photographs and the negatives are safe. You'll have them by the end of today. Then you can get on with your life.'

He kissed her neck. 'You deserve better Pat.'

They both looked down towards the harbour. It was low tide. The police were dragging the seabed. Behind them, the jagged outline of the Vincent Black Shadow poked through the shallow waves, skeletal and macabre. There would be some explaining to do. Calloway would think of something. He had good reason now.

THIRTY

They took some convincing, but in the end the police bought Calloway's story. Fenton's death had sent Simkins off the rails. He blamed himself for the accident. His behaviour became erratic, he had taken to drink and in a fit of melancholia had set fire to the stadium, before stealing a teammate's motorcycle and attempting to flee to France. The club's owner, Patricia Moxon, had signed a statement corroborating these facts, so too had McArdle, the team medic, and the rider, O'Donnell.

It was Wednesday and Pat was at the stadium coaching Riley before the evening's fixture. She had a new star rider and intended to keep him at his peak. Calloway watched from the stands. He was growing to understand the sport.

When Riley took a break, Calloway called him over. He handed him an envelope. Inside was the five hundred pounds he had taken from Simpkins at Fenton's workshop.

'That should go some way to replacing your lost winnings.'

Riley counted the money. He looked quizzically at Calloway and opened his mouth to speak but the track security boss cut him short.

'Don't ask questions. Your slate is clean, Billy. There's nothing holding you back now.'

He turned his back on the young rider and walked towards the turnstiles. Birkett was there, his arm in a sling. He clicked his heels in lieu of a salute.

'As you were, Les,' said Calloway as he passed.

He took a trolley bus along the Old Kent Road and jumped off at the Bricklayers Arms. Liz Francis walked towards him as he approached the soot-black tenement buildings, returning from her shift at the nightclub. She looked tired and drawn.

'I'm glad I caught you. I won't keep you long.'

She looked apprehensive. 'I suppose I've got five minutes. Can we talk here though? I don't want you coming up when Mum's in the flat.' She looked coy for a moment. 'Embarrassed I s'pose.'

'You've no need to be.'

She snorted. 'So you say, but I'd sooner be far away from this place, believe me.'

He smiled with genuine warmth and she noticed. 'Open your bag a moment.'

'Are you being funny?'

'Don't make a fuss, Liz, just do as I ask.'

She did, in spite of the obvious suspicion that was showing on her face. He palmed an envelope into the bag discreetly, and she snapped the bag closed.

'That's rightfully yours,' he said. 'The money Fenton had been putting aside for the flat. You can get as far from this place as you like now.'

He had Sammy Mackay to thank for the fact the money was still in his safe. All Sammy's goons had taken when they arrived with a warrant were Wood's SS photographs. They had left the cash.

'But how?' she's asked.

'Let's call it balancing the books.'

She looked blankly for a moment then small tears welled in her eyes. They were beautiful eyes, he thought. She leant forward, placed a hand on his shoulder and kissed him lightly on the cheek. Then she turned, looked up and down the busy road and flagged an oncoming taxi. The cabbie pulled up, set the meter running and said, 'Where to miss?'

'Up West,' she said.

Calloway returned to the stadium on foot. He enjoyed the walk. Pat was still coaching Riley, using his motorcycle to demonstrate cornering. Calloway caught the familiar smell of Castrol R as he ducked under the shower of cinders. Pat completed the lap and let the bike slow up alongside him. She pulled off her helmet and untied her hair. It shone in the light of the late morning sun, which had broken out from behind the cloud.

She shouted over to Calloway, 'Turned out nice again!'

He smiled, surprised that for once the catchphrase didn't irritate him. He gave her a wave as he crossed the track, then strode over the centre green. There was a lightness in his step that was pleasantly unfamiliar to him. But beneath the pleasure of the moment was fear. A terrible nagging fear. Reg Calloway was a violent man. A violent and unpredictable man. And one day that violence would erupt again. When it did, he wanted to be as far away as possible from anyone he cared about.

He climbed the steps to his office and closed the door behind him. He lugged the big Remington typewriter from the top of the filing cabinet beneath the frosted glass window and set it down on his desk. He wound a sheet of paper onto the roller and typed the address of his basement room in the top right-hand corner. He typed the date beneath it. Then he wrote:

Dear Miss Moxon,

I hereby tender my resignation as Track Security Officer for Bermondsey Stadium...

He withdrew the letter from the roller and signed it R Calloway. Taking an envelope from the drawer, he sealed the letter inside. Webber's western novel lay at the bottom of the drawer. Calloway picked it up and slid it into his jacket pocket. Then he left the office, locked the door behind him and placed the envelope and key on Pat Moxon's desk.

He walked to the turnstiles and saluted Birkett as he passed. It was the last time he would see the stadium.

THE END

BOOK TWO: PILLS & SOAP

ONE

When the phone rang, Calloway sat bolt upright in the old iron bed. The sheet clung to his back. It was soaked with sweat. He'd been dreaming again, the dream from the war.

He looked at the clock. It was one in the morning. The shrill bell of the phone pierced his skull. He wanted to ignore it, go back to sleep, hope this time he wouldn't dream.

He crossed the cold linoleum floor in his bare feet and picked up the receiver. Old Arthur, the night watchman, was panting down the line.

'You'd better get down here,' he said.

Calloway dressed and pulled a comb through his hair. He tugged a mackintosh over his big frame as he descended the stairs that led to his attic room, slamming the door behind him. There were no neighbours to wake. The rest of the three-storey factory building was empty this time of night.

The air in the street was damp. The starter motor of his car rasped through the silence before the engine spluttered into life. The drive took less than ten minutes. The road was dark and empty.

As the studio loomed into view, Calloway saw the cause of old Arthur's panic. Young women hobbled over the cobblestones in their heels. They looked distressed. They wore low-cut evening gowns showing plenty of cleavage. Their bare shoulders glowed white against the soot-black brickwork of the old brewery buildings that were home to Centurion Pictures. Rich-looking men bumbled around them, confused and indignant. The women were eighteen, nineteen, twenty-one at the most. The men were forty-plus. They were mostly overweight and bald, squeezed into expensive dinner suits, some with lighted cigars still in their pudgy hands.

Calloway pulled up, killed the motor and eased himself out of the small car. Fire engines appeared ahead of him, their bells drowning the distressed cries of the party guests as they stumbled through the studio gates. He spied Arthur in the crowd.

'It was the guvnor's car,' the old boy said.

The guvnor was Sidney G Spelthorne, head of Centurion.

'Blown sky high.'

He was gasping for breath, the tarry phlegm of the chain smoker bubbling audibly in his chest.

'An explosion?' said Calloway.

The old man nodded, struggling to speak over the chatter of his dentures.

'Must have been. Blew the glass of my hut right in. If I hadn't had my head down, the shards would've cut me to ribbons.'

Sleeping on the job, thought Calloway. He let it pass.

'Was Spelthorne in the car?'

Arthur shook his head.

'He was still at the dinner. Soon as the blast went off, his men shuffled him off the studio floor and up to his office. He's inside there now. There's blokes minding the door.'

Arthur was trembling with shock. Calloway pulled a hip flask from his pocket and pressed it into the night watchman's bony hand.

'Sit in my car and have a nip of that. I'll call you if I need you.'

The old boy complied. Calloway pushed through the fleeing bodies and into the studio courtyard. Spelthorne's Bentley burned brightly. The fuel tank had ignited in the blast and flames now lapped around the twisted metal of its mutilated bodywork. There were expensive cars either side, damaged but not yet on fire. In moments they would be.

The firemen had dismounted their tenders and were now urging the crowd back. Their oilskin over-trousers gleamed black in the light of the flames, and the silver buttons on their heavy wool tunics glistened like tiny stars. Two of them rolled a hose through the gates towards the burning motor and signalled to their colleagues to start the pump.

Revellers were still emerging from the big double doors of Studio A, amongst them musicians from a dance band clutching instruments to their chests. Calloway pushed his way towards the doors. The best he could do was to help get everyone off the premises. He stopped dead as a fleeing body slammed into his. It was a woman, dressed to the nines like the others, her makeup smeared and her platinum hairdo unravelling. As their shoulders collided, a small lamé clutch purse fell from her hand onto the cobblestone yard. She glanced down at the purse, hesitated, then fled. It seemed odd to Calloway. He slipped the purse into his pocket, looked around, but she was gone.

The scene inside Studio A matched the chaos outside. The room had been dressed for a gala, draped in rich red velvet with gilt trimmings. Inside this opulent shroud was a mess of upturned chairs and tables, shattered wineglasses and wine-stained tablecloths. The dance band stage had been abandoned like a sinking ship, strewn with bent and tangled music stands and big black instrument cases left open like empty lifeboats. It was the wake of a three-hundred-strong stampede fleeing the boom of the explosion, memories of the Blitz still all too clear in their minds.

Calloway ushered a dozen stragglers out through the doors. The women were blind drunk, stumbling knock-kneed as their male companions led them away with an outward gallantry that to Calloway seemed little more than an excuse to paw at their curves. From behind one of the upturned tables he heard a groan. A man lay on the ground clutching a champagne bottle which dripped its contents between the fleshy lips of his open mouth.

'On your feet, pal,' Calloway shouted down to the man on the ground, who responded with an inebriated giggle.

'I think I'll just stay here a little while longer chum, if it's all the same to you.'

He then began to sing a dance band hit, holding the dribbling neck of the bottle like a microphone. Calloway planted his heavy leather shoe into the reveller's fleshy backside with such force the man jumped to his feet and staggered towards the doors.

Calloway had no time for drunks. He didn't much like being called chum either.

He left the studio and doubled timed across the courtyard towards the main gate. The firemen had cleared the area and were training hoses onto the flaming car. The car was a mess, its bodywork splayed, its windows shattered and its paintwork bubbling. Only the personalised number plate seemed to have survived intact: CP1.

Passing through the gates Calloway saw an ambulance crew handing out blankets to the evacuees, who now perched on the kerb or leaned against the big boundary wall smoking and swigging from wine bottles they had grabbed as they fled.

From the end of the street he heard the metallic clang of police car bells. The cars screeched to a halt ahead of the guests that filled the road. Two big Wolseleys and a Black Maria. They disgorged uniformed flatfoots who set about looking important without really knowing what to do. The fire crew and the ambulance had the scene under control, the firemen training hoses on the last of the flames that burned stubbornly around the melted tyres of the blown-up car. Calloway spied Sandy Phelps, Chief Inspector at Hackney Central, who was giving orders with an air of authority that obviated the need for a plan. He recognised Calloway and strode in his direction adjusting his peaked cap as if he meant business.

'Well this is a right bloody mess,' Phelps said. He nodded towards the dinner guests. 'Who are these swells, and where'd all the skirt come from? I'm guessing it's not their wives.'

The young women had formed their own group, talking nervously and sharing cigarettes. They seemed relieved to be away from the men.

'The annual Producers Club dinner,' said Calloway. 'The boss throws a party once a year for the money men. The girls are bussed in from the charm school.'

Phelps frowned, not understanding. 'Charm school?'

'The Centurion Company of Stars, if you want its official title. A hot house for starlets.'

'So how come I don't recognise any of them?'

'You might call their duties largely ceremonial. Once in a blue moon they get a couple of lines in a B picture.'

Phelps gave a grunt in acknowledgement.

'Were you here when the car went up?'

Calloway shook his head. 'I was stood down for the night. The boss brought in private security for the event.'

'To make sure the guests keep their hands off the merchandise?'

Calloway scoffed. 'I rather think that's the whole point of the evening.'

'Show the money a good time, eh?'

'It seems to work. This place is churning out quota quickies like there's no tomorrow.'

With the fire extinguished and the site made safe, the firemen had dropped the air of urgency. They clumped around in their gum boots, loose limbed and relaxed, reeling up the hose and stowing away their equipment in lockers on the side of the fire tenders. Phelps's men set up a cordon around the burned-out cars. Some worked the crowd outside, taking names and addresses while sneaking looks down the dresses of the women.

'Where's your boss now?' said Phelps.

Calloway nodded towards a three-storey wing that adjoined Studio A. It was Centurion's administration building. Only now he noticed half its windows had shattered.

'Holed up in his office. Third floor.'

'We'll need to talk to him, but it can wait. Any idea what caused the blast?'

Calloway shrugged.

'Faulty engine? A discarded fag perhaps?'

Calloway doubted either. A blast enough to shatter two dozen windows suggested more than an engine fire.

'I'll get a forensic team over tomorrow. Can you secure this place overnight?'

'I don't think that's beyond me. I've got keys to the gate. They came with the job, funnily enough.'

'Alright, alright. No need for that. We'll get the folk outside packed off home. You lock the place up. I'll put a couple of lads on duty outside and we'll be back in the morning.'

'It is the morning,' said Calloway.

'Then we'll be back when you've had a shave. You look like a sack of shit.'

The chief constable turned on his heels and went back to ordering his men around. Calloway rubbed the stubble on his chin. Phelps had a point. He needed to clean up, but that would have to wait. He crossed the yard to the administration block and climbed the three flights of stairs. The anteroom where Spelthorne kept his secretaries was empty. The door to his office was shut. Two goons stood sentinel. They wore dinner suits that looked more expensive than they did. One smoked a Wills while the other perched on a desk, leafing through last month's Picturegoer.

'Who are you?' the smaller of the two demanded. He tossed the magazine onto the desk. His pal pinched the fag between his thumb and forefinger and drew hard on it with tensed lips.

'Calloway, studio security.'

The big goon smirked and blew smoke in Calloway's direction. 'A fat lot of use you were then.'

'I could say the same about you. Tonight was your lookout.'

The big goon bristled. 'Wind your neck in.'

Calloway let this ride. 'I need to see Spelthorne.'

The smaller goon grinned. 'He's not at home to callers.'

He's at home to someone, thought Calloway, judging by the sounds from behind the door. Spelthorne was calming his nerves with some female help.

'Enjoy listening, do you?' Calloway said.

He left them to it. One of the goons muttered 'prat' under his breath.

The courtyard was empty now. The fire tenders' engines rumbled in anticipation of departing, as the crew mounted and took their positions in the cabs. The fug of the burned-out Bentley hung in the damp air. Water from the fire hoses had spread over the cobbles and collected in pools which reflected the neon light from the illuminated studio sign. A quiet had descended.

Calloway pulled out his old gun-metal cigarette case and lit a Navy Cut. In the calm of the moment, the woman who had dropped the purse flickered into his consciousness. The face was wrong somehow. The woman was dressed the same as the others, she wore the same shoes and had the same hair, but the face didn't fit. It wasn't a charm school face. Those girls all had a look. Spelthorne handpicked them and he definitely had a type. High cheek bones and watery blue eyes with lips just full enough to pout. Redheads and blondes, and only delicate brunettes. Nothing too bold, nothing that smouldered. Spelthorne liked a hint of vulnerability, with just the promise of something more. Girls who looked like they would yield, then ignite. If they didn't have the look when they joined the Company of Stars, they had it when they came out. The woman who ran into Calloway was different. No one owned that face.

The two constables Phelps had stationed outside helped Calloway pull the big iron gates closed. They slid the bolts into the ground and Calloway locked up. Spelthorne and his boys could use the tradesman entrance if they planned to leave anytime soon. He told the coppers that the boss was still inside. They seemed uninterested and grumbled something about a waste of bloody time.

Arthur was asleep in the car, the hip flask still in his hand. Calloway drove him the half mile to the prefab he shared with his wife. She was awake when they pulled up, her hair tied up in a frayed and faded snood, a drab housecoat cinched around her old bird-like frame.

'I've been so worried,' she said.

Arthur put a mottled hand on her shoulder and explained that everything was alright. He was calm now. The shock had passed. He offered Calloway tea, which Calloway declined.

'Funny old night, eh?' the old man said.

Calloway had an inkling the coming days would be funnier still, but he didn't feel much like laughing.

TWO

There were two of them in Calloway's office. Both plain clothes. One was smoking a pipe. He'd been there long enough to fill the ten-by-ten-foot room with sickly sweet smoke. His colleague flicked through yesterday's Daily Sketch, which Calloway had left on the plain utility desk the previous day. Vice gang boss gets eight years, the headline read. A mugshot glared from the page, a criminal face straight out of Centurion's casting office. Both men rose as Calloway entered. The one with the newspaper glanced at his watch.

'Half day, is it?'

It might have been a joke, but he wasn't smiling. 'It was a late night.'

The electric clock on the wall said it was nearly ten. Calloway had overslept. The clock ticked like a termite to remind him.

'You show-business types need your beauty sleep, eh?'

Calloway ignored this. He crossed the small office and opened the metal window. A dirty mist blew in on the breeze and mingled with the pipe smoke. It was a small improvement. Calloway gestured to the men to sit and did the same. He leaned forward in the swivel chair and laid his big fists on the ink-stained desktop.

'And you are?' he said.

He knew they were police, but they weren't the usual sort. In his line of work he was used to visits from regular coppers. They turned up when things got nicked and looked bored. These were keen types. Straight backed and serious. They had an almost military demeanour.

The pipe smoker flashed a warrant card. 'Special Branch. I'm

DI Belcher, this is DS Bryant.'

Calloway opened his battered cigarette case. He'd carried it all through the war and it showed. Every dent and scratch told a story. Some were stories he wanted to forget. He lit a Navy Cut and blew more smoke into the small room.

'You here about last night?'

'Tell us what happened.'

If they were Special Branch, they'd be here because of the explosion. In the no man's land between regular policing and MI5, Special Branch stomped around in their oversized boots. Explosions were very much their business. Belcher refilled his pipe and sucked audibly to light it. Calloway hated pipes. His old commanding officer smoked one. That relationship didn't end well. He decided not to like DI Belcher, at least for the moment.

'The boss threw a party. Someone flicked a dog-end under his Bentley. It went up like a Roman candle.'

Belcher and Bryant exchanged glances. Belcher leaned forward.

'We doubt that very much.'

Calloway doubted it too. In the studio courtyard he'd seen men in white coats picking over the debris of the burned-out car. They weren't looking for dog-ends.

'We're you at the studio when the explosion happened?'

Calloway shook his head. 'There were private security guards on duty. It was a special event. You'll need to speak to the boss about that. What are you boys going to be doing here?'

This was his turf. He wanted them to know it.

'We'll check what's left of the car for fingerprints and tool marks, see if we can get comparisons. We can forget footprints. We're told there were more than three hundred guests on the premises.'

Calloway nodded.

'We'll need to interview witnesses,' said Belcher, 'so we're going to be hanging around here for some time yet. If we get anything useful from the interviews in terms of a suspect, we'll get an artist in to do sketches.'

Belcher changed tack. 'What's in production here at the

moment?'

'You a film fan, DI Belcher?'

The detective inspector gave a small, grudging smile.

'I like a good western, seeing as you ask.'

'That figures. Good guys versus bad guys and a right old punch-up at the end, eh? We don't make those here. No room for the horses.'

Calloway paid little attention to what Centurion produced, save for the information necessary for his job. But he answered the question.

'At Studio A it's a family melodrama. Studio B is some thriller or other.'

'Tell us about the thriller,' said Bryant. He had crossed to the window and was watching the forensic men beetling around the blackened carcass of the Bentley.

'Moonlighting for Picturegoer?'

Belcher sighed and dug into the bowl of the pipe with a matchstick. 'Just answer the question, Calloway.'

Belcher's pipe was really irritating Calloway now. Not just the stomach-turning fug. It was the ritual of smoking, like some signifier of confident manhood. It said authority and surety far too loudly.

'It's called The Rebel Gun, I believe, although the title might change. They often do. About two assassins on the run.'

Bryant turned away from the window and looked Calloway in the eye. He had a flattened nose and a scar running through his upper lip. Done a bit of boxing in his youth, Calloway surmised. He looked the sort.

'IRA assassins,' Bryant said. It wasn't a question.

'Sounds like you know more than me. I think there's a republican thread running through the plot, yes. I don't pay much attention to the productions themselves. No call for it in my line.'

'Who are the writers?' asked Bryant. He was leaning against the filing cabinet. Calloway gestured for him to shift. He opened a drawer and rifled the files, then pulled out a hundred-page document in a manila cover.

‘Cedric Dryden and Michael Balfour, according to the shooting script. They write social dramas mostly.’

Belcher stopped sucking the pipe. ‘Social dramas? Communist sympathies would you say?’

Calloway shrugged. ‘I wouldn’t know. The likes of me don’t move in their circles. But we don’t start many revolutions here. That would be bad for Mr Spelthorne’s business. I’m pretty sure he’s not a communist.’

Calloway stifled a yawn. He’d not slept well. He’d been turning the events of the previous night over in his mind. It had kept him awake. He kept seeing the face of the woman who had dropped the purse. The woman whose face didn’t fit the charm school mould.

‘Keeping you up, are we?’ said Bryant. Belcher asked, ‘Do you have a list of the cast and crew?’

Calloway nodded. He always asked for a list so that he knew which stars would be on set. The bigger the star, the bigger the crowd around the gates. Autograph hunters, kids mostly, but less-salubrious types too. The obsessives. The creeps. The ones you had to keep an eye on. He took another file from the cabinet and passed it to Bryant, who ran a finger down the list, raising his eyebrow when he saw a name he recognised. There were two male leads. Both were name actors. A veteran and a pretty boy. The female lead was an unknown. Not from the charm school. She’d come from the theatre. She was Dryden’s suggestion. He didn’t like the charm school girls, apparently.

‘We’ll take this, if that’s okay.’

Bryant had already unclipped the list from the folder and was slipping it into his inside pocket.

Then he asked the question he’d clearly been waiting to ask. ‘Which part was Terrence McCaffrey due to play?’

Calloway knew the name. A jobbing character actor and a handful. He’d been asked to escort McCaffrey off the premises when he’d turned up to Spelthorne’s office, stinking drunk and spoiling for a fight. He’d taken a swing at Calloway then regretted it. Calloway’s fist had added a little more character to his face. That was a couple of months back. He’d not been seen since.

Calloway shrugged in response to Bryant's question. 'I'm head of security, not the casting director. How should I know?'

Bryant bristled. He stepped forward, squaring up.

Belcher cut in. 'Cut the act, Calloway. We're immune. And we've handled bigger than you.'

'Much bigger,' Bryant added. Calloway was deciding not to like Bryant too. He leaned back in his chair and peered down at the burned-out car. The forensics men were packing away their kit. A uniformed copper at the gate was waving through a glaziers' van. There were two dozen windows to mend.

'Am I a suspect? You think I flicked that fag butt under the boss's car?'

Belcher laid the pipe on the scorched Bakelite ashtray. 'No, but you're being a pain in the neck. We know the difference between an accidental fire and a suspicious explosion. So do you. Don't pretend otherwise. You're also savvy enough to know that when something explodes at a studio that's making a film about republican gunmen, that's too much of a coincidence for us to ignore. We've looked you up Calloway. Ex-Intelligence Corps. Field security background. Stop playing the dumb night watchman.'

Calloway conceded the point. 'What's your interest in McCaffrey?'

Belcher and Bryant ignored the question.

'When did you last see him?' said Belcher.

'A few weeks back. He'd been to see the boss.'

'What about?'

'A role, I assume. From his demeanour I judge he didn't get it.'

'A role in...' Belcher glanced at the cover of the folder on Calloway's desk, 'The Rebel Gun?'

'Possibly.'

Calloway worked the timings backwards in his head. The picture would already have been cast by the time McCaffrey visited Spelthorne. Shooting had already started. It was unlikely McCaffrey's beef with Spelthorne would have been over a casting decision.

'Do you know where we could find him?'

Calloway shook his head. He knew McCaffrey wasn't under contract to Centurion. 'I can check with casting. They should have a file on him. Why the interest?'

'You know better than to ask,' said Bryant. His scar showed white against his tensed lip.

'Oh I think we can cut Calloway a bit of slack,' said Belcher. 'He used to be a copper, of a sort.'

Calloway shrugged. 'I was Military Police until 1940, when field security was transferred to the Intelligence Corps.'

'You see Bryant, a former Redcap. A brown-job copper.'

Bryant gave a grudging nod. Belcher pulled a file from his case. He passed it across the desk to Calloway. It had McCaffrey's name on it. Calloway flicked through it.

Belcher continued. 'This McCaffrey is on our watch list. A known republican sympathiser with some high-powered friends. See that photo?' He gestured with his pipe to a shot of McCaffrey seated at a dinner table next to a well-dressed man, guests at what appeared to be a gala dinner. 'It was taken last year in Chicago. The other man is Martin O'Driscoll, a well-known fundraiser for Irish republican causes in the United States.'

Calloway closed the file and passed it back. 'So you suspect McCaffrey of blowing up the boss's car.'

'I'm not saying that. But you can see how it looks. Your studio is making a film about the IRA, a republican sympathiser has a beef with the boss whose car is blown sky high a week or so later. Smells a bit, doesn't it?'

Not as much as that bloody pipe, thought Calloway. 'Last time I saw McCaffrey, he couldn't plant one foot in front of the other, let alone plant a bomb. I was stationed in Belfast in the thirties. I've known a few of the boyos in my time. That clown McCaffrey doesn't fit the mould.'

'Then I'm glad you're just a glorified night watchman and not the investigating officer on this case.'

'Why don't you speak to McCaffrey? If he's on your watch list you must have his address.'

'We have his address. He's just never there.'

'Party animal,' Bryant chimed in with a sneer.

'We were hoping you might tell us his regular haunts.'

'I wouldn't know. I don't move in the same circles. He's a film star. I'm just a glorified night watchman.'

Belcher passed Calloway a card. 'Find out, then call me.'

Calloway nodded without enthusiasm. He held the door open for the two detectives.

'Centurion Pictures will do everything it can to assist in your enquiries, Detective Inspector,' he said, like he'd mislaid his sincerity.

As the two detectives turned to leave, Bryant leaned forward and spoke quietly into Calloway's ear.

'You should go back to bed, son,' he said. 'You look tired.'

THREE

The casting office was down a long corridor at the rear of the administration building. The door was open. A man and woman sat at adjoining desks arguing. The man was in his late twenties with a weak face and too much forehead for someone his age. He wore a tweed sports coat with leather buttons and a yellow cravat, the kind horsey folk wear. The woman was pushing forty and not to be messed with. Buttoned tightly into a pre-war two-piece, with wiry greying hair that was devouring the pencil she kept in it. She gave off an aura of elegant hostility. She held a short tortoise shell cigarette holder between her teeth as she spoke to the young man opposite her.

'Jack Warner?' she said. 'Far too long in the tooth, darling.'

'But the part calls for an everyman,' said the young man. 'They don't come more every than Warner. He's the nation's father figure.'

'The part calls for a romantic. Warner can't do romance, unless you think a peck on the cheek and a bunch of daffs on Mothering Sunday counts.' She impersonated Warner, '"There you go, Ma, picked 'em from me garden",' then switched to a matronly cockney, '"Bless you, Jack, you aaare thoughtful." No, no, no.'

The young man thought for a moment, tapping his teeth with the barrel of a fountain pen.

'Jack Hawkins then. He can turn on the suave when he wants to.'

'Too gruff. Too military,' the woman said. 'At his best when barking orders on a ship.'

The young man made a plaintive face. 'Stanley Holloway?'

'Oh Fuck off, Tony!'

Tired of being ignored, Calloway cleared his throat and rapped on the open door.

The woman looked up, irritated by the interruption.

'And you are?' she said.

'Reg Calloway. The everyman that looks after security.'

The woman removed the lunettes from the bridge of her nose and looked Calloway up and down. Her hostility ebbed away.

'You know what? You might just do, darling. Can you act?'

'Only tough, when the role calls for it. Usually when I'm throwing someone out of somewhere they shouldn't be.'

The woman replaced the lunettes and leaned back in her chair. 'The screen tough-guy type. That might work. Can you do romantic?'

'Tried it once. Didn't work out.'

She smiled. 'Poor, poor you. Now come and sit over here,' she said, her tone softening even more. She patted an old stacking chair next to her side of the desk. 'Tell Marjorie how she can help.'

Calloway sat then immediately wished he'd stayed standing. He felt foolish. Like an oversized lapdog. The woman called Marjorie leaned into him and whispered, 'Is it about this explosion business? It's the talk of the studio this morning. Tongues haven't wagged this much since Stewart Grainger threatened to punch Sidney G's lights out for goosing Jean Simmons.'

Calloway's responded with his habitual stone face. 'Last night's incident is in the hands of the police. The studio will be helping them with their enquiries in any way it can.'

'Pah!' she said. 'That sounds like a press statement from the publicity office. Did Ivor tell you to say that?'

Ivor Cole was head of the publicity department. A slick-haired, fast-talking type who carried a lot of clout at Centurion. Calloway shook his head.

'I managed it all on my own.'

'You clever boy.' She removed the lunettes on the bridge of her nose and looked him up and down again as he sat awkwardly in the chair. 'They're shooting a thriller in Studio B. I'm sure they could find use for another heavy. You should have a go, darling. The camera would love that lantern jaw of yours.'

She took his chin in her hand and turned his head from side to side as if examining an object d'art she was considering purchasing from Portobello Road. The man called Tony tossed his pen onto the desk and let out an irritated sigh.

'I'm sure the gentleman came here for something other than your personal amusement, Marge. Put him down.' He turned to Calloway. 'What is it you want, squire?'

Calloway was grateful for Tony's intervention. Marjorie had a way about her that was uncomfortably engaging.

'Do you have a file on an actor called Terrence McCaffrey?' he said.

Marjorie looked quizzical. 'Tearaway Terry? What would a fine upstanding man like you want with that reprobate? Has he been a naughty boy? Oh do tell.'

'Just a routine enquiry,' said Calloway.

Marjorie rolled her eyes. 'You're sounding like a press statement again.'

She took a long draw on the cigarette holder and placed it in the ashtray, then stood and crossed the room towards a battered grey filing cabinet that stood in the corner. Calloway followed her with his eyes. Somehow he couldn't help it. Opening a draw, she rifled through the tightly packed hanging files.

'Mason, McGoohan, McCaffrey, here he is.'

She passed Calloway the file and as he reached to take it, their hands brushed. Calloway pulled back his hand too quickly and Marjorie noticed. She raised an eyebrow. Her painted lips twisted into a predatory smile. He returned to the stacking chair and leafed through the file, which held only a few typed sheets, with a portrait of McCaffrey paper-clipped to the inside cover. He was younger in the photo by a good ten years. When Calloway had ejected him from Spelthorne's office, he'd looked older and wearier, his face puffy from drink and his jet black hair peppered with dry, wiry streaks of grey.

'Is this his current address?' Calloway said. It was the fifth address listed in the file, the previous four struck through with a red pen.

Marjorie glanced over his shoulder. 'Yes, if he's not been kicked out already.'

'Bad payer?'

'Hellraiser.'

'And where does he raise hell when he's not at home?'

The young man Tony piped up. 'Where doesn't he? The Mandrake, The Gargoyle, The French, The Torino, The Swiss. But mostly you'll find him in the Feldman Club. He loves bebop.'

'Where's the Feldman Club?' asked Calloway.

'One hundred Oxford Street, in a hell hole of a basement with a soundtrack to match.'

Marjorie peered at the young man over her glasses. 'Tony doesn't believe in jazz,' she said, like it was an accusation.

'Neither do I,' said Calloway.

The room darkened as two studio hands passed the widow carrying an oversized panel of painted scenery. Calloway looked out towards the rolling green hills and brooding purple sky as it passed. The Irish film, he guessed, suspecting the scenery had been used many times over to evoke anywhere from Hungary to the Hebrides.

'It's like sitting in a railway carriage,' said Tony to no one in particular as the scenery rolled past.

Marjorie leaned into Calloway and whispered again, 'I hear old Terry stabbed Sidney G with a letter opener and got a punch in the kisser for his trouble.'

'No one stabbed anyone,' said Calloway.

'But he still got punched. Was that you, you big brute?'

'It generally is,' he said.

She looked distracted for a moment, as if turning something over in her mind. Something about him.

'Don't worry, darling, he probably didn't feel it. I heard he was roaring drunk at the time.'

'Does he usually throw his weight around when he doesn't get a part?'

Marjorie corrected him. 'Oh, he got the part alright. Third

from top billing in The Rebel Gun. He just didn't keep it. They'd been shooting for a fortnight when he got the news he'd been dropped.'

'Why was that?'

Marjorie shrugged. 'Search me, luvvie.' She winked and held out her arms. 'That's an invitation by the way.'

Tony scoffed. 'Stop it Marge. You're incorrigible.'

She patted Calloway's leg. 'I'm only teasing, darling.'

Calloway rose to leave. In the yard outside the window he saw three young women in costume hurrying towards Studio A. Extras, he imagined, and late by the looks of them. As he watched, the face of the woman flickered into his consciousness, the woman that had dropped the purse the previous night, the one who seemed more afraid of him than of the explosion and the burning car.

'Do you keep files on the Company of Stars?' Calloway asked.

'The charm school girls?' Marjorie looked disappointed again. 'Oh really, Reg. Is that what you came here for? A telephone number? Has someone caught your eye? I suppose I shouldn't be surprised. We get a steady stream of chaps through here looking for the same thing. But frankly, Reg, I thought you'd be above such a thing.' She wagged a finger. 'A man of your age too.'

He was not yet forty but six years of war had aged him, like most men of his generation. He looked fifty and worn out, with thinning hair and a pale complexion, a less corpulent version of the producers at last night's dinner, although age didn't seem to have stopped them taking more than a professional interest in the charm school cohort.

'One of them dropped her purse last night and I need to return it. I don't know her name. I only have a face to go on. If I could see their file portraits, I could identify her.'

'Lost property?' Marjorie sounded suspicious. 'Alright, I believe you, but we can't help you here. The charm school has its own office, at the back of an old gymnasium in Islington. It's where they teach the girls deportment and RP. But beware of Rene on the front desk.' She pronounced it re-nee. 'A veritable

Cerberus at the gates.'

As Calloway headed for the door, Marjorie looked at her watch and said, 'It's nearly noon, darling. Would you care to join me for lunch? The canteen toad-in-the-hole is more than passable. My shout. I'll even bring Tony along as a chaperone.'

'For me?' Calloway said.

Tony cracked a smile and nodded. 'Believe me, Mr Calloway, she can't be trusted.'

'Afraid I'll have to decline,' said Calloway. 'Explosions on my watch tend to upset my social calendar.'

Marjorie had risen from her chair and was checking her make-up in a compact mirror. Satisfied, she snapped the compact shut and said, 'You're forgiven. But I'll make sure there's a next time.'

FOUR

Calloway returned to his office. It reeked of Belcher's pipe smoke. He lit a Navy Cut to take away the smell, then reached down to his desk drawer and pulled out the purse the woman had dropped. It was a lamé clutch purse with a gold clasp. He snapped it open and emptied its contents onto the linoleum desktop, then laid the contents out in a neat line. A lipstick, a powder compact and mirror, a silk handkerchief with lipstick stains, a ten-bob note, some loose change and a tortoise shell propelling pencil.

There was a knock at the door and a woman in her early twenties entered. One of Spelthorne's secretaries. She had the Centurion look. A redhead with blue eyes and lips just full enough to pout. She stood in front of Calloway's desk with her hands clasped in front of her and spoke as if to a script.

'Mr Spelthorne says he'll see you in his office.'

She spoke with the plumminess of a suburban girl trying to sound sophisticated.

Calloway gathered up the items on his desk and put them back in the purse, then locked it in his desk drawer. He followed the secretary as she clip-clipped on her heels down the echoing corridors towards the lift. Calloway slid back the lift's cage door and stepped into the small panelled carriage behind her. It was just big enough to take the pair of them, with Calloway's own big frame wedged into one corner, the secretary into another, with an inch of space between them.

'Tight squeeze,' she said, her arms crossed tightly across her chest. He pressed himself harder against the sides of the lift carriage.

The lift opened onto a well-lit corridor leading to the office he'd encountered Spelthorne's goons in the night before. Three secretaries sat at small desks: a blonde, a brunette and a redhead.

Spelthorne had hired one in every colour. The brunette was typing, the redhead was on the telephone and the blonde just looked bored. Four different perfumes fought for mastery of the air supply in a fug of femininity. The roomed smelled like the ground floor of a department store. The secretary at the typewriter paused her typing and told Calloway that Spelthorne would only be a moment. She asked him to take a seat. Calloway sat on a studio couch and picked up a film magazine from the coffee table. That new young actor Dirk Bogarde gazed out from the cover looking perfect. Calloway had never seen his movies but he somehow looked familiar. He read the Bogarde article. He'd no interest in the show-business flannel, but the young actor's war record caught his eye. Intelligence officer, photographic interpreter, Normandy, Holland, Germany. The same theatres of war as Calloway. Both of them in intelligence. Then a paragraph that stopped him abruptly as he read. It mentioned the camp. The camp Calloway and his section had discovered. The actor claimed to have visited it in 1945.

'Nothing has very much really mattered to me after that experience', the quote read. 'When you've seen twenty thousand bodies in a heap, just lying in the sun like wax, you begin to wonder what life is.'

Calloway had been first man into that camp. His section were used to being first in, but never to anything like that. It had changed him for ever, in the way it changed so many others that had seen those places first-hand. He fought down a painful memory. The secretary's voice brought him back to the present.

'He'll see you now,' she said.

Calloway knocked and entered. Spelthorne's office was darker than the airy anteroom that led onto it. The walls were papered in a deep green flock, with wall lights like miniature chandeliers dangling from gold fittings. A pair of plum-coloured velvet curtains hung down to the floor, looking incongruous next to the metal-framed industrial window that overlooked the studio courtyard. There was a drinks trolley beside the window so overloaded with bottles it looked like it might crash through the parquet into the offices below. It was a night-time room, somewhere you'd smoke cigars and swill scotch around crystal glasses. Calloway's shoes sunk into the deep-pile rug until it tickled his ankles.

Spelthorne sat at a desk that was almost as big as his car. He ignored Calloway while he busied himself with papers. He went through a repertoire of expressions as he read them. Satisfaction, concern, disbelief, surprise. The expressions said he was an important man. Calloway by implication was not. He waited in silence, looking at the framed photos on the office wall with bored disinterest. Spelthorne had met a lot of people and liked being photographed. The people were old, male and important, or young, female and beautiful, but no other combination of those qualities. Calloway thought about clearing his throat to signal his presence, but Spelthorne would be waiting for that. It would just be a cue to look at the paperwork some more. He stood at ease and waited. After a few minutes Spelthorne spoke without looking up from his desk.

'Are you the security Johnny?' His accent sounded London Italian.

'Calloway, sir.'

'New, aren't you?'

'Three months now.'

'Good at your job, would you say?'

'I believe so, sir.'

Spelthorne glanced up from his paperwork. 'Then why was my Bentley blown to kingdom fucking come in the car park of my own studio?'

He rose from his desk and crossed the room to the drinks trolley. He wasn't a tall man, but he was powerfully built, with a broad chest, short arms and stocky legs. He was balding, with a prominent forehead creased with worry lines, his remaining hair heavily oiled and combed back behind his ears forming wiry tufts that tickled his shirt collar. His nose was flattened against his oval face, his top lip thin and mean, his bottom lip fat and moist. He wore a crisp white shirt, a silk tie in a Windsor knot with narrow braces holding up his impeccably cut flannel suit trousers. He poured a large slug of what looked like whisky from a cut-glass decanter and dropped in two ice cubes from a silver bucket. It was shaped like a barrel with a gold horseshoe on the front.

'Well?' he said, turning to face Calloway.

'The police suspect terrorism.'

'I know that. I spent half the morning with them. I'm asking what you were doing last night when you were supposed to be stopping things blowing up.'

Calloway looked him in the eye and spoke without apology. 'I was asleep, sir.'

The veins on the side of Spelthorne's bald head pulsed visibly. He looked like he could kill someone. Someone like Calloway.

'On my payroll?' He spat the words. Calloway felt saliva on his chin.

'On my own time,' said Calloway. 'There were private security on duty for the event last night. I was stood down.'

'By who?'

'By you, sir.'

Spelthorne's nostrils flared.

Calloway continued. 'I received a memo from your office three weeks ago, setting out the arrangements. My men cleared the car park for the VIP cars as instructed, then handed over to your men.'

Spelthorne looked less like he could kill someone, just hurt them in places the bruises wouldn't show. It went with his reputation. They say never ask a producer how he financed his first film. Actually, they only said it about Spelthorne.

The studio boss returned to his chair and sat. He'd calmed down. He kicked back and loosened his tie, then swallowed half the whisky in a single gulp.

'It's the last thing I fucking need. My investors are shitting bricks. This kind of thing doesn't inspire confidence, now does it? And the production in Studio A is all over the fucking place. It's over time and over budget. Broken cameras, broken lights, spoiled film. I buy new equipment but it still manages to break down. Same in Studio B. They can't look after the stuff either. Then all this business.' He waved a hand towards the courtyard where the police were still busying around. 'I had to sack that big

Mick from the gunmen film and pay him off, then cast the new fella, so that's more time and money.' He knocked back the rest of the scotch and poured himself another, shaking his head. 'I've hired a bunch of cowboys.'

'Perhaps you should make a western,' said Calloway.

Spelthorne shot him a look. 'Don't be smart with me son,' he said. Then he laughed. 'Yeah, maybe you're right.'

Spelthorne glanced over at the framed photos on the wall.

'I met John Wayne once. His real name's Marion. Didn't like him. All mouth, and about as tough as my old mum. Actually mum could handle herself pretty well, so that's not a good comparison.' He nodded at the drinks trolley. 'Help yourself. You probably need one as much as I do. It's been a rum old couple of days.'

It was early, but Calloway did as invited. Spelthorne perched his generous backside on the windowsill and looked out over the courtyard. The last of the police were climbing into a van, gesturing to the commissionaire at the main gate to open up. Spelthorne swilled the ice around his glass.

'Do you think he did it?' he said.

'He didn't strike me as the type,' Calloway said. 'And it's not an easy thing to do. You need the materials, and you need to know that you're doing. You can't just go into an ironmonger's and buy a stick of TNT. I don't know McCaffrey but I doubt he's going to go to these lengths just to get even with you. He's an actor, a bon viveur by all accounts. Why would he care that much?'

'The police reckon he's connected,' said Spelthorne.

'To the IRA? It's not their MO. Centurion's not a symbol of British authority.'

'But he's a sympathiser. That's why I sacked him.'

'How did that come to light?'

'He was doing an interview, something Ivor had set up to promote the picture. The journalist asked what he thought about the Irish problem. McCaffrey started mouthing off. Saying how he'd always supported the republican cause and that the IRA were freedom fighters not terrorists. Ivor had his work cut out getting that one buried. He bought off the journalist with some dirt about a starlet at a rival studio. That and a night on the town with a charm school girl. Ivor arranged that.'

Spelthorne crossed the room and took a cigarette from a silver box on his desk.

'I had to sack McCaffrey,' he said, lighting up. 'He was a liability.'

Calloway swigged the scotch. It made him lightheaded, on top of the sleepless night.

'Then what happened?' he asked.

'You were there. He tried to kill me.'

'He waved a letter opener at you.'

'One man's letter opener is another man's shiv,' said Spelthorne, sounding like he spoke from experience. 'Where is he now?'

'The police say he's gone awol from his flat.'

'On the run?'

'On the lash is more likely. Special Branch wants me to find out his regular haunts. I've just been down to casting to see what they know. He likes jazz apparently.'

Spelthorne drew hard on the cigarette. Calloway felt light lighting up too, but this wasn't the moment.

'Find him for me,' said Spelthorne. 'Tell him I want to talk to him.'

'This is a police matter,' said Calloway.

'It was my studio, my car and my party. It could have been my fucking hide spattered all over Hackney. This is my business and if that half-cut Mick is behind it, I want a word with him.'

He looked at Calloway. 'A friendly word, naturally. Before the police get their hands on him.'

Calloway took another gulp of the scotch. It gave him time to think. 'Wouldn't this be better handled by your private security people?'

He meant the goons that were minding Spelthorne's padded door the previous night.

'Franco and Giordano? They're just gorillas in dinner suits. Don't get me wrong, they have their uses. But I've heard about you...'

He grappled for the name. Calloway supplied it.

'Calloway, yeah. Intelligence Corps, weren't you? I bet you've felt a few collars in your time. This should be right up your street.'

Spelthorne was right, but it was a street Calloway tried to avoid. In his years in field security he'd interrogated German prisoners. He'd earned a reputation for not sticking to procedure. Once his adrenaline started flowing, the Geneva Convention became more of a guideline than a rule. Sometimes prisoners got hurt. He wasn't proud of it. He blamed war but knew there was more to it. He had a short fuse. It was best not to be around once you'd lit it.

Calloway shook his head. 'It's not the kind of work I signed on for.'

Spelthorne waved his hand dismissively. 'A hundred quid says it is.'

Calloway turned to leave.

'Wait,' said Spelthorne. 'Let's call it double or quits.'

'Meaning?'

'I give you two hundred quid to find the Mick. If you refuse, you quit.'

'I quit?'

'Well, not exactly. I fire you, for letting someone plant a bomb under my car.'

Spelthorne offered up his hands. 'I mean it doesn't look good, does it? You being my head of security.'

Calloway's stomach knotted. He felt nauseous. It may have been the lack of sleep or the scotch he'd just tipped down his throat onto a breakfast of phlegm and Navy Cut. More likely it was the threat of losing his job less than six months after he'd left the last one. That had ended when he'd agreed to moonlight for his former boss as a snoop. It felt like he was about to make the same mistake.

'Here's a hundred in advance,' said Spelthorne, pulling cash from his wallet. 'That's yours to keep. You get the next hundred when you bring me McCaffrey.'

Spelthorne could read the reluctance on Calloway's face. 'Like I said, I only want a friendly chat with him.'

Calloway could imagine Spelthorne's idea of a friendly chat. It would probably involve Franco and Giordano and not much chat.

Calloway folded the sheaf of crisp white fivers and put them into the inside pocket of his jacket.

'There's a good boy,' said Spelthorne with a wink. He sat back in the chair, stretched and sighed. 'Christ I'm tense,' he said.

He craned his neck until the sinews showed though his pudgy skin. 'I need to loosen up. All this stress can't be good for a man, eh Calloway?'

He pressed the palms of his bloated hands together in a half-hearted attempt at calisthenics, then wove his fingers together and cracked his knuckles.

'I really need to loosen up,' he repeated to himself, nodding like he'd just decided how. He leaned forward and pressed the buzzer on the intercom on his desk. 'Send Miss Hope in,' he said into the device. Spelthorne was the type that never said please.

There was a knock at the door and the bored-looking blonde secretary entered. Unlike the others, she wasn't from the Centurion mould. She was five foot five in heels with the kind of body advertising agencies use to sell corsets, her cashmere sweater stretched taught and the seams of her skirt looking ready to snap like overwound violin strings. She had the air of someone who already knew why she had been summoned, with a rigid smile and eyes fixed on an imaginary point in the middle distance.

'Would you like me to take a letter Mr Spelthorne?' she said like she was trying to sound keen. Calloway noticed she had no pen or notepad.

Her boss nodded then said to Calloway, 'You can go.'

Calloway crossed the room and opened the padded door by its ornate gold handle. Before he'd closed the door behind him, he saw Spelthorne taking off his tie and getting comfortable on the couch.

FIVE

Oxford Street, past midnight. Calloway had worked his way through the list of bars and clubs that Tony in casting had reeled off. He'd met piss-heads, poets and ponces and plied them with drink. They'd talked about themselves. He'd talked with tarts who recited their repertoire of sickly small talk for the price of a gin-and-It. He'd even been propositioned by a merchant seaman in full drag, which was a first for him. Everyone knew McCaffrey but no one had seen him. There was one dive left on the list. The Feldman Club.

Calloway stood outside the anonymous doorway in the light of the restaurant windows beside it. A neon sign above the restaurant said Mac's in bright red letters. Through the windows, a tired kitchen hand swept beneath tables and upturned chairs. Calloway entered the side door. The sounds of jazz oozed up from the basement. Halfway down the grubby linoleum stairs a woman in a black sweater with a red neckerchief sat behind a hatch reading a Penguin edition of Homer's Odyssey. She was twenty at most with short black hair and a fringe which looked home cut. She made Calloway buy membership. It cost him five shillings. She said, 'If you want to drink you need to bring a bottle.'

'I can live without a drink,' he replied, wondering where he was supposed to buy a bottle in the early hours of Sunday morning. She shrugged and returned to her paperback. He continued down the stairway. A heavy black door at the bottom held back the nerve-shredding sound of saxophones. As he pulled the door open, a wall of heat hit him. It reminded him of stepping onto the airstrip in Palestine in forty-five, after an eight-hour flight from the chill of a Baltic morning. Only this heat was damp, the dampness of two hundred sweating bodies crammed into the low-ceilinged space. The room was vibrating. Bebop bounced off the ceiling and ricocheted off the dripping walls. A mixed race crowd had formed a circle to watch a young couple jitterbug. The boy wore a powder blue zoot suit with a gaudy spiv's tie and slip-on shoes worn rough from dancing. The girl wore a loud print dress cinched tight by a red leather belt. Her hair was piled high above her face, a corral necklace swinging in time with her moves. The crowd watched intently, studying their steps. White youths stood side by side with young black men who smoked cigarettes and pipes, dressed in the same heavy wool suits as the Caribbeans Calloway had seen on the newsreels arriving at Tilbury docks. Calloway pushed through the crowd. A young woman blocked his way. She was leaning against a column and nodding in time to the music. She dressed like an art student, studiedly shabby. A pungent plume of smoke rose from the Gauloises she held between slender fingers with chewed-down nails. He recognised the smell from the bars in Normandy whose grateful owners had poured him and his comrades weak red wine to toast their liberation. She held the cigarette packet in her other hand in full view, in case anyone doubted her avant-garde credentials. He tried to push past her.

'Loosen up, big man. Listen to the band,' she shouted over the noise, her eyes directing him to the stage. She spoke in faux American, but her home counties roots showed through in perfect vowels. Calloway looked towards the stage. Six white men with hair en brosse played with intensity. Sweat-sodden shirts clung to their skinny young frames. Calloway's unease at the sound they created showed on his face. The young woman misread his expression.

'Okay, so it's not Club Eleven, but at least the cops haven't closed it down,' she shouted.

'Why did they close Club Eleven down?' Calloway shouted back.

She stared into his eyes and took a long draw on the Gauloises, this time holding it between her thumb and forefinger, then mouthed reefer as she blew smoke into his face. She looked him up and down and laughed.

'You don't dig jazz, do you?'

'I dig the German romantic composers.'

She scrunched up her face as she thought about this.

'That's okay,' she said, offering him a cigarette from the decorative French packet. 'Square, but okay.'

'You've just written my epitaph,' he said, taking one from the pack and accepting a light.

'So why are you here? You're not a cop, are you?'

He thought of DS Bryant and shook his head. 'I failed the IQ test. I scored too high.'

'I'm glad,' she said, and laughed again. She noticed he was empty-handed. 'You need a drink,' She reached for a slender wine bottle from the shelf behind her.

'It's German. Like your taste in music.'

She picked up a used glass and shook the dregs onto the sticky wooden floor before pouring him some wine. He ignored the lipstick on the rim and took a sip. The wine was as warm as the room.

'I'm looking for a friend,' he said. 'A big bebop fan. He's an actor. Terrence McCaffrey.'

One of the saxophonists on stage stood to take a solo. The woman whooped and clapped her hands. Without taking her eyes off the band she shouted, 'The table in the corner, to the left of the stage. He practically lives there.'

Calloway drained the wine and nodded his thanks before losing the dirty glass and pushing his way to the corner. McCaffrey sat alone, lost in the music. He had the same trance-like expression the young woman had. Calloway pulled up a chair and sat at his table. It jolted McCaffrey into awareness. He recognised Calloway.

'Did you come here to hit me again?' he said, in a soft Irish brogue.

'Will you give me cause to?'

'Not after last time. I had three loose teeth for a fortnight. What brings you here? You don't strike me as the bebop type.'

Calloway looked towards the stage. The saxophonist had finished his solo. Now it was the trumpet player's turn. The sound pierced Calloway's skull like a dentist's drill.

'I'm more the Mahler type,' he said.

McCaffrey raised a thick black eyebrow. 'A man of culture,' he said. 'A quality not usually found among studio henchmen.'

'You'd be surprised,' said Calloway. 'We studio henchmen are an unpredictable lot.'

McCaffrey laughed. 'You can say that again. I didn't see that right hook coming.'

'That's because you were blind drunk.'

McCaffrey held up his hands. They were big and work-worn. The actor had had a real life before show business.

'I'd just been sacked,' he said, 'for my beliefs.'

Calloway played dumb. 'What beliefs are those?'

'I'm an Irishman, Mr Calloway. Ireland is a divided country. I believe it shouldn't be so.'

'So not typecast then?'

'On the contrary,' said McCaffrey. He pulled a cigarette from a gold case and lit it with a Zippo. 'Apparently it's alright to play a republican but not to be one.'

'So you turned up drunk at the studio to give Spelthorne a mouthful.'

McCaffrey drew hard on the cigarette and nodded. 'I was in full swing when my jaw collided with your fist. That's quite the hammer you've got there.'

'You were threatening the boss with a letter opener.'

McCaffrey laughed. 'Assault with office equipment? That's quite the offence.'

'It was shaped like a dagger.'

The Irishman gave a grudging nod. 'Fair point. But I'd never have used it.'

McCaffrey was talking now. Calloway pushed him. 'So instead you put a bomb under Spelthorne's Bentley. Did your republican friends provide the explosives?'

'That explosion? If you suspect me then you're a bigger fool than you look.'

‘Special Branch suspects the IRA. They’re guessing you had a hand in it.’

‘Oh, Special Branch is it? I must have made the big league.’ McCaffrey shook his head. ‘They’re barking up the wrong tree. It wasn’t a bomb. Not on the mainland.’

‘They’ve done it before,’ said Calloway. He remembered the bombing campaign in thirty-nine and forty. The S-plan, they called it. S for sabotage. The IRA blew up power stations, pylons and public lavatories. Then they started bombing tube stations. It caused a handful of deaths and a lot of panic. By the time the Luftwaffe arrived that September, everyone forgot the S-plan. It was small beer compared to the Blitz.

‘That was then,’ said McCaffrey. ‘They’ve more to worry about at home. Their priority is the border right now.’

‘You seem well informed.’

‘I follow current affairs.’

‘Closely, by the sound of it.’

‘I won’t deny I’ve met a couple of the boys. Show me a Tyrone man that hasn’t.’

‘More than a couple I’d say. Word has it you’ve been fundraising for the boyos in America.’

‘Now who told you that? Special Branch was it?’

‘They showed me your file. You take a good photo.’

‘I’m a film star, Calloway. I always give ’em my good side.’

‘I saw photos with you and a man called Martin O’Driscoll.’

‘Ah, Martin. He’s an old friend.’

‘He’s Sinn Fein’s bagman in Chicago.’

‘Did Special Branch tell you that too?’

Calloway looked up. A man had approached the table looking like he was about to join them. Six foot, slender and black. His suit suggested African not Caribbean.

‘Now then Mr Calloway. I’d like you to meet my lawyer. This is Mr Ndungu,’ said McCaffrey.

‘Please, call me Paul,’ the man said, shaking Calloway’s hand. ‘It’s true, I am a lawyer. Well, law student at least. But I don’t represent this reprobate.’

He’d brought a bottle of wine, already uncorked. McCaffrey

picked up his glass and pointed it in Ndungu's direction. The young law student filled it, then poured a glass for Calloway and himself.

'Reprobate, he calls me. And this from the man that lured me into the darkest corners of London to listen to ungodly music at unholy hours.'

'I gave you jazz, Terrence. You should thank me.'

McCaffrey gave a small bow. 'I am forever in your debt, sir. Now Calloway here, he's more the romantic composers' type.'

'We'll have to convert him,' said Ndungu.

'Don't waste your time,' said Calloway. 'Someone already tried that.'

McCaffrey gave Calloway a knowing smile. 'From the tone of regret in your voice, I'd hazard a guess that someone was a woman.'

'Not a bad guess,' said Calloway, taking a sip of the wine. It was colder and better than the glass the student girl had offered him. 'I didn't come to talk about jazz,' he said.

McCaffrey turned to Ndungu. 'Mr Calloway here thinks I'm a terrorist.'

Ndungu laughed. 'You are certainly forthright in your views, Terrence.'

'Forthright enough to plant a bomb?' said Calloway.

It never hurt to stir the pot. McCaffrey rose from the table. 'Don't talk shite, Calloway.'

He headed towards a door marked lavatory. When he had gone Calloway said to Ndungu, 'How did you meet Terrence?'

'He was giving a talk at the university. Something about Ireland and Africa under the yoke of British colonialism.'

'A good talk, was it?'

'Poorly argued, but beautifully spoken. Afterwards a few of the students came here. Terrence has been a regular fixture ever since.'

Calloway looked towards the stage where another saxophonist was soloing. 'He must actually like this music.'

'This music?' said Ndungu. 'You make it sound distasteful. Come on, Mr Calloway. Listen to that saxophone. Pure poetry.'

'It's a mercy it doesn't have a smell,' said Calloway.

Ndungu let out a roar and slapped Calloway hard on the back. 'I like that,' he said. 'I'll use that line.'

'You're welcome to it. Was Terrence here last Saturday night?'

'Are you testing his alibi?'

'He hasn't given me one.'

'Then I will,' Ndungu said. 'Yes, Terrence was here and I was with him. From around ten until they threw us out.'

'When was that?'

'Three in the morning, give or take.'

'And then?'

'I put him in a taxi. He'd had a good night and was, let's say, unsteady on his feet. What is all this? Bombs, terrorists, what is it you think my friend is mixed up in?'

'Someone blew up my boss's car. Thankfully he was pawing a young actress at the time so was nowhere near.'

'That's shocking.'

'The bomb or the pawing?'

'I could make a case against both, if the client so wished.' He poured Calloway another drink and smiled. 'At least I might, if I wasn't studying company law.'

'Your friend Terrence had a flaming row with my boss a few days earlier. He threatened him. He had just been sacked from a role in a film about the IRA. He's a known republican sympathiser who, according to the police, raises money for the cause in America. The boss didn't like this.'

'And you've put all of this circumstantial evidence together and found Terrence guilty, or near as dammit.'

'I haven't,' said Calloway. 'I can't say the same for the police.'

McCaffrey returned to his seat shaking water off his hands.

'Bad-mouthing me to my friend, Calloway?' he said. 'Shame on you. So the question is, do you believe your friends in the Special Branch, or do you believe me?'

'They're not my friends.'

'You seem to care what they think,' said Ndungu.

'I care about a bomb going off on my watch. For what it's worth, I don't think you or the fanatics you rub shoulders with planted it.'

'May I ask why?' said Ndungu.

'I was army intelligence. I spent time in Northern Ireland. I know a thing or two about McCaffrey's friends. The MO doesn't fit. The IRA bombs factories, utilities and military targets, or civilian targets that will cause disruption, not film studios and certainly not for something as trivial as their pal losing a part in a picture.'

'So why the grilling, Calloway?' said McCaffrey.

'This is a friendly chat. You'd know if you were getting a grilling.'

'I'll take your word for it. When were you in Ireland, may I ask?'

'I was posted to Belfast in 1935 with the Military Police.'

'You were there for the riots?'

Calloway nodded.

'Your republican friends caused a lot of trouble.'

'So you stamped your size ten boots all over them, like a good occupying army.'

'We tried to maintain order.'

'With a fleet of armoured cars training their Vickers guns on innocent civilians. I bet that was a proud day.'

'We kept a lid on it.'

'That's the problem, Reg. When you keep a lid on things, the pressure builds up.'

Calloway knocked back the wine in his glass. The band was playing a new number. The noise assaulted his senses.

'I'm not totally immune to the problem. I saw the other side of the story too. I watched a Protestant mob going house to house, kicking out Catholic families. The mob threw their furniture into the street and burned it.'

'And did you try to stop them?'

'Our orders were not to intervene.'

'So you obeyed them.'

'I was a soldier.'

'Then may your God forgive you,' said McCaffrey, raising his glass. 'Why did you come looking for me?'

'Special Branch wants to know your regular haunts.' Calloway didn't mention Spelthorne's double or quits proposition. 'You have a habit of being out when they call.'

'It's a habit I've cultivated, believe me.'

'What are you going to tell them?' said Ndungu to Calloway.

'He can tell them that Terrence Patrick McCaffrey doesn't give a flying fuck,' said the Irishman.

Calloway rose to leave. 'It was a pleasure to meet you, Paul,' he said. He turned to McCaffrey. 'For what it's worth, you may want to lose yourself for a while.'

'Thanks, Calloway. I might just do that.'

Ndungu pushed the half-full wine bottle across the table towards McCaffrey.

'I must leave too,' he said. 'I have an exam first thing on Monday morning. I need to study tomorrow. I'll walk out with you, Mr Calloway.'

They pushed their way through the mass of sweating bodies. The dancing couple were jitterbugging with fury, the boy flinging the girl around dance floor effortlessly, like she was part of him. The crowd loved them. They clapped and cheered. Some copied the couple's moves. When Ndungu and Calloway had made it to the relative quiet of the stairs, the law student said, 'Terrence is no terrorist. He's a passionate republican and a hot-headed orator, but candidly, I get the impression he's playing at it. He doesn't have the stomach for killing.'

'How can you be sure?'

'I'm from Kenya. I've seen first-hand the carnage of the Mau Mau and the violence of the British response. Terrence is not in that league.'

'His fundraising work in America seems to be real.'

'I'm sure it is. And I'm sure he knows people. Perhaps there's no difference morally between facilitating a struggle and actually taking part in it. But in Terrence's case, it's an act of naive enthusiasm, not sedition.'

The street outside was deserted, save for the odd taxi whose diesel engine tick-ticked through the hush as it passed. The pair walked south through Soho. It was quieter now, its pubs closed, its shops dark, the only signs of life being the warm and enticing glow of red lights in windows of flats above and the footsteps of the furtive callers plucking up the courage to ring their doorbells. As they turned into Broadwick Street, there was a shout from behind.

'Where'd you think you going?'

There were three of them. None of them looked more than eighteen. They wore high-cut trousers and long sports jackets over check shirts with greasy hair piled up on their heads. They were looking at Ndungu, who kept walking.

'Ignore them, Reg,' he said.

'Perhaps you didn't hear me,' the youth said, gobbing into his fingers and flicking spittle in their direction.

Calloway turned to face them. 'Alright, lads. That's enough.'

Ndungu spoke softly, 'Leave them be, Reg, please. It will only aggravate them. Nothing will be gained.'

'We'll see about that,' said Calloway. He leaned in towards the leader of the three and lowered his voice to a whisper. 'You need to calm down, boys. Go have your fun somewhere else.'

The lead youth looked to the others for encouragement.

'Or else what?'

Calloway grabbed his ear, digging his fingernails into the soft flesh, and pressed his face against the boy's.

'Or else I knock seven shades of shit out of the lot of you.'

Ndungu stepped forward and took Calloway's arm.

'Let's go, Reg. These boys are really not worth the trouble.'

'Who asked you.' said the leader.

Den grinned, then jumped. A blade flashed in his hand under the streetlight. A cut-throat razor. Calloway shifted his weight and stamped hard on the boy's shin. He grabbed his arm and smashed his hand against the lamppost. The blade fell. Calloway kicked it into the gutter. A second boy lunged towards him, his fist raised. Calloway tripped him, pushed him onto the pavement and kicked him in the stomach. From the corner of his eye he saw Ndungu take a punch to the side of the face. A boy slap, no force behind it. The lad squared up for a second punch. Ndungu balled his fist and landed an undercut beneath the boy's jaw with a crack. Ndungu had done some boxing. As the boy reeled, Ndungu grabbed his lapels and threw him to the ground. Ndungu winced. His hand bled. The boy had razor blades sewn under his lapels. Calloway kicked the boy on the ground as a police whistle shrilled from the street corner.

'Scarper,' the boy called Den shouted, before turning on his heels. The other two scrambled to their feet and followed him into the darkness. Ndungu fumbled with a handkerchief to bandage his hand. The copper approached him, his truncheon raised. The copper shouted at Ndungu.

'Stay right where you are.'

Ndungu froze. The copper was rattled. His voice trembled. Without taking his eyes off Ndungu, he said to Calloway, 'Are you alright, sir?'

Calloway stepped in front of Ndungu to face the policeman, who was no older than the boys who'd just run off.

'Put it down, son,' he said. 'He's not the attacker, he's the victim.'

The copper looked confused. 'Then who are you?'

'I'm his friend,' said Calloway.

This seemed to throw the young copper completely. Calloway watched the little cogs in his brain working overtime. Calloway explained, 'We were jumped by three lads,' he nodded at Ndungu's hand. 'They had razors.'

Calloway pulled his own handkerchief from his pocket and helped Ndungu bind the wound.

The cogs in the young copper's brain finally clunked into gear. He turned to Ndungu.

'Are you alright, sir?' he said, sounding not quite apologetic enough.

'I'm fine,' said Ndungu. 'No harm done. Just a nick.'

The copper fidgeted, looking for an excuse to leave.

'I'll go to the police box on Regent Street. Put a call out to all cars. See if we can pick the boys up.'

Ndungu waved the suggestions away with his good hand. 'Please don't go to any trouble constable. It was just high spirits.'

The copper eyed him suspiciously. 'If you say so, sir.'

Ndungu spotted a passing cab and flagged it. When he and Calloway were in the cab, he said, 'There was no need for that Reg.'

'The lad pulled a razor,' said Calloway. 'I'd say there was every need.'

'It doesn't help.'

'Are you sure? You're not lying in the gutter with your belly sliced open, are you?'

'They'll do it again. To someone else. And now they've got a score to settle. Your intervention has solved nothing.'

'You'd have just stood there and taken it?'

'We have a saying in Kenya: only scratch where you can reach.'

They sat in silence until the taxi pulled up outside an address in Maida Vale, a tired stucco-fronted house with an array of doorbells beside its peeling black door. Ndungu stepped out of the taxi into the street.

'It was a pleasure meeting you, Reg,' he said. His face said he meant it. 'Go easy on McCaffrey. Under all that bluster is a good man.'

SIX

A young man in a shawl-collared cardigan and cavalry twills shouted at Calloway.

'You're standing on my mark, love!'

He held a clipboard as a statement of his authority. Assistant director or some such, Calloway guessed. He'd still not figured out how it all worked. He stood on a set built to look like an Irish inn, at least in the imaginings of a set designer who'd quite possibly never crossed the Irish Sea. It looked nothing like the Belfast bars Calloway had drunk in as a Redcap in the mid-thirties. Those were Victorian palaces, panelled and glazed to excess. This place looked more like an American tourist's idea of a pub in what they would no doubt call the old country. Fake beams, low ceiling and tiny windows looking onto a backdrop painted to look like distant heather. Calloway stepped off the mark, an X chalked onto the concrete floor presumably marking the spot where one of The Rebel Gun's stars was to stand. Around him, technicians busied themselves with lighting and cameras and microphones on booms that resembled Bofors guns. He walked towards the edge of the stage, treading carefully to avoid the dolly tracks that cut across his path. At the end of the track, two technicians, one in tweeds, the other in a brown store coat, were digging around in the metal bowels of an opened camera.

'I don't bloody believe it,' the technician in tweed said. He was clearly the senior of the two. 'Same problem as last time. Grit in the workings.'

'But this one's new isn't it?' said the man in the store coat, taking one of the four pens clipped to his breast pocket and prodding it gingerly into the workings of the camera.

'Yep, arrived from Studio Equipment Co. on Friday. We tested it on delivery. Had it open and everything. It was clean as a whistle.'

For some reason unknown to Calloway, the man in the store coat leaned forward and sniffed at the workings.

'And it's been sitting here all weekend?' he said.

The man in tweed nodded and looked upwards, as if expecting to see a hole in the roof and a cloud of grit threatening to rain again from the sky above.

Calloway cut in. 'Is this the same trouble that's been affecting the equipment these past few weeks?'

Startled, the man in the tweeds looked him up and down. 'You heard about that?' he said.

Calloway nodded. 'Spelthorne's been ranting about it.'

'Ranting?' said the man in the store coat. 'I'll say he was. You should have heard where he threatened to stick my pen.'

He reddened at his own reference to the unnamed orifice.

'Sorry, squire, I don't believe we've met,' said the man in tweed, frowning at Calloway.

'Reg Calloway. Head of studio security. Our paths haven't crossed up to now.'

'Security, eh?' said the man in tweed, with a hint of suspicion. 'And what might this have to do with studio security?' The implication being that this was a technical matter that was beyond the ken of a glorified night watchman. To Calloway, everyone on the studio floor was a self-important technocrat. They reminded him of the REME boys from his army days, the ones who treated you like you'd broken your field radio on purpose and behaved like they were paying for those replacement valves out of their own pocket.

'I take a professional interest in anything irregular,' Calloway said.

He figured that by looking into the broken equipment, he might at least find something to keep Spelthorne at bay on the McCaffrey matter.

'How many times has this happened?'

'This is the third time we've found grit in a camera in the last three weeks.'

'And then there's the water in the lights,' his colleague chipped in. 'Taken us over a fortnight to dry them out.'

'Very real risk of electrocution, you see,' the tweed man said, as though Calloway couldn't have worked that out for himself.

'Very real, I'm sure,' said Calloway. 'What's the cost of the damage?'

The man in tweed shook his head and tutted. 'It's not about the cost of the damage, it's about the cost of the time. A delay to shooting is an expensive business. You can't just stand the cast and crew down. They still need paying. And some of the cast will be contracted on other films afterwards. It throws everything out, you see.'

Calloway saw, funnily enough. He said, 'So, all this damage. Too much to be put down to chance?'

The tweed man shook his head grimly. 'Search me, squire. All I know is I've never seen anything like it in twenty years in the trade.'

His pal echoed, 'Nothing like it. Twenty years,' as he fiddled with the pens in his breast pocket, evening out the spaces between each, as though the gesture might bring some order to the situation with the lights and cameras.

'What type of grit is it?' said Calloway.

The man in tweed looked incredulous. 'What type of grit?' he said. 'I know my cameras chum, and my lights, but an expert in grit I am not.'

Calloway gestured towards the bright red fire bucket that hung on the wall a few feet away from them. 'That type of grit?'

The tweed technician looked over towards the bucket full of sand. 'It could be, I suppose,' he said, sounding reluctant to acknowledge the possibility.

'And you first discovered this latest incident today?'

'This morning, yes. We were double checking before loading.'

'And the other times?'

The store coat technician perked up. 'Mondays,' he said. 'The grit in the cameras and the water in the lights. We found out on a Monday.'

'And the equipment had been fine the previous Friday?'

Both men nodded.

'Who's on set at the weekends?' Calloway asked.

'No one,' said the man in tweed. 'The studio's dark at the weekend.'

'Apart from the cleaners,' said his colleague. 'They come in Saturdays. They're not allowed on set though, in case they move anything about.'

'Continuity, you see,' said the tweed man.

Calloway saw, again. He knew about the cleaning staff. It was his commissionaire's' job to let them through the gates.

'They clean the canteen, the offices, the lavs, that kind of thing,' said the tweed man. 'They're meant to do a quick spruce up around the stages, although sometimes they don't bother.' He shook his head. 'Some Mondays I've had to empty the bins myself.'

Calloway tutted.

'A man of your qualifications too,' he said.

Not knowing which way to take this, the tweed man returned to examining the eviscerated cameras, while his colleague withdrew a pen from his pocket and started to poke around some more.

Calloway returned to his office. He took a big lever arch file from the shelf and laid it on his desk. The file held copies of personnel records. He turned to the section on cleaning staff and read down the list of names. There were eleven in total. Against each name was written the days of the week on which they worked and the times of their shifts. Four worked weekends. He took out the small black police notebook from the inside pocket of his suit jacket and noted the four names and their contact details. Addresses only. None had telephones. As he snapped the notebook shut there was a tap on his open door. Marjorie from casting stood in the doorway in a trench coat that looked old enough and dirty enough to have fallen at The Somme. She spoke with the tortoise shell cigarette holder gripped between irregular teeth to one side of her mouth.

'You snubbed my lunch invitation so I'm trying again. Join me for a scotch and soda in the Star and Temple?'

'Will Tony be my chaperone?'

'He's taking his mother to the Empire. Another of those ghastly Huggetts pictures. So it'll be just you and me.'

She gave him a sly wink. 'Go on, live dangerously.'

He'd spent six years living dangerously in places like Normandy, Arnhem and the Ardennes. He reckoned he could risk a scotch and soda with Marjorie and whoever might have died in her trench coat. He wasn't one for company, not normally. But some evenings he felt the need to fill the big empty space in his soul with conversation. Occasionally, something more. It could never replace what he'd lost. But sometimes a distraction was enough, even in the unlikely form of the lady from casting with the pencil still stuck in her hair.

SEVEN

The Star and Temple was the remaining half of a pair of buildings, its mirror image levelled in the Blitz leaving only a flank wall of bare brickwork. It had the bottle green glazed brick frontage that characterised half the pubs in the neighbourhood. Inside it was cosy, with ornate tiling and dark wood panelling beneath a nicotine-brown ceiling. A gaggle of drinkers had already gathered. Storemen from the Lipton's tea warehouse talking football and politics. A couple of technicians from the studio talking shop, one sketching a scene on a beer mat. Two old retainers still in their heavy black coats, staring at the rows of dominoes in front of them. At the bar, a small man in a market trader's apron held court. He spoke loudly, like someone who spends his days shouting for a living. Two off-duty bus conductors nodded along with his rhetoric. A drayman from the Truman's brewery shook his head and looked doubtful.

Marjorie knew the landlady, a small, dark-haired woman with tired eyes and a face full of sadness. They exchanged pleasantries. There was a framed photo behind the bar, Calloway noticed. A signaller in uniform. Little more than a boy. The kind of photo with only one meaning: dead or missing in action.

Marjorie ordered two large scotch and sodas and insisted on paying. Calloway accepted but felt awkward. In his world, the man always paid. Not that he had much opportunity to these days. He seldom socialised. The landlady took the big white pound note from Marge and dispensed change from an ornate till which resemble the gilded sarcophagus of a tiny emperor. There was an empty table by the window with a bench seat and a couple of bent wood pub chairs. Marge laid her coat and bag on the bench and slid alongside. Calloway sat in the chair opposite her. He wasn't playing lap dog again.

Two men entered the pub. One noticed Marjorie. He was in his sixties, tall and straight backed, wearing a clerkly suit with shiny elbows and a faded bowler hat. He managed to look dapper in spite of his frayed shirt cuffs.

'Alright young Margie? How's your mum?' he asked cheerily.

'Not so bad, Mr Franklin. Her sciatica comes and goes, you know how it is. Nice of you to ask though.' She'd dropped the theatrical RP, Calloway noticed.

Mr Franklin said, 'Send her my regards,' then looked Calloway up and down before adding, 'and be a good girl' with a wink. He joined his friend at the bar.

Marjorie rolled her eyes.

'I'm thirty-nine and he still talks to me like I'm eight.'

'So you're a regular here?' said Calloway.

'You sound surprised,' she said and he was. 'What were you expecting? A trip down to the riverside at Kew Bridge in Daddy's MG?'

She waved the idea away. 'I grew up round here. I've known this place since my mother used to send me in to tell my father his dinner was on the table.'

'Seriously?' said Calloway.

'Don't let the studio accent fool you, love. I've cultivated that over many years. Believe me, Marjorie Moss didn't start out speaking that way.'

'Ashamed of your roots?'

She looked around her. 'Never ashamed. I just knew that if I wanted to get on in this business, I needed to sound the part. We're all at it, love. You won't hear many genuine accents on the Centurion lot.'

'Apart from Spelthorne's.'

She laughed. 'Ah yes, apart from Spelthorne's. That accent's genuine. It's his name that's not.'

Calloway had figured as much.

'So what is his name?'

'Search me, darling. Something Maltese and ending in 'i' I

suppose. Like everyone else born in Saffron Hill.'

Saffron Hill, nestled between Hatton Garden and Farringdon Road, once a wretched, stinking place immortalised by Dickens as the site of Fagin's den, now one of London's Maltese and Italian quarters.

'And what about you, Reggie? Sounds to me like you've taken trouble to lose whatever accent lurks beneath that overtone of grammar school respectability.'

'You said yourself, we're all at it,' he said.

'But you're not from round here.'

'I live round here. But it's not home. No pits, no working men's clubs, no chapel on Sundays.'

'Son of a coal miner?'

He nodded. 'And you? What was your father, when he wasn't drinking his wages in here?'

She gripped her lapels like a music hall comedian. 'Morris Moss, hatter and tailor,' she said, adopting the local accent and taking a small bow. 'We lived over the shop on Bethnal Green Road.'

'Shame he couldn't make you a new raincoat,' said Calloway, nodding at the stained and crumpled mackintosh on the bench.

'He's long dead, Reg, poor old boy. And I'm wearing that mac because I'm going somewhere later where it's advisable not to wear your best schmatta.'

Calloway tried to imagine a date where a dirty raincoat would be de rigueur.

'I like it here,' he said, looking around the pub, which had filled up since they sat down.

Marjorie nodded in agreement. 'You can only hang around film people for so long before you go crazy with all the pretension.'

'And this from the woman that calls everyone darling.'

'You've got me there,' she said, laughing. 'Of course, you'd never put on airs like that. You strike me as ever the pragmatist. The big stoic brute that keeps everything in order for the rest of us flakes.'

She took a sip of the scotch. Her lipstick left a perfect now on the rim of the glass.

'What made you take the job?' she said.

'I walked out of the last one.'

She looked intrigued and leaned forward across the battered pub table.

'Do tell,' she said, almost in a whisper.

'I got too close to the people I worked with.'

She leaned back against the bench seat. 'Then I shall keep my distance.'

'You've no need,' he said.

He didn't want Marjorie to keep her distance, at least not at that moment. He was enjoying the company. It didn't often happen.

'I won't make the same mistake twice,' he said. But he already had. He'd taken Spelthorne's shilling, or at least succumbed to the threat of its removal. There was a part of him that wasn't stoic, or a pragmatic. There was a part of him that was a bloody fool.

'And before that?' she said.

'Army. Thirteen years. Military Police then Intelligence Corps. Field Security.'

Marjorie's interest was piqued. 'Intelligence Corps,' she said, 'Were you now? Tell Marjorie all about that. It sounds awfully exciting.'

'Anyone who says war is exciting is a psychopath or an idiot.'

And there were plenty of both. Calloway had met his fair share. Public school types with something to prove. The ones who used words like dash and elan to describe the senseless rush into a melee of blood and screaming. Or the brawlers, the ones who treated combat like a Saturday night punch-up. And the trophy hunters. The sick bastards.

'It was rough work,' he said. 'We'd often go in first, or close as dammit. We'd grab enemy files, take prisoners to interrogate, round up collaborators from local towns and villages. Establish order.'

'Interrogation?' She rolled the r's and savoured the word. 'Were you a smooth talker Reg? Did you charm them into giving away their secrets?'

There was nothing smooth about Calloway. Others may have played good cop, as the yanks call it. He had used menace, coercion and the threat of brutality. Sometimes the threat was fulfilled. He had a reputation for it among his section. Some of his comrades gave him a wide berth. Others stuck with him as a good man to have around. His old CO compared him to an oversized terrier sent in after the hounds to finish the job. It was a good description.

'I was a bastard,' he said. 'A right rough bastard. Not something I'm proud of.'

After the camp he had tried to change. He'd realised he was little more than a secret policeman. Not so different from the butchers who ran that place. And he had met someone there. A prisoner. A woman. A woman who had changed him in the few precious, all too short weeks he had known her. She hadn't changed him completely though. And when he'd lost her, the brute inside him had stepped right back into the space she left in his soul.

Calloway downed his scotch with a thirst he'd not come in with.

'Can we change the subject?' he said.

Marjorie had seen the change in him. Calloway felt she was reading him. He clearly fascinated her, but she said, 'Gladly.'

He bought them two more drinks. When he was back at the table, Marjorie said, 'So the chat in the canteen is that the IRA blew up Sidney G's car for sacking Tearaway Terry from The Rebel Gun. They say Terry is a sympathiser.'

'The police seem to think so.'

As a subject changer this was hardly light relief.

'And you don't?'

Calloway shook his head. 'McCaffrey's a clown. The IRA are serious boys. They're not going to deploy an active service unit on the mainland because one of their pals got his cards. The police reckon he's a fundraiser for the cause in America and that might be the case. But the IRA's not going to put on a firework display and draw attention to the fact. They operate in the shadows and strike where it hurts. Military targets, civil disruption. Spelthorne's Bentley is an irrelevance.'

'Who do you suspect then?' she said.

'It's a police investigation. It's not my job to suspect anyone.'

But in his mind he saw the face again, the face of the woman who'd fled from the scene. The dolled-up Cinderella who'd drop the purse. For an instant he thought about describing the woman to Marjorie. She seemed to know everyone. He dismissed the thought.

'And what about you, Marge?' Do you have a past?'

She laughed. 'We all have our stories, darling. Some of them are even true.'

'What's yours? Truthfully.'

'I grew up three streets from here. One of three girls. We lived three to a room over the shop. As I said, my father was a tailor.' She corrected herself, 'Hatter and tailor. Mother was a cleaner at a bank in the city.'

'How did you get into the film business?'

'You make me sound like Sam Goldwyn. I'm just a little old casting girl in Spelthorne's tin pot little studio.'

'You've got an office with your name on the door.'

'So have you. Aren't we both important.'

She took a packet of Capstans from her handbag and offered him one. He leaned in to accept a light. Her closeness in that moment felt good.

'When I was eight my mother signed me up for Brady Club,' she said. Calloway looked quizzical. 'It's a youth club for Jewish kids. I was one of the first girls to join. They put on club shows. My mother pushed me to the front whenever they were casting. She was convinced I had talent.'

'And had you?'

'Oh I've got many talents, luvvie.' She gave a mischievous grin. 'Sadly acting isn't one of them. But I tried. Tried and failed, and in the process I found myself on the fringes of the film world. One thing led to another and within a few years I was Marjorie Moss, casting director, spinster, and a great disappointment to her mother.'

She took a small bow, then looked at her watch. 'And with that,' she said, 'I need to leave.'

She seemed to notice the small look of disappointment on Calloway's face. She picked up her coat, hung her bag over her shoulder and said, 'Fancy making a night of it?'

'Won't your date mind?'

She laughed. 'Oh, he'll mind alright. That's the whole point of you coming.'

EIGHT

They walked through the late autumn evening towards Dalston. As they walked, they were joined by others, like a crowd heading to a football match, but without scarves or rattles. Working men, some still in their overalls, store coats and aprons. Clerkly types too, and women home from shop work or cleaning. One woman holding a baby. Some people Marge clearly knew, and they exchanged nods of recognition, although they didn't speak. By the time they had reached the corner of Kingsland High Street they were among perhaps fifty men and women, walking as a group with a clear sense of purpose. As they turned the corner into Ridley Road, Calloway heard the distorted crackle of an amplified voice and the rumble of a collective response.

At the far end of the street a crowd had gathered. In front of them was a platform draped in union jacks and flanked by two big Tannoy speakers. The speakers were blasting out the words of the man at the microphone. Sharply dressed in a grey suit with blonde hair and a long, chiselled face, he spoke with intensity to the two hundred people gathered in front of a cordon of grim-looking stewards. The stewards dressed uniformly, although not in uniform. They wore grey suits, with black shirts and white ties. The closer Calloway got to the platform, the better he could make out the speaker's words. Nationalist rhetoric. Aliens in our midst. Britain for the British. His followers cheered. But others heckled. They shouted 'fascists out' and 'never again'. The hecklers started to shove; the supporters shoved back. Faces tensed. Words were spat not spoken. The anger was palpable. There were more supporters then hecklers, but the balance changed when the mob of fifty or so that Marge and Calloway walked with arrived.

'Who is he?' Calloway shouted into Marge's ear, gesturing towards the speaker on the platform.

'Jeffrey Hamm,' she replied. 'Leader of the British Union.'

Hamm shouted his words now, so that his voice could be heard above the din of the crowd. Nationalistic vitriol poured from him. His brow furrowed, demonic eyes beamed from his face, the sinews in his neck stretched as if they would snap at any moment.

'The aliens waxed fat in the black market, while our boys died in a pointless war!'

Calloway and Marge were pressed together by the mass of bodies now jostling each other. 'You believe in all this?' he said, nodding towards Hamm on the platform.

Marge laughed. 'Hardly, darling. I rather think those aliens he's ranting about include me. Come on,' she said. 'There's someone I want you to meet.'

She pushed forward and Calloway followed. They got closer to the front and Marge stopped. A well-built man in a blouson jacket and a brown trilby that had seen better days stood with his back to them, facing the stewards. Marge tapped his shoulder and he turned to face Calloway.

'Hello Reg,' he said, with a mischievous smile.

Johnny Suskind. Sergeant Johnny Suskind, Parachute Regiment, Sixth Airborne Division. At least that's what he was last time Calloway had seen him. Big, tough, fearless Johnny Suskind, who could fire a PIAT from the hip. Big Johnny, who'd taken out the crews of two Flak 88 guns singlehandedly. Earned himself a DSM. Tasty with his fists too. Regimental boxing champion three years running. Slammer Suskind, the Hackney heavyweight. A good man, but never to be messed with. Johnny turned back to face the platform, nose to nose with the stewards. He shouted 'Fuck off you fascists' in their faces. The stewards bristled. They stood their ground, challenging the crowd to have a go.

Hamm raised his fist and hollered. He spat his hatred into the crowd, sweat dripping from his hairline. Johnny Suskind turned back to face Calloway and spoke into his ear.

'You're in my wedge, Reggie. The first wedge. When I give the signal, we push forward and tip the platform over. The second wedge moves in and smashes up the Tannoy. Then it's free for all. Crack as many fascist heads as you can. If you hear a referee's whistle, it means police. That's the signal to scarper.'

Calloway looked around. Half a dozen other men had been listening to Johnny's instruction. They nodded acknowledgement. Suskind said, 'On three,' then counted down with his fingers until they formed a clenched fist. On three he shouted, 'Go, go, go!'

The six-man wedge surged forward. Calloway's instinct took over. He went in with them. It was a reflex, the conditioning of six years of war. The collective consciousness of military men. They grabbed the platform by the nearest plank and heaved. The Tannoy crunched and crackled. Hamm toppled. The stewards kicked off, fists flailing. Some had slipped on brass knuckles. Others drew coshes. Johnny's wedge fought back. They were unarmed but they were fearless. Seasoned fighters by the look of them, with little regard for their own safety. They served up bloody noses, broken ribs and bruises. Calloway spied Marge among them. She was tearing up copies of a newspaper called East London Blackshirt, a dozen at a time.

The whistle sounded. Johnny shouted, 'Here come the Chuter Ede bus company. Job done folks, time to leave.'

Calloway looked back. Police disgorged from Black Marias. Fascists lay on the ground nursing wounds. Hamm was gone. The platform was in pieces, the banners ripped, the fascist papers torn. Suskind's mob were bloodied too, but they walked tall as they quick-stepped down the street, away from the scene. Calloway and Marge walked with them. Calloway's knuckles hurt. One hand bled. The fracas was a blur in his memory, but clearly he'd used his fists. There it was again. The short fuse. The hair trigger. The quickness to violence, the nature barely suppressed. And the memory. The memory of the camp. What he'd seen. What he'd lost. When Suskind's wedge surged forward, Calloway had needed no encouragement. Hamm and his band of thugs were the same bastards he'd fought for six years to defeat. Only this lot were British. And they'd lost no time in regrouping after their wartime internment. He put the wounded fist to his mouth and licked it clean of blood. Somewhere on the ground behind them was a fascist missing his front teeth. Not a great look for Britain's answer to the master race.

He felt Marge's arm slip into his as she walked beside him.

'Not the date you imagined, eh Reg?' she said.

They regrouped in the Star and Temple. Johnny Suskind and his crew took over a couple of the tables and the landlady gave them drinks on the house. She pulled a dozen pints from the tall, ceramic-handled beer pumps which stood like sentinels along the polished bar top.

'It's good to see you, Reg,' Johnny said.

'You too, Johnny. And something of a surprise.'

'I bet,' said Suskind. 'You've got Marge to blame for that.'

Marjorie raised her pint glass and winked at Calloway.

'You boys are well organised,' Calloway said. 'That was like a military operation.'

'Course it was,' said Johnny. 'Hardly surprising, seeing as we're all ex-servicemen on our commando.'

'Commando?'

'We're the front line.'

'Front line of what?'

'Suskind pulled a pamphlet from the inside of his blouson jacket and pushed it across the table. The cover read The 43 Group Fights Fascism Today with 43 inside the Star of David.

'43 Group, eh? I counted more than forty-three back there.'

'We were just forty-three when we started.' He downed half his pint in one then said, 'It started spontaneously. A few of us ex-services lads were having a drink in a pub up near Hampstead, when we clocked Jeffrey Hamm and his boys setting up a podium on the heath opposite. We went over to have a gander. They were selling copies of Britain Awake and ranting on about 'aliens'. Meaning us. Us lads were all British, born and bred, and proud of it. We'd all fought for this country, in the paras, the infantry, the Raff, even one lad with the merchant navy on the Arctic convoys. Then one of the lads just went for it. He said, 'I'm not having this', and started pushing through the crowd. The rest of us followed like we were some kind of unit. The old military state of mind,' he looked Calloway in the eye with admiration. 'I saw that in you today,' he said. 'We banged some heads together, tipped over the podium and sent Hamm and his boys packing. They were scrabbling around, gathering up what was left of the podium and their papers and stuffing them into their little van, shouting, 'We'll get you fuckin' Jewboys. You wait and see.' We were buoyed by it. We'd done something, you know. Achieved something. We'd stood up to the fascists right here in our hometown in the same way we'd stood up to them at El Alamein, or in Normandy, or crossing the Atlantic. And we knew if we carried on others would join us. If we got organised, we could win. We started meeting regularly at Macabi House, that's a sports club where Jewish ex-servicemen hang out, and people kept turning up, volunteering themselves, or their services and skills. Men and women. Mostly ex-services. Cabbies offered us transport, printers offered to print our leaflets. Now there's about five hundred of us.' He gestured towards the other men at the two tables. 'My lads are the commandos. We do the rough stuff. But we've got a headquarters on the Bayswater Road, that's where the planning and decision making happens, and an intelligence section which finds out when and where the fascists will be speaking next, or where they're printing and distributing their literature.

'How do you gather intelligence?' said Calloway.

'Looking and listening obviously,' said Johnny. 'But the most effective gen comes from our undercover boys and girls.'

'Undercover?'

Suskind looked around him and lowered his voice.

'I know I can trust you, Reg, so I'll tell you. We put group members into fascist organisations, and there are plenty of them, believe me. The Union Movement, The Order of St George, The Gentile-Christian Front. We use Aryan-looking Jews. They join up and act like they believe in the whole fascist ideology. They become really committed. They spout the anti-semitic bullshit and even fight with 43 Group members at rallies. It's not pretty work, Reg, believe me. But they do it for the cause. And clearly, all the time they're feeding gen back to group headquarters.'

'Sounds like a very effective set-up,' said Calloway.

'Oh, it is. But the trouble is, the undercover boys and girls can only do it for so long before their tumbled, or before we withdraw them when things are getting too risky. Frankly Reg, we're running out of group volunteers that can pass for fascists. We need more non-Jewish members. That's why Marge tapped you up. She's one of our recruiters.'

Calloway turned to Marge. 'So I've been played.'

Marge gave him a devilish smile. 'I guess so, luv' she said. 'But I enjoyed the game.'

There was an awkward moment. Suskind cut in.

'Marge told me about this ex-services type working security at her studio. Reckoned he had potential. She's got a good instinct, Marge has. When she told me your name, well, it seemed like a shoo in. I know you Reg. I know how you think. I know what you saw.'

Calloway and Suskind were both Sixth Airborne. Suskind was there the day Calloway's field security section was sent to reconnoitre a barracks that had been spotted in aerial reconnaissance photographs. The barracks turned out to be the camp. Johnny knew this. He'd seen the effect it had on Calloway when he rejoined the unit.

Suskind downed the rest of his pint. He looked Calloway in the eye. 'I want you in the group, Reg. I want you to help us crush British fascism, for good this time.'

Calloway had never been one for joining in. He kept himself to himself, mostly. The times he didn't were the times he found himself in trouble. Like his last job. He thought up a reason to decline.

'I'm not political,' he said.

'Nor are we,' said Suskind. 'We're anti-fascist but we're not partisan. The group's got members of every political leaning.'

He tapped the 43 Group leaflet on the table in front of

Calloway. 'This isn't about politics. This is about humanity. You of all people know what fascism can do. You've seen it. Politics ain't in it. It's down to us, Reg. The government's refusing to do anything about it. Chuter Ede the Home Secretary won't stop the meetings. They're perfectly legal, you see. That's why the police show up when we kick off. The fascists have effectively got police protection, while us protesters are treated like criminals.'

'And the Labour government's allowing this?'

Suskind nodded and took out a crumpled packet of Woodbines from the pocket of his blouson jacket. He offered one to Calloway and Marge.

'That's about the size of it,' he said, as the three of them shared a light. 'There are individual Labour MPs who speak out. And the local councillors are generally on our side. Good sorts, most of 'em. And the trade unions help by refusing to print the fascist literature. But the government? Nah, mate. They're sitting on their hands. The group, the communists and the local people, we're the only ones fighting back. But we need more help. Help from men like you, Reg.'

Suskind downed the last of his pint and set the glass down on the table. 'Never again, Reg. That's what we say. Never again.'

Calloway heard the words of the actor in his head.

When you've seen twenty thousand bodies in a heap, just lying in the sun like wax, you begin to wonder what life is.

'I'll think about it, Johnny,' he said. 'No promises.'

NINE

He offered to walk Marge to the bus stop. She may have retained a grudging pride in her origins, but she had long since given up the thought of living in the area where she was born. She was heading west. She slipped her arm into his as they walked.

'I did enjoy our chat, you know,' she said, sounding apologetic. 'It would be nice to do it again.'

'At least until I agree to join your group?'

She gave him a gentle punch on the arm. 'Don't be like that.'

'I'll say to you what I said to Johnny. I'll think about it, provided it's not another scotch and soda with a punch-up for a chaser.'

'Perhaps we can think up another kind of chaser,' she said and kissed him full on the lips. It was a lingering kiss. A kiss with intent. Calloway was taken aback, but not so much so that he wanted her to stop. He fought the urge pull her closer. It was a hard fight, won by a slim margin.

'You're forward, I'll say that,' he said.

Marjorie slipped her arm into his again and they continued walking.

'I like to get off with people, I like to lay their arms,' she said, with poetic cadence. 'I like to be held and lightly kissed, safe from all alarms.'

Calloway laughed. 'Is that from one of Spelthorne's pictures?'

'Good god, no. That's Stevie Smith, the poet.'

'Good, is he?'

'She, darling, she. And yes, she is. She understands women, which is more than can be said for most male poets.'

'Sounds a bit strong for a lapsed chapel goer like me.'

She looked up at him. 'Darling, that all depends how lapsed you actually are.'

She held his gaze long enough to see him look embarrassed. He was grateful when the bus arrived, and he could carry on his walk alone. But deep down, a part of him wanted to join her on her journey west.

It was past nine when Calloway returned to the tiny cobbled lane off the Kingsland Road. A pea-souper was blowing in from the river which had filled the narrow street with a haze of sour-tasting soot. There was a car parked opposite the entrance to his building. A black Austin 12 by the look of it, although it was hard to tell the colour in the monochrome streetscape. Two men leaned against the car smoking in silence in the half light of a lone street lamp. A third man sat behind the wheel.

People didn't park on Calloway's street. Not at this time of night. They didn't pass the time by smoking in silence either. His 'brown job' copper's instinct told him something wasn't right. There were warehouses further down the street. He had no idea what they held, but it would be something of value to someone, with the black market still thriving and rationing showing no sign of ending anytime soon. But if the three men were there to knock off a warehouse, why advertise their presence so blatantly?

One of the men glanced up at Calloway as he passed the car. He was a brute. Five-eleven and thick-set with a mop of dark curly hair on top of a big misshapen head. He exchanged glances with the other man, who was lean and slight. He wore a cheese-cutter cap pulled down over his fine-boned face. The peak of the cap couldn't quite hide his angelic blue eyes that shone even in the half light. Their clothes were mismatched and shabby, the uniform of working men on their uppers. Blue eyes nodded at Curly, flicking the butt of his half-smoked cigarette into the gutter. Men on their uppers don't flick away a half-smoked fag. Calloway braced himself.

Blue eyes spoke. 'Mr Calloway, is it?'

His voice was low and husky with no discernible accent. Before Calloway had a chance to answer, the brute Curly had him in a body lock. Blue eyes opened the door to the big Austin saloon and pushed Calloway towards the back seat. Calloway struggled. He slammed his head backwards into his assailant's nose, like they trained you in the army. Curly yelped and loosened his grip. Calloway turned and landed a fist on the side of his misshapen jaw, but it was a panic punch with no force behind it. In return he got a kick to the back of the knees from Blue Eyes. As Calloway buckled, the two men bundled him into the car. This time he complied. A cold prodding sensation in his ribs told him it wasn't a good idea to resist. The Colt automatic he could see from the corner of his eye wasn't a thing to be argued with. He sat in the middle, Curly on his right, Blue Eyes sliding into the back seat on his left. Blue Eyes tapped the driver on the shoulder with a worn but slender hand. The driver put the Austin into gear, gunned the engine and turned left towards Shoreditch High Street, then right into Great Eastern Street.

'You boys going to tell me what you want?' Calloway said.

Blue Eyes replied, 'Bernie wants to see you.'

The muzzle of the automatic dug deeper into Calloway's ribs. They drove in silence. They headed west for ten minutes or so, then turned north off Euston Road. Somewhere between Chalk Farm and Kilburn they pulled up alongside the pavement. A prod from the automatic told Calloway to get out of the car. Curly and Blue Eyes got out too. The illuminated facade of a dance hall cast a dim, tobacco-coloured glow over the three of them. The muffled sound of a second-rate dance band banged against the insides of the building's two double doors. Billboards either side advertised dancing to Paddy Paige and his Popular Band, all for three and six. A doorman in a uniform with grease stains on the collar and rings around the armpits gave Curly and Blue Eyes a deferential nod.

'A visitor for Bernie,' Blue Eyes said.

The doorman stood aside to let the three men enter. The decor was deep red-and-gold-painted stucco, scuffed and peeling. Calloway caught the ingrained smell of a half century of dust and the faint odour of disinfectant from the gents. Blue Eyes had by now pocketed the automatic. He guided Calloway up the stairway with an insistent shove. They climbed three twisting flights and entered through a half-glazed door into a small narrow bar room. It was empty and the bar was closed. Calloway guessed it only opened at weekends. The tables had upturned stools on them to allow for cleaning. The cleaning had yet to happen. Calloway felt the stickiness of a hundred spilled pints through the soles of his brogues. Two figures sat in a booth at the far end of the bar room with a bottle of Johnny Walker and three glasses in front of them. One was a woman, forty perhaps, small and slim, with hair dyed a colour blacker than liquorice. She wore a raglan-sleeved raincoat buttoned to the collar. The other was Terrence McCaffrey.

'I'm guessing you're not here for the music,' said Calloway to McCaffrey.

The band was murdering 'Little Brown Jug' from the dance hall below them. McCaffrey looked fearful of Calloway. Perhaps it was the memory of the three loosened teeth. He didn't seem reassured by the presence of Curly and Blue Eyes standing guard over the studio's big security boss.

'For musicians, they'd make very good panel beaters,' McCaffrey said with forced good humour.

'So you're going by the name of Bernie now?' said Calloway.

'I'm Bernie,' said the woman. Her voice was an octave deeper than her small frame implied. If McCaffrey was a Tyrone man, Bernie was from somewhere much further south, Calloway reckoned. She nodded to Curly and Blue Eyes to stand down and gestured for Calloway to join her and McCaffrey in the booth. It was clear who was in charge here. She uncapped the Johnny Walker bottle and poured three glasses. She passed one to Calloway. McCaffrey took another and drank half the generous measure in one mouthful. Beads of sweat popped on his hairline.

'Thank you for coming, Mr Calloway. It's good of you to make the time for us,' the woman called Bernie said, sounding like she almost meant it.

'I generally do when there's a Colt automatic digging into my ribs,' he said. 'I assume this is about the car bomb.'

'Terry tells me you don't suspect him.'

'I'm beginning to change my mind,' he said, looking

McCaffrey full in the face.

The woman called Bernie laughed.

'I wouldn't trust Terry with a box of matches, let alone a stick of dynamite.'

McCaffrey managed a weak smile. Gone was the confident, booze-fuelled bon viveur of the Feldman Club. In present company, he was cowed and anxious.

'So who would you trust?' said Calloway.

'The question's irrelevant. Special Branch are barking up the wrong tree.'

'You seem very sure of that.'

'I'm in a position to know,' she said.

'So what's this got to do with me?' said Calloway.

'I've got a job for you,' she said.

'Whatever it is, I'm not in the market.'

Bernie continued undeterred. 'These people Special Branch suspect. Call them friends of mine, if you will. They've no intention of starting a mainland campaign, and they're certainly not minded to indulge in petty vendettas on behalf of gobshite actors who shoot their mouths off.'

McCaffrey gave a self-conscious laugh. Bernie shot him a look that shut him up.

'My friends' priorities are, shall we say, closer to home right now.'

'McCaffrey told me,' said Calloway. 'A border war.'

Her frustration with the loose-lipped actor showed even more.

'I wouldn't know,' she said, meaning she knew full well. 'Let's just say my friends are more interested in the B Specials than B pictures.'

B Specials, the Ulster Special Constabulary. A reserve police force, armed and run on military lines. Calloway had patrolled alongside them in Belfast in the thirties. Loyalist hard men with blood on their hands.

'My friends have no time to be worrying about their friends and relatives in London,' she said.

'Why would your friends worry about relatives in London?' Calloway asked.

'Because sooner or later MI5 will have Special Branch turning over every Irish pub, club and tenement flat from Kilburn to Camberwell looking for a bomb factory that doesn't exist. Innocent people will get hurt, unnecessarily.'

'That's very community spirited of you,' said Calloway. 'But like I said, I'm not in the market.'

He downed the whisky, pushed the empty glass back towards her and rose to leave.

'I know your friends,' he said. 'They bomb cinemas and tube stations. They put innocent people in hospital, unnecessarily. They put some in the mortuary. Sometimes they put bullets through the heads of my former comrades.'

He wanted no part of Bernie and her scheme. He had enough to worry about, with Belcher and Bryant breathing down his neck and Spelthorne threatening him with a regular appointment at the labour exchange.

'Oh, I think you're in the market, Mr Calloway,' she said, slipping a hand inside the raincoat and pulling out a Webley service revolver. It was old and tarnished but no less deadly for it.

'Find out who planted the bomb under your boss's car,' she said to Calloway. 'Then hand them over to the police. I want their investigation brought to a swift conclusion.'

Curly and Blue Eyes appeared again. Curly gripped Calloway's arm and pushed him in the direction of the door. Calloway shook him free and turned back to face Bernie.

'Why me?' he said.

Bernie glanced at McCaffrey, then turned back to Calloway. 'Because you once stood by and watched a family thrown into the street while their possessions burned on the fire.'

TEN

Belcher and Bryant were taking witness statements at the studio. Calloway had given them his office for the morning. Belcher was filling it with pipe smoke. Interviewees hung around the corridor outside, smoking and speculating on what they might be asked. They found it all very exciting, Calloway judged by their rapid, animated conversations. Having provided the Special Branch men with lists of those present at the dinner, at least those that worked for Centurion, there wasn't much for Calloway to do. He left the studio and took a bus along the Hoxton Street. It was a crisp autumn day with an impossibly blue sky and an arc-light sun. Plane trees had shed a layer of golden leaves, which mottled the grubby pavements like freckles on the face of an urchin. The bus windows reverberated with the cries of the barrow boys, like the soundtrack of a Centurion social drama. And the gilt signage above the shop windows behind the barrows glistened in a way that Centurion's painted scenery never could, no matter how skilled the scenic artists.

He jumped off the bus near the corner of De Beauvoir Road and headed towards a small, soot-blackened, municipal-looking building that from its architecture he judged had once been a bright red terracotta. The building was almost black now, but the stone steps were newly scrubbed and the brass work on the ornate doors was polished so it shined. It stood alone among the rubble of what had once been adjoining buildings but were now an alien landscape of jagged bricks, charred timbers and the torn fragments of wallpaper. Half a dozen kids were playing war in the rubble, holding sticks like rifles and arguing over who'd be the Germans. It was a familiar scene, which Calloway had seen in every neighbourhood he'd visited in the few years he'd lived in London since the war. Bomb-site playgrounds had become unplanned amenities, dangerous and rat-infested, but fun. Places for unrestrained Blitz kids with bleeding knees below all-year-round shorts to smash things up.

He pulled open the heavy door and entered.

'You'll have to wait,' a croaking voice said before the door had closed behind him.

Marjorie's description of Rene was spot-on. Cerberus at the gates, minus two of the heads, which she made up for with a ferocious stare and a Park Drive gripped between her teeth like the thigh bone of a tiny man she'd recently savaged. She sat at the front desk in a cloud of tobacco smoke under a sign that said Centurion Company of Stars. This was Sidney G Spelthorne's famous charm school, in reality a former boxing club. Neither the vase of roses on the windowsill nor Rene's Park Drive could mask the ingrained smell of sweat. Through the door she was guarding, Calloway could see a dozen young women in swimsuits and high heels walking in a circle around the old gymnasium. Each one balanced a hardback book on their heads. In the centre of the circle, a middle-aged woman in twin set and pearls sang out instruction in a plummy Scottish accent.

Rene cleared her throat to get Calloway's attention. 'Mr Cole has been delayed.'

She nodded towards a plush sofa in front of the window. 'Sit over there. No gawping at the girls.'

Calloway took a seat as instructed and refrained from gawping. As he leafed through one of the magazines on the coffee table in front of him, he heard the plummy voice sing out, 'Straighten that back, Barbara Bennett. You look like Quasimodo at a swimming gala.'

Through the door to the gym Calloway saw Barbara Bennett's small lips tense with frustration.

Calloway stared at the cheesecake photos in the magazine and tried not to think about Curley, Blue Eyes and raven-haired Bernie with the raglan sleeves and the Webley revolver inside her coat.

Through the open door Calloway heard the sound of a book falling onto the wooden gymnasium floor echo around the hall. The plummy voice shouted, 'You, girl, pick that up this minute. I'm not surprised you dropped it, shuffling about like a pregnant camel. You're a disgrace the studio, the lot of you.'

'They're for it,' croaked Rene, seeming to enjoy the moment.

Calloway was halfway through an article about an actress he'd never heard of when Cole arrived. He walked through the door with a lightness of step that defied his short but heavy frame. He was mid-forties with a face that looked like the rest of him lunched well. His hair was a swirl of tight black curls, heavily oiled and glistening in the light. His eyes glistened too through the lenses of his modern-looking glasses. He wore a well-cut worsted suit, with a yellow silk tie pinned with a jewel. His pocket square was ironed to a point which poked cheekily upwards from his breast pocket. He crossed the small reception room towards Calloway his hand already extended.

'Sorry, sorry, sorry,' he said. 'You're here, I'm late. All my fault. Have you been waiting long?'

'Long enough to know that Barbara Bennett is for it.'

Calloway nodded towards the old gymnasium. Cole gave a knowing smile. 'Ah yes, the lovely Barbara. Heavy on her feet but built like a goddess. Looks great in a swimsuit, and that's what counts.' Calloway saw him leer slightly before saying, 'Please, please, come in.'

He gestured to a half-glazed office door that led off the reception. It said I. Cole, Publicity in neat gold letters on the reeded glass.

If Spelthorne's office looked like a place where people gambled and drank hard liquor, Cole's at least looked like a place where work was done. There were filing cabinets with manila folders stacked on top, sheafs of photographs strewn across the desktop and a wall of framed publicity portraits, some even Calloway recognised. Cole seated himself behind his desk and gestured to the chair in front. As Calloway sat, the publicist pushed a gold cigarette box across the table and lifted the lid. Calloway helped himself.

'Now I've seen you around the studio. You're the new security fella. What d'you make of that explosion business?'

'The police suspect a bomb. My money's on a stray dog-end and a leaky petrol tank.'

'Shame. A bomb would have made a great story for The Rebel Gun.'

He tapped an imaginary newspaper and pointed to an imaginary headline. '"Fenian plot fails to thwart film mogul's must-see thriller".'

'I thought Spelthorne wanted to play down the republican angle. That's why he sacked Terrence McCaffrey.'

'It's true, he did. And I had the devil's own job keeping it out of the papers.'

Cole thought for a moment, like a sudden thought had piqued his interest.

'But what if it was a bomb?' he said. 'Do you think McCaffrey's capable?'

'Not in the slightest,' said Calloway. 'He seems the type that shoots his mouth off on any subject you care to mention. And I don't doubt his views on Ireland are heartfelt, but a bomb? Not a chance.'

Perhaps he was overdoing it, Calloway thought.

'So why exactly are you here?'

'Something far more prosaic. Lost property. One of your starlets dropped her purse when she fled the Producers Club dinner after the explosion. I want to return it but I don't know her name. I was hoping you might have photos of the cohort I could look at. Or better still allow me to see the girls next door.'

Cole laughed. 'Some of them are girls next door, at that. But that's what the charm school's for. We weed those ones out. Not the Centurion look.'

'But you're making social dramas.'

'Yes, and have you noticed how every tenement in Britain has a beautiful daughter at home?'

Calloway hadn't. He didn't go to the pictures.

'Do these girls really star in films? From what I've heard they don't get more than a walk on part in one of Spelthorne's B pictures.'

'One or two get near the top, but you're right, most don't. It doesn't matter a jot. Their role is to go out among the great unwashed and add a little Centurion sparkle. The folks out there want to believe these girls are stars. They crave glamour in their grey little lives. Look out of the window, Calloway. Tired little people living among amid the rubble. A decade on the ration eating powdered egg and pork brawn. The greatest luxury the poor sods enjoy is an extra rasher of bacon with their Sunday breakfast. The charm school girls take them away from all that. When I take them to a flower show, or a garden fete, or the opening of a swimming pool, that small corner of this worn-down world is lifted out of its post-war drudgery. The women swoon at their frocks, their husbands drool at their pursed lips and pert little arses. Centurion gives them glitz and glamour. You can't get that on the ration.'

'So you're selling empty promises to girls with dreams.'

Cole looked offended. 'Some of them do make it, really.' Then he waved away Calloway's suggestion. 'Anyway, it's not like the idea is original. Gainsborough pioneered the charm school idea by developing their young stars, you know, Stewart Granger, Phyllis Calvert, Pat Roc, then Rank went for it big time with their Company of Youth. But Spelthorne really knows how to work it.'

Calloway thought of the Producers Club dinner and the cohort of young, would-be starlets fastened into their tight-fitting, low-cut evening dresses being groped by middle-aged financiers. He presumed that's what 'working it' meant.

There were raised voices coming from the gym. Deportment class was not going well today.

Cole said, 'You'll never get into the room next door. Rene would chew your balls off and spit them back in your face. That's why Spelthorne hired her. She looks after the merchandise.'

'Then some files perhaps. I could go through them and see if I can recognise the face.'

'Yes, yes of course. We have the Company of Stars Book.'

He reached into a desk draw and dropped an over-stuffed

lever-arch file onto the desktop.

'They're all in there. Starlets from the past five years, since Sidney founded the charm school. Photos, vital statistics, biographies, all grossly exaggerated of course.'

He cleared a path through the piles of photos on the desk and slid the file over to Calloway. 'Have a flick through. The Cinderella that dropped her purse could be in there.'

Calloway opened the file. 'How did you get into this business?'

'It was the war,' said Cole. 'I worked for the Ministry of Information, writing scripts for propaganda films. They were appalling, but Duff Cooper took a shine to me and moved me into his press relations group. When the war ended, one of the directors I'd worked with on the films told me of an opening with Spelthorne for a publicist. I had the right skills. Seemed a waste not to use them.' Cole nodded in the direction of the deportment class.

'And the subject matter was far more appealing.'

The door flew open and the plummy Scottish woman in the twin set entered the room.

'Ivor, you absolutely have to speak to those girls. They're the most appalling shower that's ever been through my deportment class. No better than Limehouse harlots, good for nothing but leaning in knocking shop doorways, with not an ounce of class between them.'

Cole winked at Calloway and rose from his chair. 'Time for a pep talk.' He gestured to the file. 'I'll have to leave you to it. If you find who you're looking for let me know.'

When Cole had left, Calloway continued turning the pages. They were full of soft-focus portraits and swimsuit shots. Each girl had a story that Cole had no doubt concocted. He looked at each face in turn. There was a monotony to them. The charm school was a production line. A few pages before the end, one face jumped out. Brunette, not blonde. Finer features, perhaps. Younger by several years. But the eyes were right. The same eyes that had looked up at Calloway on the night of the explosion with the wrong kind of fear. Eyes that had been staring at him in his mind since that night. Her name was Joyce Rose, she was twenty-two and loved horse riding and romantic walks in the country. She graduated from the charm school two years previously. Calloway removed the portrait photo from the file. He slipped it into his inside pocket and left the office, nodding to Rene on his way out.

'You done then?' she said.

She looked indignant and suspicious. 'Tell Mr Cole thanks, but I didn't find her.'

Rene scowled. He got the impression no one was brave enough to tell her what to do.

Calloway caught a bus and retraced his route back to the studio. The sky had clouded over and there was the threat of rain in the air. The neighbourhood looked suddenly depressed. Grim and grey again, with the detritus of the market stalls spattered over the streets.

He nodded at the commissionaire at the studio gates as he entered and walked over to casting. He was hoping to see Marge. He had reason now to ask her about the woman who'd fled the dinner on the night of the explosion. And he had a name to go on. It was hardly a lead, but he trusted his gut feeling. The frightened face fleeing the scene was as good a place to start as any. And he needed a lead because like it or not, he was working for Bernie and her friends, and the only way they were going to take their Webley revolver and disappear from his life was if he got Special Branch a result.

To Calloway's disappointment, Tony sat alone in the office.

'Margie's out I'm afraid. You'll have to content yourself with me.'

The young man sat on his side of the utilitarian partners' desk smoking a French cigarette and leafing through a folder of photographic portraits. He held one up for Calloway to see.

'What d'you reckon?' he said. 'A passed-over major who claims credit for his sergeant's gallantry?'

'That reminds me of someone I know. He doesn't look like that though.'

Tony tossed the photo back into the file. 'So what can I help you with?'

‘What can you tell me about Joyce Rose?’ said Calloway.

The name gave Tony a start. ‘Joyce?’ he said, looking visibly perturbed. He thought for a moment and relaxed a little. ‘One of the studio’s most promising starlets. Quite beautiful, and a genuinely good actress too. Not typical charm school fodder. Leading lady material. A good friend, actually. We knew each other when we were younger. Our fathers were both French and we used to keep each other company to relieve the boredom of endless social gatherings.’

‘French then, not English?’

‘Half French. Her mother was English. She was a telephonist at the Granchester hotel. That’s where she met Joyce’s father. He was the concierge. Of course, she wasn’t called Joyce Rose originally. That was Ivor Cole’s idea. He wanted to sell her as a typical English rose. She hated the name. She was christened Celeste Leclerc. It suited her far better I always thought. But Cole didn’t know her like I did.’

He was quiet for a moment, as if distracted by a pleasant childhood memory. Then he said, ‘Why are you interested in Joyce?’

‘I think she was the starlet who dropped the purse on the night of the explosion,’ said Calloway.

Tony frowned. Lines furrowed deep into his oversized brow. He shook his head. ‘You must be mistaken, Mr Calloway. Joyce died more than a year ago.’

ELEVEN

Joyce Rose was found dead in her flat in Bayswater's fashionable Cypress Court. She had swallowed down two bottles of pills with a full bottle of gin the previous evening. The cleaner found her in the morning and called an ambulance, but by that time the young actress had been dead for several hours.

Police had found a large quantity of prescription drugs in the medicine cabinet of her bathroom. They were prescribed by a Harley Street doctor known to dispense medicines quite liberally to London's film actors. The coroner concluded that she had been living on a diet of stimulants and barbiturates. Uppers for the day, downers at night. Witnesses had reported that she had also been drinking heavily for at least six months. In the final months of her short life, Joyce Rose had been far from the gay young girl that supposedly enjoyed horse riding and romantic walks in the country.

Centurion's casting department kept a file on Rose. In fact, it looked more like a scrap book compiled by an adoring fan. Calloway suspected that Tony had compiled it, or at least embellished it following the actress's death. It was a brown manila shrine to a tragic Madonna.

Calloway had made a visit to the cutting room which was next to the casting office, on the pretence of inspecting the window locks. He'd waited until Marjorie and Tony went for lunch in the canteen. He had noticed that they never locked up behind them and that they also didn't lock their filing cabinet. Calloway found the Joyce Rose file and slipped it inside the jacket of his grey worsted suit, before returning to his office which had now been vacated by Belcher and Bryant and smelled strongly of Belcher's sickly sweet pipe tobacco. He threw open a window and lit a Navy Cut.

Clipped to the inside of the file were three press cuttings, all from the Daily Sketch. The first headline read MYSTERY SURROUNDS DEATH OF STARLET. A second headline read ACTRESS'S DEATH WAS SUICIDE SAYS CORONER. Both news reports featured the stock portrait of Rose from Cole's Book of Stars. There was a third cutting with a lengthier article under a headline that read STARS GATHER AT SUICIDE ACTRESS' FUNERAL. There were photographs from the funeral with actors and actresses that Daily Sketch readers would presumably recognise, although Calloway didn't. Jimmy Hanley, two actresses called Hermione and two young unknowns from the Rank charm school, Christopher Lee and Peter Murray. Centurion's official press release on the death was attached to these cuttings, carefully drafted no doubt by Cole to head off any suggestion that being under contract to the studio may have contributed to her state of mind at the time of her death. You'd be forgiven for thinking she was the happiest actress in the history of film making. Much of this messaging made it into the Daily Sketch copy, such was the strength of Cole's contacts in Fleet Street and his ability to influence them. The report instead dwelt on the celebrity of the mourners and the fact that no family were present at the funeral, both her parents having died in 1944, the result of a doodlebug hit on the Granchester Hotel. The remainder of the file was padded out with press coverage from her short but successful career. At least it was successful compared with the other charm school hopefuls, who no doubt spent their days parading around county shows and opening municipal swimming pools. There were fair-to-middling reviews for supporting roles in soon forgotten romances and photos in the gossip pages, mostly pictured with better known stars.

Calloway stuffed the file into his desk drawer and left the office, locking it behind him. As he walked down the corridor, Bryant appeared, blocking his way. The detective looked at his watch.

'Knocking off already? I s'pose that's what you lot call a day's work.'

Calloway looked at his own watch and said, 'The working day ended an hour ago. I've already notched up an hour's overtime.'

It was just after noon.

'Smart arse,' said Bryant. 'You got that list of McCaffrey's regular haunts?'

Calloway shook his head. 'No one knows where he goes, or at least if they do, they're not telling me,' he lied. 'He's a dark horse, that one.'

'He'll be a shade or two darker when we get hold of him,' said Bryant.

'So that's how you boys operate, eh?' Calloway said, but he was in no position to criticise. 'Does DI Belcher know you talk like that?'

'Just my little joke.'

'Mine was better.'

Calloway pulled out a cigarette and offered one to Bryant, who took it and accepted a light. He mentioned the name of one of the clubs on the list he'd visited.

'He's been spotted there a few times.'

It was the place Calloway had been propositioned by the merchant seamen in the frock. A trip there should keep Bryant busy for a while, he thought.

They exchanged competitive small talk while they smoked, the one-upmanship of males not used to giving ground. Calloway excused himself, left the studio and walked for twenty minutes towards Liverpool Street. The autumn sun was out again, but the sky was a haze of half smog. The streets looked as though they had been brushed with diluted watercolour, blurring the lines of the buildings into an amorphous grey-brown.

As he turned onto Bishopsgate, the buildings grew larger. These were the temples of commerce, the fruits of imperial prosperity, with their classical features and heavy materials. Bold and imposing to inspire confidence in their occupants to invest inconceivable sums for acceptable returns. Not all the buildings had survived the bombings. Some were half-standing ruins of stone, their columns and cupolas protruding painfully from the rubble around them. The overall impression was of an ornate wedding cake that had been trampled underfoot during a fight at the reception.

He took the Central Line to Queensway and then walked the quarter mile to Cypress Court. It was one of those typical pre-war mansion blocks that managed to remain exclusive while lacking any hint of grandeur. It was the kind of block that kept the Crittall Window Company in business. Calloway walked up the shallow travertine steps which led to a set-back entrance under a simple concrete portico. He entered the glazed doors into an ungenerous lobby whose house plants failed to mask an underlying smell of cooking. There was a small counter and behind it a wall of pigeon holes for residents' mail. A bland-sounding orchestra was playing a forgettable tune behind an adjacent door marked Manager. Calloway tapped the brass bell on the countertop and waited. The forgettable tune stopped abruptly and the door opened. A harassed-looking woman old enough to be a Boer War widow said 'Yes?' in that extended nasal tone ordinary folk use when putting on airs. She had cat hairs on her cardigan and biscuit crumbs at the corners of her parched-looking mouth.

Calloway passed his calling card across the desk. 'Calloway, Centurion Pictures. I've come to inspect flat 309.'

He'd found Joyce Rose's last address in the file he'd taken from casting. It was a Centurion flat, one they maintained for stars under contract that were valued enough to warrant special treatment. He'd been surprised that she qualified, having never had the chance to graduate beyond supporting actress to leading lady. The manager put on a pair of spectacles that hung on the chain around her neck and looked at the card. She nodded a series of barely perceptible nods as she read each word in turn. She looked up at Calloway, scrutinised his face for enough seconds to make him uncomfortable - he had no official reason for being there - before looking back at the card and turning it over on in her mottled, arthritic hands. He'd crossed borders with lesser inspections.

Seemingly satisfied, she said, 'I'll fetch the key,' which she took from a neat row of hooks just inside the door of the office.

'Anyone at home?' he said. It occurred to him only now that the flat might be occupied.

The manager frowned. 'No one has lived there since...' she hesitated, unsure of the words to use.

'I understand,' he said.

Calloway took the small cage lift to the third floor. Flat 309 was down a windowless corridor with a well-worn parquet floor that made his footsteps echo off the bare walls. Pink glass wall lights in the shape of clam shells cast a dim glow of ersatz cosiness. The key turned stiffly
in the lock of the highly polished door marked 309 in brass numbers. Inside, the flat was warm and the air dry, a stark contrast to the cold, damp world Calloway tended to inhabit. The communal heating flowed through heavy iron radiators with a comforting gurgle. Though not cold, Calloway warmed himself against hallway radiator just because he could. It was a rare treat.

The hall opened onto a lounge with a large bay window, through which sunlight would have poured were it not for thick net curtains. Instead, the light inside the room was as muted as the pastels of the decor. The lounge was roomy, but not cavernous, giving the impression of understated comfort. A chintz three-piece suite filled much of the space, making it look safe and suburban, while side tables and standard lamps added daring hints at modernism. A door to the right led onto a modern, fitted kitchen, just large enough to prepare breakfast in the morning and perhaps canapés for cocktails in the evening. To the left was a bathroom with bold green-and-black tiling, angular chrome taps and a bath deep enough to drown in. A cork-topped stool with tubular chrome legs stood beside it. He imagined the freshly bathed starlet, her skin pink and smooth, wrapped in the fluffiest of bath robes as she sat painting her toenails. But when he tried to imagine her face, he couldn't.

There was one bedroom, a large room with the same bay window as the lounge, wide enough to take an elaborate dressing table with numerous drawers and mirrors. Ornate perfume bottles like religious icons stood decoratively on lace doilies on top of the dressing table's shining walnut veneer. It was an altar for the worship of beauty. A rose-pink silk eiderdown resembling a giant Turkish delight covered the double divan bed. Matching pillows were plumped like marshmallows. Calloway tried to imagine the woman in Cole's publicity photo lounging on the bed, flicking idly through a film magazine as she waited for her nails to dry. But when he did, it was the face of the woman fleeing the gala dinner. Older, harder, more worldly, no longer the type for those romantic walks that the publicity department concocted for her. A different face and yet the same. He couldn't make it fit. Not in these surroundings. This place was seductively safe, full of conventional comforts, somewhere for an English Rose to grow more fragrant and more lovely. The face in Calloway's consciousness could never fit here.

He made a search of the place, not entirely sure what he expected to find. The wardrobes and drawers were empty, the cupboards bare. There was no space beneath the divan bed, no sign of prescription drugs in the bathroom cabinet. There were no magazines in the rack nor books on the sleeves. No records beside the gramophone, no drinks on the trolley. The place had been emptied and scrupulously cleaned. It was waiting for the next Joyce Rose.

He locked up behind him and took the stairs this time. The manager was waiting for him in the lobby. There was a small and cheap-looking cardboard suitcase on the countertop in front of her, the kind travelling salesman take on overnight stays.

'I've been waiting for someone to collect this.' It sounded like an accusation. 'It was on top of the wardrobe,' she said, as if he should have known this. 'Pushed right to the back.'

'It belonged to Joyce Rose?' he said.

'It's not my business to say who it belonged to, but it came from flat 309. They should have taken it way.'

He wasn't sure who they were supposed to be but said, 'I'll take it off your hands.'

She looked suddenly reluctant to hand it over, but then said, 'I don't have much room, you see. Just a small office.'

Calloway looked over her shoulder into the hutch-like room. An electric heater glowed from its enamelled frame while an old tin kettle on a two-ring gas burner sent a small plume of steam from its spout as it started to boil.

'Did you know her well?' he said.

The manager wasn't expecting a question and paused before answering. 'Quite well,' she said. Quite meaning perfectly. 'Delightful girl, at least at first. She changed, you know.'

'Changed how?'

She thought for a moment, brushing the biscuit crumbs from her mouth. 'The joy went out of her.'

Hardly surprising, he thought. A diet of stimulants and barbiturates is no recipe for joy. He'd seen it during the war, seen men become dependent on the little helpers the medics gave out when sleep wasn't an option, then watched them counter the effects with drink when it was. Some became erratic, unreliable and reckless. They were the dangerous ones. Others became morose, a liability, a drag on morale.

'When did this start?' he said.

'When she started getting visitors,' the manger replied.

'What kind of visitors?'

'The wrong kind, if you ask me.'

'Wrong how?'

'Well,' she said, folding her arms in front of her. The sleeves of her cardigan had picked up more cat hairs since he'd been upstairs. 'Twice her age, by the look of them. Rough mannered too, although they tried to hide it with airs and graces. They couldn't fool me,' she said, tapping the side of her nose. 'Too smartly dressed for my liking. One wore correspondent shoes.'

'These visitors,' he said, 'did they come alone?'

She nodded. 'Their drivers would wait outside. Big expensive cars they had.'

'How long did they stay?'

'Sometimes an hour or two. Sometimes they were in and out very quickly, especially towards the end. That's when the trouble started.'

'What kind of trouble?'

'I heard one of them call her names as he left. Names I won't repeat. On another occasion she was in tears for hours.'

'How do you know she was in tears?'

'I don't listen at doors,' she said.

He hadn't suggested she did.

'I was taking a parcel up to 307 and happened to hear her from the corridor.'

'Were these men her only visitors?'

'Not at first. When she first moved in, friends would call on her. I would call them the kind of people she should be mixing with. Nice young girls.'

'Any male friends?'

'Some,' she said. 'They always left at a respectable hour.'

'Anyone in particular?'

'Yes,' said. 'I'm not one to talk about these things, but seeing as she's...' she hesitated before saying the word.

'No longer a resident,' Calloway said.

'Indeed.'

She looked down as an over-fed tabby cat brushed past her legs and walked into the office. She brushed the cat hairs from her sleeves, tutting as if she'd just noticed them.

'There was this one young man. A nice boy. She seemed happy enough when she was around him.'

'Can you describe him?'

'A bit skinny for my liking.'

He wondered what her liking was.

'Intelligent looking. Tweed jacket and cravat. Very high forehead.'

Tony from casting.

'He stopped visiting after...'

She hesitated.

'Did something happen?' said Calloway.

'The young boy was there when one of those rogues came visiting. There was an argument. The man's driver, well I didn't see, I only heard. A physical exchange.'

'A fight?'

She shook her head. 'I don't think the boy was the fighting

sort.'

'He was attacked? By the man's driver?'

'I didn't see, I only heard. After that, the boy stopped visiting.'

The kettle on the gas ring started the whistle.

'I can't offer you tea,' she said, as if he'd been rude enough to ask for one. 'I don't have enough coupons for two.'

With this she walked back into the office and closed the door behind her. Calloway took the case from the countertop. It was light, perhaps half full. As he left Cypress Court, he took a last look up to the windows of flat 309. He tried to imagine the face that had fled the Producers Club dinner looking down at him, crying. Crying after being called names by rough men in correspondent shoes. But he couldn't. The face he'd seen that night wasn't a face that cried easily.

TWELVE

'Going on holiday?'

It was Bryant again. He was looking down at the suitcase in Calloway's hand. Calloway avoided the question by lobbing one back.

'Still hanging around then?'

Bryant was leaning against the unmarked Special Branch car that had been a permanent fixture in the studio's cobbled courtyard since the morning after the explosion.

'Like the proverbial bad smell,' he replied, and took a long drag on his cigarette.

Calloway held up the case for Bryant to see. 'I'm returning it to props. Someone left it on location.'

'You lead an exciting life,' the copper said.

You don't know the half of it, thought Calloway. 'You finished your interviews?' he said.

'For now' said Bryant.

'Learn anything?'

'Yeah. That half the people you work with are right up their own arses.'

'And that's news?'

'S'pose not. I don't know how you stomach it. All the pretension and the fancy talk. Bunch of fakes.'

'Of course they're fake. That's what we do here. Create fanciful imitations of life.'

'Not so fanciful when actors playing IRA thugs start planting bombs.'

'And you can prove that?'

'We've got to find the bugger first. And some help you're

being. You're dragging your feet I'd say. McCaffrey a friend of yours, is he?'

'Sure. The kind of friend I punch in the face and chuck through the main gates.'

'So you say.'

'Spelthorne was there. Ask him.'

Bryant flicked his cigarette onto the cobbles. 'I'm watching you, Calloway. You interest me.'

'Is that one of your little jokes again?'

'Might be.'

Bryant grinned an unfriendly grin, the kind you give a man when you're relishing the prospect of punching him one day. He climbed inside the car, started the powerful engine and drove out through the main gates.

Calloway crossed the courtyard towards the administration building. The two technicians he had spoken to in Studio B were unloading a new camera from the rear of a Morris van.

The technician in the store coat nodded at Calloway and rolled his eyes. 'We've had to hire in a replacement temporarily. Costing us an arm and a leg.'

His colleague in the tweed jacket frowned at him and said to Calloway, 'It's not the money. It's the lost time. That's the real trouble.'

'Got it,' said Calloway. He took the suitcase to his office and pushed it under his desk out of sight. One of his commissionaires appeared at the door, announcing himself by clearing his throat. 'A visitor to see you, Mr Calloway,' he said. 'A Mr Suskind. Shall I send him up?'

Calloway glanced down at the grazes on his knuckles. They had healed but were still a visible reminder of the fight in Ridley Road. He wasn't convinced he wanted an unplanned visit from his old pal Johnny. At the same time he was curious.

'Go ahead,' he said. 'Send him up.'

Suskind's big frame filled the doorway. He was wearing his demob suit, which had lost its shape through too much wear. But his shoes were polished brightly Calloway noticed. Old habits. He held a black trilby hat in his big hand.

'I was passing so I thought I'd drop by.'

'I don't believe that for one minute, Johnny.'

The big ex-paratrooper grinned. He pulled out a pack of Woodbines and offered one to Calloway who lit up with a desk lighter he'd inherited from the previous occupant of the office. It was a present from Weston-super-Mare, apparently. Suskind looked around the office.

'Not a bad little gaff you've got here, Reg.'

Calloway gestured to the chair opposite his desk. 'Take a seat, Johnny, seeing as you're here.'

Suskind sat awkwardly on the edge of the chair, as if getting comfortable would have been a bigger liberty than showing up uninvited.

'I've looked at a couple of security jobs myself, as it happens,' he said. 'I'm working at Lipton's at the moment, lugging tea chests around the Tea Building, but I reckon my talents are wasted there.'

He was right. Johnny had been a good soldier and a good NCO. A natural leader who had earned the respect of his men. But he wasn't the only one. The war had created thousands of men like that and there weren't the jobs for them now that they were back. Calloway had been lucky, twice. Centurion was his second job as head of security and he couldn't complain. He just hoped he didn't mess it up like the first one. Don't get involved. That should have been his motto. Should have been.

'Not at work today?' Calloway said.

'Half day,' said Johnny. 'I wanted to see you, actually. Thought it would be nice to have a chin wag. For old times' sake.'

'That's very touching. But the old times weren't pretty, were they, Johnny? You know damn well neither of us is the kind to reminisce.'

Calloway and Johnny had fought side by side in the final stages of the war. By that time the Germans were putting guns in the hands of children and old men. There was no glory in emptying the magazine of a Sten gun into an enemy like that, no matter what insignia they had on their uniforms.

Suskind held up his hands like he'd been tumbled. 'I can't fool you, can I, Reg?'

'Say your piece Johnny.'

'I've come to ask for your help.'

When Calloway helped, things had a habit of not ending well.

'Carry on,' he said.

'No rough stuff, I promise.' Johnny looked his old comrade up and down. 'Although I know you're good for it,' he said. 'Just a little shopping trip, that's all.'

'Shopping?'

'Something I need you to buy.'

Something for the group, Calloway thought. His mind raced forward several steps. Guns? No, Johnny's war was being fought with fists and boots. Guns weren't their style.

'I'm not one for shopping. There's nothing I want.'

'I get that. And it's nothing you'd want, believe me. I still need you to buy it though. It's something we can't buy ourselves.'

Calloway pulled a bottle of Black & White from his desk drawer and two cups filched from the canteen. He poured two generous measures and passed one to Suskind.

'Black & White, eh? Don't mind if I do. L'Chaim,' said Johnny, raising the cup.

Calloway presumed this was for effect. He remembered that Johnny's usual toast was 'to wives and girlfriends, may they never meet.'

'So spit it out, Johnny. What is this thing you want me to buy for you?'

As he heard the words tumble from his mouth, he was already wishing he hadn't asked. Johnny leant forward in the chair, lowered his voice and explained. It wasn't rough stuff, but it wasn't going to be an errand Calloway relished. There would be a risk in everything Johnny's group did. That was the nature of their operation. Dare to do what others seemed content to avoid. Calloway's reluctance to join in fought with his conscience, but his conscience fought harder. He and Johnny were too alike, their experiences too similar.

'I suppose saying "just this once" would be a waste of time,' Calloway said.

'Probably, yeah,' said Johnny. He downed the rest of his whisky. 'You're a good man, Reg. Marge will pick you up from your place Saturday and take you down there. She'll brief you properly on the way.'

Another date with Marge. Joining in had at least some benefits, Calloway found himself thinking, then cursed himself inwardly. He was still being played.

Calloway rented a room on the top floor of a garment factory off the Kingsland Road. It was an attic space above three floors of workshops which by day were filled with machinists, making ladies fashions sold under the name Da Costa of London. Da Costa of Hackney didn't have the same ring to it. He paid Mr Da Costa a reduced rent for his cold-water room, which had its own gas meter, a gas fire and an old stone sink. In return, he kept an eye on the factory at night. It was a good deal. The room was nothing to write home about, not that he ever wrote home, but it was dry, watertight and private. Calloway didn't like neighbours. He'd never liked digs which meant sharing. Solitude suited him. At least that's what he told himself.

Mr Da Costa was locking up the factory floors when Calloway arrived home that evening.

'You have a suitcase Mr Calloway.' He spoke as if Calloway didn't know this. 'I hope you're not thinking of leaving.'

He prodded Calloway's chest mischievously. 'You are a very good watch dog.'

'Not leaving, Mr Da Costa. Just bringing work home.'

Da Costa gave him a sympathetic look. 'You work too hard. You look tired.'

'So they keep telling me.'

'You don't sleep well,' said Da Costa.

He didn't. He hadn't since the war. And having Belcher, Bryant, Spelthorne and Bernie on his case didn't help him sleep any better.

'Work worries,' Calloway said, suddenly feeling he needed to explain.

Da Costa gave him a wry look. 'And no one to share them

with, eh? No lady friend?'

'No,' said Calloway. 'Well...' He shrugged. 'Who knows?'

'Ah,' said Da Costa with a knowing look. 'So there is someone. That's good.'

'It's complicated.'

Da Costa gave a sage nod. 'Women are complicated, Mr Calloway. If they weren't, they would be very dull indeed.' He prodded Calloway's chest again. 'And who wants a dull wife, eh?'

Da Costa finished locking the big steel door to the factory floor and said, 'Get some rest. You'll be needing your strengths for that complicated woman.'

The old man laughed to himself as he walked down the dark stairway and out into the street.

Calloway's room was cold. The autumn temperature was dropping. He put a shilling in the meter and lit the gas. The small fire set into the wall spluttered into life. He watched the blue flame turn the ceramic plates to a comforting orange. He loosened his tie and took a bottle of gin from the shelf above the sink and poured a slug into his tooth mug. The gin tasted faintly of cloves from the tooth powder he used. It wasn't unpleasant. He kicked off his shoes, plumped his pillow and sat up on the iron-framed bed that doubled as a studio couch, the only place in the room to sit, apart from a hard kitchen chair. He dragged the small suitcase onto his lap and clicked the clasps. They were unlocked and popped easily.

There were papers, books and photographs inside. Mementoes. Colourful scraps of a girl's former life. Joyce, when she was Celeste. Small things, not in themselves remarkable, but significant enough to keep. Family photos. A handsome-looking couple in hotel uniform. Her parents, he assumed. Celeste as a child playing on a beach somewhere in England. Ice creams and donkey rides. Family holidays in France, a sun-tanned Celeste in a sundress and a big straw hat, legs dangling over the edge of a café chair. A school report from 1935. A pleasant and popular girl...must learn to concentrate in class...a chatterbox...could achieve higher marks if she set her mind to it...her Mary in this year's nativity play was a revelation. Two photos of Celeste in her teens, posing like a movie star with a boy that looked very much like Tony from casting. There was also an Oxo tin, the kind people kept cotton reels and sewing kit in. This tin was heavy. Inside was a small 8mm cine camera and two reels of film. The handwritten labels on the film reels read Film star diary 1/3 and Film star diary 2/3. He examined the camera. It was loaded and the film supply indicator showed that film had been taken. Calloway replaced the reels and the camera inside the tin and set it to one side. He rifled through the remaining contents of the suitcase. There were half a dozen postcards from Paris with recent post marks. He turned the postcards over and read them. Pleasantries from a young woman abroad, the signature Yvonne written with a creative flourish. The most recent card sent six months before the actress's death. And a copy of an earnest-looking magazine called London Poetry Review. He leafed through the pages. The editor's introduction was provocative. He was turning the world of poetry on its head. Challenging the poetry establishment. The editor signed himself Mephisto. Next to his signature, a satirical illustration of the devil reading William Blake. Then thirty-two pages of poetry by poets whose names meant nothing to Calloway.

Except for one.

THIRTEEN

Saturday. Marge was leaning against a borrowed Ford Pilot she'd parked opposite Da Costa's factory. She wore the same tatty trench coat she had worn on the night of the Union Movement rally. The tortoise shell cigarette holder was clamped between her teeth.

'Well, you certainly look the part,' she said, as Calloway emerged from the building.

He wore his old army boots, trousers from a suit that was now too shabby to wear, a dark roll neck jumper and a brown leather blouson jacket.

'I feel like a B-movie thug,' he said.

'I may have a part for you, love. Come and see me on Monday.'

She leaned forward and kissed him on the cheek.

'Now let's go shopping,' she said.

They drove south down Bishopsgate, then west onto Lombard Street. The roads were empty, the city deserted at the weekend, the directors, managers and clerks of its financial institutions enjoying their Saturday in the suburbs. Marge drove fast, although they were in no hurry. She clunked through the gears of the small car, changing up to get more power from the tentative engine. Then she fished for something in the pocket of her trench coat.

'Put this on,' she said.

She passed him a small enamelled pin with the Union Movement symbol on it. Calloway did as she asked. He felt slightly grubby all of a sudden. Marge looked at him and smiled.

'It completes the look, darling,' she said. 'Johnny told you the plan?'

Calloway nodded and recited the instructions he had been given.

'I go into the bookshop, browse for five minutes, then ask the man behind the counter whether he has any patriotic literature. He will ask me what kind of thing I'm looking for and I will say "books like My Answer". He will recognise this reference to Oswald Mosley's new book as a coded request to buy fascist literature and will then fetch a selection from a locked storeroom. I will note the place he keeps the key, the location of the storeroom and any other useful intelligence that can be used when your group returns to the premises at night to remove the aforementioned literature for destruction. I will purchase a selection of literature and leave the shop. I will report all intelligence gathered back to you.'

'Clever boy,' she said, taking a hand off the wheel and pinching his cheek. As much as he was enjoying Marge's company, the lapdog treatment irritated him.

They drove past St Paul's Cathedral, standing proud among the ruins that surrounded it. Some said the Luftwaffe spared it because they used it as a landmark for navigation. Others said it was divine intervention. Calloway reckoned it just got lucky. Ninety percent of war was about luck, in his experience.

He said to Marge, 'What do you know about the London Poetry Review?'

She laughed. 'Has that Stevie Smith quotation been playing on your mind?'

It had, but that wasn't his reason for asking the question. He figured anyone that could quote a modern poet might know the magazine he found among Joyce Rose's mementoes.

'I've read it once or twice,' she said. 'It's published by this bohemian sort who hangs around North Soho. He has a coterie of admirers who follow him around. They drink in the Fitzroy Tavern on Charlotte Street. Why on earth do you ask? Are you looking to broaden your mind, Reg?'

'Would that be so odd?' he said.

'You don't strike me as the type,' she said.

He didn't often take offence, but he was close to it this time.

‘So what type am I?’

She thought for a moment, as if assembling everything she had learned about him in these last few days into a coherent character. She frowned and said, ‘You’re full of contradictions.’

‘I’m straightforward enough,’ he said, doubting himself as he spoke.

She shook her head. ‘You’re the type that puts on an accent that’s not his own but stays loyal to his kind. You’re the haunted type that wants to forget yet keeps their memories alive.’ She glanced at him for a second. ‘Especially the bad ones. And you’re definitely the type whose instinct gets the better of his judgement.’

‘A trait you’re quite happy to exploit,’ he said.

‘In the face of very little resistance,’ she said, crunching through the gears and accelerating down the Strand. ‘Oh,’ she said as an afterthought, ‘and you’re the type that doesn’t like jazz.’

She turned up her nose and shook her head with disapproval. ‘How can you not like jazz?’

‘Easily,’ he said. ‘Especially the saxophone. It’s like wind from the devil’s backside.’

She laughed and muttered ‘philistine’ before fishing in the bag beside her and pulling out a packet of Park Drive.

‘Light us both one up, darling,’ she said.

His hand glanced across hers as he took the packet. He felt less offended.

They drove around Piccadilly Circus, its neon signage alight again after years of blackout. Guinness was good for you, Wrigley’s gave you vim and vigour and Bile Beans kept you heathy, bright eyed and slim. With stout, gum and laxatives, you could conquer the world.

‘Tell me more about this bookshop,’ he said.

‘It’s owned by a fascist called Victor Dodds. He was a leading light in the BUF in the thirties and is now a pivotal figure in the Union Movement. He’s not your typical Mosleyite thug. Educated, intellectual you might say, and very influential among the myriad fascist groups that have sprung up around the country in the last few years. A good speech writer and a frequent contributor to far-right magazines. The shop itself is unremarkable. A normal second-hand bookshop that earns Dodds a modest living.'

'Will Dodds be behind the counter?'

She shook her head. 'He doesn't work there on Saturdays. We've been tailing him for some time so we know his movements. He spends his weekends in the Union Movement offices on Arundel Gardens. There'll be a slack-jawed Saturday boy in the shop today. Should make your job easier.'

Easier than what, he thought. He couldn't see anything difficult in buying a few magazines and keeping his eyes open.

Dodd's bookshop was in a side street off Hammersmith Broadway, between a painter and decorator and a tobacconist. Marge parked a few yards farther down the street. She killed the engine and reached into her handbag.

'Now you'll also need this.'

She put a small tobacco tin into Calloway's hand. One side of it had been cut away. He opened the tin. It was filled with a smooth layer of plasticine.

'It's likely that wherever Dodds keeps the key to the locked storeroom, he will also keep other keys,' said Marge. 'We're hoping one of them will be the key to the front door of the shop. There might even be a duplicate of the storeroom key. Most locksmiths provide a spare key when they fit a lock. When the boy disappears into the storeroom to get the literature you've requested, we want you to take impressions of as many keys as you can by pressing them into the plasticine. You will need to take an impression of both sides. We've done a trial run and reckon you should be able to do half a dozen keys inside a minute.'

Calloway didn't like the sound of it.

'Johnny said I'd be observing and reporting back. He said nothing about taking impressions of keys.'

Marge faked innocent in a way that told him he'd been duped. 'Poor Johnny,' she said. 'He's so forgetful.'

A big part of him wanted to slap the tobacco tin back into her hand and walk away. Buying a few pamphlets was one thing. Risking arrest, or even a beating by Victor Dodds' bully boys, was something else. The trouble was, Marge was right. He was the type whose instinct got the better of his judgement, and his instinct told him to take impressions of those bloody keys so that Johnny and his 43 Group commandos could put a match to the filth that Dodds and Hamm and Mosley and every other tin-pot little fascist were spurting to a nation still hurting from a six-year fight against people like them.

He leaned across to Marge, took her face in his big hands and kissed her full on the lips.

'Wish me luck,' he said, pocketing the tobacco tin and easing his big frame out of the small car.

The bell above the door rang as he entered the bookshop. The place smelled musky, like a tom cat had sprayed the walls. There was a chemical tang in the air from the paraffin heater that burned beside the counter. It was too hot inside. At least Calloway felt hot, conscious of the tiny beads of sweat forming under his hairline. He shouldn't have worn the roll neck jumper. The boy Marge had described sat behind the counter reading PG Wodehouse. Ironic, thought Calloway, who knew through his old intelligence circles that the gullible fop author had agreed to make propaganda broadcasts to America for the Nazis after he was interned in France during the war. He wasn't a fascist, MI5's investigation established that. He'd just suffered a dim-witted aberration that anyone with an ounce of political savvy would have avoided.

The shop was empty apart from the boy, much to Calloway's relief. And the boy wasn't a thug. He was stick thin and white as a sheet. If things went sour, Calloway could snap him in half. The bookshelves were arranged in rows, making a series of darkened cul-de-sacs. Calloway rummaged among them, trying to look like people who browse bookshops look. He'd explored all three cul-de-sacs and seen no sign of a door to a storeroom. In fact, the place appeared to be a lock-up shop with only the street door for access. He was beginning to think he'd been given duff intelligence.

The five minutes Johnny had told him to spend browsing took an age. He flicked through books he'd no interest in, all the time checking his watch. The boy tore himself away from Jeeves & Wooster and peered at Calloway through the gloom. Calloway took this as his cue. He stepped over to the counter and gave the boy the agreed spiel. The boy took it in his stride, which suggested this type of routine was a regular occurrence. He noticed Calloway's lapel pin and looked reassured. He stood up and said, 'You'll have to wait a mo,' then opened what looked like a cash drawer under the counter. The drawer opened with a ding of a small bell inside it. Calloway cursed inside. In his mind he'd pictured a key on a hook on the wall, not inside a cash drawer with a bell. The boy pulled out a key from one of the drawer's compartments. There were other keys in there too. Johnny and Marge's hunch had been right. The boy pushed the drawer shut. There was another ding from the bell.

'I won't be a minute,' the boy said.

Take all the minutes you want, pal, thought Calloway, flicking away a small bead of sweat running down the side of his face to join more sweat under his collar. The boy walked into the third of the three cul-de-sacs and fumble with the key, pushing it through a gap in the row of hardbacks on the third shelf from the bottom. There was a click and the bookcase swung back on concealed hinges, opening onto a room lined with stacks of cardboard boxes. The boy stepped into the room and closed the concealed door behind him.

Calloway stepped behind the counter. The cash drawer was the size and shape of a shoebox, with a semicircular brass pull handle on the front. Calloway thought hard. He recalled that there had been a momentary delay between the boy opening the drawer and the bell ringing. Calloway eased the drawer open a fraction, slid his fingers into the gap and felt along the underside of the lid. His fingers felt the cool metal of the bell's circular dome and the small bell hammer beside it. The hammer was pulled back on a taught spring. Holding his breath, he slid his forefinger between the bell and the hammer and gently eased the drawer out with his free hand. The drawer opened silently. He breathed again. Beads of sweat dropped off his forehead onto the countertop and he wiped them with the sleeve of his jacket. He listened hard and heard the muffled sound of the boy rummaging through cardboard boxes behind the bookshelf. There were three keys in the drawer. A large mortise, which could have been the front door, a smaller key that looked like the one the boy had taken, and a tiny key, the kind you use to open a desk drawer. The boy wouldn't be long. The boxes looked easily accessible. Calloway made a snap decision to take impressions of the two larger keys and leave the small key. Desk drawers could be opened easily with a jemmy. Pulling the tobacco tin from his pocket, he took the first impression. A figure darkened the glass-fronted shop door. The bell rang as the door opened. Calloway jumped and dropped the first key. He bent down by reflex and retrieved it. When he straightened up, he was looking up at a stout, bald man in a suit that had long since become too small for him.

The man said, 'Got anything on ham radio?'

Calloway tried to recall the sections he'd browsed through on the shelves. He heard muffled rummaging again from behind the hidden door. It seemed more decisive this time, like boxes being closed and put back in their place. He waved a hand in no particular direction and said, 'Under hobbies and interests.'

The stout man tried to follow the direction Calloway was pointing in. He frowned and was about to ask again. Calloway said, 'Third row along, two shelves down, next to artistic photography.'

This piqued the stout man's interest. He looked the type, thought Calloway. This time he followed the directions. A furtive look had come over his pink, pudgy face. While his back was turned, Calloway took an impression of the second key, replaced both in the compartment of the drawer and eased his fingers under the lid again. In his haste, he fumbled and the hammer snapped on its taught spring. In a split second he muffled the bell with his hand. It made an audible thud, but not a shrill ring not loud enough to penetrate the books that lined the hidden door. The radio ham heard the thud and turned. Calloway repeated, 'Next to the artistic photography,' and gestured to a random shelf. The boy appeared with a sheaf of pamphlets and magazines just as Calloway was returning to the front of the counter.

'I think you'll find these of interest, sir,' he said, looking around to see if there were other customers in the shop. The stout man looked over, trying to see what the boy was showing Calloway. The boy nodded to Calloway to follow him into one of the cul-de-sacs, out of view. He showed him copies of Britain Defiant, London Attack, Gothic Ripple and Unity. Calloway pointed to two of the titles at random and said, 'I'll take those.' A bead of sweat dripped onto Gothic Ripple making a dark spot on the newsprint. The boy appeared not to notice. He gave an uninterested nod and returned to the counter. He slid the chosen magazines into a brown paper bag and took the money Calloway handed him. The stout man gave Calloway a perplexed look as he left the shop with the bag under his arm.

Calloway crossed the street and climbed into the passenger seat of the Ford Pilot. Marge already had the engine running.

'Well?' she said.

Calloway tossed the magazines onto her lap and laid the tobacco tin on top of them.

'I need a drink,' he said.

FOURTEEN

He borrowed a projector from the cutting room. They had an old 8mm Bell & Howell in their store. He returned to his office and threaded the flimsy film he'd found in the suitcase into the projector and ran it until he felt the cogs start pulling at the perforations in the celluloid. He pulled down the blind on his office window and focused the two-foot-square beam on his office wall.

There was Joyce Rose. She gave a coquettish nod and beckoned him to follow her. She wore a summer dress that was respectably revealing. There was enough of the English rose on show to turn heads but not enough to shock. The young actress was among a crowd at a public event. The opening of a cinema. Commissionaires held open the chrome-and-glass doors and Joyce cut the ribbon. Then there were photos, the cinema manager's arm firmly around the starlet's waist, his fish-lips pressed against her cheek for a posed kiss. Ivor Cole was there. He orchestrated the proceedings. Joyce beamed and waved. She was good at this.

The projector clack-clacked. He smelled the burning dust on the valves. Illuminated dust specks floating in the beam. The film cut to an interior. Studio A at Centurion. Joyce on set, taking direction from Bobbie Brand, the lone female director among the studio's all-male roster. Joyce looked nervous. She stood awkwardly. She fussed over the script in her hand. She snuck a look into the lens of the cine camera and bit on her knuckles mugging comic anxiety.

Cut to an evening event, a reception in an over-decorated ballroom. Glimpses of films stars more famous than Joyce would live to be. Joyce excited, however much she was overshadowed. Meeting and greeting studio luminaries with a deferential smile. This is the big time, her eyes said.

Drinks on set. A wrap party with co-stars. Horseplay. Joyce joining in. Then a word from Bobbie Brand, a glass in her hand. Applause and well done all round. A handshake for Joyce from a sheepish crew member. A peck on the cheek from the leading man. A hug from his co-star. Encouraging words from Bobbie, just for Joyce.

A young woman's first steps towards the career of her dreams.

The film ended. The screen turned brilliant white, the full reel spun a celluloid tail like a Catherine wheel. Calloway rethreaded it and rewound it at double speed. He replaced it in the Oxo tin and cued up Film star's diary 2/3.

The projector clack-clacked once more. Joyce winking to the camera in the make-up room mirror. A more confident Joyce this time. The film showed her in a sequence of similar settings as the first, but her demeanour suggested she was in the ascendant. And Spelthorne featured this time. Joyce on his arm and a proprietary look on his face. The studio boss showing off his latest asset.

Calloway replaced the second reel into the tin and let the blind up. He lit a Navy Cut, took a long drag on the hot tobacco and sat back in the chair behind his desk. He closed his eyes and recalled the night of the explosion. It played like a cine film in his mind, silently, the clack-clack of his mental projector the only sound that accompanied it. He saw the face of the woman. Blonde not brunette, older than the Joyce in the home movies, more world-weary. And tougher. The fear Calloway had seen on her face that night was a pragmatic, not vulnerable fear. She didn't want to be seen there, nor seen by him. And it wasn't the face of Joyce Rose. Of course it wasn't. Joyce had been dead for a year or more. Yet the resemblance was too close to be insignificant.

He picked up the small cine camera and left his office, locking the door behind him, then stepped out into the courtyard. A damp mist hung in the air giving the old brewery yard the look of a period melodrama, the kind Centurion made in its early days. He called the commissionaire over as he passed out of the main gates.

'Take this down to the lab when you get a moment. Ask them to bring the developed film up to my office. I'll be back this afternoon.'

'Righto, sir,' the commissionaire said, taking the small box from him.

Calloway jumped a trolley bus and found a seat. He pulled a list from his jacket pocket. It was the list of cleaners that worked weekends with names and addresses. One name and address in particular interested him. He didn't know that neighbourhood, but it wasn't far. He'd checked the AtoZ before leaving his office. The nearest trolley bus stop was a quarter of a mile from the street he was looking for. The neighbourhood had suffered heavy bomb damage. He walked past building sites where new blocks of flats were going up. Homes fit for heroes was the promise. He wasn't convinced. Time would tell. In between the building sites were the remains of Victorian terraces, substantial homes now divided up for multiple occupation. Washing hung out of the widows on makeshift lines. The smell of unappetising cooking billowed from the windows. Kids sat on the steps, scratching their names in the blackened brickwork or seeing how many steps they could jump down without falling onto their dirty hands. Some of the houses still had visible street numbers. Others Calloway had to guess at. He was looking for twenty-seven. The remaining houses were the odd numbers. He found twenty-one, he guessed the next was twenty-three, which it must have been because twenty-five came next. There was no twenty-seven. There had been, once. All that remained was a scattering of brick rubble next to the bare flank wall of the adjacent house. He pulled the list from his pocket and checked just to be sure. He was in the right place. He looked around for any remaining houses but there were none. The rest of the street had been flattened and cleared. A gathering mist billowed over the cratered rubble landscape.

A husky, high-pitched voice said, 'Who are you looking for?'

Two had crept up on him. Both around ten, he reckoned. He gave them a name.

'What's it worth?' one boy said.

Calloway took a shilling from his trouser pocket and flicked it, letting it spin long enough for the boys to see the glint of silver. He snapped it back into his fist.

'A bob,' he said.

'Each?' said the boy, figuring he was onto something.

'Between you,' said Calloway.

The boys conferred.

'Alright,' one said, and held out his grubby hand. Calloway withheld the coin and said, 'So do you know them?'

The boy who'd negotiated the deal grinned at his pal and said, 'Nah, mate. They don't live around here.'

His pal said, 'We'd know. We know everyone.'

Calloway didn't doubt it. They were the type who didn't miss a trick.

'Now give us our fuckin' shilling.'

'Does your dad know you talk like that?' said Calloway.

'My dad's dead. Rommel killed him. I've got his medal,' the foul-mouthed boy said proudly.

'North Africa Star?' said Calloway.

'Yeah,' said the boy. 'D'you want to buy it?'

'Clear off, the pair of you,' said Calloway, handing over the shilling and miming a cuff round the head. The boys sniggered then scarpered.

Calloway checked his watch. It would be opening time in twenty minutes. He jumped a bus to Tottenham Court Road. Smog hung heavy in the air. Visibility was poor. The busses and taxis had their lights on even at this early hour. They lit up the streets like glow worms. Calloway jumped off the bus and headed into North Soho on foot.

The Fitzroy Tavern was a bohemian zoo. A watering hole for charlatans, misfits and flakes. The pub was already filling up ten minutes after opening. A motley collection of drinkers with nowhere else to go. A place to sit, to keep warm, to pass endless time for want of a proper job to go to or a conventional life to live. Others used the libraries, but this place served booze. He ordered a half of Courage and propped up the bar. Spinster twins in their sixties sat immobile at a corner table in a matching ensemble that resembled mourning dress. They looked like they'd been there since Armistice Day. A rakish bachelor, long since past the age it was acceptable to be such, sat on a bar stool in a faded blazer, stained flannels and brown suede brogues that were scuffed to a shine. He sipped at a gin and something like he was making it last till closing time. Three rouged-up good-time girls cackled over port and lemons. They seemed happy to be themselves, without male company to entertain. That would come later. A couple of bums, at least that's what the new slang term for them seemed to be, read matching copies of Being and Nothingness in complete silence, as if oblivious to each other's presence. She had eyes painted black as anthracite and hair that shone like raven feathers. She wore a man's tweed overcoat cinched tight with a worn leather belt. He wore corduroys and a college scarf. He hadn't combed his hair since his last school photograph. Calloway nursed the half pint and watched the place fill up with more human oddities. As he was ordering the other half, the doors flew open. A man entered wearing a Bud Flanagan fur coat and a Nehru hat on his shaved head. The coat was moulting and the hat was askew. He wore old cricket whites and suede chukka boots with thick crepe soles. His eyes were rimmed with a fine line of kohl, although he was in no way feminine. His skin was dark, his race indeterminate, and he was built like a tighthead prop. Half a dozen acolytes followed in his wake. Most were puny and pale. He dispatched one of them to the bar while he commandeered two tables by the window. His booming voice drowned out the muted chatter of the pub and the acolytes hung on every word. He talked poetry and publishing.

Mephisto.

Calloway watched them from the bar. Mephisto held court while the acolytes proffered opinions on TS Eliot, Stephen Spender and Cyril Connolly. He berated them or endorsed them depending on whether their views conformed to his own. They seemed happy with his judgement. He was their intellectual compass.

Calloway took the copy of the poetry review he'd found in Joyce Rose's suitcase from his pocket and walked over to their table.

'Mind if I join you?' he said.

The man in the fur coat glanced up at Calloway as if he couldn't care one way or the other. Then a look which said you could be interesting came over his face. He told an acolyte to budge up and gestured to a chair. Calloway sat. He put the poetry review on the table in front of them.

'I'm taking a guess that you're Mephisto?' he said, pointing a finger at the magazine.

'And you are Dr Faustus,' Mephisto said.

'I'm Calloway. I work at Centurion Studios.'

The acolytes exchanged glances. Mephisto's eyes lit up. 'A film mogul. Will you give me your soul in return for the best story never told?'

'I've heard all the stories,' said Calloway.

He looked Calloway up and down, as if judging him by a set of diabolical criteria. 'I doubt that.'

'I'm not a film mogul. That's a man called Spelthorne. I look after security.'

Mephisto suddenly looked bored. He glanced at the acolytes and rolled his eyes, as if to say why is this inconsequential man wasting my precious time? They gave him knowing looks in return, without really knowing at all.

'I wanted to talk to you about one of the poets you publish. Eve Clark.'

Mephisto thought a moment.

'Evie?' he said, as if recalling a dim memory. The acolytes tried to recall dim memories too. 'And why would you be interested in Evie?'

'I like her poetry.'

Mephisto looked him up and down again and shook his head. 'No, you don't,' he said.

First Marge, now this. What was it about him that looked so

lacking in intellect?

'Alright, I don't. She's a cleaner at the studio and she hasn't shown up for work. We've had some trouble lately.'

Grit in the cameras and water in the lights, found on Mondays after a cleaner called Eve Clark had worked the weekend shift.

'I'm head of security. I'd like to speak to her.'

Mephisto let out a laugh that made heads turn on the bar. 'So Evie Clark's a char lady? How terribly fucking proletarian.'

A voice said, 'How do you think she affords to buy you all those drinks, Phisto? You haven't bought a round since VJ Day.'

He was tall and distinguished, with big bushy hair and strong, chiselled features. He wore a belted tweed jacket and buff twills, with a pair of old brogues that looked like family heirlooms. Mephisto's manner changed. This man didn't defer to him like the acolytes did. In fact Mephisto seemed a little scared of him. The tall man pulled up a chair and put his pint down on the table.

'You're a new face,' he said to Calloway. 'I'm Julian.'

He held out his hand and Calloway shook it.

'Reg,' said Calloway. 'Are you a poet too?'

The tall man shook his head. 'A writer,' he said. 'Novelist.'

'Published?' said Calloway, expecting the answer to be no.

'Some short stories. I'm punting a novel around the houses.'

'Any luck?'

Julian took a sip of the pint. 'A few sniffs. Nothing definite. A bit too soon after the war for what I write.'

'How so?' said Calloway.

'I've based it on my experiences in the army. There's not much glory in it.'

'You're telling me,' said Calloway,

'What were you?' Julian said.

'Intelligence Corps.'

'Ah, a rampant pansy resting on its laurels.'

It sounded like poetry but Calloway knew it wasn't. It was army slang for the Intelligence Corps cap badge, with its red rose and two laurel branches.

'I was light infantry.'

'An Arfur,' said Calloway. The light infantry had 'alf a cap badge', because it lacked the usual crown and laurels

Julian nodded. He said, 'Does your studio normally send its head of security when a cleaner goes AWOL?'

'We've had a couple of incidents. Damaged equipment discovered after Eve Clark's shift. She's not the only one we want to talk to. There were others on the shift.'

But Eve was the only one published in a poetry magazine that Joyce Rose had kept as a memento.

'Does she drink in here?'

Julian nodded. 'Sometimes. Quite often, actually. And she normally stands Phisto a round or two. He's a total scrounger. Completely shameless. I don't think he's eaten a meal or drunk a pint in his life that someone else hasn't paid for. That's how he lives.'

Mephisto had turned his back to the two big men and was playing to his crowd at the other end of the table. He dispatched two of them to the bar. They rifled through their pockets trying to piece together the price of a round from loose change.

'Why don't you call on Evie at her place?'

'I did,' said Calloway. 'Her place has been a hole in the ground since the Blitz.'

Julian looked confused and shook his head. 'Eve has a flat off Goodge Street. Well, just a room really, with a how's-yer-father on the landing shared by the rest of the inmates. Horrible place, but a good spot.'

'Do you know the address?'

Julian looked hesitant. 'I don't want to get the old girl in trouble.'

'Are you friends?'

'Barely, but she's a good sort. She started coming here a year or so ago. She'd been living in France, writing. She fell in with this crowd of charlatans,' he waved a large dismissive hand towards Mephisto and his acolytes, 'but I don't think she completely likes them. She's certainly not in the thrall of him, like the others. I think she saw them as a route to being published. His poetry review is one of the few outlets for this new generation.'

'I just want to talk to her,' said Calloway.

Julian thought it over. 'Alright,' he said. 'Just so you can eliminate her from your enquiries, as they say.'

'You read detective fiction?'

'I do. Not the chintzy country house rubbish. The new American stuff. It's raw. It's honest.' He glanced over at the man in the fur coat and Nehru hat with a hint of disdain. 'Of course, snobs like Phisto dismiss it out of hand.'

Julian pulled a fountain pen from the inside pocket of his tweed jacket and wrote an address on a beer mat.

'I'd be very surprised if she's got anything to do with this trouble your investigating,' he said. 'Like I say, she's a good sort.'

A good sort who gave a false address when she took the cleaning job.

Calloway pocketed the beer mat.

He nodded towards Julian's empty glass. 'Buy you another?'

Julian shook his head. 'Don't bother. I can't buy you one back and I don't have Phisto's lack of scruples.'

Mephisto was berating an acolyte loud enough for the whole pub to hear him. It was something he seemed to enjoy.

FIFTEEN

The address Julian had given him was a corner building with a pawn shop on the ground floor and three pairs of filthy windows above. Next to the pawn shop window, with its wedding rings and wristwatches, was a side door whose peeling brown paint and cracked panels left no doubt as to the state of the rooms above. Calloway pressed the bell. An angry buzz sounded from behind the door, followed by stumbling footsteps on bare wooden stairs. The door opened and a sleepy-looking youth with unkept hair and a dressing gown over his jumper and corduroys said, 'Yes?'

He sounded vague, still half asleep. 'Who do you want?' he said in the accent of someone not born to these shabby surroundings. He sounded like one of Mephisto's acolytes. A well-bred brat that was slumming it. He looked at his wrist for a watch that wasn't there.

'Do you have the time?' he asked.

'Almost two. Sorry to wake you. I'm looking for Eve Clark.'

'Eve?' the youth said, yawning. 'Wait there a moment.'

He climbed the stairs. Calloway heard knocking on a first-floor door and Eve's name called several times. There was no reply. The boy descended the stairs.

'Evie's out I'm afraid. Can I take a message?'

'Do you know where she is?'

He shrugged and said, 'At work, I suppose.'

Calloway knew she wasn't. It wasn't her shift.

'Tell her Reg Calloway from the studio wants to speak to her. Tell her I'll call again this evening. Can you remember that?'

The boy ran a skinny hand through the mop of blonde hair

above his fine-boned face and nodded.

Calloway returned to the studio. Giordano, Spelthorne's personal security goon, was leaning against the big iron gates, a cigarette between his thumb and forefinger. His suit was as sharp as his boss's, but with more muscle inside it. He narrowed his eyes as Calloway approached and flicked the butt into the gutter.

'Where've you been?' he said.

'Looking for McCaffrey,' Calloway lied.

'So did you find him?'

'If I did I'd be handing him over to your boss right now.'

'Sounds like you should look harder.'

'Why don't you try looking for him?'

'Not my job.'

'That's right. Because your boss told me you don't have the brains for it.'

'Don't push your luck.'

'Then don't waste my time.'

'We fucking own your time.'

'In that case, get out of my way. I've got work to do.'

Giordano put a palm like a side of beef on Calloway's chest and said, 'You need to wait here. Boss wants a word.'

Calloway heard tyres rumbling over the cobbles of the studio courtyard. The snout of a Bentley poked round the gates. A newer model than the car the bomb destroyed with a new number plate: CP2. The Bentley pulled up alongside Calloway and the window wound down. Spelthorne looked up at him from inside and said, 'Come for a little ride'.

It was an instruction not an invitation. Calloway opened the passenger door and climbed in beside Spelthorne. Giordano took the passenger seat. Franco was driving. He had big hands too.

Spelthorne wound up the window and stroked the lacquered walnut trim of the Bentley's door, as if stroking the face of a new girlfriend.

'New car, Mr Spelthorne?' said Calloway.

Spelthorne smiled. It wasn't friendly

'Yeah, funnily enough,' he said. 'Someone put a bomb under

the last one when my head of security was tucked up in his fucking bed. You felt that big Mick's collar yet?'

Calloway shook his head. 'He's gone to ground. He's not daft. He'll know the police will want to talk to him and if he does have the connections they say he has, they're the last people he'll want to run into. He'll be across the Irish Sea by now. Or halfway to Boston.'

Spelthorne tutted and shook his head.

'Sounds like you'll be looking for a new job then, son,' he said.

'With respect, sir, I can't find a man that's done a bunk abroad. Unless you want to pay my passage across the Atlantic.'

Spelthorne gazed out of the window, weighing up whether the return would justify the investment. Calloway needed to buy time. If he lost his job now, there would be no way he could stay at the studio long enough to find a bone to throw Special Branch. A bone that would get Bernie and her friends with guns off his back. He took a chance and played the Eve Clark card.

'I'm following another lead,' he said.

Spelthorne looked confused. 'What other lead?'

'Something that connects a studio employee to the damaged equipment.'

This piqued Spelthorne's interest. 'Which studio employee?'

'If I tell you there's a risk they'll do a runner too, and then we'll be no further forward.'

'And you think the damaged equipment is connected to the bomb under my car?'

'I don't know. But I want to look into things further. See if the pieces connect.'

Calloway gathered the evidence in his mind, as if to convince himself that what he'd just told Spelthorne might possibly hold water. There was the woman fleeing the dinner after the explosion, so keen to avoid Calloway, the head of studio security. A woman that bore a striking resemblance to the dead actress Joyce Rose, who kept a copy of a poetry magazine featuring a poet who was also a cleaner at the studio. A cleaner that worked shifts on the weekends before damage to expensive studio equipment was discovered the following Monday.

'Alright,' said Spelthorne. 'You carry on for now, but if you don't bring me something...' he grappled for a word, '...something meaningful, then our deal still stands.'

Before Calloway could enjoy a tiny moment of relief, Spelthorne added, 'Giordano and Franco will be keeping an eye on you for me. You don't mind, do you?'

Another question that wasn't a question at all. Spelthorne wasn't the type that sought approval.

'As you wish, sir,' said Calloway. The 'sir' hurt. 'Actually, I've been meaning to ask something. A security question, if you will. Why do you feel the need for...'

This time Calloway grappled for a word. A word that wasn't goon or gorilla.

'Private security,' he said, nodding at the two knuckle heads that were filling the front of the far from small car. 'What are you afraid of?'

There was a silence, a big hostile silence. Calloway half expected to be turfed out of the car there and then. Possibly without it stopping first. Spelthorne sighed. He turned to Calloway and smiled a tolerant smile, like it was costing more than he wanted to spend on it.

'Not all of us inherited our father's industrial empire like J Arthur Rank,' he said. 'I was raised six to a bed in a hovel off Saffron Hill. My family were Maltese immigrants. Do you know Saffron Hill, Reg?' Calloway shook his head. He'd lived in London less than a year, only three months of that north of the river. 'It's a shit hole. And a lot of the boys from that shit hole have ended up on the wrong side of the law. You must have read the papers.' Calloway nodded. 'That bloke Azzopardi that's just been put away? I grew up with him. And you know what? I reckon he deserves all he gets.' He pointed at Franco and Giordano. 'You want to know why I keep those two dogs close at heel? I'll tell you. I've made a lot of money, Reg. The kind of money boys like Azzopardi and the rest of them would love to get their hands on. Giordano and Franco are there to make sure they don't. You asked what I was afraid of? Try extortion, perhaps even kidnapping. I wouldn't put anything past them.'

He turned away and looked out of the window. They were passing through a bombed-out area to the east of the city. Two tramps with smoke-blackened faces were burning a brazier in the knee-high remains of what could have once been a townhouse. It wasn't especially cold. They just needed a reason to be somewhere that wasn't an alley or a doorway. Some place they could call theirs, in that moment of time.

'I've got where I am the hard way,' said Spelthorne. 'I didn't even have an education, not like that Jewboy Balcon over at Ealing. At least he had some schooling.' He laughed to himself. 'I started out as a stand-up comedian in third-rate variety halls.' He looked at Calloway. 'You can't imagine that, can you?'

Calloway couldn't. Spelthorne didn't strike him as a barrel of laughs. Especially when he was holding the threat of, at best, unemployment and, at worst, a difficult conversation with Giordano and Franco.

'I was the warm-up man for the foot jugglers and the female impersonators. I wasn't the best on the circuit, I have to admit. And I realised it was a mug's game. The club owners were the ones making the money. So I quit. I borrowed a few quid and opened my first club. We had blue comedians and fan dancers. Very pretty girls they were. The punters loved 'em. Soldiers, sailors, travelling salesmen. All sorts. Just wanting a bit of harmless fun. After a while I noticed the boys would hang around the stage door after the show had finished, asking the girls for autographs. Autographs, yeah. Like they were Hollywood stars. Well, I thought, there's an angle here. So I started a sideline selling photographs of the girls. Very artistic they were,' he said, as if hearing Calloway's thoughts out loud. 'We started making as much money from the photographs as we did on the door. I ended up selling the club and building up the pin-up business. I bought a little studio off Dean Street and went out looking for the prettiest girls in Soho. I paid 'em a proper fee,' he said, sensing Calloway's unvoiced thoughts again. He was in his stride now. He shifted on the leather seat to face Calloway. 'Now I'm ambitious. Well you can see that, can't you?' he said, waving a hand around the brand-new Bentley. 'So I expanded into films. Little 8mm reels of fan dancers. Nothing tasteless, just a bit of tease. I did pretty well, what with the films and the photo sets. That's when I started feeling the heat. You start selling films and sooner or later the vice boys at West End Central start taking an interest. Now I wasn't crossing the line, hand on heart. But I still got grief I could have done without. Then,' he said, 'in nineteen twenty-seven, I had a stroke of luck. The Cinematograph Films Act.' He spoke the words in proper RP. 'It required cinemas to show a quota of British films. The yanks had too much hold on the market and the act was supposed to prop up the British film industry. The films didn't even have to be any good. They just had to be made over here. I thought if I can sell fan dancers I can sell something with a few more clothes on. Especially in a market where the supply and demand equation was in my favour. And it would certainly keep the vice boys off my back. So I traded up the studio to something bigger, moved from 8mm to 35mm, got some old frocks from Angels & Bermans and started making historical romances. I already had a stable of pretty girls and some of 'em could act.' He reflected a moment. 'Well, they could at least deliver a few lines while looking the part. I advertised for writers, and there's no shortage of those needing a hot meal. Then someone introduced me to Roberta.' Bobbie Brand, the director in Joyce's home movies. 'She'd been making silent films, but since the talkies came in, she couldn't get the work. Not for love nor money. The studios didn't want women directors once the stakes were raised. Didn't trust 'em to be good enough. But I didn't have any choice. I was a nobody. So I offered her a job and she bit my hand off. She directed my first production.'

Spelthorne gazed out of the car window, remembering, with a satisfied look on his face. He turned to Calloway and pointed at him, as if accusing him of an unspoken criticism.

'Now others will tell you that the quickie was the lowest form of the film maker's art. Turned out as a necessity with no care or attention. The yanks would fund them just so they could get their Hollywood stuff in British cinemas. Some of them were so bad they didn't bother advertising. They used to screen 'em at breakfast time until the magistrates put the block on that. People in this business will say no one made a penny out of quickies. Not true.' He prodded his chest. 'I did. Yeah, I did alright. How? I took 'em seriously. Granted, the first few weren't so good. I was still using show girls as leading ladies. They couldn't act for shit, if I'm honest. But then I started getting some decent actors. Like Neville Wilde. You know him?'

Calloway did. Since taking the job, he'd dispatched a succession of women home in cabs who'd found themselves abandoned in Wilde's dressing room in a state of post-coital ambiguity.

'That boy Wilde was on his uppers when I spotted him. I knew the club scene, you see, and I knew he was selling himself at dance halls to middle-aged women whose husbands had long since lost interest in them. But Bobbie told me he was good. She remembered him from the theatre in the twenties. So I got him on contract. He still put it about with the old birds now and again, mind you. I guess he'd just got a taste for it.' Giordano sniggered. His big shoulders moved in time with his laughter. 'I got some good writers too. You can always get them cheap but you need to get the good ones. Terence Rattigan, Eric Ambler, Noël Coward? They've all written for Centurion. And I'd got Bobbie. Now she may be a girl, but she's a real asset. Knows her craft. She can make a better picture for ten grand than other studios can make for fifty. The other studios? They were spending three times what I was on quickies and not making a penny. I was making real money. I knew where to get the talent cheap and...' He paused for a moment and looked Calloway in the eye. 'Now this is really important. I knew the audience. They don't want to go out and watch high art. They want escape. In fact half of 'em just want three hours in a heated room with velvet seats.' He tapped his chest again. 'I know poverty, you see. I've lived it. I know what it means to seek respite from the squalor. Warmth, velvet seats and something just engaging enough to take their minds off the drudgery of life. That's what I sell, Calloway. Not dreams, or whimsies. I offer them escape.'

He pulled a cigar from his breast pocket and passed it to

Giordano. The big goon unclasped a knife, the kind that's far too big for sharpening pencils, and cut the nub off before passing it back to his boss. Spelthorne lit up and sank back into the soft upholstery, in a cloud of his own smoke.

'A stroke of luck, a lot of hard graft and here I am,' he said.

He drew on the cigar and rolled the smoke around his puffy cheeks.

'And no fucker, Maltese, Irish or otherwise, is going to take it off me.'

SIXTEEN

The Bentley rumbled over cobbles in a narrow side street somewhere near Tooley Street. They drove alongside the high warehouse walls which cast long shadows across the road in the fading light. Franco turned off the road towards a set of dock gates. A Port of London policeman recognised the car and waved them through. Franco steered the Bentley between wharfside buildings towards the quay.

The Pool of London. The black heart of London docks through which flowed the flotsam and jetsam of six continents. Seamen from Marseille to Macao. Transient and rootless. At home in any port, yet strangers where they dock. All nations, all races. Liberians, Lascars and Latvians. Saint Lucians, Swedes and Senegalese. Hardened by the sea, loosened by drink, quick with their fists. And the dockers. Local men with a strict code. A law unto themselves. The pulsating arteries of the black market.

The Bentley looked incongruous. Franco parked and the four men climbed out. Spelthorne slipped a ten-bob note to a docker to mind the car. He looked up at the big dock crane that loomed over them.

'Don't go dropping any bales on it,' he said.

Calloway followed the three men along the quayside. Lights shone ahead of them. Then he saw the cameras. Cast and crew on location. Shooting at night. Bobbie Brand was wearing a sheepskin coat over heavy tweed trousers, with warm wool socks tucked into hacking boots. She conferred with the camera operator, peered through the range finder, consulted with the continuity girl. Calloway recognised the girl. Her name was Liz Francis. He knew her from his last job. She'd helped him, and in return he'd handed her a decent sum of money that she was owed. She'd used it to start a new life. She deserved one. She'd had more than her share of knocks. This life looked good for her. She looked up and saw him. She smiled and waved. Bobbie Brand dismissed her and returned to the set. Liz walked over to Calloway, beaming.

'Hello you,' she said.

'Hello you too,' he said.

She gave him a polite peck on the cheek.

'So how's the job going?' she said.

Liz had tipped him off that Centurion needed a new security boss. That was a few months back. Calloway was more than grateful. Liz said she owed him that at least. He'd not seen her since though.

'It's three months in and I'm still here,' he said. But for how much longer, he thought. 'Is this The Rebel Gun?'

He gestured towards the cluster of bodies under the harsh lighting.

She nodded. 'The continuity girl went sick so I got the job. I'd been pestering Bobbie long enough. She asked me if I'd fill in.'

'Going well?'

'I'm a bag of nerves,' she said.

'You look like you know what you're doing.'

She laughed. 'Well that's a start, eh?'

She fished in the pocket of her coat and pulled out a pack of Craven A. She offered Calloway one and lit up for the pair of them.

'So what brings you here?' she said. 'I see you got a ride in Sidney's car.'

'The perks of the job,' he said.

Perks that came at a price, he thought. He glanced over at his boss. Spelthorne was conferring with Bobbie Brand. They perched side by side on canvas chairs marked Director and Producer. Spelthorne had a cigar in one hand and a hip flask in the other. He took a nip without offering one to Bobbie.

Bright lights shone on the freighter moored along the quayside in front of them. One of the stars of The Rebel Gun stood on the gang plank with a kit bag on his shoulder. He was dressed in a reefer jacket and watch cap. He was skinny and fey. He made an unconvincing seaman. Bobbie Brand was discussing the composition of the scene, gesticulating and shouting instruction to the cameraman. The assistant director scurried back and forth between Bobbie and the engineers in the sound van. Another man was measuring the distance between the actors and the camera's lens with a tape measure. Bobbie returned to her chair. The microphone on its boom swung into place over the lot. The clapper boy positioned himself between the camera and the actor. Bobbie shouted, 'Roll 'em!' The clapper boy called out the scene number and snapped the clapper shut. The fey-looking actor stumbled on the gang plank, dropped his kitbag and swore. Bobbie shouted, 'Cut!'

'I reckon you're better off on this side of the camera,' Calloway said.

'Well I was never going to get anywhere on the other side, let's face it.'

When Calloway first met Liz, she'd just dropped out of the Centurion charm school. To him, the continuity job sounded preferable to a life spent parading around Ivor Cole's publicity pageants.

'Did you know Joyce Rose at the charm school?' he said.

'Joyce?' she said. His question seemed incongruous and she frowned. 'Why d'you want to know about Joyce?'

'She's connected to something I'm looking into. A problem at the studio. I'm not sure how she fits in exactly, but there are some coincidences I need explanations for.' He took a long draw on the cigarette. The tobacco tingled his nerves. He exhaled and said, 'It's not like she's around to ask.'

'No she isn't, poor cow. Whatever possessed her to do what she did?'

'From what I've read in the press reports, she was in quite a state in the months leading to her death. Living off pills and hard liquor. So did you know her?'

She looked concerned. 'You're not getting involved again, are you?'

She knew enough about his last job to know that he was the type that got in deeper than was good for him.

'It's fine,' he said, not at all sure that it was. 'Just studio business.'

'If you say so, Reggie,' she said, looking dubious.

She took a last drag on the cigarette and threw the butt into the dock. 'Joyce and I crossed over at the charm school for a couple of months. She was getting ready to leave when I joined. She'd just got her first role.' She laughed. 'She was one of the few girls that actually appeared in a film.'

She pulled her coat collar tight. It was dark now and the damp air was cold. She took his arm and they walked along the dock edge.

'She was Spelthorne's favourite,' she said.

'He seems to like a starlet on his arm.'

Liz shook her head. 'Joyce was different. She was his special one. He took her everywhere. Premiers, gala dinners, parties. He had the cigars, he had the car, he had the whole studio. Joyce completed the look.'

'Were they lovers?'

Liz thought for a moment. 'You know, I was never really sure. I suppose I just assumed so, at least at first. Especially given his fondness for having pretty girls on his arm, as you so delicately put it.'

Calloway felt a twinge of awkwardness as they walked arm in arm. She sensed this and looked up at him.

'This is different. We're pals,' she said and gave him a friendly nudge. 'Thinking about it, I'm not sure anything was going on. Joyce didn't seem the type. She was always slightly aloof. Focused on the job, you know. Especially when she got her break on her first film. Some of the girls just go along with it. Like it's expected of them. Especially the needy ones. The ones whose insecurities get the better of their judgement.'

She read his thoughts.

'Yeah. The ones like me,' she said.

He gave her arm a squeeze. 'We've all got pasts Liz. Now you've got a future, if you play your cards right. I reckon Bobbie likes you.'

She held up crossed fingers. 'Here's hoping.'

They walked for a moment in silence. It was dark now and they were in a quiet part of the docks. A steam whistle sounded in the distance. Liz shivered with the cold and leant into him.

'Did Joyce have any family, apart from the parents she lost in the war?' he said.

Liz thought about this for a moment. 'She mentioned once that she had a sister. She lived in France, I think.'

'A sister called Yvonne?'

The name on the postcards from Paris.

'That rings a bell.'

A sister in Paris. Where Eve Clark lived until eighteen months ago. Another coincidence that brought him no closer to an explanation.

'Did you ever meet the sister?'

'No. I hardly knew Joyce to be honest.'

'Ever see her later, when she was going off the rails?'

She shook her head. 'I'd quit the charm school by then. All I know is what was in the papers.'

They'd done a circuit of the wharfside and were now walking back towards the cast and crew. The cameras were running. Bobbie Brand sat in the director's chair, her eyes fixed on the action. Two actors were playing out their scene on the quay while their tall shadows danced on the rust-streaked hulk of the freighter. Calloway noticed that Spelthorne's Bentley was gone. He swore under his breath.

'Looks like you're making your own way back,' said Liz.

Bobbie Brand shot Liz a look which said get yourself over here. Liz gave her a quick, apologetic nod.

'I've got to go,' she said.

Calloway looked at his watch. There was just time to get back to the studio to check whether the cine film from Joyce Rose's camera had been processed before he returned to North Soho.

'It's been good to see you, Liz. I'm glad to see things starting to work out for you.'

She squeezed his arm. 'It's all thanks to you Reg. Without that money you passed me I'd still be holed up in that tenement on the Old Kent Road. Now I've got my own bedsit north of the river. Who knows, I might even make a go of all this,' she said, nodding towards Bobbie and the crew before giving him another peck on the cheek.

He walked out of the dockyard, down Tooley Street and over Tower Bridge towards Wapping Wall. The sky was black and the meagre street lighting ineffective against the darkness. He entered Wapping station and descended the dark, spiralling staircase, with its dripping brick walls lit by flashes of electricity from the electrified rails of the East London Line below. If Centurion ever made a horror movie, they should film it here, he thought. He rode the line until it terminated at Shoreditch, then walked through the chill to the studio. The main gates were locked. He let himself in the small side entrance that the big stars used to avoid the crowds out front. The cobbled yard of the old brewery was empty, the cars of the more senior staff gone for the evening. Studios A and B were dark, filming stopped for the day or, in the case of The Rebel Gun, on location down at the docks. The only sound was the eternal hum of the six diesel generators in the powerhouse.

His footsteps echoed along the corridor of the now empty administration building. There was a light on behind the door of his office. There shouldn't have been. He'd left the studio in daylight. He listened at the door. A faint scratching sound came from inside. He clasped his hand around the door handle slowly, swearing under his breath as the lock clicked loudly in the silence. The scratching behind the door stopped. He heard light footsteps. He braced himself, then gave the door a shove and stepped inside. A hand grabbed his wrist and twisted his arm until he felt his elbow joint was about to snap. He doubled over with the pain and felt a sharp chop to his forearm and again to his upper arm. He cried out in anticipation of his bones snapping. He took a harder blow to the back of the neck and another to his kidneys. The pain was intense, like his nerves were being stripped from inside him. He couldn't think. He hadn't the strength in that moment to respond. He slumped to the ground and lay on his side, doubled with pain. Then he took a boot in his guts which made the bile rise in his throat until he choked. He forced his eyes open to see his assailant, but they were gone, their swift footsteps echoing down the empty corridor. He tried to raise himself from the floor, but he couldn't summon the strength. He lay back, limp, and let the black cloak of unconsciousness engulf him.

He lifted his arm as best he could and checked his watch. He'd been out cold for half an hour. He checked the arm for a break. It was in still in one piece. He raised himself onto his hands and knees and cried out as a searing pain shot through his kidneys and neck simultaneously. Whoever had clobbered him knew what they were doing. Once on his feet he limped over to his desk. The drawer was still locked. A pair of lock-picking tools lay on the floor beneath it. Whoever he'd interrupted had not had the chance to get the drawer open. He pulled out his keys. Pain shot up his arm and he winced. He unlocked the drawer, gritting his teeth. The purse the fleeing woman had dropped on the night of the explosion was still there. So were the cine films and the bottle of Black & White. He pulled out the stopper and drank from the bottle. The warm liquor soothed him. He sat back in his chair. The hard wooden chair back pressed into his kidneys. He let out a squeal. Damn them. Whoever the hell they were, they were fucking experts. He swallowed down more of the scotch, trying to make sense of things.

What had the intruder wanted? The films? They were innocuous enough. The purse? There was nothing in that you wouldn't expect. He pulled the purse from the drawer and emptied its contents. Everything was there, just as before. Lipstick, compact, mirror, handkerchief, a little cash and the tortoise shell pencil. He ran his fingers around the lining of the purse, thinking there may have been a compartment or opening of some kind. But there was nothing. He scooped everything back into the drawer and locked it. Twisting the key hurt his wrist. Lifting the whisky bottle hurt his forearm. Leaning back in the chair hurt his kidneys and his neck felt like someone had yanked out both his collar bones and tied them in a knot. It was a miracle, or at least a testament to his thick hide, that nothing was broken.

He swallowed down more of the scotch. He didn't hurt any less, but he felt better. He eased himself out of the chair, switched off the desk lamp and left the office, locking the door behind him. There was no point making a search of the studio. Whoever had floored him would be long gone. He abandoned the idea of returning to Eve Clark's North Soho digs and took a bus home. The bus rumbled over cobbles and jolted at potholes, its every movement hurting Calloway somewhere. He alighted at Kingsland Road and walked to Da Costa's factory. Climbing the three flights of bare concrete steps to his attic room was an endeavour. If they ever conquered Everest, the last hundred feet couldn't feel worse than this, he thought.

Once inside the room he lit the gas fire, poured a hefty measure of gin into the tooth mug and collapsed onto the iron bed. The springs creaked under his weight. The sound they made was how his bones and muscles felt. Through the pain he tried again to make sense of events over the last few days.

Bernie and her republican friends weren't the bombers. He had figured that much, even if Special Branch hadn't. He couldn't shake the thought that the woman who'd dropped the purse was the key to everything. The dead actress, the postcards from France, the poet-turned-cleaner and the damaged studio equipment. Instinct told him they were all connected.

Sleep tugged at his eyelids. The air was warm and dry, the gas fire sucking the oxygen from the room. He tried to rearrange the pieces into a pattern that made more sense, but the gin he'd gulped from the tooth mug conspired with fatigue from the beating to drag him into an uncomfortable sleep.

SEVENTEEN

They stood at the southern end of Kingsland High Street. Calloway, Marge, Johnny and around thirty members of the 43 Group. A real tough-looking mob. Two ex-commandos, three paras, a burly chief petty officer and a platoon's worth of ex-soldiers, sailors and airmen. Johnny introduced Calloway to some of his comrades. There was Reg Morris, an ex-guardsman who was so good looking he worked as a stand-in for Stewart Granger. There were the Goldberg brothers, a tough and intimidating pair who were veterans of pre-war battles against the Mosleyites. And there was a neat and keen-eyed youth who worked as an apprentice hairdresser called Vidal Sassoon.

'You want to watch Sassoon,' Johnny said to Calloway. 'Always carries a pair of scissors.'

The lad patted his breast pocket and winked at Calloway.

Two dozen locals had also turned out in support, including a formidable-looking man known only as Big Arthur. The East End was the fascists' stomping ground but there were plenty there who'd sooner see the back of them.

Calloway still hurt from the beating. A street fight was the last thing he needed. But something compelled him to be there. It wasn't Marge this time. She hadn't needed to persuade him. When she told him about the next fascist meeting, he'd said he would be there without a second thought. Whether it was memories of the camp stirred up by that article, or the ease at which Spelthorne made Jewboy comments about his competitors, he couldn't tell. He felt it was right to be there, plain and simple. But no, he thought, it was more than that. He was feeling the pressure, from Bryant, Bernie, Franco and Giordano.

The pressure needed an outlet. He knew himself well enough to know it was only a matter of time before the pressure turned to anger and anger turned to violence. That's how he was. It wasn't good to be around him when it happened. He hated himself for it, but he knew no way to avoid it. If the violence broke through at the wrong time or with the wrong person, he'd be in deeper trouble than he was already. Tonight seemed as good an opportunity as any to get it out of his system.

He'd met Johnny and a few of the group members in Lyons Corner House. That's where they always did their planning so that they looked innocuous. A handful of pals meeting for coffee. Johnny suggested tactics. The others had agreed. This time Calloway would lead the first wedge. First in, he thought. Johnny's wedge would follow up once the podium was upturned.

Jeffrey Hamm was on the stage, a repeat performance of his last speech in full flow, only this time he was upping the ante. Instead of euphemisms for the targets of his hate, he was coming straight out with it, showing true colours as he stood between the union jacks that flanked the stage. He spoke of the Great Jewish Plot, the Jewish terrorists killing 'our boys' in Palestine and the need to break the hold of the Jews running Britain.

A fascist in the crowd shouted, 'Let's finish what Hitler started.'

Johnny turned to Calloway. 'Can you fucking believe this?' he said. 'It's like we fought six years for nothing.'

'It wasn't for nothing,' said Calloway. 'But it looks like we didn't finish the job.'

Johnny clapped him on the back. Calloway should have winced. The bruising from the beating had come up badly overnight, but adrenalin must have been surprising the pain.

'Ready?' said Johnny.

Calloway nodded. He looked into the eyes of every man in his wedge. There were thumbs-up all round.

They went in hard, shoving Hamm's supporters over like a wrecking ball through a bomb-site wall and thumping them as they toppled. Hamm hesitated as the wave of fascists parted and Calloway's wedge advanced. But he resumed his rant, whether through bravado or stupidity Calloway couldn't tell. There was only one way this was going to end, he thought, and Hamm would wish he'd jumped from the platform sooner. Why was he standing there shouting and looking smug? Then Calloway heard a scream. The kind of scream he'd not heard since the war. He looked to his left and saw one of his wedge, the burly chief petty officer, clutching his bleeding face. Another scream, this time to his right. One of the ex-commandos had stopped on his tracks. Blood gushed from a three-inch gash on his face. He was looking round, eager to get his hands on a fascist with a blade, but there was none to be seen. This time Calloway felt it. A sharp nick to the side of his head, an inch or so from his eye. Moments before he'd seen something scudding towards him from the direction of the stage. Now he saw the attackers. Behind the platform big men in sharp suits were hurling potatoes with razor blades stuck in them. Dirty bastards. Calloway's wedge and Johnny's behind them were taking heavy casualties. There was blood everywhere and it wasn't fascist blood. Hamm's supporters had thinned out, as if the whole operation was orchestrated. He heard Johnny shout, 'Get the fuck out of here.' He was about to turn and run when he saw two faces he recognised.

Giordano and Franco.

Spelthorne's two goons were part of the mob throwing blades. Calloway froze. It didn't make sense. Two worlds had collided. Spelthorne's and Hamm's. Why should they connect? He heard Johnny shout, 'Cab. Get your wedge out of here.'

The two wedges ran down Ridley Road away from their attackers. Some of the fascists pursued them, but not many. The rest seemed happy to let the men with the blades do the dirty work. Two Black Marias appeared ahead of them. Their doors flew open and two dozen police ran towards them, whistles blowing and truncheons raised.

'Double back and head down Dalston Lane,' Johnny shouted. This took them headlong into the half dozen fascists pursuing them. The two wedges set about them hard. Their blood was up. So was Calloway's. The switch had flicked. He grabbed one by the lapels and butted him so hard the sound of his nose breaking echoed off the walls. He smacked the fascist's chin up with the flat of his hand and planted his knee in his groin, just like he'd been trained. The fascist slumped to the pavement clutching his balls. Calloway kicked him hard in the kidneys. The fascist bellowed in pain. Then he summoned courage. From the ground where he lay he shouted up at Calloway, defiant.

'Wir kommen wieder!'

We will be back.

The accent was guttural Bavarian. Calloway had interrogated enough enemy prisoners to know. For a second he was confused. His past enveloped him. He was at war again. He raised his boot and stamped hard on the German's face.

'Reg,' shouted Johnny. 'Transport. Let's go.'

Three taxi cabs were heading towards them down Dalston Lane. Marge stood on the running board of one of them, clinging to the cab with one hand and beckoning Calloway, Johnny and their boys with the other. They piled into the three cabs, which each turned on a sixpence and headed east towards Dalston Junction. When they were clear of the action, he heard Marge shout, 'Pull over, Solly.' The cab driver obeyed the instruction and Marge climbed in the back of the taxi.

'Room for a little one?' she said.

She squeezed into the back seat next to Calloway.

'What the fuck was that all about?' said Johnny.

'Ted just got word from our man,' said Marge.

Ted Nathan, one of the group's intelligence officers. He'd been at the briefing in Lyons Corner House. 'Our man' was one of the group's agents.

'The boys with the blades were from a Maltese gang,' she said. 'Hired muscle.'

A Maltese gang. The very people Spelthorne employed Giordano and Franco to protect him from.

'Maltese?' said Johnny. 'Are they Hamm's supporters?'

'Ted reckons not,' said Marge. 'He says the Italian fascists supported the pro-Italians in Malta before the war, but there's no evidence of London's Maltese having fascist affiliations. They were just guns for hire.'

'Spuds for hire more like,' said one of the wedge, holding a handkerchief to his face to stem the flow of blood. Everyone laughed. It broke the tension.

Calloway said, 'One of the fascists was German.'

The others showed little surprise. Marge said, 'He'll be a POW from the camp in Victoria Park, most likely. The fascists sometimes set up on the corner of Gore Road to tap up the inmates when they're let out in the evenings.'

'Some of them were Waffen SS,' said Johnny. 'There's supposed to be a de-Nazification programme in the camp.' In the darkness of the taxi Calloway saw Johnny roll his eyes. 'Yeah,' he said. 'Like that's gonna work. The fascists are recruiting them. They've been turning up to the meetings for a few months now.'

Calloway shook his head. It was too much. British fascists and German Nazis, in London, side by side. Swastikas daubed on local walls, Nazi stickers on shop windows. Beatings and fire bombings. Six years of fucking war and now this, in his adopted neighbourhood. He shifted in his seat and winced. He remembered that he hurt all over. And now he had a gash on the side of his head.

Marge read his pain.

'Let's have a look,' she said, taking the hand he was using to press a handkerchief to the wound and pulling it away gently. She peered at the wound. 'You'll live,' she said. 'But you need to get that cleaned up. Then I'll find you a part as a Prussian officer and we can pretend it's a duelling scar.'

'You'd make a good Prussian, I reckon,' said Johnny. 'All straight backed and strait laced.'

'Someone's got to be,' said Calloway. 'This world's more rotten than ever.'

'You can say that again,' said Johnny.

The cab turned off Dalston Lane into Kingsland Road.

'Do you have any iodine?' said Marge, looking at Calloway.

'I think so,' he said.

He had what was left of a first aid kit somewhere.

She tapped on the glass behind the driver. 'Drop us here, Solly,' she shouted. 'I'm going to help patch up Reg.'

‘Alright for some,’ said one of the group, from the darkness on the cab.

Marge took his arm as they walked into the narrow cobbled lane. There were no lights on in Da Costa’s factory ahead of them. The machinists had clocked off for the night. She nuzzled into him as they walked through the gloom of the lone street lamp.

‘I’m sorry I got you onto all this,’ she said.

‘You didn’t,’ he said. ‘I got myself into it. And don’t be sorry. What you and your group are doing needs to be done. I know. I’ve seen where this leads if it’s not stopped. Like Johnny said, never again.’

‘The Maltese gang is a new twist,’ she said.

‘Hamm and his boys are rattled. It means what you’re doing is working.’

‘What we’re doing,’ she said, correcting him.

They stood in front of Da Costa’s door.

‘This is your place, isn’t it?’

‘I’m three floors up and there’s not much to look forward to when you get there,’ he said. ‘I’ve got a bottle of gin and a tooth mug. The tooth mug tastes of cloves.’

‘I adore cloves,’ she said.

‘I’m quite keen on gin. Especially after a night like tonight.’

Their footsteps echoed off the bare brick walls as they climbed the darkened stairway. Marge held his arm tightly. He unlocked the door to his attic room and flicked on the light. For the first time he saw the room through another’s eyes. It was dismal. A single bare bulb hung from the ceiling casting a dingy glow over old utility furniture. His two suits and best overcoat hung on hooks in an alcove. There were no pictures on the walls, no ornaments, no personal touches. Even a barrack room had pin-ups. Calloway’s attic had nothing. It wasn’t damp, being so high up, but the cold air smelled faintly of gas from the fire and coal tar soap from the bar he washed with over the old stone sink. The only sign of any pride in his surroundings was the presence of a pair of worn but highly polished leather shoes that stood beside his bed. He felt Marge shudder.

'I'll light the fire,' he said. 'There's a bottle of Beefeater on the shelf. Perhaps you could pour us a couple of large ones.'

She found two mugs, poured the gin and passed one to him. He knocked it back in a single gulp and she did the same. She refilled the mugs and they drank the gin straight down again. His adrenalin subsided and the alcohol took its place. It calmed him. It heightened his senses. He smelled her scent and felt her warmth. Being close felt good. It was what he needed. He wanted to hold her. No, to be held by her. In that moment he felt a vulnerability that only she could soothe. It frightened him. He craved closeness but he feared himself too. His volatility. He drew away.

'I'll get that iodine,' he said.

She laughed. 'Don't bother. The cut's just a scratch.'

'But...'

'A ruse, darling. Remember that poem?'

'I remember.'

'You look tired, luvvie,' she said.

She nodded towards the bed. 'Go and lie down.'

He gave in. He was tired. He wanted to lie down. With her. The fear could go to hell.

She switched off the overhead light, crossed the room and started to undress in the orange glow of the gas fire. He lay on the bed watching her.

'Lucky for you I'm not shy, isn't it, darling,' she said, holding his gaze.

'I figured that out some time ago,' he said.

He unbuttoned his shirt and threw it into the corner, then pulled his vest over his head, trying to ignore the pain from the bruising. Marge noticed the dark patches on his flesh where the blows had struck him. She must have assumed he'd picked them up during the fracas in Ridley Road.

'Poor Reg. Look at you. I still can't help thinking this is my fault.'

He would maintain the pretence that he'd been hurt scrapping with the fascists. Telling her about the beating in his office, and the threats from Bernie, and the threats from Spelthorne and the obsession with the woman that fled the explosion, was all going to be far too complicated to explain.

'I told you,' he said. 'I know what I'm doing.'

She climbed onto the bed next to him. He felt her warmth against his hurting body. She kissed him full on the lips, hungrily, intrusively, leaving no doubt that she knew what she was doing too.

'Am I still being played?' he said.

She pressed her lips against his ear and whispered, 'Yes, darling. But this time it's a different game altogether.'

EIGHTEEN

There was a queue around the block. It was always the same when Centurion advertised for extras. Two hundred men and women, shabby and in need of a free meal, lined up along the old brewery walls waiting to be checked in by the commissionaires. The wardrobe department had set up trestle tables in the studio's courtyard. Each table held a different item of clothing. Coats, jackets, trousers, skirts, hats. Wardrobe girls handed out the appropriate items as the extras filed past the tables towards the dressing rooms. Kitchen staff from the cafeteria handed out cardboard lunch boxes from a large metal trolley. A pork pie, bread and cheese, tart and bicarbonate of soda for indigestion. Calloway saw the looks of relief on the hungry faces as they took the boxes in their hands. The sight of it disturbed him. The scene had echoes of his war. Prisoners, refugees, the wounded. They were all made to queue.

He left the courtyard and climbed the stairs to his office. It was still tainted by the lingering smell of Belcher's pipe. He opened a window and lit a cigarette. There was a package on his desk. The processed film from the laboratory. He still had the projector. He wound the film onto the spool and ran it through the machine, then closed the blind to shut out what passed for daylight on the overcast and misty autumn day. The film flickered into life.

Joyce looked older. Heavily made up, masking a tired face that had lost the sparkle of the previous two reels. Forced smiles. Hum-drum openings and graceless exchanges. Glad-handing dignitaries. A flash bulb. Recoiling slightly. Not on form. Cut to a party. A small event. An apartment or hotel room. Half a dozen starlets. A handful of men, middle-aged, suited, flash. One wearing correspondent shoes. Arms around the girls. Girls sitting on the men's knees. Squeezing girls. Pawing girls. Girls with tolerant smiles. Professional smiles. Joyce among them. Staggering. Drunk or pilled. The man in the correspondent shoes grabs her. Squeezes her. Calloway reads his lips. Have a drink. Don't be a kill-joy. Let your hair down. It's a party. How about a dance? They dance. Joyce is clumsy. Flaccid. Dazed. The man's annoyed. He turns full face to the camera and rolls his eyes.

Calloway's arm shot towards the projector. He flicked the switch. The frame froze. Joyce stared out at him, her face set with a pained smile. The man she danced with stared out too. Hair slicked back from a widow's peak. Neatly trimmed sideburns framing a long, mean face. The eyes of a reptile with a bird in its sights. Calloway recognised him from the newspapers.

Alfredo Azzopardi. Vice ring boss. Jailed for eight years.

He snapped up the blind and lit another cigarette. He waited for the nicotine to soothe him so he could think. First Spelthorne tells him he lives in fear of criminals from the London Maltese community he grew up with. Then Franco and Giordano show up at the fascist meeting, part of a Maltese gang hired as muscle. Now a convicted Maltese gang boss is dancing with Joyce Rose, Spelthorne's favourite starlet, in the final reel of the dead actress's cine film diary. For a man claiming to fear such people, Spelthorne seemed uncomfortably close to them. Calloway's brown-job copper's nose told him things didn't smell right. He rifled through his wastepaper basket and pulled out the newspaper. There was Azzopardi's face. A mug shot, cold and detached, but undoubtedly the same face as the man in the film. He rolled up the paper and pushed it into his jacket pocket, pulled the plug on the projector and left the office.

Tony from casting was organising the extras in the courtyard.

'Spare me a moment?' said Calloway.

The young man gave an apologetic wince, as if he was too busy to speak.

'I need to get this lot into Studio A. They're tucking into their lunch boxes already and we've not even started.'

Calloway gripped his arm and moved him away from the crowd. Tony looked nervous. Calloway walked him towards the power house where the hum of the generators would shield their conversation from passers-by.

Tony said, 'Look here Mr Calloway, I really don't have time for whatever this is.'

Calloway gripped his arm tighter. 'Humour me,' he said.

He felt like the school bully, intimidating this weak little man. But he needed some answers.

'I visited Joyce Rose's old flat,' he said. 'The manager told me that you once got yourself roughed up by the driver of one of her visitors.'

This gave Tony start. 'Why the hell are you bringing that up?'

'Studio business. There's a few things I need to make sense of. Let's call them irregularities. I need to know about your late friend Joyce and her trouble with ugly men in fancy shoes.'

The description of the men struck a chord with Tony. He side-stepped it. 'Why drag up Joyce's past? Good god, man, she's been dead for over a year. Can't you let her rest in peace?'

Calloway ignored him.

'Tell me about the men that called at Joyce's flat. Tell me why you confronted one of them and why it earned you a beating.'

Tony looked uncomfortable. He tried to pull away. Calloway squeezed his arm harder.

'That's none of your business,' he said with unconvincing bravura. Calloway leaned in towards him and pressed his mouth to the young man's ear.

'Everything's my business, son,' he said.

The humming from the power house was relentless. It rumbled like nearing thunder, ominous and unsettling. Calloway raised his voice above it.

'I need to know how Joyce was connected to those men.'

He pulled the newspaper from his pocket and held up Azzopardi's picture for Tony to see. 'This man in particular.'

Calloway loosened his grip on the young man's arm. 'Now be a good lad and tell me what happened.'

Tony looked as if he was about to run. His eyes darted towards the crowd of extras, as if they might offer him some sanctuary from Calloway's questions. Then he sighed and looked defeated. Calloway felt the puny arm muscles relax beneath his grip.

'Alright,' Tony said. 'But not here.'

'Where then?'

Tony thought for a moment. 'Do you know the S&F Grill on Denman Street?'

'I can find it.'

'Meet me there at five o'clock. I'll be finished here by then.'

The S&F Grill was a coffee shop in a side street off Piccadilly Circus, a few yards from the Windmill Theatre. It was light and airy and sold good coffee, for which Calloway was grateful. He had arrived early and nursed a cupful until Tony showed. As he waited, a gaggle of bright young things took up their regular tables. They were noisy and animated. The place attracted a film and theatre crowd, Calloway had heard, and these types looked the part. He recognised some of the faces, although he couldn't name them. A handsome jack-the-lad with black hair piled high on his head was hamming up a crafty cockney routine a little too obviously. A platinum blonde held court among a table of admirers, one of whom held her arm possessively, her boyfriend, Calloway assumed. Another boy, athletic looking with a long face and overly large chin, complained about losing a much-needed part in a new comedy to a worn-out has-been twice his age.

When Tony arrived just after five, he noticed the young film types immediately. They recognised him, waved and said hi, beckoning him to join them. He smiled back but looked uncomfortable. He squeezed past their tables towards Calloway.

'We can't talk here. I know these people. We'll have to go somewhere else.'

Calloway nodded. 'Alright,' he said, pulling two shillings from his pocket and leaving them on the table. 'Any suggestion where?'

Soho was unfamiliar to him. He didn't socialise. He didn't go to clubs or theatres or the girly shows. Since living in London, he'd never had much call to frequent the capital's seedy playground.

‘I know a place,’ said Tony. ‘A few minutes from here.’

He nodded at the young actors. ‘Somewhere this crowd doesn’t go.’

They left the grill and walked east through the busy Soho streets. The light was fading and the neon signs glowed through the gloom like beacons. They lured expectant punters with the promise of excitement that would, in Calloway’s experience of such places around the world from his army days, turn out to be an expensive disappointment.

The two men turned left off Old Compton Street and walked a few yards until Tony pointed to an anonymous-looking doorway set back from the pavement behind two dustbins overfilled with beer bottles.

‘Up here,’ he said, leading Calloway up a darkened staircase whose meagre lighting failed to illuminate its dirty, peeling walls. Calloway caught the smell of damp, mingled with cigarette smoke and a hint of cheap cologne. They reached a door. Behind it there was noise. Tony led Calloway inside. The decor was fake colonial, with bamboo screens, high stools and tropical houseplants spilling over the mirror-backed shelves of a tiny cocktail bar that ran along the wall towards two tall windows. A stern-faced diva who was perched on the nearest bar stool glared at them between deep drags on the cigarette she held high between long, slender fingers. She was masculine and feminine all at once, part Googie Withers, part Robert Helpmann. Tony gestured towards Calloway and said, ‘This is Reg. He’s my guest.’

The diva looked Calloway up and down, weighing up whether to admit him to her club.

‘And Reg is...?’ she said.

Calloway answered. ‘I run security at the studios where Tony works.’

She raised her plucked and pencilled eyebrows. She could have been sceptical, impressed or bored. Calloway couldn’t tell. He wasn’t used to these types. He looked around the club. Rakes, rogues and reprobates the lot of them. He doubted any of them were holding down steady work. Artists, writers, actors, that sort. Cadgers and scroungers, who compensated for their financial embarrassments with flamboyant dress and camp exuberance. Homosexuals, men in suede shoes, women in berets with cigarette holders. A black pianist clunking thorough jazz standards that no one seemed to be listening to. A Liverpudlian seamen talking jazz and telling filthy stories. And all of this at five-thirty in the afternoon.

'Head of security, eh?' said the diva. 'We could do with someone like you. Keep the wrong sort out.'

Calloway glanced around the room. 'And what do you consider the wrong sort?'

The diva frowned at him. 'The police of course, cunty.'

Tony winced and felt the need to interject. 'That's her term of endearment, by the way,' he said, looking apologetic.

'I'd hate to hear her term of abuse,' said Calloway.

'They're much the same, actually,' said Tony laughing too hard.

The diva nodded and blew smoke at Calloway. 'In you go,' she said and turned away, as if utterly bored by their brief exchange.

Tony bought two bottled beers and gestured to an empty table by the window which offered a degree of privacy. The background hubbub would be loud enough to drown their conversation.

'So you're a member here?' Calloway said.

Tony nodded. 'For a few months now. It's not been open long. I used to drink at the White Room until the Rank crowd took it over. That lot back at the S&F,' he said, to clarify who he meant. 'Too full of themselves. Not really my type. I like it better here. The members are a rum lot but it's easy enough to fit in once you've had a few.'

'Not very pukka though, is it?' said Calloway. 'I thought you were the more the country club type.'

'Don't let the tweeds and cravat fool you, Mr Calloway. I'm just another film business flake that acts above his station. My parents were strictly below-stairs folk. In service all their working lives. Mother's too old for domestic work now. Since father died we've been sharing a basement flat at the back of Euston station.'

'Not the marrying kind then?' Calloway said, using a

euphemism he'd heard around the studio.

Tony looked embarrassed, then laughed. 'Actually I'm very much the marrying kind. I've just not had much luck. Living with mother doesn't help, but it's a financial necessity.'

'I'm sure it is, at these prices,' said Calloway, nodding towards the bar.

Tony laughed to himself. 'I'm surrounded by beautiful girls all day long. It's ironic isn't it?' He took a sip of the beer. 'I just can't get one to notice me.'

Calloway thought of the file he'd taken from the casting office, the file on Joyce Rose that read like the scrapbook of an obsessive fan.

'Too hung up on a dead actress, eh?'

Tony sighed and gazed out of the window into the neon glow. 'You might be right,' he said. 'Joyce was wonderful. She was beautiful, talented, ambitious. I suppose I'd been in love with her since we were children.' He thought a moment. 'If not in love, then certainly in awe. She was the most wonderful person to be around. Her joie de vivre was infectious. Spelthorne saw that. He recognised that she was different. Not like the glorified swimwear models that the charm school churns out. She was Centurion's English rose. A breath of fragrant air that this damp and dusty country was so desperately in need of. God, I sound like Ivor Cole. Spelthorne took her everywhere. Showed her off wherever it would bring him some advantage. She was always on his arm, in his car, at his table.'

'In his bed?' said Calloway.

Tony looked hurt. He shook his head. 'It was a business relationship. For both of them. Joyce wasn't daft. Like I say, she was ambitious. She knew that being the young queen to Spelthorne's king was good for her career. They weren't lovers. She wasn't Spelthorne's type.'

'What is his type?'

'Have you met Miss Hope?'

Calloway nodded. The blonde secretary, bursting the seams, who could take a memo without a pencil or a pad.

'He's not one for subtle beauty,' said Tony, with a nervous

laugh, as if Spelthorne might be listening. 'The problem wasn't that Spelthorne was interested in Joyce, well not in that sense. It was that someone else was.'

'Who?'

'The man in the newspaper.'

'Alfredo Azzopardi?'

Tony nodded. 'He'd seen Joyce in the press and in her film roles and asked to be introduced to her.'

'Who did he ask?'

'Mr Spiteri, one of Spelthorne's fixers.'

Calloway had not heard the name. He looked quizzical.

'Giordano Spiteri,' said Tony. 'He told Joyce she should host a party at her flat. She had no clue as the reason.'

'But she agreed?'

Tony sipped his drink and nodded. 'She assumed this was something that Centurion wanted. She thought it might help her career.'

'What happened at the party?'

'Nothing much, apparently. She was the perfect hostess. Everything was perfectly proper. The party wasn't the problem. The trouble started when Azzopardi started calling.'

'At the flat?"

Tony nodded.

'It didn't take long for Joyce to realise his intentions. He didn't waste time. She refused of course. Giordano got to hear about it and told her she should be nice. That's what they call it in this business, isn't it?'

'Giordano put pressure on Joyce to sleep with this man?'

'He did. At first he was subtle, making out that he was matchmaking. When that didn't work he was more direct. He let her know that unless she agreed to sleep with Azzopardi, she wouldn't have much of a career.'

'What did she do?'

He seemed affronted by the question, as if it was improper. 'She said no, naturally.'

'And then what?'

'The studio dropped her.' He clicked his fingers. 'Just like that.

Giordano called on me one morning and said that Joyce's popularity was waning and that we weren't to consider her for any more roles. It was nonsense. She was a star in the ascendant. Her press was getting better all the time. She was photographed wherever she went. Even the critics seemed to be warming to her.'

'And you agreed on Giordano's say-so? You didn't put any more roles her way?'

He looked shameful and nodded. 'He's the sort of chap you don't argue with,' as if this might absolve him.

'What did Marjorie think of this?' said Calloway.

Tony seemed reluctant to answer. Calloway pressed him. He needed to know.

'Did Marge agree to dropping Joyce?'

Tony picked at his fingernails, considering his answer. When he responded he sounded reluctant.

'Marge didn't know,' he said. 'Giordano told me to see to it personally. He told me under no circumstances was I to involve Marge. He knew he'd get a different response if she got to hear about it. Marge is one of the few around here that's not afraid of him.'

Calloway could believe it. Somewhere inside he felt a bristle of pride.

'After that, Joyce's work was strictly charm school. Public appearances, openings, fucking swimming galas. Ivor Cole even leaked a story she was engaged to one of Centurion's actors and made sure she was seen with him in public. She had to go everywhere with him. Even spent the night at his flat once, just so the gossip columnists would find out.'

Calloway looked confused.

'It was a cover, you see? In reality he was what they call a confirmed bachelor. Not the marrying kind, to borrow your phrase.'

'And it was around that time that she started going off the rails? Drinking and taking pills?'

'She was a different person after that,' said Tony. 'Bitter. Nasty sometimes. She'd lost her confidence. She used the booze and the pills to compensate, but she wasn't the same. And Azzopardi kept calling.'

'And she kept turning him away?'

'If she could, yes, but sometimes she ran out of excuses. She'd let him in the flat for a drink. Sometimes he'd bring his friends. Sometimes Spelthorne sent other charm school girls around too, to make up a party. I don't know what went on. She said he just showed her off. Made out there was something between them.'

'Do you believe her?'

'I've no idea either way. She wasn't the Joyce I knew. Not the girl I grew up with.'

Calloway remembered the school report. A pleasant and popular girl...her Mary in this year's nativity play was a revelation.

'I'm not sure I'd have trusted what she told me. It would have been the drink and drugs talking.'

'And how did the fight start?' said Calloway.

Tony laughed, incredulous. 'Fight?' he said. 'Look at me. You think I can fight? I can't fight my way out of a paper bag.'

'But they did rough you up.'

Tony nodded. 'I'd called on Joyce one evening. I was worried about her. Azzopardi arrived and I told him to leave. I'd had a couple of drinks and I suppose it was Dutch courage. He just laughed. I lost my rag. There was pushing and shoving and the next thing I know his driver was dragging me down the stairs of the apartment block, using his fists along the way.'

Tony picked up his glass and drained the last of his beer.

'A fortnight later Joyce was dead,' he said. He looked across to the bar. A moustachioed rake was edging himself closer to a tired-looking woman whose glaze of inebriation gave no clue to her interest in his advances. 'She was a fucking commodity. That's all she meant. A tradable asset.'

'Aren't they all commodities, the charm school girls?' said Calloway.

Tony shrugged. 'I suppose so. But usually there's a line that isn't crossed. You can look, you can touch within limits, but you don't get to have. With Joyce they crossed the line. Offered her to Azzopardi like a tribute. It killed her.'

'Yes, it killed her,' said Calloway. 'Well, that and someone ending her film career because he didn't have the guts to say no to Giordano.' Calloway fixed Tony's stare. 'That couldn't have helped, could it, Tony?' he said.

The skinny man was on the verge of tears, but he held them back. Calloway was grateful. He wasn't good with emotions. Especially men's. He went to the bar and bought another round. A young man, shabbily dressed with a face crumpled beyond his years, slipped off his bar stool and swore loudly.

'That fucker can't paint for shit, but he gets an exhibition on Cork Street...' He held up his beer glass like Hamlet with the skull. 'While I'm raiding the gas meter for the price of a drink.'

His drinking partner frowned, grappling for words of consolation.

'The art world is as corrupt as its favoured artists are inept,' he said.

The artist seemed not to hear.

'Perhaps I should sell my arse,' he said, to no one in particular.

Calloway paid for the drinks. He was glad he had Spelthorne's cash to cover them. A woman in a beret touched his arm. When he turned to face her, she seemed to wake from a trance and said, 'I'd like to paint you naked.'

'What colour?' he said.

She gave a disinterested shrug, shifted on her stool and stared into the mirrored glass behind the bar. Calloway returned to the table and set the drinks down. Tony had composed himself now, but he drank the beer eagerly.

'Joyce had a sister,' Calloway said. 'Did you ever meet her?'

Tony hesitated before answering. He gulped his drink like it was a condemned man's last request. Calloway must have frightened him as much a Giordano.

'Yvonne?' he said quietly. 'Of course. But I haven't seen her since we were children. She lives in France, I think.'

Yvonne. The name on the postcards from Paris.

'Did she go to the funeral?'

Tony shook his head. 'If she did, I didn't see her. Not sure I'd recognise her. It's been a long while.'

'Did she resemble Joyce in appearance?'

'A little, at least when they were young. Look, what's all this about? What's this got to do with studio security?'

'Best you don't know. And keep this chat to yourself.'

Calloway's tone left no room for doubting these instructions. Tony nodded like he'd got the message.

They finished their drinks and rose to leave. As they approached the door, the artist was on his knees begging for credit and the diva was responding with language Calloway hadn't heard since leaving the army.

NINETEEN

He took a bus to Aldwych, then the 569 trolleybus eastwards. He jumped off at Broad Street station and walked towards Shoreditch. As he turned into his street, he noticed a black Austin parked outside his building, its engine running. The door opened as he passed.

'Get in, Calloway.'

It was Bernie. She sat in the back, the raglan coat pulled tight around her neck. Curly sat at the wheel. Blue eyes was in the passenger seat. He was pointing the muzzle of the Colt automatic in Calloway's direction. Calloway eased himself into the back seat beside Bernie.

'You can put that down,' he said to Blue Eyes.

'I'd rather he didn't,' said Bernie.

She nodded to Curley, who took the gear stick in his big mitt and pushed the car into gear. He drove slowly westwards, the same route they'd taken when they'd bundled Calloway into the car.

'Are you taking me dancing again?' he said.

Bernie shook her head. 'We're going to a little place I know. I want to show you something.'

Somewhere off the Kilburn High Road they pulled up at a crossroads. Curly cut the engine. There was a wide street opposite them running south to north which Calloway didn't recognise. He wasn't a Londoner. There were huge swathes of the capital he'd never visited. The road was lined with the usual collection of shops you found in the city's Victorian suburbs. A greengrocers, a drapers, a Home and Colonial store. The shops were closed - it was past seven - and their windows reflected the glow of the street lamps. On the corner opposite was a pub. He couldn't read the pub sign. Place looked full and cheery. It was Friday night. End of the working week for most.

'Do you hear that?' said Bernie.

He heard singing.

'That's 'The Mountains of Mourne'. A lament for a country they left behind. Lured by the NHS and London Transport with the promise of a pay packet and a better life. Plucked from the poverty of De Valera's isolationism by your desperate and opportunistic government. They're the mailboat generation, Calloway. They came here via Fishguard and Holyhead to build your roads, drive your busses and nurse your sick. Those homes for heroes they keep telling you about. You know what they're made of? London bricks and the sweat of the Irish.'

'And I'm sure we're very grateful.'

'Are you now? Have you seen those signs outside the boarding houses?'

He had. No blacks, no dogs, no Irish. A good old British welcome.

'What's your point, Bernie?'

Something distracted her. She held up a finger to silence him.

Curly said, 'They're coming, Bernie.'

He gestured to the far end of the street. A Black Maria and two police cars were turning the corner, their bells silent but their engines roaring. They sped past the row of shops and pulled up outside the pub. Their doors flew open. Police dismounted. Uniformed and plain clothes. Grim faced. Meaning business. They piled into the pub, slamming its double doors back like a blue tornado. The singing stopped. There was shouting and screaming. The smashing of glass. The crash of furniture. Half a dozen drinkers were pushed back out of the doors and dragged into the van. Roughed up. Some were bloodied.

'We had a tip off,' she said. 'A sympathetic lad on the force.'

'And this is what you brought me here to see?'

'I don't expect your support, Calloway. We're old adversaries. You served the army of occupation. But I do credit you with enough common sense to know that we can all do without this.'

'I'm working on it,' he said.

It was true. He needed to find the real car bomber for the sake of his own neck.

'Then work harder,' she said, sliding the Webley out of her coat pocket just far enough for him to see.

Blue Eyes tensed suddenly. He sat bolt upright in the passenger seat looking through the windscreen at three men in trench coats heading up the street towards them.

'Christ Bernie. It's the Branch.'

Curley started the engine and slammed the car into gear. He accelerated hard towards the three detectives. One drew a pistol but leapt sideways out of the car's path before he'd had a chance to aim. As the big Austin neared the junction of the main street, a police Wolseley pulled up blocking the way ahead. Curly stamped hard on the brakes. The four of them lunged forward inside the car. Curly's forehead slammed into the steering wheel with an audible crack. His body slumped, lifeless. Bernie flung the door open and rolled onto the damp bitumen of the road. She scrambled to her feet and ran. Blue Eyes followed, swivelling his body as he ran and loosing off three rounds in the direction of the detectives. One detective took cover. Another kneeled and took aim at Blue Eyes. He fired two rounds. Both went wide. Calloway piled out of the nearside door of the Austin and crouched on the pavement, shielded from view. He figured all eyes would be on the sound of the gunfire. He lifted his head and peered through the Austin's windows to the opposite side of the street. The three plain clothes men were on their feet now, pursuing Bernie and Blue Eyes up the street. Two uniformed officers had dismounted the Wolseley and were following them. Calloway looked back towards the police car. The way ahead was clear, for now. There was no one between the abandoned police car and the commotion outside the pub on the far side of the junction. He stood upright and double-timed towards the Wolseley, adopting the manner of a concerned passer-by keen to get away from the shooting. No one challenged him. He turned left and continued past the parade of shops. On the opposite side of the road, uniformed officers bundled the last of the pub goers they had rounded up into the Black Maria and slammed the doors shut. A metallic clang echoed down the street over the hubbub of aggrieved voices coming from the gaggle of angry punters that had spilled onto the pavement outside the pub. Calloway stayed close to the shopfronts. He tried his best to stay in the shadows. He was thankful this wasn't the kind of neighbourhood where shopkeepers kept their lights on. He glanced back down the street towards the pub. The police were leaving, cars and vans heading in the opposite direction. He sighed, relieved to be clear of them. As he turned back again there was a figure blocking his path.

'And where the fuck do you think you're going?'

Before he could answer, DS Bryant jabbed him in the guts with a truncheon.

TWENTY

Calloway's eyes adjusted to the gloom. This wasn't a police station.

He judged from the old bed frame, the basin in the corner and the set of dog-eared fire instructions pinned to the door, it was a disused room in a guest house. A cheap and shoddy one. The walls were stained with damp and the carpet was as threadbare as a mongrel with mange. There was a strong smell of dead rodent coming up from the floorboards.

They'd sat him in an old metal chair. Bryant stood behind him, casting a shadow across the room from the bare and inadequate bulb in the ceiling above him. Belcher sat in front cowboy style, the chair reversed and his arms draped over the back rest.

I like a good western as it happens.

No sign of the pipe. It would have masked the putrid smell that clung to Calloway's nostrils.

'So no chance of a phone call then?' said Calloway.

'We thought we'd keep this informal,' said Belcher.

Calloway swore he heard Bryant crack his knuckles behind him. No, that would have been too melodramatic, even for Bryant. He felt in his pocket for his cigarette case.

'Mind if I smoke?'

'Be my guest.'

Belcher looked up at Bryant. 'Give mister Calloway a light, will you? He must be gasping.'

Bryant flicked open a lighter. As Calloway leaned towards the flame he smelled cologne. He'd not noticed it before. Something soapy with a sailing ship on the bottle. Perhaps Bryant was on a promise.

‘So, Calloway,’ said Belcher. ‘Here’s how it is. There’s us lads from the Branch and our uniformed pals, out to feel some collars in a well-known Irish pub. Round up a few of the boyos and see what they know about this car bomb business. Then all of a sudden, you pop up like an oversized leprechaun. What’s that all about, eh?’

Give them something close to the truth, Calloway thought. And stick to it.

‘I was looking for McCaffrey.’

‘Were you now. And why would you be doing that?’

Calloway glanced back at Bryant, who was stubbing a cigarette out in the basin.

‘Because your DS told me to.’

‘Don’t give me that,’ said Bryant, flicking the butt in Calloway’s direction. ‘I asked for his known haunts, not for you to go stomping all over Kilburn in your old army boots.’

Calloway shrugged. ‘I like to go the extra mile.’

Belcher raised an eyebrow. ‘It seems you do,’ he said. ‘And along that extra mile you met one Bernadette Doyle and her big Mick boyfriends.’

‘Never heard of her.’

‘You were sitting in her car.’

Calloway took a long drag on the cigarette. ‘If you say so,’ he said, exhaling.

It looked bad, he knew that, but there was no law against it as far as he was aware. Then again, he wasn’t in a police station. This was big boys’ rules. A different kind of law.

‘Bernadette Doyle is known to us. She’s believed to have been part of an IRA active service unit operating on the British mainland during the war.’

The time of the S-Plan

‘That’s news to me. Like I say, I was looking for McCaffrey. I didn’t get to choose who I ran into along the way.’

Bryant cuffed Calloway across the back of his head. ‘Stop fucking us about, son. You’ve been seen with Doyle twice in the past fortnight.’

Calloway swivelled in the chair. ‘Keep your bloody hands off me,' he spat at Bryant.

'I mean it doesn't look good, does it?' said Belcher, taking out his pipe and filling it from a small leather pouch.

'I don't care how it looks. I was looking for McCaffrey. Same as you. He's a potential threat to the studio. I want him caught and quickly. I was making my own enquiries.'

'And did you find anything?'

Calloway shook his head. 'Nothing yet. My money's on him skipping across the Irish Sea, or even to America.'

'Let's say we believe you,' said Belcher. 'We could just give you a slap on the wrists and leave it at that.'

The sentence hung in the air. There was a but coming.

'The trouble is you're a complicated sort, Calloway.' He nodded to his colleague. 'Show him, Bryant.'

The DS picked a brown foolscap envelope off the old bed frame and passed it to Calloway. Inside were photos. The surveillance kind. Taken at the fascist meeting at Ridley Road. There was Calloway, fists raised, piling into Hamm's cordon of semi-uniformed stewards.

'You didn't strike me as the political sort.'

'I'm full of surprises.'

'Do you consider yourself,' he thought for a moment, 'an anti-fascist?'

'Don't you?'

Christ, thought Calloway, we'd been at war with the bastards for six years. Belcher ignored the question.

'We keep an eye on the likes of Mosley and Jeffrey Hamm.' He gave Calloway a sympathetic look. 'I mean we can't have that sort of thing, can we?'

'You said it.'

'But these anti-fascists are a rum lot too. There's the Jews of course. Well you can't blame them, can you? But we can't have them fighting in the streets. What we're more concerned about is the communists. They seem to be mobilising against these fascists too and frankly, that worries us. I mean, they're the real enemy now.'

'So why don't you drag them off the street and sit them in this chair?'

Belcher dropped the chummy act. 'Don't be smart with me, son. You're in no position.'

Stand your ground, he thought. Don't be cowed. He has nothing on you. You've done nothing wrong.

'So what position am I in? What the hell has this got to do with me?'

Belcher took a long drag on the pipe. 'I'm one of those coppers that doesn't believe in coincidence. Everything's connected in some way or another.'

'Get to the point.'

'We've been looking into your story Calloway. You have an interesting background. Raised by a family of socialists. Your father was a trade union activist.'

'Like every other coal miner. That doesn't make him a communist.'

Belcher smiled. 'Well in his case, it does. He was a member of the Communist Party between 1933 and 1946. Don't tell me you didn't know.'

Calloway didn't know, but it didn't surprise him. 'The last time I saw my father I was sixteen.'

'Yes, you left home to join the army. Military Police. Posted to Belfast in 1935. Tense times, I imagine. Plenty of time for a someone with communist sympathies to make new friends, especially if he was sympathetic.'

'I wasn't sympathetic.'

Belcher frowned. 'Is that so?' He puffed on the pipe. The sickly smell was marginally better than the dead rat under the floorboards. 'Do you remember a Private Alfred Tallis?'

'Vaguely,' said Calloway.

Alfie Tallis. He knew him alright. A nasty piece of work.

'Only vaguely? I'm surprised. I'd say you knew him better than that. You reported him to your commanding officer in Belfast, claiming he'd used undue force on a Fenian during a house search.'

'You're wrong about that,' said Calloway.

But he was only half wrong. It was the height of the rioting.

Things kicked off during the Orange parades and quickly escalated. Beatings, shootings, looting. From the start, the Catholic neighbourhoods bore the brunt of it. Catholics were sacked from their jobs, turned out of their homes and attacked by the mob. But intelligence reports suggested more than thirty IRA men were on their way back to Belfast from their training camp in Dundalk. The RUC feared reprisals.

Tallis and Calloway were sent to a house in Sailortown. The police planned to raid it. They had information that a man called Redmond was hiding a cache of arms on the premises. The two soldiers were there to back up the police but the police failed to show. They'd been caught up in rioting near the Customs House.

Calloway told Tallis they should wait. Tallis ignored him and banged on the door. Redmond wasn't there, but his wife and ten-year-old son were. His wife was uncooperative, although not any more so than was usual in that neighbourhood at the time. She stood in the doorway refusing them entry. Tallis pushed her to the floor. The ten-year-old went to the defence of his mother in the way that ten-year-olds do. He kicked Tallis in the shins with dirty unshod feet and started beating on the soldier's legs with his small fists. Tallis smashed the child in the face with his rifle butt. The child fell backwards onto the bare floorboards screaming. His urchin face gushed blood. Tallis shouted at the child to shut up. The mother was on her feet now and shrieking at them. By this time neighbours had rushed into street and were closing in behind the two soldiers. Calloway grabbed Tallis and dragged him backwards through the crowd. Tallis was swearing. Baying for blood. Calloway told him to shut up, but Tallis kept taunting the crowd. The neighbours were grabbing at them, shouting and screaming. Calloway made a run for it and Tallis followed.

They made it to the end of the street. A Rolls Royce armoured car was passing on a routine patrol. A mean-looking beast, all rivets and plating. Its turret swivelled, training its Vickers gun on the mob. It fired a burst of .303 rounds into the crowd. The mob stopped in their tracks. Two of them lay dead on the ground. Then they kept coming. Calloway and Tallis scrambled onto the rear of the vehicle. The driver accelerated hard along York Street as the two soldiers clung on to the turret. Calloway shouted to Tallis that he was bang out of order. Tallis told him the family were Fenian scum and deserved what they got.

They got in a fight back at the barracks. Tallis wouldn't let it go. He told Calloway he was soft. He hadn't got what it takes. A crowd of squaddies had formed around them, egging them on. Tallis played to the crowd. He kept digging at Calloway. All the old jibes. Calloway snapped. He fought like a beast. He beat seven shades of shit out of Tallis before two NCOs pulled them apart. The next day they were called before their commanding officer. Calloway broke an unwritten rule. He ratted on Tallis. He didn't care.

'Tallis was a liability,' Calloway said to Belcher. 'He was the type that get you killed.'

He took a last drag on the cigarette and ground the butt into the leg of the chair. 'I'm not a Fenian sympathiser. I never have been.'

'That's not how it looks.'

'So how does it look, Inspector? You tell me?'

Belcher answered as if reading a report. 'Reginald Calloway, raised by a communist, sympathetic to nationalist Catholics, fighting fascists in the street shoulder-to-shoulder with communists, fraternising with republican terrorists. And his boss's car blows up after he sacked an angry paddy from a film about the IRA. It paints quite a picture, doesn't it?'

Calloway shrugged. He opened his cigarette case and put another Navy Cut in his parched mouth, gesturing to Bryant for a light. Bryant gave an indignant snort and pulled out his lighter. Belcher changed tack.

'How do you know Bernie Doyle?'

'I don't know Bernie Doyle.'

'You were in her car.'

'I mistook it for a taxi.'

'Don't play the fool.'

'Then don't treat me like one.'

'I'll treat you how I damn well please.'

'I've done nothing wrong. Why don't you let me go?'

'Why were you at the pub tonight?'

'I was looking for McCaffrey. I already told you.'

'Why that pub?'

Calloway glanced at Bryant. 'It's one of his known haunts.'

'Who did you meet there?'

'No one. You lot turned up and spoiled everyone's evening.'

Belcher kept up the questioning and Calloway kept batting them back. They couldn't touch him and they knew it. They wanted information, not him. If they had anything on him, he would be in a police cell by now. Nothing they got from this informal interview would be admissible. He guessed they used the guest house for grilling sources, not sweating suspects.

'Did your anti-fascist friends introduce you to Doyle?'

'No. Why would they?'

'They're all communists, after a fashion.'

'Now you're clutching at straws.' Calloway took a deep drag on the cigarette. 'Anyway, I don't follow politics.'

'You were seen smashing up a political rally.'

'A man needs a hobby.'

'You're not a Jew, are you?'

'Would it matter if I was?'

'Does it matter to your lady friend?' said Bryant.

'I don't have a lady friend.'

'Come off it. You're knocking off that old bint in Casting.'

'And what's that to you?'

'Nothing, mate.' Bryant sniggered loud enough to ensure Calloway heard him. 'I wouldn't touch her with...'

Calloway was on his feet before Bryant finished the sentence. He grabbed the detective by the lapels and head butted him hard. The noise of the impact filled the room. Bryant clutched his face. Calloway kicked his legs from under him. The copper fell. Calloway was about to aim a kick at the copper's head when he heard a click. The cocking of pistol. He felt its cold metal barrel against his temple.

'If you move so much as an inch, I'll blow your fucking brains from between your two jug-ears.'

Special Branch was one of the few branches of the police which carried guns routinely. But putting one to Calloway's head was a dumb tactic on Belcher's part. At that distance Calloway could have batted the gun away in a single move before the detective could squeeze the trigger. But he did as he was told. These were coppers and wrestling a gun from a copper could end very badly.

Belcher spoke calmly. 'Now sit down and don't budge. We haven't finished.'

Calloway complied. Belcher pulled his chair closer and sat. He leaned in close.

'You've done it now, mate,' he said. 'Assaulting a police officer. I doubt you'll get another security job. Not to mention the prospect of a few years inside.'

He was right. Calloway had messed up. Up to that point he'd being playing them at their own game and winning. He could have kept that up all night. They would've let him go eventually. But when Bryant mentioned Marge, the switch had flicked.

'There's a very big question mark over you, Calloway,' said Belcher.

'So ask the fucking question and let me out of here.'

Belcher rose from his chair. He tapped his pipe out on the chair back, pocketed it and stood in front of Calloway.

The blow hit him hard in the jaw before his eyes could tell his brain it was coming. Christ, Belcher was fast. Calloway tasted the ferric tang of his own blood. Belcher leant forward and shouted in his ear.

'Stop lying to me boy and tell me everything you know about the explosion.'

Calloway spat blood onto the bare boards. He turned his head sideways until he was nose to nose with the copper.

'What I know is that it wasn't me. I'm almost certain it wasn't McCaffrey and I doubt very much it was Bernadette Doyle.'

He stopped himself there. He wasn't telling them about the woman that had fled the gala dinner, or the damaged studio equipment, or what the connection might be between Spelthorne and his Maltese gangster minders. He was keeping quiet about all of that. In Calloway's experience it never paid to play an incomplete hand. There was still more he needed to find out. To do that he needed to be out of this rat-infested room and away from Belcher and Bryant.

'Pass me a pencil and paper,' Calloway said.

Belcher exchanged looks with Bryant. This time Bryant's knuckles cracked for real. Belcher looked at the DS and shook his head. He took a police note book from his inside pocket and ripped a page out. He passed it to Calloway and handed him a pencil. Calloway wrote down a name and number. He passed the paper back to Belcher.

'Call him. He'll vouch for me.'

It was a gamble. A big one. He was calling in a favour that arguably wasn't owed to him. He was relying on old loyalties. Belcher stared at the paper. He sucked on his empty pipe while he thought it over. Then both men left the room. Calloway heard a bolt sliding into place on the outer side of the door. He looked over at the dirty windows. He looked through the moth-eaten net curtains and saw that the windows were barred. He'd not noticed before. He wondered what happened at the other informal chats Belcher and Bryant had here.

TWENTY-ONE

'You better have a damn good excuse for this, Cab.'

Only Sammy Mackay called him by his old army nickname. Cab Calloway, after his Jumpin' Jive namesake. In fact Sammy had coined it during the war when they were both in army intelligence, part of 316 Field Security Section, attached to the 6th Airborne Division. Sammy had been his commanding officer from Normandy to the Balkans, then onto Palestine in forty-five. They'd seen each other once since then. That reunion hadn't ended well.

'I figured you owe me a favour,' said Calloway.

'I owe you a favour? For God's sake man, last time I had anything to do with you I spared you from the hangman's noose. You owe me a debt you'll never repay.'

'That's all in a day's work in your world.'

Sammy was a civil servant now. The kind that spied on our enemies and occasionally removed them. Last time Calloway met Sammy he'd stumbled into some bad business. The kind of business where people get killed. Sammy had got him clear of the law in return for some very deniable freelance work. It was a moot point who owed who the favour.

They drove west through the night. Sammy gripped the wheel of the car, a brand-new MG roadster - in racing green, naturally. Its engine growled like a puma about to pounce. The car suited Sammy. It would have suited any ex-army major with the same camel coat, cavalry twills and ridiculous moustache.

'Where are we going?' said Calloway.

'Chelsea. My place. We need to talk.'

Sammy lived in a mansion block off Sloane Square. One of

those places where single gentlemen share a man servant who enters each morning via the back stairs and wakes them with breakfast. Sammy would like that, Calloway thought.

Sammy parked the MG outside his block and pulled the tonneau cover over the cockpit. It was quiet on the street. Getting late. Calloway had lost track of time. Nine o'clock perhaps. A cool autumn breeze found its way up from the river between the ornate blocks of blackened terracotta. Calloway took a big lungful.

Sammy's flat was small but well furnished. Paintings in gilt frames hung from the picture rails above deep green walls. Oils and watercolours, traditional styles and safe subjects like horses, ships and landscapes. The landscapes looked Scottish. The furniture was old but expensive. There were antique pieces polished to the point of obsession and books of a kind no one read. Leather-bound editions of Scott and Thackeray. The carpet was Persian and suitably worn. It looked like an heirloom. A generous sofa covered with an Arabic throw nestled between the full-height windows with their Juliet balconies. Beside it, a sagging armchair with a side table just large enough to take a tumbler of scotch and an ashtray. Sammy's chair he guessed. The fireplace was ornate, with art nouveau tiling. There was an ormolu clock ticking on the mantlepiece, flanked by a pair of foot-high Greek statues, a male and female nude.

Sammy poured two whiskies from a bottle of single malt and passed one to Calloway.

'How the hell did you end up in a Special Branch safe house?' he said.

It hadn't felt all that safe to Calloway. As he started to reply, the phone rang. Sammy cursed and picked up the receiver. Calloway heard squawking down the line.

Sammy said, 'No, not tonight. I can't.'

More squawking. The caller wasn't taking no for an answer. Sammy looked uncomfortable. He glanced over at Calloway, then turned his back to him. He pressed the receiver closer to his mouth and said quietly, 'I have a visitor. Unexpected.'

Calloway could make out the caller's quizzical tone.

Sammy replied, 'It doesn't matter who. We will have to rearrange. No,' he said emphatically, 'don't come over.'

The caller sounded irate.

'Look, it's work, alright? I can't explain right now but...'

The caller cut him off.

Sammy said, 'Damn,' and slammed the phone down. He took a big gulp of the whisky and gestured for Calloway to sit.

'What have you got yourself into, Cab?' Mackay said.

'Not what Special Branch thinks.'

Sammy tutted and shook his head. His frustration showed.

'Alright, so tell me what they think, then tell me what you think.'

'They think I'm mixed up with an IRA cell in London. They think that cell's behind a bombing at the film studio I'm working for. They're wrong.'

Sammy let this sink in. 'Why so sure?'

'Because the IRA cell dragged me off the street, stuck a Webley service revolver in my guts and told me to find the real bomber.'

'Presumably there was an "or else" at the end of it.'

Calloway nodded. 'They want the Branch off their case as quickly as possible. They're using me to make that happen.'

'It doesn't mean they're not involved. They could just as easily be using you to find a scapegoat. To cover their tracks.'

'The IRA's got nothing to do with it. The Branch believes the bombing was revenge for my boss sacking an Irish actor for his republican links. That's ridiculous. They wouldn't mount such a high-risk operation for such a trivial reason. There's no strategic or tactical benefit.'

'The Branch can't ignore it though. It's too much of a coincidence.'

'Yes, but that's all it is. And unless I find the real bomber, the police will have a murder to investigate. Mine.'

Sammy calmed down. His earlier frustration ebbed.

'I know people who can help with that, Cab.' he said.

Calloway shook his head. 'I'll deal with it.'

Sammy shrugged as if to say Calloway was a fool for refusing the quick fix he was offering. He topped up Calloway's glass.

'You know I had to pull strings with the Irish desk at Curzon Street to get Special Branch off your back. They'll want to know what's going on.'

'Tell them to get lost.'

Sammy glared. 'It may be some great personal adventure for you, Cab, but this is my job. My contacts and connections are hard earned and I don't want to foul them up over some wild goose chase you've taken on as your next noble cause.'

'Nothing noble about it. It's just where I've found myself. And telling you more than you need to know isn't going to help me any. Tell your friends at MI5 to whistle. You used to be good at that.'

Sammy was not averse to cavalier behaviour when Calloway knew him. Arrogance and swagger carried him a long way. And when it didn't, Calloway was there with the muscle to fix things.

Sammy shook his head. 'I can't do that. I've got to throw them a bone. You can't interfere with a police investigation without consequences, Cab. The old boy network does have its limits, you know. It's bad enough having to deal with Special Branch at the best of times. I never did like policemen. Rude mechanicals in mackintoshes. But pulling favours from MI5 to lean on the Branch to let you go is well beyond what passes for friendship between us. I need to know what the hell you're up to. You can't keep secrets from me.'

The doorbell rang.

Sammy said, 'Oh, Christ'.

He sat for a moment as if weighing up whether to answer the door. The bell rang again, twice this time. Two long, insistent rings. Sammy rose and crossed the room towards the hallway. He looked afraid of what might happen next.

Calloway heard Sammy open the door. He started to speak.

He said, 'You can't...'

A voice interrupted. 'Fix me a drink love, my throat's dry as a witch's tit. They were such a rowdy lot tonight. I really had to belt out the closing number. I'm all husky.'

The visitor laughed. 'But then you quite like that, don't you luvvie?'

Calloway heard Sammy say, 'Look, I told you, you can't be here tonight, it's not...'

The visitor carried on, oblivious to Sammy's pleading. 'I had to get a taxi here like this. There was no room to change. The dressing room was full of dwarves. Dwarves! That show gets cheaper by the week. I said to Ronaldo, this is not a fucking circus and I'm not a fucking clown. He never listens. It'll be performing chimps next week. I must sit down, these heels are killing me.'

Sammy said, 'Look you can't go in there...'

He was too late. The visitor appeared in the room.

Framed in the doorway was a vision worthy of a screen goddess. Eyes, lips, hair, curves, legs, and an evening gown with sequins that shimmered like liquid gold. Calloway didn't know much about this kind of thing, but he had to admit, for a man, this young chap made a very beautiful woman.

'Oh, hello,' the vision said, raising a perfectly painted eyebrow. He looked Calloway up and down then turned to Sammy and said, 'Who's your handsome friend, Samuel?'

Calloway rose and said, 'It's a pleasure to meet you, Miss...?'

Sammy's visitor gave him a mischievous smile, then cackled like a fish wife. He held out his hand.

'Margot Montmartre,' he said. His voice dropped an octave, 'But you can call me Barry.'

'The pleasure's all mine,' said Calloway.

Barry gave him a wink.

'Cut it out, Cab,' said Sammy. 'This is awkward enough.'

There was a cold silence. Sammy was seldom lost for words. This was the exception. His face tensed and he stared into the mirror above the fireplace as if hoping to see the reflection of a very different scene playing out in the living room of his bachelor flat. Barry seemed oblivious. He pulled off his wig, kicked off his heels, crossed the room in his stockinged feet and helped himself to a drink.

Calloway leaned in to Sammy and whispered in his ear.

'Don't worry, Sammy,' he said. 'We all have our secrets. You keep mine...' He looked Barry up and down. 'And I'll keep yours. But I need a favour.'

Sammy scoffed. 'You've had more favours than a whore on payday.'

Calloway ignored him. 'I need to know about a man called Giordano Spiteri. If he has a criminal record, who his known associates are. He may be connected with organised crime.'

'That's not my bailiwick and you know it.'

Barry cut in, 'Sammy, what's this all about?'

He'd dropped his female act and sat ungainly in Sammy's chair, rubbing his feet, a cigarette dangling from his painted lower lip. With his pale powdered face and tight black hair net, he looked like Pagliacci.

'Shut up, will you,' Sammy shouted.

Barry scowled. He looked Sammy in the face and pointed a perfectly manicured finger at him. 'Don't you talk to me like that, Samuel. You know what happened last time.'

He took a swig of scotch and continued rubbing his feet.

Calloway said, 'You've got clearance to access Scotland Yard records. Use it, will you. Just this once.'

Sammy rolled his eyes. 'You don't know the meaning of "just this once". I'm not lifting a finger until you tell me what's going on.'

Calloway looked over at the young man in the chair. Consorting with female impersonators wasn't high on the list of qualities the secret service considered desirable in an operative.

'Like I said, Sammy. You keep my secrets and I'll keep yours.'

Calloway didn't give a damn who Sammy chose to share his evenings with. He was surprised, of course, but since the war he'd learned to divide life into things that mattered and things that didn't. Life and death mattered. Love and sex didn't, at least they weren't reasons to judge people. He'd seen the worst the world could do when judgement was let loose. Everything else was trivial now. But he needed a reason for Sammy to back off and he'd used the beautiful night-time caller to shut him up. Until Calloway had made sense of the past week's events, he wasn't letting anyone in on his investigation.

He slept badly that night. He was bruised from Bryant's truncheon blow and Belcher's fist. He still ached from the beating he'd received in his office. A professional beating hurt for longer. And he couldn't purge the woman's face from his mind. The scene of her fleeing the gala replayed over and over as he fought for sleep. He was convinced she was the key to everything. The IRA angle was irrelevant. He was satisfied of that, even if others weren't. It was the fear on the woman's face. Different to the others. The dinner guests were fleeing danger, the woman was fleeing the scene. The difference was subtle but significant. His brown-job copper's instinct told him so.

When he slept he dreamed again. The same dream, but with scenes from the present merging with the film loop of his past. And an incessant soundtrack of insinuating voices.

Twenty thousand bodies in a heap, just lying in the sun like wax.

A family thrown into the street while their possessions burned on the fire.

Wir kommen wieder!

TWENTY-TWO

Giordano was sitting at Calloway's desk when he arrived at work the following morning. His bulk almost fit into the chair. He was leaning back, smoking, his big feet in his big Italian-looking shoes up on Calloway's desk.

'Make yourself at home,' Calloway said, hanging up his mackintosh.

'Boss wants to see you,' Giordano said.

He stood up and gestured to the door. Calloway shrugged. As he turned to leave, the phone on his desk rang.

'Leave it,' said Giordano.

Calloway ignored him. He lifted the receiver. It was Sammy.

'You're early, Sammy.'

'Well it's not the sort of loose end I want hanging, Cab. I have what you want. Luckily for you, the duty liaison officer at Scotland Yard knows me. I caught him at the end of his night shift. He read the file over to me. Can you take this down?'

Calloway wedged the phone between his head and shoulder and wrote in his notebook. He shielded his notes from Giordano's view with his free hand. When Sammy had finished, Calloway pocketed the book and said, 'Thanks Sammy. I'd say we're square now.'

'And I'd say you're the worst kind of shit, Calloway.'

The phone went dead.

Calloway and Giordano walked in silence down the empty corridors. Outside, stage hands were dressing the flank wall of Studio B with fake foliage. Ivy leaves cut from cloth which even at a distance failed to look convincing. One of the hands was nailing a pub sign onto the jamb of the doorway, while another rolled empty barrels into position. A painter was doing his best to daub a thick coat of brown paint onto the metal-framed windows in an attempt to make them rustic. None of it worked. Calloway thought the whole scene looked as fake as everything else in this tawdry dream factory.

Spelthorne's selection of secretaries was as fragrant as usual. Two were typing. They looked up when Giordano entered the office. Calloway felt them tense, only slightly, but enough for him to notice. It told him a lot about Giordano. The third secretary, who he now knew as Miss Hope, was leafing through a film magazine. She looked bored. She didn't react as the two men passed.

Spelthorne was at his desk reading paperwork. Giordano pointed to a chair opposite. Calloway sat. Giordano remained standing. Looming. That's what he did, Calloway had noticed. Giordano loomed.

'I've just had the bills for the equipment we had to replace,' said Spelthorne.

He tapped the papers with his thick fingers.

'Arm and a bleedin' leg it's costing me.'

He stretched so that the sinews stood proud through the layer of well-fed flesh on his neck. 'So what have you got for me?' he said.

It was too early for an offer of a drink. Calloway could have done with a cigarette though, but the silver cigarette box on the desk stayed shut.

'I need to speak to you in private,' said Calloway.

Spelthorne looked like he didn't understand. 'We are in fuckin' private.'

He looked down at the foot well under the desk.

'You think someone's hiding down here?'

It was entirely possible, had Miss Hope not been sitting in the next-door room.

'I need to speak to you personally. Just you.'

Calloway nodded at Giordano. The big goon bristled. He looked at Spelthorne for a steer on what to do. Spelthorne waved his hand at Calloway dismissively.

'We're all friends,' he said.

Calloway rose to leave. 'I'm not sure we are.'

He felt Giordano's beefy hand on his shoulder, pushing him back into the chair. Spelthorne shook his head. Giordano released his grip. Spelthorne gave an irritated sigh and signalled for Giordano to leave. Giordano shot him an aggrieved look then left. When he was gone Calloway said, 'How long have you known him?'

'Giordano? Long enough. We grew up together. Both Saffron Hill boys.'

'And you trust him?'

'I wouldn't have him around if I didn't. Get to the point.'

'You told me you had your own security because you believed that you were at risk personally from organised criminals.'

'I did. So?'

'Criminals from London's Maltese community.'

Spelthorne pulled a cigarette from the box and lit it with a desk lighter. He didn't offer one to Calloway. 'That's what I said. What's that to you?'

'I told you I'd investigate the damage to equipment at the studio. In the course of my enquiries I learned two things that might trouble you. I feel it's my duty to report them.'

He had Spelthorne's full attention now. The studio boss took a long drag on the cigarette and pushed the cigarette box towards Calloway, who helped himself.

'Go on,' said Spelthorne.

'About a year ago Giordano Spiteri was leaning on the actress Joyce Rose to sleep with an associate of his. When she refused, he ensured she was no longer offered roles by Centurion.'

Spelthorne shook his head, incredulous.

'What the hell are you digging around in Joyce's past for? The poor girl's dead and gone. Nothing anyone can do about that.'

Calloway ignored the question.

'The associate Spiteri wanted Joyce to sleep with was Alfredo Azzopardi. You know, the gangster jailed last week for running a vice ring. I've reason to believe Spiteri and Azzopardi were both members of a Maltese gang.'

Spelthorne frowned. Irritation showed on his face. 'I'm really not following this, son,' he said.

'It means the man you've entrusted to protect you and your money from Maltese gangs is actually part of one.'

Spelthorne sat back on the chair. He closed his eyes as if to let this sink in. When he opened them he was looking daggers at Calloway.

'I know that boy better than you know your Saturday night finger. Someone I trust more than my own mother, God rest her soul. Are telling me I've been duped? Are you telling me I'm stupid?'

'I'm just telling you what I've found out. If you're worried about people being out to get you, then a gangster on your payroll is the first place I would be looking. Especially when someone just turned that nice car of yours into a shower of scrap.'

Spelthorne shook his head and smiled, as if Calloway was the stupid one.

'You've been misinformed, son.'

'How do you explain him matchmaking for the gangster? Although that's not what I'd call it.'

Spelthorne waved his fleshy hand, dismissing the question.

'Listen. We're in a business that attracts all sorts. And we deal in glamour. Yeah, girls. What do you think Ivor's charm school is for? We're not looking for the next Vivien Leigh. We're dressing the shop window. Pretty girls attract window shoppers. You throw a party. People gate-crash it.'

Calloway hadn't mentioned a party. He wondered why Spelthorne had.

'They want to get their hands on the merchandise. That's what Giordano's for. He doesn't just watch my back. He keeps an eye on the starlets.'

'Which would make him well placed to coerce them into being nice to his criminal friends.'

'I doubt he's got criminal friends.' He laughed. 'I don't think he's got any friends. Apart from Franco, but even they're not close.'

They were pretty close when they were standing side by side with the fascists cutting up Johnny's commandos, thought Calloway.

'If you expect me to take this seriously, you're gonna need to do better than that.'

Calloway took his notebook from his pocket. He flipped a page and read his notes aloud.

'Giordano Mario Spiteri, born Saffron Hill, London, 23rd September 1913. Served three years for grievous bodily harm in 1937. Laced up a whore he was pimping, apparently. Then a two-year stretch for grievous bodily harm in 1941. He'd beaten up a punter who'd racked up a big debt with the owner of an unlicensed spieler. The owner got his money. The punter never walked again. Then six months in March 1945 for living off immoral earnings. Known associates in the criminal underworld, Salvatore Vella, Emmanuel Camilleri...' He paused. 'And Alfredo Azzopardi.'

Calloway put the notebook back in his pocket. Spelthorne sat back in his chair. He was silent. A full minute passed. Then Spelthorne said: 'Giordano is no saint. He's got a past, like the rest of us.'

'We don't all have that kind of past.'

'He was a bad lad in his youth. He's different now.'

'Can you be sure?'

'Like I said, we go way back. I know that boy. I trust him.'

Calloway thought of the intelligence report from Ted Nathan. The Maltese gang hired as muscle by Hamm and his fascists. Giordano and Franco in the thick of it with them.

'I think your trust is misplaced. My sources suggest that Giordano and Franco are mixed up with a Maltese gang. It's possible they may have been involved in the bombing and the damage to the studio equipment.'

This last part was pure speculation on Calloway's part. He wanted to see how Spelthorne reacted. The studio boss's eyes narrowed. Behind them, he seemed to be weighing up whether Calloway could be right.

'Why would they do something like that? What would their

motive be?'

'A show of strength as a prelude to extortion. Demonstrate what they're capable of, then squeeze you for money.'

Spelthorne shook his head. 'Ridiculous. Not Giordano. He doesn't have the brains and Franco's barely smart enough to read the road signs when he's driving.'

'They don't need to be smart. The gang bosses would be the ones with the brains. All your two goons need is muscle and menace. They've got both of those in spades.'

Spelthorne glanced at the ornate clock on the wall. It looked like something you'd give to a retiring employee you didn't rate much. It was not yet ten. Spelthorne shrugged and eased his bulk out of the seat. He gestured to the drinks trolley.

'Need something?'

'Too early,' said Calloway. It wasn't. His mouth was dry, and he could have easily downed a large one. But he wanted to remain sharp.

'Suit yourself,' said Spelthorne, pouring himself a generous measure of Johnny Walker. He knocked it back in one.

'Let's just say you're right, that they're naughty boys and their friends have got their eyes on some of what I've made. What then? I'm not going to the police with something like that. I can't have that kind of stink hanging over the studio. My investors would run a mile.'

'I could help,' said Calloway.

He wasn't yet sure how, or indeed whether he was barking up the right tree. The gang angle didn't tally with his hunch about the woman fleeing the gala. He had little actual evidence of her involvement, but his instinct was strong. She was significant somehow. The only reason he had for playing the gangland card was to buy time with Spelthorne.

'Let me speak to Giordano in private,' said Calloway.

'You mean brace him.'

'I mean speak to him.'

He meant brace him. Part of him looked forward to it.

Spelthorne poured himself another large measure of the scotch. He mulled Calloway's suggestion over.

'Why would you do that? I mean, what's it to you?'

'I'm your head of security.'

'You're just a night watchman with an office.'

At least he knew where he figured in Spelthorne's empire. It came as no surprise.

'I sort this out for you,' said Calloway. 'You let me keep my job. And the two hundred pounds.'

Spelthorne scoffed. 'Now who's squeezing me for money?'

'It's a fair trade. The police aren't going to sort this out for you. They're still obsessed with the Irish connection. There is no Irish connection.'

Spelthorne nodded. 'Seems a bit far-fetched. That McCaffrey's not got it in him.' He laughed to himself. 'Fucking pisshead with a gob on him, that's all he is.'

He set his glass down and looked Calloway in the eye. 'Alright, son,' he said. 'You've got yourself a deal. But do it quickly. I want this over with. I want Gio in the clear. That's the only reason I'm agreeing to this.'

'And I'm sure he will be,' said Calloway, not sure at all.

TWENTY-THREE

Water rushed from the pipe. The level rose around him, past his chest, his neck, then up over his head until he was fully submersed. He held his breath. Beneath the water the muffled sound of metal handles cranking and water pouring. He lay still and counted the seconds, then the minutes. He felt the tightness in his chest, his lungs aching as he held onto the single breath he'd gulped down before the water covered his mouth and nose. His counting reached two minutes. He struggled against the urge to breathe. His fists clenched by his sides. He counted to three minutes before bursting upwards through the surface of the steaming water, gasping. He let out a loud grunt, which echoed around the terrazzo tiling of the bath house cubicle.

It was Saturday morning. The public baths were part of his weekly routine. And right now he needed to cleanse himself of the filth that clung to him, the whole dirty business he'd fallen into. He scrubbed with carbolic until his flesh burned.

Mornings were better at the baths. Quieter. By Saturday afternoon the place was full of noisy young blades scrubbing up for their night at the Palais. Big bars of foul-smelling soap scrubbing away a week's worth of grime. Then preening with hair oil, crafting their hair into a poor imitation of the latest movie star's style. Kings for a night.

He'd treated himself to a first-class cubicle at the Gainsborough Road baths. It was a thirty-minute bus ride, but was newer and cleaner than the local alternative. A confident Art Deco building opened before the war, with separate wings for men and women, and a public laundry. The first-class baths had their own changing rooms and lavatories.

Calloway needed some time alone. He needed to soothe the

bruises from the beating in his office and scars from the melee at Ridley Road. It gave him time to think. Time to plan. He needed a plan now. He'd played Spelthorne along with the gangland angle to buy time, but also to test him. He wanted to know how much his boss knew about the goons that followed him around. But he'd found him too hard to read. Spelthorne was a practised manipulator, at least that's how he seemed the closer Calloway got to him. He guessed you needed to be to succeed in films, as much as in any business. Spelthorne wasn't one of the big names. He wasn't a Rank or a Balcon. But he'd done alright, from humble beginnings. You didn't get that way by wearing your heart on your sleeve. People like that got taken advantage of. Calloway couldn't imagine anyone taking advantage of Spelthorne, with or without his goons in tow.

He needed to get Giordano on his own, away from Franco. That wouldn't be easy. Most of the time they were a double act. Like Flanagan and Allen without the songs and jokes. In the meantime he would try Eve Clark's place again. Catch her in this time. Find out why she'd gone AWOL from her shifts as cleaner and why Joyce Rose had a poetry magazine with her poems in it. It could have been a coincidence, but like his Special Branch friend Belcher, Calloway didn't believe in them. He was grateful to Sammy for getting those two off his back, however little choice Calloway had given him in doing so. It was one less complication.

He heard Mr Da Costa's voice in his head. 'Women are complicated, Mr Calloway. If they weren't, they would be very dull indeed.' He thought of Marge. Should he call her? Hell, he didn't even have her number. Each time they'd met she had reeled him in. A part of him felt like being reeled in again. It was the kind of complication that he was prepared to tolerate.

He dressed in the small changing room that came with the first-class cubicle. Then he rolled up his towel - you had to provide your own - and let himself out into the corridor. Sweat, soap and steam hung in the air like mist. The sound of bathers echoed down the tiled corridor. Some sang, some coughed and spat. He was glad he'd paid the extra to go first class.

He heard a familiar voice from behind.

'Nice bath? I can't get enough of them since the war. Trying to wash the stink of death off me, I guess.'

It was Johnny Suskind. His hair was wet-combed into a severe parting and he held a rolled up towel under his arm. His shirt was unbuttoned to his chest, under his old blouson jacket.

'Nice coincidence, meeting you here,' Suskind said.

'I don't believe in them, Johnny,' said Calloway.

Johnny gave an impish grin. 'You're a creature of habit, Reg. I figured you might be here.'

'You figured right then.'

Johnny was a pal, but it didn't stop Calloway being suspicious.

'I need a quick chat,' said Suskind. He nodded towards the end of the corridor. 'We can go to the caretaker's office. He's a good friend.'

'A member of your group?'

Johnny put a finger to his lips. 'Walls have ears, Reg, like the posters used to say.'

Calloway followed Johnny down the corridor towards a door marked Resident Engineer. He heard Liz Francis's voice saying, 'You're not getting involved again, are you, Reg?'

Johnny knocked on the door and a voice behind it told them to come in, as if he already knew who was knocking.

'Borrow your room for half a mo', Sid?' said Johnny.

Sid was five foot one and easily half has a wide. For a short man he had the musculature of a heavyweight. A proper mighty atom. His jaw was an anvil covered in leather. His nose was flattened like a pug's. He stubbed the last of a Woodbine out in an old tin ashtray and picked up a battered tool tray.

'One of the hydro-extractors in the wash-house is playing up,' he said. 'I need to go give it a whack. Take your time and help yourself to tea.'

He nodded towards the kettle on the gas ring in the corner of the small wood-panelled room. There was a calendar on the wall from a company that manufactured toilet cleaner. This month's photo was of a gleaming lavatory cubicle. Next to the calendar some postcards pinned to the panelling with drawing pins.

Southend, Margate, Weston-super-Mare and somewhat incongruously, Jaffa. Sid left the room, shutting the door behind him. Johnny placed a big hand on the kettle and nodded, satisfied the water was still hot enough. He spooned tea into Sid's teapot and added the water, then stirred it around with vigour.

'Time for a brew,' he said to himself.

Johnny poured the tea into two tin mugs without waiting. He spooned in three sugars each without asking.

Calloway took one of the mugs from him and sipped the pale, lukewarm liquid.

'You never could make proper tea, Johnny.'

'I know,' the big man said. 'Too impatient.'

'Sid seems like a good sort,' said Calloway, giving Johnny time to work up to whatever he had brought Calloway into the small room to say.

Johnny nodded. 'He was a lightweight contender in his day. Fists like dumbbells. He once knocked out Jackie Berg.'

Suskind took a sip of the tea and winced. 'Yeah, I never could make tea,' he said.

'What's up Johnny?' said Calloway.

Suskind looked relieved at the opportunity to get to the point. 'We've got to step it up, Reg. That episode with the Maltese and the blades. The fascists have upped the ante. We need to as well.'

'Why are you telling me?'

Johnny looked around as if the panelled walls might have ears too. He lowered his voice. 'We're planning a raid. Catch 'em off guard. Hit 'em where it really hurts. Make a statement. Instil some fear.'

Calloway didn't like where this was going. Protest was one thing. A few fisticuffs and a few sore heads, maybe. Whatever Johnny had up his sleeve sounded like the group might be going a step too far. Something Belcher and Bryant's friends at Scotland Yard might take more than a passing interest in.

'Tell me you're plan, Johnny.'

Suskind laid it out for him. It was a simple plan. It required audacity, brute force and very little else.

'We need you to front it, Reg. To go in first.'

Calloway didn't like the sound of this. It was crossing a line.

'Why me? You've got plenty of big lads who could do that kind of thing, not that I'm endorsing it.'

'We can't put Jews up front. The fascists would tumble to that straight away and we'd never get through the door. We've got one man who's put his hand up already. A Welshman. Methodist. Lives local. But it's a two-hander. You're the other man, Reg. We need you.'

'I'm not your man, Johnny. Not for this one. I'll fight on your front line at the rallies and I'm not afraid to crack a few heads in the heat of battle. But you're going to need someone else for this one.'

Suskind nodded. He was trying hard not to show his disappointment. Not disapproval. It was clear he respected Calloway's decision. But Calloway sensed that there wasn't a ready supply of non-Jewish group members with what it was going to take to front the operation Johnny had planned.

Johnny supped the last of his tea. 'Fair do's Reg,' he said. He put the mug down and crossed the small room to the door. He turned before leaving and looked Calloway in the eye.

'They daubed a swastika on mum's door last night,' he said.

The light was fading when Calloway crossed the Regent's Canal towards Ndungu's street. He was calling on the off chance, hoping that the young law student would be home. There were four bell buttons beside the door. He'd no idea which was Ndungu's flat. He pressed them all. He heard an inner door open and heavy footsteps descend a single flight of stairs. He also heard coughing and swearing. A balding middle-aged man opened the door. His stained vest and unbuttoned fly were clues to his temperament. He grunted at Calloway.

'Who are you?'

'A friend of Paul Ndungu. Is he in?'

The man sneered as if he could suddenly smell an odour worse than his own.

'See for yourself. Third floor,' he said, pulling a grey, mucus-filled handkerchief from his trouser pocket and blowing something green into it. He showed no signs of stepping aside. Instead he stood for a moment examining whatever he'd produced from his red raw nostrils. Calloway flattened himself against the hallway wall and edged past, trying not to pick up anything slimy on his suit.

The hallway was damp, but no more so than usual for such a property. It had a familiar smell. Damp, gas and boiled veg. The odour of multiple occupancy. Calloway knew it well. He'd served his time in such places since leaving the army.

He knocked on the door of the third-floor flat.

A voice said, 'Let yourself in, I've got my hands full.'

It was Ndungu. He was standing on a flimsy-looking stool reaching for the light fitting in the high ceiling, plugging in an electric iron which stood on a stained wooden ironing board beneath him. Calloway saw tiny blue-white sparks coming from the ceiling rose. They made Ndungu jump. The stool tottered ominously beneath his bare feet.

'What's that expression you mentioned?' said Calloway. 'Only scratch where you can reach?'

'This bloody house should be condemned,' said Ndungu.

Calloway looked around the room. It was shabby and cheerless, with dark wallpaper two decades old. But it was clean and tidy and Ndungu had done his best to make it his own. A new-looking gramophone stood on a plain wooden cabinet in the corner. Next to it, two long rows of records, Ndungu's jazz collection, Calloway imagined. There was a modern desk and chair and above it more shelves, with books on law and business. A portion of the room was divided by a half partition to create a kitchenette, with a gas ring and stone sink. A pile of freshly washed breakfast dishes stood on the drainer. The bed doubled as a studio couch with brightly patterned cushions. Three suits and a sports jacket with flannels hung from a rail beside the bed, together with five crisp white shirts. Ndungu liked to iron, in spite of the risk of electrocution. Two un-ironed shirts lay on the ironing board waiting.

'I've lived in worse,' said Calloway.

'Did you meet my delightful landlord on the way in?'

‘If he was part man, part mucus, then yes.’

‘He’s pretty unsavoury. But less selective than many round here, if you know what I mean.’

Calloway had seen the signs on neighbouring buildings. No coloureds.

‘I get your drift,’ he said.

Ndungu clicked the iron’s Bakelite plug into the ceiling socket with a concerted shove. The socket stopped sparking. He climbed down from the creaking stool.

‘I’ll put on some music, but I know you hate jazz.’

‘I like Mahler.’

Ndungu smiled. ‘I have Mahler,’ he said, looking pleased. He took a shellac disc from a plain sleeve and placed it on the turntable, laying the needle down with an expert hand. A soothing symphony filled the room. To Calloway, it brightened it. He’d lost most of his own record collection in a break-in at his last digs. He seldom listened to music now. He missed it. He missed the memories it evoked.

Ndungu made coffee from an Italian percolator and passed Calloway a cup. He tested the iron with a spit ball, which hissed back at him. Satisfied, Ndungu started ironing the first of the shirts.

‘It’s a pleasure to see you, Reg, but I suspect this call isn’t social.’

‘It’s not. I’ve come to ask for your help. Something that might just clear your friend Terrence McCaffrey’s name.’

‘I’m not sure what I can do, but if it helps Terrence, then I’m willing to try. I’ve not known him long, but we’ve become good friends. His mouth runs away with him, but his heart’s in the right place. I’ll help, on the condition of course it’s strictly legal. I have a career in law ahead of me. I can’t risk blotting my copy book at this early stage.’

He put the iron down and took a sip of his coffee. ‘What do you have in mind?’

‘I need someone who knows their way around company accounts to look in to Centurion Pictures’ business. You said you were studying company law.’

Ndungu nodded. 'What should I be looking for specifically?'

'Who its shareholders are and where the money comes from.'

Ndungu considered this for a moment. 'There are places I can look. Companies House for a start.'

'Good. Come straight to me with what you find.' Calloway took a pencil and paper from the desk and wrote down his number. 'Speak only to me about this. No one else. Especially no one from the studio.'

Ndungu looked apprehensive. 'I'd like to know more. Can I ask what the context is?'

'Best you don't. Leave that to me. If you can look at the names and numbers, I can do the rest.'

Calloway sipped the coffee. It was good. He missed good coffee too.

'You've got your career to think of.'

'I have. More to the point I have my father to think of.' He waved his hand at the law books on the shelf. 'He's paying for this education.'

'Is he a lawyer too?'

'A civil servant. And mother's a teacher.' He laughed. 'Terrence calls me bourgeois.'

'Terrence would. So would my father.'

'A communist?'

'Apparently so.'

'But you're not.'

'I'm not my father's son, put it that way.'

'I fear I am.'

He glanced over at the records. 'Apart from my love of jazz, of course. Father hates it. He suspects I spend all my money on records.'

Calloway looked along the two long rows of discs. 'I suspect he's right. Thanks for the coffee. And the music. Call me when you've got something to tell me.'

The two men shook hands and Calloway left. He heard the landlord hacking up phlegm as he closed the front door behind him.

TWENTY-FOUR

Saturday evening, after seven. He walked up Tottenham Court Road. It was already busy. Couples queueing outside the Dominion for a dance band. Women in their best coats, worn over their going-out frocks against the autumn chill. Higher heels and more made up than usual. Men with hair that glistened, combed flat against their heads in neat rows, ending abruptly just shy of the base of their skulls where the barber shop clippers had shorn them near to bald. The more dapper ones coiffured it up into a neat, cheeky quiff. Some had pencil moustaches, mere lines of darkened bum fluff hinting at their prowess.

It was the kind of Saturday night normality that Calloway avoided. A night of mandatory good humour, obligatory fun, accepted inebriation. People letting go. Calloway didn't let go. Not of his own volition. His episodes of abandon were beyond his control. They chose when they came. When they did, things generally ended badly. But there was something in the mood of the crowd that cheered him on this night. Just for a moment or two. He imagined Marge and him in the queue. Her arm through his. No talk of 'getting off', just warm and undemanding chatter. Like the other couples. A reassuring normality. Something he seldom enjoyed, not since the war, at least. He shook the thought off. It would do him no good.

He quickened his pace as he headed north to the junction with Goodge Street. He hoped to catch Eve Clark at her lodgings. He didn't see her as the dance hall type. He didn't imagine her kind headed out until well into the night.

He stood in front of the pawn shop and looked up at the windows above. Eve's first-floor room was dark. The second-floor window above was lit. The well-bred poetry brat's room, he guessed. He rang the bell. Its electric rasp seemed angrier than last time. He heard the sound of feet thumping down the wooden stairs. Fast, with a sense of urgency.

The brat was fully dressed this time, after a fashion. The same corduroys, worn with a check shirt and brown flannel jacket a size too big for him. Shoes he may have owned since school, scuffed with fraying laces. He'd combed his hair too. Or at least shown it the comb.

'Oh, you again,' he said. 'I was expecting someone else.'

He frowned, like a child denied a second iced bun.

'Sorry to disappoint you,' said Calloway. 'I was hoping to catch Eve Clark.'

'She's out. Been out for an hour or so. I heard her leave.'

'Do you know where she went?'

He shrugged. 'The Fitzroy, probably. That's were her gang are usually found.'

'Buying drinks for Mephisto.'

The brat looked surprised. 'You know Mephisto?'

'He publishes my work,' Calloway lied.

The brat seemed about to laugh, then stifled it. Perhaps it was Calloway's big frame filling the doorway that stopped him.

'I'll check there,' said Calloway. 'But if she comes back in the meantime, tell her I called, will you?'

The brat sulked at the thought of such responsibility. 'Not much point. She'll be out for the rest of the night. They'll go to someone's place after the pub.'

He shuffled, showing some impatience at Calloway's presence. 'Anyway, I'm going out myself later.'

'What time?'

The boy gave a petulant shrug. 'I don't know. Just later. When I feel like it.'

This last line spoken as if to a nanny he no longer had to take instruction from. Calloway had had enough. He left the boy to his sulking and tried the Fitzroy Tavern. No joy. He walked back towards Tottenham Court Road. He'd give it an hour or two. He thought about a drink but he didn't relish the joviality of a pub.

The neon lights of a cinema pierced the smoggy haze that hung over the street. Now showing: Dangerous Beat. A Centurion Pictures Production. The poster showed two young hoodlums fighting a uniformed policeman. The sell-line read: In the battle for the streets, the heroes wear blue. In the few months since taking the job, Calloway had not seen a Centurion picture, at least not all the way through.

There was no queue outside the cinema. He read the showing times on the board and checked his watch. He could catch the next showing, wait out a couple of hours and return to Eve Clark's lodgings.

A voice from behind him said: 'Get us in, will ya?'

There were two of them. One short, one lanky. Both skinny in their hand-me-down jumpers and shapeless flannels. Calloway reckoned they were eight or nine, ten at a push, if you allowed for a decade of poor nutrition. The lanky one stood with his hands in his pockets looking sheepish. The short one stuck his hand out, proffering a shilling, the price of two tickets.

Calloway glanced up at the film poster in the case beside the cinema doors.

'It's certificate A,' he said.

A for adult. Not U for Universal. Nor U for urchin, unkempt, untrustworthy.

'I'm eleven and he's twelve,' the small one said. 'We just don't look it, that's all. Can't help that, can we? The old cow in the box office won't sell us a ticket 'cause she doesn't believe we're old enough.'

Calloway raised an eyebrow. He didn't believe they were old enough either.

'It's true,' the lanky one said. 'And the commissionaire said he'd cuff us if we came back.'

'He's a right bastard,' the short one said.

'Does your mother know you talk like that?' said Calloway.

'Ain't got a mother. She ran off with a sailor. I live with me gran. And she swears like a trooper.'

'It's true,' the lanky one said, like it was his catch phrase.

Calloway looked around him. The commissionaire stood

sentinel outside the two large chromium doors. He was at least sixty, with a sallow face that hung loosely from a bony skull. His uniform was a size too big for his wizened frame. The braid on his epaulettes was unravelling. He didn't seem too alert.

There was no queue at the box office window. Calloway told the boys to stay where they were then bought a ticket for the circle and two for the stalls.

'Here,' he said, handing the small boy the two cheaper tickets. 'I'll distract the old man, you slip in when his back's turned.'

The boy gave him a conspiratorial wink. Calloway walked up to the commissionaire, flipped open his cigarette case and asked for a light. The old boy rifled in the pockets of his sagging uniform trousers and pulled out a box of Bryant & Mays. Calloway leaned in for the light, his broad back shielding the boys from view. He heard the doors open behind him and the faint scuffle of small feet. The commissionaire seemed not to notice.

The circle was half full. He took a seat two rows back from the balcony. The seats smelled musty. Above him, the beam of the projector illuminated dust. There was a faint metallic whir of film reels turning in the projection room. They were still showing the short. Popeye was downing spinach and beating hell out of a villain three times his size. Calloway could see the two boys in the stalls below. They jiggled in their seats and cackled.

The main feature opened to a menacing score. Strings and brass. The titles appeared over the shadows of darkened backstreets. A lone constable pursued two figures in silhouette, their footsteps smacking the cobbles and echoing above the music. The names of the writers Cedric Dryden and Michael Balfour appeared on the screen. Then the title: Dangerous Beat. The silhouetted figures appeared in the street light. The copper blew his whistle, its shrill tone jarring with the music. Cut to a quayside, steamers moored alongside, their masts puncturing the skyline. A steam whistle blasted in the background. The young copper leapt over a parapet onto the foreshore, the river glistening like hot tar. His helmet fell onto the stones and rolled towards the water. The hoodlums were an arm's length away now. One turned. Light shone on the pistol in his hand. The copper stopped in his tracks, truncheon raised. He was young, fresh-faced and blonde, his jaw clenched, fighting down the fear. The hoodlum was younger still. His hair was piled high, his face scarred. The score reached a crescendo. The pistol filled the screen. There was a flash from the muzzle. A gunshot echoed. Cut to the face of the copper, shocked, his jaw tightening as he feels the creeping pain. Then he fell. His dead eyes filled the screen. The score tailed away. The screen went dark. Words appeared: Director, Bobbie Brand.

Calloway was no expert but he had to hand it to Centurion. They knew how to make a picture. He looked down at the boys. They were silent and still. Transfixed. Calloway smiled. He settled into his seat and stared at the screen. He followed the plot for the first hour before sleep tugged at his eyelids.

He woke with a start. The end credits were rolling. He looked at his watch. Enough time had passed.

There was still no light in Eve Clark's window. The window above was dark too. The brat poet had gone out. The whole place appeared empty. He looked up and down the street. Not a soul about. The doorway was dark, the nearest streetlight a good twenty yards away. The darkness covered him. He reached into the inside pocket of his jacket and withdrew the six-inch metal ruler he'd taken from his desk. He slid it between the door frame and the lock. The door was old and loose. The lock was a simple night latch. It popped with little effort. Calloway looked around him. The street was still empty. He pushed against the door and stepped into damp-smelling hallway. It was pitch dark. Calloway flipped open his lighter. The flame lit up a gloomy stairway, with a cheerless floral print on the wallpaper. The bannister was worn and chipped. He headed up the stairs to the first floor. He trod firmly, with the footsteps of someone that was meant to be there. There may have been another tenant still in the house. He didn't want anyone to hear him creeping. Creeping would sound suspicious. He passed a lavatory on the half landing. The shared 'how's-yer-father' that the writer Julian had described. It smelled of Zal Pine with a hint of something nastier. He reached what he assumed was Eve Clark's door on the first-floor landing. He flipped the lighter shut and leaned in close to listen in the darkness. There was no noise from the other side. No light under the door. He tried the knob. It yielded to his turn. The door was unlocked. He stood there still and listened for signs of life in the rest of the building. He heard nothing but the intermittent rumble of car tyres on cobbles outside and voices of Saturday night revellers leaving the pubs and cinemas. He eased the door ajar. Its hinges creaked. The boards under his feet rasped as he stepped into the darkened room. The curtains were still open and a distant street lamp cast enough glow for him to make out furniture. A bed doubling as a couch, with a bolster and patchwork throw. A small reading light above it with a shade that looked like parchment and a braided flex leading down to a plug socket on the skirting. Bookshelves stuffed with paperbacks and magazines. A small drop-leaf table with two chairs, and a single armchair, well worn, wisps of horse hair bursting from cracks in the leather upholstery. A typical rented room, if your budget was slim and your expectations low. He guessed there wasn't much money in poetry. Especially when Mephisto was your publisher. He probably took more in free drinks than he gave out in royalties.

Calloway felt for a light switch. He found one to the side of the door. He flicked it down but no light appeared. Maybe the bulb had blown. He tried the reading light above the bed. No joy either. He flicked his lighter open again and looked for a meter. It stood on a shelf on the other side of the door, like a stout, sleeping robot with its rivets, pipes and dials. Fumbling in his pocket, he pulled out a shilling, pushed it into the slot and cranked the key until the coin dropped and the two lights came on. The faint ticking of the meter's dial irritated the silence.

With the benefit of light, the room was cheerful enough, with coloured cushions strewn around the place and surfaces draped with floral scarfs and throws. The pictures on the walls were chosen well, cheapish bric-a-brac but bought by someone with a good eye. Foreign landscapes, still life and nudes. They looked European. There were wax-encrusted wine bottles with candles in. The wine was French and reasonable. The table was covered with back issues of bohemian magazines. The Studio and Mephisto's poetry reviews. There was an old iron fireplace on the chimney breast and a plain mantlepiece above, with framed photographs in mismatched frames. Calloway examined the photos.

There was Joyce Rose, a teenage Joyce, and beside her the woman who'd fled the dinner, but brunette and younger. The picture looked at least a decade old. Seen side by side, the similarity between them was unmistakable. So too was the setting. Paris. Montmartre, by the look of it. Calloway had been there on leave from the front in forty-four. Here was Joyce and the sister from Paris. Sister Yvonne. The name on the postcards. Yvonne Leclerc. Anglicised, Eve Clark, as near as dammit. The poet and the missing cleaner. And the woman dolled up to the nines who seemed so keen to avoid Calloway on the night of the explosion. All one and the same. Deep down, Calloway had suspected this all along. The photo confirmed it.

He examined the other photographs one by one. Yvonne with friends mostly. In France again. One friend in particular. A young man. Tall and good looking. A little rugged perhaps, but distinguished too. He looked like a special friend. And he appeared in the last photo on the mantle. Just him and Yvonne. A studio portrait. Both in uniform. British uniforms from the war. Calloway picked up the photo and held it under the reading light to see better. He was looking at the insignia. The cap badges and shoulder flashes. It's what you do when you've lived half your life in uniform. He recognised both their units.

Everything made sense now.

He heard the floorboards creak. There was a figure in the doorway. Then a flattened hand struck him hard across the neck. A searing pain shot upwards to his skull. A second strike made his knees buckle. He steadied himself against the bed frame. He felt a blow to the kidneys, like a bad bruise multiplied a thousand times. Then an upper cut slammed into his jaw so that his teeth crunched together, the sound of grinding bone reverberating through his skull. He felt faint from the pain. A blanket of dazzling white light started to envelop him until only a chink of vision remained. Through it he saw the face. Eve Clark. Yvonne Leclerc.

He knew that by the next blow he'd be unconscious. He sank to his knees and thrust out his arm to grab her ankle. He jerked hard and saw her topple. Reaching up he pulled the reading light from above the bed and smashed it hard into her face. He saw sparks as the bulb shattered. Yvonne screamed, but just for a second. She recovered and scrambled to her feet. Calloway was on his feet too, a surge of adrenalin giving him a strength he'd not had moments before. Yvonne could kill him. Right there and then. He knew she was more than capable. Instead she ran. She was smart, a quick thinker. Better to flee and survive than to attempt a kill and die in the process. And she wasn't a killer by nature. He knew that too.

He ran for the door and threw his big frame down the stairs, stumbling downwards two treads at a time. He saw Yvonne, silhouetted in the open doorway. He fell into the street and looked around. He saw her twenty yards ahead, heading towards Tottenham Court Road. She wore a pale raincoat and red beret. At least it made her easy to spot. But she was fast. Faster than him. He gulped air deep into his lungs and tried to summon strength. He pushed himself on, towards her, seeing her turn left, losing herself in the late evening bustle.

He reached the street corner, panting. He looked to the left. He didn't see her, not at first. Then he caught a glimpse of the raincoat and beret. She was still running, turning right into a side street, attracting curious looks from passers-by. Women didn't run. Not unless they were caught in the rain or trying to catch a bus. Then they only ran in neat little steps. Ladylike running. Yvonne was sprinting. Calloway darted through the traffic. Angry horns blasted at him. A cabbie leaned out of his window and swore. A bus conductor hung off the pole at the back of a passing bus and shouted, 'You trying to get yourself killed?'

The side street was dark. At least darker than the road he'd just crossed. No proper lampposts, just small white lights on brackets bolted to the buildings along the street. They cast circles of dim grey light between swathes of black. Yvonne appeared in the light for a second then disappeared. She appeared again, her red beret glowing like a beacon. Calloway followed, running through the light and shade, watching her appear and disappear. Then she disappeared for good. He'd expected to see her under the next streetlamp. By the time he reached it himself, she was gone. He looked around. No doorways, no pubs, nowhere to hide. Yet she was definitely gone. He stopped and steadied himself against the wall. He gasped and wheezed, all the pain of the beating flooding back in one big wave. He drew up a gobbet of phlegm and spat between his feet. He looked around again. Yvonne Leclerc had vanished into the night.

Calloway took a taxi to the studio. He sat back in the worn leather bench seat and stretched his aching limbs. The cabbie made conversation. Calloway blanked him until he got the message. He heard the cabbie tut. Too bad. He hurt. But his brain was racing. The photographs told him everything. Well, almost. The cab reached the studio and pulled up outside the main gates. Calloway paid him without thanks. He resented being tutted. He let himself into the studio courtyard. His muscles hurt as he eased the heavy iron gates apart and squeezed between them. He nodded to Arthur the night watchman, who was pulling a Saturday shift. Arthur stuck his head out of his booth and said, 'Everything alright, Mr Calloway?'

He sounded almost guilty, as if Calloway's visit was somehow due to him and he was going to receive a reprimand. That's the type Arthur was.

Calloway said, 'All correct, Arthur. Just need something from my office.'

Arthur didn't look convinced but pulled his little frame back through the window.

Calloway unlocked the administration block and climbed the stairs. His legs ached with every step. He unlocked his office door, walked in and fell back into the chair behind his desk. He fumbled in his drawer for the last of the Black & White and swigged from the bottle. The liquor helped, just like before. He unlocked the opposite drawer with a small key on his key ring.

He pulled out the clutch purse, Yvonne Leclerc's clutch purse, and emptied the contents. He ignored the make-up, the loose change and the handkerchief. He picked up the tortoise shell pencil and unscrewed it. He was deliberately gentle. He laid the two unscrewed sections of the pen's barrel on his desk and pulled them apart to reveal a slender metal tube inside. Part copper, part brass, with a small pin and striker at one end. He'd seen something like it during the war. It was a time pencil. A fuse to trigger explosives.

TWENTY-FIVE

Ndungu called him at the office on Monday. He had news. He suggested a place to meet. Calloway slipped out of the studio early. By the time he reached Soho, the evening was drawing in.

'This place has just opened. Isn't it great?' said Ndungu as they took their coffees and sat on high stools at a chest-high bar opposite the counter. It was an Italian coffee bar, the first Calloway had seen in London. The Italians were back in Soho and this place screamed the fact. Calloway had never been to Italy. The war hadn't taken him there. He'd no way of telling how authentic the place was. The accents of the men behind the counter seemed exaggerated. But he guessed the coffee was good. It ought to be, given the size of the chromium machine that spat it out, with a roar like a Bugatti banking the corners at Brooklands.

Calloway watched Ndungu pull a sheaf of paperwork from an envelope in the reflection of the mirrored wall above the Formica bar top.

'You asked me to look into Centurion Pictures,' said Ndungu. 'Who its shareholders were, where the money comes from, that kind of thing.'

Calloway nodded.

Ndungu continued. 'The company has two shareholders. Sidney G Spelthorne owns forty-five percent. The majority shareholder is a holding company called Primipilus Group.'

Calloway looked quizzical.

'In the army of imperial Rome, the Primus Pilus was the chief Centurion.' Ndungu smiled. 'They clearly saw themselves as empire builders.'

Calloway nodded. 'What's a holding company?' he said.

Business wasn't his strong point. You tended not to worry about such things when the army gave you three meals a day, a bed and a pay-packet. You worried about being late, getting killed or losing a part of you that you'd really rather hang on to.

'Essentially it's a company that owns other businesses.'

'So what kind of businesses does Primipilus Group own?'

'Aside from their majority shareholding in Centurion, they have three operating companies. One runs a couple of dance halls in north London. Another is a private car service. Neither of those make much. The largest of the three is a property company, Mayho Estates Limited. They own a portfolio of properties in Mayfair and Soho, hence the name. Good income-producing stock by the looks of the figures, very good in fact.'

'So what do they do with the money?'

'A large proportion of their capital appears to be funnelled into Centurion.'

'To fund pictures?'

Ndungu nodded. He stirred his coffee and took a sip, pausing for a moment as if to judge its quality. He smiled, seeming satisfied.

'So Primipilus Group is crucial to the whole studio set-up?'

Ndungu nodded and took another sip of the coffee. He smiled again. The coffee must have been that good.

'Who's behind Primipilus? Who's on the board?'

Ndungu rifled thought the papers and handed Calloway a page listing the directors. One of the names struck a chord. Charles Lewis, who resigned his directorship less than a year ago, according to the list. He'd seen the name before but couldn't think where. It nagged at him like an itch he needed to scratch.

'Do you recognise any of those names?' said Ndungu.

'Perhaps. I'm not sure,' said Calloway. 'What kind of properties does Mayho Estates own?'

Ndungu looked apologetic.

'It's hard to tell from the addresses. Sorry.'

'You have the addresses?' Calloway said, surprised.

'Yes, well, some of them at least. After I'd finished at

Companies House, I paid a visit to the Land Registry. I did some digging around and found these.'

He passed over the details of almost a dozen buildings owned by Mayho. Most were walking distance from where they sat.

'Fancy a stroll?' said Calloway.

Ndungu nodded. He seemed to enjoy playing detective. Calloway placed the papers in the envelope, folded it in two, and slipped it into the inside pocket of his suit jacket. They paid and left.

The properties were easy to find. Most were on Greek Street and Frith Street. Most had shops on the ground floor. A newsagent, a hairdresser, a hardware shop. All pretty nondescript. None of them looked like big payers when it came to rent. But all had one thing in common. A shabby-looking side entrance and windows above with lamps in them. Night was falling and the lamps were on. They were all red.

The two men heard a voice from behind. 'Are you looking for a little entertainment, gentlemen?'

He was short and swarthy and dressed like he was going to sell you a stolen watch. He could have been a shady character in one of Spelthorne's crime stories. The stripes on his suit were too loud, the jacket cut too long. His shirt contrasted with his tie in a way that could induce a migraine. He gave Calloway a cursory once-over before looking Ndungu up and down more carefully. Next to Calloway's ancient demob suit, the African student was dressed sharply and well, in his brown worsted two-piece, crisp white shirt and hand-made shoes. The small man's eyes twinkled.

'Of course if you were looking for something a little more exclusive, we have an establishment in Mayfair. A private club, if you will.'

He passed Ndungu a card. It was thick and embossed. No name. Just an address. Ndungu looked at Calloway and raised an eyebrow. They recognised it as one of the properties owned by Mayho Estates.

Calloway took the card from Ndungu. 'I think this looks very suitable,' he said.

The small man gave a conspiratorial nod.

'Tell the doorman you're there at the recommendation of Mr Rossi. He'll take care of you.'

As they walked away, Ndungu said, 'Good grief. He couldn't be more obvious if he tried. How does he get away with being so blatant?'

'His bosses must have coppers on the payroll.'

Ndungu looked surprised. 'The police can't be that crooked, can they?' he said. 'I read in the papers that they've just sent down the boss of a major vice ring.'

Calloway stopped. He remembered the article in the paper. Alfredo Azzopardi, sentenced to eight years, who sometimes went by the less incongruous name Charles Lewis.

'I'll say goodbye, Paul,' said Calloway. He waved the card. 'I'm going to take a look at this place. You've been very helpful. No need for you to get involved any further.'

Ndungu looked relieved. 'Even if I did want to join you, I'm not sure my student budget could stretch to it. My father's right. I spend far too much money on jazz records.'

'A far better thing to spend your money on,' said Calloway. 'No matter how God awful that music is. Bloody saxophones.'

Ndungu laughed. 'It's a mercy they don't have a smell, as you might say.'

He clapped Calloway on the arm with genuine warmth. Calloway thanked him again.

'I don't pretend to understand what all of this is about,' Ndungu said, 'but if it helps my friend Terrence, then it was worth the effort.'

The two men parted and Calloway headed west towards Mayfair. He was glad Ndungu was gone. The man was too good to get any more involved in the business Calloway had found himself in.

You're not getting involved again, are you Reg?

No, he thought. Not much. Just up to the fucking eyeballs.

The property was a narrow, stucco-fronted town house on Curzon Street, four storeys high with a grand-looking balustrade on the roof. Two laurel trees stood in polished brass planters either side of the shiny black door, each manicured into perfect spheres. There were net curtains behind the tall windows. They were impermeable. No club interior visible through them and nothing to identify the building beyond the number on the door. No brass plate, no club name. The porcelain dome of the bell button said Push. He pushed and a grand sounding bell rang in the hallway behind the door. There was a pause and the sound of a heavy bolt being slid back. A large figure in a dark coat and striped trousers filled the frame of the open door, his chest at Calloway's eye level. His face was flat and featureless, his leathery skin stretched taught like rhino hide. His expression gave nothing away. He waited. Calloway mentioned the name Rossi and without speaking the doorman stood back to let him into the hallway.

He was greeted by a woman announcing herself as Madame Lacroix, in an accent that was too French to be credible. She looked about fifty, or forty if you accounted for the hard life she'd no doubt had. She was powdered too pale and rouged too pink. Her hair was high and brittle. She'd packed an ample body into too little dress. She led him to a high-ceilinged drawing room on the first floor and asked him to take seat. He eased his big frame onto a velvet love seat that left little room for a lover. Madam Lacroix managed to squeeze in beside him nevertheless. Her undersized dress tightened as she sat. One false move and she'd spill out all over him.

The room was dimly lit by table lamps with deep red shades. Pictures in ornate gilt frames hung on the sage green walls. Regency-style prints of bawdy scenes. Something to get the punters in the mood, as if they needed it. A gramophone played a sickly dance number. There was company in the room too. Three girls perched daintily on chairs set against the wall. They smoked and toyed with what looked like soft drinks. A fourth sat on a high stool at a small bar in the corner. They wore modest cocktail dresses, showing no cleavage and not much leg. The dresses appeared expensive. The girls looked at him and smiled well-practiced smiles. Lacroix offered him a drink on the house. He ordered a gin and lime. She clicked her fingers at the girl at the bar, who gave a tolerant nod before slipping off the barstool, straightening her skirt and reaching for a half-full bottle of Beefeater on the glass shelf behind the bar. She held the cigarette between her painted lips while she poured the gin and splashed in some cordial. No ice, he noticed. And not much gin.

The Madame explained the terms of the house. Calloway agreed. She invited him to choose a girl. There were two blondes, a brunette and a redhead. He looked at each in turn. None of them gave the impression they wanted to be chosen, not deep down. They kept smiling, inclining their heads and crossing their legs with tired coquettishness. Their dead eyes bore into his soul. It made him uncomfortable. He'd never liked these places, even in the army, where a visit to a brothel was almost compulsory. He'd make excuses, even cried off sick. His comrades saw through it, nicknaming him Reverend. The name stuck until he made sergeant.

He wanted a talkative one. Someone who'd open up, given some encouragement. He settled on the redhead. She looked less jaded than the rest. Perhaps twenty, twenty-two at most. A tinge of apprehension behind her emerald eyes. She took his hand and led him to an upstairs room. Her hand was cold. She told him her name was Claudette.

The room was fake boudoir style. Faux silks and satins and furniture with gold legs. He sat on the round, pastel-pink button-backed chair by the closed curtains and took out his wallet. It was bulging with Spelthorne's hundred, which he'd barely touched. The redhead noticed. She turned away and unfastened the hook on the back of the cocktail dress, then eased down the zip. Calloway saw scars across her freckled white flesh.

'You can stop there,' he said. 'I just want to talk.'

She turned to face him and raised an eyebrow. 'One of those, eh? It starts with talking, but they always want the rest.'

'Just talk. And not that kind.'

She shrugged with indifference. 'It's your tenner,' she said.

'How long do we get?'

'Madame Lacroix tells us to aim for ten minutes. Fifteen's alright. At twenty she knocks on the door. Any longer than that, Charlie comes up.'

'The giant downstairs?'

She nodded. 'They don't hang around once Charlie shows his face. Some of the drunk ones try it on with him. They don't come back.'

'I want to ask you some questions. About the owners of this place.'

'Who the hell are you?' she said, lighting a cigarette as if by nervous reflex. 'You're not with Vassallo, are you?'

'Who's he?'

She looked at him as if he ought to know. 'They say he's trying to muscle in, demanding protection from the street girls. If you're with Vassallo, I'm calling Charlie.'

She made for the door. He jumped up from the chair and grabbed her by the arm, trying not to hurt her. She seemed so delicate. He'd always imagined they were bigger girls, more robust. Blowsy and foul-mouthed. She looked like a doll, a brittle, china doll.

'Sit down,' he said. 'I've never heard of Vassallo.'

He let go of her and she sat down on the bed. She drew hard on the cigarette and exhaled through tense lips.

'How much do you make?' he said.

She didn't look sure that she should answer. 'A hundred a night some nights.'

A brittle, china doll taking in ten punters a night. He felt nauseous.

'How much do you get to keep?'

'Fifty quid a week,' she said, with a hint of defiance.

He opened the wallet and counted out ten fivers. 'Here's the ten, and another forty for yourself. Got somewhere you can hide it?'

She laughed. 'They don't go a bundle on privacy here.'

She tucked two of the notes under the lamp on the bedside table, before easing up her skirt and slipping the remaining eight inside her stocking top.

'And that's private?' he said.

She shot him a look. 'Just ask your fucking questions,' she said.

She stubbed the cigarette out in a tiny glass ashtray. He offered her another, which she took.

'Ever heard of a company called Mayho Estates?'

She shrugged. 'Who are they when they're at home?'

'How about Primipilus Group?

She rolled her eyes. 'We're whores not chartered accountants, in case you hadn't noticed.'

She used the word whore like it tasted sour on her tongue. Then she laughed. 'Not that we don't get the odd chartered accountant in here.'

Calloway checked his watch. Five minutes gone already.

'Ever met a man called Charles Lewis?'

She shook her head.

'How about Alfredo Azzopardi?'

The emerald green eyes bore into him. 'Of course. I do read the papers you know.'

Calloway waved a hand around the room. 'Is this one of his establishments?'

'Of course not. He's in jail.'

'But was it?'

She looked around as if someone might be listening. She lowered her voice. 'Him and the old girl go way back, they say.'

'Madame Lacroix?'

She scoffed. 'Madam Lacroix, my arse. You mean Edna. Edna Purves. She's as French as I am. Nothing special about Edna. Been on the game since she was fifteen, they reckon. Azzopardi's dad was her ponce.'

'You ever see a man called Spelthorne in here? Sidney Spelthorne?'

She thought for a moment. 'I don't think so. What's he look like?'

'Middle-aged, bald, stocky, wears smart suits.'

She snorted. 'That's most of 'em.'

Calloway looked at his watch again. He'd been there ten minutes.

'What about a man call Giordano Spiteri?'

The girl that called herself Claudette froze.

'Gio?' she said. Her tone was hostile. 'I don't want to talk about Gio.'

She stood up and said, 'You're time's up. Edna will be knocking on the door soon. You need to leave. And do me a favour.' She stuck out a hip. Her nostrils flared. 'Look happy on the way out.'

He put his hand on the door, preventing her from opening it.

'When do you finish tonight?'

She glared. 'Why?'

'I want you to tell me about Giordano Spiteri. Meet me later. There's another fifty in it for you.'

'We're not allowed to meet clients outside.'

'Another fifty,' he said.

She stared at him, silent, weighing up the risk and return.

She lowered her voice. 'I'm on a half shift today. I finish at nine. The rest of the girls will be on till at least two. Meet me in the Chez Cup Bar at the Regent Palace Hotel at nine fifteen.'

There was a knock at the door.

'He's just on his way, Madame,' Claudette shouted, patting her stocking top to ensure the money was secure before ushering Calloway out.

TWENTY-SIX

The Chez Cup Bar was in a circular room under the hotel's entrance rotunda. Its upholstered banquettes with their jazz-age fabrics formed concentric circles, rimmed by the broad horizontal stripes of the curved walls. The floor followed a similar pattern, with circles of geometric tiles radiating outwards from a bullseye. It felt like being inside a giant roulette wheel. Calloway could almost sense it spinning. The place was past its prime now, its thirties heyday as a luxury nightspot for the people long since gone. The wear and tear of a decade and a half was showing badly. And the big tills behind the bar lowered the tone. They looked like something you'd find in Woolworths. But it was full enough to be anonymous. Calloway had bagged a table and two chairs, whose covers were worn and chrome legs chipped and tarnished. He ordered a gimlet, which to him was an overpriced gin and lime. The illuminated clock above the bar said ten past nine. He waited five minutes before Claudette appeared. She was punctual but didn't seem pleased to see him. He guessed she'd be pleased to see the other fifty pounds. She ordered a drink called an 'aviation' with Tanqueray. The waiter said they only had Gordon's. She and Calloway made small talk, which was awkward. Calloway got to the point. He asked about Giordano.

'I'm going to need another one of these,' she said, gesturing to the waiter. She ordered another for both of them. 'I met Gio at the Trocadero. I was a dancer with Cochran's review. I remember that show well. The two Hermiones were top of the bill.'

Calloway sensed he was supposed to be impressed. Instead he looked blank. Claudette rolled her eyes.

'Baddeley and Gingold,' she said. 'You don't get out much, do you?'

Calloway shook his head but said nothing.

'He was there with Franco and two girls. If you know Gio you'll know Franco. Inseparable they were.'

'Still are, pretty much.'

She nodded without asking how he knew. In fact she didn't ask him anything about why he wanted to know these things. He guessed money talked and that was the only talk that counted.

'The girls weren't up to much,' she said. 'Nothing to look at really. I suppose they'd scrub up alright. I didn't realise what was happening.'

'What was happening?'

'Gio and Franco were doing to them what Franco did to me.'

Calloway wasn't following. His face said as much. She continued regardless.

'I noticed Gio straight away. His table was right at the front, almost touching the stage. I'd seen him from the wings and when I was doing the routine, I made sure I caught his eye. He was big, rugged, handsome. You could see his muscles through his dinner jacket. That's the first thing I noticed. He was a strong man. I liked strong men in those days.'

She looked Calloway up and down. Her face said he didn't measure up.

'After the show I met Gio at the bar. He'd left the girls with Franco. Us dancers weren't supposed to go out front with the diners but I never took any notice of that. I loved the glamour. Gio bought me a drink. He asked all about me, like he was really interested. Where I was from, did I have family, how I started dancing, what my ambitions were. He said I was the best dancer in the chorus line, which I knew I wasn't but I took the compliment gladly. I loved the attention he was giving me. Like no one else in the world mattered. I said, "What about your girlfriend?" He glanced over his shoulder to the girls with Franco and said she was only a date for the night. He'd agreed to make a foursome because his friend Franco was keen on the other girl. I believed him. Course I did. I wanted it to be true.'

The cocktails arrived and she took a large sip. She looked around the room, lost in her thoughts.

'I loved his accent. He told me he was Italian. Said he was a cousin of the great Caruso. I believed that too.'

She toyed with the glass, distracted. Calloway pulled put his cigarette case and offered her one. She accepted and leaned in to share the light. He smelled face powder and MaGriffe.

'He took me to the Cafe Royal on our first date. The Cafe Royal,' she said, emphasising the point. 'We had champagne. I'd never had champagne before. By the end of the night I knew that's all I ever wanted to drink. Next time we met he took me to the American Bar at the Savoy. We drank martinis and listened to the pianist. Gio held my hand and hummed along to the songs. He has a sweet voice would you believe.'

Calloway believed it, but he didn't care. A gorilla with a good singing voice is still a gorilla.

'Then he started taking me shopping. Bought me an evening dress and shoes and took me dancing. One day we met for lunch and he passed me a beautiful box tied with ribbon. You know what was inside?'

Calloway shook his head. He hadn't come here to hear about Spiteri's shopping habits.

'A mink stole. For me. A big, strong, handsome man who said he was Italian bought me a mink stole.'

'Very nice,' said Calloway without enthusiasm, wondering where this was going.

'He took me everywhere. The best restaurants, the most fashionable bars, the hottest night clubs. He lavished gifts on me you wouldn't believe.'

She stopped there. Her face hardened. She downed the cocktail and drew hard on the cigarette.

'Everything came at a price,' she said. 'That's how they work, right?'

'Who's they?' said Calloway.

'Christ. Were you born yesterday? Ponces,' she said, spelling it out. 'Get you hooked on the good life then tell you you've got to pay for it. You know the bastard even proposed to me. On one fucking knee.'

'So Giordano ponces for the Curzon Street club?'

'Club's a polite word for it. Yes, he does. Franco does too but he's not as good. Doesn't have Gio's looks and charm. God I was naive.'

Calloway couldn't say he'd noticed Giordano's looks and charm. He ordered two more drinks.

'Why do you stay?' he said.

She shook her head and tutted. 'You don't understand the game. When they've got you, they've got you. You're dependant. You've nothing to go back to. You've nothing to look forward to. You're stuck. On your back a dozen times a night, with a dozen different men. Even the Piccadilly commandos don't notch up that many in a night.'

Those he'd heard of. The whores that took pissed-up soldiers down back the alleys off Piccadilly Circus for a quid a time. They left their knickers off to make it easier.

'Have you ever tried to leave?'

'Once,' she said. 'Gio has a way of dealing with girls that try to leave.'

She put a hand across her chest and touched the back of her shoulder. Calloway remembered the scars he'd seen when she'd started to undress.

'He uses an electric light flex,' she said.

He had nothing to say to that. All he could think was what he might do to Giordano next time he saw him.

'So Giordano and Franco work for Alfredo Azzopardi procuring girls for their brothels?'

Claudette nodded. 'I've heard they provide muscle as well,' she said. 'For a few of Alfredo's friends.'

'And you've never seen or heard of a friend called Sidney Spelthorne? Think hard.'

She gave him a petulant look. The drinks arrived and she took hers straight from the tray before the waiter had a chance to set it down.

'He runs a film studio,' Calloway prompted. 'Centurion Pictures.'

She looked blank at first, stared at the table for a moment, then looked up at him. 'There's a man they call Carmelo,' she said. 'He's in pictures, I think. He came to Curzon Street once. Edna and Alfredo seemed to know him.'

'Does this man Carmelo have a second name?'

She frowned, thinking for a moment. The third aviation seemed to make it harder to remember. Then she snapped her fingers and said, 'Portelli. Edna once said that if we were good, her friend Mr Portelli might get us in pictures. It was the kind of bullshit she and Alfredo would feed us to keep us keen.'

She sat back in her chair and looked around the room for a distraction. It was a signal that Calloway's time was up. At least he'd had more than ten minutes, he thought, even if he was paying five times the going rate. He took her hand and pushed a wad of bank notes into it. Her hand still felt cold, in spite of the heat of the bar and the three aviations she'd downed. Instinctively she stuffed the money straight into her handbag.

'Not enough to retire,' she said. 'But thanks all the same.'

Calloway slid his wallet back into his pocket. That was his hundred gone. But he was a step closer to understanding the whole sordid picture.

TWENTY-SEVEN

He left Claudette at the bar. She claimed to be meeting someone. He wondered how many aviations she could hold. He already felt light-headed from the three gimlets he'd downed in the space of an hour. At least the alcohol dulled the pain of the blows Yvonne Leclerc had so expertly administered. He needed to confront her. To establish that last, indisputable fact that would connect everything. He flagged a cab to North Soho.

There was no light from Yvonne's room. He rang the bell. There was no reply, but the room above Yvonne's was lit. He couldn't risk breaking in again, not with someone in the building. He banged on the door with his fist.

The boy poet answered. When he saw it was Calloway he summoned some authority, the type they bang into you at expensive schools, and said, 'Now look here, I'm getting pretty fed up with you turning up on the doorstep. What the hell do you want this time?'

He sounded like Wooster berating Jeeves.

'Same as the last two times. Eve Clark,' said Calloway.

The boy smiled a satisfied smile. 'Too late, chum. She's cleared out and I don't blame her.'

Calloway pushed past the boy, ignoring his protestations as he climbed the stairs. Yvonne's door was unlocked. Half her possessions were gone, the rest abandoned. The place was a mess, like she'd packed in a hurry. The boy stood in the doorway muttering something about private property.

'When did she leave?'

'Sunday,' the boy said. 'I went out for lunch, came back and she was gone.'

'Where's she gone?'

The boy shrugged. 'Search me, chum.'

Calloway turned on him. He grabbed the boy's lapels and dragged him out onto the landing.

'Call me chum again and I'll throw you down those bloody stairs.'

The confidence of breeding was suddenly gone. The boy looked terrified, as if wishing he could hide behind nanny's skirts. Calloway let him go.

Out on the street he retraced his steps on the night he'd pursued Yvonne. It was less busy tonight. A week night. He crossed Tottenham Court Road into the side street where Yvonne had vanished. He walked through the circles of street light into the intermittent darkness. There were no doorways or windows. Nothing to suggest a hiding place. He felt along the wall with his hands, letting his fingertips glance over the rough brickwork and damp bill posters. In a darkened part of the street he felt a smoother surface, partly concealed by posters. It was cold metal and from behind it he heard a faint humming. Some kind of ventilation intake. They were common enough. The kind that sucked air down into the tube network. He eased his fingers around the vented metal panel. One side was loose. He pulled at it. It moved easily, being hinged on the opposite edge. Behind it was darkness. Pitch black darkness, the humming louder. Calloway flipped his lighter open. On the other side of the panel was a narrow set of spiral stairs. Some kind of maintenance shaft, he assumed. The flame of his lighter flickered on the stream of air being sucked downwards. Calloway placed his foot on the first step to test it. It was solid. He squeezed himself fully into the void behind the panel and started to descend.

The walls were filthy with years of dust and soot, the darkness sucking in all the light so that the flame of Calloway's lighter was barely enough to see by. He stepped lightly but the sound of his feet on the metal stair treads still reverberated down the shaft in a series of regular clangs cutting through the hum, which grew louder as he descended. He lost count of the number of steps, but reckoned he must have descended a good fifty feet by now. Still there was no sign of the bottom. He paused and pulled a small coin that felt like a halfpenny from his pocket. He dropped it down the shaft, hearing it clatter as it fell. There was another fifty feet to go, he guessed, although he couldn't be sure. He found a second vented panel at the bottom, opening into a tunnel which must have been at least fifteen feet high. The tunnel housed a huge extractor fan, the height of man, its oversized blades rotating with the noise of an aero engine. Calloway squeezed past the casing of the fan, the noise and vibration hurting his eardrums. Behind was a bulkhead from floor to ceiling and within it a door. Calloway tried the door. It opened onto a far longer stretch of tunnel, which was divided horizontally into two floors, a stairway to his right leading to the upper floor. The lower floor was as dark as the ventilation shaft, but there was light coming from the upper floor. He climbed the stairway into the light.

'If you move another muscle, I'll shoot you dead.'

It was a woman's voice.

She stood between two rows of abandoned bunk beds under the dim light of the bulbs overhead. There was a pistol in her hand aimed at Calloway. A strange-looking weapon of simple construction. Just two tubes, one for the grip, another for the barrel. Calloway knew this weapon. A Welrod. A six-round silenced pistol. An ugly beast. It looked like something a plumber had made but was no less deadly for it. It fired 9mm parabellum rounds that could tear a man's guts apart or blow his brains from his skull. And it could do it without a soul hearing.

'I just want to talk, Yvonne,' he said.

The name he used surprised her. 'Where would talking get me?' she said.

'Somewhere better than you'd end up if you pulled that trigger.'

'Really? You think anyone would find you here?'

'You might have killed before Yvonne, but this is different. This is peacetime.'

'There's no peace for me,' she said.

'I know what happened to Celeste. I can guess why you're angry. But what you're doing needs to stop. The only one that'll end up hurt is you.'

She laughed. 'And why would you care? Why would Sidney Spelthorne's head of security care about someone he's never met. Someone he knows nothing about.'

'I know more about you than you think. I've pieced your story together, at least parts of it. I know enough about Celeste and enough about you to know you're not a bad person.'

She scoffed. 'There's bad in everyone, believe me.'

He knew that too. War brings out the best and worst in people, but usually the worst.

'I just want to talk, Yvonne. You can keep the gun on me if it makes you feel better.'

He wasn't sure it would make him feel better, but he was short on options. It wasn't as if he could run for it. They were a hundred feet underground.

Yvonne stood silently, the gun in her hand level with his guts. That would be a slow and painful death. He'd seen enough stomach wounds during the war to know. All blood, shit and screaming.

'Turn around,' she said.

Calloway did as he was told. He braced himself. If it was going to happen, it would happen now. She wouldn't want to look him in the eye. This wasn't personal. He was just an inconvenience. One that could put her in jail for a very long time. He didn't often pray. He didn't believe. He'd seen too much during the war to believe a higher power would allow such things. Lapsed chapel, Marjorie had called him. He was way beyond lapsed. The trauma of war had instilled him with a deep and lasting atheism. But right now he found himself praying for a head shot. Quick and deadly. He heard Yvonne take two paces forward. His stomach knotted and his bowels constricted. He felt faint. A blinding white light started to envelope him. Then he heard her voice.

'You see the office?'

He saw a room built against the curved wall of the tunnel. There was a sign on the door that said Warden's Station.

'We can talk in there,' she said.

There was a light on inside. It lit up a room about twelve feet square, with official-looking posters on the walls. Air raid procedures, fire instructions, a list of telephone extensions. The posters were dog-eared and damp-stained. There was a bunk bed along the far wall like the ones in the tunnel dormitory, but this one had a makeshift mattress of bedding and cushions. He recognised the patchwork quilt from Yvonne's room.

She gestured with the pistol for him to sit on the bed. He complied. She pushed a stacking chair against the wall furthest from him and sat. There was a table beside her, strewn with a few possessions. The framed photos of Yvonne and Celeste in France, and of Yvonne and the officer in their uniforms. Some brushes, make-up and a small shaving mirror, the latter he assumed had been the warden's whenever this place was last used, probably during the war. She'd been cooking from tins on a Primus stove. There was also a bottle of wine. It was opened but still two-thirds full. She picked up a tin mug and poured a generous measure. She passed this to Calloway, the Welrod gripped firmly in her other hand. She gestured for him to drink then swigged from the bottle herself. She kept hold of the pistol but rested it on her knees.

'You wanted to talk,' she said. 'So talk.'

The authority had gone from her voice. She sounded resigned. And she looked tired. She was still beautiful, Calloway thought. As beautiful as her film star sister. But Yvonne's beauty was tarnished, turned ugly by bad experience and no doubt worse thoughts. Calloway had seen so many faces ravaged by war. Fresh-faced boys turned to tired old men. Handsome young bucks returning frail and bitter. All manner of beauty besmirched.

Calloway downed the wine in thirsty gulps. He held the tin mug in both hands and leant forward, his elbows resting on his knees.

'I saw you running from the gala dinner on the night of the bombing. I picked up the purse you dropped. You were dressed up like a charm school starlet but there was something different about you. You weren't the usual type of Centurion hopeful. And you knew me, knew I was security at least, and when you saw me, you ran. You looked afraid. But not of the explosion or the chaos that ensued. You looked afraid of getting caught. That made me curious. More than curious. I'll admit you became something of an obsession. Special Branch was chasing the IRA, but I was more interested in you. I checked the charm school files. I found a photo that I thought was you. It was your sister, although I didn't know it at the time. Then someone told me the actress in the file was dead. Killed herself with gin and pills. I looked into Joyce's story. Let's call her Joyce for now. The name the studio gave her. She was Spelthorne's favourite. I mean favourite like a racehorse is a favourite. Something you put money on. She was good too. She could act and she was starting to get the parts. The trouble was she got noticed. I don't mean by the folk that go to the pictures, although they certainly warmed to her. So did the critics. She got noticed by a man called Alfredo Azzopardi. A Maltese gangster that controls prostitution in London. A thoroughly unpleasant man that exploits young girls for money. Ruins their lives. This Azzopardi could have any number of the girls he keeps in his brothels, but he wanted Joyce. Not to whore for him, although that might have come later. I imagine he wanted her as a trophy. A symbol of respectability, or perhaps celebrity. He let Spelthorne know this. Told him to arrange it. Spelthorne didn't think twice about offering his favourite starlet to this man. He got his man Giordano, who moonlights as one of Azzopardi's ponces, to fix it. Or at least he tried to. Why? Because Azzopardi was one of Spelthorne's backers, a director of a company called Primipilus Group. Primipilus launders the dirty money from Azzopardi's brothels, via a property company called Mayho Estates, and funnels it into Centurion Pictures. You see Azzopardi and Spelthorne are old friends. They go way back. Back to the days when Spelthorne went by his real name, Carmelo Portelli. The Bentley that went up, the one with CP1 on the number plate? I bet you thought that stood for Centurion Pictures. It stands for Carmelo Portelli, a little nod to Spelthorne's roots in the Saffron Hill Maltese community.'

He saw small tears welling in Yvonne's tired eyes. She wiped them away with her sleeve and shook herself, as if disgusted by her own emotions.

'It killed her didn't it?' said Calloway. 'Being offered to a gangster as a tribute. Whether her death was deliberate or accidental, Joyce died because of these men. Spelthorne, the self-made mogul, Azzopardi, the gangster, Giordano, the ponce, even Ivor Cole, the publicist who turned a talented young woman with drive and ambition into a performing puppet for his publicity campaigns. It wasn't the gin, or the pills, or the betrayal, or the feeling of utter hopelessness that killed your sister. It was these men, and every man like them in the dirty business we call pictures.' He took another gulp of the wine. 'And you came back from France intent on doing something about it.'

Yvonne looked up at him. 'Did I?' she said. 'Why do you think that? You've got no proof.'

He nodded to the framed photo of Yvonne in uniform. 'The cap badge. I recognised it. The First Aid Nursing Yeomanry. The FANYs we used to call them. It explained everything. The explosion, the damage to the studio equipment, the fact that you carry a time pencil in your purse and keep a Welrod pistol in this underground lair you now call home.'

She smiled and put the wine bottle to her lips to drink. It was his moment. He summoned all the strength he could muster and sprang up from the bed. He threw the tin mug at the woman's head. She ducked by reflex, dropped the wine bottle, then raised the pistol from her lap. Calloway was faster. He pulled the Welrod from her hand and pushed her back into the chair. He returned to the bunk and sat, pointing barrel of the ugly weapon in her direction.

'Now you tell me your story,' he said.

TWENTY-EIGHT

A major in The Buffs called Selwyn Jepson had recruited Yvonne personally in late 1943. He had been lunching at the Granchester Hotel where Yvonne's parents worked. They had pulled strings to get her work as a waitress, after she'd proved unsuitable for a succession of jobs - secretary, telephonist, shop assistant in a florist - mostly through her seeming inability to take any instruction she disagreed with. Her sister Celeste was the agreeable daughter, she went out of her way to please. Yvonne could be most disagreeable when she wanted to. And she was proving a poor waitress. She came to Jepson's attention quite suddenly when she stumbled and spilled oxtail soup into his lap. Jepson, to her relief, didn't make a fuss. He quickly gathered up the serviette from his lap and screwed it into a ball before the sticky brown liquid had a chance to stain the trousers of his uniform.

'No harm done,' he said, smiling at Yvonne. He had an oval face with dark, piercing eyes, mischievous caterpillar eyebrows and a head of wavy hair. He friends told him he looked like Claude Rains. Yvonne thought he looked kind and she was grateful for his understanding. She had no love for the waitressing job, but this was the hotel her parents had worked at most of their lives. It was their reputations at stake as much as hers. Jepson's lunch guest, a Frenchman in a civilian suit, was less understanding. He made disparaging comments in French, suggesting that the girl should be sacked. Yvonne, conscious the head waiter was by this point looking very much in her direction, started to apologise in fluent French. Jepson raised a mischievous eyebrow and listened with interest. He sat back in his chair, his smile broadening with every word she spoke.

'Do you speak any other languages?' he asked.

'Some German,' she said, swiftly adding, 'my mother is Alsace

French' to avoid arousing any suspicion from the stranger in uniform.

'Do you enjoy your job?' he asked.

She gave an embarrassed smile and looked over at the head waiter, who was scowling at her, gesturing that she should withdraw from the table at once.

'I'm not sure I'll have a job for much longer if I carry on like this,' she said, scooping up the soiled serviette. Jepson unbuttoned the breast pocket of his uniform jacket and pulled out a calling card. He checked to see if the head waiter was looking before giving Yvonne a conspiratorial wink and saying, 'Call me on this number. I may have some work for which your abilities might be better suited.'

She had assumed Jepson had singled her out for some kind of administration or translation work. But after a series of interviews, the first by Jepson himself, she realised that what the kind-looking major had in mind for her was both top secret and dangerous. His plan was to drop her, along with others like her, into occupied France to subvert and sabotage the enemy war effort. She would be part of a unit called the Special Operations Executive. At first she thought he was joking. Some test perhaps for something altogether more prosaic. This SOE sounded like something a writer of thrillers had dreamt up. (She was unaware that in addition to his military role, Jepson was indeed a well-known writer of thrillers.) The idea of training men, and more to the point, women, to pose as French civilians while secretly carrying a pistol in their knickers and a stick of dynamite god knows where sounded too fanciful to be true. But Jepson was serious. In fact, he had lobbied Churchill personally to be allowed to recruit female agents, considering them better than men for the task due to their greater capacity for what he called 'cool and lonely courage'.

She was reluctant at first. The work sounded foolhardy and by no means assured of success. Female SOE agents operated outside the protection of the Geneva Convention and fell within the Nazi's Nacht und Nebel law, which permitted execution without trial. Once deployed she would have an estimated life expectancy of six weeks, a fact she did not learn until much later and which may have swayed her ultimate decision.

She had been brought up to consider herself as much French as English. She and Celeste had spent many summers with their grandparents during the school holidays and she considered France a second home, with not a little pride and a fair degree of patriotism. She was in time brought around to the idea that she could play a meaningful role in ridding Europe of the Nazi scourge, for the sake of her family in France. Before long, she became impatient to do her bit, something that Jepson, an enthusiastic sponsor of Yvonne's, had worked hard to encourage.

She joined the First Aid Nursing Yeomanry. It was the parent unit for female agents of the Special Operations Executive, essentially a cover that would allow them to move in military circles without giving away their true role. Anyone one who met her in her new, and to her mind rather frumpy, uniform would assume she was probably a driver, or something equally dull.

She was sent for training to a succession of stately homes in remote locations that had been requisitioned by the War Office. At each location she learned the skills of clandestine warfare. Coding, close combat, even silent killing. There were a series of schools, some with names Yvonne considered ridiculous. There was parachute school, which was fair enough, but 'toughening up school' and 'finishing school'? There was something childishly Baden Powell about it all.

Some parts of her training seemed dull and pointless. Other parts were either gruelling or quite disturbing. She'd be woken in the middle of the night and dragged off for interrogation by instructors dressed as Nazis. Or she'd be hectored by overzealous instructors into crossing the 'slack-ropes' between what appeared to be two of the tallest trees in a Scotland as the finale of the assault course.

'I can't see the point in that,' she'd said to her instructor. 'We're fighting Nazis, not bloody monkeys.'

This earned her the nickname Guenon, French for monkey, for the remainder of her training.

She attended 'finishing school' at Beaulieu House, an overbearing and draughty old pile in the New Forest. At Beaulieu she met a young lieutenant in the Coldstream Guards called Leonard Howes. At first she knew him only by his codename, Renard. By this stage in their training only code names were used. Born to an English father and French mother, he was educated in France while his father, a civil servant with the foreign office, was attached to the British Embassy in Paris. Unlike other civil service brats, he was spared boarding school in England. This was at his mother's insistence. Despite their differences in background, the attraction between the Leonard and Yvonne was obvious. Relationships between trainees were strictly discouraged, the risk being pregnancy and birth in the field. But by the end of finishing school, Leonard and Yvonne were secretly engaged. He had proposed on one knee with the ring of a dummy hand grenade. Their compatibility had been noticed by their instructors, though not their love affair, which was strange considering the extent to which their every behaviour was scrutinised. Perhaps this was testament to the clandestine skills they had developed. As a result they were paired for their first operation: Leonard as circuit leader and Yvonne - by this time codenamed not surprisingly Guenon - as courier. Their wireless operator was a female agent they knew only by the codename Souris. The fox, the monkey and the mouse. Their clandestine network would be known by the codename Menagerie.

Menagerie's first operations was to organise the resistance in a part of west-central France to sabotage French factories producing machinery for the German war effort. Yvonne's role as courier would be to liaise with the leader of the local Maquis, briefing him on targets and arranging for the supply of finance and arms.

Yvonne was dropped into France by parachute after four extremely cold hours in a modified Halifax bomber of the RAF's 138 (Special Duties) Squadron, during which she tried to keep warm with the help of a thin sleeping bag and a flask of weak coffee. She trembled throughout the flight, whether through nerves or cold she couldn't tell.

‘Five minutes,’ the co-pilot shouted down from the cockpit above the engine noise. ‘I’m putting the red light on.’ He flicked the switch and she was engulfed in a glow the colour of blood. If she’d wanted a bad omen, this was undoubtedly it. She knew it was merely the way to allow her eyes to adjust to the darkness of the night she would be dropping into. But she couldn’t help but be discomfited by it as she shivered in the cold, coffin-like fuselage of the noisy aircraft.

Her RAF dispatcher, who had sat beside her for most of the flight without saying a word, save for offering her some curled-up sandwiches, now gestured upwards with a flattened hand and shouted, ‘Red on.’ A demonic crimson eye bore into her. The dispatcher opened the circular hatch in the floor. A gust of icy air blew upwards into her face. She could see the ground below. There was France. Her second home and now her battlefield. She reached into her jumpsuit to reassure herself that the Llama .38 calibre automatic was still in her jacket pocket. She couldn’t imagine using it, despite being the best shot on the training course. Right now it was more like a lucky charm.

‘Drop your legs over the hatch, miss,’ the dispatcher shouted. She eased herself towards the hole and dangled her legs over the edge. The freezing air bit her ankles like a snarling German Shepherd. Her nerves turned to fear. An ice-cold fear that surged through every vein in her body, numbing her from head to toe.

‘Remember the drill, miss. Tuck your chin in when you jump. You don’t want to lose your teeth.’

She nodded, not sure that she’d heard or understood. She felt a reassuring hand on her shoulder.

The dispatcher leaned into her and spoke quietly into her ear. ‘It’ll be alright, miss.’

An estimated life expectancy of six weeks.

She felt a sudden urge to vomit.

The red eye closed, the green eye opened.

‘Green on. Go!’ the dispatcher shouted.

She gritted her teeth, eased her backside over the rim of the hatch and fell feet-first into the darkness.

TWENTY-NINE

The rush of night air sucked the breath from her lungs. Her parachute opened for what seemed like only a few seconds before she hit the cold ground hard in her civilian shoes. She rolled by reflex. The still-inflated chute dragged her before she grabbed the straps and wrestled it to the ground like a great billowing beast. Then she stopped, crouched on her haunches, perfectly still in the quiet. No broken bones. She ran her tongue over her teeth. Still there. She let her eyes adjust to the light of the full moon. The faint sound of the Halifax's engines faded to silence. She felt entirely alone.

She realised now that she had been blown off course during the drop and missed her reception committee. Leonard should have been there with members of the Maquis to take her into town to a safe house. But there was no one, neither friend nor foe. She concealed her parachute and jumpsuit like she'd been taught, picked up the suitcase that had been dispatched thought the hatch after her, and made for the woods at the edge of the field. She would have to rough it tonight and contact Renard by letter box tomorrow. She did her best to burrow into the mossy ground at the foot of a tree, but she didn't sleep. Every breath of wind through the trees, every rustle of leaves conjured images of Germans, their jackboots stamping through the dense woodland in search of her. But no one came. Her arrival still seemed to be a secret.

Before dawn she walked the eight miles to her final destination. The small shabby town with its worn-down flagstones and peeling walls was waking up. She could hear the sounds of early morning. The clang of milk churns, the clank of last night's wine bottles, a church bell striking six. She caught the reassuring smell of a bakery. As she passed it, she saw through its open door the baker, wearing only underpants and an apron as he shovelled perfectly formed parcels of dough into the glowing oven. It made her laugh and forget her fear, at least in that moment.

She walked to the railway station, navigating by the map she had memorised. She checked the timetable pinned to the wall and noted the time and destination of the first train. Limoges, 06.10h. If asked she would say she was waiting for the train, using the cover she had been given by her French Section handlers. She was a sales representative for a cosmetics supplier, travelling the west-central region visiting retail clients.

At eight o'clock she made her way to the cafe in the town square to send a message to Renard via the letterbox. The cafe was open but empty. She sat at one of the tatty chairs with a good view across the square. The letterbox was in reality a surly waitress called Marie-France who, she had been told, was the niece of a resistant. What she lacked in grace she made up for in discretion, apparently. Yvonne used the agreed password, which Marie-France acknowledged with a bored look. Yvonne ordered coffee and tartine and waited.

Around ten minutes later Yvonne got her first sight of the enemy. A German patrol was crossing the square towards the café. Her heart started to thump in her chest. Her mouth went dry and her limbs went weak. Then she felt a surge of adrenalin-fuelled anger. Could Marie-France have betrayed her? Was that sulky little bitch an informer? She ran her hand over the outline of the automatic in her pocket. But what use was that against four Wehrmacht soldiers with machine pistols and rifles? She looked to the rear of the café, wondering if she should make a run for it through the back. But there could be more soldiers there, waiting. She pictured Marie-France sitting on the knee of her Gestapo boyfriend, smoking a German cigarette and tucking a fifty-franc reward into her stocking top.

The patrol stopped in the middle of the square. One of the soldiers unbuttoned his fly as he walked into the little round pissoir. He stood behind the pissoir's half-screen, his boots visible below, his head bobbing up and down above them like something from a Punch and Judy show as he stood there pissing. Splashes of urine spattered his boots. His comrades laughed and made obscene gestures. Yvonne's beating heart slowed and she felt a wave of relief. It was just a routine patrol and a young soldier cut short. She needed to get a grip of herself. This was her life now.

Marie-France brought the coffee, bread and jam and placed it on the table with the merest hint of a smile. Yvonne felt a pang of guilt for the bad thoughts she'd had about the girl. Then she heard a wonderfully familiar voice.

'It's a beautiful morning.'

She fought hard against the urge to fling herself into his arms. She wanted him badly, right there and then. Fear had turned to a desperate passion, as her overwrought mind played with her emotions. Instead she did her best to give the most casual of nods towards the chair opposite, inviting him to join her. She looked into his eyes for a moment and couldn't resist a smile, and the tiniest, most provocative of pouts.

That night he stayed with her at the safe house. It was contrary to his orders but neither of them cared. They made desperate love, like the final wish of the condemned. Tomorrow they might die.

The safe house was a one-room bedsitter above a shabby, disreputable-looking bar opposite the railway station. It had a cold-water sink, a gas ring and tatty, but comfortable furniture. The privy, bizarrely she thought, was in a makeshift cubicle on the small balcony that overlooked the street. The next door flat had the same arrangement, meaning the sound of bodily functions was frequently shared between neighbours, somewhat to Yvonne's discomfort - although this should have been the least of her worries. There was one other tenant in her building, a worn-out prostitute who would take clients she'd picked up in the bar downstairs to the room above Yvonne's. Her clients were French, not German - Leonard had done his homework - and the frequent comings and goings made it easier for Yvonne's movements, and those of visitors like Leonard, to go unnoticed. This was welcome. What was less welcome was the nightly sound of drunken Frenchmen fucking to the unenthusiastic encouragement of a veteran whore. Yvonne knew France well, but this was an experience she'd thus far been spared.

She spent the coming weeks making visits to a town twenty kilometres away, taking messages from French Section in Baker Street, via Renard and Souris, to contacts in the Maquis. She was the go-between, arranging for the supply of cash and equipment to be used for sabotage. Plastique explosives, detonators, Sten guns, silenced pistols and ammunition, dropped by parachute in long metal canisters onto remote drop zones that had been reconnoitred by Leonard, who would travel many miles by bicycle using a Michelin tourist map to identify suitably remote locations.

Yvonne would travel by train in the third-class carriages, sitting on the hard wooden bench seats next to men who smelled of sweat that were carrying live geese by their necks to market. In third class she didn't need to make conversation, as she would have done in second. This meant less chance of her cover being compromised.

She suffered gut-wrenching nerves on every trip, with the foul taste of fear in her mouth, bile in her gullet and bowels fit to burst. Her papers were forgeries and only good enough to withstand cursory inspection at the frequent police checkpoints. If she were ever taken in, the Gestapo would discover her identification number was fake. She had been briefed on what would happen next. They would interrogate her, most likely torture her, so that she would give away the members of her circuit, their resistance contacts and their mission. Then she would be sent to a concentration camp, where death would follow through maltreatment, starvation or execution. The only way to avoid this fate was to swallow the death pill concealed in the lipstick she carried with her everywhere.

She saw Leonard more frequently than was safe from an operational perspective, but true to form she believed that some rules were meant to be broken. And anyway, she thought, it was her life at risk here, not the top brass back home who made the rules. If she could find some solace from the daily routine of anxiety, she was damn well going to take it. On the nights he stayed they would make love nosily and with abandon, their cries lost among the insincere moans of the whore upstairs.

Two months into the operation, the Menagerie circuit received new orders from Baker Street. They were instructed to scale up the Maquis's activities to prepare for the Allied invasion of Europe. The objective was to sabotage road and rail routes to disrupt German military supply lines and to equip resistance groups to support allied troops in their push through France. Yvonne approached this new assignment with confidence. She had excelled in the explosives and demolition course during her training. Supply drops increased, now with heavier weapons like Bren Guns and anti-tank rifles, together with thirty thousand francs to finance operations. And the circuit needed more SOE agents to coordinate resistance. Leonard, as circuit leader, was charged with identifying landing zones capable receiving the small Lysander aircraft that would bring new agents from London. He and Yvonne instructed members of the Maquis to serve as reception committees, using hand-held torches as landing lights on the improvised runways, in reality flat fields in remote locations, their fences pulled up and other obstructions removed.

Yvonne took part in these night-time operations with Leonard, leading the reception committees and driving newly arrived agents to their safe houses in an old truck powered by an improvised charcoal burner, the kind that had become a necessity due to the shortage of petrol for civilian use.

One such operation proved disastrous for the Menagerie circuit.

It was a clear night with a full moon. The wind was moderate and the ground conditions good. The pilot of the Lysander had no trouble making out the two rows of improvised landing lights. He put the small aircraft down without a hitch. His passenger, a twenty-four-year-old SOE agent codenamed Blaireau, slid back the plexiglas hatch at the rear of the cockpit. As he stepped onto the fixed ladder on the port side of the aircraft's fuselage, the sound of gunfire cut through the night above the din of the Lysander's engine. Blaireau fell to the ground with a thud. His body lay motionless. Yvonne heard Leonard shout 'Christ.' He pointed towards the edge of the landing field where a dozen armed men were running towards them. They wore oversized berets, belted tunics and baggy trousers tucked into high-laced boots. By the light of the moon Yvonne saw that the uniforms were blue, not the field grey the Germans wore. They carried Berthier carbines and captured Sten Guns. They were Milice, French fascist paramilitaries loyal to Vichy. They were viscous bastards. Yvonne knew this. The Milice were easily more feared than the German Wehrmacht. They were said to be more ruthless than the Gestapo. You didn't want to get captured by the Milice.

Leonard dropped to one knee and raised his Sten Gun. He fired at the advancing Miliciens in short, controlled bursts, then gestured to the Lysander to leave. Yvonne heard the rapid fire of a light machine gun as a Milicien FM 24/29 tore into the cockpit of the aircraft. She saw the pilot slump. The Lysander continued to taxi across the landing field towards a copse of trees at the edge of the field, the dead pilot at the joystick. Gunfire echoed around her. She was disorientated. The sudden surge of adrenalin made her head spin and her knees weak. A bullet buzzed like a hornet past her ear, close enough for her to feel its heat against her flesh. It snapped her back to attention. She looked around her for cover, but there was none. The landing field was flat, the trees that surrounded it too far away. There was no chance of running. The Milice were too close. She remembered her training. She drew the Llama .38 from the waistband of her trousers, gripped it with both hands and raised it to eye level, bending her knees as she'd been taught. She selected her target and loosed off two rounds, double tap. The Milicien fell. He lay on the ground clutching his belly and screaming obscenities. A tremor of satisfaction shot through her body. Almost sexual. She selected another target and again fired twice. The shots went wide. She heard Leonard shout, 'Guenon.

Run. I'll cover you.' He was gesturing towards the truck. 'Go to Souris and send a message that Menagerie is blown.'

She shook her head. 'I'm not leaving you.' She raised the .38 and fired all five of the remaining rounds in the magazine towards the militia soldiers. She pulled the spare magazine from her jacket pocket and snapped it into the grip of the pistol. She heard Leonard shout, 'Just fucking go, will you. Contact London.' He was right. If she stayed she would die and London would continue to send agents, only to be captured, tortured and killed. The circuit would be rounded up, Souris would be found and forced to send false information back to Baker Street. Many would die. But love fought with duty. A part of her wanted to die right there with him. Not leave him. Be there, together, as they gasped their last breaths, their bloodied bodies intertwined in one last embrace.

An explosion lit up the night sky. The Lysander had hit the copse. Its fuel tank was ablaze. The Milice were distracted. She saw Leonard throw down the Sten Gun. He ran for the cover of the woods behind them. He shouted, 'I'll be fine. Get to the truck. Go to Souris. We'll regroup at the fallback.' Their fallback location was a farmhouse nine kilometres from the town, owned by an old farmer who had two sons in the Maquis.

Yvonne ran towards the truck. She pressed the starter and prayed. The starter motor rasped and spluttered. She heard gunshots. Rounds pinged off the rusting bodywork of the old truck.

She swore at the motor, pushing the starter button over and over. A round pierced the windscreen, which shattered like a sudden hailstorm. Glass shards lodged in her clothes and her hair. She felt pinpricks of pain on her face. She pressed the starter button again and again. She heard the engine rumble into life, slammed the truck into gear and pushed the accelerator pedal so hard her foot might break through the rusting chassis. She swung the truck towards the road. The Milice were just yards away, raising their weapons. Two of them fired in her direction. A round glanced off the truck's bonnet. It sent a shower of sparks into the night. She looked back and saw one of the Miliciens turn and aim his weapon towards the woods behind her. She saw Leonard running, still on open ground, only a few yards from the cover of the trees. A single rifle shot cracked. Leonard jerked and fell. Yvonne gasped. She lost control of the truck. She wrestled with the wheel, only just managing to pull the lumbering old vehicle back onto the farm track that led to the road.

She looked back once more and saw two Miliciens dragging Leonard's limp body across the ground.

A Milicien sat on the bed. An officer with an 8mm Lebel revolver in his hand. The revolver was pointing at her belly as she stood frozen in the doorway of her room. Bundles of French francs lay beside him. The thirty thousand destined for the Maquis. She'd come back to collect it. It was a big risk, but without that money, she would not have been able to fund Maquis operations. That was her plan. Escape to the countryside, team up with one of the more remote resistance units and lead sabotage operations against German supply lines, as per Menagerie's orders. This was to have been Leonard's role, but Leonard was dead. She would take his place. She would instruct the resistants in the use of explosives and blow up railway lines. If the circuit was blown and the location of Maquis hideouts discovered, they would just have to fight it out with the enemy. It was worth a go. But that wouldn't happen now. The Milice officer was a step ahead of her.

He said, 'Come in. Close the door.'

He nodded towards the bulging hip pocket of her jacket. 'Don't think about reaching for the pistol.'

She complied. He would have shot her before her hand had touched the pocket.

'If you're going to shoot me, then do it,' she said.

She'd rather be shot than taken to the Gestapo for interrogation. The officer smiled. It was a smile with intent.

'I'm not going to shoot you. For one thing, you're far too pretty.'

So that was the deal. He intended to have her. He'd bank on her thinking compliance would save her skin. She wasn't that stupid. He'd have her and shoot her.

'And for another?' she said.

He considered his answer. 'And for another thing, I'm going to keep this money. No point handing it to the Gestapo.'

'So shoot me and take it,' she said.

He made a face. He waved his head from side to side, as if considering this option.

'It's not quite that easy,' he said. 'There's a problem you see. My men will be outside now. If they hear a shot they'll come running in and they will see the money. Then I'll have no choice but to hand it in. Instead I'm going to give you enough money to disappear and let you go. You can leave through the back. It will give me time to conceal the bundles of cash inside this loose and rather unflattering uniform. I'll go down to my men and tell them that you weren't here. No one will be any the wiser.'

'So toss me one of those bundles and let me go.'

He stood up from the bed and crossed the room towards her, the gun still pointing at her middle. She didn't move. She thought of the Milicien she'd shot in the guts. She heard his curses and screams in her head. She wasn't going to go that way if she could help it.

The officer stood facing her. He leaned in close. She smelled cognac and tobacco on his breath. She felt the barrel of the Lebel pressing into her abdomen. The officer raised his free hand and stroked her cheek. He kissed her lightly on the forehead.

'We have a few minutes,' he said.

She gritted her teeth. 'I'll break your neck before you're all the way. I know how.'

She did. She'd excelled in silent killing techniques during training. She never thought she'd need it under such circumstances.

He laughed quietly to himself. He pressed his lips against her ear and whispered, 'If you do, you'll never see your boyfriend again.'

Her stomach tightened. The veins at the side of her head pounded.

'He's alive,' the officer said. 'Your agent Renard. He's hurt but he'll live. I've not reported his capture to the Gestapo yet. If you're nice to me I'll let him go.'

He was clever. He knew she wouldn't strike a bargain for herself. But for her lover? That would be different. Her head reeled. She couldn't think straight. She knew she should reject him. Sacrifice Renard. Not submit to the enemy, not least to this crooked French collaborator. But the urge to save her lover's life was strong. To see him one more time at least. To hold him in her arms.

She pressed her lips against the foul-breathed Milicien and kissed him.

'Let me make myself nice for you,' she whispered. He put his head to one side, as if weighing up her suggestion. Then he smiled, satisfied. She felt the barrel of the revolver pull back from her stomach. The officer stepped back.

He nodded towards the gun in her pocket. 'Take off that jacket first and throw it into the corner.'

She did as he asked. She unbuttoned her blouse so that he could see the silk of her underwear beneath. She had dressed for Leonard. Now she was baiting this animal. She stepped towards him and looked into his eyes. They were lustful and aggressive. She held his gaze and pursed her lips. She slipped her hand into the pocket of her trousers and drew out her lipstick. She pressed its blood red tip against her lips and traced seductive lines. The Milicien smiled. A wolf's smile. The gesture excited him. His hungry jaws opened. She leaned into him, pushed the lipstick into his mouth and slammed his jaws shut with the flat of her hand. The lethal pill cracked. Cyanide gushed into the Milicien's mouth. His face contorted. His lips bubbled. His eyes rolled like a rabid dog. He spasmed and fell to the floor with a thud. She put the heel of her boot into his groin, ground it down hard and heard the last breath of life seep from his from his pale, dead mouth.

THIRTY

'Leonard died in Dachau concentration camp. That's where they sent captured SOE agents. They told me when I returned to London after the Allies had liberated France. Vera, the French Section's intelligence officer, met me at Victoria station and bought me tea and a slice of fruitcake at the buffet. That was all the welcome I got. She asked how I was, told me what had happened to the rest of the Menagerie circuit and then said goodbye. Just like that. It was the last I saw of her or anyone else from the section. I'd served my purpose. I was no longer needed. I suppose they thought I would just settle down to civilian life and make some young chap a pretty young wife.' She laughed. 'A wife that could kill with her bare hands, fire any infantry weapon you cared to hand her and blow up a railway line, should the need arise.'

Her face tensed. She bit her bottom lip. She picked at her nails and shifted in the chair.

'I could have saved him,' she said. 'Not a day has passed that I haven't wished I had chosen to go along with that pig Milicien. Given him what he wanted, taken the money and gone to Leonard.'

'Chances are he was spinning you a yarn,' said Calloway.

'Perhaps. I'll never know, will I?'

'What happened then?'

There was a pack of cigarettes and a lighter on the table next to her. She nodded towards them and said, 'May I?'

'Alright,' said Calloway. 'But slowly.'

She did as he asked. She took a long drag on the tobacco and blew a plume of smoke upwards towards the dim bulkhead light above them. The light flickered.

‘I looked for Celeste. She was all I had. Mother and father were dead. I had no other family in London. I tried all of the film studios and found her at Centurion. She was doing well. My little sister a film actress. Just bit parts at that time, walk-ons, but I could tell she would amount to something special. She had it in her. Something pure. Something magical. We spent some time together. We talked about old times and future plans. She told me about the charm school and I told her the little I could about what I’d been up to, which was little more than a cover story. The one contact I’d had from the War Office since Vera left me at the station was a letter reminding me that I had signed the Official Secrets Act. It was lovely to see Celeste doing well, but it was clear there was no room for me in her new life. I didn’t resent that. I was pleased for her. There was nothing else keeping me in London and I had no idea what I was going to do with my life, so I went back to France. To Paris.’

‘What did you do there?’ he said.

He didn’t like Paris. He’d been on leave there once. It seemed to him like a city living off a reputation it didn’t deserve. A colourful myth, but a miserable reality. Perhaps that was just the effects of the war.

‘I fell in with a bohemian crowd. Writers, poets, artists. You know the type. They were outsiders. It suited me. I’m not sure I’ll ever be able to live what you’d call a normal life. Not now. Not since the war. I started writing poetry as a distraction and it turned out that I was actually quite good. One of the crowd I went around with knew a publisher in London who was interested in new British poets. He was starting a magazine. He was a pretentious and conceited arse, in truth. Called himself Mephisto.’

‘I’ve met him,’ said Calloway. ‘He didn’t take to me.’

She laughed. ‘No, I don’t imagine he did.’

She drew on the cigarette and blew another wisp of smoke towards the bulb. It flickered again.

‘The power down this end of the shelter is not so good,’ she said. ‘Most of it’s disconnected. I fiddled with some of the wires and managed to get some of the lights working. It’s a bit hit and miss though.'

'What is this place?'

'It's a deep-level shelter. Built during the war for civilians to escape the air raids. But it proved too expensive to run so it was never used. At least not by civilians. The Americans took it over and billeted a signals unit here. Most of it is still in military use. This section of the tunnel was sealed up as surplus to requirements.'

'How did you know about it?'

'I came here during the war. The Americans were putting Jedburgh teams together to drop into France and carry out similar operations to ours. Some of the agents from French Section acted as liaison with them before we were deployed ourselves.'

He gestured with the pistol. 'Carry on with your story.'

She stubbed the cigarette out in an empty Spam tin. The hot tip made the leftover fat hiss.

'Mephisto published my work under an English-sounding pen name. He wanted his magazine to feature exclusively English poetry. I wrote to Celeste and asked her to send me some copies. You couldn't get them in Paris. Celeste and I started writing to each other regularly. We were both building new lives and we had a lot to tell each other. Her letters were a joy to read. She was so excited. Full of ambition, loving the life. Her dreams were starting to come true. But the letters started to change. The joy went out of them. It was when Spelthorne's friends showed up. She became more and more uncomfortable with that side of the job. You know, putting on a pretty face for her boss's financiers. But it didn't stop at a pretty face, did it? She told me what happened. With that bastard Azzopardi. And the drink. And the pills. Her last letter arrived a week after they found her dead.'

She lit another cigarette without asking him and took a long, desperate drag.

'So you decided to kill Spelthorne.'

She shook her head. 'Not kill him, destroy him. Destroy what he held dear. His empire, his money, his backers. Sabotage and intimidation. That was my plan. I went back to the region I'd operated in during the war. We'd buried a cache of arms and I knew they might still be there. Guns, explosives, detonators. I smuggled what I needed back to Britain and got myself a job as a cleaner.'

'Using your pen name.'

She laughed. 'I thought that was a nice touch.'

'So you set about sabotaging the studio equipment and worked your way up to a bomb under Spelthorne's car. On the night of the annual Producers Club dinner, when you knew all his backers would be there. You could have killed everyone.'

She shook her head. 'But I didn't. I knew what I was doing. I'd had enough first-hand experience with detonators in the field to time it just right. When everyone was half cut and stuck into their sherry trifle.'

The light flickered again. The room went blank for a full two seconds before coming back on. The light flex was buzzing.

'What are you going to do?' she said.

'I should take you in. Hand you over to the police.'

He'd be off the hook then. He'd keep his job, Bernie would leave him alone and Special Branch could close their file. It would be the best result for him.

Again the light flickered. The flex buzzed louder.

Then he heard the bulb pop.

The room stayed dark this time. It was pitch black. He couldn't see a thing. He heard the legs of Yvonne's chair scrape on the ground. He heard the door open and the sound of running. He stumbled through the darkness towards the noise. His shin slammed into something hard. He heard the clang of metal and the rattle of springs. He fell forwards over one of the old iron cots. His head hit the hard concrete of the floor. Light flickered, this time behind his eyes. Then it went dark.

He came to an hour later. His skull buzzed with pain. He flipped open his lighter. The tunnel lit up like a Dickensian scene from a better class of film than Centurion made. He scanned the floor. The Welrod had gone. She must have come back and taken it when he was out cold. He pulled himself to his feet, stepped between the abandoned cots and headed for the staircase in the half light of the lighter's flame.

It felt cold in the street. He shivered and pulled his jacket tight around him. His ears were ringing. His eyes couldn't adjust to the street light. He felt like throwing up. Concussion. Nothing he could do about it. He flagged a taxi and told the driver to take him to the studio. He slurred his words. The cabbie thought he was drunk. He gave him the once over, deciding if his fare was going to vomit in his cab. He satisfied himself and swiped the taxi meter. The engine tick-ticked as they headed east.

Old Arthur was asleep in his watchman's hut. Calloway left him to it. Better that way. He headed for the administration block. He wanted the purse and the detonator from his desk drawer. It was evidence. It corroborated the real story. He saw that the lights were on in Studio B. He crossed the courtyard and pushed open the big double doors. The Irish pub set was lit. Giordano sat at the table pouring champagne. It looked incongruous. He had company. She couldn't have been more than seventeen. She was dolled up. One of his swanky nights out, Calloway thought. Show her the high life. Play the movie mogul to impress. Give her a late-night tour of Centurion. Champagne on set. Fill her head with notions of movie glamour. She'd be upstairs at Curzon Street before the year was out.

'You need to leave,' Calloway said to the girl.

Giordano bristled. 'You need to fuck off,' he said.

Calloway ignored him. He stepped onto the set and took the girl by the arm. He led her towards the door. He said, 'Wake up the old boy in the hut and get him to call you a cab. The studio will pay.'

The girl looked back at Giordano confused. 'Gio, what's going on? You said we'd make a night of it.'

Giordano shrugged and smiled at the girl. It was the kind of smile that said he couldn't have cared less.

'Maybe next time,' he said. 'I'll call you.'

The girl walked towards the exit doors in quick uppity steps. Her heel caught a cable that snaked across the floor to one of the cameras. She tripped. She steadied herself and shot Giordano a backwards look.

The big Maltese rolled his eyes. He knocked back his drink and poured himself another.

Calloway waited until the girl had left. 'Does she know you're a ponce?'

Giordano rocked on the back legs of his chair and lit a cigarette. 'Not yet. The penny will drop sooner or later. By that time she'll be a busy girl. Fifteen quid a go, I reckon. They pay more for the young ones. She's good for a ton and a half a night.'

Calloway pulled a chair up to the table. 'Enjoy your work, do you?'

Giordano smirked. 'It has its benefits.' He made an obscene gesture. 'And it pays well,' he said, stroking the lapel of his jacket with the back of his thick, manicured figures. 'I don't see you wearing a suit like this.'

'Clothes maketh the man, that's what they say, don't they?' said Calloway. 'In which case you're made of something loud and very vulgar.'

The goon snorted through his flat boxer's nose. 'I should skin you for that.'

He pulled the knife from his pocket, the one he'd used in Spelthorne's car, and stabbed it into the tabletop.

'Careful,' said Calloway. 'You might need that later, if your boss wants another cigar. He gets you to run around him all day long doing all the little jobs. He knows a lackey when he sees one.' The big goon's face stiffened. 'I bet you'd wipe his arse if he asked you.'

Giordano heaved his big frame out of the chair and grabbed Calloway by the lapels. He threw back his head to butt him. Calloway slammed his flattened hand upwards and deflected the blow. Giordano's jaw crunched. Calloway grabbed the lapel of his wideboy suit and spun him around. He rabbit punched the back of his thick neck before grabbing a mop of oily hair and slamming his head down hard on the tabletop. He punched his kidneys and threw him back in the chair.

'Don't ever think your anything special, son,' he said. 'You're the shit on my shoes. You're a gangster and a ponce. No better than the villains you work for, just cheaper and more obedient. Like a dog at their heels.'

Giordano lifted his head and spat blood from his mouth. He reached for the knife. Calloway had been a fool to leave it stuck in the table. He'd let anger cloud his judgement. He went to bat Giordano's hand away, but the gangster was quicker. He grabbed the knife in his big hand and slashed at Calloway. The blade ripped through his jacket. It drew blood. Calloway made to grab the big Maltese's wrist. His foot snagged a cable. He stumbled. The gangster had him by the throat, one hand pressing his windpipe into his spine, the other pushing the blade into his solar plexus. Calloway felt the cold metal puncture his skin. It was heading for his heart. He flailed his arms. He punched the air. He choked. He heaved his chest, trying to draw air into his lungs. His windpipe was shut tight. The big gangster's thumb had it sealed. He felt faint. He felt nauseous. His heart pounded, fit to burst. He forced his hand between their two bodies and balled his fist. It stopped the blade going further. Giordano gripped the knife and pushed harder. Calloway tensed his arm and squeezed his fist. He tried to push the goon away. Giordano put the full force of his weight behind the knife. He lay on Calloway. He sandwiched him between his body and the tabletop. Calloway felt dizzy. Bright white light engulfed him. He gasped and gasped but couldn't draw a breath. Suffocation summoned unconsciousness. He started to fade out. The bright white light was turning to darkness. The gangster pressed harder. The blade was easing its way towards Calloway's heart. He felt Giordano's lips against his ear. He heard his voice.

'I ain't shit on no one's shoes.'

There was a violent spitting sound. White heat singed Calloway's ear. The gangster jolted. He went limp. He lay on Calloway like a dead weight. Calloway summoned strength and pushed back. The gangster rolled to the floor. He landed on his back. The crash echoed around the studio. Calloway looked down at him. Black-red blood trickled from a perfect hole in his temple. The left side of his face was missing. Brain and bone oozed onto the studio floor.

Yvonne Leclerc stood in the doorway, knees bent, arms outstretched, gripping the butt of the Welrod in both hands.

'The bastard deserved it,' she said.

THIRTY-ONE

She lowered the pistol.

'You came back for the detonator,' he said.

She nodded. 'I tried before, but you caught me in the act.'

'I've still got the bruising.'

He saw something catch her eye.

'You're bleeding,' she said.

The gash in his sleeve was wet with blood and a deep red stain was forming on his shirt front. They were flesh wounds. No blood vessels cut.

'I'll live,' he said. 'Have you got the detonator on you?'

She tapped her hip pocket. He saw the glint of the lamé purse protruding from the pocket flap.

'Give it to me,' he said.

She laughed. 'Why the hell would I do that?'

He looked down at Giordano's body. The gangster's head lay in pool of vivid red that glinted under the studio lights.

'Because you and I are in more trouble than each of us has ever been. I can fix that if you give me that detonator. You've got to trust me.'

'Why would I ever trust you?' she said.

'We're cut from the same cloth, you and me,' he said. 'We've lived the same lives. We know what war does. We know what loss is. We know the value of happiness, especially when it's ripped from us, and from those we loved.' He nodded at the body on the floor. 'We know good from evil. We fought gangsters. Gangsters in uniforms. People like him, but smarter and more powerful. We've killed and we've maimed and we might even have enjoyed it sometimes. We've done terrible things. In some ways we're just as guilty as him and his bosses. The difference is that somewhere deep inside us we know right from wrong. That earns us the right to live. I've cheated the hangman's noose by the skin of my teeth. You can too. Just trust me.'

She stood silently, thinking, then slipped the pistol into the waistband of her trousers.

'I need a cigarette,' she said.

He tossed her his cigarette case and lighter. She lit up and took a long hard drag.

'I've not finished with him,' she said.

'Meaning you've not destroyed Spelthorne?'

She nodded.

'I can do that,' he said. He looked around him at the studio. 'I can bring his empire tumbling down. I can reduce him to nothing.'

They stood in silence in the glare of the lights. Up close the film set looked as fake and flimsy as Spelthorne's ill-gotten grandeur.

She reached into her pocket and brought out the purse.

'Here,' she said, holding it out for him.

He snapped open the clasp, took out the pencil and unscrewed the barrel. He slid the time pencil into his hand. He passed the purse back to her.

'You'd better lose this,' he said.

She nodded and pushed it back into the pocket of her jacket. Calloway knelt beside the body on the floor. He slipped the time pencil into the pocket of Giordano's suit.

'Did the night watchman see you arrive?'

She shook her head. 'He was asleep in his hut. I slipped past him.'

Good old Arthur, thought Calloway. He could be relied on for something.

'You need to get away from here. Away from London. Tonight. And you need to be out of the country tomorrow.'

'That's easier said than done,' she said.

'Come with me,' he said, walking towards the door.

She took a last look at the body and followed him. He killed the studio lights on their way out. He didn't want old Arthur waking up and being suspicious. If Giordano's body was found while they were still on the premises, they were in even deeper trouble.

They crossed to the administration block and climbed the stairs in darkness. The lock on his office door was broken. There was a size-five boot mark on the door panel.

'That's one way of doing it,' he said.

She shrugged and said, 'Needs must.'

He switched on his desk lamp. The top drawer of his desk was open. No lock picking tools this time. Just jemmied, good and proper. He opened the lower drawer and pulled out the bottle of Black & White and two glasses. He slid them across the desktop.

'Pour us two large ones,' he said.

She took the bottle, poured the drinks and downed hers in one. Then she poured herself another. He picked up the phone and dialled a number. He knocked back his scotch while he waited for an answer. It rang for a good half minute before he heard a male voice, woozy with sleep.

'Johnny, it's Cab. I know it's late but listen. I'll do that job. The one you told me about at the baths. But I need a favour in return.'

He explained what he wanted.

Suskind said, 'Alright, Reg, I'll be there in thirty minutes. I'll bring Solly. He's a good man.'

Calloway thanked him and put the phone down. He put his hand in the desk drawer. Yvonne saw him slip a package into his pocket. He reached in the drawer again and pulled out a newspaper. He rifled through it and ripped out a page. He took a big bunch of keys from a row of hooks behind his desk and said, 'Where's your passport?'

'I have it on me,' she said. 'When you've lived in an occupied country, you get used to carrying your papers everywhere.'

'Good,' he said. 'You're going to need some other things too. Follow me.'

He took her to the props store and picked out a suitcase.

'This do?' he said.

She nodded and smiled. It was Joyce's smile, from the first reel of her home movies.

'I've travelled with less,' she said.

Their footsteps echoed down the corridor. He pulled out the keys and unlocked the door of the wardrobe department. He flicked on the lights.

'You need to pick out some clothes. I've no idea what's where. You'll have to poke around but be quick. We've got less than thirty minutes.'

'I know my way around. I used to clean in here. It's how I knew where to find the dress I wore for the gala dinner. It's back on the rails now.'

He'd not thought that she might have borrowed her ball gown from the studio.

'The purse too?' he said.

She nodded.

'Put it back then. Take your personal effects out first.'

She emptied the contents into her pocket and put the purse with the others that were lined up tagged and numbered in a row along one of the shelves.

He watched her pack clothes into the case. Two dresses, a suit, trousers and a jacket. A belted mac. Heeled shoes, flats and sandals. Silk underwear and stockings. A handbag, two berets and a handful of scarves. She was a fast shopper, he thought. Not that he'd really know. He'd never been shopping with a woman. Never been close enough, at least not in peacetime. The woman he'd loved hadn't survived the war.

She pushed the lid of the suitcase down hard and snapped the clasps shut. She patted the bulging lid and said, 'Ready.'

He pointed to the Welrod in her waistband. 'You'd better give me that,' he said.

Arthur was still asleep as they passed the watchman's hut. Johnny was waiting in a taxi outside the main gates. Solly, the cabbie who had transported them from the last dust-up with Hamm's fascists, was at the wheel. He gave Calloway a nod of recognition.

Calloway introduced them to Yvonne. He called her Eve. Best she kept her real name out of this. Johnny held the door for her. He said, 'Solly and me will take you to the coast tonight. I've got a mate in Deal you can hole up with until first light. He'll take you to Dover. You can get the first boat the France.'

Suskind handed Yvonne a small roll of bank notes. 'Don't worry,' he said, with a wink. 'Reg says he'll pay me back.'

'There's enough there to get you to France and buy you a fortnight in a hotel. The rest is up to you,' said Calloway.

Yvonne climbed into the cab. Johnny noticed the blood on Calloway's clothing.

'Do you need that looking at? I know a doctor. He's discreet.'

Calloway shook his head.

'I can fix it. Drop me at my place on the way.'

The taxi rumbled over the cobbles. Its diesel engine tick-ticked through the silence of the night. It was past one o'clock. The streets were empty. They passed a row of shop fronts. A baker, a delicatessen, a kosher restaurant. There were fascist slogans daubed on the restaurant's shutters. Fresh paint ran from the points of a swastika.

'Bastards,' Johnny muttered under his breath.

Solly parked the cab outside Da Costa's factory.

Calloway said, 'Keep the engine running, Solly. I'll be right back.'

He returned with the case full of mementoes he'd found in Joyce's flat.

'You should have this,' he said. He slipped his hand into the pocket of his jacket. 'And this.' He put the first reel of Joyce's home movies into Yvonne's hand. She looked at the film reel, confused at first. She opened the case and saw the letters and photographs and the copy of the poetry magazine. He saw a small tear well in her eye. She leaned out of the window and kissed him on the cheek. She put her lips against his ear and said, 'Destroy him. You promised me.'

He clapped Johnny on the back and said, 'Over to you.'

Suskind gave him a mock salute. 'I'll see you later, Reg,' he said. 'I'll let you know the time and place.'

Solly turned on a sixpence and headed back up to Shoreditch High Street. Calloway saw the two red tail lights glare at him, like the eyes of a devil taunting him. He'd struck two deals tonight. Made two promises. He would enjoy keeping the first. The second he wasn't so sure about.

He walked the length of the factory floor in the semi-darkness. A lone street lamp outside cast a web of shadows through the metal window frames onto the worn wooden floorboards. Sewing machines stood in rows on one side, cutting tables along the other. Dressmakers' forms stood sentinel. They reminded him of the straw-filled dummies he'd used in the army for bayonet practice. He felt his chest. The blood stain on his shirt was damp but the bleeding had stopped. He pulled a key from the fob in his pocket and opened the door to Da Costa's office. As caretaker he had keys to all the doors in the building. He switched on the desk lamp. He took a telephone directory from the shelf behind the desk. London A to E.

He slid the directory into the rectangle of light under the desk lamp and leafed through the pages. He reached the Ds. He ran his fingers down the dense column of names until he found the Daily Sketch. It was a populist conservative rag. It abhorred immorality. It revelled in lurid tales of villainy. He noted down the address. He took a foolscap envelope from Da Costa's drawer and on it wrote the name of the journalist whose byline had appeared on the articles about the death of Joyce Rose. He reached into his inside pocket and pulled out the papers Ndungu had passed him. The Companies House files and the Land Registry lists. He ringed names in red ink, blew on the ink to dry it, then slipped the papers into the envelope. He took a sheet of Da Costa's note paper, ripped off the letterhead and slipped it onto the roller of the typewriter on the secretary's desk adjacent to Da Costa's. He cranked down the roller and two-finger typed. Then he slipped the finished note into the envelope with the cutting he'd ripped from the newspaper, the story about Azzopardi and the vice charges. He reached into his pocket and pulled out the final reel of Joyce Rose's home movies. He stuffed it into the envelope and sealed it.

It was two a.m. The roads were empty as he drove east towards Fleet Street. The night was damp. Mist hung in the air. Street lamps cast a putrid, smog-yellow glow. He pulled the car over. The Daily Sketch offices were lit like a fairground. There was life in every window. He heard the printing presses rumbling from the rear of the building. He walked up the steps and into the foyer. It was decked out like a grand hotel. A rugged-looking commissionaire with a row of campaign ribbons sat behind a reception desk the size of the Queen Mary. He glanced at the clock on the wall and gave Calloway an inquisitorial look.

Calloway put the envelope on the desk and jabbed the name of the journalist with his finger.

'See this gets to him will you,' he said. His tone had authority. The commissionaire deferred. He gave Calloway a respectful nod and said, 'Right you are, sir.'

He left the car where it was and walked south towards the river. While the rest of London slept, this small quarter of the city was alive. He could hear the shouts of print workers as they loaded bundles of newspapers into the liveried vans that waited at the loading docks of the big newspaper buildings. Early editions heading for the hotels and railway stations. Closer to the river it was quieter. He did his best to blend into the mist and shadows. He crossed the street and walked towards Blackfriars Bridge. He stood at the centre of the bridge and leaned on the railings looking down onto the blackness of the Thames. He smelled the damp, rotten smell of the river. He slipped his hand inside his jacket, pulled out the Welrod and dropped it into the dark waters below.

THIRTY-TWO

It had hit the papers. Calloway sat in the canteen reading the headlines.

Film mogul linked to gangland murder

Vice ring profits fund Centurion productions

Studio car bombing was 'gang feud' revenge

Marge pulled up a chair and joined him at the table.

'How terribly exciting,' she said.

'I expect we'll all be out of a job soon,' he said.

'I'm not so sure. Rumour has it that J Arthur Rank is already circling.'

He leafed through the pages of the paper. Joyce Rose's face stared out from the centre spread.

Maltese 'ponce' drove starlet to suicide

'Poor Joyce,' she said.

You should speak to your pal, Tony, he thought. There was no mention of him in the story.Or of Ivor Cole or any other movie Mephistos that worked behind the scenes trading dreams for souls. They sullied the young and innocent for publicity and profit. Underneath the gloss and the glamour they were as viscous and corrupt as any gangster. Joyce was the leading lady of an un-filmed epic. Romance, melodrama, tragedy. And no amount of pills could take away the hurt and no amount of soap could scrub away the filth.

He left these thoughts unvoiced. He wanted out. Bryant and Belcher had their man. McCaffrey was off the hook. Bernie was off his case. He had one thing more to do.

'I'll be taking a holiday, Mr Da Costa,' he said. They stood on the factory floor amid the locust-clicks of a dozen sewing machines. Plumes of smoke rose from cigarettes that hung from the lips of the seamstresses. It was past eight p.m. They were pulling a night shift on time-and-a-half. Da Costa had a big order to fill. A radio played dance band music above the din.

Da Costa gave Calloway a knowing look. 'A holiday is good. You are tired, young man.' Calloway caught a twinkle in the old boy's eye. 'Will you be holidaying alone?'

Calloway shrugged. 'Maybe not.'

'Then maybe not is also good.' He frowned and thought for a moment. Then he looked up and smiled. 'I can spare you for a week or two. My nephew can keep an eye on the place. That lazy schlemiel needs something to do with himself.'

Calloway packed a case. He didn't pack for a holiday. He packed everything. Then he pulled the flex of the telephone out of the wall. He took a last look at the attic room. He thought of Marjorie naked in the orange glow of the fire.

He left the building and dropped the case onto the back seat of his car. He walked to the call box on the corner of the street, pushed tuppence into the slot and dialled Marjorie's number.

'Marge, it's Reg.'

'Reggie, darling. I hear you're going to be a very brave boy tonight.'

'I'm doing that job for Johnny. I thought we could meet afterwards.'

There was a pause. He heard a voice in the background. A man's voice.

'I'm so sorry, Reg, darling, but I'm busy tonight. A friend of mine is visiting and he's taking me to Mirabelle for dinner.'

He felt stupid. Why did he think he had some claim on her? They'd slept together. Once. No dinner beforehand, no dancing, just an opportunistic fumble on sweaty sheets by the light of a spluttering gas fire.

'Of course,' he said. 'I'm sorry.'

He put the phone down. He felt empty and alone.

Johnny was waiting for him at the corner of Ladbroke Grove and Arundel Gardens. A stocky man with tight black curls and a heavy brow stood next to him. He wore a grey demob suit with a black shirt buttoned to the collar.

'This is Dai the Dairy,' Johnny said.

The stocky man turned to Johnny and said, 'Fuck off.' Calloway recognised traces of a rich Valleys accent from just those two syllables. He'd known a lot of Welshmen in the army. It was that or the pits for most of them, just like it was for him. Calloway nodded at the stocky man and said, 'Why's he call you that?'

'Because I'm a Welshman and I run a dairy.'

He aimed a cuff at Suskind's head. The ex-paratrooper ducked then grinned. The stocky man grinned back and offered Calloway his hand.

'I'm Gruffydd,' he said. 'You can call me Griff.'

Johnny said, 'Griff's family have been delivering our daily pint for generations. He's an honorary East Ender.'

Griff nodded. 'I moved to London when I was demobbed and took over my uncle's business. I'd been dairy farming with my father in Wales before the war.'

'Griff could have missed the whole shout if he'd wanted to,' said Johnny. 'He was in a reserved occupation. He could have avoided service altogether.'

Griff sneered. 'I wasn't having that. On the first day of the war I took the bus into town, told a few fibs and signed up. Royal Marines.'

He rolled up his sleeve and showed his tattoo, a winged anchor crossed by a Tommy gun, the emblem of Combined Operations.

Johnny said, 'Griff was a commando.'

Griff reeled off names of famous raids. 'Lofoten Islands, Bruneval, St Nazaire...'

In other words, a right tough bastard, thought Calloway.

Johnny went over the details of the plan. He pointed to a house on Arundel Gardens. A tall townhouse, typical of Notting Hill, shabby and smog-blackened.

'That's the Union Movement headquarters. Jeffrey Hamm has an office and flat on the fourth floor. He lives there with his bodyguard. He's been shitting himself ever since we stepped up operations. Don't forget boys, they're more scared of us than we are of them.'

Griff nodded. He puffed out his barrel chest. His muscles

bulged in the sleeves of his jacket. Calloway doubted he needed reassurance.

Johnny continued. 'You need to get in there, sort out the bodyguard and teach Hamm a lesson he won't forget. Then grab as many files as you can and get the hell back here.'

He nodded to a taxi parked at the corner of the street. Calloway recognised the driver.

'Solly will get us clear before Hamm and his boyfriend have noticed you're gone.'

Calloway saw Griff slip a knuckle duster onto his muscular fist.

They knocked at the door. They heard heavy footsteps on the stairs. The door opened and the bodyguard blocked it with his oversized frame.

'Who the hell are you?' he said, in heavily accented English.

It was the German from the rally. The Nazi POW who'd shouted his battle cry before tasting Calloway's boot. He showed no signs of recognising his erstwhile opponent.

Griff clicked his heels, gave the fascist salute and said, 'Hail Mosley!'

The bodyguard looked bemused.

Calloway said, 'We need to speak to Hamm. We have an urgent message.'

The two of them pushed past the bodyguard and ran up the stairs.

Hamm was in his office. He sat at a desk reading papers. Calloway took in the scene. Fascist heraldry. Flags, shields and posters. Slogans screamed at him.

Mosley speaks! Tomorrow we live! Keep out alien Jews!

Hamm read their faces. He looked alarmed. He stood up and said, 'What the hell do you want?'

Griff shut him up. He slammed brass knuckles into the fascist leader's face. Hamm went down. Griff struck again. Hamm whimpered. He spat blood through loosened teeth. Griff hit him twice more, good and hard. Hamm was out cold. A piss stain spread across the trousers of his suit. Behold the master race, thought Calloway. Griff grabbed files. Calloway rifled the desk.

He found a book. A big ledger. He flicked through it. Names of every Union Movement member. Johnny's going to love this, he thought. He stuffed the book into his waistband. The two men headed for the stairs.

The bodyguard was blocking their way. He gripped a lead pipe in his hand. He swung at Calloway. Calloway parried the blow. Pain shot through his arm. The bodyguard spat obscenities and swung again. Calloway side-stepped this time. He kicked at the bodyguard's legs. The bodyguard buckled. He teetered on the top step and lost his footing. Calloway grabbed his lapels. He channelled his anger and summoned strength. He lifted the big German off the ground and heaved him down the stairs. Bang, bang, bang. The bodyguard hit every step. He smashed through the stair spindles. He sent the bannister flying. Calloway picked up the lead pipe and piled down the stairs after him. Griff followed close behind. The bodyguard lay on the ground, his limbs contorted. He raised his head and sneered. Calloway swung the pipe. He heard the snap of bones. The bodyguard squealed. His jaw jutted sideways like a gargoyle. Calloway fell on him, full weight. The bodyguard looked up at his two attackers. All three men had fought the same war. Two had driven fascism into the ground. One was trying to revive it. Calloway grabbed the Nazi by the hair and yanked his head up. He leaned in and whispered, 'Wir kommen wieder.'

We will be back.

THE END

BOOK THREE: ROPE & CANVAS

ONE

When the drunk took liberties with the barmaid, Calloway broke his nose.

He should have lost his job. But the barmaid was a friend of Trudi Trauber and Trudi had a lot of influence at the arena. The drunk was lucky. If Trudi had got to him first, a broken nose would have been the least of his worries.

Calloway tossed the drunk a beer towel to wipe the blood from his face. Then he yanked him by the collar of his threadbare jacket and dragged him down to the foyer and out through the big double doors. The drunk stumbled down the steps cursing, the blood-soaked towel muffling his empty threats. As Calloway turned to re-enter the building, he heard a familiar voice.

'I expect he deserved it.'

'They generally do,' Calloway replied.

A small, bow-legged man stood in the light of the red neon sign in a well-cut suit that clung to his wiry frame like it was nailed to him. He had the dry parchment skin of the lifelong chain smoker which aged him beyond his forty-odd years. He looked like a jockey with cash in his pocket, which wasn't a million miles from the truth. He grinned at Calloway through his crooked yellow teeth.

'So you're in the wrestling game now?' the small man said.

'I'm in the nose-breaking game, Bert.'

'You should be in the ring.'

'It's lady wrestling.'

The small man chuckled. 'Might be a laugh.'

Bert Webber nodded towards the poster in the glass display case beside the main doors. Fierce painted faces glared back, their muscled bodies squeezed into swimsuits above tightly-laced wresting boots. Trudi Trauber was top of the bill.

'They're a rum lookin' bunch, mind you,' said Webber.

'They'd chew you up and spit you out, Bert.'

Webber pondered this. 'I don't think my Elsie would approve.'

Calloway pulled a Navy Cut from a battered gun-metal case and offered one to Webber.

'It's been a while, Bert.'

'Over a year, I reckon.'

'You don't strike me as the lady wrestling type, so I assume this isn't a chance encounter. How did you find me?'

'Called round your old gaff. There's Irish living there now. They had a forwarding address. So I called there and they told me you was working here.'

'You've clearly been to a lot of trouble.'

This made Calloway uneasy. Webber was part of a life he'd done his best to leave behind.

'Yeah, I had to go round the houses. Didn't think it was a good idea to ask Pat.'

Patricia Moxon. Speedway promoter. Former boss, former lover and the cause of a whole lot of trouble for Calloway. Bert was one of her riders. Calloway had been her head of security.

'Does she know I'm here?' said Calloway.

Webber dragged on the cigarette. He shook his head. 'Look, can we go inside?' he said. 'I don't really want to be seen outside this place. If the *Sunday Pictorial* caught me on me tod hanging around lady wrestlers, Pattie would do her nut.'

Webber was a proper star now. Pulling in six thousand a year, Calloway had read.

He nodded and looked at his watch. 'My shift finishes in twenty minutes. Wait for me in the bar. Tell the barmaid you're a friend of mine. She'll serve you after hours.' Calloway noticed blood spots on his cuff. 'She owes me a favour,' he said and returned to the arena.

The last bout had finished and the punters were leaving. Calloway was there to ensure an orderly exit. They were an odd bunch. Old biddies with a blood lust, couples on a night out, single men of certain tastes. Those were the ones you had to watch. The ones with their hands in their pockets all night and shameful looks on their faces when you caught their eye. There was the odd drunk, like you get anywhere hard-working folk gather to let off steam. If they got punchy, Calloway would turn up with an arm lock or a sly jab to the guts.

He met Bert in the bar. It was closed now and Trudi's friend was clearing the tables and emptying the ashtrays. A fug of bitter beer, body odour and cigarette smoke hung in the air. Bert sat at a table in the far corner smoking a cigar. In his well-cut suit and handmade shoes he looked like a mobster from an American B movie. That's what happens when the boy from Bermondsey gets six grand a year, thought Calloway. He was pleased for Webber. He was one of the good ones. A fearless little rider and everybody's friend. He also knew everyone's business, which had been an asset to Calloway in his former job.

'You're looking well, Bert.'

Webber swilled what looked like scotch around in his glass and took a sip. 'Can't complain. I've had a couple of good seasons.'

'Still in the prefab?'

Webber rolled his eyes. 'Elsie won't leave it. She hated it when the corporation first moved us in. Now she says it's home. I keep telling her, we can live anywhere now. Bromley, Beckenham, somewhere decent. She won't have it.'

A cleaner was clanking around the floor with a can of bleach and a bucket, smearing the dirt around with his sodden mop. A roll-up fag dangled from his lower lip. The smoke from the fag aggravated the tick in his eye.

'Lift yer feet,' he grunted in Webber's direction. The small man took one look at the grey swill heading in the direction of his handmade shoes and put his feet up on the chair opposite him. When the clang of the bucket had died down, Calloway cut to the chase.

'This isn't a social call, is it Bert?'

Webber looked sheepish and shook his head. 'I came to ask a favour.'

Calloway was done doing favours. They'd never done him much good. He nodded towards the arena. 'Need a few wrestling tips? I reckon I can get you those.'

Webber glanced back at the posters pinned to the varnished wood panelling behind them and winced.

'I'll pass, if you don't mind.'

He drained the whisky glass and lit another cigar, puffing at it instead of getting to the point. It irritated Calloway.

'Say your piece, Bert. We've both got homes to go to.'

'Yeah, I've seen yours. Not much of a place, is it, if you don't mind me saying.'

'I do mind,' said Calloway.

Webber realised he'd crossed a line, but he was right. Calloway was all but on his uppers. The big man lived in a single room in a rat-infested building that should have been condemned. When he'd taken the job at the arena two years ago, he'd argued for the title head of security. In reality he was a bouncer and a cheap one at that. His shoes were down at heel and his dinner suit smelled of damp. The once proud military man had lost much of the fastidiousness that had been second nature. What spare cash he had, he gave to Doreen. Her need was greater.

'It's me brother-in-law, Stan,' said Webber.

Calloway had a vague recollection of the man. He'd eaten with Webber at the cafe where Stan's wife Vera worked. Vera was a blowsy brunette with big curves and a dirty laugh. The stuff of shameful thoughts.

'What about him?'

Webber spat out a shard of tobacco and stubbed out the cigar out like it suddenly tasted bad. 'He's dead.'

Calloway's meter flickered red. He tried not to let it show. 'Sorry to hear that, Bert.'

Webber drained the last of the whisky and looked like he needed another. The bar was empty and Trudi's barmaid friend had clocked off for the night. Calloway crossed the room and helped himself to two doubles from the optics. When he returned, Webber took a large slug before continuing.

'Stan's a short-haul lorry driver. Well, he was. He was working away from home. Running ballast from the quarries to the building sites at that new town they're building up at Stratton-Fenwick.'

Calloway had read about the new towns. They were building them around the country to relocate families bombed out of their homes during the war. Entire towns built from scratch. All modern and orderly. Homes with indoor bathrooms, heating and hot water. A far cry from the close-knit, oppressive pit villages of his own upbringing.

'He told Vera he'd be away for a few months. He'd never been away that long before, apart from the war. Vera didn't like it, of course. Kept on at him to come home weekends. Stan told her the fares home would cost too much. And he said he needed the overtime. He was saving to buy her a television. Vera's been on at him for ages to buy one, even more so when she heard I'd bought one for Else.'

The little man looked sheepish, as if owning a television made him a traitor to his class. 'Anyway, after a couple of months this bloke turns up at her door. Stan's boss, he said he was, although Vera says Stan had never mentioned him. He had a copper with him. They sat her down and told her they had some bad news. Stan had been killed in an accident.'

'What kind of accident?'

'Crashed his lorry, they said, on the fourteenth of last month.'

Calloway shrugged. 'These things happen, Bert.'

Webber shook his head like his big friend was missing the point. 'They sent his things back to her, his wedding ring, his watch, his clothes. All wrapped up in a brown paper parcel. She went through everything, wanted it clean, wanted him to look his best when they laid him out. I told her, don't bury him in his wedding ring. I know them undertakers. They'll have that down the pawn shop before he's gone cold and have pissed the proceeds up the wall by the time they put him in the ground. She wouldn't have it. "He's keeping it on," she said. "Wherever he's going next I want them to know he's married." Never really trusted him, see. Not since the war. Old Stan had a good war, if you know what I mean. Vera knew it. She knew he'd been putting it about in Egypt for starters. He was stationed in Alexandria. Got a liking for the local bints. His love letters home were all sweetness and light, but she knew. Knew him of old. After he was demobbed she kept him on a short leash.'

Calloway glanced at his watch. He should have been clearing the place and locking the gates by now. The punters had all left but through the open doors of the bar he could see lights on in the wrestlers' dressing room at the end of the corridor.

Webber noticed him looking and gave him a nudge. 'She found this in the lining of his best suit. It had slipped through a hole in the pocket.'

Webber passed a printed card to Calloway. It was crumpled and garishly coloured. It said *Club Continentale* in lettering cheap establishments think looks sophisticated. Below it were cheesecake images of pinup girls dancing with feathers.

'So Stan found a clip joint on his night off. Hardly surprising, given his past form.'

Webber shook his head. He looked around him to see who might be listening, even though the bar was empty. He behaved as if he and Calloway were conspirators. He nodded at the card, like he was saving the best for last.

'Turn it over.'

There was an address on the other side, on Potsdamer Strasse, Berlin.

'That ain't no new town, Mr Calloway.'

Calloway passed the card back. He wanted rid of it.

'So?' he said.

'Why would he have that in his pocket?'

'Could be any number of reasons. Could have been there for ages. Had he ever been to Berlin? Was he ever stationed there?'

Webber shook his head. 'Just North Africa. Before that, Blandford Camp. He was Royal Signals. He was demobbed by forty-six. He was never posted to Germany.'

'So maybe a pal passed him the card. Recommended the Club Continentale. Maybe he was planning a holiday by himself. Slip the leash for a bit.'

Calloway knew this was unlikely.

Webber scoffed. 'Do you think our Vera would have let him go to Berlin? On holiday by himself? She did all she could to stop him going to Brighton for the races on bank holidays. It was only 'cause it was his job that she let him go. It was good money and she knew it.'

Calloway drained the last of the scotch. It still had the previous customer's lipstick on the rim of the glass. The arena was that kind of establishment.

'There's any number of ways that card could have ended up in Stan's suit. The man's dead, Bert. What does it matter? Can't you leave Vera to mourn him in her own way, suspicions and all?'

Webber sulked like a child that thinks it's been chastised unfairly. 'Vera's not having it.'

The small rider dug into his pocket again. He pulled out half-a-dozen postcards and pushed them across the table. 'He sent her these.'

Calloway leafed through them. They were picture postcards of the sights of Stratton-Fenwick. There weren't many sights yet, clearly. Three of the six postcards were the same: a collection of boxy, flat-fronted buildings and a couple of rows of saplings which they called the town square. The rest showed the town sign next to some kind of sculpture Calloway couldn't make out. The messages from Stan were bland. 'I'm alright', 'how are you?', 'how's the weather?', 'missing you'. They were written by someone who felt obliged to write but had nothing to say.

Calloway's irritation showed. 'What's your point, Bert?'

'Six postcards in the six weeks before his accident.'

Calloway shrugged.

Webber rolled his eyes in frustration. 'Stan wouldn't write that often. He's not like that. He wasn't the romantic type, not in that way. He'd have been happy to be away, not missing her enough to write to her once a week.'

'You know what they say about absence, Bert.'

'Yeah but in Stan's case it usually meant a fondness for playing away.'

They both looked through the bar windows towards the arena as the lights went off one by one. Calloway looked at his watch again. He was tired and his knuckles hurt from the punch he'd given the drunk.

'Go home, Bert,' he said, as kindly as he could muster. 'It's late and you're a good hour from your place. Give your sister-in-law time to grieve. There could be any number of reasons Stan had that nightclub leaflet. It doesn't mean anything.'

Webber wasn't having it. He reached into his pocket and pulled out a small slip of printed paper and slid it across the table.

'Then what's this about?'

It was a ticket for the Berlin U-Bahn.

'Why did Stan have a Berlin underground ticket in his pocket, dated when he was supposed to be in Stratton bleedin' Fenwick?'

Calloway picked up the ticket and turned it over in his big hands. Webber sat back in his seat and shook his head repeatedly.

'Vera's beside herself and I don't blame her. All she's had from Stan's boss is flannel. They seem to think that because she'll get a pension now, she don't have to worry.'

'Is it usual for short-haul lorry drivers to get a pension?' said Calloway.

'Search me, squire.'

'Has she mentioned Berlin to Stan's boss?'

'Of course she has.'

'What did he say?'

'Told her he didn't know what she was talking about. Made out she was hysterical. Offered to take her to one of those Harley Street doctors for her nerves.'

'Harley Street?'

Webber raised his eyebrows and gave a knowing by nod. 'Yeah, that's what I thought. That's pushing the boat out, innit? They could send her up the Maudsley on the National Health for nothing. Something ain't right.'

'Who's she been dealing with at the haulage company?'

'A fella named Denton. Oily git, by all accounts. He was the one that turned up with the copper to give her the bad news. He said she'd be well looked after, if she didn't make a fuss.'

The whole business smelled rotten. Calloway knew that smell. It followed him around.

'What did you come to me for?'

The little man smiled. He knew he was getting somewhere. 'Sniff about, that's all. See if you can get some proper answers. You've got a knack for it.'

It was a knack Calloway could do without. But ten years in the military police and six in the Intelligence Corps gave a man certain talents. Talents which can get you into a lot of bother in civvy street. That's how he and Webber had become friends. A bad business at the speedway stadium they'd both played a part in fixing.

'Vera needs peace of mind, Reg,' said Webber. 'All this not-knowing is tearing her apart. Just see what you can find out. I'll pay the going rate. I've got money and it looks like you need it.'

Calloway bristled. 'I'm not for hire, Bert, unless you want me to throw someone out of somewhere. That's what I do these days.'

Webber looked Calloway up and down. 'Yeah, and it don't pay much, I can tell. When I first met you, you was straight out of battledress and straight into Moss Bros, like they used to say in the adverts. Sharp as a pin.'

'I was straight into Allkits, Bert. My commission was temporary, remember?'

'Suit, yerself. But, no offence, Mr Calloway, you look like a sack of shit.'

Calloway had knocked men out for less, but Webber was right. The past year hadn't been kind to him. A succession of scrapes and lost jobs. His standards had dropped.

'Look, there's no shame in being down on your luck,' said Webber. 'And there's no shame in accepting good money for a job, neither. That's what I'm offering. I'm good for it.'

He looked Webber up and down. Handmade shoes, chalk-stripe suit, a showy signet ring with the initials *AW*. Webber was good for the money and flash with it too. Qualities not normally endearing to a man like Calloway, who should have sent the little rider packing the moment he showed up at the arena doors. But Webber ranked among the very few that Calloway considered a friend, to the extent that he'd ever had real friends. And the money was tempting. Doreen could do with some help. The pound or two Calloway gave her every other pay day didn't go far.

'I'll talk to Vera,' he said, regretting each word the second it formed in his mouth.

Webber beamed. 'That's the ticket.'

He reached into his inside jacket pocket and pulled out a wad of pound notes. He peeled some off and passed them to Calloway.

'That'll get you started.'

Calloway nodded and pocketed the money, but unlike Webber, he wasn't smiling.

TWO

There were boys playing cricket in the street, in spite of the weather. They had a dustbin for stumps and a charred plank scavenged from a bomb site for a bat. Fielders in hand-me-down shorts shivered in the chill of the damp afternoon while a lanky lad in oversized corduroys walloped a tennis ball towards Webber's car. The wet ball scudded across the windscreen leaving a greasy smear.

'Little sod did that on purpose,' said Webber through a wheezy cackle. A cigarette dangled from his lip as he wound down the window.

'Oi, Dennis Compton,' he shouted. 'Watch where you're hitting that ball.'

The boy flicked a V-sign. His entourage giggled.

'Serves me right for driving a flash car I s'pose,' said Webber. 'Especially round here.'

Webber had picked Calloway up in his new motor. A pale grey Buick with red leather seats. Calloway had watched pride fight with inverted snobbery on the speedway star's face when he wound down the window and asked Calloway to jump in. Webber still wasn't quite used to that six grand a year.

They'd driven south along the Old Kent Road towards Deptford. They'd taken a left down Canal Road, past the speedway stadium where Webber and Calloway had met. Where Calloway had met Pat Moxon. He felt his stomach knot as they drove alongside the old tin fencing around the stands. He remembered the day over a year ago that he'd walked out on all of them. It was a memory that pained him. He was grateful when Webber turned into the grubby backstreets of Deptford.

‘I can’t promise she’ll be up and about,’ said Webber. ‘Been sleeping odd hours since the news about Stan. The place’ll be a tip too. She’s all but given up on housework, my Else says. Not that she was a big one for it in the first place. She was happier with a milk stout inside her and a fumble on the couch with Stan. They was always like that, even when they was courting.’

‘I’m surprised she wanted a television,’ said Calloway.

Webber sniggered. Then he looked thoughtful. ‘She’s a good girl, Vera is. Solid, you know. Won’t take no truck from anyone.’ He shook his head. ‘This business with Stan has changed her. She’s losing her grip, if you know what I mean. She flips from being angry half the time to being all maudlin. And she’s necking gin like the country’s running out. Starting early too.’

Webber turned into a narrow, cobbled street. Only half the houses remained. Mean little two-up, two-downs. Old dockers cottages by the look of them. They stood in a row along one side of the street. The other side was still a mess of rubble. Deptford had taken a pounding in the Blitz. Two little girls with mucky chops pushed a rusty doll’s pram over the cobbles. An impudent-looking fox terrier sat upright in the pram, like he was lord of this manor. Webber pulled the car up by the kerbside. He looked over at the two girls with the dog. One gave him a disingenuous smile. The other stuck her tongue out. The dog gave him a mischievous look.

‘Reckon I’ll lock the car,’ said Webber, pulling out his keys.

Vera came to the door in her housecoat. She’d lost weight since those few times Calloway had seen her in the caff. The kind of weight loss that trouble brings. The housecoat hung on her like it fitted, rather than straining at the seams like it used to. She looked tired and drawn. She’d made an effort with her hair, but it was half-hearted. Her bold, saucy cheeriness of old had packed up and moved out.

‘Bert,’ she said, her voice flat. ‘And Mr Calloway. I’ll get the kettle on.’

She turned and walked into the small dark hallway, leaving Calloway and Webber to follow. Calloway smelled gin on Vera’s breath amid the rancid fug of unwashed dishes. The two men stood in the kitchen in the awkward silence as Vera filled the kettle from the tap above the stone sink. The sink had three days' washing-up in it, Calloway reckoned.

'How've you been?' said Webber, like he couldn't decide whether to sound cheery or concerned.

'How d'you think?' Vera replied, without emotion. She rinsed cups from the sink and put them on a tray.

'Mr Calloway's going to help us, Vera,' said Webber.

Vera looked Calloway up and down but said nothing. She carried the tray into the front room. The curtains were closed and the room was dark, lit only by the half light of the hallway through the door. She turned on a standard lamp in the corner. It cast a sepia glow over the cheerless surroundings. Webber and Calloway sat on the small two-seater sofa, each balancing their cups and saucers on their laps. Vera slumped in an armchair and lit a cigarette. She put the spent match in the saucer of an un-drunk cup of tea on the side table. Webber stirred his tea unnecessarily, for something to do.

Calloway broke the silence. 'I'm sorry to hear of your loss, Vera. I really am. Bert here has asked me to help make sense of some things that are troubling you. I'll do my best.'

Vera sniffed. 'Good luck,' she said, 'because they don't make an ounce of sense to me, luv.'

Bert nudged Calloway. 'Ask her about the man who came to visit, the one with the copper.'

Calloway tried not to show his irritation. This was going to be hard enough without Bert chiming in.

'This man Denton said he was from Stan's employer. Had you met him before?'

Vera shook her head. 'Stan worked all over. I never really knew who he worked with. They weren't the sort of jobs where you get to take your missus to the annual dinner dance. I'd never heard of this Denton until he turned up on the doorstep to tell me my Stan had been killed in an accident.' She pursued her lips and drew smoke through the gap in her clenched teeth. 'Said he came off the road on a bend. Going too fast, swerved to avoid a car coming the other way. The weight of the ballast in the tipper had him over. Cracked his head on the side of the cab, Denton said. I asked if I could see Stan's body, you know, say goodbye, but they told me I couldn't. Can you believe that?'

'It would have been quick, Vera,' said Webber. 'He wouldn't have felt nothing.'

Vera shot him a look. 'Oh, yeah?' she said. 'And how the hell would you know?'

Webber stuttered. 'I was only trying to...'

'Well don't,' she said. 'I'm a big girl, Bert. I don't need you to kiss it all better.' She looked at Calloway. 'My Stan's dead and someone's not telling me the truth. I'll grieve for the poor sod later, God rest his soul, but right now I want to know why this Denton said Stan was killed in an accident in Stratton-Fenwick, when I know he was in Berlin, of all the places.'

'We don't know that Vera. Not for sure,' said Calloway, half-wishing he hadn't.

'Then how come he had a Berlin train ticket and a flyer for a local girly bar in the pocket of his best suit? Explain that, if you're supposed to be so smart.'

Bert shuffled, looking uncomfortable. He said, 'Mr Calloway used to be...'

Calloway stopped him. 'There's a dozen reasons Stan could have had those things.'

'What reasons?' she said, pinching the butt of the cigarette and grinding it into the saucer on the side table. 'Find me a reason that makes sense and I'll buy you a toffee apple. Nothing makes sense, apart from the fact that I'm a fucking widow and I'm being fed a load of bullshit.'

Bert backed into the sofa. Calloway heard him whisper, 'She's proper angry now.'

Vera stood up and crossed the room. She lit another cigarette and held it in her mouth while she reached for the bottle of gin on the sideboard. She poured herself a good-sized slug.

'What else did this man Denton say?' said Calloway.

'He said I'd get a payoff. That the company's insurance would pay out, even though the accident was Stan's fault. Reckless driving, he said.'

Bert rolled his eyes. 'They all drive reckless, those short-haul boys. It's not like Stan was any worse than the rest.'

'Has there been an inquest?' said Calloway.

Vera shrugged. 'If there has, nobody told me.'

'That strikes me as unusual.'

'Does it?' she said. 'How would I know? I've never lost a husband before.'

She was agitated. Tense. On the edge of snapping.

Calloway adjusted his tone. He summoned up what passed for a bedside manner. 'I know this is difficult, Vera, but if I'm going to help, I need to ask questions.'

Vera knocked back the gin and poured another.

Webber said, 'Go easy, Vera girl.'

'Don't lecture me, Bert Webber. You haven't been through this. You've still got your Elsie. Nice and cosy in your little prefab. I've lost my Stan. It's just me now. And I'll bloody well drink when I want.'

She took another gulp of the gin. Bert and Calloway lit up cigarettes. They both needed one.

'He was no angel,' said Vera. 'He could be a right old devil when he wanted. I mean I could never really trust him. He was a good-looking man and he got the attention. He liked it an 'all. But I kept him close. Kept him fed, made him laugh, made sure he didn't go short of the other.'

Bert shuffled in his seat. 'Steady on, girl,' he said.

Vera waved it away. 'He was a rogue, my Stan. An opportunist. Always a bit sly.' She laughed. 'I mean, he'd done a stretch, hadn't he?'

'Stan had been to prison?' said Calloway.

'Glasshouse,' said Bert. 'An army prison in Egypt. Got caught selling the signals corps' radio valves on the black market to local shopkeepers. They banged him up for a bit. Must have behaved himself 'cos he got out early, as I recall.'

'He was no angel, my Stan.' said Vera. She drew on the cigarette. 'But he was mine.' Her voice wavered and her eyes welled up.

Webber stood up and put his arm around her. She pushed him

away.

'You've no need, Bert. I'm alright.'

Her stoicism looked skin-deep to Calloway. It was to be expected. But there was anger too. Plenty of it.

'What else did Denton talk about when he visited you?'

'Funeral arrangements,' she said. 'He said the company would arrange it all and that I didn't need to worry about the cost. They'd pay for a nice send off.'

Webber whistled. 'They must've liked him, Vera. Not many firms offer perks like that.'

They certainly didn't, thought Calloway.

'He had a load of questions too. About Stan,' she said.

'What sort of questions?'

Vera sat back in the armchair. She was calmer now. Must be the gin, thought Calloway.

'He asked if I'd seen Stan since he first left for Stratton-Fenwick. Had he come home to visit at weekends? That kind of thing.'

'Anything else?'

'He asked if he'd written me letters or called. I told Denton I'd had regular postcards, which surprised me to be honest, although I didn't tell him that. Stan wasn't the writing kind. I can't recall him ever writing me a love letter, even when we were courting. He expressed his affections in other ways, if you know what I mean.' She rolled her eyes and shook her head. 'I got six postcards in as many weeks. Part of me suspected it was guilt. That he'd been up to something while he was away.'

The room was getting stuffy. The earlier drizzle must have cleared up and the afternoon sun was shining on the front of the house. Calloway wished Vera would open the curtains, but he knew she wouldn't, and it would be impolite to ask. It was tradition. You closed your curtains when there had been a death in the family. Like flying the flag at half-mast.

'Bert tells me this man Denton offered you help from a private clinic when he visited?'

'That was the second time he called,' she said.

Webber and Calloway exchanged looks.

'You didn't tell me he'd been again, Vera,' said Webber.

'Last week,' she said. ''Cause I'd been calling him up. Demanding to know what was going on. He kept fobbing me off, but I wasn't having that. Told him if he didn't give me answers, I'd take it somewhere else.' She looked across at Bert. 'You know, David,' she said.

Webber read Calloway's quizzical expression. 'One of her nephews,' he said. 'He's a reporter on the *Mercury*. The local paper.'

'That got their attention,' Vera said, with satisfaction. 'Two of 'em turned up on the doorstep.'

'Two of them?' said Calloway. 'Did Denton bring the policeman again?'

Vera shook her head. 'He brought a doctor. Talked to me about how I was feeling, how grief plays tricks with the mind. Gave me some pills for my nerves.' She scoffed. 'Nerves, I said. What nerves? I've just lost my husband. I'm not likely to be in the best of spirits, am I? I haven't got nerve trouble, I said. I'm tough as old boots.' Calloway didn't doubt it. 'But this doctor, he kept on about it. Like he was trying to convince me I was losing my marbles, you know, because of the grief.'

'Private doctor?' said Calloway.

Vera shrugged. 'Smartly dressed. Blazer, cavalry twills, nice striped tie. Good looking sort.'

'Did he give his name?'

'If he did, I can't remember. I was all at sixes and sevens.'

'Have you still got Denton's telephone number?' said Calloway. 'And the name and address of the haulage company?'

She stood up and crossed the small room to the sideboard. She was a good woman, Calloway thought. Confident, engaging and smart as buffed-up buttons on a tunic. Even in the half-caring dishevelment of grief, she retained an innate dignity. Stan had been lucky to have her. Whether she had been lucky to have Stan was another matter. She opened one of the sideboard drawers and rifled around.

'Here,' she said, passing him a business card with Denton's name and number on it. There was no address or company name.

She also handed him a payslip on headed paper.

'Thank you,' said Calloway, slipping both into the pocket of his suit jacket. 'Just one more thing,' he said. 'What does Denton look like?'

She thought for a moment. 'I don't know. Skinny fella, I s'pose. Dark hair with a widow's peak. Bit big in the chin.'

She turned her back to them and poured herself another large measure of gin.

They left Vera's house and stepped out onto the street, their eyes adjusting to the late autumn sun. The two little girls were sitting on the running board of Webber's Buick. The fox terrier stood sentinel by their side.

'We minded your car, mister,' one of the girls said.

'Give us a shilling,' said the other.

Webber pulled a coin from his pocket and tossed it towards them. As he unlocked the driver's side door, the dog cocked its leg against the Buick's wheel.

THREE

It was full house at the arena. A rough-looking lot too. All the local chancers, with their women in tow. Adult artful dodgers in too-wide suits, their hats pulled down over their eyes, their faces set firm. None of them smiling, except to greet others like them with a mean little grin and a nod. They sat close to the ring, at tables with tablecloths and candles in wine bottles. Mr Finnegan's nod to nightclub sophistication, and an excuse to charge half as much again for ringside seats. The men stared through the ropes, their eyes fixed on the action. It excused them from chit-chat, or any other concession to perceptible enjoyment. These were the local hard men, in their own eyes at least. They gave no quarter where emotion was concerned. They weren't much of a date for their women, these local faces, thought Calloway. Their dates sat there in their vulgar faux-couture, sipping their gin-and-Its, looking bored. It was a different story in the cheap seats, the long, hard benches you had to excuse-me along to get to the bar or the peanut stall. This crowd were packed in and revved up. They hollered encouragement and abuse in equal measure, singling out their heroes and villains from the night's bill. Couples, groups of lads and girls in pairs. The lads stared transfixed at the fighters in the ring, their hungry eyes devouring the female flesh, as it grappled and bounced. They would nudge each other, winking, eroticising the contortions of the fighters in their oversexed young minds. The girls sought a different pleasure from the display, projecting the rivalries of their everyday lives onto the women on the canvas, like living voodoo dolls. For the couples it was a way of just being together, sharing in the fun, such as it was, holding hands and nuzzling up, lost in the throng.

And the smell of the crowd. God, thought Calloway. It was

enough to turn your stomach. Five hundred unwashed bodies, basting in their own sweat, stale inside their overcoats. A monstrous odour, and more than a match for the cloying scent of the Brylcreem in their hair, or the lavender behind their ears, or the smoke of the Woodbines that hung from their lips.

A man in a loud check suit emerged from the office that overlooked the arena and adjusted his garish, fat-boy tie.

'Mr Finnegan,' said Calloway with a deferential nod.

Frankie Finnegan was the promoter. He ran the arena.

'Good crowd tonight, eh, Mr Calloway?' he said. He shot his cuffs and rubbed his hands. 'Bodes well for the title fight.'

The two men looked down onto the ring from the gallery.

'Trudi's on form,' said Calloway, for want of something to say. He watched Finnegan's star attraction bouncing a fighter half her size off the ropes, to the boos of the crowd.

'They love a good villain,' said Finnegan. 'That's what they pay to see, and Trudi's the best.'

The big fighter slammed her opponent onto the deck, like a butcher slapping meat on the block. The crowd hurled abuse. Trudi deflected it with a shaking fist. She bared her teeth and snarled.

'She certainly puts on a show,' said Calloway. How they called this a sport, he couldn't fathom. Finnegan pulled a gold cigarette case from the inside pocket of his dog-tooth suit. He offered Calloway a cigarette and lit it with a shiny new gold lighter.

'Hand-rolled,' he said. He was a flash bastard, Finnegan, thought Calloway. But he had to admit, he'd never smoked a fag so good.

George the cleaner scurried up to the two men, panting, an expression of disgust on his old, sagging face.

'There's one in the gents again,' he said.

'I'll deal with it,' said Calloway. He ducked through the fire door and walked along the corridor at the back of the first-floor gallery. The smell of cheap pine disinfectant hit him as he approached the lavatories. There were three stalls inside, opposite a row of rank-smelling urinals. Two stalls were empty, one was occupied. Calloway kicked the closed door open.

'You should put that down, pal,' he said. 'Before it goes off in your hand.'

A middle-aged man in a gabardine mac let go of his manhood and scrabbled to pull up his trousers. The man stepped out of the stall, his face flushing red. He edged past Calloway's big frame, avoiding eye contact.

'Don't forget to wash your hands,' said Calloway. 'And don't come back.' He left the man in the mac to it. His work was done.

At the end of the night, Calloway made his rounds of the arena, turning out lights and testing the doors. The light in the wrestlers' dressing room was still on. Calloway knocked and entered.

The room smelled of sweat and cheap talcum powder. Trudi Trauber was alone in the room packing her kit into a shabby canvas hold-all. She wore high-waist American jeans with a check shirt rolled up at the sleeves and men's penny loafers on her size-nine feet. Her dark hair was up, with a roll at the front and a ponytail behind. At just shy of six foot with big square shoulders, she looked like a bobby-soxer crossed with a fire door. Someone you wouldn't want slamming into you.

'Reggie, *liebchen. Wie gehts?*'

It took someone of Trudi's height and build to speak German so openly. Wounds still ran deep in these post-war years.

Calloway shrugged. He'd just taken on a new burden and it showed in the lines chiselled into his face. He answered in German. He was out of practice and barely fluent, not like during the war when he interrogated German POWs as a sergeant in a field security section. But he could still hold a conversation.

'I've just agreed to something I may live to regret,' he said.

'The story of my life,' said Trudi. She kissed the fingertips on her man-sized hand and touched his cheek. 'Thanks for defending my friend's honour. I'm glad chivalry is alive and well.'

'I'm not sure the man whose nose I broke will agree when he wakes up tomorrow. Or Mr Finnegan, for that matter. I'm waiting for him to haul me up on the incident.'

'Frankie won't do anything. I've had a word,' said Trudi.

Trudi was the star attraction. She was worth a lot of ticket sales to Finnegan, which meant she could call the shots.

'I'm grateful,' said Calloway. He changed the subject. 'You started wrestling in Berlin before the war, didn't you?'

Trudi laughed. 'Mud wrestling. Not so much a sport as a sideshow.' She looked around the dressing room. 'Back then we wrestled in nightclubs, not arenas.'

'Ever hear of a Club Continentale?'

Calloway passed Trudi the flyer Bert had given him. She looked at the gaudy image on the front. She shook her head. 'I don't recall it,' she said, then turned the card over. She gave Calloway a wry smile.

'Potsdamer Strasse. I can guess what kind of club that is.' She handed back the card. 'Are you planning a little holiday, Reggie?'

Calloway flushed red. He shook his head. 'Enquiring for a friend,' he said, and then regretted it.

Trudi raised an eyebrow. 'If I didn't know you better...'

'I trust that you do,' said Calloway, cutting her short. 'Give you a lift home?'

He could barely afford to keep a car on the road these days, and it wasn't much of a car at that, a 1938 Morris 8 with more dings and dents than a panel beater's workbench. It was a small car for a man Calloway's size, smaller still once the six-foot wrestler had climbed in. The pair of them wore it as much as rode in it.

'So what have you agreed to that is causing you so much angst?'

A good German word, *angst*, thought Calloway. The feeling of fear that comes from the immense responsibility of the power of choice. He'd chosen to help Bert against his better judgement, against his instincts even. And now he was committed. He had Vera's expectations to think of too.

'I have a habit of getting involved,' was all he said.

It was a twenty-minute drive to Trudi's place that time of night. The roads were deserted, save for the odd cab and a street cleaning bowser spraying disinfecting water to dilute the filth in the gutters.

'How does a Berliner end up wrestling in East London?' said

Calloway. He had often wondered this since taking the job. This was the first chance he'd had to ask.

'When the national socialists came to power, they closed down the clubs. The Resi, the El Dorado, the Heaven and Hell. They all went. Too decadent for the new German ideology. The Nazis turned the El Dorado into a headquarters for the Brownshirts. Can you believe that? After that, I found it hard to work. I wasn't cut out for a regular job.' She laughed to herself. 'Or a regular life, for that matter. Not regular enough to fit in with the expectations of the thousand-year Reich. I'd never been one for *kinder, küche, kirche*. And I had no intention of producing offspring for the master race.' She paused, thinking for a moment. 'You know they gave a medal to any woman that could produce more than four children for the fatherland.' She shook her head. 'My talents lay elsewhere.'

'Like throwing young girls around the ring to entertain the populous?'

'They're not so young, believe me. And don't dismiss all-in wrestling as entertainment. It's strictly Lord-Admiral Mountevans rules.'

Calloway wasn't convinced. Trudi's ironic tone said she wasn't either, although she was quite happy to play along. Admiral-Lord Mountevans and his radio-star pal, Commander Campbell, may have created sportsmanlike rules, weight divisions and formal championships, but Calloway couldn't help sharing the more sceptical views of the press. From what he'd seen at the arena, the sport still relied on fakery and gimmicks, as much as sportsmanship.

Trudi pulled a cigarette case from her hold-all. She lit two cigarettes, passed one to Calloway and wound down the window a couple of notches.

'So did you leave Germany for Britain?' he said.

'No. I went to Paris first.' She laughed. 'I didn't have much choice. Ideology wasn't the only reason I had to leave Germany. There were more pressing considerations.'

'Such as?'

She took a long drag on the cigarette and blew smoke out of

the half-open window. 'Let's just say I found myself on a side of the law that wasn't conducive to a long and fruitful life.'

He was curious, but it was idle curiosity.

'In Paris I met a French promoter,' she said, changing the subject. 'He was taking wrestlers to Portugal, to fight at the Campo Pequeno in Lisbon. He added female wrestling to the bill.' She looked reflective for a moment. 'The Campo Pequeno was some arena, I tell you. A grand old bull ring. The atmosphere at the fights was electric. The best I've known.'

'So you sat out the war in Portugal?'

She nodded. 'A neutral country seemed the best place to be. I moved to London in forty-seven, when the formal championships started up. That's when Finnegan picked me up.'

She stared out of the car window, as they passed row after row of bombed-out buildings, their remains still to be demolished.

'I miss Berlin,' said Trudi. 'Or whatever's left of it.' She turned to Calloway. 'Have you been there?'

Calloway had been there in forty-six, when he was still in the army. He had been recalled from his posting in Palestine to support the war crimes trials that were just starting up. He had experience with war criminals. Too much experience. He'd been part of a unit that had liberated one of the first concentration camps the British forces found. He'd interrogated members of the *kommandantur*. He'd read their files, files recording the camp's procedures and processes, cold and meticulous in their detail. His role in Berlin was escorting prisoners to Nuremberg for trail. One of them spoke out of turn, justifying himself, sneering and remorseless. Calloway had punched out his front teeth and broke three of his ribs. He avoided a charge but was advised by his CO to leave the army, quickly and quietly. Since then he'd been scraping a living as a jobbing security boss, in jobs that had a habit of turning sour. He didn't share Trudi's affection for Berlin.

'I've been there,' he said. 'There's not much left of it.'

He dropped her outside a block of flats. One of those low rectangular blocks with curved metal windows and a portico over the entrance. Not a palace, but not half-bad either. Trudi was pulling in a few bob as Finnegan's star attraction.

'See you Thursday,' he said. 'Big night.'

Thursday was the Southern Area title fight. Mr Finnegan would be upping the ticket prices. Trudi climbed out of the car and raised herself up to her full six feet.

'I'm big every night, *liebchen*,' she said, with a deep, throaty laugh.

It was past midnight when he arrived at his street.

'You've got a visitor,' his landlady said. She stood beside the stairs in a dressing gown that had seen better days. Her arms were folded.

'No visitors after ten,' she said. 'That's the rule.'

Calloway looked at his watch, although he knew the time.

'I'm not expecting anyone,' he said. 'Not my fault if someone turns up when I'm not about.'

'Rules are rules,' she said.

He looked around the hallway, with its peeling wallpaper and brown stains on the ceiling. The smell of cat piss hung in the air.

'A house in this state doesn't deserve rules,' he said, shaking the loose banister in his big hand. He felt her eyes boring into him as he climbed the stairs.

Doreen stood outside his door, half-hidden in shadow, little Maggie cradled in her arms. The toddler was asleep. Doreen looked relieved to see Calloway. She also looked scared.

'I'm so, so sorry Reg, but I had nowhere else to go.' Her voice quivered, on the verge of tears.

'It's alright,' he said, as softly as his gruff voice would allow. 'What's happened?'

She hesitated, backing further into the shadow of the door well. She was turning her head to one side, shielding the right side of her face from his view. Calloway stepped towards her. She flinched. He cupped his hand under her chin and turned her head towards the insipid light from the bare bulb in the hallway. The side of her face was swollen. A bruise was coming up under her eye.

'Jimmy,' she said. 'He's been round again.'

FOUR

Calloway had set off early for the drive north, dropping Doreen and young Maggie home on the way. He'd let them stay the night. His landlady could go to hell. Doreen and Maggie shared the bed in his small room, while he'd slept as best he could in his armchair. It wasn't the best night's sleep he'd had. Doreen had woken him with a cup of tea around six-thirty. Her black eye was up good and proper. He knew he would have to pay Jimmy a visit, set him straight, but that would have to wait. He was on Webber's time now and had to fit in his enquiries between shifts at the arena.

Drinkwell's Haulage had a depot eight miles outside Stratton-Fenwick. The address was on the payslip Vera had given him. The depot was a collection of wartime huts behind a high fence, most likely part of a decommissioned RAF station. He drove through the open gates and pulled up outside the building that looked like an office. There was a sign by the door that said 'no soiled boots' and a scraper set into the concrete step caked in congealed clay mud.

The office was warm inside, despite the chill of the morning. A three-bar electric fire radiated dry and dusty heat. A young female voice from behind the counter said, 'If you're looking for work, we've no vacancies.'

'I'm not looking for work,' said Calloway. 'I'm looking for Mr Denton.'

She stood up from behind her desk and peered at him over her cat's eyeglasses. She wore a candy-stripe shirt tucked into high-waisted trousers that buttoned down one side. Her kitten heels would have been no match for the boot scraper. She looked out of place in the run-down Quonset hut, with its grubby box files and posters advertising spark plugs. He guessed this wasn't the kind of place she'd always dreamed of working.

'Is he one of the drivers?' she said, running her finger down a clipboard.

'One of the managers,' said Calloway.

'I've not heard of a Mr Denton,' she said. 'But then I'm new here. Only started a fortnight ago.'

'Could he be at another office?'

'We've only got the one,' she said.

He passed her Denton's business card. She took it and frowned, then shook her head.

'Doesn't say Drinkwell's on it,' she said. 'Have you tried calling the number?'

He had. Three times. He couldn't get past the switchboard operator.

'Perhaps I could speak to someone that's been here longer.'

'Mr Drinkwell's here, but he's over at the workshop.'

'Then I'll wait, if you don't mind.'

'Suit yourself,' she said and returned to her desk.

Calloway called after her. 'You could do me a favour, while we're waiting. I'm actually here about one of your drivers. Stanley Deakin. I heard he had an accident. I wanted to get some details.'

She thought for moment.

'Are you sure he's one of ours?' she said. 'He's not on the current roster.'

'He was working here for a few months, running ballast up to the building sites at the new town. Perhaps I could see his file.'

She hesitated. 'I'm not sure I can do that. Personnel files are private.' She held the clipboard close to her chest. 'And I don't even know who you are.'

'Rude of me. Sorry. My name's Calloway. Army field security,' he lied. 'We think a deserter might have signed on with you in the name Stanley Deakin. Heard rumours he'd been killed in an accident. Clearly we need to look into it.'

She looked uncomfortable. 'I think you need to speak to Mr Drinkwell.'

Calloway looked at his watch. He gave her a plaintive smile. 'Looks like he's going to be a while and I've only got till noon before I need to be back at the barracks. I won't half get it if I'm late. Are you sure you can't help me out?'

She looked out of the window towards a hut he assumed to be the workshop. 'I'm not sure,' she said, her voice wavering.

'I've already been late twice this month. Three times and they'll dock my pay. Not to mention the balling out I'll get from my Sergeant-Major. Terrifying he is. A giant of a man with a violent temper.'

He tried to look forlorn, in spite of his bulk. She frowned, weighing up the options. Then she smiled. 'Alright,' she said. 'But quickly. I don't want to get in any trouble either. Not this soon into the job.'

She pulled down a box file marked H to J from a shelf behind her and laid it on the counter. She opened the lid and walked her fingers through the manilla folders.

'Here he is,' she said. 'S Deakin.'

Calloway took the folder and opened it. He read down the entries. Stan's start date tallied with Vera's account. He'd received a pay packet every week, with deductions for damage and speeding fines. His last payday was the day of his death. There was a pencilled entry beneath this final pay date. It said, 'Terminated following accident.' There were no other notes on the file.

'Who said you could look at that?'

A stout man in his fifties stood in the doorway, in a worn tweed suit and bowler hat. He didn't look pleased.

'I'm sorry, Mr Drinkwell,' the secretary said. 'This gentleman's from the army. He's asking about one of the drivers.'

Drinkwell peered over at the file, reading the name on the front. 'And what would the army want with Stanley Deakin?'

'Possible deserter,' said Calloway, already worried that the lie was wearing thin.

Drinkwell eyed him suspiciously. 'Do you have identification?'

Calloway reached in his pocket and handed over his old army identity card. He'd smeared the date with spit so you could no longer see that it had expired more than four years ago. He was far from convinced it would hold up to scrutiny. Drinkwell looked at the card, frowning. He handed it back to Calloway.

'Our personnel records are confidential,' he said. 'Even to the army.'

He glared at the secretary, who looked on the verge of tears.

'Miss Fisher, please escort Sergeant Calloway off the premises,' he said. 'And ask Wally to lock the gates. He shouldn't be leaving them open.'

Miss Fisher walked beside Calloway across the hard standing towards his car.

'I'm for it now,' she said.

'I reckon his bark's worse than his bite,' said Calloway, not convinced that it was. 'Anyway, you've done nothing wrong, not really. He'll probably forget about it by tomorrow.'

She looked at him and smiled, only half-reassured.

'I hope you're right,' she said.

'I hate to ask you one more thing,' he said, 'after you've been so helpful, but where can I get a decent lunch round here? An army marches on its stomach, as they say.'

'I'm not sure,' she said. 'I bring packed lunches.'

'Then where do the drivers eat?' he said. 'I bet they love a good fry-up.'

She thought for a moment. 'There's a transport caff a couple of miles up the A1. I've heard them talk about going there.'

Calloway thanked her and opened the door of his car. He glanced back at the office before climbing in. He saw Drinkwell through the window, looking back at him and speaking into the telephone.

The caff was in a pull-in, set back from the main road. A low slab of a building, little more than a box, but with black timbers fixed to the facade in a misguided attempt to give it a cosy, mock-Tudor feel. The red gingham curtains that grinned through the steamed-up windows did little to add to the effect. Nor did the tin signs advertising Coca-Cola, Lyons Cakes and Capstan cigarettes. But he was in the right place. There were five Dodge tippers lined up in the car park. They each had Drinkwell's livery.

The fug of frying grease hit Calloway as he entered. Somewhere beneath it, the smell of bacon and chops. He ordered tea and an egg banjo. He'd not eaten yet today. He'd given the last of his bread to Doreen and Maggie for toast. The five Drinkwell's drivers sat at a chipped Formica table by the window. They were unmistakeable, in their brown leather jerkins, gum boots and berets. Calloway sat at an adjoining table. He looked across to them as he ate. One of them caught his eye, a parchment-faced old timer with a red nose and thick black hair in his ears.

'Hungry work, eh?' said Calloway, above the din of their chatter. 'You Drinkwell's boys?'

The old man nodded. 'For our sins,' he said, jamming a fork full of pale pink bacon between his yellow teeth.

'Know my mate, Stan Deakin?' said Calloway.

Four heads turned to face him. None of them were smiling. The fifth driver sat at the head of the table with his back to Calloway.

'Who wants to know?' said one of the four, a small, weaselly man, with keen black eyes and a sharp, oversized nose.

'Just a mate. The name's Calloway.'

The driver with his back to Calloway stood up and turned to face him. He took out a pack of Woodbines and offered one. Calloway accepted.

'They call me Spanner,' the man said. He was Calloway's height and just as broad, with wiry red hair and a face like a mastiff. 'I know Stan.'

Calloway held out the cigarette for a light from the Zippo the man called Spanner was holding in his tattooed hand. Spanner shook his head. 'Not here,' he said. 'Outside.'

They stepped through the caff towards the door, the other four drivers watching them. Calloway saw one grimace. Another grinned. It wasn't reassuring.

Once they were outside, Spanner held out the lighter. Calloway leaned in to accept the light.

The first blow knocked him sideways. The second one floored him. Spanner was on top of him, big hands gripping his lapels and slamming him against the hard gravel of the car park.

'Where's my hundred and fifty?' he spat. 'Where's my fucking money?'

The four other drivers were outside now. Calloway heard cries of encouragement. Amid the cries, a heavily-accented voice said, 'For Christ's sake, Spanner, you'll bloody kill him.' The owner of the voice leaned forward and pulled Calloway's attacker off him. Calloway scrambled to his feet, spitting blood and gravel dust from his mouth. The driver with the accent took Calloway's arm and led him towards one of the trucks. Spanner and his three pals shouted abuse. Spanner picked up a fist full of gravel and hurled it at the two men. Calloway felt chippings sting the back of his bloodied head. He heard Spanner and his pals advancing towards them.

'You'd better get in,' the man with the accent said, holding the passenger door of the Dodge truck open. 'Quickly, if you know what's good for you.'

FIVE

The truck driver floored the accelerator and drove out of the car park, spraying gravel in his wake. Calloway looked back and saw Spanner shaking his fist, while his little gang of acolytes shouted obscenities.

'Thanks,' said Calloway, 'whoever you are.'

'Marek,' the driver said. 'Mad Marek, they call me.' He laughed. 'I'm a crazy, mad bastard.'

He spoke broken English with a Central European accent.

'Your pal Spanner looked like the crazy one.'

'Different kind of crazy. I'm crazy behind the wheel. He's crazing in the head.'

'I got that impression,' said Calloway. He felt the back of his head with his hand and winced.

'I'll pull over,' said Marek. He bumped the Dodge up onto the roadside verge and slammed on the brakes. The wheels slid along the damp grass before the truck jerked to a halt. Marek reached under his seat and pulled out a canvas haversack. It had a faded red cross on the front inside a circle of blanco. He fished inside and pulled out a bottle of iodine and some sticking plaster.

'Lean forward,' he said. He cleaned the wound on the back of Calloway's head and stuck the plaster on it. 'Just a nick,' he said, 'but head wounds bleed more. I got the dirt out. Now you won't get sepsis, eh?'

'Thanks, Marek. I'm Reg, by the way,' said Calloway. The two men shook hands. 'So what was all that about?'

'Stan did a bunk owing Spanner money,' said Marek.

'One hundred and fifty pounds?'

Marek nodded. 'That's a month's wages for a short-haul driver. A lot of money Stan owes.'

'What do you mean, Stan did a bunk?'

Marek pulled a pocket watch from his jerkin and checked the time. 'I must drive. Must get my runs in. You ride with me, I tell you about Stan and Spanner.'

Marek revved the engine hard and let out the handbrake. The heavy truck shot forward, throwing Calloway back in his seat. Marek pushed the pedal to the floor and the truck gathered speed. The speedometer hit sixty. They gained on an old Austin Seven. Marek pounded the horn.

'Slowcoach bastard,' he shouted.

He yanked the wheel and swung the truck over the white lines into the right-hand lane of narrow the two-lane road.

'Christ,' said Calloway. A single decker bus was heading straight for them. Marek pounded the horn again. He revved the engine and changed down. When he was within feet of the oncoming bus, he heaved the truck back into the left-hand lane. The two vehicles clipped mirrors as they passed. Calloway caught the ashen face of the bus driver through the window. Marek laughed.

'Like I tell you. Crazy mad bastard.' Calloway had to agree. 'I beat every driver for the most runs in a shift. Today I need to make time on account of stopping to fix your damn head.'

'For which I'm very grateful,' said Calloway, 'along with saving me a kicking from your mate Spanner.'

'He's not my mate,' said Marek. 'He's mad in the head. Stan saw him as soft touch. Tried to win his money. Stan underestimated Spanner. He's a canny bastard, Spanner is. He looks like a big orang-utan. Orang-utans are smart monkeys.' Apes, thought Calloway, but he wasn't inclined to correct his crazy mad bastard saviour.

'How did he try to win Spanner's money?'

'Cards,' said Marek. 'In the back of the workshop, after their shift. Kept losing, kept trying to win it back. Night after night. Spanner is a good card player. Ran rings around Stan. Took him for a hundred and fifty quid, before Stan threw in the towel.' Marek sat upright, suddenly alert. 'Bastard truck's blocking the road.' One of Drinkwell's trucks was overtaking another ahead of them, taking up both lanes. 'Hold on tight, my friend,' he said.

Calloway saw what was coming, although he hardly believed Marek was serious. He gripped the sides of the passenger seat and braced himself. Marek pushed the accelerator to the floor until he was almost rear-ending the left-hand truck. He tugged the steering wheel to the left. The truck mounted the narrow verge. Marek let out a battle cry. He drove through the gap, trees scraping his left flank, an inch to spare on his right. Calloway heard the squeal of metal on metal as the two trucks scraped wheel arches. Sparks flew upwards. Marek went rigid as he pushed the accelerator through the floor. He swung his truck back onto the road, cutting up the truck behind him from the inside.

'Ha,' Marek shouted in triumph. Calloway's heart thumped harder than during his first parachute jump.

'Do you know why I am the fastest driver? Because I have no fear. I lost my fear during the war.'

He pushed the speedometer to seventy-five, as if to prove the point.

'Did you serve?' said Calloway.

'I was a partisan, in Slovakia. I am Slovak. I lived in the mountains for a year attacking the Germans.' He went quiet for a moment. 'When I returned to my village, all my family were dead. The Nazis killed them all in reprisals.'

Calloway had lost a loved one to the Nazis. *The* loved one. Lost to their brutality, their bestial self-entitlement. He shook the thought from his head. 'How did you end up in Britain?' he said, in an attempt to shift the conversation to something less painful.

'After the war, some of us partisans fell out of favour with the new Czech government. It was a good time to leave and I had no reason to stay. I worked my way through Europe taking what little work I could. It wasn't easy. Then someone told me about a displaced workers' scheme, where you could work in this country. Proper wages. I lived in a workers' camp outside town called King's Lynn, with Poles, Latvians and Ukrainians. Do you know Kings Lynn? They talk funny there. We spoke better English than they did. I took a driving job. Got my license, all proper. But I fell out with some of my fellow workers. It was best I left the camp. I ended up here, at Drinkwell's. Mr Drinkwell is a miserable sod. But the pay is okay.' He smiled to himself. 'I like it.'

Marek swung the lorry into some kind of works. There was a conveyor belt dumping aggregates into a big, rusting hopper. The whole area was caked in a thick layer of dust.

'Good,' he said. 'I beat the others.'

He reversed the truck, expertly positioning the tipper right under the spout of the hopper.

'Are all the drivers this competitive?'

'Of course. We make four shillings an hour and seven shillings a load. More loads, more money. Simple mathematics. Everyone competes, but I am the best. Other drivers make ten runs a day, I make fourteen. I do crazy mad speeds, eh?'

'Do you ever get caught? For speeding?'

Marek shrugged. 'Sometimes. We all pay our own fines. That's the rule.'

He gestured through the widescreen to a worker standing near the hopper. 'You wait here,' he said to Calloway, climbing down from the cab.

Marek exchanged a few words with the worker. Then he grabbed a shovel and headed towards the rear of the truck. Calloway heard an almighty crunch as a big load of gravel landed in the tipper. A cloud of dust billowed around the truck. Calloway looked behind and saw Marek standing on top of the gravel, evening out the load with the shovel. Then he jumped down and climbed back in the cab.

'Quick, yes? I am the quickest. Now hold on.'

Calloway gripped the seat again and braced his legs against the sloped floor of the footwell. The Dodge's engine growled like a cornered beast. Marek reversed away from the hopper. He took the corner out of the depot and onto the road at such a speed that a thick spray of gravel crashed onto the kerb. Calloway wondered how much of it would be left by the time Marek reached his destination.

'We make good time,' said Marek, satisfied.

Calloway lit a cigarette and offered one to Marek.

'When did Stan do a bunk?' he said.

Marek thought. 'Maybe two months ago.'

'That long ago? Are you sure?'

According to Drinkwell's file, the haulier had been paying Stan until three weeks ago, up to the time of the accident. He'd also sent postcards from Stratton-Fenwick more recently than that.

'I'm sure,' said Marek.

The Slovak driver hadn't mentioned any accident, let alone Stan being dead. He was talking about him in the present tense. So was Spanner, who was still wanting his money.

'Did Stan have an accident?' said Calloway. 'A road accident?'

'Stan? Speeding yes, accident no. He was a good driver.' He laughed. 'Lousy card player, but very good driver.'

'Did he give you any clue as to where he was going when he disappeared?'

'He said he knew how to get the money he owed Spanner. He told me there was more to him than driving trucks, whatever that meant. Frankly, I thought it was bullshit. Just an excuse to welch on his debt. But who knows?'

'Did Stan ever say anything about going to Berlin?' said Calloway.

Marek screwed his face up, as if Calloway question was nonsensical. 'Berlin? No. Why would he go to Berlin?'

'That's one thing I'm trying to find out,' said Calloway.

Marek dropped Calloway at the transport caff on the way to the new town site. He gave a cheery wave and shot out of the pull-in, narrowly missing a school bus heading in the opposite direction. Crazy mad bastard thought Calloway and smiled. He crossed the car park to the Morris. It was slumped on the gravel, lower than it should have been.

Spanner and his gang had let all four tyres down.

SIX

He arrived back at his digs as the sun was setting. He'd had to wait at the transport caff for a driver that would lend him a pump for his tyres. A salesman who travelled in cleaning products obliged him, insisting he buy Calloway tea and an Eccles cake afterwards. He subjected Calloway to an hour of mindless chat on the relative merits of powder and cream for cleaning sinks.

When Calloway stepped into the hallway of the rooming house, he found his belongings sitting at the foot of the stairs. Two battered suitcases and an orange crate, hastily packed, and not by him. The landlady stood beside them, her arms crossed and her face like granite.

'No overnight guests,' she said. 'It's a house rule. The penalty is forfeiture of lodgings.' She snorted through her nose, like it hurt to do so. 'A woman too,' she said.

She pushed the orange crate towards him with her carpet slipper.

'This is a respectable establishment,' she said.

'The only thing respectable about it is the money I pay you to live in this hovel,' he said. 'I'll be happy to see the back of it.'

She shot him a look like she'd just been slapped. He piled the two suitcases on top of the orange crate and carried them to his car.

His bravura had ebbed by the time he reached the kerb.

'Congratulations, Reg,' he muttered under his breath. 'You've just joined the ranks of homeless ex-servicemen.'

He had keys to the arena. There was no wrestling that evening. He let himself in and carried his belongings up the darkened rear stairs to the second floor, where he had a small office, in reality an unused store cupboard with a desk and chair. He dumped the cases and crate in the corner and went back down the stairs to the small gymnasium behind the auditorium, where Finnegan's wrestlers trained. The ingrained smell of sweat and embrocation stung his nostrils. He took a floor mat back to his office. It would serve as a bed until he sorted himself out. There was an old army blanket and a Primus stove in the crate he'd brought with him. This wasn't the first time in the past year or so he'd roughed it between lodgings. He switched on the wireless and tuned it to the third programme, for the classical music. He listened to Mendelssohn while he heated a tin of oxtail soup. Home sweet home, he thought.

There were footsteps in the corridor. Soft and tentative. Like someone was creeping. Odd, he thought. It was past eight now. He put his canteen of soup down and reached for the door handle, then yanked the door open, quick as a flash.

George the cleaner gasped. His dentures came loose. His mottled hand shot up by reflex, to push them back in his mouth.

'Sorry to make you jump, George,' said Calloway. 'I thought I had the place to myself.'

'I'm putting in a spot of overtime, Mr Calloway,' the cleaner said, clenching a rolled-up fag in the corner of his mouth. 'Mr Finnegan wants the place spick and span for the regional championship fight.'

Spick and span was a tall order, thought Calloway, especially for an old boy armed only with a mop and bucket. The arena's grime was ingrained. George peered onto Calloway's office and saw the floor mat and blanket.

'Staying over tonight?' he said, with a degree of suspicion. The tick in his eye went double time.

'Let's just say I'm between lodgings,' said Calloway. 'My landlady and I didn't see eye to eye.'

George nodded, like he was familiar with the scenario. 'Kicked you out, eh?'

'Strictly speaking I walked out, but the end result is the same.'

'Hard to find places these days,' said George, drawing on the wet end of the roll-up. 'People bombed out, still not rehoused.

Servicemen back from the war, still with nowhere to go.'

'Tell me about it,' said Calloway. Since the war he'd gone from one dingy boarding house to another. One job to another too, usually leaving under a cloud.

'How long you planning to kip here?' said George.

Calloway shrugged. 'As long as it takes.'

It wasn't going to be easy finding a place. Calloway knew that much. He'd been a fool to walk out of his digs. He could have smoothed things over with the landlady. But impulsiveness was ingrained in him like the dirt in the nooks and crannies of the arena. Sometimes his impulse got ugly. It was best he backed off, even if it did leave him homeless. It wasn't as though he couldn't afford new digs. He had Webber's money in his pocket. But he had other plans for that.

'You like this music,' said George, inclining his head towards the wireless.

Calloway nodded. 'Reminds me of happier times.' All too brief times. A few precious weeks. Learning to love music. Learning to love. And then learning loss.

'I prefer a dance band, me'self. Bennie Goodman. I used to cut a rug to Bennie back before the war.' He tapped the side of his leg. 'Before Jerry knackered this for me.'

George took another drag on his cigarette, thinking. 'I might be able to get you a room. Up Kensington way. Hotel.'

Calloway raised an eyebrow. 'A Kensington hotel? Sounds way beyond my slender means.'

George tapped the side of his nose with a grubby finger. He gave a conspiratorial wink. 'Not beyond the means of old soldiers like us.' He picked up his mop and bucket. 'Give me a couple of days,' he said, then clanked his way back down the darkened corridor, dragging his leg.

Calloway hadn't noticed George's limp before. There were enough damaged men around since the war for things like that to be unremarkable. Everyone was damaged in some way. Calloway's damage was the kind you couldn't see. At least not until it raised its ugly head.

He drove south of the river the following morning. He'd slept badly and his eyes were bleary. Even the coffee he'd drunk from Syd's stall in Shoreditch couldn't compensate for a cold night on the old gym mat. The weather didn't lift his spirits either. The meagre wipers on the Morris struggled to maintain a clear view of the road through the thick drizzle.

Bert lived in a prefab between Peckham and New Cross. The six grand a year he trousered as one of Bermondsey Bullets' star riders couldn't prize him and his wife Elsie from the little flat-roofed building, one of thousands thrown up by the Ministry of Works to house families bombed out by the Blitz. Bert's Buick glistened in the rain outside his temporary home. It looked as incongruous as pearls on a washerwoman. Bert had at least made some concessions to stardom.

Elsie opened the door to Calloway like he was some kind of royalty. Odd considering he was still wearing his demob suit and his car looked like scrap compared to her husband's.

'Oh do come in Mr Calloway,' she said with an unconvincing plumminess in her voice. 'Would you care for some tea?'

He heard Bert shout, 'Ooh, listen to her swank,' from inside.

Elsie held the door for Calloway, undeterred. A small table beneath the living room window was laid for tea. They'd brought out the best china by the looks of it. A small television, little bigger than a large wireless, took pride of place on a stand in the corner. Elsie saw Calloway looking at it.

'Our television,' she said, to confirm the fact.

'Leave it out, Else,' said Bert. 'Mr Calloway didn't come here to listen to you boast about your worldly goods.'

Elsie frowned at him. 'Says the man that got up early this morning to polish his trophies.'

Bert's speedway cups sparkled on the mantle of the tiny, tiled fireplace.

Elsie poured the tea and Calloway made a show of enjoying it. It was a good cup of tea. She dropped the frown and smiled at him. He could see the likeness to Vera, but the differences were obvious. Elsie had chosen well. He knew Bert doted on his missus, in spite of the ribbing he gave her, and it seemed like the feeling was mutual. The little house and the little couple in it radiated contentment, and the pair retained the spark that must have drawn them together in the first place. Vera, by contrast, had picked a bad boy.

'Well,' said Bert. 'Find anything out?'

Calloway hesitated before reporting on his enquiries at Stratton-Fenwick. He wasn't sure how much Bert had shared with his wife about the situation with her late brother-in-law. Bert sensed this and said, 'You can talk in front of my Else, Mr Calloway. It was her idea that I come to you in the first place. She's as worried about her sister as the rest of us.'

'I've never known her like this,' said Elsie. 'She's swinging from tears to tantrums at the drop of a hat. Sometimes she rambles and doesn't make any sense. What with that and the drinking, well...'

Bert lit up and Calloway joined him. Elsie lit one of her own filter tips with a box of Swan Vestas. Calloway said, 'I asked for the man called Denton at Stan's workplace. They hadn't heard of him. I managed to get a look at Stan's personnel file, which showed that the firm had been paying him up to the date of his accident. Then I got short shrift from his boss, Drinkwell, and had to leave.'

'So he couldn't have been in Berlin when he died,' said Bert, in a way which suggested relief that the matter might have quickly been resolved.

'On the face of it, you're right. But then I met some of Stan's workmates. Other drivers for Drinkwell's. They were adamant Stan did a runner about two months ago, owing a one-hundred-and-fifty-pound gambling debt.'

Bert whistled. Elsie looked surprised, but not exactly shocked.

'Cards, was it?' said Bert.

Calloway nodded.

'Figures,' said Bert. 'He weren't ever much of a card player. But that never stopped him. Wouldn't be the first time he'd tried to take a bloke's shirt and ended up losing his own.'

'He was a silly sod,' said Elsie, shaking her head. 'Nice looker, mind, and a lovely dancer.'

Bert gave her a disapproving look. 'Steady on, girl.'

‘Oh don’t give me that, Bert Webber. It’s not as if you never snuck the wrong sort of look at my sister.’

Bert reddened.

Calloway continued, to spare the little man more embarrassment. ‘I spoke to one of the drivers, a chap called Marek, a Slovakian, a decent sort. He said Stan claimed to know a way to make the money back and settle his debt. Stan had told Marek there was more to him than driving short-haul trucks. Any idea what he could have meant?’

Bert shrugged.

‘Had he always been a driver, since being demobbed?’ Calloway asked.

‘Yeah,’ said Bert. ‘Different firms, but always driving.’

‘And before that?’

Bert glanced over at his trophies. ‘He was a rider. Rode up Hackney, in the thirties, with the Hawks. That’s how me and Else met him. He was alright, but nothing special.’

‘How easily could he get back into speedway racing? Could he make decent money in a hurry?’

Bert didn’t hesitate before answering. ‘Nah, mate. No one would have him. He got himself a bit of a reputation, see. Disruptive influence on the other riders, if you know what I mean. Things like that follow you around in speedway.’

Calloway thanked them for the tea and left. He told Bert and Elsie he’d keep working on making sense of things, but short of trying the man called Denton’s number again, he was unsure what to do next. He checked his wristwatch. The pubs would be open. It was as good a time as any to pay a visit to Doreen’s friend Jimmy.

SEVEN

He pulled the car up outside a pub called the Lord Nelson, at the corner of Doreen's street. He'd been there just the once. The night he'd met her.

He'd been especially down that night. A real black mood. The kind he fell into more and more since he'd returned from the war. Sometimes he slept them off. Sometimes he drank them away. That night had been a drinking night. He'd wandered into the pub after walking aimlessly for an hour. He was already half-cut when a young woman who looked no more than twenty introduced herself as Doreen and asked if he wanted company. He did, and he told her so. It was unlike him. He'd normally decline, even in the army. That night was different. He responded willingly to her contrived flirtations. He drank pint after pint while she nursed a gin and lime, cheering him along with compliments and impressed looks on her pale, pretty face. While they talked, he caught the eye of a well-built young lad in a flashy suit sitting at the bar. The lad kept looking at them. Sometimes the young woman Doreen caught the lad's eye too. Through his increasing inebriation, Calloway sensed something conspiratorial between them. When the landlord called time, Calloway went with Doreen to her lodgings, a few doors up from the pub. He swayed as he walked, with her clinging to his arm, steering him in as straight a line as he could manage. Inside the dim hallway of the tall, terraced house, she made him wait while she went upstairs. He heard another female voice, old and croaky, then footsteps and the shutting of doors. She whispered down the stairs for him to come up. He stumbled through the door to her room and slumped on her bed. He leaned forward and grabbed her arm, pulling her towards him. She pulled away.

'Not so fast, you,' she said. 'Good things come to those who wait.'

The line sounded fake. Part of a repertoire she'd grown tired of delivering. She stepped back and stood in front of a shabby chintz curtain that divided the room. He watched her slip off her heels and take off her skirt and sweater, revealing a slight, undernourished body. She turned for a second and peered behind the curtain. A hint of caution crept into Calloway's beery consciousness, subsiding as she stepped forward and sat beside him on the bed. She started to unbutton his shirt.

There was a sound from behind the curtain, movement, someone else in the room. Calloway thought of the well-built lad in the pub and the conspiratorial looks he exchanged with Doreen. Was it a setup? Was he being rolled? He jumped up and lunged across the room, tugging the curtain aside. Behind it was a cot. In it was a girl of eighteen months, two at most. She called for her mother.

Calloway felt sick. Bile rose in his gullet. Doreen grabbed the child and held it to her. Only then he realised how threatening he must have looked. He'd squared to his full height, to see off the lad from the pub, expecting a cosh or a knife. Expecting to be robbed. Now he was terrifying a woman he'd never met, as she stood half-naked and vulnerable, fearing for herself and her baby girl. He put his hands up to signal he had no bad intent. He stepped back and fell on the bed like a heavy sack, apologising, telling her not to be afraid, disgusted with himself. Doreen was whispering to her little girl, trying to calm her. Then Calloway started to weep. Doreen looked down at him with pity.

'I should never have come here,' he said. 'I don't do this.'

She looked confused. Moments ago he'd been pulling her onto the bed, a boozy lust coursing through his veins. Now he was a mess. A weak, pathetic mess. He poured out more apologies and opened the door to leave.

The lad stood on the landing, blocking his path.

'You're not running out on us now, are you, big man?' he said, with a confidence that defied his youth. 'Don't seem like you've sealed the deal.'

The lad looked past Calloway into Doreen's room. He leered

at her as she stood framed in the doorway, still in her underwear.

'That's a nice little piece,' the lad said. 'Worth the price.' He held out his hand. 'Ten bob and you can finish the job.'

Calloway snapped. He clamped his big hands around the lad's arms, lifted him a foot in the air and threw him down the stairs. The boy bounced off the banisters like a ball in a bagatelle, banging his head on the bare wood stair treads and crashing onto the hard tiles of the hall floor. He let out a yelp and clutched his arm. Calloway went back into Doreen's room. He reached in his pocket and pulled out his wallet. He took out all the cash he had and laid it on her bedside table. It was payday at the arena and he had a week's worth of wages on him.

'For you and your daughter,' he said. 'It doesn't excuse anything, but I want you to have it.'

He closed the door behind him and walked down the stairs. He felt stone cold sober now. The lad lay on the floor, nursing one arm and squealing though clenched teeth.

Calloway leaned down to him. 'I'll be round this way a lot now. And I'll be watching you. You're going to leave that young woman alone. If I hear or see otherwise...'

He stepped on the lad's injured arm with his full weight and walked into the street to the sound of screaming.

Since that night, he'd called on Doreen and little Maggie once or twice a week. She was cautious at first. In time they became friends, of a sort. He had no intentions, and she came to realise it. He insisted on helping her out. He'd leave her money, what little he could afford. She'd protested at first but took it by necessity. She couldn't make ends meet with her part-time job, and working full time was not an option. Mrs Grant, the old lady across the landing, would only watch Maggie three days a week, as she had her own work, Doreen had explained.

It was a strange arrangement, him calling and helping her out, watching her go about her life with her daughter, listening to her chit-chat while she poured him weak tea. It was just something he felt compelled to do. A compulsion rooted in his past. In the war. In his profound sense of loss. It went a little way to filling the great emptiness he felt every day.

The pub was half-full, in spite of it being Saturday. The smell of last night's beer hung in the air. Sad faces sat at scuffed tables nursing half-pints and killing time. Folks with nothing in their lives save for the work they did to pay for dingy lodgings, fags and enough tinned food to subsist.

'How's the arm, Jimmy?' said Calloway.

Jimmy Jenks stood at the bar with two young girls who were seventeen at most. He was holding court. The girls were giggling. This was the first time Calloway had got a good look at him. He was barely twenty, with hair piled up high on his head and swept back at the sides so that it touched his collar. It was smeared with enough grease to open a chip shop. His jacket looked American. The style matched his hair.

'Getting better, no thanks to you.'

Calloway snapped his fingers and ordered a pint.

'A multiple fracture, so I heard,' said Calloway. 'Quite debilitating. Taking a long time to heal.'

Jenks made a fist with his left hand and punched the air.

'Lucky I'm a southpaw.'

One of the girls laughed. Jenks told her to shut up. Calloway shook his head and took a mouthful of his pint.

'You want to watch this one,' he said to the girls. 'He'll charm you one day and have you taking punters down alleyways the next.'

Jenks mouthed an obscenity.

Calloway cut him off. 'Oh and don't upset him. It'll take a lot of make-up to cover the bruises.'

Jenks coughed up a gobbet of phlegm and spat at Calloway's feet. Then he told the girls to get lost. He slipped his good hand in his pocket. Calloway grabbed his wrist.

'Don't be silly, lad,' he said. 'I just want to talk.'

Jenks withdrew his hand from his pocket. He pulled himself up to his full height and looked Calloway in the eye.

'So talk,' he said.

Calloway took a swig from his pint and set it down. 'Next time you give a woman a black eye, you'll get two from me. And a kicking for good measure. Next time you so much as open your mouth to Doreen, I'm going to fill it with my fist. Do you understand?'

Jenks sniggered. 'What I understand,' he said, 'is that you're trying to install yourself as Doreen's ponce and you want me out of the picture.'

'Don't drag me down to your level, son. I'm not the sort that thinks living off the immoral earnings of a girl is an acceptable career choice.'

'It's not all one way. A girl gets a man in her life. Someone looking out for her. Not to mention a bit of company.'

'There's better company in a cellar full of rats. The only thing a girl gets from vermin like you is bruises, and no more money in her purse than before she was coerced onto the game in the first place.'

Jenks forced a sigh, for effect. 'Spare me the moral crusade, will you.' He squared up. 'You don't get to tell me what I can and can't do. I've got more sway round here than you have. If I want to talk to Doreen, I'll talk to her. If I want to take a few quid in return for keeping an eye on her, I'll take it. If I want a bit of the other, well that's up to me. And if you know what's good for you, you'll keep your nose out of my affairs.'

'That's big talk from a snot-nosed little Caesar in a jacket he's not grown into yet. What exactly do you plan to do if I don't?'

'Someone might get hurt,' said Jenks.

'You? Hurt me?' said Calloway. 'I've had bigger than you with chips.'

Jenks summoned his nastiest grin. 'I didn't mean you.'

That flicked the switch.

Calloway grabbed Jenks' good arm. He lifted the heavy wood flap in the bar top and brought it down hard on Jenks' hand. Jenks cried. The punters in the pub stared. One punter winced. Another gave Jenks a *serves-you-right* look. Jenks looked down at his crushed fingers and tried to form a fist, before squealing in pain.

'Try hitting a girl with that,' said Calloway.

EIGHT

They heard it before they rounded the corner. The chiming and clanging of carnival music and the diesel roar of engines powering the rides. Then the sickly smell of toffee apples mixed with the electric tang of ozone from the sparks above the dodgems. Then barkers husky from years of shouting. Hook a duck, blue picks a prize. Rifle range, five pellets for sixpence. Calloway hated fairgrounds. He recoiled from their insistent energy. It was distracting, disorientating. It reminded him of battle. Flashes, screams and the fierce growling of engines. A mechanical hell.

Webber didn't share Calloway's distaste. The nearer they drew to the fairground, the more his excitement showed. Calloway saw a glimpse of how Webber must have been as a boy. Too much energy, overexcited, talking thirteen to the dozen, eyes alight with anticipation.

Webber had phoned Calloway at the stadium the previous evening. He'd remembered something. A time just after he'd first met Stan, when Stan, then a speedway rider, was moonlighting. Earning extra cash to pay off a debt.

Webber led Calloway through the crowd. Kids ran around at knee height, fingers sticky with candy floss. Courting couples dallied, boyfriends daring their girls to go on the most daunting rides. Ex-soldiers showed off on the rifle range, aiming at overly tightened tin-man targets that refused to lie down. The fortune teller in her fake gypsy garb caught Calloway's eye. 'Read your future, luvvie?' she said in a flirtatious tone, her slender finger beckoning. Future? thought Calloway. It's difficult enough coping with the past. A gaggle of men in caps and coats were huddled around the front of the boxing booth. A fighter emerged onto a small stage in his robe, dancing around, shadow boxing. The name *Slammer Suskind* sewn on his back in gold silk letters, above the epithet *The Hackney Heavyweight.* Well, well, Johnny Boy, thought Calloway. A fighter now, are we? Last time Calloway had seen Suskind, he'd been lugging crates at the tea building by day and roughing up fascists in the East End by night. Calloway stopped and watched, as the boxing booth barker set up Johnny for the challenge.

'Who'll take on the Slammer?' he shouted in hoarse cockney. 'Which of you fine gentlemen is man enough?' He put on a show of surveying the crowd, his eye cocked. 'Go three rounds, you win five pounds.'

'What's up, Reg?' said Webber. 'You thinking of having a go?'

Calloway shook his head. 'He's an old pal of mine from the war. Ex-paratrooper.'

Webber looked on, his face showing admiration. 'Good strong lad, by the look of him. You wouldn't catch me having a go.'

'Some fool will,' said Calloway.

Some fool stepped forward. He couldn't have been more than five foot eight, but he was broad enough. Young too. He'd have youth on his side. Johnny was only a couple of years off forty, Calloway knew. The crowd gave the boy a cheer as he stepped up. He was pretty, but hard looking with it, with a shock of white-blonde hair and a sparrow tattoo peeking through the open neck of his shirt. The mark of the sailor.

'Let's get a couple of tickets,' said Webber, like the excitable child he resembled, in spite of his own forty years. 'The other business can wait. It ain't going nowhere.'

They joined the crowd around the small ring in the low-roofed tent. The air was thick with the smell of sweat and cigarettes. Suskind was in the ring now, sparring an invisible partner. The young challenger was getting gloved-up in the opposite corner.

Calloway looked at the crowd. They were rugged working men, their faces hewn by toil or adversity. One face stood out though. Different to the rest. Smooth and good looking, in spite of a prominent jaw line. He wore a blue blazer beneath his raincoat. His dark hair was combed back from a widow's peak. Just like the man Vera described. His eyes were fixed on the fighters readying themselves in the ring. Calloway stared at him. In Calloway's experience, when you stare at people long enough, they'll catch your eye eventually. It felt as if this man was making every effort to avoid that happening.

The bell rang. The crowd cheered, shouting encouragement to the pretender. Johnny took a few punches to the head and body, but he took them in his stride. He was letting the lad show what he'd got. He was playing the crowd, softening them up, opening up the prospect of a win for the tattooed sailor boy. Letting him show his good right hand. Johnny kept this up for the first two rounds. The tension mounted inside the tent. It was hot. The sailor dripped sweat in spite of his youth. Johnny hadn't popped so much as a bead. Neither had the man with the widow's peak, Calloway noticed. He was too cool by half.

The bell started round three. The fervour of the crowd grew. A blood lust. They cheered the young blonde David as he took on Johnny's Goliath. Johnny went for an inside slip towards the challenger's right hand and planted an uppercut to his body. The sailor really felt it. Johnny had turned the tables, right on cue. They spun around the ring, before Johnny knocked the young sailor down with three hard punches to his head. The sailor fell to his knees. The referee started the count.

'One, two...'

'Your mate's pretty tasty ain't he?' said Webber. 'Young lad didn't stand a chance.'

'Three times regimental boxing champion,' said Calloway. 'He's used to decking six-foot paratroopers.'

'...eight, nine...'

The challenger gave up any pretence of a comeback. He flopped onto the canvas, resigned to his loss.

'...ten!'

The referee grabbed Johnny by the glove and raised the big fighter's fist in the air.

Johnny caught Calloway's eye. A flicker of pleasant surprise crossed his face. He gave his old pal the wink. Calloway gestured with a nod towards the back of the tent that they should meet.

'Stone the crows, Reggie, old son,' said Suskind, stepping out of the ring. He gave his former comrade a bear hug with his gloves still on.

'You've still got it, Johnny,' said Calloway. 'How come you're back in the ring?'

Suskind grinned. 'Got fed up with lugging tea chests all day long. Decking people is a whole lot easier and it pays better.' He glanced over at the ring. The ref and the barker were lifting the flaccid sailor boy through the ropes. They handed him to his mates, abdicating all responsibility.

'Felt sorry for that one,' said Suskind, unlacing his gloves with his teeth. 'He had a bit of technique. But he was cocky. Fancied himself and let it go to his head.'

Calloway noticed the man with the widow's peak was hanging around. It made him uneasy. He introduced Suskind to Webber. The small speedway rider seemed in awe of the big boxer.

'Any friend of Cab's, as they say,' said Suskind. He rubbed his shoulder and winced. 'Not as young as I used to be,' he said. 'I need to get this a rub before the next bout. You've got my number, haven't you?' Calloway nodded. 'Give me a bell, eh? We'll have a drink.' He turned to Webber. 'You too, mate.'

Calloway said he would, adding, 'I hate to ask, Johnny, but can you do us a favour?'

'Anything, Cab,' Suskind said without hesitation.

'There's a fella over there we don't want to meet, if you get my drift. Can you distract him so Bert and I can slip out?'

Bert looked confused. He'd clearly not noticed the smooth-looking man in the crowd.

Johnny didn't ask for details. He said, 'Anything, Reg, you know that. You risked your neck for me not so long ago. It's the least I can do.'

Johnny had recruited Calloway into his band of anti-fascists. They'd cracked some heads at Mosleyite rallies in the East End.

'Good man,' said Calloway, clapping the ex-paratrooper on the back.

Suskind approached the man with the widow's peak and gave

him some spiel, telling him he looked like a fighter and challenging him to step up for the next bout. Calloway and Webber slipped through a vent in the canvas at the back of the tent.

When they were outside, Webber said, 'Good bloke, your mate. But what was all that about us slipping out?'

Calloway looked over his shoulder. They were clear for now.

'There was a man in the crowd that fitted Vera's description of Denton. Normally that wouldn't be unusual. There must be hundreds who do. But not in a boxing booth full of working men that we happen to be in too.'

'Blimey,' said Webber. 'You sure? It's all a bit Dick Barton, innit?'

'Not sure,' said Calloway. 'But when things don't add up, like your brother-in-law Stan's death, it's best to trust your instincts.'

They wove their way through the crowds between the rides and sideshows. It was busy now. Easier to lose themselves. Calloway kept alert, casting an eye around the faces. Bert pointed to a sideshow at the edge of the fairground.

'There it is,' he said.

It was a brightly-lit, double-height structure, edged with rows of lightbulbs, illuminating a gaudy, painted sign which read, *The Devil's Drome – defying gravity and death!* It had tall open stairways on either side. Between them was a small stage where a motorcyclist was riding a motorcycle on rollers while a barker gave the spiel.

'Roll up, roll up, to the greatest show on wheels. Be amazed as the fearless Cyclone Sid rides the entirely vertical, totally diabolical, Devil's own drome! Witness the sensation of the century for only a shilling.'

Webber was eyeing the bike on the rollers. 'That's an Indian Scout,' he said. 'Or was. They've stripped off the lot. Mudguards, speedo, lights. They've just left a stub pipe for the exhaust. They've shortened the frame and bent the forks back, an'all.'

Calloway knew nothing about motorcycles but he could see the bike on the stage was little more than a skeleton, on which its rider was balanced, his hands in the air. Webber bought a pair of tickets and they climbed the stairway, ducked through the doorway in the tented cover and took their place among the punters on the viewing gallery that lined the rim of the high, circular wall below. They were packed in tight. Perhaps this really was the sensation of the century, thought Calloway. The rider, Cyclone Sid, appeared, wheeling the stripped-down motorcycle through a hidden trapdoor at the base of the drome. He was stocky and muscular, with slicked back blonde hair, an impish grin and a gap between his teeth. The crowd cheered as he entered. The barker followed him, picking up a microphone and continuing his patter, this time through the small Tannoy speakers in the dome of the tent. Cyclone Sid kickstarted the bike, signalling to a third man, his mechanic, who crouched behind the machine and gave it a good push off. The scream of the engine echoed off the planked wooden sides of the drome. The crowd leaned forward as far as the safety wire would allow. Webber did too, and Calloway followed his lead.

'Watch yer hat,' said Webber, pushing his trilby down on his head. 'You don't want to lose that down there. You could have him off.'

The rider made circuits of the gently sloping base of the wall, revving hard and building speed. With a jerk of the long, cow-horn handlebars, he mounted the vertical sides and immediately sped up to the rim, his tyres missing the noses of the crowd by inches. They recoiled, gasping. He fixed them all with his impish grin as he passed them at speed. Their heads circled with every circuit, and each time they relaxed and peered back down into the hole, he shot up to greet them, to more gasps and screams. The barker worked his spiel, building the anticipation and announcing each new trick the rider performed. No hands. Side saddle. Backwards in the saddle. Backwards with no hands. And Cyclone Sid's pièce de résistance, side-saddle, lying flat on the seat with arms flung outwards and legs in the air. The crowd cheered and applauded. Their exhilaration was palpable, their excitement infectious. Calloway felt himself drawn willingly into the collective delight of the moment. He had to admit, the show was thrilling, even to a tightly-wound brute like him. Webber nudged him with his elbow.

'Great, innit?' he said, beaming like a small boy again.

After the show, they hung around until the punters had dispersed.

'Let's grab 'im before they start over again,' said Webber, tugging Calloway by the sleeve and leading him to the stage. The barker looked down at them. He recognised Webber.

'Bert?' he said. He scraped his hand through the big tuft of greasy black hair on his square head.

Webber nodded and gave him a smile.

'Bert Webber, as I live and breathe,' the barker said. 'Gawd, it's been a while.' He climbed down to meet them. 'You still riding?'

'With the Bullets, down Bermondsey,' Webber replied.

'The Bullets, eh?' he gave Webber a knowing look. 'Pretty Patty Moxon's mob, you lucky boy.'

Webber shuffled, looking slightly awkward. 'She's alright, as it happens,' he said.

The barker gave him a sleazy look.

'A good guv'nor, I mean,' said Webber.

The barker gave a grudging nod. 'She was a great show rider in her day, I'll grant you that. Had some balls on her.' He looked at Calloway. 'We've not met, squire,' he said, offering his hand. 'I'm Alfie Shuman. Shuman the showman.' He cackled, shaking Calloway's hand. 'So what brings you here, Bertie Boy? You found that brother-in-law of yours?'

Webber frowned. 'What d'you mean found him?'

Shuman took a Woodbine from behind his ear and lit up. 'Your Stan did a runner, so I hear.'

'From Drinkwell's?' said Calloway. 'The hauliers?'

Shuman pulled a face. 'Never heard of no hauliers. He did a runner from our tour of Germany. Left me right in the lurch. I've got a girl rider over there and fuck all else right now.'

'What tour of Germany?' said Webber.

'Stan didn't tell you?' Shuman frowned at Webber then shrugged, meaning he didn't care whether Webber knew or not. 'I run two dromes,' he said. 'One here, and one for touring. Stan came to see me a few months back saying he needed to get his hands on some money real quickly. I guessed what was up. He'd been gambling, as is his wont, and he'd been losing, as is his habit.'

Webber turned to Calloway. He said, 'Stan used to moonlight for Shuman when he was riding with the Hawks. This was back before the war.'

Shuman nodded.

'Anyway, he showed up a couple of months back looking for work and it just so happened I was starting a tour of the bases in Germany, so him popping up was a bit on the convenient side,' he said. 'I bit his hand off. Signed him up to ride as a double act with this German bint I've got on the books. Hannelore and Herman, we called them, with Stan being Herman, if you know what I mean.'

'What do you mean bases?' said Calloway.

Shuman took a drag on the fag, exhaled and belched. 'US bases,' he said. 'Army, air force, you know. Entertaining the yanks. My business partner's a yank, as it happens, and he fixed it all up. Nice little earner too. Them yanks'll pay through the nose. It's like they don't know what the money's worth.'

'And Stan disappeared?' said Calloway.

Shuman nodded. 'It was all going great guns. The yanks loved the show and we got more bookings and extensions. It was promising to be a nice long run. The show arrived in Berlin where we had a string of dates in the American sector. Next thing I know,' he said, nodding at Webber, 'I'm getting a telegram saying that his toe-rag brother-in-law had done a runner. Didn't show up for a show and hasn't been seen since. When you turned up just now I thought maybe you had some news for me.'

Webber looked down at his feet. He looked up and was about to speak. Calloway cut him off.

'We came here thinking you might know where Stan had got to,' he said. He didn't want Webber mentioning that Stan was dead. 'He's not showed up at home or anywhere, and his wife is beside herself.'

'Perhaps he's run off with a *fräulein*,' said Shuman. 'He always had an eye for the skirt, eh?'

Webber forced a grin.

'When did he fail to show up?' said Calloway.

Shuman dragged the last of the nicotine out of the butt of the Woodbine and flicked it onto the ground. He thought for a moment. 'A month back. The fourteenth or fifteenth, I reckon.'

The date Stan was supposed to have died in the accident, thought Calloway.

Shuman squinted at Webber, furrowing his brow.

''Ere, Bertie Boy,' he said. 'Speedway season'll be finishing any day now, won't it? Don't fancy a nice little trip to Germany, do you? Wouldn't take much to get a rider like you trained up on the wall. The money is handsome, like I said. You could line your pockets and treat your Else to something nice. Not to mention a bit of oompah, oompah, with a local Helga and a couple of her flaxen-haired friends. I've heard they're pretty broadminded over there, Bertie.'

Webber flushed red. He shook his head. 'Nah, mate. Sorry. You won't catch me risking me neck in that contraption,' he said, nodding towards the drome. 'The cinder track is one thing, that's second nature to me, but that bleedin' drome is a mug's game.'

Shuman lent back, faking offence.

'Yes Bertie,' he said. 'It's a mug's game that's putting my two boys through a very good private school, if you don't mind.' He pulled another cigarette from a pack in his pocket. 'Anyway, son,' he said, 'let me know if you change your mind. And if you know of any other mug who fancies a trip to Berlin and a pocket full of Deutschmarks, you know where to find me.'

NINE

'I want you to go to Germany,' said Webber, as they were walking back to his car.

'You're not serious, are you?' said Calloway.

'It's the only way we're going to find out what happened to Stan. I can pay your passage and expenses. You need to get over there and start asking around.'

'You make its sound easy, Bert. Even if I went to Berlin, I can't just go walking into US military bases asking difficult questions.'

Webber considered this for a moment.

'No, I suppose you're right,' he said. 'It's a shame you're not a rider. You could take that job Shuman's offering.' Webber caught the look on Calloway's face and laughed.

'That's never going to happen,' said Calloway. 'I've not ridden a motorcycle in my life and I don't intend to start.' Calloway thought for a moment. 'If anyone's going to join that German tour, it should be you, Bert. Shuman seemed pretty confident you'd shape up as a wall rider.'

As he said this, Calloway was doubting the sense of it. Berlin seemed very far away. The idea of going into a strange city to investigate the mysterious death of an indebted gambler, fairground stuntman and all-round ne'er-do-well seemed ridiculous.

'Shuman's being a bit ambitious,' said Webber. 'It ain't that easy to learn them tricks, no matter how much of a natural you are on a bike. I would if I could, but I don't have what it takes.'

Webber ground through the Buick's gears. His frustration showed in his driving.

'I hate to say it, Bert,' said Calloway, 'but we may have hit a dead end.'

Calloway knew he should have left it there and then. And perhaps he would've done, were it not for the appearance at the fairground of a man matching the description of Denton. Calloway reckoned he knew when something wasn't right, and that wasn't right. The official line on Stan's death made no sense at all. It didn't tally with the facts, as Bert and Calloway had uncovered them. It was a loose end. Calloway hated loose ends. They were the bane of his life. They led him down paths that he knew he should avoid.

Webber dropped him outside the arena and drove home. The little man couldn't have looked more down in the mouth. Calloway climbed the dark stairway to his office and turned in, grabbing what sleep he could on the uncomfortable floor mat. He was awoken the next morning by a tap on the door. George the cleaner stepped in the small room and said, 'I found you a place.'

Calloway was barely conscious. He sat up, rubbing sleep from his eyes. 'What place?'

'A new gaff. Somewhere to live. Somewhere better than this,' he said, gesturing around the pokey office room.

Calloway said thanks and agreed to meet George once he'd freshened up. He washed and shaved in the gents' lavatories, combed his hair in the cracked and mottled mirror and made himself a plate of beans from a can for breakfast. He met George on the pavement outside the arena doors, with his two suitcases and orange crate full of belongings. The two men set off in Calloway's car. They headed west.

Kensington was alive and bustling at this time in the morning. The pavements were already busy with gentrified folk, or shabbier types that aspired to be, heading to work, shopping or walking ridiculous dogs. George gave directions. They turned the corner into a wide side street of tall and ornate buildings. Calloway saw a gaggle of people at the far end of the street.

'What's going on there?' he said.

George said, 'Oh, Christ, they've come for us. It was only a matter of time.'

'What was?' said Calloway, pulling the car over just ahead of the crowd. He saw two dozen policeman, a news crew with a camera and an angry-looking bunch of men and women of a class not normally found in this part of town. They were shouting slogans at the policeman while some threw what looked like food parcels up to the first-floor windows of the corner building, where men were reaching out to catch them.

'The Scott Hotel,' said Calloway, reading the sign above the entrance.

George nodded. He said, 'We've been squatting in it for a year now. The Vigilantes took it over and moved a dozen families in.'

'Who are the Vigilantes?' said Calloway.

'They organise squatting for homeless ex-servicemen and their families. There's enough empty buildings in this city to house the lot of them, but you can't get your hands on them through official channels. Too much red tape and stupid regulations. The Vigilantes started squatting in them after the war.'

'What do you mean "squatting"?' It was an unfamiliar term to Calloway.

'Breaking in, claiming it and moving in those that need a roof over their heads.'

'Why the police?'

'The building's owner wants it back. We knew this was on the cards but wasn't expecting it so soon.'

'So who are the people on the ground, the ones chanting?'

George looked over at the crowd. 'Supporters, other squatters. And the Communists of course, although if you ask me, it's none of their business. This ain't political. It's about respectable people needing a home, like Mrs Churchill said. Good old, Clemmie. She supports us, you know. The reds have jumped on the bandwagon and they're a pain in the neck.'

Calloway watched as the squatters fielded the upward barrage of packets and tins thrown from the crowd below.

'Why the food parcels?' said Calloway.

'It's a siege. Like the Berlin airlift. The squatters can't leave, or they'd lose their spot. The folk on the ground are their lifeline.'

'And that's where I'm supposed to live? Seriously?' said Calloway.

George nudged him. 'Go on with you,' he said. 'You're an old soldier. You've faced bigger challenges. And once you're inside, it's a bit of alright. Proper high class, as squats go. Better than the old military bases they're squatting outside London. All we've got to do is sneak round the back to the service entrance. My pal Jimmy is manning the barricade. He'll let us in.'

Jimmy was a burly man in his mid-thirties. He wore a reefer jacket and flat cap, with a pair of steel-toed boots on his oversized feet. He nodded to George, and eyed Calloway with suspicion.

'This is Reg,' said George. 'He's moving in. Ex-airborne. He'll be useful.'

Calloway didn't like the sound of that. But as he walked through the corridors of the former hotel, he had to admit that as digs went, this place was a cut above. It had retained much of its grandeur, with deep red carpeting, panelled walls and high stucco ceilings. Even the chandeliers were intact. Children were chasing each other up and down the corridors, while their mothers chatted cheerfully from their respective bedroom doors. Men were piling the supplies thrown up to them onto a trestle table, where a studious-looking young man in horn-rimmed spectacles noted down each item in an exercise book.

George said, 'The lifts are out, so you'll have to put up with climbing a few stairs. Your gaff is on the top floor.'

The 'gaff' that Calloway had been allocated was a double bedroom with two floor-to-ceiling windows overlooking the street. It had jazz-age wallpaper and thick velvet curtains, which looked dusty but warm. There was a door in the far wall. Calloway peered in. The room has its own bathroom, with vivid green and black tiles, and angular chromium taps.

'This is what you call a squat?' Calloway said.

'Good, innit?' said George. 'Normally we'd put a family in a room this size, but the roof leaks. You'll have to keep changing the bucket when it rains.'

Calloway spotted the galvanised pail in the corner of the room, beneath a brown stain on the ceiling. He shrugged.

'I can live with that,' he said. He threw his cases on the bed and George lifted the orange crate onto the walnut dressing table.

'Everyone gets chores,' he said. 'It's how we run the building. Yours will involve lifting and carrying, I reckon, seeing as you're a big lad.'

Calloway said this would be fine. A small price to pay in return for free lodgings, even if they were under siege. The chanting below was still going. Calloway glanced down. The police were trying to move the protestors on. Two constables grabbed one of the ringleaders by the arms and led him to a Black Maria. The protestors booed and hissed.

'What are the neighbours like?' said Calloway.

'Most of the building is full of London families. From north London and the East End. People who were bombed out and had nowhere to go when their old men came back from the war. Your corridor's different. They're Poles mostly. Blokes who fought with the free Polish army and air force and didn't fancy living in Poland under the Soviets.' George lowered his voice. 'A word of advice. The Poles don't like the Communists, for obvious reasons, so if any reds show up here, it's best to keep your head down and let 'em get on with it.'

Calloway had met plenty of free Polish serviceman during the war. He'd fought alongside the Polish 1st Independent Parachute Brigade in Europe. He didn't rate the Communists' chances much.

George left Calloway to it.

'Me and the missus are in room 106 on the first floor, if you fancy dropping in,' he said.

Calloway said he might. He returned to the window and stared down at the protest below. Even from this height he could see the faces of the crowd. They were a mix of ages and types. Working-class men and women in their work clothes or their Sunday best, skinny student types, organisers with earnest faces busying around in their raincoats.

And a smooth-looking man in a blazer, with dark hair and a widow's peak. He was looking Calloway straight in the eye.

TEN

'Call for you, Mr Calloway.'

Young Charlie Fowler, Finnegan's gofer, popped his head into the bar, where Calloway was steering a drunk back to his seat. The drunk had been overly familiar with one of the female bar staff, who had complained. He wasn't worth kicking out yet, just sitting down with a warning.

Calloway left the bar and climbed the back stairs to his office. The phone's receiver was lying on his desk.

'Calloway,' he said.

'Reg, it's Bert.' Webber sounded excited. 'I've found a wall rider.'

'Go on,' said Calloway, trying to conceal the apprehension in his voice.

'I can't talk now. Meet me tomorrow night.'

He gave Calloway a place and time.

The following evening Calloway drove out to Custom House, near the Royal Albert Dock. He parked his car in a side street of mean little dockers cottages. His was the only car in the street, apart from a grey Nash which had pulled up a hundred yards behind him. Two men got out and nodded, then turned and walked towards the noise in the distance. They wore belted macs and woollen scarves, like typical sports fans. Calloway followed in the same direction, the noise getting louder. He turned the corner at the end of the street. He could hear the roar of engines, even from this distance. It was a familiar sound, from his days as head of security at Bermondsey Stadium. But this wasn't Bermondsey. This was West Ham. Bigger, grander, almost palatial by comparison. With its Art Deco gates and neon lighting, it resembled a Hollywood studio more than an East London dirt track. He caught the unmistakeable smell of methanol and Castrol R in the damp night air. The smell of speedway. It sparked memories, some he'd sooner forget.

He bought a ticket and a programme and took his place in the crowd. There must have been forty thousand in tonight, if he was any judge. The toffs had Ascot and motor racing at Brooklands. The working man and woman had the dogs and speedway. Dogs for gambling. Speedway for thrills. Dirty, fast and dangerous. Maniacs on machines.

It was the Bullets away to the Hammers tonight. Bermondsey versus West Ham. The last fixture of the season. Webber was riding, alongside others Calloway knew. 'Six Gun' O'Donnell, Billy 'Boy' Riley and Chip 'Clanger' Bellman. Calloway looked in the programme. It was heat nine already. Webber and Riley riding for the Bullets, against West Ham's two Aussies, Lawson and Watson. Calloway checked the scoreboard on the opposite side of the big oval track. It was still close. Everything to ride for tonight. And the Bullets and the Hammers were neck and neck in the league table. Tonight would decide the champions.

Calloway let the atmosphere wash over him. He tried to lose himself in the scream of the engines and the chanting of the crowd. But all the time, his thoughts drifted back to the man with the widow's peak hairline that was following him. He was sure of it.

He snapped to as they announced heat fifteen over the Tannoy. Webber was up again, with the tall American, O'Donnell. The scores were close. This was the deciding heat. Calloway watched the riders line up at the tape, digging in with the heels of their lead-soled boots. A hush descended. The atmosphere was electric. The tape flew up and the four bikes shot forward, revving hard into the first bend. O'Donnell claimed the lead, the Hammers were second and third with Webber a hair's breadth behind them. They broadsided round the bed and into the back straight. Webber let rip, passing both of the Hammers and tucking his bike in behind O'Donnell, as the pair of them entered the second bend. The conditions suited the Bullets. They were used to riding the tightest circuit in the league at home. More circular than oval. A big track like West Ham gave them time to breathe, time to think, time to steal a lead and hold it. This they did. The Bullets fans went wild. Webber and O'Donnell grabbed each other by the shoulders and slapped each other's backs.

Calloway killed time. It would be a while before Webber changed out of his race leathers and could meet him in the bar. His stomach churned. Was it hunger or the jitters? He bought a hot dog, realising he'd not eaten since lunch. The churning didn't stop. He sat at the back of the stands and smoked a half pack of Navy Cut.

He looked at his watch. Time for a drink. He crossed the stands, going against the tide of punters leaving the stadium. He climbed the stairs to the bar, a generous affair more suited to a modern hotel, at least in comparison to the bar at Bermondsey, as he remembered it. And it was full too. Rammed to the gills. Calloway elbowed his way in and ordered a scotch and soda.

Webber was seated at a table by the big windows that overlooked the track. Webber wasn't alone. Someone sat drinking with him, with their back to Calloway. Calloway downed the scotch and ordered another. He picked it up and crossed the bar towards Webber.

'Reggie,' said Webber, his face lighting up. 'Come and celebrate.' He gestured to a seat he'd clearly been saving. He'd had a few already, judging by the glazing of his eyes. If he'd been sober, he might have sensed Calloway's apprehension. Calloway hesitated before sitting. Webber's drinking companion turned to face him.

'Look what the cat dragged in,' she said.

Pat Moxon. Pretty Pattie. Queen of the dirt track. The Bullets' promoter and Calloway's old boss.

And the lover he walked out on without saying a word.

'Hello Pat,' he said.

Webber's smile dropped, as if suddenly realising the significance of the meeting.

'Sit down, Reg,' said Pat. Her tone was gracious. And ice cold.

‘Have some champagne,’ she said. ‘Like Bert says, we’re celebrating.’

‘Thanks,’ said Calloway. ‘But I’ve got a drink already.’

Pat smiled at him. She had a lovely smile when she chose to use it, but right now he struggled to see any warmth in it.

‘I’ll pour you one anyway,’ she said. ‘As a chaser. I’m sure your mouth’s dry.’

Dry and sour, thought Calloway. He swigged the scotch to take away the taste.

She huffed with mock impatience. ‘Well, aren’t you going to join us?’ She patted the chair beside her. ‘I mean, I’ve saved you a seat.’

Calloway sat. Bert caught his eye. Now he realised. He looked apologetic. Too late for that, Bertie Boy. Calloway downed the scotch and picked up the champagne.

‘To the Bullets,’ he said.

Pat raised her glass. ‘I’d prefer to drink to absent friends, Reg,’ she said. She gave an insincere laugh. ‘Absent without leave, as I’m sure you used to say in the army.’

She chinked his glass and looked him full in the face. Her eyes were beautiful, and as hard as diamonds. The air turned brittle. Webber cut in to break the tension.

‘Pat’s gonna ride the wall,’ he said, taking a gulp of his champagne. ‘She’s agreed to do the tour.’

‘In Germany?’ said Calloway. He found this hard to grasp, in spite of his suspicions. It was hard enough meeting the woman he’d walked out on. Now Webber was suggesting they go to Berlin. Together.

‘I told Pat all about it. About Stan and how Vera’s doing her nut.’

Pat nodded. ‘I know Bert well. I know he’s not going to let this go. I can’t risk his mind not being on the job.’

Webber shuffled in his seat, looking slightly offended.

Pat responded. ‘I know you got a result tonight,’ she said. ‘Especially in the last heat. But if your mind had been on the job, you’d have taken that first bend and held the lead for all three laps. Instead you played catch-up and scraped second place by the skin of your teeth. I'm not having that carrying into next season. You need to get this business with your brother-in-law sorted out once and for all.'

She was serious. Calloway had hoped Webber had been overplaying Pat's willingness to join the wall of death tour. But she was deadly serious.

'Can you really ride the wall?' he said.

She scoffed. 'Oh ye of little faith, Reggie. How do you think I got set up as a speedway promoter in the first place?' She rubbed her thumb and forefinger together. 'It takes dough, you know. I earned it on the wall. When they banned us girls from speedway in the thirties I became a show rider.' Calloway remembered her telling him this. 'After a couple of years as a warmup act, doing stunts at speedway fixtures, I got offered a crack at the Kursaal drome in Southend. Girl riders were a novelty back then. I made a packet.'

'And you're prepared to join a wall of death tour in Germany, just to get me in there to investigate Stan's death?'

She poured herself another glass of champagne and sipped it. Her lipstick left a ruby red bow on the glass.

'No,' she said. 'Not just to get you in there.' She lit a cocktail cigarette and drew on the gold filter. You didn't see many of those in West Ham. She exhaled with a wistful sigh. 'If you want to know, Reggie,' she said, 'I'm bored. The season's finished and for now I've had enough of wet-nursing the likes of Bert and his cowboy teammates.' She looked at Bert. 'No offence,' she said. Webber gave a small bow, as if to say *none taken*, although Calloway suspected he was hurt by the comment. Pat waved the cigarette in the air. 'I'm bored with the stadium, and the press, and the accountants, and the interfering busybodies at the association. I fancy a thrill. A real thrill.' She cocked her head to one side and looked at Calloway. Her diamond eyes twinkled. 'Not a cheap thrill, Reggie,' she said. 'I've had enough of those.'

She snapped her fingers and a steward brought another bottle. Calloway drank more champagne. The booze calmed him. At least it calmed his churning stomach. Deep down he'd guessed this would happen, the moment Webber told him on the phone he'd found a wall rider. Patricia Moxon. Pretty Pattie. The moniker didn't do her justice. She was bold, confident and handsome. Well-dressed, well-coiffured, well-manicured. She worked hard at being a class act. For a moment Calloway felt something more than the drink.

Pat raised a glass. Calloway and Webber did the same by reflex.

'To Berlin,' she said. They chinked glasses. 'So what's the plan, Reggie?'

'Seems like you're the one with the plan, Pat,' said Calloway. 'I'm just the fella doing the dirty work.'

She leaned into him and pinched his cheek.

'Perhaps that's all you're good for, lover,' she said.

ELEVEN

It was almost midnight when Calloway returned to the hotel. The crowd was gone, and the only police presence was two weary-looking beat coppers at the far end of the street. He parked the car and walked down a side alley to the rear of the building. The service entrance was dark. Burley Jim would have knocked off for the night, now that the police had thinned out. They'd be back with a court order, George had said. But the Vigilantes would hold out. This was their home now and they had plenty of supporters. Clemmie Churchill for one.

He let himself in. The Vigilantes had changed the locks and given everyone a key. The hotel was quiet as he climbed the stairs, save for a baby crying in a distant corridor. The Poles were awake on his corridor. He could hear their chatter and the muted sounds of a gramophone through the heavy door to one of their rooms. He missed his gramophone. He still had a handful of records in the orange crate. Mahler, Mendelssohn, Brahms. He'd learned to love the romantic composers. He had a wonderful teacher, for an all too brief moment in his life. He'd bought gramophone records to remember. He would ask the Poles if he could play them.

He kicked off his shoes and laid out his blanket, rolling up a towel to use as a pillow. The streetlights outside cast a bright glow across the bed. He crossed the room to close the curtains and looked down from the window.

There was a grey Nash parked opposite the hotel.

When he arrived at the arena the following morning, there was a message for him on his desk. Webber had called again. He said they should meet at Vera's house. Calloway sighed. It wasn't that he didn't like the little rider or want to help him. Webber and Johnny Suskind were the closest thing he had to friends. But this business with Vera and her late husband was getting too strange by half. His meter was nudging red all the time now. The Grey Nash turning up in Kensington only made it worse. But Webber's money was good. He had a use for it and there would be more to spare, now that he had free digs at the squat. He looked at his watch. He reckoned he could get to Deptford and back in time to catch Finnegan before the wrestling that night. He didn't relish breaking the news that he'd be taking some leave.

Webber had heard Calloway's car pull up outside Vera's house and was waiting for him on the doorstep. He was smoking and looking anxious.

'She's really bad today,' he said, shaking his head. 'My Else is in there with her now.'

'Bad how?' said Calloway.

'Off her rocker. Speaking in tongues.'

They went inside. The curtains were open, the obligatory darkness of mourning over. Vera was anything but over it though, as Calloway looked at her. Her eyes were glazed, but not like a drunk's. She was staring at the wall, at the wallpaper, concentrating hard, enthralled. She pointed with a limp hand, tracing the outline of the pattern, and giggled to herself.

'Hello, Vera,' said Calloway. 'Bert says you're a bit out of sorts today.'

Bert's wife Elsie looked up at him from the sofa, where she sat holding Vera's hand.

'She's been getting worse all week,' she said. 'Sometimes she's fine. Other times she's away with the fairies.'

'She's been taking them pills for her nerves, but they don't even touch it,' said Webber.

Calloway picked up the pill bottle from the sideboard. It was half-empty. He read the label. Common barbiturates, from his limited knowledge.

Vera snapped to.

'It's that nice Mr Calloway,' she said, crossing the room and taking his hand. She turned to Elsie. 'Handsome devil, ain't he.'

She let go of his hand, returned to her armchair and drank some tea from the cup on the side table.

'Are you going to find my Stan?' she said, in a sing-song voice.

Bert looked at Calloway, uncertain, then turned to his sister-in-law. 'Stan passed away, Vera. Remember? An accident, they said.'

Vera thought for a moment then huffed. 'You don't need to remind me, Bert Webber.' Her tone was suddenly rational. 'I know my Stan's dead. What do you think I am, gaga?'

Webber shrugged.

Calloway had to admit, Vera's mood had deteriorated since his last meeting with her. She would switch from whimsical, to angry to completely lucid within only a few minutes. The nearest Calloway had seen to it was battle stress. That could alter men's minds in strange and disturbing ways. He'd seen it happen.

'Reg is going to Germany, Vera,' said Webber. 'To Berlin. He's going to find out what happened to Stan. It'll settle your mind, girl.' He looked at Calloway with plaintive eyes. 'It will, won't it, Reg?'

It was a tall order. Calloway doubted a few facts about Stan's death would fix Vera's current condition. She needed proper help.

'I'll do what I can,' he said.

He drove north back towards the stadium. He took a left turn at The Nelson into Doreen's street and parked.

She stood by the sink making him tea. Her tightly-cinched dressing gown clung to her skinny frame. She'd lost weight. She had the body of a boy. She played with her hair self-consciously knowing she looked a mess. He wanted to hug her but he couldn't bring himself to, not when he knew she'd had a caller. The small amount of money he was able to give her wasn't enough to make ends meet. She was still relying on other means.

'I'm sorry, Reg. I wasn't expecting you,' she said.

'I should have called first.'

There was a phone in the shared hallway but he didn't know the number.

'How's Margaret?' he said.

'Alright. She's across the hall with Mrs Grant. Mrs Grant is very understanding. She looks after Maggie while I'm...'

Doreen looked shameful. Calloway smiled.

'She's a good girl,' he said.

They perched on the unmade bed. The lone armchair she used to own had gone. Pawned, he assumed. They sat in silence for a while before Calloway spoke.

'I have to go away,' he said.

'Away?' There was a tremor in her voice. 'Where to?'

'Not far,' he lied.

'But for how long, Reg?'

She took his hand in hers and held it tight, like he was a lifeline. He understood. She would be scared Jenks would be around when he heard Calloway was gone.

'I've taken care of Jenks,' he said.

He let go of her hand and kissed her lightly on the cheek. Her skin felt cold on his lips. She stood and paced the room, her thin arms clasped tightly around her.

'If he comes back here, Reg, I swear I'll kill him.'

Calloway stood to leave. 'He won't.'

He pulled out his wallet and put a few notes from Webber's advance on the bedside table. It made him feel uncomfortable, like the first time he'd been there.

'I expect Maggie needs new clothes. She'll be growing.'

She lit a cigarette and drew hard on it with tensed lips.

'Thanks,' she said, not looking him in the eye.

Finnegan took Calloway's request for leave better than he had expected.

'You could do with a break, Reg,' Finnegan said. 'I can't remember you ever having taken one since you've been here.'

It was true. What would Calloway have done with a holiday? He preferred to keep busy. Holidays meant time to think. And thinking brought thoughts he'd sooner forget. There were plenty like him in his generation. The generation that fought. A life of thoughts not thought, and words not spoken, gathered up, nailed down and buried in the war grave of the mind.

'Growler Grimes is looking for work. He's one of my old wrestlers, before I started in female wrestling. He can fill in while you're away.' He looked apologetic. 'I'll have to pay him you're wedge, though.'

Calloway nodded his agreement. He'd be using Webber's money anyway.

'You're going away?' said Trudi, when he told her Grimes would be around for the next couple of weeks.

'Berlin,' he said. 'Your old stomping ground.'

'Marvellous,' she said. 'Assuming there's anything left of it.'

'I'll be working,' he said. 'After a fashion.'

He told her about Vera, and Stan's death, the man called Denton and the dates that didn't tally. It was indiscreet, but in that moment he couldn't help relieve himself of the burden of discretion. Maybe he was growing weak. Not the stoic, tight-lipped type he'd been since first joining the army as little more than a boy.

Trudi frowned. 'Be careful, Reggie,' she said. 'Berlin is a rotten city if you meet the wrong people. Believe me, I know.'

'I'll get by,' he said.

She shook her head.

'Don't be too sure. You'll need to keep your guard up. Do you have friends there?'

'I don't know a soul,' he said.

She smiled. She unbuttoned her shirt halfway. She had a thin gold chain around her neck. A signet ring hung from it. Calloway hadn't noticed it before. She didn't wear it when she fought. She reached behind her head and unclasped the chain.

'Take this with you,' she said, handing him the ring on the chain. 'For luck.'

She reached in her hold-all and took out a wrestling flyer. She wrote a name and address on the back.

'You may need a friend,' she said.

TWELVE

D-Day minus one, somewhere over Normandy. Eight young, tense men huddle in a glider, its wood and canvas creaking. The engines of the Dakota tow plane throb ahead of them. There's a smell of piss. Warren kicked over the Elsan. His nervous bladder again. Turbulence sends streams of cold piss in rivulets along the glider's grooved wooden floor, reflecting the red safety light, glowing like rivers of blood.

The glider pilot signals to the men hunched up in the long tubular fuselage behind him.

'Gentlemen, we're about to lose our tow.'

There's a jolt as the tow plane releases the cable, then a bump as the flimsy Horsa glider hits the air beneath and starts its downward glide. It's quiet now. The tow plane's engine noise fades and the airstream whispers around them. The men check their weapons and adjust their webbing.

There's a massive, bone-shaking thud as they hit the ground, throwing them every which way, bouncing their brains around their skulls like snooker balls off the cushion. They scramble over each other, out of the glider and onto the damp earth below.

They approach the radio hut, affixing silencers. Lofty Small dons knuckle dusters. They blow through the door like a hurricane. There's five in the room, a Waffen SS signals unit. Four men, one woman. Lofty floors the officer with a jaw breaker from his brass knuckles. Choc Brown kicks the chair from under the NCO and stamps on his face. Warren, Reece and Cauldwell loom over the other three, pistols held two-handed like Shanghai police. Brown disarms the men. Calloway, their sergeant, opens a canvas duffel bag and starts stuffing in the signals unit's files.

The woman jumps from the chair, her arm raised. She squeezes the trigger on a small Walther pistol at point-blank range and blows Cauldwell's arm from his shoulder. Cauldwell screams. The arm dangles limply in the sleeve of his Denison smock. Blood seeps through the camouflage fabric forming a pool of crimson the colour of his beret.

Calloway raises the Browning automatic in his hand. It spits through the silencer. The 9mm round takes off half the woman's head.

A hand gripped his arm, shaking him.

'Reg, Reggie.'

He awoke, screaming.

'For God's sake Reggie, pipe down. You're scaring the passengers.'

Faces were watching them from the aisle.

'It's the engine noise,' he said. 'It's a DC-3. We called them Dakotas during the war. They towed the gliders to Normandy, the night before D-Day.'

He didn't need to explain any further. People were well used to the hangover of war. They tried to ignore it, deny it, put it behind them, but it wasn't going away. Pat snapped her fingers and summoned the stewardess.

'He needs a large gin,' she said.

The stewardess smiled with forced grace. 'We're not actually serving drinks yet, madam.'

Pat shot her a look.

'It's medicinal,' said Pat. 'And it's Miss.'

Calloway downed the gin in a single gulp. It grounded him. The other passengers had lost interest in the commotion now. Half the seats were block booked for government officials and members of the occupation forces. They remainder of the sixteen passengers looked like business travellers. They had boarded at the new London airport. Calloway remembered when it had been a military airfield sending long-distance flights to the Far East towards the end of the war. Now it had a smart modern terminal, with a bar and cafeteria. They were flying BOAC to

Frankfurt, where they would change to a flight to Berlin. Shuman was all for sending them by boat and train, to save on the fares. Webber had bought Calloway an air ticket. Pat had insisted on paying for herself.

On landing in Frankfurt they transferred to a smaller aircraft operated by the new British European Airways. It was a pre-war twin-engine biplane, an anachronism among the smart new Stratocruisers and Constellations lined up on the tarmac of the airport.

'Christ,' said Pat. 'Is that ours? It looks like something out of a flying circus.'

'We called them Dominies during the war,' said Calloway. 'I think the civil airlines call them Dragons.'

'Well if it starts breathing fire, I'm bailing out,' she said. She pointed to her luggage on the tarmac. 'Take those will you, luvvie.'

He obeyed by reflex, then felt irritated by his own compliance. She was making him pay and he knew it. She strode across the tarmac drawing admiring looks from the ground crew. A steward held her hand and helped her up the small steps into the door at the rear of the plane.

They took two adjacent seats from the half-dozen inside the cramped fuselage. Pat pulled a silver hip flask from her handbag and took a nip before offering it to Calloway.

'Thirsty work carrying my bags, eh?'

He declined.

'Suit yourself,' she said, taking another drink and putting the flask back in her bag.

The little biplane taxied along the runway and glided up into the chill autumn air. Its twin engines made little more than a whisper in comparison with the DC-3. Calloway sat back in the bucket seat and lit a cigarette.

What the hell was he doing?

It was dusk as they made their approach to Berlin. The city lay spread out beneath them, with its endless blocks of gutted buildings and new construction sites. The streets were lighting up, revealing a latticework of routes punctuated with the red and blue neon of cafes and gaudy advertisements. Halfway across the city, the neon stopped abruptly. The Soviet sector, Calloway assumed.

He slid back the window next to his seat and breathed in the cool air. He could see the grand crescent shape of the airport terminal ahead. They were landing at Tempelhof, a swaggering monument to Germany's air superiority. Calloway remembered it from his last visit. If the Roman Empire had airports, they would look like that, he thought.

Tempelhof buzzed with activity. Affluent-looking civilians, sales representatives with sample cases and servicemen in the uniforms of the western allies, all swarming over the mosaic floors, between the travertine columns under the high-vaulted ceiling. The building inspired awe, without a doubt. All part of Nazi architect Albert Speer's megalomaniacal vision for Germania, the new capital of the thousand-year Reich. A liaison officer had given Calloway the history the last time he was here. Calloway had just come through six years of war and couldn't have cared less.

He took a last draw of his cigarette, flicked it to the floor and ground it into the mosaic tiling with the sole of his shoe.

A long line of Volkswagen taxis was lined up outside the terminal like obedient insects. The driver, a worn-down man in his fifties, struggled to get their luggage into the boot at the front of the car. Calloway and Pat eased themselves into the meagre back seat. He felt her warmth against his thigh as they squeezed together.

'This is cosy,' she said. 'Don't get any ideas.'

He ignored her and lit another cigarette, offering one to her.

She waved it away.

'I prefer my own,' she said, taking a brightly-coloured cocktail cigarette from her case.

She made small talk with the driver in English, which he responded to with a series of polite grunts. Calloway looked out of the window and watched the city pass by. This was the American sector. Its bright cafes and illuminated shop windows detracted the eye from the blackened carcasses of the windowless, bombed-out blocks behind them. They passed the derelict stump of the Kaiser Wilhelm church, which stood stubbornly, as if righteously indignant to the damage inflicted on it by the RAF. The arrogance of it struck a nerve in Calloway. In an instant his experience of war surged through him like a current. He stared at the bombed-out church. Serves you bloody well right, he thought.

The driver turned into Kurfürstendamm, a wide boulevard of shops and cafes that seemed oblivious to the damage that encircled it. Neon advertisements for German radios, American cars and French cosmetics cast a glow as bright as daylight. People promenaded, window shopping, or sat at cafes drinking beer and eating ice cream. Last time Calloway was here it was a dim and decaying strip of half-lit windows, where war-ravaged Berliners pretended life was normal again. What a difference a few years of American occupation makes.

The driver asked for the name of their hotel. He drove another hundred yards and pulled the Volkswagen over. Pat gave him a generous tip. They stood under the faded awning, beneath a sign which said *Hotel Pension Ritz*. The stonework either side of the double doors was peppered with bullet holes from wartime street fighting. Calloway ran his fingers over the damage. It sparked memories of war. Pat peered through the doors into a darkened lobby.

'Not my idea of the Ritz,' she said. 'And they say Germans don't have a sense of humour.'

Calloway carried their bags into the lobby and up a flight of stairs. The reception, such as it was, was on the first floor.

A thin, sad-looking woman, who looked sixty but was probably in her forties, handed them two keys.

'Klaus will show you to your rooms,' she said. She smiled for no longer than was courteous.

Klaus shuffled up to them wheezing. He had one arm. He picked up one of their cases and led them down a dim corridor. Calloway rolled his eyes and picked up the other bags. Pat sniggered. It didn't help his mood.

Klaus showed them to two tall doors that faced each other

across the corridor. Pat tipped him the same as the taxi driver. Her largesse irritated Calloway. She flicked the light switch inside the door and peered in. She wrinkled her nose.

'Smells like someone died in there,' she said.

'Someone probably did,' said Calloway, thinking of the bullet holes around the hotel entrance.

Pat shrugged.

'I'm going to freshen up,' she said. 'I'll meet you downstairs in an hour. You can buy me dinner.'

They ate at Cafe Wien. A passenger on the flight from Frankfurt had recommended it to Pat. It was just warm enough to sit outside.

'I want to watch the world go by,' said Pat. 'That way I don't have to talk to you all night.'

She winked at him. Her tone had softened, at least he thought so. The aggressive coldness of their reunion at the stadium had been replaced by a tolerant courtesy, with the occasional joke at his expense. It might just be enough to get them through this ridiculous escapade.

A chubby waiter with a pencil moustache made a fuss of them as they ordered. At least he made a fuss of Pat. He offered Calloway the wine list. Calloway waved it away.

'Beer for me,' he said.

'And I'll have the strongest thing you've got,' said Pat.

The waiter concealed his surprise with an ingratiating pout.

'That would be *Doppelkorn*,' he said, with a small bow.

'Make it a large one,' said Pat. She looked at Calloway. 'If I'm going to get through the evening looking at your ugly face, I'm going to need Dutch courage.'

'I believe *Doppelkorn* is German courage,' said Calloway.

She looked out across the busy street and sighed.

'I reckon we both need it,' she said. He sensed this wasn't one of her quips. Perhaps the penny was dropping. Two ex-lovers come to a strange city seeking the truth behind the mysterious death of a man they hardly knew, who was at best a chancer and at worst God only knows. This wasn't a holiday by any sane person's measure.

Pat frowned at the menu and asked the waiter for a recommendation. He suggested *Konigsberger Klopse*, a local meatball dish with potato. That would at least soak up the *korn*, thought Calloway. He ordered schnitzel with asparagus for himself. The schnitzel when it came was tasteless and the asparagus was tinned, but he ate it eagerly. He'd not eaten since leaving London.

Pat ordered more liquor and insisted Calloway join her. He didn't refuse.

'Does this relieve the boredom?' he said, waving a hand towards the city life in front of them.

'Ask me tomorrow,' she said. 'When I've tackled the wall.'

They made small talk as they ate and kept it civil. Calloway let the *korn* relax him. He started to feel better, if not something approaching good. Pat excused herself, asking the waiter for directions to the bathroom. Calloway's eyes wandered over to an adjacent table where two women sat drinking and smoking, wearing sunglasses like Hollywood starlets, despite the sun having set more than two hours ago. One was blonde, with shoulder-length hair, plump lips and a rounded face. The other was brunette, her hair falling over her shoulders in waves from beneath a small black felt hat. She wore a belted herringbone trench coat with shoulder pads and elaborate pleating, and a skirt cut short enough to show off the legs she was stretching in Calloway's direction. She drew on a cigarette with red-painted lips and tapped her peep-toe heels in time with an imaginary dance tune. She caught Calloway's eye through her tortoise shell sunglasses and smiled.

Pat returned to her seat.

'Put your eyes back in, Reg, or they'll fall in your schnitzel,' she said.

She gave the woman in the trench coat a predatory smile. The woman took the hint and turned back to make conversation with her friend.

They ordered strudel for dessert and *Underberg* as a digestif, which the waiter took great pride in saying was back in production after its cessation during the war. Pat took a sip of the digestif.

'It's bitter,' she said. She held Calloway's gaze. 'A bit like me, really.'

He'd been waiting for it. The more she'd drunk, the more they'd forced polite conversation, the more he knew it was coming.

'Why did you walk out, Reg?' she said.

He felt a knot in his guts. He took a slug of the bitter liquor.

'I wouldn't have been good for you,' he said.

'Shouldn't I have been the judge of that?'

'By the time you'd realised, it would have been too late. There's a side to me that isn't pretty.'

She laughed, incredulous. 'Who are you, Dr Jekyll?'

There was more than one Calloway, he knew that much. His stoic, dependable facade masked the violence inside him. It had always been there. The war had made it far, far worse.

'I'd settle for Mr Hyde, some days,' he said.

'And what made you think I wouldn't?' she said. She reached over and put her hand on top on his. 'I'm made of sterner stuff than you think, Reg.'

He drew his hand away and lit a cigarette. The brunette in the sunglasses looked over at him and made a sad face.

They walked back to the hotel in silence. Pat unlocked the door to her room and stepped over the threshold. She turned to wish him goodnight. In the half light of the corridor he thought he saw the hint of a smile.

Someone pulled the knot in his guts tighter.

THIRTEEN

The snowdrop at the gates examined their papers. Snowdrop because of his white helmet, British army slang for an American military policeman that Calloway knew well. It wasn't a term of endearment and usually preceded a fight. The snowdrop called them 'sir' and 'ma'am' in that insincere tone every US serviceman seemed to use when dealing with civilians. He asked them to wait while he returned to his sentry box and made a phone call. Satisfied their papers were in order, he waved them through.

It was a typical barracks. A confident, two-storey building which stretched the full length of the parade ground. Imperial German architecture was little different from its Victorian counterparts in Britain. Places like this had been Calloway's world, but perhaps without the level of amenity these Americans seemed to enjoy. Calloway read the signs. Snack bar, club, indoor ranges, gym. Craft shop, library, swimming pool, cinema. This place was better appointed than a holiday camp.

A platoon practiced drill on the parade ground. They drilled well, with precision and flair. They wore peaked caps and white silk scarves tucked into the tunics of their dress uniforms.

'Now there's something you don't see every day,' said Pat, looking at the soldiers.

Calloway had to agree. There were about fifty of them and all of them were black.

The drill lieutenant dismissed his men and walked over to Calloway and Pat.

'Your men are good,' said Calloway. He knew good drill when he saw it. He'd done enough himself.

'We should be,' the lieutenant said. 'It's the only reason we're here.'

'What d'you mean?' said Pat.

The lieutenant smiled. He looked around as if to check whether other soldiers were within earshot.

'The 7800th Infantry Platoon is an honour guard. All we do is greet visiting dignitaries.'

Pat raised a pencilled eyebrow.

'I never knew I was that important.' She nodded at Calloway and laughed. 'And he certainly isn't.'

'Sorry, ma'am,' said the lieutenant. 'We're just here to practice. I'm afraid it's a coincidence you arrived at the same time.'

'I'm only pulling your leg,' said Pat.

'Sometimes I think General Clay is pulling ours,' said the lieutenant, lowering his voice. 'He keeps us here to counter Soviet propaganda about segregation.'

Calloway watched the honour guard leaving the parade ground. Some white soldiers stopped what they were doing and stared at them as they passed. The lieutenant straightened his cap, although it didn't need straightening.

'I came to ask if I could direct you anywhere. You looked pretty lost.'

'We're here with the fairground,' said Pat, holding out her papers.

The lieutenant waved them away. He said, 'The show's out back. On the training field. Are you a performer?'

'Stunt rider,' she said. 'On the wall of death.'

The lieutenant whistled. 'Then you're some brave lady.'

She gave him a wink. 'Come to the show and find out,' she said. 'It's a thrill a minute. You'll have a great time.'

The lieutenant looked apologetic. 'I don't think so, ma'am.'

'Oh well,' she said. 'We've got passes to the NCO's mess. Maybe we can buy you a drink sometime.'

The lieutenant smiled with regret. Calloway guessed what was coming.

'We have our own mess,' he said. He turned and pointed. 'The training field is behind the main building. Turn left at the chapel and walk on past the motor pool. You can't miss it.'

He turned on his heels and followed his men.

The drome was pitched at the centre of a ring of stalls and sideshows. It was identical to Shuman's drome in London. Same lights, same slogans, same gaudy signage, but instead of Cyclone Sid, the main attraction was Hannelore von Hölle.

Calloway laughed. 'Hannelore from hell,' he said. 'There's your double act partner.'

'It got a ring to it,' said Pat. 'Who shall I be?'

Calloway thought. 'Heidi Himmel.'

'*Himmel* means heaven, yes?'

He nodded. She huffed.

'Well, I reckon that's the nearest I'm going to get to a compliment from you.'

A man appeared at the top of the stairs that led into the drome. He was around forty, wearing a voluminous flat cap, a vivid shirt under a sleeveless Fair Isle jumper and high-cut trousers.

'Pattie?' he shouted.

'That's what they call me,' Pat shouted back.

The man slid down the stairway with his hands on the rails and his feet barely touching the treads. He bounded over.

'Pretty Pattie Moxon, Queen of the Dirt Track.' Pat winced. Calloway knew she hated the name. The man held out his hand. 'Milt Harper,' he said. 'I run this show.'

'Call me Pat,' she said. 'And this is my mechanic, Reg.'

Harper looked Calloway up and down. 'You don't look like a grease monkey.'

'I'm still learning,' said Calloway.

'You want to watch this guy,' said Harper, looking at Pat. 'One loose bolt and you could be over the safety line and through the roof of the officers' mess.'

'If they sever a good Manhattan, I shan't complain,' said Pat.

Harper slapped his thigh. 'Atta-girl.'

The sound of engines rumbled out of the drome.

'Hannelore is working out a new trick,' said Harper. 'Backwards, no hands.'

Pat nodded. She looked unimpressed.

'I need to get some wall time in,' she said. 'Can I use the drome for the afternoon?'

He waved a hand towards the sound of the engine. 'Be my guest. You can work with Hannelore. She's got a couple of two-handed routines she wants to try out with you. Tricks she used to do with Stanley, before the sonofabitch did a midnight flit.'

The three of them climbed the wooden stairs, ducked through the doorway of the brightly-coloured tent and stood in the gallery leaning over the safety rail. Hannelore was circling the drome. She stood on the footrests and raised her arms with a flourish, as if to welcome them to her world. Her long red hair flowed behind her. She crouched back down onto the seat of the motorcycle, swivelled until she was facing backwards. Then she threw out her hands again.

Harper clapped his hands. Pat put her fingers between her teeth and whistled. Hannelore gave a small bow. She swivelled forwards and brought the bike down the ramp and onto the ground, before killing the engine and handing the machine to a grease monkey in overalls who stood ready to receive it.

'She's good,' said Calloway.

'Nothing I haven't done before,' said Pat. 'I just need to get my wall head back. It takes a few good rides to get over the dizziness.'

Hannelore joined them in the gallery. She stood next to Pat. She was the same height and build, with the same hard diamond eyes. Only the hair colour was different.

'Look at you two,' said Harper, beaming. 'You're gonna make an A1 double act.'

Hannelore leaned down and took a Zippo lighter that was tucked inside the top of her knee-length lace-up boots. She pulled a pack of Lucky Strikes from the pocket of her jodhpurs and lit up.

'Welcome to the Devil's Drome,' she said. Her German accent had hints of cockney.

Harper made the introductions. The two female riders eyed each other, as if sizing the other up. Pat lit one of her cocktail cigarettes. The four of them exchanged pleasantries until Harper suggested Hannelore show Pat the ropes. He shouted down to the grease monkey to get a second motorcycle ready.

Pat whispered to Calloway, 'They've got their own mechanic. Looks like you're off the hook.'

Calloway was relieved. His knowledge of motor mechanics was rudimentary at best. Hannelore led Pat by the arm to the stairway. Calloway offered Harper a cigarette and lit up for the pair of them. Harper took a good look at Calloway's suit. Hardly Savile Row, but it wasn't a pair of overalls.

'You really her mechanic?' he said.

'More of a chaperone,' said Calloway.

Harper screwed up his face then gave a nod of understanding.

'I getcha,' he said. 'The lady didn't want to travel alone to a strange city. And boy is this a strange city.' He gave Calloway a sly grin. 'Are you and her, you know, are you…?'

Calloway shook his head.

'Just old friends.'

Even that was stretching a point. She may have shown signs of thawing after a skinful of Doppelkorn, but there was still an inch-thick layer of frost between them.

'Did you know Stan Deakin?' said Harper.

'We were on nodding terms.'

'The bastard sure dropped me in it when he left.'

'Did he give any hint he was leaving?'

'None whatsoever,' said Harper. 'We started the tour here in Berlin, at the McNair Barracks in Lichterfelde. Then moved out to Frankfurt, then Heidelberg, then back here. By that time I'd lined up extra dates at the British and French barracks in their sectors. It was gonna be a long tour for good money.'

'Were there any signs something might have been wrong with Stan? Did he seem troubled, or bothered by anything?'

Harper shrugged. 'You know Stan,' he said. 'He's the life and soul. A joker, a charmer, a real showman.'

'How did he get on with the crew?'

'Okay, I guess. He's a likeable guy.'

'No trouble? No fallings out?'

'Not that I know of.'

A motorcycle started up in the drome below them. The

mechanic held the bike for Pat as she mounted it. She'd changed into a check shirt and leathers, with knee-length motorcycle boots. She revved the engine and stated circuiting the circular ramp. When she'd picked up enough speed, she let the bike glide up the wall. She made it look effortless.

'Looks like she's still got it,' said Harper.

Calloway watched her making circuits. She gave him a wink as she passed. She was pleased with herself. He shared her satisfaction. He enjoyed watching her ride. Harper caught the expression on Calloway's face. He grinned again.

'You sure there's nothing between you two?' he said, above the noise of the engine.

'Sure,' said Calloway, hearing the hint of doubt in his voice. He changed the subject.

'Stan was a gambler,' he said. 'Is it possible he got into debt with one of the crew?'

Harper frowned and shook his head. 'I don't allow it. This whole setup works on trust. There's lives at stake. I can't have debts or grudges getting in the way. If Stan had a card school going, I'd have known and I'd have stamped on it.'

Calloway didn't doubt it. Harper was no flake.

'How did Stan get on with Hannelore?' he said, knowing that gambling wasn't the late Stan Deakin's only vice.

'Fine, I guess,' said Harper. 'They were a good double act.'

'And that's all they were?'

Harper looked surprised at the question. Then he smiled, as if realising what Calloway was implying.

'I get you,' he said. 'I kinda made him for a pussy-hound. He'd disappear on his free nights and I could guess where he was heading. But Hannelore? No, nothing doing. I would have known. If anything there was a little tension there. Something I sensed as the tour progressed.'

'I thought you said they got along fine.'

'And they did, for the most part.' He drew on his cigarette and thought. 'There was this one time, though. They had some kind of argument. They were a little cool around each other after that. Nothing terrible, but I noticed it all the same.'

'Do you know what the argument was about?'

'Something stupid. Hannelore got pissed at Stan for taking tools from her toolbox. I put it down to stress.' He gestured towards Pat. She was doing circuits with no hands. 'Riders can get pretty uptight taking these kinds of risks night after night.'

Calloway reached in his pocket and passed Harper the nightclub flyer that Vera had found in the pocket of Stan's best suit.

'Did Stan ever mention this place?' he said.

Harper looked at the flyer and shook his head. 'Looks like a typical Berlin titty bar. Why are you so interested in Stan anyway? Was he a friend of yours?'

Hannelore joined them on the gallery. Calloway pocketed the flyer, ignoring Harper's question. Harper gestured towards Pat. She was sweeping up at full speed, crossing the safety line then plunging down again.

'Fräulein von Hölle, it looks like you've got competition,' he said.

Hannelore gave him a tolerant smile, the kind you give a child that's playing up.

'I got to leave you guys for moment. I need to speak to the entertainments officer over at the mess.'

Harper disappeared through the door in the tent and descended the stairs.

'Let's go down too,' said Hannelore to Calloway. 'I need a break from the noise.' She looked down at Pat. 'She's not so bad,' she said.

Once they were away from the noise, Hannelore said, 'I have coffee in my trailer. Would you like some?'

Her tone was courteous, but there was a coldness behind it. Calloway said yes, he would like coffee. They walked to the rear of the drome. Hannelore's trailer was in fact an old war-surplus radio truck, stripped out, refitted and painted in Shuman & Harper's red and cream fairground livery. The fit-out was modern, with veneered panelling, a small kitchenette and a table between upholstered benches that Calloway assumed converted into a bed. It was neat and tidy inside, with framed photos of

Hannelore in action fixed to the walls. There were also flyers pinned to a small, felt-covered pin board, one for the current tour of the bases, another for a recent tour of eastern England. An illustrator had drawn Hannelore on a motorcycle, exaggerating the size of her thighs and breasts, and picking out her lips in bright red ink. Beneath the illustration were the words *Hannelore von Hölle, the Devil Queen of Danger.* She saw Calloway looking and said, 'They make me look like a hooker.'

'I wonder what they'd make of Pat?' he said.

Hannelore took him literally. 'It is too late to have posters made,' she said, turning to fill a coffee pot and place it on a small gas ring in the kitchenette.

He read the place names on the English fairground tour. Peterborough, Bury St Edmunds, Newmarket, Cromer.

'You certainly get to see the sights,' he said, with a hint of irony she seemed to miss. Perhaps it was lost in translation. He switched to speaking German. 'You live in England now?' he said.

She nodded. 'And you speak German?'

'They taught me in the army.'

'Isn't that unusual?' she said.

'Not if you're in the Intelligence Corps.'

He caught a flicker of something more than causal interest in her face. She busied herself with the coffee.

'Why brings you here to Berlin?' she said.

'I'm keeping Pat company.'

'Milt told me you were a mechanic.'

'I dabble,' he said.

'A wall rider needs more than a dabbler for a mechanic,' she said. 'I would prefer if you didn't touch my motorcycle.'

'I'm happy to oblige,' he said, meaning it. 'How about you? You speak perfect English. What's your story?'

'I live in England now. I came there after the war.'

'After the war?' he said. 'Not an obvious move for a German at that time.' Unless you were built like Trudi Trauber, he thought. 'There was a lot of bad feeling. There still is.'

She shrugged. 'I had bad feelings too. I wanted a new start.'

'It couldn't have been easy getting travel documents.'

She poured the coffee. The aroma filled the trailer. She settled herself in the bench seat opposite him.

'When the British army came to my town in 1945, I worked for them as a translator. My family had been circus people. They travelled and spoke many languages. They taught me English. Because of the work I had done for the army, I was able to get a special permit to move to England. Germany wasn't a place for fairgrounds just then, but I had heard there were dromes up and running again in England. I had saved enough money from the translation work to pay my passage. I travelled to London and met with Alfie Shuman. He gave me a job touring with his second drome.'

Through the open window they could hear the sound of a motorcycle. Pat was riding the wall again.

'So what was Stan like as a wall rider?' said Calloway.

'Stan?' she said and laughed. It was derisive. 'Stan was reckless. An egotist. The show was all about him. But we were a double act and there is no room for ego in a double act. Ego can be a dangerous thing when you're riding a motorcycle ninety degrees from a vertical cylinder at fifty miles an hour.'

'It sounds like you were glad to see the back of him.'

She sipped her coffee without answering.

'Any idea why he left?' said Calloway.

Hannelore shook her head.

'It was a week or so into our second run in Berlin,' she said. 'He just failed to show one afternoon.'

'Was that after you and he had an argument?'

She looked put out by the question. She raised her eyebrows.

'You've learned a lot in a morning,' she said.

'Just something Milt said when we were chatting about Stan.'

She dismissed the subject with a wave of her hand.

'It was nothing,' she said, in a tone which made clear this was the end of the matter. He persisted.

'It must have been something,' he said. 'A man doesn't just walk away from a well-paid job like this for no reason.'

She put her coffee cup down and stared at him. 'Did I say he left after we argued? No. Then why do you think the two things are connected? In fact, why are you asking this at all? Is that why you came here? To find out where your friend Stan went?'

He was playing this badly. Too heavy-handed. She was no pushover and he'd made her suspicious.

'Just making conversation,' he said.

She went to speak, then paused a moment. 'Then make a different conversation.'

He dug deep for some idle chit-chat and she seemed to soften. She reminded him of Pat. The steely eyes, the commanding personality, the handsome face. In fact, only her flame red hair and the absence of jibes at his expense separated them.

'What's it like being back in Germany?' he said.

'Is this Germany?' she said, looking out of the trailer window in the direction of the city beyond the barracks. 'It's the carcass of a city torn to pieces by the occupying armies. They all have their piece of it, with their flags flying and their soldiers patrolling, to remind the Germans of their place.'

'Their place?' he said. 'They're alive and they're no longer at war. All things considered, that's not a bad place.'

'Maybe,' she said. She was quiet for a moment. He caught a faraway look, as if in her mind she was somewhere else. 'Germany will be a better place one day. Perhaps then I will return.'

There was a knock at the trailer door and Pat stuck her head through the doorway. Her hair was tied back and she had a grease smudge on her face. She looked at Hannelore and then at Calloway.

'Well isn't this cosy,' she said.

FOURTEEN

There were two goons minding the door. One was ruddy-faced and rustic-looking. If it weren't for the dinner suit, he could have been a pig farmer. The other just looked like a pig. The piggy one opened the door for Calloway and ushered him in without any hint of welcome. It was dark inside, lit only by candles in wine bottles on the dozen or so tables in front of the stage, where a bored-looking stripper was performing a half-hearted routine under a single spotlight. The audience were mostly men, although some were accompanied by women who looked like they came with the house. A waitress in a cheap, revealing cocktail dress showed him to a table. He declined the house champagne and ordered a beer. The waitress looked disappointed. She asked him if he'd like company, gesturing to two young women seated on stools at the bar. He said no. She said perhaps later then.

He imagined the late Stan Deakin in the place. He'd built a picture of the man in his mind. He would be sitting near the front, talking himself up to a hostess that was sipping watered down *Sekt* from a reused champagne bottle. He might flash the cash, or invite another girl to join them. He would try to impress them with his wall riding stories and they would feign interest and order more of the exorbitant sparkling wine on his tab. He'd ogle the strippers and feel up the hostesses. Stan was the kind of punter they would remember.

Calloway gestured to the women at the bar to join him. They exchanged looks as if agreeing whose turn it was. One of them crossed to floor and sat at his table. She smiled a practiced smiled and said her name was Magda. He offered her a drink and she asked for champagne. He had a pocket full of Webber's money, so he agreed.

My friend recommended this place, he said. He was here a few weeks ago.

That's nice, said Magda, looking slightly surprised that anyone would recommend Club Continentale.

'Name of Stan. He was here with the fair. A motorcycle stunt man.'

'I don't remember,' she said, without thinking first.

He took the photo of Stan from the inside pocket of his jacket and showed her. He saw a head turn from the corner of his eye. The piggy doorman was eyeing him with suspicion.

'I bet you wouldn't forget that face, eh? He's a handsome devil, Stan is.'

She took the photo and looked at it by the light of the candle.

'Maybe,' she said. 'I don't know.'

Calloway saw the doorman speaking to the barman. The two of them were looking at him now. Piggy walked causally past Calloway's table and glanced at the photo. Then he returned to the bar and conferred with the barman. The barman left and disappeared through a door next to the stage.

'Perhaps one of the other girls remembers him,' said Calloway.

'Ask one over, why don't you?' she said, in a tone that dismissed the suggestion. She wasn't sharing her commission on the overpriced *Sekt* with another girl. He took the hint, for now, and put the photo back in his jacket pocket. One of the hostesses drinking at another table rose, taking her punter by the hand. The punter walked with her to a curtained doorway at the back of the house. They disappeared and Calloway heard footsteps on stairs above the piped music. Club Continentale had private rooms, which didn't surprise him.

Piggy the bouncer appeared at Calloway's table.

'The manager invites you to join him for a drink,' he said. He stood over the table waiting, until Calloway accepted. Calloway's hostess looked disappointed. He left the price of the *Sekt* and a generous tip on the table. By the time he stood up, the tip had disappeared and the hostess was on her way back to the bar.

Calloway followed the bouncer through the door by the stage. Behind it was a dim corridor with an anteroom leading off it, where half-naked strippers were changing into their costumes for the next routine. There was another door at the end of the corridor. Piggy knocked and entered.

The room inside oozed cheap opulence. Deep carpet, flock wallpaper, chandelier wall lights and gilt-framed prints of American pinup girls. The air was thick with cigar smoke. There was a large desk by the far wall. From behind it, a man in a dinner suit rose and bowed. He had longish grey hair swept back over his ears and a matching kaiser moustache. His eyes were a steely blue. He fixed Calloway with a calculated smile and beckoned him to sit. Piggy the bouncer stood with his back to the door. Calloway sat and accepted a cigarette from a jewelled box, the kind of tat they sell in Egyptian bazaars. The manager poured two generous measures of whisky from a bottle Calloway recognised. PX whisky, supplied to the US army, and clearly black market. He took a large sip. The whisky was good enough.

The manager sat. He lit a cigarette.

'Thank you for joining me, Mr...?'

'Calloway.'

The manager nodded and repeated Calloway's name, as if trying it out for future use. He swallowed the *w*, rather than pronounce it with a *v* like German stereotypes in films.

'I understand you are asking about a friend of yours. A visitor to the club.'

'Yes. Someone I know in London who recommended this place. I was just making conversation with the young lady.'

The manager put on a look of apology. He flicked ash from his cigarette into a heavy glass ashtray on the desktop.

'I'm afraid that's not the sort of conversation we encourage at Club Continentale. Discretion is very important to us, as I'm sure you will appreciate. Our clientele are discerning gentlemen who come here to enjoy our glamorous stage shows and stimulating company. We respect their privacy.'

The only thing those punters out there could discern would be a blonde from a brunette, thought Calloway. The manager continued. 'You must understand that for us to comment on any gentlemen that might or might not have visited us, would be a gross infringement of the trust they place in us.'

'I'll be straight with you, Mr...'

'Vogel,' said the manager. He gave Calloway an ingratiating smile.

'Mr Vogel, I'm keen to find Stan Deakin. He's gone missing.'

Vogel frowned. 'You sound like a policeman, Mr Calloway. Or perhaps a military official. Are you with one of the occupation armies?'

'I'm with the fairground,' said Calloway.

Vogel looked surprised, then feigned delight. 'Ah,' he said. 'So we are both in the entertainment business.' He dropped the look of delight and frowned again. 'To me, you sound like a policeman.'

Calloway heard piggy behind him grunt.

'You're a shrewd man, Mr Vogel, but I'm not a policeman. I'm with a travelling fairground and so is Stan Deakin. He's a motorcycle stunt rider who rides the wall of death.' He kept it in the present tense. He was keeping Stan's death to himself, at least for now. 'He disappeared from the fair and hasn't been seen since. I'm just asking after him. His family is concerned.'

Vogel gave a knowing nod. 'Men tend not to mention visits here to their families.'

'And I'm sure he didn't. But he told me.'

Vogel appeared to think for a moment. 'The name means nothing, but I understand you have a photograph. May I see it?'

Calloway handed the snap over. Vogel made a show of looking at it. Then he shook his head.

'I'm sorry,' he said. 'I've never seen this man.'

'Perhaps your doorman has,' said Calloway, turning in his chair and holding up the photo for piggy to see. The bouncer looked to his boss for a signal. Vogel gave a small nod. The bouncer glanced at the photo, grunted then shook his head.

'There, you see,' said Vogel. 'I think it very unlikely this man Deakin is one of our clientele.'

Calloway reached in his pocket and pulled out the leaflet Vera had found in Stan's best suit.

'He gave me this,' he said.

Vogel recognised the leaflet and waved his hand dismissively.

'Our leaflets are distributed freely in Berlin. He could have picked one up anywhere.'

Vogel gave the bouncer a look. It was a signal. Calloway heard piggy step towards him. He sensed the big man's presence looming over him. Calloway stood up. The manager spoke. He'd dropped the obsequious tone.

'Berlin is a dangerous town, Mr Calloway. And its entertainment business is not without its, shall we say, criminal elements. I, of course, run a respectable establishment.' He stood and walked around his desk until he was eye to eye with Calloway. 'Not all businesses like mine are as respectable. You should exercise caution before continuing with your enquires. You are not, after all, a policeman.'

'No' said Calloway. 'But I can smell bullshit when I'm served it. You run a cheap strip joint with a knocking shop upstairs. Hardly respectable, by any standards. And if you were telling the truth about Stan never having visited here, you wouldn't be playing the intimidation card right now. You know something, Vogel. You're just keeping it to yourself.'

Calloway pushed past the bouncer and opened the door. He turned back to face the two men.

'And for the avoidance of doubt,' he said, 'I'll ask what the bloody hell I want, to whoever I want, until I get a straight answer.'

He walked back down the corridor. A stripper in a revealing *Brünnhilde* outfit gave him a smile which he didn't return.

The air outside was damp. There was a slight mist through which the dirty neon of Potsdamer Strasse tried its best to glow. Calloway walked towards the U-Bahn station at Kurfürstenstrasse. It was the station on the ticket found in Stan's pocket. The fact cast even more doubt on Vogel's claim not to know anything about Stan. Calloway felt light-headed. The beer, the diluted *Sekt* and the black-market whisky were mixing up a sickly cocktail in his empty stomach. The smell of bratwurst from an *imbiss* kiosk at the corner of the street reminded him he needed to eat. He ordered sausage in a bread roll and stood at the counter smearing on the mustard. He heard footsteps on the cobbles behind him. The sudden look of fear on the *imbiss* vendor's face told him something bad was coming. He felt a hand grab his collar and yank him backwards. The bratwurst hit the cobbles. From the corner of his eye he saw his assailants. Piggy and the farmer were dragging him into a side street. The street was dark and stank of bins. Calloway lashed out but his punches failed to connect. The two bouncers bundled him to the end of the side street and onto a bomb site, well away from the glow of the streetlights. He stumbled over the rubble and lost his footing. He fell face down onto the floor of jagged bricks. They started kicking. He felt their boots in his ribs, guts and kidneys. He grabbed at their legs but the kicks kept coming. He took a kick to the head. Lightning flashed behind his eyes. He felt himself falling. The onset of unconsciousness pulled him down into the rubble.

A shrill whistle pierced his eardrums, then another, then the rumble of boots on cobbles. The kicking stopped. His attackers ran. Someone knelt beside him and put a hand on his shoulder.

'Can you hear me, sir?'

A man's voice, with an American accent.

'Sir, can you hear me?'

Then darkness and silence.

He came to in the rear seat of a jeep. The same voice said, 'Easy, sir. Take it easy, now. We'll get you some help.'

A snowdrop. A US military policeman in a white helmet sat next to him on the rear seat of the patrol jeep. Another MP was at the wheel. Calloway swallowed hard, blinked his eyes and felt his jaw. He felt his ribs and rubbed his back. His head hurt like crazy but he was in one piece.

'I'm fine,' he said. 'Just take me to my hotel.'

'I don't think so,' said the snowdrop, concern in his voice. 'You took quite a beating. You ought to see a doctor.'

'I told you, I'm fine,' Calloway growled. He just wanted to

crawl into bed.

The snowdrop ignored him. 'Do you know the men that attacked you?'

Calloway shook his head. 'I was lost. They followed me. Tried to take my wallet,' he lied. 'I was just unlucky.'

The snowdrop gave a knowing nod. 'It's that kind of neighbourhood,' he said. 'That's why we patrol it. It's the kind of place trouble finds GIs.' He looked at Calloway and smiled. 'And the occasional Englishman.'

The MP at the wheel took a left. Calloway recognised the street.

'This is Kurfürstendamm,' said Calloway. 'My hotel's just there on the left.'

The snowdrop looked doubtful. 'Well, if you're really sure you don't need a doctor, I guess...'

'I'm sure,' said Calloway. He pointed out Hotel Pension Ritz. 'Just drop me there.'

It was late and the hotel doors were locked. One-armed Klaus was on the night shift and let Calloway in. He seemed not to notice his guest's bloodied face. Calloway asked for a bottle of liquor. After some initial reluctance, Klaus agreed to charge a bottle of Bismarck to Calloway's bill.

He locked the door of his room behind him and poured himself a large measure of schnapps in the glass from the wash basin. The liquor burned his throat. It sedated him. He kicked off his scuffed-up shoes and fell onto the bed. His head was fuzzy. He heard the voice of the snowdrop.

'It's the kind of place trouble finds GIs. And the occasional Englishman.'

One thing was clear. It was the kind of place trouble found Stanley Deakin.

FIFTEEN

There was a tap at his door. He lifted his head from the pillow and looked at his watch. His head hurt and he couldn't focus. He lifted himself off the bed. Everything hurt. The tapping persisted.

'Reg, Reggie. Open the bloody door.'

It was Pat. He unlocked the door and flopped back down on the bed. Pat came in the room.

'Christ,' she said. 'What happened to you?'

'Just God's way of telling me girly bars are evil.'

'Looks like he struck you down good and proper,' she said, sitting on the bed beside him and pulling his blood-caked hair off his face.

'He had two gorillas in dinner suits to help him.'

She tutted. 'Where the hell did you get to?'

He'd left Pat and Hannelore in the trailer to discuss their wall routine. He'd killed an afternoon in what was left of the Tiergarten, Berlin's war damaged central park, then found a cafe on Fasanenstrass to kill time, before making his way to Club Continentale.

He passed Pat the nightclub flyer.

'Let's just say Stan's favourite gentleman's establishment didn't welcome me with open arms.'

She looked across the room and through the tall window onto Kurfürstendamm. It was past ten and the street was already buzzing.

'What the hell are we doing here, Reg?' she said.

'Relieving the boredom of your unsatisfied life.'

She looked at him with a half-smile. 'There was a time when

nothing would have given me more pleasure than seeing you beaten to a pulp.'

'I'm glad you've changed your mind.'

'Don't take it for granted,' she said. 'Now get your clothes off. There's a bathroom down the corridor. I'll take your suit to reception and see if they can get it cleaned.'

The soak did him good. He padded back to his room half dry, leaving footprints down the corridor. He dressed in his only other clothes, a sports jacket and trousers, and his remaining clean shirt. It hurt to put the shirt on. He slapped Brylcreem in his hair and combed a parting. He looked at himself in the wardrobe mirror. Despite the pain of the bruising, he could pass for man who hadn't been used as a football by two nightclub goons.

Pat returned with a tray of coffee.

'Don't say I never do anything for you,' she said.

The coffee was good. Better than the ersatz muck he'd had to drink last time he was in Berlin. The strength of it revived him.

'The nightclub manager was hiding something,' said Calloway. 'He claimed never to have seen Stan, but he was lying. He set his two bouncers after me, to give me a good kicking down an alleyway. If it hadn't been for a military police patrol passing, they would probably have finished the job.'

'You think they did the same thing to Stan?'

'Perhaps. The question is why.'

'Did Hannelore have anything to say? Or Harper?'

'Harper knows nothing. That was pretty clear. Hannelore? I'm not sure. Harper mentioned she'd had an argument with Stan not long before he disappeared. He said it was something about taking tools from a toolkit, although I don't buy that. I asked her about it. She shrugged it off, but I got the feeling there was more to it than she was letting on.' He drank more of the coffee. 'How's the routine going?'

'It's the greatest show on earth,' said Pat. 'If you drag your bruised behind up there tonight, you'll see it for yourself.'

'I will,' he said. 'I mean it can't be any more dangerous than Club Continentale.'

She cocked her head. 'Speak for yourself.'

Pat poured more coffee and Calloway gulped it down.

'Do me a favour, will you?' he said.

'Depends what it is.'

'If you get the chance, have a look through Hannelore's toolkit. Just in case there is something in this argument that Harper told me about.'

'What am I looking for?'

'Something other than tools.'

The training field was packed. The autumn sun had set behind the main barracks building and the festoon lights of the fairground cast a vivid glow over the crowd that gathered around the rides and sideshows. The men were American and uniformed, their dates for the night were local women. There were families too, from the married quarters. Well-nourished American kids with freckles and hair shorn short. Dutiful army wives making the most of an evening out. Harper was standing on the small stage at the front of the drome with a bullhorn to his lips. He was giving the crowd the spiel.

'Hannelore von Hölle and Heidi Himmel. The all-girl daredevil double act. There's glamour, there's danger, there's devilish dames on bikes.'

Calloway stood by the side of the stage listening to Harper's pitch. Pat was sitting astride her motorcycle, showing off her no-hands riding as the bike's wheels spun on the rollers, just like he'd seen Cyclone Sid do at the fairground in London. A crowd had gathered in front of the stage. Calloway saw an American officer and two military policemen squeeze their way through the jostling bodies. The officer came up to him.

'Excuse me, sir. Would you be Mr Milton Harper?'

Calloway gestured to the stage. 'The fella with the bullhorn is Harper. He's the boss.'

The officer looked apologetic. 'I don't want to disturb him. Could you maybe pass him a message?'

'Sure.'

'You need to tell your people to stick to the training field while you're here. If you need to leave at any time, just cross the parade ground to the main gate. We've had reports of someone from the fair wandering around the barrack buildings, places that are restricted to US military personnel.'

Calloway nodded. 'I'll tell him,' he said. 'It shouldn't be a problem.'

The officer looked relieved. He didn't strike Calloway as the most robust member of the warrior class. He was puny and pale, with round, gold-rimmed spectacles. He had freckles like the kids from the married quarters. A typical shiny-arse.

'Do you know who it was, this person that was wandering around?'

The officer shook his head. 'The enlisted man that stopped them didn't take their name. It was a woman apparently. A redhead. Quite a looker too, by all accounts.' Calloway caught a slight flush of embarrassment. 'Not that that makes any difference.'

'I'll make sure they get the message,' said Calloway.

The officer nodded.

'We'd be much obliged. While you folks are here we'll put a couple of MPs at the entrance to the field, just to direct people coming and going.' He smiled. 'To keep them on the path of righteousness.'

The American officer saluted by reflex, before realising his mistake. Calloway had been out of the army for five years and he'd only been an officer by grace of a short-lived battlefield commission. But he still had a natural authority. He gave the American a forgiving smile and returned the salute with a wink.

Harper had finished his spiel and was selling tickets hand over fist from the booth. Pat's big night was looking like a sell-out. Calloway felt a pang of vicarious nerves. Then he felt a sharp pain in his ribs, a reminder of the treatment Vogel's boys had dished out the previous night. He wasn't finished with Vogel yet.

He squeezed through the crowd in the arena above the drome. The timbers creaked with their weight. Harper had said with pride that this was an old drome from the nineteen twenties. This didn't sound reassuring. Pat and Hannelore entered through the trapdoor in the base of the wall. They wore matching outfits. Knee-length boots, jodhpurs and tight sweaters. From this distance they looked like the pinup illustration on Hannelore's tour poster. Pat played to the crowd. She blew kisses and wiggled her hips. It drew wolf whistles. She slipped her arm through Hannelore's and the pair of them promenaded around the wall, smiles beaming and eyes twinkling, like two gals looking for a date. GIs hollered. They blew kisses back. The two riders split up and crossed the circular floor to their motorcycles. Pat flung her leg over, wiggled into the seat and kicked the starter. She bent over slowly, as if to make an adjustment to the engine. She looked up at the crowd and winked. The cheers and whistles crescendoed. Harper was in the drome now. He gave dramatic safety warnings to build the sense of danger. The riders kicked into gear and started circling, building up speed, Hannelore ahead of Pat. They needed a good thirty miles an hour to create centrifugal force. By the time they were up, they were doing fifty. They started the tricks. Standing, no hands, side saddle. He had to hand it to Pat. A day's practice and she was on peak form. She matched Hannelore for skill, and beat her on elegance. Calloway felt a tremor of pride, then cursed himself. The pièce de résistance was a no-hands backwards circuit in opposite directions. The crowd went wild. Pat looked ecstatic. If there was ever a cure for boredom, this must surely have been it.

As the riders descended and gave their bows, the crowd threw money into the drome. Yankee dollars fell like autumn leaves in a gale. Harper beamed like the cat that got the cream.

Calloway pushed ahead of the crowd and descended the stairs. Pat was emerging from the drome. She ran to him and flung her arms around his neck. He felt the smack of a kiss on his cheek.

'God, that was incredible,' she said. 'Did you see it? Did you see how good we were?'

She was buzzing with excitement.

'I saw,' he said. He touched his cheek. 'I even got a kiss.'

She let go of him and lit a cigarette. She took a long, deep drag and blew smoke in his direction.

'Adrenalin,' she said. 'That's all. Don't get any ideas.'

She closed her eyes and let the nicotine take effect.

'How long until the next show?' he said.

'An hour.'

'Time for a few adjustments. You'll need to borrow some tools.'

She got his meaning. She nodded towards Hannelore, who was encircled by autograph hunters.

'I'm sure I'll get a chance at some point.'

A cluster of GIs were looking in Pat's direction. All smiles and better teeth than any British soldier Calloway had met.

'Go and talk to your fans,' he said. 'You're a star now.'

She walked towards the soldiers, then turned to blow Calloway a kiss.

'I've always been a star, luvvie,' she said. 'Shame you never realised it.'

SIXTEEN

Calloway stood in the shadows beneath the S-Bahn viaduct and smoked his fifth cigarette. He had a good view of the street. It was late and punters were starting to leave the club. The pig farmer in the dinner suit stood outside the illuminated door nodding a curt good night to everyone that left. He was there to ensure an orderly exit. The last thing a business-like Club Continentale needed was to attract too much attention from the police or a military patrol. Calloway checked his watch by the light of a passing cab, appearing for a moment like a ghost in the headlights. He stepped back behind the big iron pillar of the elevated railway. The darkness swallowed him. He carried on watching as the trains rumbled overhead every few minutes.

He waited another half-hour and smoked another cigarette. His throat felt dirty and his chest tight, but the tobacco kept him alert. Piggy appeared, exchanged words with the farmer and walked away in the opposite direction. A few moments later, the barman and half-a-dozen hostesses left the place for the night. They walked heavy-footed with fatigue after their shift. Then Vogel appeared. He pulled a set of keys from the pocket of his astrakhan coat and locked the door behind him. Calloway peered through the darkness and held his breath. He willed the two men not to leave together. He'd banked on it. Vogel didn't seem the type to treat staff like friends. He was too self-important. Calloway wanted Vogel alone.

Vogel reached in his pocket and drew out a wad of banknotes. He reeled some off and passed them to the farmer. Wages for the night. The farmer gave a surly nod and walked away by himself. Vogel stepped forward to the edge of the pavement and looked up and down the street, searching for a cab, Calloway assumed.

Now was the time. Calloway ran across the street, then edged his way to the entrance of the club, hugging the walls of the neighbouring buildings and treading as lightly as his big frame would allow.

'Herr Vogel,' he said. It startled the club owner, who turned around. Calloway gave him a hard punch to the guts. Vogel doubled over. Calloway grabbed his coat collar and dragged him across the street and into the darkness of the viaduct. He pushed Vogel against one of the big iron pillars. Even in the darkness he could see the fear in Vogel's eyes, the calm assurance of their first meeting absent. Vogel looked around as if hoping that piggy and the farmer might appear.

'Your goons are long gone, Vogel. It's just you and me.'

An S-Bahn train rumbled overhead. Calloway grabbed Vogel's lapels and slammed his head against the iron pillar. The screech and rumble of wheels on rail drowned out Vogel's cry.

Calloway leaned in. 'Hurts, doesn't it?' he said. 'Every time a train passes overhead, I'm going to slam your head into that pillar. If you want me to stop, you'd better give me answers. Straight ones this time.' He lifted Vogel an inch off the ground and leaned into his ear. 'Stan Deakin came to your club. I want to know what happened to him.'

Vogel stammered. 'I don't know this Stan Deakin, I swear.'

'You know him, and you sent your men to give me a good kicking after I'd I asked about him.'

Vogel shook his head. Then his ears pricked up. The next S-Bahn train was approaching. Calloway nodded towards the sound of the train. 'I'd try again, if I were you.'

Vogel's voice went up a tone. 'I know nothing,' he said. 'On my honour, Herr Calloway.'

'Men like you have no honour. Try again.'

The noise of the approaching train grew louder. The train was right above them. Calloway banged Vogel's head against the iron. Vogel winced and started to weep.

'Spit it out, Vogel. I want the whole story, while you've still got a brain that works. If I keep this up, and believe me I will, you'll be a basket case before the night's out.'

He lifted Vogel off the ground again.

'Alright, alright, I will tell you. Just let me have a cigarette.'

Vogel reached in his pocket. Calloway stopped him.

'No you don't,' he said. 'Keep your hands where I can see them.'

Calloway gripped Vogel's lapel with one hand and opened his own cigarette case with the other. He put a cigarette in Vogel's mouth and lit it with his lighter. Vogel drew hard on the tobacco. He exhaled through trembling lips.

'Your friend Stan came to the club,' Vogel said. 'He came several nights running. Stayed a long time. He liked the girls. He went with them, upstairs, you know. Spent a lot of money enjoying himself.'

Vogel stopped. He heard another train approaching.

'I'd carry on if I were you,' said Calloway, cocking his head in the direction of the train noise.

'He was talkative,' said Vogel. 'About why he came to Berlin.'

'He's a wall of death rider with a touring fairground,' said Calloway. 'Tell me something I don't know.' He tightened his grip on Vogel's lapels and lifted him. 'Train's coming.'

Vogel nodded, desperate. He blurted words as the rumble of the train approached.

'I told Baumann,' he said.

'Who's Baumann?' demanded Calloway, although there was something about the name that was familiar.

Vogel looked around him, as if checking they were alone.

'He buys information,' he said. 'Things the girls pick up, you know, from soldiers.'

'This man Baumann pays for intelligence?' said Calloway.

Vogel nodded. 'The men are drunk. They boast to the girls. The girls tell me. I tell Baumann. It's just business.'

The train was overhead. Calloway smacked Vogel against the pillar. Vogel screamed but no one heard.

'What kind of intelligence would Stan Deakin have? He rode a motorcycle with a fairground. What did you sell this Baumann?'

Vogel looked hesitant. Calloway cocked his head as if he could hear a train in the distance.

'It was something he was doing, here in Berlin,' said Vogel. 'Something he'd been asked to do for...'

Vogel hesitated.

'What was he doing? Who for?'

Calloway was shouting now. His words echoed under the viaduct. Something caught Vogel's eye. His head twitched sideways towards the street. Two policemen had stopped and were looking over towards the viaduct.

Vogel shouted. 'Help. Thief.'

The policemen came alert. They looked in the direction of the shouting. They ran towards the viaduct. One was unholstering his pistol.

Calloway let go of Vogel and ran. He ducked between the pillars of the viaduct and stumbled onto a bomb site behind it. It was a cleared site, with an open foreground lit by the half-moon above. Calloway ran towards the line of jagged building facades silhouetted against the sky at the edge of the site. He heard the rumble of boots fifty yards behind him.

One of the policemen shouted, 'Halt.'

Calloway reached the building facade and flattened himself against the walls. He was in deep shadow and he could see the police peering over, looking for him but not seeing him. He edged along until he found a doorway. It led to the remains of a basement. It stank of damp earth and rat piss. He scrambled down inside it. He tried to breath quietly, despite the heaving in his chest. The police were overhead. Their boots clunked over the rough ground above him. They were shouting, telling him to show himself. They found the entrance to the basement and shone their torches in. Light played on the charred walls. The policemen whispered between themselves. He sensed their reluctance to enter the basement, to risk being jumped by a thug with a knife or cosh. They debated whether to continue the search, whether it was worth it for a street thief. It was late after all and they were nearing the end of their shift. They agreed to give up the chase and he heard the sound of their boots retreat in the direction of the viaduct and onto the street behind it.

Calloway let out a big sigh.

'Stanley Deakin,' he said to himself. 'What the hell did you get yourself mixed up in?'

SEVENTEEN

He woke to the sound of knocking on his hotel room door. It was insistent. He climbed out of bed and opened the door. Pat pushed past him and entered the room. She looked him up and down.

'Sleeping in your clothes?' she said.

He looked down at his vest and suit trousers. 'It was a late night.'

He walked to the window and opened the curtains. Kurfürstendamm was bustling. People sat drinking coffee at cafe tables. Others peered keenly into the glass display cases that stood at intervals along the wide pavements, at cosmetics, lingerie or travel posters. Every other car that passed was a shining, egg-shaped Volkswagen. And amid the scene of happy prosperity, reminders of a troubled past. The one-legged street vendor, aged beyond his years, the ravages of war still showing on his face. Old men with hand carts, pulling meagre possessions along the street. The windowless facades of bombed-out buildings, marring the fashionable streetscape with their angry presence.

'Sit down,' she said. 'I've got something to show you.'

He stepped back from the window and sat next to her on the bed. He smelled her perfume. He liked the feeling it gave him.

'I did as you said,' she said. 'I found an excuse to borrow tools from Hannelore's toolkit, when she wasn't around.'

'So you found something?'

She shook her head. 'Nothing you wouldn't expect. But later in the evening I was redoing my make-up before the last show. My lipstick broke as I was applying it. I hadn't got another one with me so I went to Hannelore's trailer. I'd noticed she had a fancy looking make-up box, the proper show business type.' She reached into the pocket of her trousers. 'When I was rooting around inside I found this tucked in one of elasticated lipstick holders.'

It was silver and not much longer than a lipstick, with an aperture along one edge, two circular dials on top, with a small button protruding between them. Calloway took it and examined it. He'd seen something like it before.

'It's a camera,' he said. 'A Minox camera.'

Pat looked doubtful. 'A bit small for a camera.'

'That's the point,' said Calloway. 'Small enough to be concealed. I saw one during the war. We were working alongside the Special Operations Executive, who operated behind enemy lines clandestinely. Their agents were issued with cameras like this, to photograph documents, plans, that sort of thing.'

'Why would Hannelore have one?'

Calloway shook his head. 'I've no idea, but the longer I'm here, the more I'm coming to realise that there was more to Stan Deakin and his associates than motorcycle stunts.' He handed the Minox back to her. 'Do you reckon you could put this back where you found it? I don't want to set hares running.'

'Or stunt riders,' said Pat. She pocketed the camera. 'I'll find a way. I'm on my way up there now. We'll be getting some practice in. I'll put it back when Hannelore's riding the wall.'

They sat in silence for a moment on the unmade bed. He felt slovenly sitting there in his vest and trousers, the smell of the rank, bomb-site basement still on him. She turned and looked him in the eye.

'I hope Bert Webber's paying you enough,' she said.

'It's enough,' he said. 'But I'm not doing this for the money.'

He'd got other plans for that.

'What's your reason then?'

He thought for a moment and shrugged. 'Similar to yours, I suppose. I need the distraction.'

She gave him a sympathetic look. 'Life lacking a bit of sparkle?'

'It's not that,' he said. 'It's just that sometimes my head's not a good place to be. I need to keep busy.'

He'd not spoken like this to anyone about how he felt. The things he'd learned to do, to stop the bad memories filling the chasm in his soul. But he could talk to Pat. He was realising this, the more time he spent with her. A big part of him didn't like it. He shouldn't open up. Not to her, not to anyone. His business was his business, his burden to shoulder. Sharing it wasn't good for anyone.

'You need cheering up. Forget about Stan for the night. Come out with us.'

'Who's us?'

'Me, Milt, Hannelore, and Isaac and some of his men.'

'Isaac?'

'The American lieutenant we met on the parade ground. The one drilling the honour guard. He came to the show after all. He's got some tickets for tonight, to a club he knows.' She had a twinkle in her eye. She seemed excited. 'You'll never guess who's playing.'

When Pat had left, he took a bath and put on fresh clothes. Well, different clothes at least. His Berlin wardrobe was lacking, much like his London wardrobe for that matter. He decided to go for a walk. He needed to clear his head.

As he was leaving the building, the thin, sad-looking manageress stopped him.

'Herr Calloway,' she said. 'A gentleman called and left a message for you.'

She passed him a slip of hotel notepaper. The message was short.

I think we should talk. Meet me tomorrow evening at eight o'clock, Cafe Friedrich, Jägerstrasse, in the Soviet sector.

Franz Baumann

Vogel hadn't wasted time. He'd clearly been rattled enough by Calloway's questions get straight onto his contact who bought information from loose-lipped occupation soldiers.

'Did Herr Baumann call personally?' Calloway asked the manageress.

'Yes, Herr Calloway.'

'Can you describe him?'

Her face suggested she found the question odd. 'He was not a tall man like you, but not short either. He wore a loose overcoat, but I could see he was well-built beneath it. He had thick black eyebrows and a shaved head.'

Calloway pictured the man in his mind. The description had the same ring of familiarity as the name Baumann when he first heard it. But he couldn't place either.

'It was not a kind face.'

She said this as if it were purely a statement of fact, rather than a judgement. It was an odd postscript. Calloway thanked her and left.

He managed to waste the day. He made a trip to the zoo, which he found depressing. Then he killed a couple of hours at a small, newly-completed cinema called the KiKi, where he watched a new release called *Export in Blond*. It was about a young woman trafficked to Rio de Janeiro for auction. He thought it was lousy and couldn't help thinking of the hostesses at Vogel's club. He spent the rest of the afternoon back at Hotel Pension Ritz sleeping off the beers he'd drunk at a dingy bar after the film.

Pat called for him at nine. They took a cab to an address she had been given by the lieutenant called Isaac. When the cab pulled up, Pat said to the driver, 'Are you sure this is it?'

Calloway looked out of the taxi window. They had pulled up beside a cleared bomb site flanked by the remaining walls of the neighbouring buildings. The flank walls bore a familiar patchwork of mismatched wallpapers and paint colours, and the outline of rooms and stairways. They looked like a cross-section diagram that an infant had coloured in with chalks. There was a cleared path across the bomb site lit by festoon lights hanging from a rudimentary pergola which led to a small door in what Calloway assumed was the remainder of the bombed building.

The taxi driver, sensing their doubt, said, 'Yes, yes, this is the place. Most of it is gone, but the show must go on, eh?'

Pat paid him and gave him a handsome tip. She took Calloway's arm and walked with him to the door beyond the lights. They exchanged looks before entering. They were in a quiet part of the city, and this was not a typical entrance to a night spot.

Inside it was a different story. They got a friendly welcome from the doorman. Pat gave their names to a young woman behind the counter. She checked down the list and nodded with a smile. 'Please,' she said. 'Upstairs,' gesturing to the grand-looking staircase that led up towards the rhythmic beat of live music. The stairway was lit with candles, fixed with melted wax to the stone treads, casting a warm glow on the peeling paint work.

'It's a bit of a ruin,' said Pat. 'But the place has got something about it.'

Calloway agreed. In spite of its state of disrepair, the remains of this building were welcoming. They climbed the stairs, following the sound of the music. Pat gave his arm a squeeze.

'You're in for a treat,' she said.

Calloway wasn't convinced. The music emanating from the top of the building was jazz, not the classical music he liked.

A tall, relaxed-looking man in an ill-fitting tuxedo beckoned them towards a set of double doors. Calloway opened the door for Pat, and they both entered. Pat looked around the room with surprise and delight.

'I wasn't expecting this,' she said.

It was a *Spiegelsaal*. A mirrored ballroom with ornate decoration and chandeliers, dimly lit by candles on tables clustered in front of a small stage. Like the stairway that led to it, the grandeur was faded, with peeling paint and flaking plasterwork. But it exuded a warmth which engulfed the pair of them the moment they walked in. There was a band on stage, a small jazz orchestra, and its leader was a face that even Calloway recognised. He turned to Pat.

'Is that…?'

She beamed at him. 'Duke Ellington,' she said. 'It's a secret show, a warmup for his tour of Europe. Isaac has a friend at Radio Free Europe who heard about it on the grapevine.' Calloway looked around the room, through the haze of cigarette smoke. He saw Isaac and a couple of his men at a table with their dates, together with Hannelore and Milt. He and Pat pushed between the tightly-packed tables and joined them.

Isaac and his men stood and offered their seats. One of the men was dispatched to find more chairs. Isaac introduced three young German women, who dressed like the shoppers on Kurfürstendamm. Calloway spoke to them in German. They enthused about Duke Ellington. Pat looked over to the orchestra and turned to Isaac.

'I can't believe this,' she said. 'I can't believe it's really him.'

'What did I tell you?' said Isaac. 'Up close and in the flesh.'

They sat and Isaac poured them cheap German wine from one of the bottles on the table.

'You a jazz fan, Reg?' said Isaac.

'I need to be converted,' said Calloway.

Isaac laughed. 'If this doesn't convert you, nothing will.'

'Reg is a Philistine,' said Pat.

Calloway looked offended. He said, 'I enjoy the romantic composers.'

Isaac gave him an appreciative nod. 'A man of culture and taste,' he said. 'We just need to broaden your horizons a little.'

They watched the band and made idle chatter. The cheap wine relaxed Calloway. And he enjoyed the company of Isaac and his two fellow GIs. They traded the kind of stories that soldiers do. One of the men, a corporal called Joe, had been with an all-black tank battalion in the Ardennes, at the same time as Calloway's unit. Calloway remembered the battalion. It was a rare sight. Meeting Joe in a Berlin *Spiegelsaal* was one of those coincidences that happen with war. You meet a guy for the first time in peacetime and then realise he'd been in the next foxhole along from you, with the same hell raining down upon both of you. Although from the reports Calloway had heard, Joe's battalion rained a whole lot of hell of its own down on the enemy.

But Isaac and his friend had other stories. Stories that were beyond Calloway's experience of military life.

'America's a Jim Crow nation and the army's no different. We're here to promote democracy, but I tell you Reg, the army's as segregated as the Deep South. Forget democracy. We're peddling hypocrisy and the Germans know it.'

'And what do the Germans think?' said Calloway.

Isaac pulled his chair closer and leaned in. 'Here's the thing. Me and my men like it here. We like the people. Sure, there are Nazi die-hards who'll never appreciate us. But for the most part, a German posting is a pretty good thing. You won't catch me getting homesick for the South.'

He looked around the room and smiled. Calloway hadn't noticed the number of black occupation troops in the audience.

'You don't see whites-only signs in Germany,' he said. 'We go where we want, and we drink with who we want. The only people stopping us are our fellow Americans, when they decide we're not welcome some place. That's when the slurs fly and the batons come out.'

'Does that happen?'

Isaac nodded with a hint of solemnity. 'Oh yeah, that happens.'

Calloway felt Pat's hand on his arm. She leaned forward shouted into his ear.

'Go and speak to Hannelore, will you? Milt is boring the pants off her with shop talk.'

They swapped seats and Calloway ordered more wine from a waiter that was weaving his way between the packed tables. Hannelore was more relaxed than the first time they spoke. She was leaning back enjoying the band, one arm slung across the hooped back of her chair and the other raised high, with a cigarette between her fingers. She wore a long-sleeved dress, her vibrant red hair styled in a soft, full pompadour. She reminded him of Greer Garson.

'I like this place,' she said, nodding her head to the music.

'It's a shame Stan's not here,' said Calloway. 'I reckon he'd like this too.'

'Stan likes other kinds of places.'

The wine arrived and Calloway topped up her glass.

'It strikes me that you didn't like Stan.'

'We didn't click,' she said.

‘I think there was more to it,’ said Calloway. ‘I think Stan found something you didn’t want him to see. Something from your toolkit, which you then hid in your make-up box alongside your lipsticks.’

She turned her head slowly to face him. ‘Aren’t you the curious one,’ she said, taking a sip of her wine. ‘I shall have to start locking my trailer.’

She looked back towards the band, who were finishing a number. The crowd applauded, some whooped. Their leader stepped forward from the piano and announced the next number. He described it as part three of a jazz symphony. This caught Calloway’s attention. It was the musical language he understood. A trumpet player stood and played a lazy refrain which built to a taught climax, then the orchestra joined with a relaxed but confident swing. Calloway’s ear wasn’t attuned to the style but he had to admit you couldn’t fault the quality. He’d always dismissed jazz as glib and immature. The music he was hearing had a level of sophistication that challenged his snobbery. He was not quite a convert, but a barrier had fallen. Pat caught his eye. Her expression said, *See? I told you.*

Hannelore brought him back to earth. She said, ‘So, I have a camera? What of it? I take photographs for my album.’

‘People take photos for their albums with a box brownie, not a miniature camera designed to be concealed. Where did you get a camera like that?’

She took a drag on her cigarette and blew smoke above his head. ‘It was a gift, from a British officer I worked with when I was a translator. We dated for a while. I liked him. I liked him a lot. He was a nice man.’ She sipped her wine. ‘But he was married.’

She turned to face him again. ‘Would you like any more episodes from my life story?’

‘Perhaps,’ he said. ‘I’m certainly wondering about you. I worked in intelligence during the war, like I said. I was in field security. One of my jobs was to sort the bad Germans from the good. We compiled lists. Blacklists and whitelists, based on information from our sources. The blacklist was for the Nazis, the SS and the Gestapo. The whitelist was for the ones we trusted, the ones who checked out. You needed to be on it to get a job with the British occupation forces. I'm interested in what qualified you for the whitelist.'

She sighed as if his question was tiresome but she would tolerate it, just this once. She unbuttoned her cuff and pulled her sleeve back.

Calloway turned cold. He recognised the tattoo on the inside of her arm. He'd seen enough of them for one lifetime and very few of them on the living.

'You were in the camps?' he said.

She looked at him as if he was stating the obvious.

'Dachau,' she said. 'Nazi population policy extended to fairground folk which, as a wall rider with a fairground, extended to me.'

Calloway felt uncomfortable. It was hard to find things to say when presented with such a difficult truth.

'I was with an army unit that liberated a camp,' he said. 'I saw it first-hand.'

She stared into his eyes, as if reaching into his soul. 'As a liberator,' she said. 'Not as a prisoner. There is a difference.'

After that, they watched the band in silence. Pat looked over, sensing the tension. She gave Calloway a questioning look. He shrugged it off. Calloway lost himself in the music. He let it speak to him. He needed the distraction. Denton, Hannelore, Vogel and now a man called Baumann. Stan's story was clouded and obscure. He was involved in something bad, Calloway knew that much.

The band finished the number and the audience showed noisy appreciation. Calloway tried to pour more wine but the bottle was empty. He sat up and looked around the room for a waiter but he couldn't see one. What he could see was the woman in the sunglasses and peep-toe heels he'd seen at Cafe Wien. She was seated at a nearby table, her long legs outstretched, and she was looking right at him.

EIGHTEEN

A sign told him he was leaving the British sector. Ahead of him a Soviet flag flew above the Brandenburg gate. It had been there since 1945. A British army scout car was positioned at the border between the two sectors. A military policeman in a red cap peered into the Soviet zone through binoculars.

'What's happening?' said Calloway to the redcap.

The soldier looked down from the small turret of the scout car and gave a weary sigh.

'Not much, pal. Just a bit of tension over there. A strike by some of the workers over conditions. More people's police on the street and Ivans lurking in the shadows.'

'Safe for a visit? A bit of sightseeing?' said Calloway.

The redcap nodded. 'You can walk straight through the gate. Just mind yourself when you're over there. The authorities might be a bit twitchy about foreigners.'

Cars were passing freely through the gate, directed by traffic police on each side, wearing their respective uniforms. Pedestrians walked casually through beside the traffic. Calloway thanked the redcap and walked eastwards across the wide-open stretch of Charlottenburger Chaussee.

Two *Volkspolizei* eyed him as he passed under the gate. They wore murky, field grey uniforms, German in cut but styled with the peasant utility of the Soviet military. Behind them, the expressionless faces of three red army soldiers stared through the windscreen of a Gaz jeep parked at the entrance to Unter den Linden. Calloway saw the machine pistols on their laps as he passed.

He walked along Unter den Linden beside the newly-planted

saplings, there to replace the mature lime trees, from which the boulevard took its name. The old limes had been removed by Hitler to make way for grandiose Nazi parades. The new limes might have symbolised East Germany's rebirth under socialism. To Calloway they just looked sad.

The Soviet sector bore the same scars of allied bombing and Soviet artillery bombardment as the western sectors, but the pace of restoration seemed slower. For every repaired or replaced building there were two that stood derelict amid piles of rubble. Lines of women in pinafores, as if straight from the kitchen, passed buckets of debris hand to hand to others who lined the pavements chipping mortar off the bricks, preparing them for reuse. *Trümmerfrauen*, they called them. Calloway remembered them from his last trip here. In the western sectors this work had passed to commercial contractors. In the east, these 'rubble women' still cleared sites by hand for the equivalent of fourpence ha'penny an hour.

He turned off the main drag onto a side street, following directions the hotel manageress had given him. The manageress knew the restaurant Baumann had suggested. 'It was once good,' she had said with a snort, as if dismissing it as no longer relevant, being inside the Soviet sector and therefore below a standard acceptable in the west.

It was a grand street, or had been, with bold Wilhelmine architecture that echoed the ornate, stone-faced Victorian buildings of London. Every doorway and window was peppered with bullet holes from the furious street fighting of the final days of the war. No attempt had been made to repair or conceal these blemishes. They were worn like duelling scars on aristocratic faces.

Cafe Friedrich was a double-fronted restaurant on the ground floor of one of the buildings. It had an awning and tables outside, in spite of the autumn chill. Diners sat wearing overcoats, none of them smiling. Whether this was due to the cold weather or the restaurant's lack of ambiance, Calloway couldn't say. A stocky man in his thirties with a shaved head sat alone at a table for two. He was toying with a coffee cup and reading *Neues Deutschland*, the Soviet approved newspaper of the east. Stalin's face covered half the front page. Baumann furrowed his thick black eyebrows as he read. He looked up when Calloway approached his table.

'Herr Calloway,' he said. It was a statement, not a question.

Calloway nodded.

'Herr Baumann,' he said.

The man's face was familiar, just as his name had been when Calloway had first heard it from Vogel. He was sure he had never met this man in his life, but he recognised him. There was a connection between them that Calloway couldn't place. It nagged at him.

Baumann gestured to the empty chair.

'I hope you've brought an appetite,' he said, in German. 'The pork knuckle here is very good.'

Calloway glanced over at the other tables, where diners were tucking in to mean portions of insipid-looking food. Baumann pushed a menu towards him.

'Order. Then we can talk.'

Calloway ordered *jägerschnitzel* and a glass of *Radeberger* beer from a waiter, who nodded, just managing a polite smile from his dull, colourless face.

Their food arrived quickly. It was lukewarm. Set dishes plated up until they were ordered. Baumann pushed a serviette into the collar of his shirt and tucked in. He ate noisily. Between mouthfuls he said, 'Why are you in Berlin, Herr Calloway?'

'I'm with the travelling fairground.'

Baumann laughed. 'You don't look the type.'

'What were you expecting?'

'Oh, I don't know. A clown costume at the very least.'

'I'm no clown.'

Baumann thought for a moment. 'No, you're smart and inquisitive, at least from what I've heard. And quite violent.'

'Your friend Vogel's been talking. How is his head by the way?'

'Sore, I imagine. You use the interview techniques of a secret policeman.'

'How would you know? Are you a secret policeman?'

Baumann had the whiff of an official about him. A man enjoying the sanction of his role, his license to probe and pry, perhaps to coerce. He moved his shaved head from side to side as if weighing up the question.

'I'm just a man who is interested in what goes on in this city.'

Baumann's accent was curious, one that Calloway couldn't place. It wasn't a Berlin accent.

'Go and talk to Herr Vogel,' said Calloway. 'He seems like a mine of information. Especially if there's a price on it.'

Baumann smiled.

'Vogel is just a friend. I was concerned to hear that you had caused him some...' He paused as if searching for the word. 'Inconvenience,' he said. 'I'm interested in his wellbeing. You, clearly, are not.'

'Vogel is a grubby parasite that runs a strip club with a brothel above it. I couldn't care less about his wellbeing. What I do care about is how my friend Stan Deakin fits into the picture. Vogel knows more than he told me. I suspect you do too. You buy intelligence. What intelligence did you buy from Vogel? What did Vogel's hostesses tease out Stan that was so interesting to you?'

Baumann gave a theatrical shrug. 'I don't remember. I hear so much tittle tattle.'

'You remember. You're the type that remembers everything.'

Baumann looked up from his plate and gave Calloway a knowing smile. It said he knew but wasn't telling.

Calloway said, 'What's the accent? You don't speak like a Berliner. You don't have any German accent I recognise.'

'You've met a lot of Germans?' said Baumann.

'I was here at the end of the war, with the British army. Yes, I got to talk to a lot of Germans. There's a reason I sound like a secret policeman.'

Baumann smiled. 'Then we are not so dissimilar.'

'So where are you from, Baumann? I'm curious.'

'I've moved around. How's the *jägerschnitzel*?

'Less than satisfying. Like the answers you're giving me.'

'I think it would be best if you stopped asking questions, Herr Calloway. In fact, I think it would be best if you were to leave

Berlin. I'm sure your fairground can survive without you, whatever it is you are supposed to be doing there.'

'That sounds like a threat.'

Baumann scraped the last of the flesh off the pork knuckle with his fork. 'Not so much a threat as a firm suggestion.'

Calloway downed the last of his beer and rose to leave.

'Thanks for the lunch,' he said. 'I'll leave Berlin when I've got some answers. Not before, and certainly not because of any firm suggestion from you.'

Baumann smiled and spoke in English. 'Alright cocker, have it your way,' he said, in a perfect Midlands accent.

NINETEEN

The hotel manageress was anxious to see him. She scuttled over from the reception desk as he appeared at the top of the stairway.

'Telegram, Herr Calloway,' she said holding a folded piece of paper in her hand. She passed it to him and waited while he read it. It was from Bert Webber. It was four words long: *They have taken Vera.*

'They' meaning the man called Denton and his colleague that claimed to be a doctor, Calloway assumed. He tore up the telegram and stuffed the pieces in his pocket. The manageress hovered at his side, expectant for news. He turned his back on her and went to his room.

The *jägerschnitzel* lay heavy on his stomach. He felt queasy and jittery. Baumann had unsettled him. The name, the face and the accent. All familiar to him but a million miles from his grasp right now. And he was no closer to understanding what Stan had been mixed up in. It was something serious, he knew that much. Something Vogel was too scared to spill. Something that got Calloway followed, by Denton in London and by the woman in the sunglasses in Berlin. He was convinced her appearance at the Ellington concert wasn't a coincidence. His radar was good like that. He'd had a career in intelligence based on suspicions. They had proved right more times than not. And now, this character Baumann wanted him out of the way. A man who frequented the Soviet sector, read a Soviet-sponsored newspaper and acted like he owned the city. An Englishman too, or near as dammit, which just added to Calloway's unease.

Then there was Hannelore. A displaced victim of the Nazis who sought refuge in Britain, or a snoop with a spy camera? The jury was still out on Hannelore in the courthouse of his befuddled mind.

He lay on the bed staring at the ceiling, letting the sounds of the Ku'damm wash over him, a soothing soundtrack of near normality in this anything but normal city. He wanted to sleep but he couldn't settle. He crossed to the wash basin and splashed water on his face. The man who stared back at him in the mirror looked tired and drawn. He picked up the half-drunk bottle of Bismarck from the bedside table and poured a big slug in his tooth mug. Medicinal, he told himself.

He flagged a taxi on Ku'damm and told the driver to take him to the barracks. It was mid-afternoon and they'd be getting ready for the early show in the drome. He held out his papers to the snowdrop at the gate and got a business-like nod in return.

'I hope you're feeling better, sir,' the MP said. It was the driver from the patrol that pulled him from the clutches of Vogel's goons.

'Yes, thanks,' said Calloway, ignoring the ache in his ribs and gut. 'I owe you a drink.'

'All part of the service,' the MP said, smiling. 'You take care now.'

Nice guy, he thought. A Southerner by his accent. Then he remembered what Isaac had told him.

'When they decide you're not welcome some place, that's when the slurs fly and the batons come out.'

He crossed the parade ground and walked past the motor pool towards the training field. He heard motorcycle engines as he approached the drome.

Hannelore was working on her bike by the side of the drome. She looked up as Calloway approached.

'Have you come to search my trailer again, Reg?'

'No, but I need some answers. Straight ones. You need to level with me.'

'For someone who claims to be a mechanic, you sound more like a policeman.'

'I'm not a policeman. I'm not an official, or a soldier. I couldn't care less about sectors, or politics, or armies of occupation. I'm just a friend of Stan's family and I want the truth. You're hiding something.'

She threw down the wrench. 'This is ridiculous.'

'It's not ridiculous. It's deadly serious. Stanley Deakin is dead.' This caught her attention but didn't seem to surprise her. 'All the signs point to him being killed in Berlin. I need to know why. For what it's worth, I don't think you killed him. I've met enough killers to know the sort. But you know something you're not telling. And that might just be where the truth lies. I need the truth right now, because there's some people out there making it very clear they don't want me to find it. Don't be one of them. Level with me. You have my word I'll not cause trouble for you.'

She pulled a pack of cigarettes from the pocket of her jodhpurs and took the lighter from inside her boot. She lit up and took a long hard drag.

'You need to leave Berlin,' she said.

'Another threat,' he said. 'That's the second I've had today.'

'Not a threat. Just advice. This isn't the city to go prying. You mean well, Reg, I can see that. But you need to leave things be. It's not safe here.' She glanced behind her towards the sound of the motorcycle. 'Not safe for you or for Pat.'

'Then the sooner I get some answers, the sooner we can go home.'

'Answers about what?' she said.

'About what you're up to. An American officer told me a woman had been poking her nose around the barracks, in restricted areas, claiming she was lost. A woman whose description sounded a lot like you. That in itself wouldn't be remarkable were it not for the fact that you keep a Minox camera in your make-up box.' She fixed him with a look of defiance but beneath it he saw anxiety. He'd struck a nerve. He played a hunch. 'Are you selling information to Franz Baumann? Was Stan Deakin your go-between?'

'Who is Franz Baumann?' she said. The question sounded genuine.

'A man who pays for information. A man who bought information that originated from Stan.'

'I don't know this Baumann and I don't know what you're talking about.'

'Perhaps you don't. But there was more between you and Stan Deakin than you're owing up to.'

She picked up the wrench and returned to working on the bike. 'I don't have time for this.'

He felt a hand on his shoulder. It was Milt Harper.

'Are you distracting my star attraction when she's got work to do?' he said with a smile.

'Just chewing the fat,' said Calloway.

'Go see what the lady Pat is up to. She's working on something good.'

There was no point staying. Hannelore wasn't going to say any more with Milt there. Calloway was half-convinced by her denials. But only half.

He climbed the stairs to the gallery at the top of the drome. Pat was high on the wall, riding backwards with no hands. She gave him a small nod of acknowledgement. She swivelled in the seat and straightened her legs so that she was standing on the footrest, then bent forward, gripped the seat with her hands and flung her legs upwards to perform a head stand. The motorcycle trembled with the movement. Calloway felt a pang of anxiety. Pat adjusted her balance and let the bike circle the wall three times before sitting back into the saddle. She cocked her head and gave him a wink. Calloway clapped his hands and shouted, 'Bravo.' He forgot Baumann, Vogel and Hannelore in that moment. Watching Pat was exhilarating. She gave a small bow as she descended the wall onto the circular ramp below it. Calloway descended the stairs and met her by the exit hatch of the drome. She pulled out her hip flask and took a nip.

'Steadies the nerves,' she said, offering him the flask.

'You're a bloody maniac,' he said, taking a slug of the liquor.

'Living dangerously is not without its thrills,' she said. She was trembling with excitement.

'I wish I could agree. People keep telling me Berlin is a dangerous place, but I'm not getting much of a thrill.'

The light was fading and the festoon bulbs of the fairground sideshows twinkled. They cast a warm glow over the barrack blocks at the perimeter of the training field. Pat took his arm.

'Let's walk,' she said. 'I need to do something to stop my legs shaking.'

'I need to see Vogel again,' he said.

'The clip joint owner?'

He nodded. 'I'm getting nothing out of Hannelore and I've been warned off by a man called Baumann, who Vogel peddles information to.'

'What kind of information?'

'Titbits from loose-lipped soldiers.'

He offered her a cigarette and lit one for both of them. 'Vogel's the weak link,' he said. 'I need to break it.'

A man who goes scuttling off to his paymaster at the first sign of trouble is a weak man. An anxious man. The kind of man that will break if you apply enough pressure. Baumann would never give Calloway the answer. Vogel was his best chance of finding out what Stan had been involved in and how he had died.

Calloway looked at his watch. 'I'm going to miss your big performance.'

She shrugged and smiled. 'You've had a private view.'

He leaned forward and kissed her cheek. 'Break a leg.'

'Try not to do the same. But if you do, make sure it's someone else's.'

He took a taxi to Potsdamer Strasse and a found a bar which served food. He ordered beer with a schnapps chaser, and bratwurst with sauerkraut and *kartofelsalad*. The food was better than the bar's appearance implied. There were British soldiers at the counter, chatting up two young German women, although in this neighbourhood it was probably the other way around and there would be a price involved. He managed to kill an hour and a half. He checked his watch, paid the barman and walked out of the bar. The street was alive with the kind of life you'd expect in a red-light district. Servicemen of three nationalities in various states of inebriation. Maître d's lurking in doorways, luring their prey into overpriced fleshpots. Street walkers on the corners, underdressed for the chill autumn night, hopping from foot to foot to keep warm.

The neon signage of Club Continentale bathed one end of the street in a wash of sleazy red. The pig farmer was minding the door. Calloway turned up the lapels of his trench coat to conceal the lower part of his face. He pulled his hat down low over his eyes.

The pig farmer was looking in the opposite direction. Two randy-looking American soldiers were hovering ten yards up the street, summoning the courage to enter the club. The pig farmer gave his best attempt at a beckoning smile. It fell flat and the soldiers disappeared. He shrugged and lit a cigarette. He hadn't noticed Calloway sidle up to him.

The first blow bent the pig farmer double. The second floored him. He slumped in the doorway. Calloway dragged his unconscious body inside and dumped it in an alcove where punters' coats hung from a wooden pole. Calloway threw one of the coats over the unconscious doorman. He entered the door into the main room of the club. There was no sign of pig face, just a skinny barman and half-a-dozen punters showing more enthusiasm than the act on the stage deserved. Calloway crossed the darkened room as if to take one of the tables, then ducked through the door that led to Vogel's office. Two women eyed him from the open door of the dressing room. One wore a harem veil and translucent pants, the other had just left the stage and was naked, save for her shoes and a feather boa. Calloway said good evening, like he was supposed to be there. He opened the door at the end of the corridor.

Vogel was behind his desk. Pig face sat in the chair opposite, reading the sports pages of a Berlin newspaper. Both men looked up. A look of consternation spread over Vogel's face, then turned to fear. Pig face rose from the chair. Before he'd straightened up, Calloway grabbed the heavy glass ash tray from the desk and smashed it over the doorman's head. Pig face fell back in the chair unconscious.

'Time for another talk, Vogel,' said Calloway. Vogel looked towards the door. 'Your other little friend is taking a nap too, in case you were wondering.'

Vogel pulled one of the desk drawers open. Calloway reached over and grabbed him by the wrist. He slammed Vogel's hand down onto the desk. A small automatic pistol fell onto the desktop. Calloway took it and flipped off the safety catch. He pointed it at Vogel.

'I should sit down if I were you.' He nodded to the bottle of PX whisky on the desk. 'Pour yourself one of those. You're going to need it.'

TWENTY

'Who does Baumann work for?'

Vogel stared at the gun in Calloway's hand. His face was frozen. His last encounter with this big stranger was proof enough of just how ruthless the man could be. He went to speak, then hesitated as if weighing up who he was more afraid of, Calloway or Baumann. He picked up his glass and downed the whisky in one gulp.

Calloway nodded to the bottle. 'Be my guest, if it helps loosen your tongue.'

Vogel picked up the bottle. His hand was shaking. Without his two goons, he was nothing. Pig face lay unconscious in the chair, a trickle of blood running down his fleshy face from the blow of the ashtray.

'Let's try again. Who does Baumann work for?'

Vogel shook his head. 'I don't know. He just buys information.'

'Who's he buy it for? The Americans, the British, the Russians?'

'I don't know, honestly.'

His voice was trembling. He was sweating. He was also lying.

Calloway glanced around the room. There was a small sofa against the wall to the side of Vogel's desk. He crossed the room and picked up one of the cushions. He smothered the pistol with it and fired two rounds into Vogel's desktop. Vogel jumped. He spilled his drink. What remained of the colour drained from his face. Calloway gave him a satisfied look.

'No one will hear,' he said.

Vogel blurted, 'You won't kill me.'

'You're right, I won't. Well at least not to start with. I'll put a bullet through your shoulder first. That will hurt, but not half as much as the one I'll put through your kneecap. You'll wish you were dead after that.'

Calloway waited. He said nothing, just looked Vogel full in the face. Vogel breathed heavily. He reached for the cigarette box on the desk. Calloway shook his head.

'Speak first,' he said.

Vogel took a deep breath. 'Baumann's an ex-Nazi who works for East German security. A branch called the Administration for the Struggle Against Suspicious Persons. He keeps a watch on foreigners from the west.' Vogel took a gulp of the whisky and forced a wry smile. 'He wouldn't be the first Nazi thug to sell out to the Communists.'

A former Nazi thug with a perfect English accent.

The realisation hit Calloway like a truck. He knew Baumann. He knew his story. He'd recognised the name and the face but couldn't place them until now. He reached across the desk and took a slug of whisky from the bottle.

'Why was an East German spy catcher interested in Stan Deakin?' he said.

'Your friend Deakin was shooting his mouth off one night. Trying to impress the girls. He said he was a British agent who was here to crack a spy ring.'

Calloway laughed. 'Deakin was a truck driver who moonlighted for a fairground. The most he could crack was a dirty joke.'

He was speaking of Stan in the past tense. Vogel was either too scared to notice, or it was a fact he already knew.

'All I know is what the girls told me. I sold the information to Baumann.'

'Then what did you do?'

Vogel was wrong-footed by the question. He hesitated. He stared at Calloway as if trying to read him, to understand the motive behind the question.

'What do you mean?' he said.

'Come off it, Vogel. We both know Stan Deakin is dead. Did

you kill him?'

Vogel paused for a moment. He composed himself. 'Why would I kill him?' He took a sip of the whisky. 'I'm not a killer, Herr Calloway.'

Calloway nodded at the bouncer slumped in the chair. 'I bet he is, given half a chance. Him and his pal tried to kick the life out of me.'

'It was only meant as a warning. When dealing with a man like Baumann, it's best to avoid complications. I just wanted you away the club.'

'It didn't feel like a warning,' said Calloway, taking another swig from the bottle. He heard sounds from the corridor outside. Heavy footsteps getting louder.

The door opened behind him. The pig farmer piled into the room. He pulled Calloway out the chair and hit him hard in the face. Calloway recoiled from the blow. The crack of a pistol shot echoed off the walls. The farmer clutched his arm. Calloway smelled the cordite from the gun in his hand. He felt Vogel's arm around his neck. He jabbed his elbow back into the club owner's guts. Vogel groaned and fell back in the chair. The pig farmer took another swing but missed. Calloway struck him with the butt of the pistol. The farmer reeled. His legs buckled. Calloway ran through the door and down the corridor. The women in the dressing room saw the gun in his hand. One grabbed the other and pulled her away. He crossed the main room of the club towards the exit doors. The music was loud. There was a stripper on stage reaching the climax of her routine. Punters wolf whistled. Calloway pushed through the double doors into the lobby, pocketed the gun and stepped out onto the street.

He stood for a moment in the glow of the neon, catching his breath. A car pulled up and two men got out. They were broad-shouldered and ugly, wearing cheap ill-fitting suits.

'Herr Calloway,' one of the men said.

Before Calloway could reply, he felt a sharp blow across his neck. He stumbled on the kerb. Hands grabbed him and bundled him into the back seat of the car. Someone stuck a gun in his ribs.

‘I told you to leave Berlin, Mr Calloway, for your own good.’

It was Baumann. His two thugs climbed back in the car. Baumann nodded to the driver through the rear-view mirror. The driver floored the accelerator. The car shot forward, its tyres screeching. Calloway looked out of the window. Heads turned. One of the onlookers caught his eye. She was standing in the shadows at the corner of a side street, a look of shock her face. Calloway recognised her. It was the woman with the sunglasses and the peep-toe heels.

TWENTY-ONE

Calloway sat in silence. He knew better than to ask Baumann where they were going. It wasn't going to be another indigestible meal, he'd figured that much. They drove east, slowing as they crossed into the Soviet sector, getting a nod from the two uniformed *Volkspolizei* at the border. The car was clearly known to the border police. They crossed a bridge over the Spree, with its rusting barges and ink-black water, and sped down a darkened side road. The road narrowed, the carcasses of bombed-out buildings seeming to close in on the car. What little street lighting there was cast more shadow than light and only served to make the surroundings more ominous. The silence in the car was more threatening than any words Baumann might have spoken. Calloway's mind raced. The sour taste of fear filled his mouth. He knew how this story ended. He needed to act. There was a sharp bend ahead. The car would need to slow. He remembered his parachute training, jumping off a moving truck at thirty miles an hour onto hard ground. It was a damn fool idea, but he hadn't the time to think up a better one. He grabbed the door handle and yanked it, throwing the full weight of his big frame against the door.

He hit the road surface side-on and rolled into the gutter. His already bruised ribs erupted into pain. He scrambled to his feet, the leather soles of his shoes struggling to grip on the well-worn cobblestones. The car skidded to a halt and he heard the sound of its doors opening. Baumann was shouting.

Calloway stumbled over brick rubble between the facades of two windowless buildings. The passageway led to a courtyard, surrounded on four sides by what had once been a tall apartment block, four or five stories high. Now they were just shells. He darted into one of the doorways and up a flight of dark, communal stairs. The stairs led to a landing beyond which was a void. The entire rear wall of the block was missing, the jagged edge of the first floor leading to a twenty-foot drop. The remainder of the stairway had been destroyed. He couldn't go higher. There was a door to his left, a high apartment door hanging loosely by a single hinge. He pushed past the door and into the hallway of the apartment. The rooms to his right were missing, their doorways opening onto thin air. He took a door to the left, into a room the size of a generous bedroom. It stank of damp and brick dust. Two tall, glassless windows looked onto the courtyard below. Through the gloom he could see Baumann and his two heavies. They were all holding pistols. Baumann gave instructions. The three men split up, each taking a block to search. Baumann was heading towards the stairway Calloway had just ascended.

The sound of Baumann's feet crunching broken glass echoed around the empty shell of the building. Calloway flattened himself against the wall beside the door of the room. He pulled Vogel's pistol from his pocket. Baumann's goons had been fools not to search him. Calloway heard footsteps entering the apartment. He breathed small, shallow breaths, trying his hardest not to be heard. It was hard. His chest was heaving, his heart pounding. He could hear Baumann checking the adjacent room, then re-enter the hallway. He braced himself. The nose of Baumann's pistol appeared in the doorway, then his forearm. Calloway grabbed his arm and yanked it. He struck Baumann's wrist with the edge of his hand. The pistol fell to the floor. Calloway kicked it away. He slammed Baumann's head against the wall. Baumann lost his footing. Calloway shoved him to the far end of the room and levelled the pistol at him.

'Don't make a sound,' he said. From across the courtyard he could hear the goons searching the other blocks floor by floor.

Baumann spoke in German. 'You fire that pistol, my men will be here in seconds. You won't know what's hit you.'

'I've been hit enough lately not to care.'

'Then shoot me now and get it done with,' said Bauman. He looked at Calloway and grinned. 'Or don't you have the guts?'

Calloway levelled the pistol at Baumann's chest. 'You're going to talk to me first,' he said. 'After that, I might just let you go.'

Baumann scoffed. 'Why should I talk to you?'

'Because I know your story, Baumann. I know who you are.'

Baumann sneered. 'You know nothing about me.'

'Oh, believe me I do. You see I had the misfortune to meet a friend of yours a year or so back. He was a speedway rider who went by the name of Ray Simpkins.'

Baumann was suddenly alert. 'Yes, I thought that might get your attention,' said Calloway. 'I was head of security at the speedway stadium where Simpkins raced. He was being blackmailed. I was asked to look into it. Another rider had photographs you see. Photographs from an old wartime album. You were in those photos. You, Simpkins and a third man called Wood. You were soldiers. Soldiers with skulls on your caps.'

Baumann looked towards the window. 'You'd better finish your story, Herr Calloway. My men will come looking for me soon.'

'You can quit with the German. You're as German as I am. You're British and your real name's Belper. You, Simpkins and Wood were members of the Britische Freikorps, a volunteer unit recruited into the Waffen SS. You were a fascist and a traitor. Your name rang a bell when you left the note at my hotel. When I met you I recognised your face. It took me a while to figure out where from. I've seen the photographs of your exploits during the war. They were in the album being used to blackmail Simpkins. They weren't pretty, believe me.'

Baumann seemed to relax now the truth was out. 'War isn't pretty.'

'No, but your war was uglier than it's possible to be. You're a sick bastard, Baumann. You're lucky you didn't face a war crimes trial. You were lucky you were picked up by our intelligence services.'

Baumann raised an eyebrow.

'Yes,' said Calloway, 'I know about that too. I know the story.

They let you settle in the East as a German called Baumann, let you embed yourself in a nice cushy job within East German state security. You've been their man on the inside ever since.'

Baumann looked incredulous. 'How can you possibly know that?'

'Ray Simpkins wasn't our only mutual friend. I know Sammy Mackay too.'

This startled Baumann. 'Sammy was my old commanding officer,' said Calloway. 'He's now a spook. You're one of his assets.'

Baumann gave Calloway a look of grudging respect. 'It seems you are a step ahead of me.'

'I can blow your cover, Baumann. Just one phone call to a Stasi informant line and you'll be digging salt in Siberia for the rest of your life.'

Baumann was silent. He was thinking.

'So what do you want?' he said.

'I want to know how Stan Deakin died.'

Baumann gave a dismissive wave of his hand. 'Deakin was a fool. He was shooting his mouth off. He was causing trouble for everyone. Vogel's men killed him.'

'Why Vogel's men?'

'Because I told them to. It was tidier that way. In my position the last thing you need is a loudmouth that knows a little too much.'

Baumann looked towards the window again. The sound of the two other men searching the blocks was closer now.

'There's still a few more floors to go,' said Calloway. Now that he had Baumann, he should have asked more questions about Stan's death. What Baumann had told him was half an explanation. But Calloway was remembering the worst of the photographs. He couldn't shake the image from his head. It was taken in a forest somewhere in Central Europe. Simpkins, Wood and Baumann stood in a line, their pistols pointing at the heads of three kneeling figures. Two men and a young boy.

'Tell me,' said Calloway, 'what's it like to kill a child?'

Baumann seemed emboldened by the question. He appeared

to almost welcome the opportunity to give an answer. He gave Calloway a satisfied smile and composed himself.

'You make them kneel, facing away from you,' he said. 'It's how you dominate. They must recognise your superiority. You don't want to see the fear on their faces or hear their prayers. That would be...' he grappled for a word. 'Inelegant,' he said. 'It would detract from the ceremony of the act.' He looked down at his palm. 'The pistol feels good in your hand. As you squeeze the trigger the full force of your power is concentrated in your fist. You squeeze hard. You feel it. A tingle of excitement spreading through your fingers, your arms, down through your heart, your belly. It's almost sexual. In that moment your superiority is proven.'

Baumann took a long, slow breath, then continued.

'It's good to see them dead, face down and lifeless. All your bad, painful, awkward childhood memories dying with them in that moment.'

Baumann gazed into space, as if transported back to the times he was describing. Calloway could barely believe what he was hearing. The man was deranged.

'I don't like children,' Baumann said. 'Their milky smell, their soft cheeks, their careless, unkempt hair. Vulnerable, powerless and dumb.' He paused as if something had just occurred to him. 'Some survive the first shot. They lie there twitching on the ground.' He made a pistol with his thumb and forefinger and levelled it at a spot on the floor. 'You deliver the coup de grace in a single elegant move. Like a noble duellist, in your fine uniform. You light a cigarette and inhale with satisfaction. Your brothers offer congratulations and you share their sick jokes as they point at the bodies. One will have a camera, capturing the kill as a trophy. Then,' he said, 'you turn and leave. There are lesser men to drag away the corpses and sweat to dig their graves.'

Calloway pointed the pistol at Baumann's head and fired two bullets into his brain.

TWENTY-TWO

Baumann's heavies burst into the room. They grabbed Calloway by the arms and wrenched the pistol from his hand. Only then did they notice the body on the floor. Blood trickled from two clean holes in Baumann's forehead.

There was no fight left in Calloway. The heavies dragged him down the stairway, across the courtyard and out into the street towards the car. They bundled him into the back seat. One of them took handcuffs from his pocket and chained Calloway's wrists. He pushed the barrel of his pistol into Calloway's ribs. Calloway barely felt it. He was numb.

They drove for fifteen minutes, heading further east. The heavy behind the wheel pulled the car up outside the pockmarked facade of an old office building. The new East German flag hung limply from a pole above the doorway. They dragged Calloway up the steps and through the double doors. It was bright inside. The brightness of officialdom, like a police station. A uniformed officer nodded at the heavies from behind a tall reception desk, as if the appearance of a bloodied man in handcuffs was not unusual in this place. The heavies pushed Calloway through another set of doors and dragged him down a corridor. The overhead lights flickered. There were stairs at the end, leading downwards to a basement. Calloway stumbled on the steps as they descended. His legs were weak and he felt lightheaded. There was an iron gate at the bottom with a uniformed guard outside it. The guard acknowledged the heavies and unlocked the door with a key from a big ring on his belt. The clank of the key in the lock echoed off the painted brick walls. The heavies led Calloway through the gate and the uniformed guard locked it behind them. They pushed Calloway into a darkened cell and slammed the door.

The cell stank of stale sweat and urine. The smell of fear. Calloway groped in the darkness and found a hard wood bench along one wall. He lay on it, shivering.

He slept fitfully for perhaps an hour. The cell was cold. He pulled his jacket tighter around him. His eyes adjusted to the darkness. He made out a slash of dim light from under the door. There were voices in the corridor outside, then the flick of a switch. A bulkhead light filled the cell with a dazzling glare. Calloway squinted. The light hurt his eyes. He heard the slide of bolts. The door opened. Two men stepped in, one uniformed, a holstered pistol on his belt, and the other in a civilian suit. The suited man was burly, with close-shorn hair and a thick neck. He smelled of a cheap cologne with a chemical tang. He stood over Calloway and told him to sit up. The uniformed guard stood with his legs apart, one hand on the pistol holster. The man in the suit asked Calloway his name and nationality. Calloway answered truthfully. No point doing otherwise. He saw no way out. He'd killed Baumann. In Calloway's mind Baumann had deserved it. He was a sadistic thug and a traitor who'd escaped justice. But the East Germans knew nothing of this. As far as they were concerned Calloway was a foreigner and a murderer. There was only one way this was going to end.

The two men left the cell. The light went out. Calloway lay back on the hard wooden bench and closed his eyes. He thought of Bert Webber and his sister-in-law Vera, who would never know the truth, not even the fragments of truth Calloway had uncovered. He thought of Pat, throwing her arms around him, exhilarated from riding the wall. He thought of the tenderness she had shown after his bruising from Vogel's goons. He heard her voice saying, *'Why did you walk out, Reg?'* He wondered why himself. What had he feared? Why couldn't he allow himself some happiness? These were pointless questions. He knew why, deep down. He'd never let go of Miriam, the love he'd lost, the woman he'd met in the camp who had reached into his soul like no one before or since. He mourned her and he carried the constant guilt that he had survived when she had died. The guilt pained him, the anger that it spawned terrified him. That anger was the reason he was here, alone in the dark cell. When he'd killed Baumann he was taking his revenge on all the other Baumanns that had caused Miriam's suffering. The persecution, the imprisonment, the violation. The fate he now faced was a small price to pay for vengeance. The thought calmed him. He fell into a deep, dreamless sleep.

The bolts slid back and the light came on. The glare roused him. He'd been out cold for hours. It might have been the morning. He couldn't tell. The same two men stepped into the cell. The uniformed man told him to stand. Calloway complied. The man in the suit held a sheet of headed paper. He read out a series of charges, some criminal, some political. He asked Calloway if he understood. Calloway nodded. The two men left the cell, slid the bolts and switched out the light.

An hour later footsteps sounded in the corridor outside. Voices conferred. They reached agreement. A small hatch in the bottom of the cell door opened, casting a long rectangular light across the concrete floor. Calloway heard the scraping of metal. Someone on the other side of the door pushed a tray into the cell and closed the hatch. The light came on. On the tray was a bowl of weak stew, a chunk of bread and a plastic beaker full of water. Calloway ate. It was no worse than army food.

The same routine continued for several days. He tried to count them but failed. Five, perhaps six. He couldn't be sure. The lights would come on, the men would enter, they would ask questions, he would give non-committal answers. No coercion, no brutality, just procedure. Food came twice a day. The dishes varied up to a point. All of them could be eaten with a spoon.

After what could have been a week, a third man came to see him. He came twice a day. He was better dressed, self-assured, with an air of superiority. The other two men deferred to him. He spoke English to Calloway, with a strong Russian accent. He asked interrogator's questions. Calloway knew the game. He played along, feeding small amounts of information to keep the interviews civil. The questions implied Calloway was acting for a foreign power. An agent or freelancer. Calloway revealed nothing to support this assertion. He gave the Russian nothing more than the impression he was a hot-headed thug who'd messed with the wrong people. If he was to be hung, he'd be hung as a murderer, not a spy. The Russian kept his temper. His demeanour was, at worst, one of frustration and irritation. Calloway worked hard to keep it that way.

The Russian didn't come again. Calloway was left alone in his cell. He gave up any attempt to count the days. Then one day, as he slept, he was woken by the sound of the bolts sliding back once again. He peered through the doorway into the dimly-lit corridor. There were three men. Two uniformed guards with machine pistols in their hands, and the East German in the suit, with the close-shorn hair, who smelled of cheap cologne.

'Come with us, please,' he said.

It was night outside. They were in a small parking lot at the rear of the building. One of the guards ushered Calloway into the back of an unmarked van, then got in behind him. The second guard slammed the doors and locked them from the outside. Through a small portal window between the cab and the back of the van, Calloway saw the East German in the suit climb into the passenger seat. The second guard sat in the driver's seat. The engine started.

'I don't suppose you're going to tell me where I'm going,' Calloway said in German. The guard opposite said nothing. His hand tightened on the grip of the machine pistol.

They drove for twenty or thirty minutes. Calloway could make out the headlamps of oncoming traffic through the portal window. There wasn't much traffic to start with. There was virtually none as they neared their destination. Calloway felt the truck's wheels mount the kerb and bump over rubble. The driver changed down and revved. They were heading up an incline. The van seemed to bump over a threshold and level off. They drove at no more than a few miles per hour then stopped. Calloway heard the rasp of the handbrake. The two cab doors clunked open. The sound of footsteps approached the back of the van, then the sound of the rear doors being unlocked. The doors opened. The guard opposite gestured with his machine pistol for Calloway to dismount. Calloway climbed down onto the rubble floor. He let his eyes adjust to the darkness.

They were in the ruined shell of a massive oval building. Its outer walls had survived but its roof was gone. Above them a charcoal sky offered little light. Calloway looked around. The building had been some sort of arena. A *Sportpalast*. Now it was open to the elements, the smell of damp weeds and mould circulating within its walls. The van's headlamps cast two harsh, conjoined circles of light on the wall in front of them.

'Stand over there,' the man in the suit said, pointing towards the illuminated wall.

Calloway hesitated. 'Do you have a cigarette?'

The man nodded. He pulled a pack of Juwels from his jacket pocket, passed one to Calloway and lit it with a match.

'Now go,' he said, nodding towards the circles of light.

Calloway walked to the wall and turned to face the men. He squinted through the light. The two guards had stepped forward a few paces. They were training their machine pistols on him. The man in the suit lit a cigarette for himself and drew on it hard. The man checked his watch.

Calloway savoured the cheap East German tobacco. He closed his eyes and waited. This was it, he thought. No people's court. No show trial. No diplomatic complications. He would just become one of the missing. He took a last drag on the cigarette, flicked it into the darkness and watched the orange glow of the burning tip fade to nothing.

TWENTY-THREE

The sound of an engine neared. A car drove slowly over the threshold of the building and into the oval centre ground. Its tyres rumbled over the rubble, its headlamps sweeping the inner walls as it turned. The car parked. It kept its engine running. Calloway peered through the glare of the headlamps and saw three people climb out of the car. A man and two women. The light was too bright for Calloway to get a proper look at their faces. The man walked over to the East German in the suit and exchanged words. The East German nodded. The man then gestured to one of the women, who took the other woman by the arm and walked her towards Calloway. He recognised them as they approached. The woman being led was Hannelore. The one holding her arm was the woman that had seemed to be following him around Berlin, only this time she'd ditched the movie star glasses and heels. She wore trousers and boots, with a heavy reefer jacket. She had a pistol in her hand. Hannelore looked at Calloway, tired and expressionless. She stood next to him and faced the beam of the headlamps. The East German in the suit looked at her for a moment and beckoned her over.

'Goodbye, Reg,' she said. 'I hope you found what you were looking for.'

She walked over the rubble and climbed into the back of the van. One of the armed guards climbed in after her. The van revved hard and bumped over the rubble floor and out through the *Sportpalast* entrance.

No longer dazzled by the light, Calloway could make out the face of the man who'd arrived in the car. It was Sammy Mackay.

'You know, Cab,' he said, 'I had a feeling our paths might

cross. Now get in the car, will you.'

Calloway climbed into the back seat. Mackay took the passenger seat. The woman drove.

'This is Carmichael, by the way. One of my people here.' The woman acknowledged the introduction with a cock of her head as she drove. 'She's been keeping an eye on you since you arrived at Templehof. We see all the passenger manifests for the incoming flights. Your name rather jumped out. You have a habit of turning up, don't you. Like an oversized bad penny. Or perhaps that should be bad *pfennig*.'

Sammy was SIS, otherwise known as MI6, the part of the intelligence community that didn't exist officially. He'd been Calloway's CO during the war. They'd done their best not to keep in touch, but it hadn't always worked out that way.

'You really have fucked things up good and proper this time, old man,' said Mackay.

'Where are we going?' said Calloway.

'We need to debrief you. But first, I expect you'd like a drink.'

They drove west into the British sector, through the Tiergarten towards Charlottenburg. Carmichael pulled the car up outside what had once been a grand town house. Now its upper windows were boarded and its crumbling stucco bore the scars of shrapnel.

'It's not much, but it's home, as they say,' said Mackay. His conviviality would be hiding a seething resentment at the trouble Calloway had caused. Calloway knew his old CO well enough to know the signs. The three of them walked up the steps of the house and through the heavy front door. A man sat behind a desk in the high-ceilinged hallway. He was military in all but uniform.

Sammy said, 'Sign us in, will you, Geoffrey. One visitor, name of Calloway.'

The man behind the desk nodded.

'Anyone in the mess?' said Mackay.

'It's all yours, sir.'

They crossed the hallway towards a door at the far end. Sammy stopped halfway.

'You and Carmichael go ahead. I just need to get something from the ops room,' he said. He opened a door onto a busy room, where more young men with a military demeanour fussed around wirelesses and teleprinters, which crackled and clacked above the hum of voices. There were maps on the walls, divided into the sectors of the occupying forces, with coloured pins and scrawlings in chinagraph pencil. Carmichael led Calloway away, towards the room Sammy had called the mess. It was a long, narrow drawing room that looked onto what was left of the garden, now a jumble of building debris, broken crates and jerry cans from the war.

'Nice view,' said Calloway.

'The budget won't stretch to a gardener,' said Mackay, closing the door behind him and crossing the room to the window. He drew together a pair of dusty velvet curtains.

The room was furnished with a collection of salvaged armchairs and sofas, with cheerless prints on the walls. Standard lamps with frayed shades shed sepia light. It resembled what Calloway imagined a common room at some minor public school might look like. A dark and ornate sideboard served as a bar, with a row of spirits and a dozen bottled beers. Sammy poured three large scotches and set them down on a low table between two threadbare sofas. He brought the bottle with him.

'Sit down, Cab,' he said.

Calloway sat and sank into the deep horsehair upholstery. It was the most comfort he'd experienced for a fortnight. Every muscle ached, every tendon groaned with dull pain. He downed the whisky in thirsty gulps. Sammy poured him another.

'You've certainly made your presence known here, Cab,' he said. 'Berlin hasn't buzzed so much since Grigori Tokaty defected.'

Calloway had heard the name, a Soviet rocket scientist who'd walked into West Berlin with his family and applied to the British for asylum.

'I like to make an impression,' he said.

Sammy's expression changed. Here it comes, thought Calloway.

'You've done more than that,' said Mackay. 'You've made a bloody mess and I've had to clear it up.' He slammed his glass on the tabletop. 'For Christ's sake, man, you nearly started a war.'

'I just asked some questions.'

Sammy slopped more whisky into his own glass. He gulped it down in one.

'Questions that left a member of the East German security services dead in an abandoned building in the Soviet sector. They found him with two bullets through his head.'

'That must be an occupational hazard in his line of work,' said Calloway.

'Quit the bloody jokes. Do you realise where you are? Peace in our time hangs by a thread in this city. A thread that can snap with a single wrong move. You've made several, from what I've heard.' Sammy looked at Carmichael, who gave a faint nod of agreement. 'You're a bloody nuisance and I was the one that had to bail you out. It's my balls on the line if this doesn't blow over.'

Calloway thought of the exchange at the *Sportpalast*, the image of Hannelore climbing into the unmarked van.

'You made your swap,' he said. 'The slate's clean now.'

Sammy scoffed. 'The slate's never clean. You're not so long out of this business not to realise that. Forget the swap, that's just a short-term fix. As far as the Russians are concerned, we've killed one of theirs. That means one of ours in return. That's how it works here. Tit for bloody tat. You've put lives at risk.'

He knew Sammy was right, but old habits die hard and he took the dressing down from his old CO with a stone face and a hint of defiance.

'And to boot,' said Mackay, 'you've dispatched an asset we've been embedding in East German security for the last five years.' Mackay put his head in both hands. 'What the hell were you thinking, man?' he said.

The last thing Calloway remembers thinking was that Baumann's death was a small but necessary vengeance on him and his kind. He kept these thoughts to himself.

Mackay composed himself. He took a sip of the whisky. 'You recognised Baumann from that other business?'

He meant the blackmail case at the speedway stadium. That was the first time Mackay's and Calloway's paths had crossed since the war. That's when Calloway heard about the deal that Baumann, real name Frank Belper, the psychotic traitor in the blackmail photos with his Britische Freikorps comrades, had struck with the British intelligence services.

Calloway nodded. 'I remembered him from the photographs,' he said.

Mackay sighed and shook his head. 'Sod's law he'd be the one East German you ran into on this wild goose chase of yours. What the hell's it all about, Cab? What's Stanley Deakin to you?'

'A friend of a friend,' he said.

'And you came here looking for who killed him?'

'I came here to find out how he died. It wasn't in a road accident in England, like his wife has been told. Why don't you tell me what it's all about, Sammy.'

Mackay refilled their glasses. He turned to Carmichael. 'Tell him what we know. I've had enough.' He lay back into the sofas and rubbed the muscles in his neck, wincing.

'It's not an SIS matter,' said Carmichael. It was the first time Calloway had head her speak. She was well-spoken but with a cavalier air, like a bad girl from Rodean. The type Sammy would like, Calloway thought. 'This is strictly Curzon Street territory.'

'MI5?' said Calloway. 'What are they doing stomping around Berlin?'

Mackay looked up. 'Same as you probably,' he said. 'Sticking their nose where it doesn't belong.'

'We only found out about it when Deakin was killed,' said Carmichael. 'Curzon Street had to own up to Berlin Station that they had a live operation gone sour in our bailiwick. They needed our help to clean up the mess.'

'How does Deakin connect to MI5?' said Calloway. 'The man was a truck driver. A pretty unreliable one, from what I've heard.'

Carmichael exchanged looks with Mackay. Mackay nodded. She handed Calloway a file with a few flimsy sheets, copies of a file on Stanley Deakin. Calloway read in silence.

Deakin was arrested by the military police in Alexandria,

Egypt in 1940 for selling army radio valves to local civilians on the black market. This much Calloway knew, from what Webber had told him. Deakin was sentenced to six months in a military prison somewhere in the desert with an Arabic name Calloway didn't recognise. It was a hard regime. Endless PT, drill and beastings from the redcap guards. After three months he was visited by a major in the Queen's Own Hussars. He offered Stan a way to cut short his sentence. The major was recruiting for a new unit, a highly irregular one. A deep reconnaissance unit that would disappear into the remotest parts of Egypt and Libya for weeks on end to observe enemy activity. It was called the *Long-Range Desert Group* and, the major said, they were short of skilled radio operators. Despite his petty criminality, Stan was one of the best wireless men in Egypt. He agreed to join the new unit and was released from prison the same day, leaving in the major's jeep to the chagrin of the redcaps, with whom he'd developed a less than respectful relationship. There was some training to follow, on the minutiae of desert warfare, the use of weapons like the Lewis gun and the Boys anti-tank rifle, and the best ways to dig trucks out of deep sand. He also had to get to know the stripped-down Canadian Chevrolet trucks that would be their home, their fortress and their camel train for weeks at a time. He was encouraged to grow his hair and beard and was issued Arab garments to wear over his battledress, should they need to pass themselves off as Bedouin when encountering an enemy patrol. Stan adjusted well to irregular warfare. He liked its informality, the comparative equality between officers and men, and the maverick bloody-mindedness the group were allowed to exhibit in their dealings with more regular units. He was placed under the command of the major that had recruited him and the two men struck up a good working relationship with moments of friendship, in spite of the difference in their rank and social class. Stan spent the best part three years with the LRDG, before returning to the signals corps for the remainder of the war.

He received an honourable discharge in late 1945 and resumed his civilian life. He had no contact with his former comrades in the years following his demobilisation. Then, in 1948, he was again contacted by the major. They arranged to meet and Stan was offered a proposition. The major was now an operational officer with MI5 and as such he needed reliable freelances to take on arm's-length assignments suited to their experience, capabilities and type. Stan qualified on all three counts for some very deniable work and, thanks in part to the decent sums of money involved, agreed to the major's proposition. He had been used three times since then, although details of these operations were not included in the file. The report was dated and signed by the major himself. His name was Patrick Denton.

Calloway passed the file back to Carmichael. 'Do you know this man Denton?'

'Never set eyes on him,' said Mackay. 'Our dealings on this mess have been higher up the chain of command. Issues like this tend to get kicked upstairs.'

'Denton's been following me around, in London.'

'I'm sure he has,' said Mackay. 'I can imagine you've been as much of a pain in his arse as mine.'

'What was Stan doing for Denton? What was he working on when he died?'

Carmichael lit a cigarette and offered one to Calloway. 'Denton had assigned him to keep close to Hannelore Schneider, that's her real name. MI5 has been watching her for some time. A former member of KPD before the war who joined the Communist Party of Great Britain soon after settling in England. A staunch anti-fascist, not surprisingly given her experience, who saw communism as the antidote. She quit the party after a couple of years and steered clear of politics, at least as far as appearances are concerned. She was recruited by the Russians sometime around 1947 we think. Her role is believed to be gathering intelligence on the deployment of British and US air forces in the UK. Touring with a fairground takes her around the country to places within an easy motorcycle ride to our air bases. The fairground is a perfect cover.'

Calloway remembered the place names on the tour poster in Hannelore's trailer. Peterborough, Bury St Edmunds, Newmarket, Cromer. All within easy reach of bases in the east of England, places Calloway had heard of, like Alconbury, Lakenheath and Mildenhall.

'MI5 weren't interested in Schneider *per se*. She was a small fish who they could have lifted at any time. They wanted her network. It was Deakin's job to get close to her, with a view to turning her. His name showed up on MI5's radar when he applied for papers to travel to Berlin with the fairground. That's when Denton saw his chance. He hired Deakin to shadow Schneider on the German tour and thereafter on the English dates.'

And all the while, thought Calloway, Vera believed her husband was driving a truck in Stratton-Fenwick, sending the postcards that were no doubt pre-written.

'The plan was to expose her, so that Denton and his people could work on her to turn double,' said Carmichael.

'It should have been plain sailing,' said Mackay, 'as far as these things ever are. But your friend Stan's fondness for cheap champagne and the local *fräuleins* threw a spanner right in the works.'

'He blabbed, in other words,' said Carmichael. 'He tried to impress the girls with his Dick Barton story, which in this case happened to be true. He told them enough for the club owner Vogel to see the value. That's when Baumann got involved.'

'Baumann said he had Stan killed.'

'He did.'

'Baumann was your asset, Stan was working for MI5, couldn't you have stopped him?'

'Oh yes, Cab, it's that bloody easy,' said Mackay. 'We didn't even know of Deakin's existence. Curzon Street were flying solo, operating on our turf without our knowledge. Baumann saw Deakin as a complication that might compromise his position. His solution was to remove the complication. Frankly I can't say I blame him.'

'I'll tell Deakin's wife that. I'm sure it will be a great comfort to her.'

Mackay shook his head. 'Reg Calloway,' he said. 'The thug with a heart of gold. That was always your problem, Cab. You cared too much and it clouded your judgement. You let your anger get the better of you.'

'Next to your friend Baumann, I'm a fucking angel. Don't talk to me about judgement, Sammy.'

Calloway took a long drag on the cigarette. 'Was it your idea to trade Hannelore for me?'

'There's no need to thank me, if you were considering it.' Calloway wasn't. 'I did it to avoid an almighty diplomatic stink, not to save your neck. Believe me, that's of little value to me.'

'What did MI5 think?'

'They weren't happy, as you might imagine. But frankly, she was as good as blown the minute Vogel tipped Baumann off that Deakin was onto her. He might have been our man, but there are some things he couldn't have sat on. It was a fair assumption he'd have told the Russians.'

Sammy lit a cigarette and sat back in the sofa.

'MI5 can fuck themselves. They shouldn't have been operating on our patch without telling us.'

Calloway had smoked Carmichael's cigarette down to the butt. He nodded at the pack on the table. Sammy passed him one and lit it.

'So what happens next?' said Calloway.

Carmichael spoke. 'You disappear as soon as possible. We'll get you on a plane from Templehof and send you back to London.'

'And Pat Moxon, the woman I came here with?'

'She's no concern of ours.'

'I need to speak to her.'

Carmichael shook her head. 'You'll stay here until it's time to leave.'

He needed to see Pat. He couldn't walk out on her again.

'What about Denton?' he said.

Mackay shrugged and looked irritated. 'How the bloody hell should I know? He's MI5, I'm MI6. There's not a lot of love lost between us at the best of times.'

'He's taken Deakin's wife off to some kind of clinic.'

'Not my worry, old boy,' said Mackay.

Calloway downed the last of the scotch. 'I need to sleep.'

‘There’s a room upstairs with a camp bed for the duty officers on the night shift,’ said Mackay. ‘You can have that. The duty officer can sleep in here if he needs to.’

Carmichael showed Calloway to the room. It faced onto the rear garden, although its blown-in window was boarded up. There was a fresh pillow and two blankets on the rickety canvas bed.

‘Try to stay out of trouble,’ said Carmichael, closing the door as she left.

TWENTY-FOUR

Wind whistled between the cracks in the boards on the window. Calloway tested the bottom plank, which gave a little, its nails sitting loosely in the damp window frame. It came away easily as he pulled on it. He worked on the other boards until there was a big enough opening to for him to fit through. He climbed out backwards, finding a small parapet with his feet. It was just big enough to stand on. He flattened himself against the outer wall and eased himself over to a small balcony beneath an adjacent window which was also boarded. He judged that if he hung off the balcony with his hands, the drop to the garden below would be manageable. He slung one leg over the parapet, then the other, then took a deep breath and let himself drop. He fell to the uneven ground below, snagging his ankle on a broken brick. He cursed. He tested his foot on the ground. Sore but not broken. There were voices coming from the mess. Its curtains were still drawn closed. There was no sign that the garden was overlooked by any other windows.

The weak glow of the moon behind the clouds was enough to see by. He watched his footing as he negotiated the piled debris in the garden and made it to the far wall. It was six foot high. He dragged a crate over and up-ended it. It gave him the leg-up he needed. He heaved himself up with his arms and rolled over the top of the wall.

He had no money and no papers. He didn't know what time it was, other than that it was late. He navigated the dark streets by instinct, ducking into doorways or cutting across bomb sites to avoid the headlamps of the few cars and taxis that passed. It took him an hour to reach Hotel Pension Ritz. He did his best to smarten himself up. He had a fortnight's growth of beard but there was nothing he could do about that. Old Klaus was asleep behind the reception desk. Calloway reached behind him and took his room key from the rows of hooks. Klaus stirred, smacked his chops noisily, then settled. Calloway stepped lightly on the hard parquet floor down the hallway towards his room. There was light shining under Pat's door. He tapped softly. He heard stirring inside. The door opened a crack.

'Jesus Christ, Reg, look at the state of you,' she said.

She held the door open and ushered him in. He flopped on the bed, and she sat beside him.

'What the hell happened to you?'

'Been worried about me?'

'I wouldn't go that far,' she said. There was a half-bottle of whisky open on the bedside table. She poured him a glass.

'Thanks,' he said. He took a sip. 'The less you know the better.'

She looked him up and down. His suit was stained, his shoes scuffed. His shirt was grimy at the collar. His hard face was pallid beneath the growth of beard.

'You're probably right. I don't want to go the same way as Hannelore. The military police came for her.'

'I know,' he said. 'They swapped her for me. That's why I'm here and not on trial in the east.'

She paused for a moment, taking this in, then nodded. 'The less I know the better. Now go and get yourself cleaned up.'

Her room had a bathroom. He ran a bath to the rim and let the hot water soothe him. He lay there for an age, slipping in an out of a bleary half-sleep. Then he dried himself and wrapped the bath towel around his waist.

Pat had undressed. Her clothes lay on the floor. She was in bed. The cover was turned down on one side like an invitation. Her eyes beckoned him over. He sat on the bed beside her and she took his hand in hers. She pulled him towards her.

'Don't think I'm not still angry with you,' she said.

He slept through the night, the first decent sleep he'd had in days. Pat nudged him awake. She had ordered coffee. He sat up and lit a cigarette. The gravity of his situation came back to him.

'What's happened since I've been away?' he said.

'You've had callers. Two men looking for you. They've been here most days.'

'They speak to you?'

'The receptionist told them we were travelling together. She called me down to see them.'

'What did you tell them?

'That I knew nothing.'

'Did they accept that?'

'No, they looked like they were going to turn nasty. But I guess they didn't want to do anything in front of a witness. I'm just glad I wasn't on my own. I can handle myself, as you well know, Reg, but these two were bruisers.'

'Describe them.'

'Big, ugly, German.'

'Does one look like a pig?'

She laughed and nodded. 'More than I thought possible.'

'They're trouble,' he said. 'They killed Stan.'

Pat didn't often look shocked. She was made of sterner stuff. But the colour had drained from her face.

'Did they say they'd be back?'

She nodded. 'Today.'

'We need to leave. Pack some essentials.'

He climbed out of bed, wrapped a towel around his waist and crossed the room to the door.

'Listen, Reg...' she said.

He cut her off. 'We'll talk later. Right now we need to move.'

He went to his room and put on a change of clothes, all he had left. He would leave the soiled suit behind. There was a mouthful left in the Bismarck bottle. He swilled it down. He reached under the mattress and took the last of the cash Webber had given him for the trip. Then he fumbled in the drawer of the bedside table and pulled out the signet ring on the chain that Trudi had given him. He put the chain around his neck and fastened the clasp.

When he returned to Pat's room she was still in bed.

'I'm staying here,' she said. 'I'll change hotels to be on the safe side, but I'm not leaving Berlin. I'm going to finish the tour.'

'You're mad,' he said. 'These men are killers. They killed Stan and tried to kill me. They're coming back to finish the job.'

'Then perhaps it's best I keep away from you.'

There was no arguing with the look she was giving him. Pat had determination in spades.

'If I go, Milt doesn't have an act,' she said.

He looked incredulous. 'So what?' he said. 'It's a sideshow. This is life and death.'

'It's my life, Reg. It's not yours to own.'

She climbed out of bed and walked over to him. She took his head in her hands and kissed him hard.

'Now it's my turn to walk out on you,' she said. 'We're even.'

TWENTY-FIVE

The address Trudi had given him was on a street in Kreuzburg. In reality it was half a street, the other half no more than piles of rubble a good storey high. Laundry hung on makeshift lines on half-remaining first-floor rooms, which jutted out like jagged balconies from the flanks of high buildings. Children played on the rubble piles like kings of the castle. Old women in black coats huddled on street corners to gossip. Tired-looking men in the worn and dirty clothes of labourers strode purposefully to work. Mothers pushed rusting prams, toddlers played in sandpits made from the destroyed footings of buildings. The contrast with the bright shop-window hubbub of Ku'damm was striking. This was slum living, or little better.

Calloway knocked on a heavy wooden door within a tall, Wilhelmine-era apartment building. If it had been grand once, its grandeur was long gone. Its curtains were filthy and torn, half its window broken or boarded. There was no reply. Calloway knocked harder. He heard footsteps and scuffling from behind the door. A bolt slid back and the face of a man appeared in the crack of the half-open door. He had fat lips, jug ears and a toothbrush moustache. His skin was like leather, tanned to a potato-peel brown with deep lines chiselled into it. A hand-rolled cigarette dangled from his lip. He squinted into the light from beneath a Neanderthal brow.

'What do you want?' he grunted, eyeing Calloway up and down.

'I was told you could help me.'

The man frowned. 'Why should I help you?'

Calloway reached inside his shirt collar and pulled out the ring on the chain.

The man in the doorway looked at the ring and back at Calloway. He looked suspicious.

'Who sent you?' he said.

'I'm a friend of Trudi Trauber.'

The man frowned some more. Then his expression softened. He held open the door.

'Come in,' he said.

He bolted the door behind them and led Calloway up the darkened stairway to the first-floor landing. The man ushered him into a shabby apartment which looked onto the street through dirty windows.

'Sit,' he said, gesturing to a small table on which a coffee pot stood. He took a chipped mug from the shelf and poured Calloway coffee.

'Here,' he said, passing Calloway the mug. 'I am Otto.'

'Reg,' said Calloway, holding out his hand. Otto hesitated. He leaned forward and examined the ring around Calloway's neck. He glanced down at his own hand. He wore the same ring. He clapped Calloway on the shoulder and sat down opposite him.

'How do you know Trudi?' he said.

'I work at a wrestling arena in London. She's our star wrestler.'

Otto slurped at the coffee. He wiped the dribbles off his chin with his shirt sleeve.

'Trudi is the best,' he said. 'She give you that ring?'

Calloway nodded. 'For luck.'

'She must like you,' said Otto. 'That ring is important. It means a lot to us.'

'Who is *us*?'

Otto lowered his voice.

'The Kreuzburg *Ringverein*,' he said.

Calloway translated in his head.

'Ring club,' he said. 'What's a ring club?'

'They were started last century,' said Otto. 'Official clubs to help ex-convicts back into decent society. Started by some philanthropic fool who thought it was a good idea to create networks of criminals across the city.' He laughed to himself.

'What this fool created was organised crime in Berlin. Our very own mafia families.'

'And Trudi was a member of the Kreuzburg *Ringverein*?'

Otto smiled. 'Oh yes. A valued member. Loyal and strong.'

'Had Trudi been to jail?'

'Two years in Hohenheck women's prison for assault.'

Calloway was taken aback. Trudi was a devil in the ring, but outside it, she was a gentle giant.

'I expect he deserved it,' he said.

Otto was quiet for a moment. He looked solemn. 'He deserved it.'

The men drank their coffee in silence for a moment. Upstairs a couple argued while a baby cried.

'What kind of trouble are you in, Reg?' said Otto.

'A man called Vogel wants me dead.'

'Vogel the club owner?'

'You know him?'

'He was a member of *Ringverein Immertreu*, until they kicked him out. The man is a snake.'

'He set his two dogs on me.'

'Max and Günter?'

'We weren't on first name terms,' said Calloway. 'I got away from them. Now they want to finish the job. I need to get out of Berlin.'

Otto waved a hand in the direction of the door.

'So leave,' he said. 'Catch a plane from Templehof. I have money if you need it.'

'That's generous,' said Calloway. 'It's not that simple. I have no passport. I also have a friend who is staying behind in Berlin. I believe she's in danger too.'

Otto weighed this up. 'So you want that danger removed.'

'If it can be arranged. I'll also need a passport.'

'Vogel is nothing without his hired muscle. A weak and frightened man. We can deal with Max and Günter. A passport is more difficult. There are still a few good forgers in Berlin but they are busy. People want to leave the east. The wait would be too long. But,' he said, 'I can get you out of West Berlin and across to Hamburg without papers. From there you can take a boat and take your chances. We know people. People who will help us.'

It sounded risky but Calloway had little choice than to trust the criminal Otto. It wasn't just the lack of a passport. He wanted to get back to London without Denton knowing. This seemed like the only way.

'Thank you,' said Calloway. 'I know it's going to cost you. I can send money when I get home.'

Otto waved the offer away. 'Trudi has saved my skin on more than one occasion. I owe her this much. Tell her Otto says hello.'

He laid low in the Kreuzburg apartment until nightfall. Otto was gone for several hours making arrangements. At just after nine o'clock a truck pulled up outside the building. Otto introduced Calloway to the driver.

'This is Lothar. He is making a run to Hamburg to collect goods from the docks. Legitimate freight. You can ride in the cab for most of the journey, but you must hide while Lothar drives through East Germany between the two checkpoints. There's a false floor in the back of the truck, for smuggling contraband. It's just big enough for a man your size.'

'If you breathe in,' said Lothar with a grin.

'You'll be leaving West Berlin via Checkpoint Bravo in the woods at Dreilinden. Then you'll take the autobahn to Checkpoint Alpha at Helmstedt-Marienborn on the border with West Germany. It's the shortest route between east and west.'

Lothar looked at his watch. 'We must get moving.'

Calloway thanked Otto and climbed into to the cab.

Lothar offered him a slug of American PX whisky from a bottle in the glove compartment.

'For the road,' he said.

Calloway declined. He wanted a clear head. This wasn't a pleasure trip.

Lothar was talkative. Calloway could have done without company, but he was grateful to the driver for sticking his neck out to help. He wondered what Lothar's deal with Otto was. Was he *Ringverein* too, or just a hired hand? Either way, Calloway wasn't going to ask. Instead he listened to Lothar talk about football, which Calloway didn't follow, politics, about which Calloway didn't care, and family, none of whom Calloway knew. It was an ordeal of forced platitudes on Calloway's part. He was already exhausted when the truck approached the forest. Lothar pulled over.

'We must stop here,' he said. 'Go and take a piss. A good long one. It will be your last for about three hours.'

Calloway did as instructed. Lothar led Calloway to the rear of the truck and dropped the tailgate. The two men climbed in. Lothar lifted a section of planking on the wood floor. Beneath it was a sunken recess, measuring about five foot by two foot six. It was lined with an oil-stained blanket.

'Are you serious?' said Calloway.

'It's either that or you walk, my friend,' said Lothar, without his usual joviality.

Calloway lowered himself into the small space. He curled up like a foetus. Lothar lowered the planking. Calloway heard the clinking of metal then a loud banging. Lothar was nailing the planks down. Calloway shouted through the boards.

'Jesus Christ, man, what the hell are you doing?'

'If it's loose, they will discover you in an instant,' Lothar shouted back. 'This is the safest way.'

Nothing about being nailed into an undersized box felt safe to Calloway. Trusting a criminal gang was starting to seem like a dumb idea. He heard Lothar place his head against the boards and whisper.

'You must be quiet now. Not a sound.'

He heard the tailgate close and the engine restart. The truck pulled back onto the road.

It was cold in the box and the smell of diesel fumes was overpowering. He wasn't sure he'd survive three hours in Lothar's nailed-down coffin.

He felt the truck slow until it came to a halt. He heard American voices, sounding official. They'd reached Checkpoint Bravo. Calloway could just make out the conversation. The American MPs were telling Lothar the procedures to expect on the East German side of the border at Drewitz.

The procedures on the American side of the border took no more than a few minutes. The truck rolled forward at a few miles an hour then stopped again. German voices this time. More urgent, more authoritative. The wait this side seemed interminable to Calloway, crammed into the small space. He strained to hear the exchanges between Lothar and the East German *Grenzpolizei*. They sounded tense. The Grepos were questioning the validity of Lothar's travel papers. Calloway heard Lothar climb down from the cab and the sound of heavy boots walking to the rear of the truck. The slam of the tailgate dropping shook the truck. Two sets of boots climbed into the back and stomped around. The Grepos tapped and tested. Calloway's mouth went dry. His heart pounded in his chest. If he was caught here, there would be no prisoner swap this time. He'd burned his bridges with Sammy and Carmichael when he'd climbed out of the window in Charlottenburg. The Grepos were on top of him now, tapping the planks with their knuckles and comparing the sound to other parts of the floor. Calloway heard fingernails scrape over the heads of the nails in the planks. The guards' voices got louder. They seemed to be arguing with each other now, one suggesting they should get tools and lift the planks, the other complaining of the cold and saying it was late and they should get back to the warmth of their hut. Lothar was silent throughout the search. He clearly knew better than to remonstrate with the East German border police. A third voice spoke, with the tone of a superior officer. He ordered the two Grepos off the truck. Boots jumped down onto the ground. Lothar exchanged words with the officer who wished him a safe trip and walked away. Calloway heard Lothar grunt as he climbed into the back of the truck. He put his head against the planks and whispered.

'Their officer likes PX whisky.'

Calloway heard the tailgate close. Lothar climbed back into the cab and drove on.

Calloway managed some sleep. It passed the time. He woke with cramp, a searing pain through his calf muscle and no way of stretching it out. He pressed his foot hard against the edge of the box, which brought some small relief, but he had to suffer the pain for a good half-hour before it subsided.

Crossing at Helmstedt-Marienborn was more straightforward. It was late and there was no queueing. The truck rumbled over the border and was waved on by a soldier with an English accent. Lothar drove for a further half-hour and pulled over. He jemmied up the planks and helped Calloway out of the hole. Calloway stretched his limbs. His joints ground like they were rusted.

'Welcome to West Germany,' Lothar said. He shook Calloway's hand. 'Come on, you can ride in the cab now. I have some bread and sausage.'

Calloway scoffed the food. He was starving. He'd not eaten all day.

'We should reach Hamburg in about three hours,' said Lothar. 'You should get some sleep.'

Calloway complied. He fell asleep to the rumble of the engine and the sound of Lothar humming an off-key tune.

TWENTY-SIX

Calloway awoke to the sound of seagulls. It was just before dawn and the light was turning from stifling black to a hopeful blue-grey.

'Hamburg docks,' said Otto, passing Calloway a flask. 'Here, coffee.'

Calloway poured a cup. It was weak but welcome. He looked out of the truck window across the vast swathes of cold black water, criss-crossed with girder bridges and lined with cranes. A timid sun peeked from behind the funnels and masts of some of the biggest cargo ships Calloway had ever seen. The docks were busy, despite the early hour. Merchant seamen bustled around in gangs, uniformly dressed in pea coats and black caps, with shapeless kit bags slung across their backs. They smoked pipes and exchanged words through missing teeth. Otto drove the truck along the dockside road at a crawl, avoiding the cat's cradle of ropes as thick as a man's arm that held the vast freight ships in their berths. Beyond them, tugs belched smoke to a dawn chorus of steam whistles and ship's horns.

Otto gestured to one of the ships. '*The Kurtz*,' he said pointing at the name on the rust-streaked stern. 'Two thousand tons. She leaves in an hour for London.'

'Who's the captain?' said Calloway.

'A man called Steiner. A friend.'

Lothar parked the truck. The two men dismounted and wove their way across the busy quayside and up the gangplank to the ship's deck. *The Kurtz* had seen better days, its steelwork battered and rusting. Lothar exchanged words with a pint-sized deck hand who pointed up to the bridge of the ship. Lothar and Calloway climbed the stairway and ducked through the low door.

Captain Steiner was alone on the bridge. He slouched in a high chair, watching the activity on deck with a bored expression. He was perhaps fifty, with a ruddy face and a paunch beneath the straining brass buttons of his bridge coat. A mop of greasy grey hair stuck out from beneath his braided cap. He stood and looked Calloway up and down.

'Is this our cargo?' he said to Lothar.

Lothar nodded. Calloway held out his hand. Steiner shook his head.

'Best we don't do introductions. As far as I'm concerned, you don't exist.' He turned to Lothar. 'You have the money?'

Lothar reached inside the pocket of his pea coat and pulled out a grubby envelope. Steiner took it, counted the money and pushed it into his own pocket. He leaned out of the door and hollered down to one of the hands, who scrambled up the stairway two treads at a time.

'Take our guest to the fore hold,' said Steiner. The hand gave a curt, *'Jawohl, Herr Kapitan,'* then gestured for Calloway to follow him below. Calloway shook Lothar's hand and thanked him for the ride. Lothar wished him luck. Without thinking Calloway reached inside his shirt and fondled the ring on the chain. Then he clanked down the stairway after the hand.

The fore hold was damp and stinking. It didn't hold cargo so much as all the oily odds and ends that didn't have a place elsewhere on the vessel. A space had been cleared for a camp bed, over which hung a battery lamp that would be the only source of light. There was a thin blanket folded on the bed. The hand passed Calloway a small canvas bag containing a sandwich wrapped in paper and a bottle of water.

'There's a bucket in the corner,' the hand said.

Calloway could smell it.

'You stay here,' said the hand. 'We will come and get you when it's time to disembark.'

Calloway acknowledged the instructions with a nod and settled himself on the camp bed. The hand slammed the hatch shut. Calloway fumbled for the battery lamp and switched it on.

It cast a weak glow outwards for no more than a couple of feet. Shut in a box again, thought Calloway. But at least there's room to stretch. He lay flat on the bed and stared into the half-darkness. The muffled blare of the horn announced their departure from the docks. The anchor chain clanked and water slapped against the hull. The ship's huge engines sent shudders along the lower deck, vibrating the bed beneath him. He didn't relish spending the best part of twenty-four hours under these conditions. He peered through the gloom at the hatch. There were no handles on the inside. He unwrapped the sandwich and ate, then settled himself back on the bed, pulling the blanket around him against the cold and damp.

He slept a fitful sleep, incoherent dreams colliding as he tossed and turned under the meagre blanket. The wall of death spun around him, dragging him down into a vortex of screaming faces – Vera, Hannelore and Pat – all calling his name, desperate and accusing. Then pain, the fierce, intolerable pain of fists and boots pummelling into him, Max and Günter drooling from the mouths of their pigs' heads, squealing with delight.

He was woken by the slow metallic creak of the hatch opening, and the silhouette of a man ducking into the hold.

'Time to go,' said Captain Steiner.

Calloway threw the blanket off. His shirt clung to his back, soaked in a cold sweat. He peered at the face of his watch but couldn't make it out in the darkness.

'What time is it?' he said.

'An hour before dawn,' said Steiner. 'Quickly now.'

It was cold on deck. Steiner led Calloway to the starboard side of the boat. They stood looking over the side under the green glow of the navigation light.

Calloway could just make out a small vessel, a motorboat, perhaps a fishing boat, with a wheelhouse not much bigger than a call box. On the deck of *The Kurtz*, hands were stuffing boxes into a cargo net that hung from the jib of a crane. There must have been three dozen boxes, each a foot and a half square. Whatever they contained, it was something the customs men would never get to see.

Steiner saw Calloway looking towards the net.

'I hope you have a strong grip,' he said. 'That's how you're leaving the ship.'

One of the hands sniggered. Calloway didn't find it funny. He peered down into the black waters between *The Kurtz* and the fishing boat. They looked cold and rough, perhaps not rough by Captain Steiner's standards, but there was enough swell to put the fear of God into any land lubber.

'Put your feet through the squares in the net and hold onto the rope with both hands. You'll be fine if you don't let go,' said the captain with a smirk.

Calloway hesitated. The fishing boat was still far back from the ship.

'Can't they get any closer?' he said.

Steiner shook his head. 'Any closer and they risk slamming into the hull.'

Calloway did as instructed. He slipped the soles of his shoes through the net until the heels caught. He pushed his feet down to test their grip. He caught the rope from the jib with both hands and straightened up.

Steiner read the look on Calloway's face. 'If you know a better way to get to London without a passport, I suggest you do it, my friend.'

'If I did, do you think I'd be clinging onto this bloody rope,' said Calloway.

Steiner clapped him on the back. 'You'll be fine,' he said, signalling to the jib operator.

Calloway felt the rope tauten beneath his hands and the cargo beneath him rise from the deck. The filled net started to sway. The jib swivelled on the mast and swung the cargo out over the water, its momentum rocking Calloway back and forth with more violence than he'd expected. He squeezed the rope tighter. The fishing boat skipper shouted instructions to the crane operator. Wind whipped around Calloway ankles. It was a cold damp wind. It bit at his fingers as they clutched the rope. The wind sent the cargo swaying out even further. The jib operator was struggling to align the load with the meagre deck of the fishing boat. The boat's skipper was swearing, tugging at the wheel, trying to steady the tiny vessel, while at the same time shouting instructions into the darkness. Calloway felt a sudden, violent lunge, which all but wrenched his arms from their sockets. A tall wave threw *The Kurtz* upwards. The jib of the crane snapped backwards towards the ship, the cargo net following. Calloway clung on. The net hit the hull with a jolt. Calloway felt his ankle slam against the steel. He screamed in pain and lost his footing. His legs dangled above the waves, his hands clinging to the cold wet rope. The rope slipped through his grasp. His legs flailed as he tried to find a footing on the net. The jib swung again, this time out over the sea. The inertia flung Calloway horizontal. He felt the sting of rope burns across his palms. He heard shouting all around him. His body slapped back against the cargo and one of his feet snagged in the net. He pushed down hard and found a footing. He heard the high-pitched squeal of the pulley above him and looked down to see the sea rising up to meet him. Then the fishing boat lunged backwards on the waves so that its deck was directly below. The skipper gave a signal and reached up with a boat hook. He snagged the net. The pulley squealed again and the cargo landed on the deck with a mighty thud. Calloway lost his grip on the rope and fell backwards, the boxes in the loosened net tumbling over him. They were light. Lighter than he'd expected. Light enough to spare him the two broken legs a heavier cargo would have dealt him.

'You alright, chief?' the skipper said.

Calloway's subconscious audited the damage. It was a habit from the war and was seldom wrong.

'A few bruises and rope burns,' he said.

'You can help me get these below then,' said the skipper. 'Quickly now.'

The two men tossed the boxes through a small hatch beneath the open wheelhouse. Clearly, they weren't fragile. When they were done, the skipper signalled to *The Kurtz*, which picked up speed, leaving the fishing boat bumping in its wake.

The skipper wrestled with the wheel and, satisfied all was well, reached into his coat and passed a hip flask to Calloway.

'You'll need a nip of that I expect,' he said.

TWENTY-SEVEN

'What are we carrying?' said Calloway.

The boxes were too light for liquor, probably too light for drugs.

'Nylons,' said the skipper.

'Stockings?'

The skipper nodded. 'It's bloody ridiculous, if you ask me,' he said. 'Britain manufactures loads of them but exports them to Europe. The racketeers buy them in Europe and smuggle them back to Britain to sell on the black market.'

'Who's picking them up?'

'Bloke called Freddie. He'll have a van waiting by a jetty near Maldon.'

'Essex?'

The skipper gave an affirmative grunt. 'The Blackwater,' he said. He cackled to himself. 'Takes someone as old as me to navigate the Blackwater by night. I've been navigating these waters since I was a boy.'

Calloway felt reassured, at least by the skipper's confidence in getting him back on dry land. He kept an open mind about Freddie.

Dawn was breaking behind them, but the dull grey light didn't make the Blackwater any less black. It remained dark and threatening. Calloway wasn't a natural sea goer. He could jump out of an aircraft with a parachute on his back or plummet to the earth in a glider, but he'd happily leave the sea to the mackerel and the matelots, especially after his ride on Steiner's cargo net. He was relieved when the skipper gestured to a jagged black line against the low horizon.

'The jetty,' he said.

Calloway could see the van beside it and a man standing. The red glow of a burning cigarette beamed like a lighthouse. The skipper pulled alongside the jetty. Calloway picked up the ropes and jumped out of the boat. He tied up fore and aft. Freddie approached the jetty and gave Calloway a cautious nod.

'You the stowaway?' he said, drawing on the butt of the cigarette and flicking it into the water. He was about five foot eight with slits for eyes and a gap in his teeth. He wore a broad-shouldered coat that covered his knees. The coat was made of a tweed that was too loud for this early in the morning. Its lapels were wide enough to touch his arms. He wore his stingy-brimmed trilby at an angle. If the intention was to advertise that he dealt in black market nylons, he was succeeding. He looked incongruous amid the sodden marshland.

'I'm here,' said Calloway. 'Let's just leave it at that.'

'Freddie will take you to London,' said the skipper.

'I could do without company, if I'm honest,' the spiv said, looking at Calloway.

'A deal's a deal, Fred,' said the skipper, with an air of authority he'd not shown before.

Freddie shrugged. 'S'pose so,' he said, like he supposed quite the opposite. He looked at Calloway and cocked his head in the direction of the van. 'You can help me load up,' he said. 'Earn your passage.'

They transferred the boxes from the fishing boat to the vehicle. Freddie reeled off a wad of banknotes and handed them to the skipper. The look on his face said it pained him to do so. The skipper shook Calloway's hand and bade him farewell. Freddie started the van and Calloway climbed in beside him.

'What's your story then?' Freddie said, tugging at the wheel as the van bumped over the uneven ground towards the road.

'Just a man who needed to get home,' said Calloway.

'Sounds like I could get in some bother if I got found with you in my van.'

'So keep driving and don't get found.'

The van bumped onto the hard surface of the road. The boxes

thudded around behind them. Freddie took his hands off the wheel and lit a cigarette.

'Cocky sod aren't you?' he said.

Calloway ignored him. They drove in silence for close to an hour. They were on country roads. Freddie looked in his rear-view mirror and said, 'We'll stop here. Stretch our legs.' He turned off into a narrow track. He pulled the van up on the verge, in a small patch of woodland that shielded them from the main road.

'We've only been going an hour,' said Calloway. 'Hardly worth stopping.'

'I need a piss,' said Freddie. He climbed out of the van and relieved himself against a tree. Calloway got out and lit a cigarette. Freddie buttoned his fly and wiped his hands on the back of his coat. He walked back to where Calloway stood.

'Got money on you?' he said.

'That's my business,' said Calloway.

'Course you've got money. I'm going to need a fee.'

'That wasn't part of the agreement.'

Freddie scoffed. 'With the krauts? Don't make me laugh. They don't count for nothing here.'

It wasn't worth the argument, thought Calloway.

'How much do you need?' he said.

'All of it.'

'Don't be stupid, son.'

Freddie reached in the pocket of his overcoat and pulled out a pistol. A Luger. He pointed it at Calloway's belly.

'You're the one being stupid,' he said. 'Hand it over.'

He cocked the pistol.

Calloway reached into his jacket pocket for the last of Webber's cash. There was plenty left and he had plans for it. But he wasn't inclined to argue. He'd seen a single round from a Luger rip a grown man's skull in two and spatter his brains like sauerkraut. He tossed the small bundle on the ground. Freddie bent to pick it up then hesitated.

'Don't you fucking move,' he said.

Calloway looked at the gun.

‘I wasn’t planning to,’ he said. ‘I’ve seen the holes those things make.’

Freddie grinned. He reached down towards the money.

Calloway seized the moment. He took a step forward and kicked the spiv in the head. It was a good hard kick. The spiv reeled then fell flat on the ground. Calloway kicked the Luger out of his hand and picked it up. He tucked it into his waistband, retrieved his cash, then riffled through Freddie’s pockets for the keys to the van. He found the keys and a wad of five-pound notes. He left the money. No point starting a feud with a gang of black marketeers. Calloway prodded the prostrate spiv with the toe of his shoe. The spiv was out cold. He opened the rear doors of the van and chucked out the boxes of nylons. If stopped, he could say the van was borrowed. He couldn’t explain twenty-four boxes of contraband stockings. Or the Luger. He stuffed the pistol down the back of the passenger seat.

The drive to London took more than two hours. The van was a pig to drive. He had to wrestle it into top gear through a series of grinding gear changes. But it was better than hitch hiking with empty pockets.

He hit central London in the morning rush hour. The clock that told Guinness Time at Piccadilly Circus said a quarter to eight. Freddie would be conscious by now. Calloway hoped his head hurt. He parked the van in a side street in Victoria. He pulled the Luger from the back of the seat and tucked it in his waistband. He then left the van and took the tube to Kensington High Street. From there it was a short walk through busy streets to the hotel.

There was no crowd outside, nor any police. Since he’d left for Berlin, the squatters must have won a stay of execution. He went to his room, splashed water on his face and changed into his one remaining set of clothes. His guts felt queasy with hunger. He left the building, found a cafe and ordered breakfast. Then he called Webber from a phone box. Elsie answered.

‘It’s Calloway. I’m back in London.’

She sounded relieved to hear from him.

‘Did you get Bert’s telegram?’ she said.

'I did. Have you heard anything from Vera?'

'Not a peep. We're so worried, Mr Calloway. Her neighbours said those men came and took her away.'

'The man called Denton and the doctor?'

'Sounded like them. The local kiddies recognised the car. They don't miss a trick.'

'And you've no idea where Denton and the doctor have taken her?'

'One of Vera's neighbours asked, because Vera seemed distressed when they were leading her to the car. The doctor told the neighbour they were taking Vera to a clinic for some rest. That's all we know.' There was silence on the line. Then Elsie spoke quietly. 'Can you help us, Mr Calloway?'

His answer might have been no, under any other circumstances. The favour he'd agreed to do Bert when the little rider had first shown up at the arena had long since been used up. But something compelled him to help. It might have been friendship, but if he was honest, he'd long since forgotten what that really felt like. It might have been the death of Stan, a pointless casualty in a new kind of war that seemed more like a game to Calloway. Or it could have been the hatred he felt for Vogel, Baumann and Freddie the spiv. Jumped-up little caesars with guns instead of guts. They reminded him of Jimmy Jenks. Whatever the reason, he wanted resolution. He wanted to draw a line under the whole sordid business.

'Tell Bert to meet me at this address,' he said.

He gave Elsie the location of the squat and put the phone down. He made another call, dialling the number on the calling card Denton had given Vera. He knew he wouldn't make it past the switchboard, but he wanted Denton to know he was in London. Then he called the arena and asked for Trudi Trauber. When she came to the phone, he made her a proposition.

He went back to the squat and slept. He woke at dusk, the streetlamps casting a comforting glow through the widow. For a moment or two, in the mist of half-sleep, he thought Pat was beside him. He reached across the bed, finding no one. He felt a sudden, overwhelming loneliness. There was noise from the corridor. The Poles had their door open and were playing music on their gramophone. Calloway recognised Chopin. The piano music was soothing. He went to his bathroom and ran a bath. It was a luxury he seldom enjoyed. He scrubbed the oily stink of *The Kurtz* off his skin and lay there soaking. Two nights ago he had bathed in Pat's hotel room, while she undressed and turned down the bedsheets for him. He hoped that Otto had been true to his word, that Max and Günter were out of the picture and that Pat was safe. As safe as a wall of death rider could be.

He went out and bought a bottle of scotch from a wine merchant and borrowed three glasses from the Poles when he returned. He poured himself a slug and waited. Webber arrived at just after seven.

'A Kensington hotel?' he said, looking around the room. 'You going up in the world, Reg?'

'It's a squat,' said Calloway.

'A squat with hot water and a tub,' said Webber, poking his nose around the bathroom door.

'I struck lucky,' said Calloway.

'Noisy neighbours, mind.'

A crying baby was competing with Chopin in the corridor outside.

'I like it,' said Calloway.

He poured Webber a drink. Webber raised his glass.

'Welcome home,' he said. They drank in silence for a moment, listening to the muffled sounds of piano music, then Webber said, 'You going to tell me all about it?'

'You're better off not knowing,' said Calloway.

'But you went there to find out. To put Vera's mind at rest.'

'I'm not sure the truth will do that, Bert.'

Webber reached into his pocket. 'If it's more money you want...'

'Don't be stupid,' said Calloway. 'Put your money away. I'll tell you the story, but it's not pretty. I'll leave it up to you what you tell your sister-in-law.'

He told Webber everything, from Stan's debt to Spanner, to his death at Baumann's behest. The small rider listened to it all, his usually expressive face completely blank. When Calloway had finished, Webber shook his head.

'I know he's family and I know I shouldn't speak ill of the dead.' He took a large gulp of the scotch. 'But what a silly cunt.'

It took a man like Bert Webber to see the world like that. Calloway admired him.

'In truth, there's nothing silly about it, Bert. Stan had a whole other life you didn't know about. A secret life, full of deception and lies. A dangerous one too. A very deniable life, where nothing's what it seems. It's all smoke and mirrors in that world, Bert. Don't try to understand it. Stan's gone and we need to find Vera. I'm going need your help. It won't be without its risks.'

Webber looked down at the glass in his hand. He swilled the last of the whisky around then drank it.

'Well,' he said. 'It's not as if I have much to do, now the season's over.'

Calloway smiled and poured them both another slug.

'You expecting someone else?' said Webber, nodding at the third glass.

There was a knock at the door. Calloway opened it. Trudi filled the door frame. He beckoned her, introduced her to Bert and poured her a drink.

'Otto says hello,' said Calloway. Trudi smiled. He unfastened the chain with the ring and handed it to her. 'Thank you,' he said. 'It brought me luck.'

In truth, he didn't feel too lucky right now, but at least he was home. And alive. Trudi laughed and clapped him on the back.

'You are now a member of the Kreuzberg *Ringverein*,' she said, raising her glass in toast. '*Prost!*'

Calloway clinked her glass. He sensed Webber's discomfort at Trudi's presence. Whether it was because she was German or that she was a woman twice Webber's size, Calloway didn't know. He got to the point.

'Trudi's a friend, Bert,' he said. 'We can trust her. And what we've got to do is going to take more than the two of us. Trudi's agreed to help and I've persuaded her to accept a fee. I know you're good for it. What we need to do carries a level of risk that's unreasonable to expect as a favour.'

Webber looked a little confused but nodded his agreement. Trudi thanked him.

'You don't need to pay me any more,' said Calloway.

He charged their glasses and told them his plan. He adopted an air of outward confidence. It hid the grave unease he felt about what he was proposing.

TWENTY-EIGHT

For three days Calloway waited. He watched the street below from the window of his room. He eyed faces in the crowd as he moved about the city. He cast sideways glances into parked cars everywhere he went.

Then Denton appeared. He sat in a Ford Prefect parked in a side street opposite the arena, its bonnet poking out from behind a corner giving him a clear view of the arena entrance. Calloway watched him from a small window on the third floor of the building. Denton was alone. It was time.

Trudi and Calloway had prepared for this. They had agreed on a plan beforehand. Calloway collected her from the dressing room and walked with her to the foyer. They stood in the shadows of the unlit entrance and looked towards Denton's car.

'You see him?' said Calloway.

'Ripe for the plucking,' said Trudi with a grin.

'Off you go. I'll be right behind you.'

Trudi walked out into the street towards Denton's car. Calloway watched Denton pick up a newspaper and pretend to read. Did they really teach them this Boys' Own nonsense at MI5, he thought. Trudi crossed the road until she was a yard or two from the car. She glanced back in Calloway's direction. He gave her the nod. She wrenched open the car door, grabbed Denton by the arm and yanked him onto the pavement. She got him in a body lock, which probably had a name in wrestling circles although Calloway didn't know it. Calloway ran over to them. Together they frogmarched Denton into the arena. They led him through the foyer into the auditorium. It was dark inside, save for a shaft of light which struck the canvas of the ring from a skylight high in the roof. They ignored Denton's protestations. He shammed innocence and indignation. Calloway parted the ropes and Trudi tipped Denton into the ring then jumped up behind him.

'Seconds out, round one, Mr Denton,' said Calloway.

Trudi swung Denton by the arm onto the ropes. The force catapulted him back onto the canvas. Trudi fell on him, pinning him to the ground. Denton looked up at the six-foot female wrestler with a combination of fear and astonishment. Calloway leaned down and spoke into Denton's ear.

'Our friend Bert Webber wants his sister-in-law back. Where have you taken her?'

Denton gasped for breath under Trudi's weight. 'I don't know any Bert Webber.'

Calloway nodded at Trudi. She gripped Denton by the shoulders and slammed him down hard on the canvas.

'You know Webber and you know his sister-in-law, Vera. You and your doctor friend led her to a car and took her to a clinic. We want to know where.'

'I tell you, man, I don't know what you're talking about.'

'Think again, Denton. I'll give you some names to jog your memory. Stanley Deakin and Hannelore Schneider.'

The names got Denton's attention but he feigned ignorance. 'This is all some kind of mistake. You need to let me go.'

Calloway smiled. 'We've only just started,' he said, signalling to Trudi. She picked Denton up off the floor, flipped him around and slammed him back down again. The impact sucked the air out of Denton's lungs. He gasped like a beached fish.

'Where is Vera Deakin?' said Calloway. 'You took her away. Her family wants her back.'

Deakin spat.

'Fuck her family. And fuck you.'

Trudi didn't need a signal. She dragged Denton off the floor and flung him onto the ropes. He rebounded into her clenched arm, spasmed and dropped onto the canvas. Calloway bent down.

'There's no wrestling matches tonight. It's just the three of us here. We can go on like this for hours.'

Denton was dazed. He pushed himself onto his hands and knees and swayed like he was going to collapse again. Trudi flipped him over and dropped down onto him, pinioning him to the ground with her knees.

'Where is she Denton?' said Calloway. 'Where's Vera Deakin? Where's this clinic you took her to?'

Denton summoned strength and shouted, 'Get this fucking Amazon off me.'

Trudi laughed. Calloway gestured to her to move over.

'That was just a bit of sport,' he said. 'Now it's serious.'

He hit Denton hard in the face.

'Every bullshit answer you give me, you'll get another one like it,' he said.

Denton shouted through bloodied lips. 'Go to hell.'

Calloway hit him again.

'Seems like you need softening up a bit,' he said. He nodded to Trudi. Again she grabbed Denton's arm, dragged him to his feet and flung him into the ropes. She tripped him on the rebound so he fell face down on the deck. Calloway grabbed Denton's hair and slammed his face onto the hard canvas. Denton gave a muffled yelp. He went limp. He was breaking. Calloway knew the signs. A sharp blow to the kidneys bought his compliance.

'She's at the fort,' Denton mumbled. 'The clinic at the fort.'

'What fort?'

Denton mumbled words Calloway couldn't make out.

'Speak up, man,' he said. 'We're all ears.'

He cuffed Denton around the head.

'Grain Tower Battery. At the mouth of the River Medway,' said Denton.

Then he passed out.

'Take him to the dressing room and lock him in. Can you keep him here for a few hours?'

Trudi nodded. She hoisted the unconscious body over her shoulder as if he weighed no more than a child and climbed down from the ring.

Calloway went to his office. He made two phone calls. The first was to Bert Webber. Calloway told him to be ready at the prefab in an hour. The second was to Johnny Suskind, his old paratrooper comrade from the boxing booth. He made Johnny a proposition, like the one he'd made Trudi. It meant asking Webber for more money, but the stakes were high and he needed Johnny's kind of muscle on the job. He banked on Webber understanding.

Calloway took Denton's car. He met Johnny at the entrance to the fairground. There was no fair today. The rides were shrouded in faded canvas and the sideshows were shuttered. Johnny wore his old paratroopers Denison smock. He clearly meant business.

'I owe you for this, Johnny,' said Calloway.

'Forget it, mate. Sounds like a laugh, this caper.'

'I can't promise any laughs. But you'll be helping some good people out of a bad situation.'

'It'll stop me getting bored.'

Johnny was another one. Couldn't settle back into civilian life. The war had shaped him so that he no longer fitted. He wasn't a nine-to-fiver. He was neither factory fodder nor a shiny-arse. He'd lived on instinct, wits and adrenalin for nigh on six years. That kind of living doesn't leave you in a hurry. The boxing helped, Calloway imagined. It channelled Johnny's aggression. The same applied to their scrapes with the fascists in the East End. And now this mad fool plan. Any normal man would have run a mile, but Johnny didn't need persuading. A good word from Calloway and the promise of a few extra quid was enough.

They picked Webber up outside his prefab.

'Elsie's down the shops. I've left her a note.'

Johnny laughed. 'It's not like you're leaving home,' he said. 'Unless you plan to run off with her sister.'

Webber looked embarrassed, then gave an impish grin. 'Might have crossed my mind a couple of times.'

He laughed for a moment, before the seriousness of the situation struck him.

'Do you reckon she's alright, Reg?' he said. He tapped his

temple. 'You know, up here I mean.'

It was a rhetorical question, an excuse to fish for a reassuring word.

'Grief's a poison, Bert. It can turn your head inside out.' Calloway knew grief. He'd never been right since his own loss. But what he'd seen of Vera's condition troubled him more than he was letting on. He'd seen many kinds of madness. It was as much a product of war as death and maiming. Hysteria, melancholia, rage, even blindness. Vera was in a different state, like nothing he'd seen before. It was way more than grief, if he was any judge.

They drove for almost an hour, leaving the Dover Road before Rochester and heading northeast along a scrubby minor road. They pulled over in a village that was little more than a cluster of sad, isolated cottages and asked directions. They were on the right road. The three men were tense now. Conversation had long since run out. They smoked one cigarette after another looking intently through the windscreen. Heavy grey clouds hung over the flat and marshy peninsula. They could see the estuary ahead of them, a cold and murky expanse that stretched to the featureless coastline beyond it.

'There's the fort,' said Johnny, pointing across Calloway as he drove.

It wasn't so much a building as a mutation of concrete, brick and stone. From what Calloway could see, it had started life as a Martello tower, on whose round stone base newer defensive structures had been added during successive conflicts. On one side a brick-built barracks block floated on stilts, beyond that a concrete tower rose up four or five stories with open stairs up to an observation post.

Webber, who was sitting in the back seat, poked his head between the two men and peered through the windscreen.

'Fuck me,' he said. 'It's got to be a mile out to sea.'

He was right. It was something they hadn't banked on. Calloway had assumed the battery was on dry land, facing out to sea from the coast. This was a sea fort.

'I hope you can swim, Bert,' said Johnny.

'It's not funny, mate,' said Webber. 'How the hell are we going to get over to that?'

'Maybe it's walkable at low tide,' said Johnny.

'Low tide could be hours away,' said Calloway.

He'd been a fool. He'd not planned properly in his haste. He was strung out since his experience in Berlin and his judgement was way off. Bert and Johnny had trusted him. But he was leading them on a wild goose chase.

Webber drew breath, as a thought occurred to him. 'We could get a boat,' he said. 'You know, nick one.'

Calloway didn't like the idea. His experience on *The Kurtz* didn't endear him to another jaunt on the water.

The wind whistled around the car and the sea ahead of them was rough. Even at this distance he could see the white peaks of waves lapping against the base of the fort.

'We're all ex-army, Bert,' he said. 'We're not exactly seafaring types. I don't fancy our chances out there, looking at that swell.'

Bert grinned. He bristled faintly with pride. 'Speak for yourself,' he said. 'When I was in the service corps I did a stint with *No.2 Motorboat Company* over at Mersea Island.' He pointed to the other side of the estuary. 'Somewhere over there, I reckon.'

'The service corps has boats?' said Johnny, looking quizzically at Webber.

'The army's little navy,' said Webber.

'So you reckon you could handle one?' said Calloway.

Webber nodded. 'And hot-wire one too,' he said. 'I know me way around engines thanks to the Corps.'

A mad fool idea. Another one. But they were committed now. Each knew they wouldn't forgive themselves if they'd not given their best shot to bringing Vera home, whatever the consequences.

'The light's going,' said Johnny. 'If we're doing this, we'd better get moving.'

They drove in silence down to the outskirts of a small town, which stretched along the western bank of the River Medway. It was a ramshackle place, with half-a-dozen jetties with small boats moored to them.

'We'll pull up here,' said Calloway. He checked his watch. 'Half an hour till it's dark, I reckon. Then we'll see what we can find.'

They chain smoked while they waited. They had parked alongside an old marine workshop, in amongst the rusting and rotting hulls of broken-down craft which sat haphazardly on the quayside. The workshop was shuttered and dark. The boats moored along the adjacent jetties bobbed up and down on the swell, straining at their ropes.

'It looks quiet enough,' said Johnny.

Webber opened the car door. 'Come on,' he said. 'Let's do a recce.'

The three men climbed out and walked along the quayside. The air was damp and smelled of diesel fuel. The wind was up and the boats clanked together as they were jostled by the swell. Johnny stopped as they approached the first jetty.

'You go ahead,' he said. 'I'll keep an eye out.'

Webber surveyed each boat like he was hunting for bargains at a street market. He shook his head and tutted.

'Flotsam and bleedin' jetsam,' he said. 'A load of floating junk.'

They tried another jetty. This one was longer and the vessels were larger. One caught Webber's attention.

'That's more like it,' he said.

He was looking at a fishing boat, newer than the rest, about thirty or forty feet long, with a small round-fronted wheelhouse and a cabin in the bow. A tarnished name plate on the transom said *Strood Lights.*

'You keep watch,' he said. 'I'm going aboard to check her over.'

Webber hopped over the rail onto the deck and tried the wheelhouse door. It was open. He gave the thumbs up to Calloway and ducked inside.

Calloway stood waiting. Bert was taking his time. It made Calloway uneasy. He lit a cigarette and held it between his thumb and forefinger, concealing the glowing tip in the palm of his hand. His suit flapped in the wind like a sail. It was cold. He pulled his jacket tight around him.

Johnny gave a low whistle. Calloway peered into the darkness towards the sound. Two figures were walking over to the jetty. They were maritime types, with woollen caps and heavy, loose-fitting jumpers. One was sucking on a pipe, the other smoked a roll-up that dangled from his lip. Johnny said hello and gave them some chat about looking for a good pub for the evening. They bought the line. One of the men mentioned a place called the Five Bells. The other laughed and made a disparaging comment. Johnny kept them talking. Calloway heard Webber clunking around inside the fishing boat. He had no way of telling him to keep quiet. Then the boat's engine started up. It was as noisy as hell. Webber stuck his head out of the wheelhouse. He'd not noticed they had company.

'Untie the ropes and jump aboard,' he shouted above the noise of the engine.

One of the men looked over.

'Who the hell's that on the *Strood Lights*? That's not old Billy.'

The other man, the bigger of the two, grabbed Johnny by the arm.

'What the fuck's going on pal?' he said.

Johnny shook free. He jabbed the big man in the guts, doubling him over. He kicked the other man's legs from under him, sending him face down onto the boards of the jetty.

'Sorry gents, needs must,' he said, running towards the fishing boat.

Calloway was untying the ropes.

'Did you hurt them?' he said. He knew what Johnny was capable of.

'Only their pride.'

'Jump aboard and help me push us off.'

They pushed against the slippery timbers of the jetty and felt the boat move out a foot or two. The bigger of the two men was running towards them.

'Shit, here he comes,' said Johnny.

There was a boat hook pole on the deck. Calloway grabbed it. The big man was level with the boat. He made to board it. Calloway jabbed him in the chest with the pole. The man lost his footing. He slipped and plunged into the water. Calloway and Johnny watched him splashing around, looking for a hand hold.

'Christ, I hope he doesn't drown,' said Johnny. He sounded genuinely concerned.

Calloway looked around. There was a lifebuoy hanging by the wheelhouse door. He pulled it off and flung it towards the man in the water. The man grabbed it. His mate was there now, reaching down to offer a hand.

'He'll live,' said Calloway. 'Mind you, I wouldn't want to be in their shoes when they tell whoever old Billy is that they let three strangers steal his boat.'

Three strangers driving a car stolen from an MI5 operative, thought Calloway. Damn fool plan.

TWENTY-NINE

'She's got a tank full of diesel,' said Webber, tapping the fuel gauge.

The three men stood in the wheelhouse peering through the rain-spattered glass into the darkness. The boat lunged back and forth with every roll of the waves.

'You ever navigated these waters, Bert?' said Johnny. There was a hint of unease in fearless Johnny Suskind's voice.

Webber shook his head. 'We'll stay in the middle and hope for the best,' he said. 'That usually works.'

Suskind exchanged glances with Calloway. Best give him something to do, Calloway thought.

'Search the boat, Johnny. See if you can find anything useful.'

The big boxer said 'aye-aye' and squeezed himself through the hatch, down into the cabin below. Calloway stared through the arc of half-clear glass with every sweep of the fishing boat's inadequate wiper.

'You reckon we'll make the fort in this light?' he said.

'Keep looking left,' said Webber. 'She's bound to pop up.'

Calloway knew Webber's jocularity was a sham. Pure bravado. It hid the gut-wrenching nerves they were all feeling. Johnny appeared in the hatch.

'A torch, a wrench, some rope...'

'If all else fails, we can play Cluedo,' said Webber.

'Oh,' said Johnny, 'and some Dutch courage, courtesy of old Billy.'

He waved a half-drunk bottle of navy rum at them.

'Pass it round, mate. My mouth tastes like a zookeeper's boot,' said Webber.

Johnny passed him the bottle. The little man uncorked it with his teeth, spat the cork out and gulped down a good measure. He passed the bottle to Calloway.

Johnny laid his finds on the ledge in front of the wheel. Calloway pulled out Freddie's Luger.

'Just for show,' he said. 'We're not leaving any bodies behind.'

Calloway thought of Baumann, dead on the floor of the bombed-out apartment. He wasn't sure he trusted himself.

'You take it, Johnny,' he said.

Suskind was the level-headed one.

'Look,' said Webber.

They could now see the fort a few hundred yards ahead of them. Calloway felt his stomach churn. An assault on a fixed position took a certain sort of courage. Assaulting a sea fort took two dozen commandos.

Johnny coiled the rope across his chest like a mountaineer. He slipped the Luger into the pocket of his camouflage smock. Calloway put the wrench in his trouser pocket.

'There's a landing stage between the stilts,' said Webber, pointing to a concrete platform lined with old tyres as fenders, under a three-storey, brick-built block. 'I'm going to drop you two off and then circle the fort. I'm not mooring up. We can't risk them getting hold of the boat.'

Calloway agreed. He left the wheelhouse with Johnny and the two men crouched on the deck. Webber grappled with the wheel, bringing them alongside the landing stage. The choppy waters buffeted the small boat against the fenders. Calloway gave Johnny the signal. They jumped over the rail and onto the wet concrete base. There was an open staircase leading to the first floor of the block above. Johnny led the way. They climbed the stairs. There was a rusting steel door. It was locked. Johnny pulled out the Luger. Calloway banged on the door with the wrench. The sound echoed around them. They heard the bolts sliding on the other side. The door opened a chink. A face appeared. Johnny stuck his boot in the gap. Calloway put his full weight against the door. The two men barged through, Johnny first, the Luger in his hand.

'What the hell...' said a voice.

Johnny silenced him with his left fist. A second blow knocked him down.

'How many in the fort?' said Calloway, leaning over the man on the ground.

'Who are you?' said the man, his voice faltering, his eyes fixed on the pistol in Johnny's hand. He wore a white side-fastening tunic, like a doctor in an American movie.

'How many manning the fort?' said Calloway again. Johnny cocked the pistol.

'Four,' the man on the ground blurted out.

'You and three others?'

The man nodded.

'Armed?' said Calloway.

'What?' the man looked confused. 'No. Lovell, perhaps. I don't know.'

'Who's Lovell?'

'Security.'

'The rest?'

'Two orderlies and a doctor. I'm one of the orderlies.'

'Where are they now?'

'On the ward, or in the office. On the floor above.' He looked at the pistol nervously. 'I don't know for sure. We heard the boat, then the banging. They sent me down to see what the noise was.'

'How many patients?'

The orderly hesitated. He looked from one man to the other. Johnny pushed the barrel of the pistol against his temple.

'One,' said the orderly.

'Vera Deakin?'

The orderly nodded.

'On your feet,' said Calloway.

Johnny grabbed the back of the orderly's tunic and shoved him along the corridor. Their footsteps echoed off the dirt-streaked wall tiles. For a clinic the place had the feel of a public lavatory. There were stairs at the end of the corridor and the sound of voices above.

'Up you go,' said Johnny. He jabbed the barrel of the Luger

into the orderly's back. 'Quietly does it.'

There was a door at the top of the stairs. Johnny gestured to the orderly to open it. The orderly hesitated. Another jab with the barrel of the gun convinced him to comply. As the door latch clicked, Johnny shoved the orderly into the room and he and Calloway piled in behind him. Two shocked faces turned towards them. Johnny raised the gun so they could both see it. Calloway took in the scene. A large open space like a small ward in a convalescent hospital. Three empty beds along one wall, some medical cabinets and a desk. The windows were barred. One man wore an orderly's tunic, the other wore a suit.

'Face down on the ground please, gentlemen,' said Johnny, pushing the first orderly towards the other two men and gesturing with the Luger. The two orderlies complied; the man in the suit hesitated. Calloway saw him slide his hand inside his jacket.

'Johnny,' Calloway shouted. 'The suit's armed.'

Johnny slammed the butt of the Luger across the side of the suited man's head. The man's knees buckled. Johnny grabbed him and pulled a small automatic pistol from inside his suit jacket. He tossed it to Calloway, who turned off the safety catch and cocked it.

'I don't need to tell you what will happen if anyone moves,' said Calloway.

There was a door at the end of the room, half glazed with a frosted panel. Calloway walked towards it. He could make out figures behind the glass. He reached for the door handle and threw the door open.

It was a small office, like a doctor's consulting room. Vera Deakin sat in an armchair, her knees raised to her chin. She was barefoot and wearing a loose hospital gown. She looked up at Calloway, trembling. A grey-haired man of about fifty wearing a white coat sat opposite her. He had a stethoscope around his neck and a notebook on his lap. He started to stand. Calloway gestured with the pistol. The doctor sat back down. Vera stared at Calloway's face, moving her head slowly from side to side as if examining him from many angles. A weak smile spread across her face.

'It's Bertie's friend,' she said and sang, 'Burlington Bertie, I rise at ten thirty...'

'We've come to take you home, Vera.'

The doctor protested. 'She's in no fit state to...'

Calloway cut him off. 'Exactly what state is she in, doctor?'

'Who are you?'

'A family friend who doesn't think much of this clinic of yours. What the hell is this place?'

'That's none of your business.'

'I'm the one with gun, pal. I'd say everything's my business.'

The doctor peered through the open door into the ward. 'Where's Lovell?'

'Face down on the ground, wishing he was better at security.'

Vera sang, '...but my people are well off, you know.'

'What's the matter with her?'

'She's in an altered state.'

Vera was staring at the backs of her hands, reading the veins for some hidden meaning.

'I can see that,' said Calloway. 'Is she mad?'

'A kind of madness, yes. But it's temporary. Chemically induced.'

'Something in those pills you gave her? I assume it was you visiting her with Denton.'

The doctor nodded. 'A small dose, yes.'

'What for? What was wrong with her, apart from the natural grief of losing her husband?'

'I can't tell you that. I'm not permitted.'

Calloway gestured to the pistol in his hand. 'Oh, I think you are. Unless you want to see what *my* temporary madness looks like.'

Vera was staring at the gun now. It seemed to fascinate her.

'You look just like Alan Ladd with that,' she said. 'Are we at the pictures?'

She started to laugh. The doctor looked at the gun. His bravura ebbed away. He hesitated, then spoke.

'She knew too much. She was threatening to go to the press.'

‘About her husband Stan being killed in Berlin, chasing Soviet agents for your friend Denton. Yes, I know. What kind of pills do you prescribe for that?’

The doctor shook his head. ‘It’s all classified.’

Calloway stepped forward and cuffed him around the head, good and hard.

‘Classify that,’ he said.

Vera giggled. ‘You *are* Alan Ladd. I knew it,’ she said.

The doctor rubbed the side of his face.

‘Let’s start again,’ said Calloway. ‘What have you pumped her full of, and what’s it do?’

The doctor swallowed hard. ‘Lysergic acid diethylamide.’

‘What the hell is that?’

‘A hallucinogenic drug.’

‘Hallucinations?’ Calloway knew of delirious soldiers seeing things. ‘Why are you giving her hallucinations?’

‘Used in combination with hypnosis, we can create memory loss.’

‘Are you serious? Sounds more like something from a cheap B picture.’

‘A picture with Alan Ladd,’ said Vera, giggling and wiggling her toes.

‘The work is experimental. But the Americans have been achieving good results by all accounts. They have an extensive research programme. It builds on work the Germans were doing during the war using mescaline.’

Calloway could imagine who the subjects were. He felt his blood rise. The veins pounded at his temples.

‘So you’re using this woman as a lab rat?’

The doctor looked offended. ‘We work under strict clinical conditions.’

‘In a draughty sea fort, cut off from the outside world, with an armed guard.’

‘Our work is top secret.’

Calloway scoffed. ‘Not anymore, blabber mouth. Those pills were supposed to suppress her memory?’

‘We tried small doses at first, hoping that the behaviour

change they induced might discredit any allegations she was making about her husband's death. But she's strong. We couldn't be sure the smaller dose would have the intended effect, especially without concurrent hypnosis.'

'So you abducted her and brought her here for the full à la carte.'

'For longer-term treatment, yes.'

Vera rose from the armchair. She walked up to Calloway and put her arms around him. She nuzzled into him.

'I've always liked Alan Ladd,' she said.

'Get yourself dressed, Vera love,' Calloway said. 'We're going home.'

She smiled then walked through the door onto the ward, opening one of the bedside lockers and removing a pile of clothing. She continued humming the tune, seeming not to notice Johnny with the gun in his hand and the three men lying on the floor.

'Will this wear off?' said Calloway.

'It should do. In several hours.'

He didn't relish getting Vera onto the boat in her present state.

'Can't you give her something?'

The doctor shook his head. 'You'll just have to wait.'

'What are the aftereffects?'

'It's hard to say. We're in the early stages of the programme. It's possible there won't be any permanent change to her mental state.'

Calloway's switch flicked. He hit the doctor hard in the face. Blood spattered onto his white coat.

'Get in there and get down on the floor with the others.'

He grabbed the doctor's collar, dragged him through the doorway and pushed him to the ground. Johnny tied the four men together using the rope he'd taken from the boat. Calloway looked at the door to the stairs. It had a lock. He nudged the first orderly with his foot.

'Where are the keys?'

The orderly stuttered the words. 'The desk, top drawer.'

Calloway opened the drawer and took the keys. There was a

radio telephone on the desk, military issue. Calloway picked it up and smashed it onto the hard floor. He heard the valves shatter.

Vera was in some semblance of dress now. She wouldn't pass muster in the street, but it was better than the hospital gown. Calloway helped her into her coat.

'This is Johnny,' he said, nodding to Suskind, 'and I'm Reg, remember? You stick with us. We'll have you home soon.'

Vera held Calloway's arm, like they were heading out for a walk along the prom. Calloway tossed Johnny the keys. Johnny locked up.

They signalled to Webber from the landing stage. The swell was still high and Calloway sensed Bert was struggling to control the boat. Vera shivered in the cold of the night. Calloway put an arm around her and held her close.

Webber pulled the boat alongside. The swell bumped it back and forth against the fenders.

'She'll never make the jump, Reg,' shouted Johnny, looking at Vera. 'We're going to have to tie up for a mo'.'

Calloway signalled to Webber to tie up. Webber looked anxious. He brought the boat in as close as he could and ducked out of the wheelhouse, grabbing a rope and throwing it. Johnny leaned forward to grab it, but he was short. The rope fell into the water. Webber cursed. He pulled the rope in and tried again.

'Hook a duck,' said Vera. 'Blue picks a prize.'

She laughed above the sound of the engine. The boat strayed out, a good five yards from the landing stage. Webber ran back into the wheelhouse and wrestled with the wheel. He brought the boat in close again and threw the rope once more. Johnny grabbed it.

'Howzat,' he shouted.

Calloway grinned, relieved. Johnny pulled the boat onto the fenders and looped the rope around one of the concrete stilts. Calloway helped Vera onto the prow. He heard a shout behind him. It was Johnny. Calloway turned and saw him grappling with Lovell, the security man. Damn my haste, thought Calloway. There must have been another exit.

'Bert,' he shouted. 'Put Vera in the wheelhouse, then hold the boat steady.'

Bert looked gravely towards Johnny. Lovell was trying to wrest the Luger out of the big boxer's fist. Calloway felt for the automatic in his waistband. It was gone. In the bloody sea when he jumped onto the prow.

'Here,' shouted Webber. He threw Calloway the boat hook pole. Calloway caught it. He held it like a pike and jabbed at Lovell, snagging his jacket on the hook. He yanked the pole towards him, pulling Lovell to the edge of the landing stage. Johnny seized his moment. He gave Lovell a shove. They heard him scream as he plunged feet first into the swell. Johnny released the rope and jumped aboard. Calloway gave Webber the thumbs up. The diesel engine revved hard, exhaust billowing from the pipe above the wheelhouse.

'Take her below,' said Calloway, gesturing towards Vera.

Johnny took her by the hand and led her down the steps into the small cabin.

'How is she?' said Webber.

'Mad as a box of frogs,' said Calloway, 'but that quack doctor said it will pass.'

'What a bloody place, eh? Like being locked up in the tower.'

Calloway looked down into the cabin below. Johnny had his arm around Vera, who was leaning into him, muttering to herself. The whimsy was gone. She seemed distressed now. Johnny was talking her down with calm words. Calloway had never seen that side of the big ex-paratrooper.

'Good job there was a handsome prince to rescue her,' he said, nodding towards the pair below.

'He seems like a good sort, your mate,' said Webber.

'I reckon he is.'

It was pitch dark now, but Webber seemed calm at the wheel.

'It's all coming back to me now,' he said. 'You know, motorboats and that.'

'Can you get us to London?'

Webber shrugged. 'I'll give it a go. What's the worst that could happen?'

Calloway could think of a few things, but he didn't voice them.

All he could do was place his trust in Webber. Of the three of them, he was the only one who knew anything about boats.

'Here, have a nip of this,' Calloway said, passing Webber the bottle they had found.

It was cold in the boat. Calloway pulled his jacket tightly around him. The night was fully dark now and only clusters of lights from the estuary towns gave them any clue as to where they were. They were navigating by instinct, Webber doing his best to control the boat as it lurched through the water, buffeted by the swell.

In time, the clusters of lights merged into two long strips of illumination either side of them.

'We're getting close to London now,' said Webber. 'I reckon that's Tilbury.' He pointed towards the lights on their right. 'Where are we heading for, Reg?'

'We're taking Vera home. She needs to be in her own surroundings. Somewhere she feels safe.'

'What if they're waiting for us?'

'We'll have to take that chance. I smashed the radio at the fort so with any luck they will be cut off for hours yet. And I made sure Denton was out of action before I left London.'

He tried not to think how Trudi, the German gangster turned wrestler, might be restraining their guest back at the arena.

'Can you get us to Deptford?'

Webber nodded. 'But I reckon we should cover our tracks,' he said. 'I'll get us to the Isle of Dogs and tie up there. We can cross the river through the foot tunnel. It's only a short walk from there to Vera's house. If they're looking for the boat at least they'll find it on the other side of the river. It might buy us a bit of time.'

'Worth a go,' said Calloway.

He looked down through the hatch into the cabin. Vera lay on the bench, her head in Johnny's lap. Johnny stroked her hair like a mother lulling a child to sleep. Vera's distress seemed to have passed. Above the sound of the engine, Calloway could hear the faint sound of Johnny humming a lullaby.

THIRTY

Denton sat on a bench in the female wrestlers' changing room, his head down, his hands in his lap. He looked up when Calloway entered the room. He had a black eye and dark bruises on his forehead. His split lips were crusty with congealed blood.

'You are in so much fucking trouble,' he said.

Calloway lit two Navy Cut and passed one to Denton.

'I could say the same to you.'

Denton winced as he dragged on the cigarette. 'Don't you know who you're dealing with, man?'

'Yes, I do. The scum that inhabit the rotten end of the intelligence world. The grubby little men with dirty raincoats and blood on their hands.'

'Don't sound so pious. We know your record. You're no choirboy yourself.'

'Perhaps not. But I sing a different tune. And boy, have I got a song to sing, should the need arise.'

'That sounds like a threat.'

'Oh, it very much is.' Calloway pulled up a chair and sat facing Denton. 'I've been to your fort. I've seen what goes on there. Sick experiments. Treating human beings like lab rats. Sending them mad with chemicals.'

'The rules have changed, Calloway. We're fighting a different war.'

'Fuck off, Denton. You took a man's wife. His widow. An ordinary woman, grieving for her husband. You abducted her and locked her up. Why? Just because she wanted the truth? Doesn't she deserve that? Does the balance of power between east and west depend on whether Vera Deakin, a truck driver's widow from Deptford, knows her husband died on government service? Did it ever occur to you that you might be able to trust her?' Calloway shook his head. 'You underestimate people, Denton.'

'Don't be naive. She threatened to take the story to the press.'

'You could have slapped a D-Notice on it.'

'It would be no guarantee.'

'So you tried brainwashing her instead. That's what you lot call it, isn't it?' Calloway had read the term in a lurid news report from the war in Korea, claiming US prisoners were cooperating with their Chinese captors though some kind of mind control. 'I bet your doctor mate was rubbing his hands. A human subject. Widowed, working class, no old school tie, no influential friends. The sort that don't count. In other words, expendable.'

Denton sighed. He looked resigned.

'So what do you plan to do?' he said.

'Nothing, if you leave Vera Deakin alone. Same goes for the others.'

'What others?'

'Oh, there's a few of us. We can keep our mouths shut. But if you try anything, you're going to need something stronger than your doctor's happy pills to keep us quiet.'

He watched Denton weighing up the threat. There was a knock at the door and Trudi walked in. Denton flinched.

'Get him cleaned up,' said Calloway. 'We've reached an agreement. Mr Denton can go home.'

Trudi pulled a sponge from a bucket in the corner and turned on the showers.

'Wait a minute,' said Denton. 'We don't have an agreement. We have nothing of the sort. Your threats are meaningless. Who the hell would believe someone like you?'

Calloway sat back in the chair. He took a long drag on his cigarette.

'Perhaps you're right,' he said. 'Perhaps I'm just like Vera Deakin. One of those people that don't count. But you count, don't you, Denton? You count a lot. Major Denton, a hero of the desert war, a chest full of medals and an old school tie. What club do you belong to? Bucks? The Naval and Military? Or the Special Forces Club? You're one of those people with a reputation that counts. So what about your little indiscretion in the ring? I mean, you didn't put up much resistance, did you? You broke good and early. Sang like a subaltern at his passing out party. Not qualities conducive to good intelligence practice. Letting the side down good and proper, I'd say. "Lacks moral fibre". You wouldn't want that in your report, would you? So let's keep all that between you, me and my big lady wrestler friend, eh?'

Denton looked at Trudi. She waved the bucket and sponge at him. Calloway rose to leave.

'I think we have an agreement now,' he said. He pulled a ten-bob note from his wallet. 'You'll be needing a cab. Your car's down by the river a mile outside Rochester. Just watch yourself when you collect it. There's an old sea dog called Billy who might want a word about his missing boat.'

When Denton had left, Calloway went to his office and slept. He curled up on a floor mat in in the corner of the room and slept in the clothes he was wearing.

He woke around eight and treated himself to breakfast at a cafe. He couldn't remember the last time he'd eaten. He went to a barber's shop and paid for a shave, enjoying the smell of the lotion and the warmth of the towel on his face. He tipped the barber well. He had a lot of money in his pocket. Webber had insisted he take it. He couldn't fault the small rider's generosity. He took a trolleybus east and stepped off at the corner of Doreen's street.

She answered the door in her dressing gown. She had bruises on her face.

'What happened?' he said.

'Jimmy brought a friend.'

She let him in and put the kettle on. 'Why did you do it, Reg? Why did you have to hurt him again?'

'So he'd leave you alone.'

'Well that worked, didn't it?' she said, touching the bruised skin with her fingertips.

'I never thought...'

'No, Reg, you didn't think.'

She poured the tea and handed him a cup. He hadn't the stomach to drink it.

'You don't know Jimmy like I do.'

'I know he's scum.'

'You won't change him.'

'But things need to change. For you and little Maggie.'

She rolled her eyes. 'You don't say.'

He took the wad of notes Webber had given him from his pocket and laid it on the table in front of her.

'This is a start,' he said.

She looked at the big white notes, expressionless. 'Keep your money,' she said. 'You can't fix things.'

'I want to help.'

She pointed to her face. 'Look what your help did.'

'It was a mistake. A big mistake. I see it now.'

'Everyone can see it now.'

She turned her face away from him.

'Take the money. It might not fix things, but it won't go amiss, eh?'

She looked at him. He caught the faintest hint of a smile. She picked up the bank notes and put them in the pocket of her dressing gown.

'What do you want from me?' she said.

'Nothing. Just to know that you're safe.'

She laughed. 'Who d'you think you are, the patron saint of lost causes?'

'I lost someone once. Someone who'd been hurt. I wanted to make things right for her, to make up for what had happened to her.' He shook his head. 'But I couldn't. She's gone and that's that. I tried to make things good for her and I guess there's a part of me that just keeps on trying.'

She put her hand on his. 'You're a good man, Reg,' she said. 'You can stop trying.'

He took a sip of the tea. He looked around the room. It was filthy and damp, in spite of Doreen's efforts to make it a home.

'Let me do one more thing,' he said.

THIRTY-ONE

Finnegan wasn't best pleased by Calloway's extended absence. But the arena boss agreed to give him his job back. Calloway suspected Trudi had had a word. She was the star attraction and she had influence. He wondered whether Finnegan knew about her criminal past. Probably not, because if he did, she would be known as Jailbird Judi, the Gangland Gorgon, or some such legend.

It had been three weeks since Webber, Johnny and Calloway had snatched Vera from the fort. There had been no word from Denton, no more figures in the shadows, no police at the door. The agreement seemed to be holding.

It was Sunday and Calloway sat in the passenger seat of Webber's Buick with little Maggie on his lap. Doreen was squeezed into the back seat along with boxes and bags filled with the contents of her rented room. She'd given notice to the landlady and handed back the keys. Maggie was thrilled to be riding in the car, staring awestruck from the window as they passed over Tower Bridge heading south. Webber was giving her a running commentary. He seemed to be enjoying himself.

'It took eight years to build, that bridge did, and takes five minutes to raise so the boats can get under. That's clever, innit?' Little Maggie nodded. 'And that street down there,' Webber's voice went up a tone with excitement, 'that's Webber Street. Same name as me, eh?'

They drove for another twenty minutes, Webber pointing out landmarks to Maggie and telling anecdotes. As they turned the corner into the narrow street of dockers cottages, they saw Vera standing on her doorstep. She was dressed in her Sunday best and her hair was newly set. She looked a different woman to the addled figure in the hospital gown they'd found at the fort.

'There's aunt Vera,' said Webber, pointing through the windscreen at his sister-in-law.

'She looks nice, doesn't she, Maggie?' said Doreen.

Calloway could hear the nervousness in her voice. He reached back and took her hand.

'It's going to be fine,' he said.

Vera had set the table for tea. A fruitcake took centre stage. Maggie stared at it with hungry eyes.

'Leave your things in the car for now,' said Vera to Doreen. 'Bert and Reg can bring them in later.'

Webber looked out of the window towards the bomb site on the opposite side of the street. The grubby kids with the fox terrier were staring at the Buick.

'I'll just nip back and lock the car doors,' he said.

The adults sat at the small table making conversation, while Maggie nibbled at the large slice of cake Vera had cut for her. The conversation was stilted, but well-meant, and by the second cup of tea the four of them were starting to relax. Calloway caught Doreen's eye. She smiled at him, looking more at ease than she had been in Webber's car.

'It's going to be nice having guests,' said Vera, taking Doreen's hand. 'It will bring a bit of life to the place.'

'It's very kind of you, Mrs Deakin,' said Doreen.

'Call me Vera, love.'

There was a knock at the door, loud and heavy. A man's knock. It startled Vera. Webber turned to Calloway, with a look of concern.

'I'll get it,' said Calloway.

Vera tensed. Webber put his hand on her shoulder.

Calloway rose from the table, stepped into the small, dark hallway and opened the door.

'Reg?'

A surprised Johnny Suskind stood on the doorstep in his best suit, holding a bunch of chrysanthemums. Calloway gave him a sly grin.

'I'm guessing those aren't for me,' he said, nodding to the flowers.

Johnny's face reddened. 'I thought I'd drop in on Vera. You know, just to see how she's getting on.'

'It's a bit of a houseful, Johnny, but come on in,' said Calloway. 'I'm sure she'll be glad to see you.'

After moving Doreen's possessions into Vera's spare room, Webber drove Calloway back to the squat. Calloway was happy to make his own way back but Webber had insisted.

'It'll be good for her, having people around,' he said. 'That Doreen seems a decent girl.'

There was a hint of uncertainty in Webber's voice.

'She needs another chance,' said Calloway.

Webber nodded in agreement. The answer seemed to satisfy him. Neither man mentioned Johnny's surprise appearance. That was Vera and Johnny's business.

'One for the road, Bert?' said Calloway, when they pulled up outside the old hotel building.

'I'll pass if you don't mind,' said Webber, yawning. 'I reckon the past few weeks is catching up with me.'

Calloway was relieved. He knew how Bert felt. He wanted more than anything to sleep a long, dreamless sleep. The two men said goodbye. Calloway climbed the steps to the hotel portico, pushed the heavy panelled door open and stepped into the hallway. The place was run down but retained a sense of grandeur, with its columns, chandeliers and wide marble staircase. There were worse places to call home and worse people to call neighbours. There was a sense of community forged by common experience. Scarred by war, spurned by peace, homeless, stateless or just unable cope in the world they'd fought to save. He was going to fit right in here.

He turned to climb the stairs when a voice called to him.

'Are you Calloway?'

It was the old boy that manned the reception desk, one of the Vigilantes. He stood in front of Calloway with his arm outstretched.

'You've got a postcard,' he said.

Calloway climbed the stairs to his floor and opened the door to his room. The Poles were playing their music. The sound of Chopin drifted down the corridor. He left the door open so he could hear it better. The bed was unmade but enticing nonetheless. He kicked off his shoes and lay down, holding the postcard to the beam of streetlight shining in through the tall window. The postcard said *Greetings from Berlin*, with a view down Kurfürstendamm towards the Kaiser Wilhelm church, in vivid, unreal colour. On the back, three words.

Miss me? Pat, xxx

THE END

About the author

DDC Morgan lives in South East London. He has written professionally as a journalist and consultant for more than thirty years. Crime writing fills the rock'n'roll-shaped hole in his life left by no longer playing in bands.

You can follow him on Twitter @DDCMorgan

Abide With Me by Ian Ayris

Abide with me is the story of two boys forced to walk blind into the darkness of their shattered lives and their struggle to emerge as men. It's also a story of loyalty, of community, and of powerful friendships shaped by adversity and celebrated on the football terraces of England.

With power, sensitivity and wit, Ian Ayris has crafted one of the most authentic snapshots of working class life you will ever read.

"Ayris brings a depth and level of emotion to his writing that most authors strive their entire career to achieve, and which many never do."

Know Me From Smoke by Matt Phillips

When Stella and Royal meet one night, they're drawn to each other. But Royal has a secret. How long before Stella discovers that the man she's falling for isn't who he seems?

A noir of gripping suspense and violence, Know Me From Smoke is a journey into the shadowy terrain of murder, lost love, and the heart's lust for vengeance.

"Two great characters here in Stella and Royal. Couple that with a psychotic villain and a grudge-bearing cop, and you're gonna be hooked til the end. Happy endings? Well, maybe..." - Paul Heatley,

Slow Bear by Anthony Neil Smith

In the oil fields of North Dakota, times were good during the boom. Some people got rich: Santana the Exile certainly did. A lot of other people got jobs. A lot of bars and strip joints got busy. Then the boom times ended and everything slowly crumbled back to the red dust from which it was built.

This is noir at its deepest, at its most savage, at its most vital, from an acknowledged modern master of the genre.

"More happens in the first two chapters of Slow Bear than in some literary novelist's entire output. Thrills, spills. Twists, turns. Heart, soul. As good as it gets." - Mark Ramsden

Black Moss by David Nolan

In April 1990, as rioters took over Strangeways prison in Manchester, someone killed a little boy at Black Moss.

And no one cared.

No one except Danny Johnston, an inexperienced radio reporter trying to make a name for himself.

More than a quarter of a century later, Danny returns to his home city to revisit the murder that's always haunted him.

If Danny can find out what really happened to the boy, maybe he can cure the emptiness he's felt inside since he too was a child.

But finding out the truth might just be the worst idea Danny Johnston has ever had.

Find out more at www.Fahrenheit-Press.com

www.ingramcontent.com/pod-product-compliance
Lightning Source LLC
Chambersburg PA
CBHW020344310726
48979CB00015B/2499/J

* 9 7 8 1 9 1 4 4 7 5 6 1 0 *